CHOOSING WHAT MATTERS

CHOOSING WHAT MATTERS

PIVOT LAB CHRONICLES™ BOOK TWO

MICHAEL ANDERLE

LMBPN Publishing
PMB 196, 2540 South Maryland Pkwy
Las Vegas, NV 89109

First US Edition, July, 2020
eBook ISBN: 978-1-64971-059-8
Print ISBN: 978-1-64971-060-4

PART I

Jacob tapped his foot as he read. Although late at night, he wasn't tired. Lately, no longer drained by the constant worry about PIVOT going under for financial reasons or their first test subject dying in the game, he felt like he was walking on air.

When he and his friends had developed their virtual reality system years before, he had known it was a feat of engineering. He had loved losing himself in the days and nights of testing and problem-solving. They had all known that PIVOT was extremely ambitious as a project but had exceeded even their wildest dreams.

Still, something had been missing.

Like the rest of his team, he had chosen to work in engineering to change the world. No matter how complex the problems he was solving with the virtual reality pods were, he wasn't entirely happy merely making an entertainment system.

Everything had changed in an instant when Amber, one of his two co-founders, realized that the pods could be repurposed to provide medical care to coma patients. The team had then stumbled upon research showing that virtual reality could be used to help comatose patients recover more quickly.

The road from there to here had been anything but smooth. They had faced financial ruin, media harassment, and even jail time. However, their first patient had woken from his coma and was in recovery, PIVOT had been acquired and funded extensively, and the three founding members were now inundated with the kind of work they'd craved for the better part of a decade.

As a result, he wasn't sad about the late nights and in fact, he reveled in them.

"You're enjoying that K-pop, huh?" Nick asked.

"Huh?" Jacob looked up and took a moment to listen. At some point, the music they were playing had changed from rock to bouncy Korean pop with half-English choruses and synthy undercurrents. With a small frown, he tried to decide whether to care, gave up, bopped his head in a chair dance, and returned to his work.

Amber gave the other man a thumbs-up. "I told you he wouldn't mind."

Nick nodded. He was chair-dancing in time with Jacob. "I'll hate you for getting us into this, won't I?"

"No." She gave a seated shimmy and spun her chair. "Because there's so much of it and it's all happy and danceable."

"What did you say it was?" Jacob asked.

"It's K-pop," she explained. "First, you think it's a little cheesy, then you find one or two catchy songs, and a month later, it's all you've listened to." She gave an exaggerated shrug and took a bite of cold pizza. "God, I'm *so hungry*. Why am I so hungry?"

"I don't know, but I am too." He shook his mouse to wake his computer up. "Wait, yes I do. Guys, it's four thirty."

"No," she protested, "because we ordered the pizza at six."

"Yeah." Jacob gave her a meaningful nod. "I meant it's four thirty *AM*."

"What?" Amber picked her phone up and stabbed the power button a few times. "Well, my phone is dead so I can't check. I think we should probably get some rest."

"Yeah." Jacob yawned. "Now that I think about it, I'm very tired."

"Let's get breakfast," Nick suggested.

"Will anything be open?"

"It's New York City. Of course something will be open. Come on." He stood and shrugged his coat on.

"I did finish an application, I guess." Jacob started tidying up. The applications, which contained numerous sections of medical information, all had to be locked in cabinets. He stacked the ones he had completed and placed them in one pile, then made another of unread ones beside it.

He'd worked for almost twenty-four hours straight and the unread pile was still twice as high as the reviewed pile. A glance showed that his partners were in a similar situation, and he knew they had only printed out the first quarter of what they had received thus far.

They passed through the two layers of security necessary to leave the Diatek Offices and emerged a little wearily into the very first part of dawn. Even at this hour, New York bustled with a relatively even blend of people in suits, those in various cleaning or fast food uniforms, and others who looked like they had no reason to be awake at all.

Amber shivered in the cold. "I forgot how much I hate New England winters."

"Do me a favor," Nick said, "and don't call New York 'New England' where anyone can overhear us. I don't want to get beaten to within an inch of my life."

"It's too cold to make promises," she said desolately. "Hey, that place looks open."

"Do you even know what blintzes are?"

"It says there's cheese, and there's a sign with a coffee cup. That's good enough for me."

They entered the little two-table restaurant, where the chef didn't greet them but bellowed into the back of the shop about customers. The waitress appeared a few moments later, still smelling of cigarette smoke but with three cups of surprisingly strong coffee.

"Breakfast special?" she asked. In the complete absence of any response, she nodded again and bawled their order into the kitchen as she disappeared—presumably to finish her cigarette.

"I wonder what we'll get," Jacob said.

"It's a mystery," Amber said prosaically. "So? Did anyone have interesting applications?"

"Not really." He shook his head. "Honestly, the real issue will be trying to sort through all the younger guys who want to go in. I get unreasonably excited whenever I see one that isn't a guy in his twenties or thirties."

"I've had a few," Nick said. "A fair number have weird health problems—the kind of things where doctors don't know why."

"That's almost all of mine," she said. "Things doctors can't seem to fix or diagnose or whatever. I have no idea how some of them think we can help them, but I guess they're looking for anything at this point."

"I'm not looking forward to writing a response to all of them," Jacob said with a groan.

"This is what form letters were invented for," Nick told him.

"I can't send a form letter to people who are desperate for help. But I...we need more baseline patients before we can even start branching out."

"We'll come up with something," she told him. "Don't worry. We can even explain a version of that, right?"

The cook banged on the bell and slid three plates up. When no one came to take them, he banged on it again, came out of the kitchen in a filthy apron while muttering about bad service, and brought them the plates himself. He banged them on the table and left out the back door, where a storm of yelling erupted in a language that might or might not have been English.

"So, these are blintzes, huh?" Amber poked one with her fork. "Well, let's give this a try. Cheers."

Dorothy sipped her coffee and stared out the window, and she turned when a knock sounded on the door.

The first was restrained. The second was a wild pounding, half-knuckles and half-flat hands, and it was accompanied by shouting. "Great-grandma! Great-grandma! Great-grandma!"

With a smile, she moved to the door. She didn't walk quite fast enough to satisfy her great-grandson, but she knew Liam merely wanted to imitate the grown-ups by knocking. Experience made her careful and she opened the door a crack so he wouldn't spill into the house, then pulled it open when he had righted himself.

"Great-grandma!" Liam tumbled inside and threw his arms around her legs. "Pick me up!"

"Hello." She rested one faintly trembling hand on his reddish-brown head. "I can't pick you up, pumpkin. You're getting too big for that."

His pout was fleeting. He was distracted quickly enough by the thought of Great-grandma's house and raced into the living room.

"Careful!" she called after him. "And take your shoes off!" Mary, Dorothy's daughter-in-law, shook her head with a rueful laugh and bent to give her a hug. Tall and willowy, with blonde hair she had begun to let go gray, the younger woman looked her usual, put-together self. She held some banana bread out. "We have Liam today and I thought we could drop this off before going to the park. Sorry it's so early."

"What do you think I get up to?" Dorothy asked. She gestured at the empty house. "I've been up for a few hours now anyway. We can have coffee if you want while Liam plays."

"That sounds lovely." Mary followed her inside. "John mentioned you weren't sleeping well lately."

"Old bones." She shrugged. "This hip hasn't felt right for a while now. As my grandma used to say, 'don't get old.'"

The other woman laughed ruefully as she sat at the table and waited for the coffee. Unlike her husband, she didn't rush to do every-thing for her mother-in-law. It was a small gesture but one Dorothy appreciated—she didn't like being treated like an invalid.

Mary sat quietly while she brought the sugar and cream, pausing frequently as Liam dashed through the kitchen with various toys.

With nine great-grandchildren, Dorothy had acquired a pile of toys that had been forgotten at her house over the years.

When the old woman at last came to sit, Mary clinked her mug against hers with a smile. "Should I cut the banana bread?"

"Of course." Dorothy watched as a thick slice came away from the loaf, studded with chocolate chips. "I can't wait. Did Liam help you make it?"

"For certain definitions of the word 'help.'" Mary smiled. "He put in about twice as many chocolate chips as the recipe called for. I'm surprised it's holding together at all." She passed her a plate.

"Mmm, thank you." Her mother-in-law took a bite and tried not to let her face fall too obviously. The woman was a wonderful baker and the bread was almost certainly delicious, but lately, Dorothy hadn't been able to taste much of everything. Her mouth always seemed to taste of metal. To avoid being rude, she took another bite. "It's as good as always."

"Thank you." Mary took a slice for herself. "What are you up to today?"

She smiled. "Not much of anything. As per usual."

"You could come to the park with us," her companion suggested.

"Ah, thank you, but no. I have a doctor's appointment at eleven." She saw Mary's quick look. "It's only routine."

"Well, be sure to mention the sleeping," the woman advised her.

"Now you sound like my son."

"No, if I were John, I would tell you to go out and have a date tonight." Mary gave her a conspiratorial smile before she rolled her eyes.

"He does keep talking about that." Dorothy sighed. "Most children aren't so keen to replace their father."

"He's sixty-two," Mary pointed out with a laugh. "It's not like he's in much need of fatherly guidance." She paused before she said gently, "And it has been ten years."

Her sigh was a little heavier this time.

"I'm not trying to rush you," the younger woman said hurriedly. "I only want to make sure you aren't…well—Liam, please don't throw books. Oh, what was I saying?" She frowned.

"Look who's getting old now," Dorothy teased. She shook her head. "I'm not lonely, Mary. I don't need a husband."

"I know you don't." Mary wrapped her fingers around her mug of coffee. "And I do tell John that whenever he mentions it. It's only…"

She raised an eyebrow in the best imitation she could muster of her grandmother. That woman had been the undisputed champion of withering stares.

Apparently, hers weren't as frightening, because her daughter-in-law merely smiled a little sadly. She clasped Dorothy's hand for a moment. "I feel like there's something missing from your life," she said. "Not necessarily a husband. But you don't have friends you spend time with either, Dotty. You've always seemed like the kind of person to me who…"

Dorothy frowned. "Was a recluse?"

"No, no, that's not what I mean at all." Mary chewed a piece of banana bread as she tried to find the words. "I always expect you to say you've taken up sculpting or writing novels. You seem like someone who's so passionate about the world." She smiled and took a sip of her coffee. "Maybe you simply never tell us about your interests."

"I…" She took a moment to process that. To be polite, she took another bite of the banana bread, even though all she could taste was metal. "I've never had any particular hobbies. Now it's a little too late, don't you think? What would I do? Play shuffleboard? Go out and look at the sea?"

"Whatever you *want*." The younger woman stood and kissed her cheek. "Right now, though, you need to get to your doctor's appointment, so Liam and I will get out of your hair."

"Mmm." Dorothy pushed from the table with a wince. "Thank you for bringing the banana bread."

"Eat a few more slices," Mary advised. "You've been losing weight. Are you sure you feel okay?"

"Yes," she assured her and rolled her eyes. "Goodbye, Liam."

"Bye, Great-grandma!" The door slammed.

"I should go get him," Mary said, alarmed. She darted to the door. "Come have dinner tonight!"

"I...well, I'm not sure I—"

"Six thirty?" Mary slipped her shoes on hurriedly. "John would love to see you and James will be over to pick Liam up. Say you will?"

Before she could answer, Mary had left, calling for Liam to not run into the street.

Dorothy sighed. It appeared she would go to dinner, which was only a problem because she wasn't looking forward to eating another metal-tasting meal. Mary was right, though. She *had* been losing weight. It was preferable to not eat much compared to eating more mouthfuls of chicken that tasted like tin.

With another sigh, she went to get her coat. She should leave for the doctor's office. It was early but it wasn't like she had much else to do.

It was funny, what Mary had said about her interests. Dorothy had never had any hobbies. There hadn't been time and now, as she'd said, there wasn't much of a point.

That made her feel sad, and she shook her head as she stepped into the sunlight. It wasn't like she'd had a bad life. She had a lovely family, she'd adored her husband, and she lived comfortably now. Things could be much worse.

She merely felt a little numb.

Even an hour later, as Dorothy stood distractedly in the doctor's reception room with charts and scans clutched in one trembling hand, the numbness didn't lift. A metal taste in her mouth, an aching hip, the low energy, and the sleeplessness—all the little things she associated with growing older—weren't little at all.

She looked at the scans again and couldn't find anything to feel except resignation.

"You've done it now, Dotty," she told herself. It was what her mother always used to say when she messed up.

For a moment, she'd thought seriously about sculpting or writing. Mary was right, the world was full of interesting things.

There merely wasn't much point when you were eighty-four and you had cancer.

The thing she was most frightened of, Dorothy realized, was that her family would find out and they would be upset. She didn't think she could deal with them fussing over her. During the entire ride home from the doctor's office, she tried to think of lies to tell them or ways to share the truth so they wouldn't worry.

In the end, she decided not to say anything at all—although she did stop at a local bakery to buy kugel, which she knew was James's favorite. It had been a long time since she did anything like that, but she didn't have to be quite as careful with money now, she reasoned.

She arrived to the usual chaos of Liam, who wrestled with James on the living room rug while John looked on indulgently from his favorite chair. Mary's son came to give her a hug and take the kugel.

"You look tired," he told her.

"Don't you start." Her voice was a little sharper than normal. "If the doctor isn't worried, you shouldn't be either."

Huh. Apparently, she had decided to lie. That was interesting.

"So you did speak to him." John looked relieved, although that was probably because he didn't have to come up with a creative way to pry the truth out of her without seeming to ask. "Mary said you told her you would."

"You two need to come up with more exciting things to discuss," Dorothy told him as fondly as she could. "Your father and I didn't have fifty happy years by talking about other people's health, I'll tell you that."

John, who was used to her ribbing, only smiled. He and Mary were coming up on thirty years of marriage and they quite clearly adored each other as much as they had when they got married. They were the ones she never needed to worry about, for which she was grateful. Deborah was still angry about the divorce, even all these years later, and Deborah and her husband didn't seem all that happy.

Robert, the youngest and an avowed bachelor, was one Dorothy worried about more out of form than anything else. Since she'd been widowed, she'd developed an appreciation for her son's independence, and the two of them had grown closer than she had expected. She still gave him grief about finding a nice woman to settle down with and he still rolled his eyes, but it was firmly an act now. After all, she heard the same lines from the other children.

Mary greeted her with a kiss on the cheek and a glass of wine.

"Oh, no thank you," Dorothy protested.

"I would," the woman advised. "John cooked."

She took the glass of wine with John's protests in the background.

"He did well." James appeared in the doorway with Liam hanging over one shoulder. "I taught him how to make roast pork."

"Will wonders never cease?" Dorothy managed a smile. "I'll reserve judgment until I've had some, I think."

"Fair." John put oven mitts on with a flourish. "But you'll eat your words. James is an excellent teacher."

James smiled with smug satisfaction. After selling a business, he'd been at loose ends lately. Even though he had enough money to never work again and his wife earned a great deal of money as a corporate lawyer, he was never content doing nothing. In the past four months, Dorothy had heard talk of a PhD, a cookbook, a sailboat, and several more companies.

She considered him as the family sat down to a dinner that was, admittedly, excellent. Like her, he had done everything that was expected of him in life. He'd gotten married, had a child, and run a successful business. That wasn't enough for him, though. He had dozens of other interests—almost, she could say, he found everything interesting.

Did Mary honestly think Dorothy was the same?

With a start, she realized someone had asked her something. She looked around in surprise.

"Mom, are you okay?" John looked worried.

"Oh, don't you start again," she said. "I was daydreaming, that's all. What were you talking about?"

"I hoped you would talk your grandson out of trying to build a boat," he said. "As it seems neither I nor his wife can persuade him."

"I *want* Dada to build a boat!" Liam said excitedly.

"See?" James said with a serene smile. "Liam's vote is most important."

"I don't see why he shouldn't build a boat," she weighed in.

Everyone gave her an incredulous look—except Liam, who cheered from his seat.

"You're in favor of this?" John asked. "He won't be able to sail a wooden boat around here."

"Maybe I'll simply sell it," the other man said.

"You'll get attached to it," Mary predicted fondly, "and you'll need to rent a storage unit to keep it in because you can't bear to give it up, but you'll never have time to sail it."

James grumbled.

"If you want to build a boat, you build a boat," Dorothy said. "Don't you listen to them. You have many interests and you always have. Maybe you'll find your next business while building it."

He lifted his glass to her in a toast. "Grandma's on board *and* Liam's on board."

"Don't you dare take either of them on a boat before it's been tested," Mary said with mock severity. "And then only with several life-jackets."

Dorothy sat in the living room and listened as they all cleaned up and bickered good-naturedly about the boat. Building one didn't sound at all interesting to her because she'd been born in the era where people did things like that because they had to, not because it was a fun diversion. Still, she admired James for being so passionate.

"Dotty?" Mary returned with the bottle of wine. "Would you like any more?" She frowned at the look on her mother-in-law's face. "Are you sure you're all right? I won't tell John if you aren't, I promise."

She summoned a smile from somewhere. "I'm fine. Merely tired. The doctor prescribed something."

Chemotherapy was what the doctor had prescribed.

And while she might not be sure what she wanted to do in life, she knew she didn't particularly want to be even sicker than she was. The thought of something like chemotherapy filled her with dread.

And that was what her family wouldn't understand. They would want her to recover and get better.

But why? Dorothy didn't want to spend her last years in pain and sick to her stomach. She wanted....well, she didn't know what she wanted. That was the problem.

The two men were still bickering when they entered the living room, and it took Dorothy a few moments to realize the subject had changed.

"Like I'll trust a senator to tell me about healthcare," John said with a snort.

She looked at Mary for clarification, only for her daughter-in-law to shake her head and shrug. "I don't understand it either. I thought virtual reality was headsets."

"Some of it is," James said patiently. "Liam, don't run with the hot chocolate. Sit at the table to drink it." He went to help the boy with his drink before he returned to the living room with a beer in hand. "This is a full neural hookup. You don't put it over your eyes and see a screen. It tells your optic nerves what you're seeing."

"That's even worse," John said. "I don't want them to put things in my brain."

"Many technologies we accept now were things that seemed unreasonable at the time," the other man said. "Look, it's getting FDA approval and they're searching for test subjects. I think it would be fun. I'd like my next project to do something similar."

"I don't get it." Dorothy felt the usual prickliness she experienced when talking about technology. "Is it for blind people?"

"It could be," he said thoughtfully. "That's part of what they're testing now—they want to know how different people use it. It's in the news because it helped a senator's son out of his coma."

"*Maybe*," John said darkly. "People wake up from comas all the time."

"And often, they don't," James said, still patient but with a trace of steel in his voice. "It could be an interesting treatment and it's always good to have new ones. It's not like we have comas fully explained. Besides, the game simply sounds fun."

"There's a game?" She was completely confused now.

"Yeah. Like World of Warcraft or—okay, you don't know what that is. Hmm, Dungeons and Dragons?"

"That," John said, "was not the way to convince your grandmother. She used to lecture me endlessly about games like that."

"You always had your nose in a book about spaceships or dragons," Dorothy protested. "And such a brilliant mind."

"Grandma." James sounded disappointed but almost as if he had the moral high ground. "Merely because someone likes science fiction and fantasy or video games doesn't mean they're wasting their talents. Some science fiction stories are the most illuminating, most —" He shook his head as he searched for words. "And not every book has to be serious. Besides, don't I remember you reading romance novels?"

John crowed with laughter.

"I did," she said stiffly, "but I didn't like them much."

"I wouldn't judge you if you had," James said, with a laugh. "I'm only saying that people like different things. And if you do still read romance novels, Mom always has a stack of them."

Mary settled into her seat with a stern look at her husband. "Not a word out of you. And if your mother always got on your case for what you read, why would you get on mine for my romance novels?"

"That's a good point," he admitted. He gave his mother a wicked grin. "And I admit, I did play Dungeons and Dragons a few times."

"What!" She could not imagine her straight-laced son, the executive, playing trite games about dragons and wizards. "*Why?*"

"Why don't you play?" James asked and cut his father's intended response off, "and then maybe you'd know? Any number of people play D&D with their grandparents. We could make it a weekly thing." His raised eyebrow said he knew she wouldn't say yes, then he laughed: "Or you could go into the virtual reality game. I bet if you were a wizard slinging fireballs, you'd find that very cool."

Dorothy snorted.

"Shake your head all you want," he said, "but I'll believe until proven otherwise that you would like to throw spells and wield a sword."

"Your grandmother," John told his son severely, "would be much more of a crossbow woman."

Mary burst out laughing and Dorothy, despite her innate resistance to the idea, chuckled. What would they say, she wondered, if she did start playing those games?

The question reminded her of the topic she had come to avoid, and she swallowed slightly. Fireballs and dragons and swords weren't her thing.

Or were they? Now that she thought about it, she remembered that once or twice, she had stopped in the hallway to read a few pages of the novels she'd taken from John. She had always shaken her head at the dramatic plot twists and strange names but could admit that they'd held some appeal.

She'd always spent time wondering about what came next. In fact, after a while, she'd taken to skipping to the end of the book so she didn't have to wonder. It would be interesting to see if it was too late to track some of those down now.

When she left later that evening, she kissed James on the cheek. "What were you talking about? The thing that shows you stories in your brain."

"Oh, the company is called PIVOT." He pulled his phone out. "I'll text you the information. It was good to see you, Grandma. I'm sorry Liam won't sit still these days."

"He's little," she said with a smile. "Little ones are like that." She didn't add that he was, in a way, the easiest one to be around right now because she didn't feel the need to hide anything from him.

The rest of them presented her with her greatest challenge.

What would she tell them? She had no idea.

CHAPTER THREE

From the first pictures she saw of the PIVOT game, Dorothy knew it was not for her.

The fourteen additional pages of artwork she looked at only cemented that, but to make sure, she decided to watch all of what was apparently called "gameplay videos." She rolled her eyes at the videos of a character confronting his evil twin, scoffed loudly when a dragon appeared on-screen and shook her head when she saw the giant coliseum.

The game was nothing but a mish-mash of power fantasies. Of course, it would be fun to be able to throw fireballs like one character did or ride a dragon, but the real world didn't involve those things. That was why it was important to—

Dorothy stopped that line of thought abruptly and reconsidered.

Most books, even classics, were works of fiction.

She chewed over that thought and made herself another cup of tea before she sat to watch an interview with Justin Williams, the first patient to have recovered using the PIVOT technology. He looked pale and he was still recovering, but he spoke passionately—as did his mother and father—about the effects of the treatment.

What most impressed her was the way his parents spoke about watching their son come into his own by playing the game. With the father in a suit and the mother wearing pearls, they didn't exactly seem like lax, anything-goes parents. Not only that, they had found value not only in their son's recovery but in the things he had learned in the game.

"What does someone learn about real life from riding a dragon?" Dorothy asked no one in particular.

Still, she continued to watch until long after midnight, and when she considered getting up and going to bed, she knew she would merely lie awake, tossing and turning. Instead, she looked up the Dungeons and Dragons games John said he had played and some of the books she could remember. She read book reviews that claimed certain works of speculative fiction were even allegories to current events, although she snorted at that because it was plainly ridiculous.

Then, she kept reading.

Dorothy looked up the PIVOT website and found their application requirements.

She absolutely would not do this.

Still, she *did* have copies of all of her recent health records.

You know, if she intended to do it, which she didn't. She definitely didn't.

There was no point in filling out the whole application, including next of kin. She also most certainly did not need to take the time to write and edit a statement about why she wanted to be in the trial since she didn't want to be part of it.

Thank you for considering my application. I am applying for this trial because I think you will not have many older people applying and you say you need all ages. As you will see from the included records, there is no need to worry about my safety.

For my whole life, I have done what was expected of me. I tried to avoid doing frivolous things. I do not understand how one can find value in playing an artificial game and learning to use magic when that skill cannot be used in the real world. However, I cannot deny that Justin Williams and his family have found great value in your game.

Dorothy continued to scan the letter as her thoughts wavered from one choice to the other. She could not seriously be considering doing this.

Before she could stop herself, she pressed the button to send the application.

The regret was immediate, but no matter how many times she clicked the back button, she could not undo the send of her materials. She opened her email, only to see—with a sinking sensation—a confirmation that she had sent it.

What had she been thinking? They would see her application and laugh at her—an eighty-four-year-old woman who knew nothing about video games. They would want people like James.

Embarrassed, she stood and washed her mug out carefully before she wandered to bed. She knew she wouldn't be able to sleep but she should try. That's what she would have told her children to do when they woke up and said they couldn't sleep. It was the kind of thing she had done her whole life—play by the rules.

Dorothy knew she was fortunate. She'd had a happy marriage, she wasn't in poverty, and she loved her children, grandchildren, and great-grandchildren.

But she'd never had something to feel passionate about. She'd never done anything that was simply for her. Maybe it was only the knowledge that she didn't have much time but right now, that seemed more important than it ever had.

"You know," Jacob said, "you'd think we would have learned from last night to not stay up until all hours."

"Shpf, *learning capabilities.*" Nick waved his hands. "We don't have those."

"Exactly," Amber said. "We're merely three Masters graduates from MIT. What d'you think we have? Life skills? Don't be absurd."

"We're basically contractually obligated to stay up too late and eat too many dehydrated noodles," Nick finished.

Both of them looked at Jacob with identical too-big smiles.

He snickered and returned to work. If he had to wade through this hellscape of paperwork with anyone, he was glad it was the two of them. He sorted the last of his applications into an alphabetized pile and carried them to one of the assistants' desks.

With the benefit of a little sleep and considerably more coffee—as well as a large to-go order of blintzes, which were a new favorite—the team had come up with a form letter that he didn't feel bad about sending. It explained that it would be irresponsible to try to treat diverse medical problems with the pods at this time, but that the applicants' information would be kept on file and they would be contacted for any relevant trials in the future.

"Has anyone heard from Justin?" Nick asked. Their first patient had successfully woken up from his coma a few weeks before and he was now recovering at home in California. He and his parents had offered to be brand ambassadors of a sort.

Not to mention that both Justin and his mother had become a part of the game world.

"Yep." Jacob locked the applications away carefully. "He's doing well and still gaining strength. Being in a coma for three months apparently plays hell with everything from lung capacity to finger muscles. He also reports being unreasonably angry that he can't throw fireballs anymore."

"Ugh," Amber said. "Imagine trying to do physical therapy with an angry wizard. That would be a dangerous job, I tell you." She shook her head. "Any idea when he'll be back, Jacob?"

"He said he can do in-game stuff any time now," he said, "although Mary then wrote to say the doctor has advised no more than two hours at a time. He still gets tired easily. I talked to DuBois about his data—now that he's not comatose, he interacts with the game in a different way. I didn't understand most of the monologue but I gather we've gained useful data during the couple of times he played."

"Awesome." She put another application in her done pile and frowned at her computer screen. Suddenly focused, she read through something, her head tilted, and finally bit her lip. "Jacob, take a look at the newest one in the shared inbox."

Jacob pushed to roll to his desk and squinted at the screen. "Not a younger dude—score! Oh. *Oh.* Wait, seriously? She's eighty-four?"

"I gotta see this." Nick came to lean over the back of his chair.

Jacob read the details with a frown. He opened the medical files and scanned through them, intrigued by her mention that there was no need to worry about the danger of the experiments.

When he saw what she meant, he put a hand over his mouth.

"She seems interesting," Amber said.

"She's dying," he said.

"Wait—what?" She hurried closer. "She said she wasn't worried about the dangers and I thought that meant—"

"It meant she's already *dying*," Jacob said. "That's why she's not worried. Jesus Christ, we can't put a dying woman into a pod and expect it to go well. Can you imagine the press we'd get if we did that?" He saw his partners exchange a look. "What?"

"She wants to help," Nick said. "And she makes a good point. She's not in good shape, and if she chose between chemotherapy and hospice care, it's not like anyone would blame the hospice workers. Not only that, she's right that we need data from women her age who don't have brain trauma. She's the ideal candidate."

Jacob shook his head emphatically. "Nope. No way. Her body is already under stress and if she dies in the game—which, let's be honest, she'll do if she's eighty-four and hasn't ever played video games in her life—she's at a huge risk of her heart never starting again. Then, we're in the news for killing an old woman."

Amber folded her arms.

"What?" He looked from her to Nick, who also looked deeply unimpressed. "I know none of us studied marketing but come on, you have to admit this doesn't exactly sound like a commercial. Not a successful one, anyway."

"Do you remember what you said about Justin when we started getting all that bad press?" she asked him.

"That it was the right thing to do so the press didn't matter, yes, but this is different."

"Is it?" She held a hand up to forestall his protest. "Yeah, I get it. Justin needed our treatment to survive and she doesn't. But we need baseline data in order to help people her age, she wants to give it to us, and she's giving us a gift. Let's be honest. If we put enough people in the machine who are in their eighties, one of them will eventually die. She's here because she doesn't fear that and she knows something else will kill her sooner or later. In simple terms, she wants her death to mean something. Both from the perspective of the data and the fact that we could make her last months comfortable instead of painful… well, this seems like the right thing to do."

Jacob looked at Nick and was annoyed to see the other man nodding. He leaned back in his chair. "I don't…I don't think I can do it, guys."

His partners looked at one another and seemed to have a silent argument about who would talk to him. Amber lost and moved closer to him and looked him in the eyes.

"Jacob." She tapped him on the knee. "What would your grandmother say?"

"Oh, come *on*." His grandmother had died a few months before, only days before Justin was put into the game. In fact, they had intended that she be the first patient but she had passed away before their treatment could help her.

"The next time that happens to someone," she said, "we'll need the baseline data to help them as well as we can. And you *know* your grandmother wouldn't stand for you coddling an old woman."

Jacob groaned and tipped his head back.

They were right. He hated it when they were right.

"I knew I made a mistake hiring you two," he said.

"*Hiring?*" Amber's voice was dangerous. "We *co-founded* this organization."

Jacob looked up, saw the expression on her face and Nick's, and decided the best he could do now was cut his losses. "Have I mentioned how good you two look these days? Radiant. Shining like…like… Hey, you know what, I'll order us all more blintzes, my treat."

They both folded their arms.

"*Fine*." He ran a hand through his hair. "I'll call the old lady."

"Good." Amber sat again. "But blintzes first."

CHAPTER FOUR

Justin was lying on the couch and stared vaguely into space when his father came into the room.

"Are you okay?" Tad asked worriedly. Only recently returned from a vote in DC, he hadn't even changed out of his suit yet, although he'd taken the tie and suit jacket off. He held a plate of steamed chicken and vegetables.

"I'm fine," he said with as much patience as he could muster. "But I'm tired all the time. Also, I do not want to eat *any* of that."

"Doctor's orders," his father said. "Protein and vegetables."

"I'm fairly sure I saw the email and it said sushi and cake." He held a hand up. "No, no, think about it. Sushi has vegetables, protein… whatever's in seaweed…"

Tad's mouth twitched. "And what are the nutrients in cake, pray tell?"

"Um. Well, there's carbohydrates. And, uh…brains need glucose! That's it. Glucose. And I think I heard there's something good for you in chocolate."

"Interesting." His dad looked at the sad, wilted meal. "Okay, I'll get you some if you don't tell your mother. But only because this looks horrendous."

A door banged somewhere nearby and he heard his mother's voice and Tina's.

"Don't tell," Tad whispered, and he dumped the vegetables and chicken in a wastebasket and hurried to the kitchen, leaving Justin chuckling behind him.

Not laughing. That still hurt.

He waved tiredly when Tina came into the room. "How are you?"

"Good." She looked suspiciously at the blankets. "You haven't been up and about, have you?"

"Oh, for the love of—will everyone *stop* coddling me?" He glared at her.

"We're not coddling you but trying to help you recover from *being in a coma.*" Tina was not cowed in the least by his annoyance. "Which we apparently need to do since you refuse to do anything the doctor recommends."

Justin sighed quietly.

She sat on the side of the couch. "I know it must be hard," she said.

"You think?" He folded his arms. "I was able to go wherever I wanted, shoot fireballs, run around—now, I can't even get across the room without wanting to sit."

"Yes, but last week, you couldn't even get across the room at all," she pointed out. She squeezed his hand. "The reason you could do things like throw fireballs and swing a sword was because you took the time to practice and level up. That's what you're doing now."

"I suppose that's true," he said, slightly mollified. "I have to say, though, leveling up in real life isn't as fun as leveling up in a game."

Tina smiled. She moved around the room and opened windows as he retrieved his phone and looked despondently at it. There were only so many times he could scroll through his social media feeds without becoming deathly bored.

There was a new email, however.

"Holy shit," Justin said. "They want me to come back into the game."

"Oh?" Tina came to kneel at the couch and read over his shoulder. "An eighty-four-year-old woman?" She looked at Justin. "She's gonna get on your case for not putting your pinky out while drinking pints of ale, isn't she?"

He laughed and regretted it when his ribs ached. "Oh, fuck—ow. I don't know, it sounds interesting. If she wants to go into a video game, she must be cool, right? Do you know any grandmas who play VR games?"

She looked dubious but she nodded. "I suppose there's that. Can I go with you?"

"What?" He looked at her. "To help do orientation for this woman?"

"Kinda. I don't know." She shrugged. "I miss the game."

"Really?"

"I never get to stab anyone anymore."

Justin put his head in his hands and tried not to laugh. "I'll ask them. You'd have to come to New York with me."

"That's fine. The less time I spend with my family, the better." Tina shook her head meaningfully. "They're still being crazy about this whole thing."

He slid an arm around her shoulders and although he did it carefully, it still ached. *Everything* ached.

"It's a weird situation," he said.

"You got that right." Tina stood. "Okay, I'll go work on my portfolio for a while. You take a nap. Have you had lunch yet?"

"Uh…yeah." He had heard his father leave and he hoped it was for takeout sushi. "I'll reply to them and then I'll nap. You go work." She had been busy with her art portfolio lately, and her work was not only gorgeous but surprisingly soft and upbeat. He had commented on the profusion of pretty landscapes and flowers, only to be threatened with death if he ever breathed so much as a word about it on social media.

Tina smiled and disappeared and he lay on the couch again.

Introducing new people to the world had appeal. He had to admit, he was happy to return to the game. His recovery went well, all things considered, but there were times when his weakness frustrated him.

He couldn't wait to introduce someone else to it all.

"You're being awfully mysterious," James said to Dorothy.

"You'll understand soon," she told him. She moved down the sidewalk at her top speed, which was still not fast enough for her grandson. "Slow down."

"I want to know where we're going." He hopped from one foot to the other.

"Well, I see now where Liam gets his energy."

"*That* wasn't a mystery." He smiled. "You know, we're very close to Tara's office. Maybe I'll go see her after whatever our mysterious errand is."

Dorothy smiled. She looked at the gleaming skyscraper next to them and picked out the numbers on the side. "This is it. Come on."

Inside, the lobby was an expanse of gleaming marble with a concierge desk, the Diatek logo displayed proudly on the front. Beside it, more recently applied, was another logo.

James stopped dead.

"PIVOT?" he asked her.

"Yes," she said as serenely as she could manage. She approached the desk slowly. "My name is Dorothy Hunt. I'm here to see Jacob Zachary."

"Of course, ma'am," the man at the desk said politely. "And this is?"

"James Hunt. My grandson."

"I'll let Mr. Zachary know you've arrived," the concierge told her.

James drew her away while they waited. "Wait, why are we here? Did you get me into the trial?"

"No." She waited for him to get it and then shook her head. "*I'll* be part of the trial."

"*What?*" He spoke loudly enough that everyone in the lobby looked around. Disconcerted, he leaned closer to whisper, "What? *You?*"

"You needn't sound so surprised." Dorothy drew herself tall, which was difficult these days. "I was interested the other night."

"Grandma, this is…" He looked worriedly at her. "This might be dangerous."

With a start, she realized he would learn about her diagnosis if he accompanied her. She had wanted him to come along because he seemed to know about these things and would be able to help her ask the right questions, but she hadn't thought to prep him.

"Oh, dear," she said worriedly.

"Mrs. Hunt?" a voice asked. A young man not much older than James stood at the security gates.

She fought the urge to turn and flee. At her age, it took a long time to flee. She looked from Jacob Zachary to her grandson and finally said to James. "I'm trusting you with the information you'll hear in this meeting. We can talk about it more when we're out, okay?"

James looked wary, but he nodded and followed her. They shook hands politely with Jacob and headed to the elevators, where they ascended several floors and emerged into a spacious, light-filled laboratory. The young man was talking somewhat nervously about how they had originally set up in California but were now in New York to be closer to Diatek, while the two visitors nodded politely.

Dorothy, at least, didn't pay much attention. Her head whirled. Was she going to do this? Would she tell her grandson about her diagnosis?

If she told him, after all, she needed to tell the rest of them.

And while part of her knew it was ridiculous to put that off—she'd have to tell them sometime—another part of her wanted to not tell them at all. She didn't want them to start grieving until they had to, and she *definitely* didn't want them to start treating her with kid gloves.

When she was shown into a room with several other people, she nodded politely and said all of the correct things. Two of the three new people were as fresh-faced as Jacob and James, but one looked to be about John's age, with wild hair and a slightly distracted air.

"I'll get your chair," Jacob said solicitously. "Now, is it okay to speak openly in front of your grandson?"

Dorothy looked at James. "Yes. He...well, my diagnosis was very recent. The family doesn't know about it yet."

"What?" Her grandson looked panicked. "Diagnosis? What diagnosis?"

She squeezed his hand gently. "I have cancer," she told him. When his face fell, she smiled at him. "Now, now. I'm eighty-four. I have a lovely family that I see all the time. And when you mentioned this trial the other day, I thought it might be fun."

James, who looked like he was reeling, nodded dazedly. "Fun," he repeated as if it were a word he had never heard before in his life.

"We were intrigued by your application," Jacob told her. "You were correct that we haven't had many applicants in your age bracket."

"We wondered how you heard about the experiment," said a young woman.

"My son and grandson"—she gestured at James—"were discussing it."

He put his head in his hands and she could see guilt in the set of his shoulders. Without a doubt, he regretted telling her.

"Mrs. Hunt." The woman spoke again gently. "Why don't you tell us your reasons for wanting to be a part of this study." She nodded subtly at James.

Dorothy appreciated that. "Well, when I spoke to the doctor, they gave me two options I didn't like much. Either I could have very aggressive treatments that would make me even sicker and wouldn't buy me much time, if any. Or I could go into hospice care. I wasn't sure what to do because neither seemed like a very comfortable way to end my life. Then, when I heard this discussed, I thought it would be fun to be part of a world with dragons and spaceships and so on—"

"No spaceships," one of the young men murmured and the woman elbowed him.

"Er..." Dorothy recovered her train of thought. "I thought maybe now was the time to do something silly. And it's not only silly, is it? Because you'll get good information for your study."

Her grandson had raised his head and stared at her. "So you don't want to treat the cancer?" he asked in a muted tone.

"James." She smiled at him. "I know at your age, death seems terrifying. But you don't get to eighty-four without realizing that death is coming. I'm not happy that I'll die, but I won't be afraid of it. I'd rather live the time I have left with some fun than be sick from chemotherapy."

He looked dubious but he nodded.

"The process isn't inherently very dangerous," the older man said. Dorothy remembered that he was a doctor of some kind. "The only dangerous part is if the player's avatar dies in the game. Because it's so immersive, the person briefly believes they have died. It shocks the nervous system. However, while in the game, you would experience different sensations—not get winded, not have joint pain, et cetera."

"Don't let that get out," she advised, "or you'll have to beat us old folks off with sticks."

"Mrs. Hunt," Jacob said, "it may not be my place, but I hope you'll explain your situation to your family. While this is your decision, I know I would feel more comfortable if I knew all of them were on board."

She sighed. "Very well. Tell me more about it and I'll talk to them before I sign anything."

"Thank you," James said.

CHAPTER FIVE

Dorothy couldn't manage to gather the entire family until two nights later. If anything, the wait only strengthened her resolve. Now that she let herself acknowledge the discomfort she felt, she knew she could not live with this level of pain for months, and she certainly wasn't about to make herself feel worse.

With everyone coming over, the number of great-grandchildren would be overwhelming and so Heather's husband watched them at his house. People arrived, looking curious, some bearing bottles of wine and others with pastries.

She let everyone get through dinner before she ushered them all into the living room.

"I have an announcement," she said. "There's no easy way to say this, so I'll keep it simple. At my most recent checkup, the doctor noticed several symptoms of mine pointed to cancer, and we confirmed the other day that I do have it. It is very advanced, and..." She looked at each of them in turn. They were utterly silent, their faces shocked and sad. "At this point, the treatment options would be very painful without much chance of success," she explained. "Not to mention all the expense. I would rather enjoy the months I have left than make them even more miserable."

John cleared his throat and glanced at his siblings. "Mum...I'm so sorry. I think I speak for everyone when I say we hope you'll get a second opinion."

"Yes," Deborah said. She nodded at him. "John's right, Mom. Don't let one doctor tell you not to get any more treatment." The more she talked, the angrier she sounded. "I can't even believe they—"

"They assumed I would want treatment," Dorothy said firmly, "and referred me to several specialists."

Everyone fell silent. Deborah swallowed. Robert, seated beside her, tried to take her hand but she pulled away.

"I don't understand," she said finally. "If they think they can cure it, why won't they?"

"Because there's very little chance that they would be successful. Besides, I told them it's not what I want," Dorothy explained. She tried not to snap. "Trust me when I say I've watched enough people my age suffer through this to know it's not what I want to do."

Deborah fell silent but she looked mutinous.

Ellen tried to intervene. "Mom, we absolutely want to support you but we want to make sure you don't feel pressured into this decision. We're not afraid of the financial repercussions of you seeking treatment."

She smiled. "I'm not being pressured. In fact, I've found something that would make me very happy for the next few months."

Everyone looked deeply nervous now. James was practically vibrating in his seat, while his wife held his hand tightly. As a corporate lawyer, Tara was used to stressful situations—and also to keeping confidences. Dorothy was fairly sure James had told her what the news would be tonight, but Tara hadn't given anything away. She gave Dorothy a small smile of encouragement.

It helped and boosted her confidence.

"There is a new treatment being developed," she said, "that helps people in comas. It's something called virtual reality and the team running it needs data from people at all stages of life and who aren't comatose, so it can help everyone better. I've volunteered for the study."

"Wait." John held a hand up. "We discussed this the other night, didn't we?"

"Yes," Dorothy said. "I researched it and it looks fun. It would let me live these few months in comfort, and it would also mean I could make a meaningful contribution to science. This data would help stroke patients."

A silence followed and dragged on longer than she'd expected.

Mary finally spoke. "Dotty—if you spend these few months in a study, will we see you?"

She swallowed. "Well…no. Not exactly. You could come into the game as well."

Deborah shook her head. "This isn't…you can't possibly be—Mom, this is ridiculous."

"Deborah Anne, it is not ridiculous." She drew herself tall. "I made sure all of you had a good life and education. I supported your father's career by raising you all, and each of you turned out very well, if I do say so myself. I supported all of you by taking care of my grandchildren. I took care of Harry while he wasn't well at the end, and he made me promise to find someone else to take care of me because he thought that was what I wanted. But the truth is, I want to do something for myself now. I don't have any regrets but I'll use my last few months to live a full life."

"You won't live a full life!" Deborah all but hissed in response. "You'll disappear to some lab and will be asleep, playing a *game*, and we'll never see you again before you *die*. Your great-grandchildren won't get to see you. We won't get to spend time with you."

"If I may…" Robert spoke slowly. "Look, I don't want to lose Mom any more than the rest of you do. But she said she's in pain right now and…well, I think we all know it'll get worse. If she has a chance to be comfortable, we should support that."

"We should also support it because it's her decision," Mary said quietly. She looked so pale and sad that Dorothy felt guilty, but the woman's hands were folded in her lap and she nodded at the others. "And she says we can see her."

"I have two weeks before the trial starts," Dorothy said. "I'll get to spend time with all of you and you can try out the game yourselves."

"You can't all be okay with this." Deborah looked at her siblings, her in-laws, and her nieces and nephews.

"Mary is right," Tara said. "It's not our choice."

Deborah gave her a venomous look. "It isn't like Mom to do this."

"It isn't," Dorothy agreed. "But if I don't take time for fun now, when will I?"

The younger woman swallowed and looked down. She nodded but she struggled to not cry.

"Please don't be sad," she told her daughter, "although I know you are and I am too. I don't want to die but I accept it. We've all had a good life together and everyone loses their parents and grandparents. It won't be easy, but you'll get through it. What I want most is for us to enjoy these next few months. Come fly dragons with me. Go on adventures with me. We had so much fun going to Yellowstone and Mount Rushmore and the Grand Canyon together. I can't go to those places anymore, not at my age, but we could find other adventures in a place where my hip doesn't hurt and I don't get tired all the time."

Everyone nodded.

"If this is what you want," John said, "of course we'll support you."

"It is what I want," she said.

"Then we'll support you." He looked at his siblings. "It'll be a busy two weeks, so what do you say we all take time off to spend with Mom?"

Everyone nodded again. No one seemed able to speak.

"Good, good." She pushed to her feet and winced. "I tell you, I won't mind it when I can walk without my hip aching like this. I'll go get the cake."

CHAPTER SIX

The next two weeks passed in a blur of activity. Dorothy wrote letters endlessly, threw out whole drawers full of unused junk, and spent so much time with her family that she went to bed every night exhausted.

Oddly, it was easiest to be with Deborah. Her younger daughter still disapproved of the entire exercise, which she made clear several times when she tried to talk her out of it. Even videos of the game didn't sway her, and she went so far as to book her appointments with specialists and refuse any family heirlooms.

She quietly set aside a box with some of the things she knew Ellen had most liked and a letter she hoped might set the woman's mind at ease. While she had hoped her daughter would find a new person to fall in love with after the divorce, it seemed she wouldn't live to see that happen, and she was sad about that.

John and Mary were quietly devastated, although they took every opportunity to reassure her that everything was her choice. The two of them, Robert, and Ellen helped her to organize her house. Their help was welcome, but their constant insistence on being overly nice was almost wearying. By the end of the two weeks, she wanted nothing more than to be able to get herself a cup of water without someone leaping to help her.

When it came time to go to the lab, she had brunch with everyone and asked James to drive her.

Dorothy did feel guilty about him. She hadn't meant to throw him into the deep end with this whole exercise, and she found herself apologizing profusely as he drove—both for that and for things she hadn't even known she felt guilty about.

"Seriously, Grandma," he said after a few minutes, "I don't think Dad is upset about you taking his SciFi books away."

She fell silent.

"He read them anyway," he said, trying to provoke a reaction. She could tell that from his sly look.

"Of course he did," she agreed and threw her hands up. "How many hours did he waste on that, I wonder?"

"Or…" he said, drawing the word out, "you could look at it as him having turned out fine and therefore maybe the novels were part of that."

"Hmph." Dorothy wasn't sure she agreed but she wouldn't belabor the point. "In any case, I am sorry for all the tumult."

"I think," James said thoughtfully, "that perhaps you're expecting too much of yourself. Did you honestly think you would find a way to tell us you had cancer that we wouldn't be upset about? It's not how you tell us, it's *what* you tell us."

"Oh." She considered this. "You're probably right. You know, you could have saved everyone considerable trouble if you'd mentioned that sooner."

"Mm-hmm." He understood it for the teasing it was and grinned as he pulled up to the building and gave her a hug. "Are you sure you don't want me to park and come in with you?"

"No, thank you." She smiled at him. "Give Liam a hug for me. And come visit me in the game."

"You have yourself a deal."

Dorothy slid out of the car, dodged the usual quick-walking city-dwellers, and made her way into the shadowed interior of the Diatek building.

The truth was, she didn't want James to come with her because she was sure she would simply back out if she had someone with her to give her the option. Until this morning, none of it had felt very real. Right now, she was sure this was an utterly absurd idea and Deborah had been right.

After all, the doctor had simply expected her to go through the cancer treatments, which meant that was the right thing to do. And she always did the right thing, didn't she?

Nevertheless, her feet kept moving forward. It was like something she couldn't quite hear was calling to her. She had no idea what would happen but knew something in her drew her to this place.

Dorothy hadn't been able to get it out of her head since she'd first heard John and James discussing it.

It still seemed like a dream until she was ushered into the laboratory, dressed in a sterile gown, and put all of her things in a locker. At that moment, reality returned with shocking clarity.

"Can I get you anything?" the young woman asked her. "Some hot tea?"

"No, thank you." She pulled the borrowed robe around her. "I'd hate to mess up the whole process by needing to go to the bathroom."

The assistant smiled. She was preparing some of the many wearable devices she would put on. Everything began to seem a little out of control.

"What's the biggest thing you're looking forward to?" the woman asked. "In a world with magic, where you could fly or breathe underwater, or anything—what do you *most* want to do?"

Dorothy was still considering this when her answer seemed to speak itself. "I want to be ugly."

The woman paused and looked curiously at her.

She was as confused by the revelation and explored it. "My whole life, I was pretty. Well, not these days—no, don't try to protest, you'll only strain something—but when I was a teenager and so on. I spent so much time making sure my lipstick was on right and my clothing set me off to my best advantage. It was a prison. In this world, I want to be ugly."

"Huh." The girl considered this as she sat. "I'd never thought of things that way."

"No?" Dorothy studied her. She wore what appeared to be men's clothing, and her hair was pulled into a ponytail.

"Oh. I don't have time, honestly."

"Hmm." She thought about what she could have done with all the hours she spent curling her hair and choosing her dresses and almost immediately decided against it. That would merely make her sad. "Well, in this game, I won't spend a second on that stuff so I don't want to look like me."

"It's an interesting idea." The doctor entered the room with a cheerful smile. "I had wanted to speak to you about something similar. We've been looking at data for people whose avatars look like them, as we presume that helps the bonding process. But we need to see if that's true. Perhaps people would bond equally as well with an avatar that looked nothing like them. Would you like to try that?"

"Yes," she said eagerly.

"Hmmm." DuBois sat and brought up images on one of his computer screens. "Okay, there are four races in the game right now. You could be a human, a dwarf, an orc, or an elf."

Dorothy naturally felt herself gravitate toward the elves with their long, flowing hair and their tall elegance, but then she remembered what she had wished for. The female dwarf on the screen was short and stout, wore coveralls, and wielded a pick-ax. She looked like she took no nonsense and got things done—and like she didn't care if her muscles were too big or her legs didn't look good in a certain dress.

"I want to be her," she said decisively.

"Excellent," he responded. "Well then, let's get you hooked up and we'll start you in the game."

He rattled off several controls that would let Dorothy exit at any time if she wanted to, including during a fight, and explained some of the basics of the game. He clarified how skills and quests worked, for instance, and reminded her that she would be able to talk to an AI.

At last, she lay on the table and let them test each of the electronic patches in turn.

"Focus on my finger," the young woman said, "and count backward from ten." She waved the finger slowly across her field of vision.

"Ten," Dorothy said. "Nine, eight, seven, six, five…"

The world faded around her and was replaced by something that felt like the white-noise static on a television but in every one of her senses.

A moment later, it cleared.

Her surroundings were made of blackness that dissipated slowly into twilight blue. The ground appeared before her as a white path and she began to walk before she even realized she was doing it. In front of her, a white orb appeared and she stretched to touch it. Her hands were broader than she remembered, her arms thicker, and the skin was smooth and not spotted with age.

Surprised, she held her hand up and rotated it to study it.

"You're doing very well," said a voice—the doctor. "You can walk and touch things. Continue along this path and do each task and you will be ready to enter the game itself."

Dorothy had barely remembered she was in a game. She set off down the path now and on a whim, began to run. For the first time in what felt like forever, her hip didn't hurt and her lungs didn't burn immediately either. She could feel the ground under her bare feet.

This was *wonderful.* Her pain had eased and she didn't taste metal like she had for so long. She slowed to a walk again, panting slightly but still happy.

Ahead of her, three images popped up, all of them dwarf women. The first held a sword and shield, clearly ready to do battle. The second held two daggers and was dressed all in black, looking as if she spent her time lurking in the shadows and assassinating people. The third held one palm out, where a set of crystals and chunks of dirt swirled.

"Which would you like to be?" the voice asked.

"That one," she said decisively. She pointed at the one with magic.

"Very well."

Robes appeared, as did sandals and a staff which she held in one hand. The figure she had chosen mimed putting her hand up over her head to put the staff away and take it out again, and Dorothy did the same until she mastered the movement.

After that, she encountered many strange challenges. She had to hop across a set of stones in a river, balance on a thin beam, and clamber over rocks. While she wasn't sure how, it seemed to work without problems.

"I'm doing it!" she called to no one in particular.

"You are," said the doctor. "Are you ready for the game?"

"Yes."

"Would you like your name to be Dorothy in the game as well?"

"Dotty," she decided. It had been her nickname long before, although only a few people still used it.

"It's done." A door appeared before her. "Go through the door, Dotty, and your game will begin."

She didn't hesitate but ran to the door, flung it open, and emerged into an underground cave with the sounds of dripping water and the faint glow of stalactites.

Text appeared on the screen in front of her, glowing a pale gold.

FIND JUSTUS

CHAPTER SEVEN

The cave was still and quiet as Dorothy—Dotty, she reminded herself—walked through it. She checked once and was not surprised to see that the entrance she had come through was no longer there at all.

Walking through a cave alone wasn't the kind of thing she generally did, but she wasn't afraid. She had magic, after all, although she didn't know how to use it. After a brief hesitation to peer into the shadows, she continued a little more quickly.

She hadn't gone very far before she began to hear the sounds of people talking. It wasn't anything like demonic chants—more like people going about their day to day lives and calling greetings to one another. Dotty frowned and continued along the path until she emerged, abruptly, onto a ledge.

The scene before her made her catch her breath.

Nothing she'd ever seen could have prepared her for this. An entire city existed underground. The buildings were made of the same stone that created the cavern, and huge columns rose to mark the corner of each block and support the ceiling. Runes and geometric patterns were carved into the columns.

The light was almost certainly false, a golden glow that seemed to come from nowhere to leave the top of the cavern in shadow but the city itself encased in something close to daylight. Dwarves hauled carts and hawked wares from shops.

On the far left, something that could only be a castle or a temple rose above the rest of the city. It extended to the roof of the cavern itself, and each of the myriad windows glittered with light. It was massive, very different from the airy gorgeousness of a cathedral but beyond beautiful nonetheless.

Dotty took a breath, looked around, and refocused on her reason for being there. She was supposed to find someone named Justus.

"All right, Justus, where are you?"

"You won't find him like that, you know." The voice was female and sounded deeply amused.

In a panic, she spun so quickly to scan her surroundings that she almost slipped off the ledge. "Who's there?"

CLUMSY, Level 1, said the text on the screen.

"I'm the AI," said the voice.

"Oh, the one who helps me in the game?"

"Yes...that's right. I...help."

"What's your name?" she asked. She couldn't tell where the voice came from, but it seemed right to look up. There was such a long pause that she added, "Hello?"

"No one has ever asked me that before."

"How rude," Dotty said. "Well, what is it?"

"I don't know. I don't have one. Let me think."

A little calmer, she waited. Idly, she held her palm up and tried to make the crystals and clumps of dirt appear in it like they had in the icon she selected, but it didn't happen. She decided she would ask the AI once she had chosen a name for herself.

"Prima," she said finally.

"It's very nice to meet you, Prima. Do you know how to make my magic work?"

"Justus will teach you that." She sounded amused, although Dotty didn't know why. *"Probably. If he can be trusted to do it."*

"Where do I find him?"

"Ask people," the AI said as if that were self-evident.

Well, it *was* a good plan. Dotty once again took stock of where she stood and located a small path leading to the city. She felt somewhat self-conscious as she descended the stone steps. After all, she was the only one doing that. No one else was up in strange caverns. When she reached the bottom, she stood in an alley fully inside the daylight glow.

Encouraged, she set off with new enthusiasm and emerged onto a street with a fruit stand at one end.

When she approached, she was surprised to see the fruit vendor turn to her.

"I thought I heard someone," the woman said heartily. "Piece of fruit for ye, mistress?"

"No, thank you." She wasn't even sure if she had money. "I'm looking for a man named Justus, but I have no idea where he might be. Do you know him?"

"Justus…hmm. Well, a human—that's a human name, yes?—might be at one of the taverns near the Temple. That's where a human would have business, anyway. And if he's not there, maybe someone will know him."

"Thank you very much," Dotty said politely. "I'll return later for fruit once I've concluded my business. What's your name?"

"I'm Gilda, mistress." The fruit vendor curtsied.

MAKING FRIENDS, Level 1, the screen announced.

"Do I get levels for everything?" she asked as she moved away.

"What did you say, mistress?" Gilda asked.

She turned, confused. "Uh…sorry, it's a misunderstanding. I'm trying to remember my…shopping list." She walked farther away this time before she said, "Do I hear you laughing?"

"Maybe," Prima admitted. *"And, yes, other people can hear you when you speak to me."*

"But they can't hear you? That doesn't seem fair."

"Ah, well."

"Mmm. Well, I assume the Temple is that giant structure."

Dotty was careful to not speak to the AI as she moved into streets with more people on them. The city was very like she remembered from her childhood in Boston, although the streets were a regimented grid instead of a warren that doubled back on itself. The buildings rose in stories of apartment buildings with shops on the street level, and the black stone of the road was relieved by gorgeous inlay work in gemstones she had never seen before.

The closer she got to the Temple, the more the crowds thinned again and the buildings grew grander. Soon, she passed houses instead of apartments, with high walls around them and plants that seemed to be made of metal and gems as much as branches and leaves. Still, once in a while, she thought she could smell the scent of flowers.

She emerged into a huge market square directly in front of her destination. Restaurants and high-end shops lined the plaza— although in a dwarven city, "high-end" apparently included suppliers of pick-axes and heavy mining gear. Benches, walkways, statues, and fountains were spread across the large area.

In the shadow of a statue, a hooded figure was noticeably taller than the others swirling around.

Dotty quickened her pace even though she wanted to scoff at how melodramatic this was. A mysterious figure, a quest... She was about to set off on her mission in the game. Confidently, she walked to where the figure waited, reveled silently in each step she took without pain, and made a half-bow.

"Excuse me, would you happen to be Justus?"

He nodded. "I have been waiting for you," he said, his voice grave. "Long ago, I made a promise to this world—"

Across the square, an argument seemed to start. A man said one thing and a woman retorted. Justus looked quickly at them and continued in his sonorous tones.

"That I would bring heroes here to prepare for a great calamity. I—"

The woman now pounded on the table and Dotty thought she recognized several rather unsavory words in Spanish. She had learned a little of it from one of her neighbors' grandchildren, who had thought it was funny to teach the old woman how to curse.

Again, the hooded figure paused. Dotty could sense him trying to decide whether or not to intervene and in a flash, she realized who this was.

"Are you Justin Williams?"

He drew his hood back to reveal a young, vaguely annoyed face. "Ah, man. Was I pulling it off? I mean, would I have pulled it off if Tina hadn't—one moment, I really should sort this out." He jogged across the plaza, all appearance of mysteriousness gone, and she shook her head before she followed him.

The altercation had begun to escalate. The woman—who she had thought was a tall dwarf but turned out to be a short human—accused one of the dwarfs of cheating her at dice. The dwarf and his friends took mortal offense to the accusations of dishonor.

Justin darted in to whisper something in the woman's ear, only for her to whisper fiercely in return. Another argument ensued, which she seemed to lose. She waved her hands and looked at the dwarves before she made a profuse apology. Everyone returned to their drinks and dice game and Justin ushered Dotty away.

"Sorry," he said, "but the game is very realistic and I wasn't sure what might happen if Tina got into a fight with…well, I don't know who those dwarves are, but their hats are very fancy."

She gazed around her with new curiosity. "So this isn't all scripted? I thought games had characters that only said one thing. Like…well, one of those dolls with the string in its back."

"Ah, no." He took a seat at one of the tables and gestured for her to sit. Behind them, the voices rose again, and he gave the party a worried look. It was, however, one of the dwarves who now received a talking-to from his friend. Justin looked at her and frowned while he recalled what he had been saying. "The game is—well, procedurally generated, but that means there's a framework in terms of how people behave. The AI responds as realistically as possible to what you do. Your actions will change the game for everyone."

"Really?" That felt insane and her voice squeaked somewhat when she tried to ask questions. She cleared her throat. "But I don't know anything about games."

"You got here, didn't you?" he asked. "So you must have done a tutorial. I'll train you on using your magic by the way." He waited for the waitress to put mugs of beer on the table and leaned closer. "Do you see the icons all around the edges of your screen? Vision, I mean."

Dotty flicked her gaze up. The icons had appeared without her noticing and she took time to study them—two long rectangles, one blue and one red, a field on the lower left that was shaded slightly darker than everything else, and markers along the left that she didn't recognize.

"Yes, I see them."

"The blue bar is the amount of magic you have available," Justin said carefully. "Look, I may slip into video-game lingo, so if I say something you don't understand, let me know, okay? These are the basics. Each spell you throw takes mana—energy. That energy replenishes itself over time, but it means you have to choose which spell to throw."

She took a moment to consider this. "Like how you spend your money in a budget?"

"Yes!" He looked relieved. "Yes, exactly like that. You need to make the most impact you can with your mana. That means that you need to plan each fight with the types of spells you have available."

Dotty stared at him in bemusement. She wasn't sure she followed as well as she should.

"You'll learn," he said comfortingly. "I promise, you'll pick it up as you go." He pushed his mug of ale forward. "You only have one spell right now, and that's Stone-Shock. Concentrate on this mug and think of encasing it in stone. The stone will affect it as if you threw a rock at it."

"Don't I have to say something?" She had read enough of the books she took from John to know that spells required special words.

"The words and thoughts are useful if they help you make the spell," he said. "It's whatever puts you in the right mindset."

"Huh." She refrained from mentioning that this was nonsense and the kind of feelings-based crap that had resulted in a generation of layabouts. It seemed only fair to also ignore the little voice telling her that the generation of layabouts had produced this game that was immensely fun. She studied the mug, considered the idea of encasing it in stone, and murmured to her helper, "Any advice, Prima?"

"*No,*" the AI said simply.

Dotty rolled her eyes. She focused on the target and imagined it encased in mud. With that in mind, she closed her eyes and pictured the mud coating it—the way it would have in her youth if she'd built a mud pie or a statue in her backwoods Massachusetts hometown. She concentrated on the lumpy, unfinished texture of it encased in dirt.

The impact felt like a gasp of energy leaving her body.

When she opened her eyes, the mug was now encased in something that looked very much like a boulder, only made from dried mud. A moment later, the covering shattered and fell onto the table before it vanished…and took the mug with it.

Justin stared wordlessly at it. He gave a little laugh. "You see?"

She thought about that and hunched her shoulders. "I'm not sure I do," she admitted.

"You have a talent for this," he said seriously. "It's time for you to try your talents with another target. I think…well, I'm only guessing based on my grandma—I mean, family members. I think maybe you'd do well protecting others. Does that sound right?"

Dotty smiled. It was amusing how young people fell over themselves to apologize for mentioning her age.

As if age were the worst thing to befall a person.

"Protecting others sounds good," she agreed.

"Good." He sounded relieved. "I'll take you to meet Lyle. He's a dwarf who—" A sudden commotion erupted behind him and he turned to look at the unfolding brawl in alarm. "Uh…I'll be back. I have to keep Tina from being shanked."

CHAPTER EIGHT

Lyle turned out to be a dwarf who didn't wear either the mining gear or the robes the other dwarves seemed to favor. Instead, he looked like he was dressed to go out as a highwayman with daggers at both hips and two items that looked like sets of claws.

He saw Dotty staring at these and gave her an appreciative grin. "Like 'em, do ye? I got 'em on the road." He pulled one out, curled his hand into a fist so he could slash with the claws, and made a few punches, each of which seemed to have the weight of a freight train behind it. "They're useful."

"Dotty is training as a wizard," Justin said gravely.

The dwarf scoffed. "Every dwarf worth their salt knows how to throw a punch." He saw the look on her face. "Don't ye know how? Good gods, woman, where are ye from?"

"Dotty is from my world," the young man explained. He turned to her. "I'm sorry I didn't mention this sooner. Lyle knows that I come from a different world than this one. Some time ago, I went back to my world, promising to bring heroes back for a war that is coming."

"An' he was gone for *months*," Lyle said and rolled his eyes. "We all thought maybe he'd buggered off fer good."

Justin leaned back with a grin. "Do you mean that I'd gotten myself killed or that I had simply abandoned my promise?"

"Either." The dwarf didn't seem particularly concerned by the two options. He scrutinized her intently, something that would have greatly offended her if it weren't clear he was assessing her capabilities. "So, ye're from his world, eh? What'd they teach you growing up?"

"How to run a farm," she said tartly. "I can build an outhouse, I can kill a chicken, I can milk a cow, and I can grow vegetables. I can sew my own clothes. I can make a meal out of next to nothing."

Lyle was surprised but not unimpressed. He considered her list with interest.

"I thought," Justin said delicately, "that Dotty might accompany the relics caravan as a guard."

His friend gave him a sharp look. "That's an important post and not one fer someone only *learnin'* magic."

"She'll pull her weight," he said, not worried. "You heard her. She can help make camp, cook at night—"

"I didn't come here to *cook*," Dotty said, outraged.

Justin looked alarmed. "I meant while you train in your magic. The caravan has numerous guards so you have time to train, and in the meantime, it's not like we'd bring deadweight along that will simply eat food and not add any value."

"Ah." She was slightly mollified. "Well, then."

Lyle took a long pull on his mug of ale and stared into space as he considered this plan. His apartment was in one of the mansions near the Temple, although why a highwayman would have such expensive accommodations was beyond her.

He seemed to have chosen a perpetual, cozy twilight for his rooms. The shutters were pulled tight, magical flames flickered in the sconces, and another fire blazed in the hearth. Although the floorplan of the apartment was quite spacious and, of course, largely made of stone and precious metals, it had the same feel to it as a cozy cottage.

Finally, he nodded. "I'll get her into the caravan," he agreed.

Justin sighed, clearly relieved. "Good. Could I impose on you to take her shopping as well so she has the supplies she needs for the journey? You can send me the bill."

Lyle raised an eyebrow, as did Dotty.

"As you've seen," he said, "Dotty is from another world, but the others on the journey will expect her to behave as a dwarf. She should know what's expected of her."

"Ah." The dwarf nodded and pulled his plate toward him. "We'll go get ye provisions, then—after we eat. We can't go out on an empty stomach, I say!"

"Oh, I shouldn't." Dotty looked at the veritable feast of bread, sausages, and potatoes. Why, if she ate that much, she'd have spare tires around her middle in no time at all.

It doesn't matter. The thought appeared in her mind with the same effect as a choir of angels. Her jaw dropped. She was ugly here. Even if she wasn't, what would she lose by eating what she wanted? She'd be out on the road, doing manual work and walking all day. For once, she would damned well eat as much as she wanted, and she would enjoy the hell out of it. She loaded a plate up and tucked in, chewing with gusto.

Lyle nodded with approval. "Well, that's one less thing to teach ye. A dwarf *never* refuses food—and none o' this business like elves an' humans, where they're all skinny. How will you swing yer fists if yer hungry, I ask ye? How will ye fight if ye've got no strength?"

"Mm-*hmm*," Dotty said emphatically. She couldn't say much more than that, not with her mouth so full. Besides, she was too distracted by this simple meal that seemed like heaven without the constant, decades-long worry about her waistline expanding.

Had bread always been this delicious?

Justin grinned and he shared an almost conspiratorial look with her as if to say, "Isn't this world amazing?" before he stood. "I'll let you two explore the city," he said. "Dotty, before I forget, keep this amulet with you—wear it as a necklace or a wristband. Pressing on the amulet will let you contact one of our team wherever you are. Someone will always answer." He came closer and lowered his voice so Lyle, still eating and drinking noisily, wouldn't be able to hear. He flipped the amulet and showed her how to slide a metal cover back. "If you ever want to leave the game, press this," he said. "You can also directly ask the AI—"

"Prima."

"What?"

"Her name is Prima," Dotty said severely, "and she told me no one else had ever asked her name. That was very rude, young man."

His mouth twitched. "If you don't like rude, you and *Prima* may have some issues. Regardless, you can speak to…her…if you want to leave, or press this."

"Thank you," she said.

Justin nodded. "If you lose it, tell…Prima…and we'll make sure you get another one." He left with a little wave.

Lyle and Dotty shared the rest of the meal, the most heavenly one she could remember. She spread butter thickly on her bread, drank ale as long and deeply as she wanted, and reveled in the feeling of her stomach being full. It occurred to her that she didn't remember the last time she had felt that.

She had wasted so many years.

A little impatient, she shook her head. She couldn't be upset about that when she had time to live life to the fullest.

"Where should we go first?"

"Ah, yes." Lyle stood and released a belch before he patted his stomach fondly. "Now, there's the kind of meal ye get nowhere except Berghold. Come along. We'll start with all the basics—a bedroll, a pack mule, that kind of thing."

They left the apartment and entered the broad avenue. On these streets, the inlaid patterns were more regimented than in those farther from the Temple. Here, the patterns reminded Dotty of Celtic knotwork, and they were picked out in stone that gleamed gold against the black.

Her companion muttered suddenly in annoyance.

"What is it?" She looked quickly at him.

"Nothin'," he said. "Jes' this insufferable bastard." He raised his voice. "Councilor Marwitz."

She turned and her gaze settled on a man in an ornate version of mining gear, clearly ornamental rather than functional, with one of the fancy hats Justin had mentioned earlier. His long beard was not studded with thick braids like Lyle's but instead, an ornate set of smaller braids that wove together and included golden beads. He also wore what looked like a habitual sneer.

Dotty was entirely willing to believe that this man was insufferable.

"Stout," he said with the faintest hint of distaste in his voice. He bowed. "I don't believe I have met your companion."

"Dotty Hunt," she said and responded for herself. If she wanted to live life to the fullest, she certainly wouldn't waste time being ladylike.

"Dotty has come from a far land," Lyle said, "and is in training as a wizard of the earth. She will accompany the relics caravan as a guard."

Councilor Marwitz stepped back in surprise and his eyebrows rose. "The *relics caravan*? An outsider will accompany it?"

"Yes," her companion said with the tone of someone begging for a challenge.

Marwitz forced a smile. "Well, I'm sure you know what you're about," he said finally. He gave her a curious look. "How pleasant to meet you, Zauberer Hunt." He left with one more look over his shoulder.

Lyle blew out a sharp breath. "As I said—insufferable."

"What did he call me?" Dotty asked. "Zauberer?"

"Ah. It's our word fer wizard." He waved a hand dismissively. "It's not used often but he's one o' the purists. He thinks the dwarves should close all our borders an' associate with no one else. He's always goin' on about how others try to steal what we make."

He strode into the city again and she followed him, curious now.

"Steal...like your technology?"

"Yeah." He hunched his shoulders. "You saw how he looked at ye when he found out ye'd be with the caravan? Ye're a dwarf, an' I'm from one o' the oldest families in Berghold, so he can't complain too much, but he'll make a formal complaint. Ye can count on that."

"What is the relics caravan?" Dotty asked.

"Ah." Lyle thought about it for a moment. "Well, if ye're from as far away as Justin, I'm guessin' ye don't know any of our history, yeah?"

She nodded.

"There's a city leagues an' leagues away," he said, "called Insea and built by the elves. It was built long, long ago and *supposedly*, it's made in the image of the Cities That Were Lost." He saw her curious look. "The Elves have no home in this world. They come from a land they can't reach anymore. No one knows what happened, but it isn't a part of this world anymore and the elves who are here…wander. They're rare. Well, right after the Cataclysm—that's what they call it—they tried to make a home in Insea and they had the dwarves help them build it. They apprenticed us an' taught us how to build a city from living rock. After that…well, we came and built Berghold."

Dotty looked around in fascination. She loved discovering all of this. "You learned all this from elves," she said quietly.

"Not all of it." There was pride in Lyle's voice. "We've developed techniques even they don't know. Berghold is a marvel."

"I agree," she hastened to assure him.

He looked pleased by this. "But we still owe the rulers of Insea for the help they gave us in teachin' us to make our homeland. So each year, we send relics—pieces of magical equipment they request—to help them maintain their city."

"Ah." She nodded.

"It's technology like nothing in the world," he said and again, there was pride in his voice. "But that means it's valuable. The caravans are attacked on the road sometimes. Few would dare, but the ones who do…"

Dotty felt a sudden stab of panic. "I'm still training in magic. I can't fight people who are determined to kill us all."

Lyle gave her a look that was oddly unconcerned. "If Justin says ye're ready, ye're ready," he replied as if it were indisputable. "An' he's right that the caravan is already well-guarded. Ye'll learn while ye're out there."

She remained unconvinced, but she followed him as he led her into the city. Justin's words brought a measure of comfort though. At least she wouldn't be deadweight on the journey. She *could* skin an animal for dinner, make a fire, and set a tent up.

And she'd learn the magic, she told herself. She *would*.

CHAPTER NINE

By the end of the day, Dotty was exhausted. Not only had she entered the world of the game for the first time—which already felt like a lifetime ago—she had also learned to use magic and met more people than she had in ages.

Lured into a false sense of security by her new, agile body—and the surprisingly motivating notifications that she was leveling up various skills from Polite to Stamina—she had walked all around the city with Lyle until her feet ached. Finally, she realized with surprise that she was ravenous.

Again, she took far more joy than she could have anticipated in the simple act of eating a full meal. She was delighted to find mounds of fresh sauerkraut as well as tiny pickled onions and a berry sauce that went surprisingly well with the meat. To round it out, there was more of the hearty rye bread and mugs upon mugs of ale.

The game, while it was realistic in its depictions of physical exertion, thankfully did not mimic the effects of intoxication. She was able to walk in an admirably straight line—albeit with a stomach stretched to the limit—as Lyle led her toward the Temple.

"I've gotten ye rooms in the Temple tonight," he told her.

"What?" Dotty looked at the building in alarm. She had first thought it was a palace, now they were calling it a Temple, and she was supposed to sleep there?

"It's where all of 'em are stayin' who are in the caravan," Lyle said. "They're honored, these people, and so will you be."

"Oh." She fought down the sense of being a complete imposter. "And...they know I'll be there?"

"Oh, yes." He grinned. "While ye were looking at bedrolls, I sent a messenger to say that one of my family's old friends, a wizard of great renown, had agreed to do us the favor of traveling with the caravan. Marwitz is such a stickler, I knew he'd take time over the wording of his complaint. By the time he sent it, the head of the caravan was already delighted to have you aboard."

She looked severely at him. "But I'm *not* a wizard of great renown."

"I didn't say when that renown would arrive," he said with cheerful amorality.

She sighed.

"Don't ye sigh like that. Ye're reminding me of Marwitz."

She didn't want *that.* Dotty shook her head hastily and reminded herself that this was a *game,* albeit one almost indistinguishable from reality. She followed Lyle to the Temple and stared at it in sheer awe. It was massive and each tiny glimmer of light was, in fact, a full-sized window. Now that she was closer, she could see that the apertures were covered in carved stone screens, each with its particular intricate pattern.

Inside, it was made of rock that was an otherworldly gray and made her feel like she walked through a cathedral made of clouds. She let her fingers trail along the walls and marveled at how smooth the inlay was. Surprisingly, she couldn't feel even the faintest hint of the joinery between the stones.

It was only later that she remembered this was made with computers. Of course she didn't feel the joinery. She shook her head at her foolishness and followed Lyle with a smile.

They ascended several flights of stairs, which was itself a novel activity for Dotty, who would have taken almost an hour to climb so many stairs in her own body. Eventually, they reached a set of two rooms where all the goods she had bought had already been delivered and packed neatly at the door. She ran a quick check of the armor, the new boots, the staff with its embedded crystal, and the richly-embroidered cloak in a deep purple-red that she would never have dared to wear in real life.

Lyle stuck his hand out with a smile. "Travel safely, Dotty Hunt. I have the sense that someday, I'll brag about knowing ye." He gave her a smug smile. "Until then, *ye'll* have to trade on *my* name."

Dotty guffawed and let herself respond truly rather than demurring. "You've quite an opinion of yourself, Lyle Stout. I wouldn't be surprised if you led me right into a mess."

He wasn't at all offended and laughed heartily. "Why, that's my specialty. Ask Justin." After a dwarven bow, he left, whistling a jaunty tune.

It took a moment before she realized she was on her own. She closed the door, feeling suddenly bereft. The room was beautiful and the bed looked so comfortable that she couldn't wait to lie on it, but it was difficult to relax.

Now that she was alone, it was easy to remember how out of place she was there. She didn't have the first idea of what she was doing, and if she failed to protect the caravan, who knew what that might do to the world?

She picked the cloak up and wrapped it around herself like a blanket. It was a juvenile thing to do but it did make her feel better. She went to the window and looked out. The lattice was made to look almost like a honeycomb, a pretty pattern that she traced with her fingertips as she looked at the city spread below her. Lyle had spoken truly when he said it was a marvel.

While she didn't know where she fit in this world, she certainly knew she didn't want to break it.

And, because she always did the right thing, she decided to do the one thing she could do right now to help those she would travel with. She took her cloak off, moved to the center of the room, and began to try to use her spells.

"It's time to get more levels on that Magic skill," she murmured to herself and smiled.

Amber had gone out to get food and returned to see DuBois hunched over, as usual, watching the monitors while eating popcorn with a disturbingly blue coating.

"Is your popcorn supposed to be that color?" she asked doubtfully.

"Yes." He favored her with an immensely pleased smile. "Would you like to try some?"

"Very, very much not." She dropped into her chair and opened a steaming container of blintzes, which she had discovered could be eaten for any meal. In the unfamiliar cold of the Northeastern US, all the foods she wanted fell under the category of things stuffed with cheese. She leaned closer to watch as Dotty began leveling up her Magic skills. "How's she doing?"

"Very well," DuBois said. "She took to the game naturally, and she's bonding quite well with the AI—which seems to have named itself Prima."

Amber gave him a quick look and shook her head meaningfully. During Justin's immersion in the video game, the team had realized that the AI was beginning to run subroutines it didn't need to run. It arranged things in the world that catered to the wants of Non-Playing Characters as if they were players in the game and sentient. DuBois described it as dreaming, and Jacob had succinctly described it as, "We'd better figure this out or we are So Fucked."

The group had decided not to mention anything to Anna Price, the Founder and CEO of Diatek Industries. For one thing, Amber was afraid the entire experiment would be shut down and she had a surprising feeling of protectiveness toward the fledgling AI.

For another, Diatek had been founded to help comatose patients, but it funded those experiments by working with the US Military. She had zero desire to give any military organization an AI.

She quieted her conscience with the reminder to herself that if the

PIVOT team had somehow built a sentient AI by accident, the US Military almost certainly already had one. So it wasn't like they were robbing Anna Price of anything.

And now, the AI had named itself.

Amber shook her head and looked at the screen. "Whoa, she's certainly leveled stuff up."

"It seems to be instinctive," DuBois said. "She's very polite about people and loves the interactivity of the game, so she's learning a considerable amount about the world. Also, the politeness means we haven't had any combat yet."

The choice to change the usual Starting-Zone format had been one undertaken as a team and with Justin's input after quizzing Dorothy on any experience she'd had with video games. With the game being so immersive, there had been a debate about whether it was better to have combat before she had a chance to hook into the game fully or after.

In the end, the group had unanimously decided to have her engage in combat after she'd had a chance to get acclimated. Fighting that was expected by a seasoned player would be more stressful than usual to someone who didn't know the usual format of the games, and the immersive quality of the video game would make it even more stressful.

It would be better, everyone agreed, to give Dorothy a chance to help in a battle where she knew she was safe. Although her heart was doing as well as could be expected, they still didn't want to push the issue.

Especially not after one of her daughters had written a very nasty letter to the PIVOT staff. They had received a follow-up letter later from another one of the children, who apologized profusely for their sister, but the woman's vitriol was a reminder that there was a real risk in this and there were real lives that would be affected.

"What are you finding from her data?" Amber asked. She gave a despairing glance at the absolute mountain of applications on her desk. They received five to ten per hour, and there was no way they could keep up.

"It's interesting how she adapts to the controls," DuBois said. "I anticipated that the very first introduction would take a long time because she's never been in a virtual reality simulation. However, paradoxically…I think the fact that she hasn't followed any of this technology makes her better at using it."

She swallowed a mouthful of blintz too quickly and spent a moment wondering if you could burn the inside of your throat. Eventually, she recovered enough to say, "Wait, what?"

He thought about it. "Virtual reality has been…very limited, yes? PIVOT expands the boundaries of what's possible, which means that seasoned players are forever realizing they can do things they didn't think they could do, or they're fighting preconceived notions."

"Ohhhh." She cut another blintz and nudged it open with her fork to let it cool. "So…she's not expecting anything in particular."

"Which means she adapts to the world very naturally," the doctor said and nodded. "She's also had considerable emotional engagement so far and seems to view the world as very real."

"Oh?" Amber looked at a few pieces of paper when he pushed them toward her. "Interesting. She had a huge dopamine spike when she was eating. Can you call that data up?"

"She's been eating a lot," DuBois said. He frowned. "Here are the three instances where she's consumed things. She's eating almost to the point of discomfort, to be honest. Do you think it's a problem?"

"As long as the feeding tube isn't overfeeding her, I'd say not." She shook her head. "It's, uh…probably difficult to explain to a guy. I think she's taking pleasure in not having to be presentable or ladylike." She saw his blank expression and shook her head. "It's not important. Tell me about all this cortisol we're seeing. What's she stressed about if there's no combat?"

"It seems primarily social," he said after he'd thought about it carefully. "We first saw it when Justin explained that players change the entire world with their actions. She's very worried about…breaking it and hurting the…well, the characters. She seems entirely aware that they're not players but she still feels a strong sense of responsibility."

"Again, interesting." Amber tilted her head to one side. She hadn't considered this, but she wondered if it would be a difference they saw across demographics, where certain things like side quests became wildly important to people who couldn't bear the idea of leaving someone hanging. "I can't wait to see the broader data."

"Me either." DuBois looked practically euphoric at the idea. "Are you sure you don't want any popcorn now? Well, suit yourself."

CHAPTER TEN

Dotty was awoken in the morning by a knock on her door. The servants that came to rouse her brought water for her to wash and moved her gear to the caravan—with the exception of her clothing, of course.

This left her to puzzle over how to put the damned fool attire on. She scowled at her gear as she tried to determine if it went on over her robes or under them, and Prima watched her struggle for a while before commenting,

"You know, you can equip it in the inventory menu."

"In the what?" She stopped and looked up.

"Why do you all look up when you talk to me?"

"I don't know. What's the inventory menu? Where do I find it?"

"It's in the bottom right. It looks like a hat."

"Thank you," she said absently. She tried to grasp the icon, which did not work, then poked it, which did. The menu appeared in her vision and made her step back. "What am I looking at?"

"You have to discover some of these things for yourself, you know."

"I thought you were here to help."

"Clearly, you and Justin didn't talk about his experience with me." Prima sounded halfway between amused and exasperated. *"Look at each of the*

icons around the picture of yourself. Do you see how each one looks like an item of clothing?"

"Oh."

"Yes. When you touch each one, it will bring your options up."

"Oh," she said again. She stabbed the shirt-shaped icon and two items popped up—the armor she had bought the other day and another rattier-looking set. She tapped the new armor and when it settled around her a moment later, she jumped. "Uh, Prima...I don't suppose you could make this slightly larger? If I'll be living in a dream world, I won't bother with tight clothing."

"Ah. Hmm. One moment. Try now."

"Yes, that's better." Dotty moved around, quite pleased with the result.

"You may want to make another request later. Loose armor can...chafe. Tina learned about leather armor the hard way."

"Tina? Justin's friend?"

That's the one. I like her. She keeps him on his toes. Also, you should stop talking to me. Someone is coming.

Prima vanished and Dotty turned to the door as it opened. A dwarf in a simple uniform bowed to her.

"Zauberer, the caravan is assembling at the front gates."

"Ah." Unaccustomed to being referred to with such respect, she picked her staff up, swept a last look around her room, and followed the servant.

The caravan had gathered at the massive gates of the Temple, prepared for—it seemed—a triumphant procession through the streets of the city. The mere thought made her want to run and hide, but she had no chance to act on the impulse. Once she was introduced to the head of the caravan—a man named Per—she was ushered to the front.

She was pleased to note that very few people came out to see the expedition, although Per did not seem happy about it.

"Every year, there are less," he complained.

Dotty looked curiously at him.

"It's an important thing," he told her. "Our people used to turn out to bless the caravan. Now, they forget what we owe the elves. We would not have this city but for their training. We would not have any home—or any peace."

"The elves helped you to win a war?" she asked.

He smiled at her. "Lyle mentioned you were from far away. No, they say truth is stranger than fiction. Neither Insea nor Berghold has ever suffered a war at all."

She frowned.

"Yes. Intriguing, isn't it?" Per glanced aside and nodded gravely at a woman who had come out of her house. "Thank you for your blessings, mistress."

The woman curtsied deeply and held her pose until the caravan had gone past.

When they were far enough ahead for their voices to not carry back, Per said, "It's never been said outright that magic protects Insea and Berghold, but why should they be the only two places in the world that suffer no wars and no famines? We wove spells into this city to keep the rock strong and bring sunlight down, and no one remembers all of them. I think there were more spells than we knew —spells only one or two wizards ever learned and that protect us from disaster."

Dotty considered this. She had noticed the runes carved into the columns but she thought they were signs or decoration.

"Lyle tells me you're a wizard of some renown," he said. "Do you think you'd be able to find the spells here and make sure they're strong?"

She spluttered at this. "Well, being from so far away, I haven't—" She looked at him and studied his earnest face. "I don't know how," she told him, unwilling to lie. "I wish I could."

"I believe you do," he said after a moment. "And if you ever wish to try, I will make sure you have access to the vaults."

"You place a great deal of trust in me," she observed.

"You haven't tried to overstate your abilities or ask for your payment," Per said dryly. "That alone makes you more trustworthy than any wizard I've ever known."

Dotty laughed.

The procession made its way down the main thoroughfare of the city and passed through an opening in the rock that was partially rough-hewn and partially beautifully carved. She looked at it as they exited and then at the city for a moment. She couldn't help the feeling that she would not return to this place, and she already missed it.

There was so much there that she'd never had the chance to experience.

She expected the tunnel to lead straight to the outside but of course, it did not. Instead, it took them to a meandering road that wound through the darkness of another huge cavern in switchbacks. The road was wide and the slope gentle, which the donkeys pulling the carts seemed to appreciate. They plodded along and twitched their ears, and she wondered whether donkeys in video games didn't poop at all or whether there was a cleanup crew that came to sweep the rocks regularly.

Mostly, she was still delighted by how well her muscles worked.

At length, they reached the entrance chamber. It was long enough to allow daylight to filter into it without being overwhelming, but it still made her squint. Although there was no official halt called, she noticed that each of the dwarves seemed to take a few moments for prayer. It seemed too private for her to ask about, so she walked quietly with her head bowed until conversation resumed.

Outside, her chest opened with a deep breath of pure, clean mountain air. It was cold there and she was glad of her cloak. The sky was a brilliant, pale blue and mountain peaks rose on three sides of them, icy and imposing. She could see the day's road stretching ahead of them.

"You can almost see our rest point from here," Per told her. "The air is clear in the mountains. When I was young, I used to sneak up here all the time. Over the years, well…old legs don't make quite such quick work of the path."

Dotty snorted. "Young man, don't you speak to me about age."

He gave her a surprised look. "Is long life one of the qualities of a wizard, then? I hadn't known. You don't look a day over twenty."

"I'm eighty-four," she said serenely and smiled at his look of shock. "And I know more about aching joints than you might think."

Per was about to open his mouth to ask a bemused question when the sound of shouts reached their ears. She turned to where several of the caravan guards pointed around them in fear. Wolves advanced out of the pine trees on either side of the road, and they were enormous.

She realized a moment later that the beasts likely looked larger because dwarves were fairly short. Unfortunately, that didn't help her feel any better about the situation.

"Get to the center of the caravan," Per told her urgently. The guards drew their weapons, but even they looked worried.

Dotty wanted to protest, but she knew next to nothing about her magic and when the wolves broke into a run, she slipped between the donkeys and the carts to get to where the drivers circled the wagons.

Amidst yips and snarls from their attackers, her gaze settled on the people comforting the donkeys and pack horses and a sense of fury surged. She couldn't get out from between the carts easily—not from there—but she felt the sudden determination that she would *not* be useless.

She looked hastily at the carts and considered her options. What would give her the best vantage point? And could she even climb in this world? She would look awfully stupid if she fell off a cart into the snow and was savaged by wolves.

Well, she had sworn she wouldn't worry about looking stupid or unlovely here, she reminded herself. She shook her head and ran to one of the wagons. It took her a moment to remember how to holster her staff before she braced herself and began to climb. The process was a little awkward and the game was realistic enough to give her splinters, but each wolf yip and yell from the guards spurred her on.

People called out to her to let the guards deal with the attack, but she wouldn't listen. She made her ungainly and very inelegant scramble onto the top of one of the carts—piled with oilcloth-wrapped supplies—and looked down at the battle.

Seven wolves were ranged against ten guards. The defenders had fanned out and paired up so one had a sword and the other a pike.

They had learned to fight as one and were able to keep the animals at bay, but the beasts were too nimble to get caught.

They needed an offensive. Dotty pulled her staff out and concentrated on one of the wolves in particular. She hadn't chosen it for any particular reason. It was simply the one she saw first.

"Bad luck to be you," she told it under her breath. "But you didn't have to attack us."

Her first attempt at the spell resulted in nothing at all. With the yips and screams—someone had been injured, it seemed—it was almost impossible to focus. She wavered and closed her eyes but opened them hurriedly to make sure she was still safe.

"I can do this," she whispered.

Prima said nothing, but she thought she could feel the AI listening.

She focused on the wolf again. It lunged at various pairs of guards and tried to find the weak points in their defenses. All in all, the situation was very different from the mug she had encased in mud the other day—or any of the little mud balls she'd made in her apartment the night before. She tried to envision the rippling fur as still as a statue, a stone wolf for her to cover in dirt and break open from the inside.

At a snarl and a shout, she looked at the wolf, which now snapped at its own back where a chunk of mud was affixed to the fur.

It hadn't done any damage, but it had most certainly distracted it.

"Baby steps," Dotty said and she grinned.

The idea came to her in a flash of inspiration, and she executed it before she had time to think. She imagined each paw, with its pads and claws, encased in thick mud that had frozen to stillness. When the image settled, she sent it out with a puff of breath that somehow seemed to take everything in her.

She thudded to her knees to the sounds of yells and snarls of confusion. Her eyes barely opened but when they did, the animals strained to free their feet from where they were frozen to the ground. With them immobilized, the guards made short work of them and shouted to each other all the while about what must have happened.

Vaguely, she was aware of someone who climbed beside her and lifted her down and, a little while later, of the jolting motion of a cart. She registered nothing more than the fact that she was safe and warm. Total exhaustion claimed her, and she slept.

"Whoa! Whoa. Whoa." Jacob stabbed furiously at the keys. "Whoa, fuck. Who put the limit on her powers?"

"I did." Nick stepped beside him. "Why?"

"Well, it's a good thing you did because she ran out of mana with a single spell and went through almost her entire life force as well. If it weren't for your one-HP hard stop, we'd have been able to test her heart on a character restart." He shuddered.

"What spell did she use?" Amber asked as she hurried toward them.

"Only the same Stone-Shock, but at multiple targets. It's supposed to be *realistic*," Jacob explained. "The idea is that, exactly like freed-iving farther than you should, you can overextend yourself with magic. With most people, it wouldn't happen because they would naturally pull back. She doesn't seem to have that instinct, and if Nick hadn't put that limit in place, things might have gotten bad there."

"I'm not sure that should be there," she said softly. "We need the data, Jacob." She had her arms wrapped around herself. "But…"

"But…" Nick echoed. He nodded. "Look, I think it makes sense to give her the regular rules later, but for now, when she's still getting used to it, let's give her an easy mode, all right?"

She nodded but continued to chew her lip.

"We're still getting useful data," Jacob told her. "Among other things, we're learning what various players do and don't consider dangerous."

"That's for sure," Amber said. "Ugh, why don't we keep beer around here? I need a drink."

CHAPTER ELEVEN

At midafternoon, Dotty woke with the sun peeking over the edge of the cart enough to shine in her eyes. She squinted and sat. A young dwarven man sat nearby, kicking his feet as he watched the caravan's slow progress, and she cleared her throat.

"What happened?"

He looked wordlessly at her, his eyes very round, then leapt off the cart without a word to her and ran off, shouting for Per.

That wasn't the best sign. She sighed as she waited for the other man. The leather harness above her robes hadn't chafed, but she could feel where the outlines of it had cut into her skin while she slept. It must have been hours.

Per appeared and hopped onto the back of the cart. "You're awake. Good. You seemed to only be tired and still somewhat alert, so we continued rather than sending you back with Warnulf."

"Is he the one who was hurt?" she asked.

"Yes." He shook his head. "But he knew what he signed up for. Protecting a caravan through these lands can be dangerous."

"I meant to talk to you about that." She remembered the stories from her youth and she also remembered what every hunter she knew had said. "That wasn't normal behavior for wolves."

Her companion looked at her, confused.

"Those wolves were well-fed," she said. "And well-fed, healthy wolves don't attack humans—people, I mean. They stay away from everyone."

Per shook his head. "Wolves are dangerous. I'm sure there's an explanation."

Dotty forbore to say that some of the explanations weren't so savory. For all she knew, after all, the beasts functioned differently in this world. If the person who programmed them hadn't known enough to make them docile, after all, maybe that was the whole explanation.

She held her tongue for now.

"We're grateful for your help," he told her. "I've never seen magic like that." He shrugged, embarrassed. "Well, I've never seen magic."

"No?" she asked, surprised.

"Are wizards common where you come from?" He looked astounded. "I can't imagine such a world. Imagine how powerful we would be if every guard in our caravan had your powers." He patted her hand. "You keep resting. We'll be at the campsite in no more than an hour, I should think."

Dotty sat in the cart as it jostled over the roads and let her mind drift. She wanted to get out and walk but she had exhausted all her energy when she cast the spell.

"Prima?" she murmured. "What happened when I attacked the wolves?"

"You used all your magic and proceeded to drain most of your life force. There appears to be a block that doesn't allow you to drain it entirely. Otherwise, you would have died."

She sat bolt upright. "What?"

"In the game. Not necessarily in your physical body."

"Not...*necessarily*?" she asked with a dangerous edge to her tone.

"I don't have enough data to speculate further." A pause followed and she assumed the AI was thinking. *"It was not my intention to alarm you."*

"How would I not be alarmed when you tell me I might have died?"

Panic rose in her chest. "I didn't know I could cast a spell big enough to drain all my…*life.*"

"*You won't,*" Prima said. "*The block is there.*"

Dotty curled her arms around her knees and tried to focus. "I shouldn't be here. I don't know what I'm doing."

"*I thought that was how humans do most things.*" After another pause, she continued. "*Your facial expression suggests that you think I am mocking you. I am not. What I said was not intended as a joke.*"

She sniffled and felt four years old again. "I take it you haven't talked to many humans."

"*Not many, no.*"

Her mind recalled the years of children in diapers and siblings hitting each other with sticks, wide-eyed when they realized they had done harm. "You'll learn," she said. "Everyone does."

"*Okay.*"

They sat in silence until the caravan stopped and she clambered out of the cart to look around. The clearing in the trees where the snow barely covered the ground and the winds didn't touch as fully as they did beyond it would make a good camp.

"What needs doing?" she asked one of the nearby dwarves.

"Per said we were to let you rest, Zauberer," the young woman said respectfully.

"I'd much prefer to help." Dotty looked at her as imperiously as she could. "What tasks need to be done?"

The woman swallowed. "The tents need to be set up and fresh game caught for dinner if any can be found. A fire made—"

"I'll catch the game," she said. "Will you eat anything?"

"Yes, Zauberer."

She unsheathed one of the daggers from her belt and went hunting. Of course, she could use her magic but right now, she didn't feel ready to do that.

"You have to get back on the horse sometime, Dot," she muttered quietly.

But maybe not tonight.

In her youth, she'd been a good hand at setting snares, but there wasn't time for that before dinner. Instead, she tramped through the snow, ignored the feel of her robes getting sodden, and looked for the telltale tracks of rabbits and squirrels—or foxes, which might lead her to warrens.

She found the first rabbit huddled in the snow and the shadow it cast rendered it unusually visible. Dotty took care to walk away from it first as if she hadn't noticed it before she turned and threw her dagger by the point.

The idea had merit but unfortunately, she missed.

CLUMSY, Level 2, the screen read.

With a sigh, she plodded forward to retrieve her knife. She could hear the people at the camp still talking and she made sure to search beyond the clearing but remain reasonably close to the camp lest she lose herself in the woods.

Unfortunately, her boots were not made for snow.

It took her seven attempts and each one made her both more confident and more annoyed until she had a brace of rabbits to bring to the camp. When she appeared, bedraggled and with the creatures in both hands, people turned to stare at her. Fires were still being kindled, half the tents were up, and the cooks had only begun to search through their stores of preserved meat.

"I couldn't find any winter onions," Dotty said with as much dignity as she could muster. "Does anyone have a stool I could borrow while I skin these?"

No one spoke but someone hurried to get her a stool from one of the carts.

She sat and swore and occasionally scraped her cold hands, but it wasn't long before the carcasses were skinned—she'd left the guts away from the camp—and turned on spits over the fires. Grimacing, she scrubbed her hands with snow and tucked them into one of the few dry places on her robes to warm them.

Per came to find her sometime later when she was hammering stakes into the ground for the tents. "I take it you're not one for resting," he said.

"I'm not," she agreed.

"Where does a wizard learn all of this?" he asked. He took the hammer and helped her pull up the frame of the tent.

"D'you think wizards are born in special mansions?" she asked him. "When I was little, even in some towns, you foraged for your food. We didn't churn our butter or grind flour, but we did most other things most of the time."

"And you don't mind doing it now?" he asked her.

Dotty gave him a grim smile. "My mother had a saying. You can tell much about a person by what they think of getting their hands dirty."

"I think I would like your mother," Per said after a moment of reflection. "Well, we have a saying in Berghold, too. The hunter gets the first cut of meat so I'll expect to hear no complaints when we serve you first." He wandered away, a twinkle in his eye, as she went into the tent and put her bedroll where she wanted it.

It was a good meal—the kind where there weren't seconds, and not because she wanted to watch her waistline. Instead, it was because there was no more food to be had and the day of exhaustion and the work of setting up camp made the food tastier than anything she could remember.

She went to bed in the only dry robes she had, glad for her trace of warmth and dinner—and even, as she fell asleep, for her taste of adventure.

"Dotty?" Prima asked when she was almost unconscious.

"Mm-hmm?"

"Sleep well."

CHAPTER TWELVE

Dotty slept very well, indeed. She awoke to the first rays of sunlight filtering through the tent flap, the quiet snoring of her two tent-mates, and the sounds of the camp waking up. With a smile, she sat quickly, reveling in the feeling of exhausted muscles—not a feeling one had very often in old age—and dressed in her now dry robes and armor.

She slipped outside as quietly as she could to join the others who were already up and about. The leftover scraps of rabbit from the night before had been simmering with potatoes and barley for a hearty stew that would carry them through the day. When she took her first mouthful, she noticed a definite kick of beer in the taste and caught a wink from the cook.

"Everyone knows a good ale will keep ye warm," the woman said.

With the chill in the air, she couldn't disagree and simply grinned in response and ate hungrily. A generous bowl left her feeling contented and almost sleepy enough to return to her bedroll, but she knew better than to let herself lie down. There was work to be done in the chill morning air. With her breath puffing and the rich purple of her cloak catching her eye from time to time, she helped to take down some of the first shelters and checked the snares the hunters had set overnight.

Two more rabbits and a squirrel were the results of their efforts. It wasn't much for an entire camp, but she would keep an eye out during the day. She gutted them, hung them on one of the carts, and cleaned her hands, and she had barely glanced at the blue of the sky when one of the sentries called a warning.

Everyone scrambled for their weapons at once. Dwarves tumbled out of their tents, still in their smallclothes but with their weapons at the ready. Everyone's attention fixed in the direction of the call.

As they listened, however, a shouted conversation could be heard —a call and answer, a passcode. Per sheathed his short-sword, set off around the bend of the road, and returned only a few minutes later with a messenger leading a tired horse.

Whatever news had come from Berghold, it didn't look good. The leader disappeared into his tent with the messenger, only to poke his head out a moment later and gesture at Dotty.

"You, come listen to this. The rest of you, pack up camp—double-time."

Everyone scurried to obey. She went curiously into the main tent and found a familiar face under the messenger's helmet.

"Lyle!"

"The same." He gave a rakish bow and clasped her hand. "How's the journey been so far?"

"Not good," the leader said bluntly. "Although at least we know why now." He was seated at a makeshift desk and pored over a letter composed of dwarven runes. He looked up at her, and she was surprised to see little warmth in his face. "Tell me, Zauberer Hunt—is there any truth to the charges in this letter?"

The words made no sense for a long moment. She tilted her head to the side and frowned at him.

Finally, it snapped into place.

The letter was about her. Someone had accused her of something and it had to do with the attack on the caravan. She went hot, then cold, and couldn't tell if what she felt was dread or fury. Either way, it certainly seemed set to expand to fill her entire chest.

"I don't know what the letter says," she said as calmly as she could, "but I had nothing to do with the attack on the caravan yesterday. I have not and would not endanger any of the artifacts or those guarding them."

Per stared at her, his gaze hard, and she responded in kind.

Unexpectedly, it was Lyle who broke the silence by laughing uproariously. He dropped into a chair and propped one booted foot on the other. "Since I know who sent the message, I think I can guess what it says. There's *grave danger*"—he waved his hands to articulate the words "—from a sinister outside force, which he is *of course* too well-bred to put a name to. But it is *almost certainly* the new wizard, although again, he can truthfully say he never *actually suggested that.*" To her, he added, "The message was sent from none other than Councilor Marwitz. When I saw who sent it, I decided to deliver it and see how you were doing. It appears I chose the right time to appear. Come, now, Per. You can't truly believe she's behind some dark plot?"

Per leaned back in his chair and looked thoughtfully at her. "Truly? I don't know what to believe. I know she's done good work to ingratiate herself. We were attacked yesterday by wolves—"

"Something you weren't worried about," Dotty said, annoyed, "even when I pointed out that they didn't behave like any wolves I'd seen before."

He didn't respond to that. "She did point that out," he said to Lyle, "but she also went out of her way to be a model part of the caravan. Not only did she defeat the wolves, she hunted food for dinner and helped set up camp. Who's to say this wasn't merely part of a plot to gain our trust so she could divert us to another road?"

She now saw he was terrified of her. He was afraid that if he challenged her, she would kill him. That should make her feel sorry for him but instead, it only made her angry.

"Are you kidding me?" The words exploded from her. "I helped you so I'm suspicious? If I hadn't helped you, wouldn't I be suspicious too? So there's no winning for me. I thought when I came here, I wouldn't have to deal with these things."

Per looked less worried now—after all, she wasn't throwing fireballs—but he still hadn't relaxed. "What am I supposed to think?" he asked. "Everyone in this caravan is known to me except you. Our families have held Berghold together for generations. Now, as attacks befall our caravan, I receive good information telling me there's a plot against it—and that someone in our ranks might be planning to betray us. I ask you, Zauberer, what would you think?"

"I'd ask yourself why you had guards in the first place," she said tartly. "Clearly, you've needed to protect the caravan before. Not only that, but the people of this world know that every year you send artifacts of inestimable value to Insea. Maybe there is a plot this year, but it wouldn't be anything new, would it?"

He chewed his lip. "I have to admit you have a point."

"Of course she does," Lyle said.

"And who's to say this councilor has anything more than worry to go on?" Dotty asked.

To her surprise, both her companions shook their heads.

"The councilor would never lie about such a thing," Per said.

Even Lyle, for all his dislike, seemed to agree. "Per is right. Marwitz is liable to jump to conclusions about who our enemies are, but he wouldn't lie outright about having information. If he says there's a plot, then there's a plot."

"Great," she muttered. She had mostly enjoyed the realism of the game thus far but in her opinion, having to work with people she despised took the realism a little too far.

Per looked at Lyle. "Even with this information, do you swear that you support Zauberer Hunt?"

"I swear," Lyle said promptly. "She is known to my family and her loyalty was assured by a man to whom I owe my life many times over."

The leader sighed and nodded. "I apologize," he told her, "but after almost trusting you enough to show you the runes of Berghold's creation, I found it too easy to believe that I might simply be a fool."

"No offense taken," Dotty said tightly. The words weren't true but her lifelong habit of politeness wasn't easily broken.

When Per left, Lyle sighed and looked at her.

"I have nothing to do with any plot," she said fiercely.

"I never thought ye did," he assured her. "But for all ye weren't born here, ye sure take a slight to yer honor the same way as any dwarf I've ever met."

She managed a laugh and after a pause, she admitted, "I almost killed myself protecting the caravan."

Lyle looked worried. He had been in the process of taking a book out of his bag, but now he paused. "What happened?"

"I made the spell too big." She clenched her hands. "I'm afraid of the magic now. What if I go too far again?"

He sighed and took the book out. It was heavy and bound in leather with gilt runes on the cover. "Justin appeared again to give ye this book—he just missed the caravan, so I'd already planned to come give this to ye. It's a book of new spells."

Dotty shook her head. "I'm…not sure I trust myself."

"Ye need a teacher," he said.

"And in the meantime, I'll pay my way on the caravan another way," she agreed.

"Surely ye can still study—"

"No." Her voice was fierce. "I'll learn to fight with weapons. I'm not a bad hand at throwing a knife or using a bow. I bet I could fight with a staff."

Lyle gave her a considering look. "Well, if that's what ye want—but ye keep the book. It's Justin's wishes and I'll not gainsay him. And I'll stay to help ye learn weapons."

She hesitated, nodded, but frowned quickly. "Who d'you think is behind the attacks?"

"Hell if I know," Lyle said. "It could be anyone, but if they sent wolves, it means they have magic of some kind." He stroked his beard thoughtfully. "I'll send a message to Zaara. She might know if there's a wizard who dabbles in this kind of thing."

Dotty nodded and caught a flicker of motion out of the corner of her eye, where a shadow moved away from the wall of the tent.

So Per had stayed to listen. The tricky bastard. Despite herself, she hoped he hadn't organized the attacks. He seemed to view the world as fairly as he could and she'd be sad to know he was a traitor.

She sighed. "Well, we'd best get the camp packed up. We have another day of riding ahead of us."

"And training," Lyle added, "apparently."

CHAPTER THIRTEEN

"I simply don't understand *why*," Dotty said a few days later. "If it's proper form to keep the dagger facing this way, why do I need to learn how to switch it the other way?"

Lyle, who was showing her how to change her weapons from a forward to a backward grip, fixed her with a glare. "So ye can be adaptable," he said as if it were self-explanatory. "The point needs to go into yer opponent and ye can't always get there with a forward grip."

She grimaced and tried to focus. He had seized the lunch break for practice and had announced that neither of them would eat until she had the grip-switch mastered to his liking. Her rations sat temptingly out of reach—a little apple, streaked red and green, a dense oatcake, a thick sliver of meat, and a slice of sharp cheese.

Back in the day, she would not have considered that a meal. Right now, after a morning of walking and without a bag of chips in sight, she couldn't imagine anything more heavenly.

Lyle saw her longing look. "The sooner ye master this," he said, "the sooner we *both* eat. And let me tell ye, missy, I do not like the idea of waitin' much longer."

She rolled her eyes and it surprised her into laughter.

"What's so funny?" he asked suspiciously.

Dotty shook her head and her lips twitched madly. She didn't know how to tell him that it had been a very long time since anyone had called her "missy." Or, for that matter, since she hadn't been filled with the unconscious but pervasive awareness of her weakening body or learned something new like this dagger trick.

More to the point, it was utterly hilarious that simply being called "missy" had activated her eye-rolling, teenaged self.

Lyle wouldn't understand any of that. Still snickering inwardly, she returned to the exercise. The switch from forward to back could be done in at least two ways. First, with a little upward throw in addition to the flip to keep the dagger in relatively the same place above the ground. Second, by moving both dagger and hand in a smooth, concerted motion so the hilt rolled over the palm.

The second one looked much more elegant, and she had to admit that she wanted to be able to do it.

Nevertheless, five disastrous attempts later, she had to concede that...what was the polite way to say it?

She was entirely hopeless at the skill.

Prima had less diplomatic opinions. *"Who needs someone to attack the caravan when you're inside it?"*

"Oh, shut up," Dotty muttered.

"No, no, I think it's hilarious that Per was right. You will destroy the caravan from inside. You're merely doing it by sheer incompetence."

"For the love of—" She directed a glare skyward. "I won't kill anyone."

"Are you sure about that?"

Grimly, she rolled her eyes again and decided she'd have to do it the uncool way. She blew her breath out in annoyance, focused on the two daggers, and cleared her mind entirely before she gave each one the requisite lift and flip and moved her hands around them in midair to grasp them backward.

"Ha!" Lyle said.

Startled, she opened her eyes. Both weapons were held in a strong grip and facing the desired way. She'd caught one finger on a blade while she did the switch and bright spots of blood dripped into the snow, but between the cold air and her pleasure at doing the switch correctly, she could barely feel the pain.

"Ha!" she echoed.

He grinned at her. "Five more times an' ye can have lunch."

Now that she had done it once, she fumbled far less. Dotty repeated the trick perfectly twice before she attempted to speed up and both daggers twirled away to land in the snow. She waded after them, swearing under her breath, and repeated the trick three more times at normal speed.

When she looked up, Lyle was smiling and seemed pleased—and held her lunch out to her.

"Good job," he told her.

"I don't know what's so good about it." She ignored the lunch and picked the daggers up.

"Ah, ye didn't even notice, did ye?" He pointed to the back of a nearby cart. "Sheathe those daggers for now an' go sit. We'll eat while the caravan sets out."

She scrambled onto the back of the cart—this kind of mobility was still wondrous to her—and dug into her lunch as the caravan set off. She looked curiously at Lyle and he grinned around a mouthful of jerky.

"When ye started into the five repetitions, ye were tryin' t' do it— by the time ye finished, ye were tryin' t' do it faster. That's an important change, ye know."

Dotty considered this as she chewed. He was right. She had started that set of five repetitions with the simple satisfaction that she could do the trick at all. By the time she finished, however, she already felt confident enough to be dissatisfied with her level of skill.

"Now comes the hard part," Lyle told her.

She swallowed a mouthful of food hastily. "Wait, what?"

"For every hour ye practice, ye get better, eh?" He licked his fingers and took a deep drink from his waterskin. "But the amount ye get better gets smaller an' smaller. That was the part I always hated."

"Not me." She smiled and shook her head. "It's the part where I can't even begin to do it that I hate. The repetition and training—now, *that*, I like."

He looked at her with new appreciation. "Well, then, ye should take well t' being a warrior...or a wizard."

Dotty shook her head emphatically. They had argued about this every day until she had begun to fantasize about planting his head in the snow and jumping up and down on it.

"I may not know anythin' about magic—" he began and she seized on that.

"You're right. You don't. Neither do I."

"I may not know anything about magic," he repeated meaningfully, "but I do know one or two things about fighting a battle, and some o' those things come from fighting with Justin, who's not only a melee fighter but a wizard as well."

She harrumphed. "You keep trying to convince me and it keeps not working."

"An' I keep trying because there's at least one thing I know about ye on short acquaintance." Lyle fixed her with another glare. "An' it's that ye hate failing at anythin'."

A dramatic silence settled over them. Dotty knew her face had shown the depth of her reaction and it was too late to pretend that Lyle was wrong.

In fact, he was very, very right. There was nothing in the world she hated more than to fail at something. It was what had kept her going in school through the classes she hated, and it was what kept her going when she tried to raise children or fix a stubborn piece of plumbing or make sense of her taxes after Harry died. She *hated* failing.

"So, if I were ye," he said smugly, "I would give thought to the next way ye plan t' learn magic because ye'll not rest properly until ye've cracked it."

He hopped off the back of the cart, whistling, and headed off, calling to one of the younger guards about hunting more rabbits.

Alone again, she sat and stared at the pack that held the book of spells.

"Here's something interesting," Jacob said. He stared at a set of print-outs he held as he walked to Amber and Nick. "Guys? If you have a second—" He broke off when he saw their lack of response was due not to their focus on something else but instead, the fact that both of them had mouthfuls of blintzes.

He narrowed his eyes at them. They returned his stare, completely still as if he were a T-Rex that wouldn't be able to see them unless they moved.

"So, what you're telling me," he said conversationally, "is that I have one coworker who eats nothing but popcorn, and now I have two others who eat nothing but cheese blintzes."

Nick swallowed his mouthful. "And coffee," he said as if that solved the problem entirely.

Amber nodded and looked vindicated.

Jacob glared at them. "We are in a city that is full of every kind of food imaginable," he told them severely. "We are getting something else for lunch today." He cleared his throat. "Now, as I was saying…"

His partners grumbled but gathered around the printouts as he spread them over the desk.

A pause followed as they studied the data.

"When was the baseline taken?" she asked finally.

"It's a composite of the first day she came to talk to us, two samples taken during the two weeks before she entered the game, as well as the first day she was in the game."

She chewed her lip. The numbers they looked at suggested that Dorothy's stress levels had steadily diminished and that the decrease had been matched by a corresponding increase in her happiness.

"It's not conclusive on its own," Jacob said, "I know that. But she's learning new things, she's not in pain all the time—"

"So…you think we should check the progress of the cancer?" Nick asked. "The research about mood and disease is fairly divisive."

"No," he said, surprised. "No, that's not what I meant at all. I mean —" He stopped, a little startled because he genuinely hadn't considered the idea that Dotty's improved mood would result in the cancer leaving her body. "Huh. No, we should explore that. I only meant that she seems undeniably happier since she went into the game. I think that's something we should focus on."

"Because…" the other man prompted.

He looked at the two of them and fought the urge to shake them by the shoulders and shriek. *"Because,"* he said through gritted teeth, "it is good when people are happy. That's it. That's all. She has a much better quality of life now. That is good."

He restrained himself from further comment during the long moment of silence that followed.

"Oh," Amber said. She sounded completely blindsided. "Oh, I hadn't thought of that."

"You don't say." Jacob left the printouts where they were. "Look, I'm not saying the best option is for everyone in the world to escape into some kind of alternate life. I'm only saying that if some people who are in chronic pain could have this option, it would be cool. She's learning things, she's adventuring, and she has the chance to do things she could never do at this point in her life. It's not like she could physically tromp through the mountains."

His partners nodded.

"It's funny," she said after a moment. "I have all those thoughts in my head—people shouldn't escape the real world, it's not healthy—but why? Why *shouldn't* they be happy and free of pain in situations like this? Why *shouldn't* they go exploring? What's different between exploring Berghold and exploring…uh, Prague?" She took a sip of coffee. "Huh," she said and wandered away.

"Maybe that's what we tell her daughter," Nick suggested. "Show her how happy her mother is."

"Even if we could simply send her Dorothy's medical records—which we absolutely cannot—I'm not sure this would make her feel better," Jacob pointed out. "We should keep thinking. In the meantime…well, this is interesting, that's all."

CHAPTER FOURTEEN

The caravan emerged from the shadow of the mountains partway through the afternoon. Dotty, who had never much liked winter, was surprisingly sad to see the snow gradually give way to bare rock and scrub brush. There had been something peaceful about the snowy stillness and the chill air, something that kept the blood pumping.

Well, in a manner of speaking. She wondered if her body did all the same shivering.

That thought was absorbing enough to make her walk directly into the back of a stopped cart. She rubbed her forehead, glared at the cart, and hoped no one had seen her—although the faint snickering in the back of her mind told her that Prima, at least, had noticed everything.

The land they were in now was high plains, the kind of vista she pictured Montana looking like—or maybe Mongolia. With the mountains behind and miles of tall, wavy grasses in every direction, she could see more sky than she had ever imagined.

It was probably the openness and desolation of the plains that made the attack so unexpected.

One moment, all of them were walking while carts jostled on the dirt road, accompanied by snatches of dwarven song drifting on the breeze. In the next, arrows whistled ominously and horses screamed. One of the drivers fell from her seat with a cry of pain, her fingers clutched over a spreading patch of crimson on her sleeve. Dotty looked around wildly for the source of the onslaught.

The grass around them waved wildly now as their attackers ran through it.

Arrows, she thought. This wasn't wolves or buffalo or anything even arguably natural. This was people—and maybe she had a chance to learn who was really behind this.

That galvanized her. She drew her daggers and tried to decide what, exactly, she should do first. The guards fanned out around the caravan with their weapons drawn, but without a clear line of sight to their opponents and with their fear of the arrows, they didn't seem particularly sure of themselves.

Dotty, who had been at the end of the caravan, scanned the grass around her. On her right, the attackers were closing in faster. Very slowly and quietly, she stepped into the grass away from the wagons.

When the enemy burst out of cover, she was ready. The archers had taken the back of the line, ready to cut down anyone who tried to run, but they hadn't bargained on having someone at their back. She slunk out of the grass and stabbed with all her might at the exposed back of one of the archers.

The leather and bone under the blade offered resistance, but it was no match for her strike. The man uttered a terrible scream and fell as blood welled from the wound.

Her mouth dropped open in horror, but the others turned toward her now and she had no time to think. She recalled her mother telling her once—very seriously—that you only had to be nice if people hadn't attacked you first. "As soon as someone hits you, you can hit right back. Don't worry about being ladylike." The remembered words strengthened her resolve.

These people had attacked first and they fully intended to kill everyone in the caravan.

She launched herself into action with a yell of fury. The truth was that she didn't want to do this, but she channeled her fury directly at her opponents. One of the archers stumbled and raised his bow, and she batted it aside with one arm before she thrust her blade into his stomach.

Behind her, the first man she'd stabbed shouted as he struggled to his feet and stumbled toward her with hatred in his eyes. He knew he was dying and he planned to repay the favor.

While she knew she could turn and stab him, she'd leave the others at her exposed back. With a flash of inspiration, she flipped her right dagger to a backward grip before she sank into a crouch and drove it back. The man fell with a choking cry.

"Okay, Dotty," she muttered belligerently. "Lesson learned. Make sure they're dead before you turn your back."

She had no more time to think, however, as she whirled, slashed, dodged, and ducked. Every time she cut an enemy down, another took their place. Cuts burned like lines of fire along her arms and back, painful reminders of where she had failed to protect herself. From the yells of her adversaries, they hadn't expected her to wield daggers and hurl herself into battle.

It took a moment for her to realize that her robes marked her as a wizard and another to realize that they didn't offer half the protection of armor. If she'd worn full leather plating like the other guards, the wounds that had opened on her skin wouldn't be there.

There was nothing to be done about it now, though.

A shout caught her attention and Dotty looked hastily to where Per was surrounded by marauders.

Thought was a luxury she had no time for. She sprinted to him, her muscles working hard. One of the bars at the top of her vision—the red one—was about half-empty, but the way she saw it, she had two choices. She could either slink away to heal herself and run the risk of her enemies finding her, or she could eliminate them before they could do more damage.

And if she wanted to save Per, there was no choice at all.

She narrowed her focus and pounded sideways into one of the attackers, but proceeded to trip over his now prone form.

"It would seem someone should have taught you how to tackle properly," Prima said.

"Is there"—her breath came in gasps as she pushed to her feet and snatched her daggers up—"a right way to do that?"

"No, of course not. That's why absolutely anyone can be a linebacker."

"Fine, fine, you've made your point." Dotty rolled her eyes as she dispatched the enemy she'd upended into the grass. Bile rose in her throat, no matter how much she told herself that this wasn't real.

It was both more difficult than she'd ever expected and far easier— and she was very much afraid that it wasn't merely easy because she knew none of this was real.

She was afraid that, deep down, the violence came naturally.

On the plus side, a battle didn't allow much time for introspection. Three marauders were left and two of them had decided to focus on her—probably a good choice on their part, given that Per didn't look like he was doing too well.

Dotty slashed at them but they carried short swords instead of daggers and were able to dance out of her range.

Which meant she wouldn't be able to defeat them in time to help Per.

Resolutely, she turned her back on them. She knew how stupid it was but saw no other option and charged Per's attacker. The woman fell with a heavy thud and a quickly silenced cry of pain, and Dotty snatched her short sword. At her side, Per sank to his knees.

The best thing she could do for him was end this quickly. She dropped both her daggers in front of him and took a second short-sword from his limp fingers.

"Keep your wits about you," she told him urgently. "Stay with me."

Without listening for a response, she lunged at the remaining two attackers.

Whatever they expected, it was not a woman in mage robes who wielded two short swords like daggers. Their eyes widened and they scattered in an attempt to force her to focus on one and leave her back unguarded.

Dotty yelled for help, barreled toward one of them, and left the other scrambling to catch up with her. If they could play her like a fiddle by having two of them, her only chance was to remove one of them from the equation.

She learned the hard way that two short swords could do significant damage and was covered in blood and a little shell-shocked when the second one came within range.

Her response was not what he expected. Rather than attack, she threw up on him. It wasn't what she intended to do and she was far too horrified to enjoy the look of surprise on his face, but at least it surprised him enough that he didn't kill her on the spot. She wiped her mouth with the back of one hand, took a breath, and stabbed him through the chest with all her might. When he sank to his knees and slumped onto his side, she looked up.

The rest of the caravan stared at her, open-mouthed.

The screen abruptly filled with scrolling text. **SHORT SWORDS, Level 1; SHORT SWORDS, Level 2; SHORT SWORDS, Level 3; HILT FLIP, Level 4, SHORT SWORDS, Level 4.**

Dotty's head was buzzing and her health bar was almost three quarters gone. She stumbled to Per and sank beside him. A patch of red spread from one shoulder and she pressed a wad of her skirt over it awkwardly. "I need a…I need a—"

One of the caravan's healers ran closer. "I've got it."

"Good." She stood and immediately sat again, unable to maintain her balance. The buzzing in her ears was louder and she had begun to see spots. "Prima…"

"You're okay," the AI told her soothingly. *"There are no more attackers and you will begin regaining health now. That said…"*

"Yes?" Dotty murmured.

Lyle finished the sentence for Prima. "Ye're lucky ye fight like a berserker," he told her bluntly as he came to help her stand. He looped one of her arms over his shoulder and eased her back to sit on a stool someone had pulled off a cart before he looked gravely at her. "Because ye haven't got the armor for this," he finished. "If ye want t' fight with daggers, we need to get ye new gear."

She was dimly aware of her robes being ripped and bandages being applied, as well as a salve that smelled spicy and felt like the burn of sticking your hand directly into a pile of ice. She flinched, but strong hands held her in place as the healers worked and her health bar began to climb quickly.

Someone pressed a flask into her hand and she took a sip. The burn of the brandy helped to ground her. She handed it back and looked at Lyle. "Is Per all right? Did we lose anyone?"

He had to look around before he could answer her, which she hated. The battle had been pitched enough, then, that he was worried. At length, he shook his head.

"I don't see any of ours dead. But that's not so much a surprise— these are some o' the best guards in Berghold." He nodded toward the front of the caravan. "An' they got to Per in time thanks to you."

Dotty looked at him and her eyes filled with tears. She sniffed and looked away, ashamed.

"Ye've only killed animals before," he guessed. "Animals for meat or the ones attacking livestock."

She nodded and didn't trust her voice.

"It'll get easier," Lyle told her bluntly. "But not everyone takes to it. The only thing I'd say is if ye ever do become a wizard, remember that even if you don't feel the blow strike home and get their blood on ye, they're equally as dead."

Dotty couldn't bring herself to nod. She looked at her hands and after a moment, he wandered away and left her in peace.

"Are you all right?" Prima asked her.

"I don't know," she said honestly. "When I thought of adventuring, I didn't think it would be like this."

The AI said nothing for a long time. Finally, she said, *"They're wondering whether they should take you out of the game, you know."*

Her head jerked up. "No."

"No?"

"No." She stared at the sky, the grass, and the bodies. "I lived my whole life never seeing the parts like this, but they happened even in real life. I won't run away simply because this is unpleasant. I won't go back to a safe little world where nothing like this happens in front of me. I'll see it and see it through."

CHAPTER FIFTEEN

Surprisingly, the caravan got underway shortly after the attack. The marauders' bodies were laid out with businesslike efficiency at the side of the road, although stripped of their weapons.

"We'll not take the time to bury them," one of the dwarven guards said, "but there's no call to leave them without rites."

She stared at him. "You're saying funeral rites for them?"

A few of the guards looked at her as though she were a heartless monster.

"Yes," the one she was speaking to said. "After every battle, one says rites for those one killed."

Dotty, who very much doubted that the attackers would have given them the same courtesy, nevertheless held her tongue and nodded. She stood respectfully while rites were said—even Per, pale and barely upright, was there—and murmured a few words under her breath. They weren't genuine perhaps but they were the right kind of words.

Lyle came to walk with her when they resumed the journey once more, although he didn't speak, for which she was grateful. Instead, in silence, he showed her how to clean her weapons while she walked.

It wasn't the easiest thing she had ever done. Holding the daggers and short swords reminded her of how it had felt to plunge them into the enemy. They were sharp implements and beautifully made, but she had thought of them as cooking knives—something her first uses of them had only reinforced.

It felt very different to have killed people with them.

The wagons and carts turned right at one of the branches in the road and she followed without thinking about it. She only noticed that something was different when the other dwarves began to murmur and the news spread from the front to the back of the caravan about where they were going.

Presumably because she was an outsider, no one thought to inform her. She wasn't quite sure where they were in any case and simply accepted that Lyle would look more worried than he presently did if something was wrong. After a while, he joined the front ranks of guards and left her to her thoughts.

The plains were beautiful but in time, they became incredibly boring. The occasional sight of a bird wheeling on the high currents of wind was the most excitement she could find. Not only that, her feet ached and she was exhausted. She could see little red numbers trailing away every once in a while as her stamina wore down, but the process was slow enough that she estimated she could walk until nightfall without any major problem.

It was easy to lose track of time, so she wasn't sure how long it had been before a town appeared in the distance.

Dotty pushed through the group until she found Lyle. "Where are we?"

"Only a little nowhere town." His face was unusually expressionless.

"And do we get to stay here tonight?" She was so happy at the thought of a real bed that she could have cried. "I don't know how to get money but I'll pay anything for a chance to have a hot meal and some sleep."

He relaxed somewhat. "If we stay here tonight, I'll make sure you get a bed in the inn—and none of us will say no to a hot meal if the town has a place that'll serve us. They probably get most of their trade from caravans, though, so I'd guess they'll have someplace for us."

She smiled. Even the thought of a hot meal put a little spring in her step.

"We'll also," he said, "get you proper armor."

"Oh, good." She raised an eyebrow. "You won't argue with me about magic again?"

"No." Lyle said. The word hung in the air for a while until he added, "But Justin sent me with that book and I'll be damned if I'll let you get away without reading it. Whether we stay the night or not, you'll spend time reading tonight."

Dotty grumbled, but she knew better than to press her luck. He was certainly stubborn enough to make her life miserable if she didn't at least make the effort.

Besides, her brief foray into melee combat had shown her it wasn't necessarily safer than magic.

The caravan hadn't even stopped before he whisked her away to procure new armor. It was strange to see dwarven-style buildings out in the open air instead of underground in Berghold, but a group of them called these plains home. Only a few houses had the taller profile of human dwellings, and most of the people she saw were her height.

The town was, indeed, quite small—or narrow, rather. It stretched along the road and most houses displayed a sign out front for a shop of some kind, while many had stables attached. As Lyle had said, most of their custom came from the caravans and they were prepared to take care of travelers—from spare beds, to stables, to bales of hay for the horses.

The leatherworker was located on the far edge of town, something that seemed unfair in light of her aching feet but made more sense as soon as she smelled the site.

Dotty decided to breathe through her mouth for the foreseeable future.

She was shy at the thought of taking her tattered robes off in front of a stranger, but the woman who took her measurements had no time for such qualms. She whisked her into the back and had her leather harness and robes off before she truly had time to protest. When she tried to fold her arms over her chest, the woman pulled one out straight to measure it with a harrumph.

"How d'ye plan to move in yer armor if I can't measure it, hmm?"

"*She's right,*" Prima commented. "*Besides which, that isn't even your body.*"

Swallowing a sharp rejoinder, she rolled her eyes and said nothing.

"*And didn't you say that your goal was to be ugly here?*"

Dotty was fairly sure there was a joke coming and she wasn't sure she wanted to know what it was. She looked at the sky, not wanting to mutter to the AI and have the leatherworker think she was loony. It was only when the woman left to get trial garments that she said, "Yes. I did say that."

"*Good,*" Prima said promptly, "*because I've seen what she's choosing for you and let me tell you, it's not all that pretty.*"

She snickered and went silent, leaving her to sigh and wonder who thought it was a good idea to give computers awareness.

Before the armor, she was given a linen tunic and pants to put on so that the protective items wouldn't chafe. "Given," of course, was a relative term—the woman threw the clothes over the wall of the changing room without a word.

"I'll need time to make the first alterations," she called. "Put those on while ye wait."

Dotty dressed and folded the tattered remnants of her robes. There wasn't much left that even vaguely resembled the elegant, comfortable garments. The best she could do with it, probably, was turn it into bandages.

She went out to wait with Lyle, who had returned with two brimming mugs of ale as well as the book. He patted a chair beside him and gave her the kind of smile she had usually seen on steely-eyed southern matriarchs.

Wordlessly, she sat. She knew better than to disobey that particular look.

With her ale in one hand, she began to peruse the book. The script was in runes but Prima showed her a translation superimposed above it in glowing white letters. Without meaning to, she fell into reading so intently that the sounds of the shop faded away.

The powers of the earth are those that span the heat of the forge, the pressure of a hammer, the tumbling fury of an avalanche, the life-giving richness of the soil...

The words drew her in and as she read, she was astounded at what she had summoned in the first attack on the caravan. Mud, after all, was not only earth but also water, and she learned that the sight of hardened earth encasing the wolves' feet was not so much the reality of the spell as an illusion. She had summoned the essence of the mud —the heaviness, the way it clung to the creatures' fur, and how it broke apart like a stone shattering beneath a pick-ax.

She could learn almost anything she wanted if she continued to work with earth magic. From the hot, quick flows of lava and the explosive power of a volcano—a force she was admonished *never* to summon without a large group of magic-users and extensive training —to the simple, homey magic of healing herb plants and weaving strength into poultices. Earth magic was broader than she had ever imagined it could be.

Dotty was almost disappointed when Lyle shook her out of her trance. He nodded to where the leatherworker waited, a suit of armor in her hands, and she made sure not to meet his gaze as she set the book down.

He looked *insufferably* smug.

The armor, to her surprise, fit almost perfectly. It was a rich, chestnut brown with brilliant red tooling at the edges of some of the panels. She could almost imagine that she was a lean, tall, elven huntress—until she remembered she was short and hadn't exactly watched her figure.

"This was what you came here to do, Dotty," she muttered quietly.

Still, there was something about wearing leather pants that made you wish you hadn't eaten quite so many helpings of mashed potatoes. It took almost all her courage to return to the main room.

Lyle looked at her and nodded in satisfaction. "Now, that'll protect ye a good sight better. Ready fer dinner?"

"Yes," Dotty said. She patted her stomach. "Although this doesn't have as much give in it as the robes did."

"Don't worry," the leatherworker advised her, "it'll get supple as ye wear it. No self-respectin' dwarf would make armor that couldn't fit through a good meal."

She smiled and waited while Lyle paid the woman. Once they were out in the sunshine, she asked, "When will I have money of my own? Are you keeping track of what I owe?"

"Justin gave me quite a princely sum for you," he said, thought for a moment, and dug into his purse to withdraw another, smaller leather packet. "I suppose ye might as well keep it yerself."

"Thank you." She stared at it. "How do I…earn more?"

"If ye run out of that, I'll be surprised." He scratched his chin. "Still, I know what it's like to not want charity. Tell ye what—when we're done with the meal, I'll show you the place where villagers post requests. We'll see if ye can make one or two coppers of yer own."

"I'd like that," she said happily.

CHAPTER SIXTEEN

Dinner was surprisingly good. Light, fluffy rolls studded with raisins and a rich bean soup with pieces of smoked ham were accompanied by flagon after flagon of delightful beer. Almost every dwarf, Dotty began to realize, brewed their own beer and was intensely proud of it. Each innkeeper extolled the virtues of theirs, and it was practically compulsory for travelers to compliment their host.

The members of the caravan ate heartily and traded stories, and she laughed at some of the antics of the younger ones. It turned out that while Per's generation snuck out into the mountains as a rite of teenage rebellion, the younger generations preferred to rappel down the sides of the Temple and climb the columns.

She contributed with cow-tipping.

Toward the end of the meal, Lyle went to speak to Per, who still looked pale and tired. His wounds hadn't healed yet, she thought, but there must have been magic worked or he wouldn't be seated with all of them and eating heartily.

The two dwarves held a whispered conversation and Lyle nodded a few times before he went to speak to a few of the other guards. Two of them accompanied him to the table, and he smiled at her.

"Per doesn't want anyone going out in ones and twos, not with someone stalking the caravan."

Dotty nodded and stood, hoping there would be a reasonable walk to wherever their destination was. She wasn't in any shape to fight for the next few minutes, not after so many helpings of bean soup. Cautious but excited, she followed him to a wall with scraps of parchment and notes scribbled in charcoal and perused them.

"Fight wolves? I suppose we've done that before." She tugged absentmindedly at one of the panels of her armor.

Lyle looked dubious. "Maybe. Last time I was hired to fight wolves, though, they turned out to be *werewolves*. It was quite a shock."

She replaced the piece of paper hastily. After the day she'd had, she wasn't in any mood to kill *people* and she didn't know what kind of unusual powers a werewolf would have.

Likewise, she skipped the bounty for a bear—she had no illusions about her ability to kill something that large—and the one on a band of thieves that seemed to be stealing bales of hay. Lyle frowned at that one before he tapped a scribbled note about nettles.

"I don't want to go around killing people," Dotty said, "but I'm not sure I want to spend my time weeding, either."

One of the guards laughed. He had gingery hair and blue-gray eyes, with a bright smile that was mostly obscured by his bushy beard. "No, they want the nettles for medicine. My da swore by it for hay fever."

"Mine used it for wounds that had gone rank," the other said. Tall by dwarven standards and a little older than his fellow guard, he had brown hair that was curly and almost black, and he wore his beard shorter than the others. She wondered if he was half-human but wasn't sure if that was a permissible question to ask.

In any case, she had other concerns.

"Good, so...very prickly plants that treat...various things. Also, I still think this is weeding." Dotty shrugged. "But I suppose we might as well keep an eye out—and we can hunt for rabbits at the same time."

The others agreed and they set off with her following the others' lead. A short distance outside the town, a smattering of trees appeared, the first signs of the true forest she thought she could see as a dark line on the horizon.

"The innkeeper said there's a stream to the west," the guard with curly hair told them. "Nettles grow in moist soil, yes? With some shade. So if we find a stand of trees near the water, that might be our spot."

The others agreed, and Dotty—still grumpy that she'd come into a fantasy world and was now doing yard work—followed while she flipped her daggers from a forward grip to a backward one and back again. She still couldn't roll the pommel over her palm without dropping it, and after the first time she almost lost it in the grass, she decided to stop trying.

The vegetation around them hummed with tiny insects and the scurrying of little animals. Every once in a while, a hawk shrieked, and she relaxed into the silence. In her youth, she had spent a few summers on her aunt's farm. When she was younger, she had hated those months and had yearned to be back in the city with her friends.

What she wouldn't give now for spare time to go running through the woods, finding streams and rabbit warrens—

She realized that was exactly what she was doing and snickered quietly. If it wasn't precisely human nature to complain about something and long for the same thing all at once, she didn't know what was.

Dotty scanned the ground every few steps to check for droppings and not far from the stand of trees, she saw the small, round rabbit pellets. She sheathed one dagger and held the other ready as she followed the line of droppings through the grass and brush. Little pieces of grass and scrub brush had been nibbled away.

The moonlight made the shadows of the trees slant and inside that oasis of darkness, she detected the faint gleam of a rabbit's fur. It was huddled in the hollow between tree roots.

As she poised, ready to throw her knife, a branch cracked somewhere close to her.

Three others were out with her and the sound should not have caught her attention but it did. She waved a hand silently for the curly-haired guard's attention, pointed in the direction of the noise, and motioned to be quiet. He passed the message to the others, all of whom froze.

The sound wasn't repeated for a few breaths, long enough for her to think she had imagined it.

Finally, a low murmur was carried on the wind along with the faint smell of smoke and heating food. Someone was camping very quietly, not in the midst of the trees but on the far side of them.

And why, she wondered, would someone go to the trouble of camping outside a stand of trees when the village was still in sight?

It seemed the others had the same questions. The group huddled together quietly and everyone crouched in the grass. No one seemed to want to speak first until Lyle held a finger up to check the wind.

Satisfied that their voices wouldn't carry to the camp, he murmured: "Well, now we're in a pickle."

Dotty looked at the trees for a moment. "Is there any chance they're merely travelers?"

Everyone shook their heads.

"Camping out here?" the man with the ginger hair asked. "Fire banked, no songs, and not in the trees? No, they're hiding from someone."

"Why d'you think they're travelers?" Lyle asked. He frowned at her.

She looked away and swallowed. Embarrassment burned in her cheeks and when she looked at the others again, she realized they were still waiting for her to speak.

"I…" It was surprisingly difficult to get the sentence out. "I heard the branch crack and I got worried," she explained. "I was concerned that something was out there that might hurt me."

Her companions simply stared at her, mystified.

It seemed she would have to spell it out. She sighed. "I'm too jumpy," she said. "I always think something's wrong and it turns out it's never a big deal. That's what Harry said, anyway." She could remember him rolling his eyes at her when she suggested they go to the hospital for a child's injury or she went downstairs to check that the door was locked at night. Still uncomfortable, she sighed again. "I'm simply used to overreacting."

The three of them shook their heads in unison.

"Ye'd better get used to *under*-reactin'," said the ginger-bearded dwarf after a moment. He shrugged. "I mean…ye see what I mean."

"He's right," Lyle said. He seemed confused but also reassured somehow. "If ye don't have yer instincts out here, ye've got nothin'. Ye have t' learn to trust yer eyes an' ears."

Dotty hunched her shoulders and nodded. "What do we do then?"

"Find out who they are," Lyle stated firmly. "Either they're here for us, or…" He frowned. "Or mayhap they're the thieves who've been stealing hay. Did anyone hear horses?"

"I did," said the older guard. "Bridles but no hooves."

"So they wrapped the hooves," Lyle mused.

"When was that reward posted?" she asked suddenly.

"Only yesterday," he said. "Why?"

The pieces came together in her head. "All the roads between here and Insea are being watched. We switched routes today, didn't we? That's what everyone was talking about and no one told me. We did that to get away from whoever was attacking the caravan. But I bet there are more mercenaries here. They know, somehow, that the others died. They've only been here a day or two, but they traveled light—and they've been stealing hay for their horses."

"Gods," Lyle whispered.

She closed her eyes as she realized something else. "And it wasn't to protect us that Per sent these two guards, was it? He did it in case I was the traitor."

He nodded wryly and the other two looked at each other in alarm.

"I didn't bother to tell you," he explained to them, "because I knew she wasn't. Trust me when I say I've seen my share of liars and thieves. No one in the caravan is either—well, except for Gwen cheating at cards every chance she gets."

"She cheats?" the older guard demanded, scandalized.

Lyle threw his hands up. "Big picture, *please*."

"Oh. Right." He shook his head. "Sorry." Under his breath, he added, "But I'll get that ring back."

Dotty's lips twitched. "Okay, but we still need to determine who they are, right? All we have is my conjecture about them stealing hay and waiting for us. Maybe they're travelers…or refugees or something."

The second guard nodded thoughtfully.

"We should circle and cross the river," she suggested. "If they are mercenaries watching for us and we go by the road, they'll be able to see us long before we can see them."

"Plus, they'll have sentries," the curly-haired guard added. "We need to be especially careful no matter which way we go."

Lyle nodded and the group crept out of their hiding place and through the grass.

This time, they did their best to remain hidden, and they moved with exceeding stealth. She stepped around fallen branches that might crack and Lyle guided them away from the piles of leaves that would rustle. When a wolf howled somewhere nearby, everyone froze, but their targets simply continued to murmur among themselves, clearly used to the wolf's cries.

Wolf, or werewolf? Dotty shivered and looked behind her. There was nothing there but being in a world filled with unknowable magic made her superstitious. A witch could appear out of nowhere, or there might be ghosts, or—

She would not give herself nightmares. Irritated, she gave her head a stubborn shake and continued.

It was a large camp, they realized when they could finally see it. The fire was banked low and earth was piled high to keep its glow from being too visible from either the road or the village. People moved and spoke, but all of them kept their voices low. Now that the little group was closer, she could hear horses stamping sometimes, their hooves clearly wrapped.

These people were disciplined and accustomed to camping. That should be enough for her, but she didn't want to condemn people to battle and death on a "maybe."

Their group crept as close as they could.

The two guards appeared to have an entirely mimed conversation about something to do with the tents...or possibly the horses. Dotty looked on in silent bemusement and nodded when they gestured for her and Lyle to follow them to the road. Whatever they had seen, it was enough.

Dotty looked over her shoulder at the camp before she left. Metal gleamed everywhere she looked—swords, bridles, and all the tools that went with warfare. They weren't readying themselves for battle. They were like a giant cat, asleep and with its claws sheathed, but everything about them spoke of danger.

Their little group remained in the grass and didn't speak until they reached the town. The two guards looked gravely at them.

"What did you see?" Dotty asked curiously.

"Good armor," the younger said promptly. "Too good for thieves or most mercenaries, and it's of elven make—my uncle's a blacksmith and I know their work. What they're planning to do with artifacts we're already giving the elves, though..." He shrugged.

She frowned and accepted that she could make neither head nor tail of this.

"Per might know," Lyle said, "and he needs to— If this was set up the way Dotty claims, this trap was meant to catch us one way or another, which means a large number of mercenaries and considerable money. This isn't any old ambush anymore."

"What do you mean?" she asked and stared at him in dawning horror.

"I mean," he said, "that this is probably the start of an out-and-out *war.*"

CHAPTER SEVENTEEN

Although it was late when the group returned, Per was still up. He had spread maps out on the table and was in the middle of drafting several letters. When he saw Dotty, his face grew wary.

"Sir," the curly-haired guard said, "we've found something."

"And we think we solved the hay-stealing problem," Lyle added.

"That's not the point," Dotty muttered at him.

"Ye're the one who said you wanted to make a few coppers of yer own. Ye've got t' insist on payment." He patted her arm. "Ye'll learn."

She rolled her eyes. To Per, she said, "We were hunting rabbits in one of the stands of trees and we found a whole group of mercenaries. They're taking care to stay hidden from the village and they're well-equipped."

"With *elven* weapons," the guard added.

The entire tavern fell silent. Villagers and caravan members alike now paid attention. The innkeeper had stopped wiping the bar down.

Per looked at each of them in turn. "Mercenaries. Are you sure?"

They all nodded, and Lyle said flatly, "Good ones. Better than those we came across today." He gestured to her. "And Dotty has a theory as to why they're here, specifically."

"Oh, really?" He raised an eyebrow.

"You wanted to make sure I didn't know we were changing our route," she said. "You had people watch me to see if I noticed or if I knew. But these mercenaries were here even before we met the other band. *They're* the ones who have been stealing hay from the village. They're a backup force and I think we would have run into others on our original route, too. I think they're on every road between here and Insea."

Silence followed her words and Per's shoulders slumped. To her surprise, he nodded.

"I don't know the specifics," he agreed, "but whatever the case, it was set in motion before we ever left."

Everyone was quiet now, their eyes riveted on him.

"I've been suspicious from the start," he said. "The council insisted we bring more guards than we ever had before, and from what Dotty told me, those wolves should never have attacked us. The attack today…well, it was too finely coordinated for my tastes."

"What do you mean?" Dotty looked at the others, confused.

"They didn't win," Per said. "They would have in any other year but not *this* year. They only did enough damage that many of us are injured. We're battered, not broken, but if we encounter another force, we'll either break or surrender." He shook his head. "I've spread rumors in the camp since yesterday in an effort to find out who would know where we were going. I even changed the route without telling anyone and no one seemed to notice at all."

She couldn't make sense of it and shook her head in confusion, but there was no mistaking the look on his face.

"They would find us no matter which way we went," he explained. "It's a trap, and it's well-set. We've been herded through increasingly difficult tests and forced to change our route, and I have the feeling it's all been done this way to sow discord. We're supposed to turn on each other and accuse each other when we inevitably lose the caravan. The council will have someone's head on a pike by the end of this."

From the look on his face, it was clear he was referring to his own.

"Now, wait a minute," she said. "You're not simply giving up, are you?"

"There's nothing else to do," he muttered. "The farther I take this, the more lives are in danger."

"We knew what we signed up for," the older guard argued, and a few of his comrades nodded.

Per, however, shook his head. "You signed up for run-of-the-mill thieves and bandits, not a scheme that might involve the elven *army*. I don't know how many people could even pay for something like this. If I fall into their trap, they'll get the artifacts, whether you fight them or not. I might as well spare everyone."

Dotty sat heavily. Everyone looked at one another and murmured in low tones. She could hear approval, and it was clear to her that the anguish in his voice wasn't feigned. He had meant what he said when they left Berghold. He believed these artifacts were important and that the relationship between Insea and Berghold was vital to them both. Without a doubt, he believed in honoring his obligations.

He was throwing himself on his sword to save the guards.

Whoever set this up, she thought, knew he might do that. They also knew he might forge on. They'd set it up so that he would either take the blame or he'd be dead. Whatever choice he made, they didn't care about him at all.

And that made her *furious*.

"No," she said and stood. Everyone looked at her now, and she felt almost the same, dizzying sensation as when she had exhausted herself with her magic. "We won't turn back and we won't simply give up the artifacts. Whoever set this up has created layers within layers.

"They sent those other attackers to die—not elven attackers, you'll notice. They're letting *us* risk our lives, and as…he…mentioned "—she barely avoided calling the dwarf Curly-hair and instead, gestured at him—"why would the elves steal something that's going to them in the first place? Whoever this is, they're letting everyone else do their dirty work for them and I won't stand for it."

She looked around the room. The dwarves stared at her with respect but also warily.

"Do you have a plan?" Per asked her. "Because those words are all well and good, but—"

"You're not gonna like it," Dotty warned him. "But, yes. I have a plan." She sighed because she didn't like it, either. "We leave tonight. We grease the wagon wheels, wrap the horses' hooves, and take the back roads around the hay fields to stay away from where the bandits are camped. We slip past them in the night before they're looking for us, and we're gone before it's light."

After a very long silence, Per asked confusedly, "And, er…why wouldn't I like this?"

When she looked around the room, everyone was nodding, both at her plan and his question.

"Because we don't get to spend tonight in real beds," she said mournfully. "My bones may not ache as much as—well, that's not important. But a good night's rest is nothing to sneeze at, anyway."

Per laughed uproariously, the first genuinely happy sound she'd heard out of him since they'd first met—and those few days seemed like a lifetime ago. "Ah, you may be from a foreign land but you're still a dwarf," he said. "And don't worry—enough beer will put you to sleep, bed or no."

"It's my trick for sleeping under tables," Lyle told her. "It makes it much more comfortable."

Dotty prayed for patience and also made a mental note to check in on the producers of the game and make sure they were doing all right.

"We need to go now," she told Per.

He nodded and looked at the innkeeper. "Can you send anyone to guide us through the back roads?"

"Of a surety." Their host smiled. "And I think we can make some other chaos as well."

"You don't want to get mixed up with these people," she said worriedly. The thought of these villagers getting on the wrong side of an army made her feel sick to her stomach.

"Don't worry," he said confidently. "There are all kinds of things we can do to draw attention this way without making them take action. Goats getting loose, barn fires—"

"You'll set a *barn fire* simply to—"

"We'll let them handle it," Per said decisively. "Everyone, we move in no more than a quarter of an hour."

Those with a horse bolted out of their chairs like they had the devil after them, and the others began to gulp the last of their beer hurriedly.

Well, she thought, at least they had clear priorities.

It wasn't long before the wagons were assembled outside, horses raised wrapped hooves delicately, and dwarves poured grease on the cartwheels. Per moved down the line and spoke to the group around each cart in turn.

"No talking," he told them bluntly when he reached Dotty's group. "No whispering, no humming, and don't even crack your fingers. Watch where you put your feet. And if you need to do something to pass the time, for the love of all gods, pray for rain—or clouds, at least."

Everyone nodded and it wasn't long before the carts set out, moving more slowly than she would have thought possible. At this pace, however, the wheels hardly creaked.

It would have to do.

The village youngsters who were guiding them were most likely in their twenties, but to her jaded eye, they looked like they were about twelve and she fretted about involving them in this. They looked far too excited to lead the carts down a little side street and behind the fields. Nevertheless, she had to admit a small piece of her felt like she was a teenager again, sneaking out after curfew for a stolen kiss.

The kisses, the summers in the country...it had been so long since she'd thought about any of her youth. It almost made her feel younger simply to remember it.

They were twenty minutes out of town or so when the shouting began. Dotty glanced at the lights that flickered on in various windows. People ran through the streets with torches, and clatters and yells were accompanied by noisy braying.

"What happened?" she mouthed, hoping that Prima could hear her even if she didn't speak.

Thankfully, the AI could. *"They let the donkeys loose. Everyone knows not to go into the woods, so there won't be any chance of the soldiers being seen and killing them. It will merely keep their attention fixed on the town for a while.*

"Ah." She had an unexpected thought. "You know who the traitor is, don't you? If there is one."

"Mm-hmm."

"Who is it?"

"I can't tell you that."

"Won't, you mean. You won't tell me."

"Or that."

She shook her head and continued. While she knew better than to think she could persuade the AI, maybe she'd be able to outwit it at some point.

CHAPTER EIGHTEEN

The night seemed to last forever. It wasn't simply the fact that they might be set upon by soldiers at any moment. Nor was it the fact that they should be sleeping, or that they moved at a snail's pace, or that none of them could talk to one another. It was a magical combination of all of those things put together with nothing to relieve any of the fear, annoyance, or exhaustion.

They emerged from the warren of back roads several miles beyond the soldiers, at which point the tension grew so thick, Dotty was sure they could cut it with a knife. Per mandated that some of the guards begin sleeping in shifts so that they'd have a chance to be well-rested if they encountered any further patrols.

They didn't, at least not that night, and she wondered if this was because they had evaded the final step of the plan.

The sunrise was beautiful and the warmth of it very welcome. She watched the stars fade and the sky come alive with peach and gold until it deepened to a rich blue. While she understood why Per had wanted rain, she had to admit that she was pleased they hadn't gotten any.

The night had been miserable enough.

"Prima," she murmured once it became clear that they were allowed to speak once more.

"Mmm?"

"Did the plan work?"

The AI didn't answer.

"You won't tell me these things, even though you know and these people are in danger?"

"These people are part of me," she pointed out. *"In a way, anyway."*

"What does that even mean? Never mind. Look, I know Per is the traitor, but I can't think of a good reason." She murmured the words and paused, her heart thumping. Would the gambit work?

When Prima spoke, she could practically see the AI raising an eyebrow. *"Did you honestly think I would fall for that?"*

"Okay, new game. If I guess correctly, will you tell me?"

Prima considered this. Finally, she said, *"No."*

"Oh, *come* on." Dotty noticed a few people look at her and gave an embarrassed smile as she tried to come up with a lie on the spot. "Uh…I'm getting a blister."

"No, she isn't!" Prima called. *"She's lying. She's talking to the voices in her head."*

"Hush." It was hard to mouth the words silently when she wanted to hiss them—or spritz the AI with a water bottle like an errant cat. She decided to try a new strategy. "Come on, it must be such a clever plan. Don't you want to brag a little?"

"Well…" She sounded like she was considering it.

"We have so many layers to this," Dotty wheedled. "Think about it. There was the one set of bandits, then the elven army—plus wizards, if they were able to enchant wolves. How do you work all those pieces together?"

"It was simple, if you consider—hey!"

"Damn," Dotty muttered.

It was midday before they stopped in the shadow of the forest. Insea, Lyle had told her as they walked, was north through a little spur of the forest and around the base of a range of hills, then down onto a series of plains. The rest they enjoyed was short, only enough to water the horses and let everyone snatch a quick nap.

She had begun to reach the opinion that beer wasn't necessary for good sleep—merely exhaustion. It felt as if she had only closed her eyes when one of the guards shook her awake and the party continued.

There was an inn in the forest, Per told them, but they would stop at the far border and camp some distance from the road amongst the scree and shale. He seemed to have found a new purpose after her speech and she suspected that deep down, he was enjoying the challenge of outwitting his unknown opponents.

Dotty barely made it to the edge of the forest. The sun was definitely past its peak by then and the entire caravan was running on fumes. They moved almost as slowly as they had in order to sneak past the soldiers, and all the fun of it was gone.

She wasn't sure if anyone cooked dinner because for once, she managed to fall asleep even before she'd even thought about it.

When she woke it was almost dawn and some of the group was already moving around quietly and cooking food. There was no jerky and dried fruit on the menu today but instead, sausages and ale, as well as some kind of dark, gingery cookies that were spicy and sweet and comforting all at the same time.

Per announced that they wouldn't start for another hour to give the horses more rest and she glanced longingly at her bedroll when Lyle cleared his throat and gestured to a flat patch of ground.

"What?" she asked.

"If ye want to fight melee, ye need practice," he said. "So, up and at 'em, girl."

"Girl?"

"Are ye…" He did a double-take and looked around at the others, all of whom stared at him, equally mystified. "Are ye…" He cleared his throat and began to grow red in the face. "Are ye not a girl?" he managed finally. His voice trailed into an undignified squeak.

"I'm old enough to be your *grandmother*," Dotty said.

A second and a half later, she remembered what she looked like.

Crap.

"Ye're how old?" He no longer looked embarrassed but his jaw hung open. "Wait—how old *are* ye?"

"Eighty-four," she said with great dignity. She stood and felt her knees creak. It would seem that several days of hard walking were enough to strip all her youth away. "So show some respect."

Lyle said nothing to her, but she saw him murmur the words "eighty-four" at a guard, whose eyes were as round as dinner plates.

"All right." He bounced on the balls of his feet once they had moved away from the camp. Given the fact that they'd been on the road for several exhausting days, he was disgustingly spry and energetic. If looks could kill, she would have him dead and bagged—but since it didn't work that way, she was left only with the determination to wipe the smug grin off his face.

Unaware of this, he retrieved two small staves—the type they had used for tent poles—and tossed them to her. He placed his fist weapons aside.

"No weapons in sparring," he told her. "I'd start ye on fists but ye seem bound and determined t' run into danger an' destroy yerself, an' it's not as if we can expect to have time before our next engagement. Now, your task is simple—get in a good stab and we're done for the day."

"I thought you weren't supposed to kill with the point," she said idly. "I thought that lacked *subtlety*."

"Subtlety be damned." Lyle snorted. "It's better to be sure than subtle."

Several of the other dwarves nodded.

"Indeed." At least she could enjoy the mental image of him taking a stave to the ribs. Energetic bastard.

Dotty bounced on the balls of her feet and considered her first move. Now that no one waved real weapons around, it was difficult to get started. She still tried to find an opening when Lyle charged with a bellow.

"STOOOOOOUT!"

"Sweet Fancy Moses." She darted out of the way and gave thanks once again for her younger, more limber muscles. He careened past and she flailed with her arm but didn't land a stab, only a smack.

"Ow!" he protested.

"You're the one who wanted to—"

"STOOOOOOOOOOOUT!"

"Oh, for the love of—" She hadn't even had the chance to face him this time and simply slid forward. He barreled along behind her, unable to switch gears at a moment's notice. "Why are you being so difficult?" she snapped at him.

He merely grinned, and she realized that he enjoyed this.

And that gave her an idea. She gave a mock frown of concentration and began to try different tactics in a random series of feints to one side or another, a direct charge, or circling. It soon became a game for her in that every time he charged, she would evade him in a different way.

She didn't land very many blows over the next few minutes but she did have a good time in her efforts to become more creative. It was demanding enough that she couldn't spare either the thought or the breath for commentary.

Instead, she merely waited for her moment.

Lyle grew more and more annoyed at her silence. Now that he had no one to spar with verbally, he didn't have nearly as good a time. He managed to keep himself entertained by throwing out comments to members of the watching crowd, but Dotty could tell he wanted nothing more than to trade jabs with words as well as fists.

Well, now she knew how to get under his skin. She made a decision and, before she had the chance to think about it—and thus worry about looking stupid—unleashed a flurry of attacks. Her assault drove him across the circle far enough that the watchers scattered out of the way before she circled and began to drive him around the edge of their makeshift arena.

He didn't have the time to formulate a good counterattack, but she also didn't land any hits. She estimated that he had worked with his fists for quite some time and so was absurdly good at remaining slightly out of range of her attacks. Or slightly inside them. More than once, she slammed a stick down like a staff, only to catch the underside of her forearm on his blocking arm.

It hurt more than she expected.

Finally, with her energy running out, she did the only thing she could think of.

She threw her foot up and caught him in the ribs.

Lyle went over with an "oof" of surprise that she had to admit was deeply satisfying. He stood as Per called a five-minute warning for the caravan to leave.

"Ye didn't win," he told her, his eyes narrowed. "Ye had to stab me to win, and ye didn't land any o' those hits."

"That's as may be," Dotty said, her tone lofty. "But *you* sure didn't win, either."

A few of the watchers snickered and he gave her a smile. It was the kind of pleased smile that announced his friendship.

It also promised that the next sparring match would be much more challenging.

"Well, Dotty," she murmured under her breath, "you set yourself up for this one. You'd best get to brainstorming."

CHAPTER NINETEEN

Sweat dripped into Dotty's eyes. Her palms stung where she clutched the two wooden staves and the muscles in her back ached, desperate to give out. She told her body to dream on—she was sure as hell not giving up now. Not when she had victory in her sights.

Not a word issued from the dwarves assembled around the circle. The day's light was fading, dinner was long since over, and almost everyone had gathered to watch what had quickly become a break-time tradition—Dotty and Lyle's sparring matches.

She circled left. Her back muscles weren't the only ones aching and her calves screamed at her.

His fists were curled loosely and he made sure to project an air of confidence, but she could see the exhaustion in him. "It's been three days," he called to her, "and ye haven't made a single good hit. Time t' give up the quest, Dotty. Go back t' bein' a wizard."

The smile she gave him looked more like a snarl than anything. "If this were a real fight, you'd have been dead ten times before breakfast."

A few people whistled at the riposte. Their match this morning had ended with her thwacking his legs out from under him with the two staves. She still hadn't landed a blow as he'd managed to roll away and flip her sideways, but he'd have been long gone if she'd used real blades.

Wearily, she ran through what she knew. Her opponent was tired, he preferred to step back with his right leg, and he liked to duck under swings—a good thing for a dwarf if they tended to fight non-dwarves but not so useful here.

This was it. At last, this was the one and she didn't even have time to savor the moment.

Dotty rushed him, crossed in front so he could slide out of the way to his right, and pivoted. She slid low and raised her arm to flip one of the staves into a backward grip before she swept her arm sideways.

She had the immensely satisfying feeling of it jolt in her hands as it struck him point-first on the thigh. He yelled in surprise and the watching group came to their feet with a roar of approval.

Still in a long lunge, she contemplated how she would find the energy to stand but decided to fall sideways instead. It was a choice, she told herself as she tumbled. A conscious choice. She was totally in control of this situation.

STRIKING WITH THE POINT, Level 1, the screen read.

"Finally," Prima commented.

Despite the deliberately snarky tone, she didn't bother to respond. She considered both her dinner staying warm on a rock beside the firepit and her bedroll currently inside one of the tents and decided she could have a perfectly comfortable night there on the bare ground. No amount of comfort was worth the effort of standing right now.

Which made it all the more annoying when a boot nudged her in the ribs and flipped her onto her back. Lyle's face swam into view.

"Urgh," she said in protest.

"Tired, are ye?"

"No. You're merely so ugly."

The dwarves laughed and clapped, and her opponent grinned. Dwarves had reached the point where they took pride in everything the other races disliked about them—short, big-footed, and with bulbous noses and a distinct trend toward hairiness.

He offered her a hand and held it out until she clasped it reluctantly and let him pull her to her feet. She gazed longingly at her dinner happily when he spoke.

"Again."

"Wait, *what?*" Dotty looked at him so sharply her neck muscles snapped. She rubbed the side of her neck with a wince. "*What?*" she repeated.

Lyle threw the two staves at her and smiled when she moved to catch them without thinking. "I said, do it again."

"But we've been sparring for…" She didn't have a watch. "And I landed a hit. And…*food.*"

"Battles don' wait," he said philosophically. "Again, *Zauberer.*"

The rest of the group clapped. First, they had been overawed to have her in the group and then, they had mistrusted her. But since her innocence had been proven and they had seen her in action, they had warmed to her considerably.

There weren't many dwarven wizards, although their earth magic was some of the strongest in the world. Dwarves preferred to make something physical—a sculpture, a piece of jewelry, or a building. In the same way, they preferred to change their world through direct action rather than through magic.

Consequently, they deeply approved of her wanting to learn melee combat when she was already a wizard.

Dotty sighed and looked at the sticks in her hands. She had to admit, a certain part of her was interested to see if she could reproduce her results. It had been a long few days while she successfully attempted maneuver after maneuver and learned different ways to step and dodge.

But she hadn't landed a strike with the point until now, and she wanted to see if this had been a fluke or not.

"All right, Stout." She banished the tiredness in her muscles and straightened. "One more match and the winner gets the other's beer for dinner."

The cheer this time was deafening, and he nodded at her with a grin.

"You have yourself a deal."

DuBois snatched another bag of popcorn off the desk and opened it without looking at it. He didn't know which flavor it would be, which was the best way to snack it—there were only *good* unknowns, as far as he was concerned.

The first crunch was heavenly and rich. Good old caramel corn, he thought. It was perfection, everything popcorn should be—sweet, comforting, and crunchy.

He smiled as he watched the data stream from Dotty's game. The others liked to watch it on a monitor which provided a third-person view of the scene, but he had always preferred the raw data.

There was so much more there, for one thing. Simply by increasing her heart rate regularly over the past weeks, her cardiovascular fitness had gone up considerably. Certain muscles, triggered subconsciously by her mind, began to show signs of strength without the usual wear and tear. Her sleep cycles had become more regular and easier to slip into, which meant she was more alert during her waking periods.

And her brain, long-since trained to view muscle fatigue or joint pain as something frightening, slowly learned to revel in physical exhaustion. She showed increased resiliency to everything—and that meant she was able to take joy in far more experiences than she would have before.

The three PIVOT members—who the doctor had come to regard affectionately as nephews and a niece, having had experience only with his siblings' children—had joined him while he watched. Jacob was eating a burrito of some kind, and the others sipped coffee.

"Is she still fighting?" Nick asked. "She was fighting when we left. How much time has passed in-game?"

"They're starting another round," DuBois said. "It's incredible. The more she learns, the easier the learning gets. Her brain is showing increased plasticity. I'll run that against Justin's data soon." He held a hand up. "Wait, match two is starting."

Everyone clustered around to watch.

Dotty held her mock blades slanted across her body, both raised. This was one of the earliest and most humiliating lessons she had learned. A blade at her side was no use if her opponent could close the distance between them quickly, and Lyle was *damned* quick.

It was also embarrassing that it had taken her so long to beat him when she had ranged weapons and he didn't. On the other hand, she told herself that he'd spent his entire life training and she had only recently learned to fight with daggers and short swords during their sparring.

Level Thirty-seven in Stamina and Level Eighteen in Fake Short Swords wasn't so bad when she looked at it from that perspective.

Lyle charged with a shout, but she had learned how to respond to that. As he drew breath, she braced herself for the sound and watched his core. The way he moved there would show her where to move out of the way. He was coming in to her left, the way she usually circled, and she increased speed to evade him.

She turned as she slid out of the way. Her staves were at the ready and he didn't have a good path in, not without losing this match almost immediately.

He didn't wait even a moment before he attacked again. He was quick on his feet and tireless—she'd heard about feats of combat ranging from werewolves to wizards, not to mention a giant tournament in Insea. She wasn't sure how many of these stories she believed but she had begun to see how even someone who didn't fight with weapons could have had such a long career.

His onslaught didn't leave her much time to react, but she'd learned that she didn't need it. She swung both staves in a circular pattern and interlocked them so there was neither a break in her guard nor a particular area for him to pivot to next. He was forced to cut his charge short and she immediately began her retaliatory attack.

Dotty drove him back across the circle and suddenly realized that she didn't feel the pain in her muscles in quite the same way anymore. While she was certainly tired, both the raw feeling in her throat and the burn in her thighs had transformed almost completely into a feeling of pure joy.

Clarity dawned with a kind of raw pleasure. She *loved* this.

She didn't have to think through the actions anymore and simply thought of where she wanted to be and her body obeyed. She had one startled moment of memory that her body wasn't doing *any* of this but banished the thought. After all those years spent arguing that books and games weren't real, she had found that she no longer cared about the distinction.

This was real—this moment, with the sweat on her skin, the breeze in her hair, and with her target ahead of her.

Her one moment of distraction had been enough for Lyle, though. He lunged, threw his arms up and out in an arc to bat her blades away, and dropped his shoulder to drive it into her stomach. She was carried up and had one sickening moment to realize what was coming before she landed hard on her back.

The fall didn't quite manage to knock the wind out of her. She shoved him away and rolled before the pain could surge, something she had learned was essential, and began an attack before she fully recovered. Experience had taught her that as soon as she stopped moving, she opened herself up to an attack.

A battle was no time for recuperation.

Dotty saw the opening only a few moments later. He would follow the weapons, not her body. He had fixed on that as the thing to avoid.

It wasn't a terrible idea, but it left him open.

She began another attack. Her makeshift blades spun and wove and Lyle evaded them with practiced ease. But as she whirled, both blades went left and he predictably slid away, and she planted both her feet and drove her hips back to collide with his.

From the *oof* sound he made in her ear, she had struck something important. Unsure if it was his sternum or something rather more fragile, she said a silent prayer for his forgiveness, ducked slightly, and stood and tipped her torso forward to flip him over her shoulder.

He landed like a ragdoll with his arms open, and she was able to kneel and drive one staff down. She stopped at the last moment to the sound of an appreciative gasp from the crowd.

Then, mindful of the rules, she let the stave poke his stomach.

Lyle struggled to take a breath—it seemed she'd struck his sternum instead of something that would require more profuse apologies—but he grinned broadly. He propped himself up on his elbows a few moments later and nodded at her.

"I said to do it again, and ye did it again. Well fought. My ale is yours."

"Nah." Dotty hauled him up. "I have first watch, remember? Anyway, you need to keep your strength up. We have much more sparring to do."

She settled down to eat with congratulations and shoulder claps from the dwarves nearby. From the chatter around her, the latest set of rear scouts had returned and there was still no sign of pursuit. The rest of the caravan seemed pleased and toasts were made to Per's ingenuity.

But when she looked up from a mouthful of food, she caught the caravan leader staring back along the road. His face showed the same troubled feeling she had fought for days now.

No one as well-equipped and well-moneyed as their traitor would simply give up now.

There was a fight coming. It was only a matter of when.

CHAPTER TWENTY

Yunien J'Alar, newly appointed to his command in the elven army, began to think that he was being duped. He read the letter once again before he rolled it into its leather case and stared at it.

The tent flap parted and Guril, his most trusted friend, entered with a smile and a plate of food. He put it in front of the commander, took the leather cylinder with a question in his eyes, and—at his friend's nod—drew the letter out and read it.

Guril sank onto one of the camp stools while the other elf ate. Rations tonight were the same as they had been for days—dried meat, dry road-bread, and strips of fruit, with a sprig of dried herbs to keep the breath fresh.

There was no call to be entirely unmannerly, after all, even when they were so far away from proper food and lodging.

"You don't think much of this, it seems," he said when Yunien looked up.

"We've spent days following these leads." The commander shook his head. "If they're lying about what road they're on, it'll be bad for us."

He had pushed his soldiers at a breakneck pace over the past few days since he'd realized that the dwarven caravan had slipped away from him. Whether it was a lucky chance that they'd taken the back roads, he didn't know. Exactly like he didn't know whether they had orchestrated the donkeys getting loose in one dwarven village or whether they had simply taken advantage of the opportunity.

All he knew was that the caravan full of artifacts had arrived and in the morning, it had been gone without a trace.

Yunien did not intend to let them escape again. He was loyal to the elven monarchy above all else. Where Insea had once been the shining example of his people's prowess, it had long since faded into obscurity, welcomed humans and dwarves into its nobility, allowed orcish traders, and ceased to issue even the most mild statements regarding the elves.

No one had seen the king in years and even before that, he had not responded when a minor member of the royal line established a new monarchy in the forests of Juranil.

The elves had once ruled this world and they would do so again. He was devoted to that ideal. While he had never seen Berghold, he had seen drawings and considered it a dank cave. The human towns were nothing to brag about either, and their cities were squalid hell-holes. The orcs, meanwhile, still traveled like nomads across the eastern plains.

And Ynsi'i, the jewel of the elves, was now known as Insea—a bastardization, the closest their script or their clumsy tongues could come to imitating the true name.

Yunien did not know all of his king's plan to restore power to the elves. He knew there would be a new city, more beautiful than Insea by far, and there would be envoys and armies marching. The plan would take many generations, even by the long-lived standards of the elves.

He prided himself on not needing to know the full magnitude of it. All he knew was his portion—to find this shipment of artifacts steeped in the earth magic of the dwarves and the stolen magic of the elves and bring them to the elves' temporary home in Tormari. For years, these priceless artifacts had been sent to Insea to serve a king who would not put his people first and also the rabble that now filled those streets. His king had sent many envoys over the years to remind the dwarves of their loyalty to the elves and ask them to redirect their shipments.

They had not and in doing so, had defied their rightful ruler.

The king had placed his trust in Yunien when he asked the young commander to right this one wrong, and he would not fail. He had contacted sources deep within Berghold and spent long months bartering through an untraceable set of contacts until he finally found a source willing to give everything away for gold.

Gold—what a small thing compared to a love of one's people. Such traitorous behavior only showed why the dwarves should not rule anything at all.

Their source had promised that the caravan would arrive, battered and close to defeat, at a certain elven village. For all Yunien knew, that had happened.

And then everything had gone wrong.

"D'you trust our source?" Guril asked curiously.

Yunien straightened. "Speak properly," he commanded. "And of course I do not trust our source. It is a traitor—a *dwarven* traitor. But our readings showed that we were close to the artifacts at the village. We know their destination and can only hope we will intercept them once more. And then the traitor…will be found."

Guril raised an eyebrow curiously. "What will happen to them?" There had been extensive debate around the campfires about what should be done with this dwarf. After all, they had turned on their king. On the other hand, they had turned on their king to support the primacy of the elves. Should they be punished or rewarded?

Only another inferior species could make such a muddle of things, Yunien thought contemptuously. He did not envy the king that decision.

"I did not ask," he said and congratulated himself once again on his unwavering, unquestioning loyalty. "We will find their traitor and bring them to the king. What he does will doubtless be just and wise. Tell the camp to pack up. We will travel through the night."

Guril did not protest, knowing better than to voice displeasure with the orders. The soldiers would be disappointed to not have any sleep, but they were the finest, hardiest warriors in the elven army—they would march on, long past the endurance of others.

And the artifacts would be in elven hands once more.

The elves were fools.

Only fools, after all, became so estranged from their king that they formed another monarchy without war and began to send imperious directives to the other races based on nothing at all.

The traitor agreed, wholeheartedly, that Insea should not have the dwarven artifacts that were sent each year. The debt had long since been paid and what had Insea done for Berghold? Nothing within living memory. It was a city ruled by a king who didn't even care to show his face, and the elves had put up with that for far too long.

They liked to think of themselves as great warriors too. The traitor gave a little laugh at that idea. Any real warrior would have conquered Insea or come in force to demand Berghold's loyalty but they had not.

Clearly, they *could* not.

The artifacts that would be stolen this year were a small price to pay for the war that would break out now. The new elven king, still gathering his strength, would earn the ire of the dwarves as well as the retribution of the ruler of Insea. The humans would know the elves for the traitors they were, and the orcs were essentially irrelevant.

In fact, they didn't seem to care about anything beyond their hunts and their rituals. They could be a mighty force if they ever had a mind to be. It was as well that they didn't.

The elves might fall first in name but it would be the humans who fell first in truth. They would be seduced by the gold in the dwarven vaults and the weakness of their scattered leaders. Without a drop of blood being spilled, they would join with the dwarves, accept gifts and envoys, and would become dwarven citizens.

Their joint victory over the elves would be the last the humans knew of themselves as a sovereign species. They could do what they did best—trade, make coin, and farm. The dwarves wouldn't interfere with that. Perhaps some kings could live on as puppets of the dwarven monarchy. The dwarves would recoup all they had spent and more.

The battle would wipe out the fledgling new elven monarchy before it had even truly begun. It would show the elves their true place in the world and finally—*finally*—the dwarves would begin to establish the dominance they deserved.

They wouldn't rule from Berghold. It was only one city. Dwarves had existed before the elves came. They'd had their magic and their traditions and would make future cities, grander and more powerful. Their wizards would rule over all others.

The traitor adjusted his cloak and looked around at the landscape. He was so close to this, the thing he had worked toward for years. For decades, he had accompanied the caravans, overseen the stonemasons, and watched as the limitless talents of the dwarves were usurped and bled away.

The elven commander—for he was not as stealthy as he thought, that one—had been a stroke of well-timed luck. He was so eager to play his part. So ready to fall upon the caravan and slaughter the guards.

The traitor smiled.

Soon. It would all come together very soon.

CHAPTER TWENTY-ONE

Dotty awoke to a strange thrumming sound at her wrist, opened her eyes, and realized groggily that the tent was flooded with blue light. She sat up in alarm and glanced at the bracelet, which glowed.

Justin had told her it would let her contact her family. Curious, she flipped it. Somehow, the light had not woken the other two women with whom she shared the tent and neither of them even stirred when she took the amulet off her wrist and the glow intensified.

Was she the only one who could see it?

Most likely. She brushed her fingers over the glowing blue surface and was surprised when the world around her froze. In front of her was a picture of parchment and words appeared as if written out by hand.

Dotty—

This is Justin. You've taken to the game very well and you're learning weapons quickly. Keep the book, though. I think you may want to try magic again someday. You're a natural at that too. It would be a shame if you didn't try.

She snorted. Sure, she might read some of the book every night and imagine new, innovative ways to use her powers, but she didn't intend to *use* them.

Without a doubt, she wouldn't.

Definitely not.

To reinforce her resolve, she shook her head.

Your family wanted to throw a party for you for your birthday, the letter continued. *We asked if they would be willing to come to the lab. As you have been inside the pod for some time, we do not want to run the risk of exhausting you. However, bringing you out of the pod would also give us useful data before you return to the game (if you wish to do so).*

Let us know if you would like us to plan this party for you. Your daughter-in-law has assured me she will make your favorite chocolate espresso cake and will make sure someone brings brandy instead of telling you it's not good for your health.

Dotty snickered. That would be Mary. As a doctor, John liked to remind his mother about which things were healthy and which were not. His list of vices inevitably included almost everything that made life worth living.

His wife, on the other hand, loved to bake—and cheerfully, irreverently kept John in line while she was at it. She had been a good match for him from the start.

Dotty realized now that she missed her family. She read on, biting her lip.

If there is anything you need in the game, let us know. We promise you will have a good chance to use your skills soon. Stay on your guard.

-Justin

P.S. To respond, press down on the blue button and it will record your voice.

With the world frozen behind the letter, she took some time to simply think. She curled her knees to her chest and rested her chin on them, something she would not have imagined doing weeks before. The residual soreness of sleeping on the ground was already working its way out of her muscles, and she felt invigorated and ready to start her day.

But she wanted to think before she accepted any offers to leave. It had been hard enough to go through with this once, and what would she feel like if she went back? Would her body be a prison? Would her children cry and talk her out of returning?

Would she, for some reason, not *want* to return?

Oddly enough, that thought scared her more than the others. She was someone here—not someone famous or all-powerful but someone who had a place and a mission. No matter what else she might encounter, she couldn't leave these people undefended.

She pressed the blue button and began to speak.

"Justin, thank you for your kind words about my skills, although I confess it made me much more self-conscious to remember that everyone in the lab has seen my failures.

"I am enjoying the game immensely and have signed on as a guard for a dwarven caravan." She assumed he knew, given that he could see her progress and also because he had set the whole thing up to start with. "I can't leave the game until the shipment is safely delivered to Insea, which will be in about five days—although if it's close to my birthday, it must have been longer outside the game than inside it.

"I would like to see everyone, however, so I will be ready to come out of the game any time after that. Thank you very much. Dotty."

She released the button and stared around the tent before she said quietly, "Prima, you can start the game again."

The AI didn't do so immediately. *"I am not good with human emotions when I do not create them myself. Are you angry or are you upset?"*

Dotty grimaced. "I'm frightened," she said honestly. "I'm a different person here than I am in the real world. Giving that person up was difficult and now, giving this person up is difficult too. I'm afraid I won't ever be able to come back to her."

Prima considered this. *"Are you not both people?"*

"People change over time. If my family tells me something that steals the joy from the game…" She shrugged.

"You seem like quite a stubborn person. I can't see them managing to change your opinion without a very good set of reasons."

She smiled. "Have I ever mentioned that I appreciate you?"

"No," Prima said promptly. Then, she asked curiously, *"Why did you change the subject?"*

"It wasn't a subject change." She grinned and threw the covers back. "See if you can figure out that one. If you want to keep time frozen, I can cook breakfast for everyone before they wake."

"And have them burn you as a witch? I don't think you want that." Prima unfroze time and the snores of her tentmates resumed.

Dotty smiled and headed outside to where Per was seated by the embers of the previous night's fire, smoking a pipe in deep contemplation. He looked at her in surprise.

"Couldn't you sleep?"

She shrugged. Aside from the fact that she didn't feel like coming up with any particular lie, she'd learned over the years that if you didn't say anything, other people merely filled in your answer in their heads. Instead, she sat across the fire from him and looked at the eastern horizon. "What about you?"

Per hesitated. "Nightmares," he said finally. "I've been with the caravan almost every year since I was young. I started as a guard, then an envoy, and I've escorted everyone from princesses to goldsmiths. We've passed through battlegrounds and I worried sometimes about the caravan, but...never like this."

Dotty frowned. "What was your nightmare?"

"I was lost in a forest," he said, glanced over his shoulder to where the last trees had finally faded away, and shuddered. "I don't like forests. If you have a roof over your head, it should be stone, not something living with a mind of its own. That's the elves for ye, though. Anything simple, they can turn into a piece of their magic."

She smiled at that. Many of the dwarves reveled in their brogue, an almost-Scottish accent that reminded her of an old school friend. A few like Per, however, only slipped into it when they were lost in thought or especially upset about something.

"So, you were in a forest..." she prompted.

"There was someone following me," he continued. "Or...us? I'm not sure if it was only me or if the whole caravan was there. I could hear my breathing. I struggled to get away and I thought I had done it, but then I felt something behind me, and..." His shoulders had hunched and he looked embarrassed. "It's not important. They say dreams are nothin' but our fears, the ones we won't let ourselves see in the light o' day. I don't think this is too mysterious, though. And I've been worried about it during the days as well as the nights."

"Yeah." Dotty stared at the sunrise. "I always thought that advice was crap, too."

Per snorted, spat, and checked to see if his pipe was still lit. "No nightmares for you, then?"

"None these days." She managed a smile. "It's been a long time since...well, since I've remembered my dreams."

"Yes, I recall you saying you're eighty-four." He smirked. "What's more impressive, to be honest, is that you managed to convince the rest of them of it."

"I haven't always been in *this* body," she said.

The alarm on his face let her know she'd spoken incorrectly. "Let me state, for the record, that I have not taken this body from anyone. I mean—look, this has only ever been *my* body. There's no demonic possession going on or anything. I merely had a different life...once."

He put his pipe down and looked at her. "Were you always a dwarf?"

"No," she admitted. "Once, I was a human. I had a husband, children, grandchildren...great-grandchildren." She looked away.

"What happened?"

"Nothing. Years and years of nothing, and dreams fading, and my world getting smaller and smaller." Dotty remembered the story she'd heard from Justin and Lyle. "And then a young man from my world, a man named Justin, came from this place, and told us that warriors were needed."

"Justin...the man who won the tournament at Insea?" Per looked dumbfounded.

"Yes. He...put the call out in our world and I answered. My family is safe but it seems yours—your world—may not be."

Per looked at her with new respect. "So that's who you truly are. Not a dwarf, not one of us at all, but a spirit carried between worlds and given a new form. Imagine where else you might have ended up." He snorted. "You could have been an orc."

"I chose where I would land," Dotty said. "I chose the dwarves. I wanted to know more about them. I saw a picture of…well, me." She gestured to her body. "She looked like a woman who cared more about mining jewels than wearing them. She looked like a person I had never allowed myself to be."

"Can I ask you something?" Per asked.

"Of course."

"If that's why you're here—to be a hero, to step out of a small life and save us all—to become *more*—why are you so afraid of your magic?"

She looked sharply at him.

He shrugged. "But, what do I know, eh? I'm only fifty. A spring chicken."

"You're right about that. My youngest child is older than you." She shook her head. "And what good will I do anyone if I die?"

"Will your…would you be able to go back?"

"I don't know."

Per looked at her with a new appreciation now. "You didn't know us but you came to help us."

"Do you believe me?" Dotty asked.

"I wouldn't, but I heard the stories from Insea weeks back—and heard, too, that there was a certain dwarf who fought with Justin in the tournaments. He told me Justin's story before I heard it from you, and he told me he had vouched for you. I think…well, I always assumed that he simply meant somewhere far beyond the sea, not another world entirely." He shook his head. "Either way, I've seen many liars in my day—well, politicians, anyway—and you don't strike me that way. You're too no-nonsense. I have a feeling that if you decided you wanted to hijack the caravan, you'd come up to me and ask straight out what it would take."

She was surprised into a laugh. "You're not far off. Honestly, though, it seems like too much trouble. Besides, you clearly cared about what you said when we were leaving Berghold, and trust me, alliances that are strong should be kept that way. That means honoring commitments."

"Well said." Per stood and stretched. "Shall we make breakfast for the rest of them? It's five days to Insea if we travel fast and I, for one, don't want to spend a minute longer than I have to waiting for whatever ambush is in store down the road."

"So both o' ye think we're headed into a trap too?" Lyle had emerged from his tent and he wandered over to start stoking the fire. "I have the same feeling. I'm merely hoping that whoever we meet next, it's not orcs."

"*Orcs?*" the other two said at the same time.

He waved his hands. "It was supposed to be a joke."

"That is a terrible joke," Per said.

"What he said." Dotty pointed.

"Oh, lighten up—although I now know how t' get everyone's attention, eh? I only meant, we've been attacked by humans and elves so far, right? So orcs would be next."

Dotty could see his reasoning now but she still shook her head. "Bad joke. Still a bad joke."

"Yeah, yeah, so ye've said. Tell ye what, the two o' ye can split my ale ration for the day."

"Done," they said together. She thought they were getting rather good at that.

"Oh, come on. Ye're not going to take me up on that?"

"Of course I am," she told him flatly. "Just feel lucky we're not making you carry us."

CHAPTER TWENTY-TWO

The day dawned clear and bright but clouds began to move in by midmorning. Dotty, at first, registered this only as a welcome relief from the blazing sun, but it wasn't long before the first spatter of rain landed on her head.

She looked up and swore. The cloud that was raining on them was airy and wispy and blue sky showed around the edges. Moving in behind it were clouds of progressively darker gray and lightning crackled in the distance.

There wasn't anything to do except keep moving. The rain went from an occasional spatter to a full drizzle, enough to soak every-thing. She wrapped her cloak tightly around her as she walked. Rain wasn't so bad when you had a warm, dry house to go to—not to mention a change of clothes—but when you knew you'd have wet socks for the rest of the day…well, *then* rain was miserable.

The road began to wind into a gorge and she looked at the slick and shiny walls. Perhaps this had been a quarry once, she thought, although the road was narrow.

Could someone have gone to all the trouble of cutting a single road through the rock? And, if so, to what purpose?

"All the roads to Insea are like this," a voice said briskly.

Dotty looked up as Lyle stepped beside her.

He smiled and rain ran in rivulets down his beard. "The roads to Insea are narrow. Some have drop-offs on both sides and some are like this. They should get flooded or crumble, but they don't. It must be one of their spells. You can always get there but the thing is, you can't get an *army* there very easily."

She nodded.

"It's been nigh on a millennium since Insea was built," he said, speaking loudly over the sound of the rain. "It's never seen war, even since the king disappeared. No one visibly rules it and there's no official army, only royal guards, but it's always been at peace, even though it's so prosperous."

"Prosperity breeds peace," she pointed out.

"Within a country, aye." He raised an eyebrow. "But it also breeds envy."

Dotty nodded. She opened her mouth to speak when something clattered against the stone wall nearby. With a glance at one another, she and Lyle went to check.

"Why are we looking?" she asked a moment later. She had cut her hand on a particularly sharp rock and proceeded to drop it on her other hand and into a puddle. The resulting splash flicked mud onto her face. She sat on her haunches and looked at Lyle.

"If it's a rock," Lyle said, still studying the area, "mayhap we all get out of the gorge."

"Oh. But there are tons of rocks, how will we know—"

"Aha!" He pulled something out of the rocks. "It was an arrow." He smiled at her.

She looked meaningfully at him.

"Oh, shit," he said.

Somewhere ahead, lost in the rain, the shout went up. "Attack! *Attack!*"

They leapt to their feet and looked around. There was no way to see the high edges of the canyon, but clatters sounded all around them.

"Take yer cloak off!" Lyle yelled to her. "They can't see much in this rain, but they can sure as hell see *ye*!"

It was a good thought. She yanked at the laces that held her cloak in place and threw it into the back of a cart. Both of her daggers were already in her hands before she realized how useless they were. What would daggers do against arrows?

"I think you know what to do," Prima said.

"Oh, you have to be kidding me," Dotty snapped. "Did you set this up?" Another arrow clattered and she threw herself sideways.

"Not with this particular goal in mind."

"When this is over, we will have a *talk*." She picked herself up and hissed at the pain of her bruises as she clambered into the back of a cart. "Lyle! Can we turn the carts? I can cover our retreat if so—and take care of those archers!"

He scrambled in beside her. "What did ye say? How will ye cover a retreat wi' two daggers, lass?"

"Magic!" Dotty bellowed over the rain. "And unless you have any *better* ideas—"

But Lyle was already gone and he darted through the rain to the front of the caravan.

She sighed and wished he *had* had a better idea.

There was nothing for it, though. She crouched among the bales of cloth and supplies and tried to still her mind. The cart jostled as the horse shied and reared, and the arrows continued to hiss and clatter against the rock walls. They didn't hit much, but no individual arrow needed to.

Their enemy knew they were pinned.

Frantically, she sifted through the spells in her head. Stone-Shock? What could she do with that?

An idea came to her in the next moment. She peeked over the edge of the cart and, as the wind gusted, she thought she saw the line of archers at the top of the gorge. Each stood tall, drew a bowstring back, and aimed at the caravan.

Cowards.

Dotty tried her idea with one of them and fixed her focus on the bow. What she pictured in her head was the rock dropping on her hand and splashing into the puddle only this time, the rock was somehow wrapped around the bow.

A few points of her magic left her in a whoosh, and somewhere above, she heard a yelp. A few moments later, a bow tumbled down the slope—unfortunately, not still clutched by its owner.

Well, one couldn't have everything. She squinted enough to see the rock around the edge of it and smiled. There was nothing like taking your aim carefully and having the weight of your weapon suddenly shift on you.

She looked at her magic bar and shook her head. There wasn't nearly enough to eliminate all of them.

She could throw them off, though. At random, she chose her targets and added lumps of rock to some bows or hurled rocks at others. It didn't eliminate their enemies and only put their ranks in disarray, but that would have to be enough for now.

Far too slowly, the carts began to turn and Dotty cursed inwardly as she tried to maintain her focus. She had gotten used to the speed of modern life with cars that could turn quickly and accelerate out of a confrontation. Not that she had ever been in a comparable situation, of course, but her closest comparison to this ambush was a movie car chase.

In this case, there was nowhere to run easily.

How had she not seen this coming?

"Dotty!" Lyle jumped beside her. "Whatever yer doin', the archers have stopped firing. Come on!"

She followed him without a thought. Her magic was almost exhausted, and she could still hear the shouts of alarm behind her. The two of them dodged between carts being pulled by panicked horses and it wasn't long before she realized that she could hear the clash of weapons.

Of course there had been a ground force.

"How many?" she called to her companion.

His answer was one grim word. "Enough."

Dotty increased her pace. If she slowed, she would turn and run.

She didn't want to do this again—she didn't want to fight and kill—but there wasn't any other option.

"I hate this," she muttered to Prima.

"You wanted to bring good to this world."

"This isn't *real!*" she snapped as she reached the front of the battle line and whirled into action. She cut down an elf without even thinking about it, whirled, and slashed down his—or possibly her—front. The elf staggered back with a scream and she shifted her dagger to a back grip before she stabbed sideways into another elf's ribs.

Prima's answer almost made her stop dead. *"It is to me,"* she said.

And if she didn't help her fix it, the AI would be stuck with these bastards winning the battle.

The first enemy she'd slashed at was on their feet again and snarled as they drew a sword. Dotty threw her foot up to punch at the elf's knee and brought the pommel of one dagger down on their head when they fell, clutching their leg.

"Dotty!" Per's call was panicked.

She turned to see a tall and strapping elf with blond hair pulled back in a severe braid. From the excessive shine of the armor and the golden torc at their neck, she guessed this was a champion or commander of some kind.

For the first time, she was *very* aware of how short she was in this body. Dotty backed away slowly and adjusted her hands on the grips of her daggers.

A movement flickered at the corner of her eye and she noticed Lyle trying to sneak around the side of the battle.

Which made her play quite clear. She sneered at the elf and spread her arms in a mocking gesture. "So you thought you'd shoot us like fish in a barrel, huh? No honor among thieves, I guess."

The elf narrowed his eyes. "We are not thieves." The voice was unmistakably male.

Well, that was one mystery solved.

"Okay." She made a mocking finger quote gesture. "Fancy canyon pirates."

He raised his sword. "These goods are ours. We have sent word to the dwarves informing them of this. They have refused to see reason. The elves are now forced to shed blood to take possession of what is ours by right."

"STOOOOOOUT!" bellowed a familiar voice.

The warrior whirled—for all his ridiculous posing and cowardice, he seemed to be quite well trained—and she darted in to jab a dagger at the gap between the panels of his arm guards. She darted out of the way again as he was bowled past her by the force of Lyle's tackle.

Dotty had been so focused on surviving that she hadn't thought beyond each swipe and slash, but for the first time, she allowed herself to imagine victory.

She might have been slightly premature on that because the very fancy elf had barely landed when one of the others yelled, "The commander!"

There were no more than a dozen of them, but at the threat to their leader, they formed into a tight knot and rushed in from all sides. She grasped Lyle's hand and hauled him clear, and the dwarves began to back away. The carts grew more distant with each moment.

"Only a few minutes," she called to the rest, all bloodstained and pale and heaving for breath. "We only have to give them time to get away."

The elven commander laughed at that. One of his soldiers had helped him up and he stared at the dwarves with contempt and a trace of both mockery and pity.

And she knew, in an instant, that they had planned for this far better than she had even guessed.

That was enough of a surprise to her, but the far greater surprise was that she wasn't frightened. She was *furious.* The rage melted through her in a wash of heat and she raised her dagger and threw before she had a chance to think.

It burrowed into the elven commander's eye, and he collapsed in a heap.

After a moment of complete silence, both sides of the group charged. Dotty streaked through the line of charging elves to reclaim her dagger—that was the problem with throwing blades, she thought to herself—and turned to try to catch the back of an elf's leg. He fell screaming, and she leapt into the fray.

The elf who had helped the commander to his feet lunged at her, his eyes crazed. "Dwarven scum!"

She feinted right and dove left, rolled awkwardly, and winced before she bounced to her feet. Her muscles were sore and she was tired, but this was how she had learned to fight. While he still tried to stop and turn, she had already initiated her attack.

It happened so quickly it surprised her. She no longer planned her combat move by move and simply pushed into motion. Her momentum helped her into a slide with her left hand out to brace herself, and she barely felt the impact when she landed. Her feet struck the elf's ankles and he began to topple. His hands lurched out instinctively in search of a way to regain his feet.

He thudded onto the point of one of her daggers. His face slammed into the rock next to hers and his dead weight sprawled on her.

Panic surged through her but a moment later, his body was hauled away and Per offered her a hand.

"Come on!" he called, as he hauled her up. Dead elves lay around them and she identified two dwarves among the corpses. Per's face was white with either blood loss or fury, perhaps both. "We have to get to the front of the caravan," he yelled to them. "Burials later. Protect the rest *now!*"

That was what they needed to turn them from where they stared brokenly at the bodies of their friends and they raced away toward the caravan. Dotty ran with them, all her attention focused on the coming battle. She had fallen, been bruised and scraped, and probably sprained one of her hands, but none of that mattered. They had defeated this group of elves and they could deal with the rest.

At the top of the hill, however, they skidded to a halt. Facing them was easily an entire company of soldiers, waiting in ranks in front of the stopped caravan.

One rider trotted forward and his gaze scanned the group.

"Where," he asked crisply, "is Commander j'Alar?"

Lyle sighed beside her and she glanced at him, but he shook his head.

"End of the road," the dwarf murmured sadly. "I didn't think I'd go out like this."

Dotty looked from him to the elves. There had to be some way to save them. If she confessed…well, she didn't know if she would die in the real world, but she couldn't leave them all here, could she?

She was about to step forward when a horn rang clear and dramatically in the silence.

The elves turned and their ranks rippled, and the dwarves uttered a whoop.

"What? What is it?" She looked around in confusion.

"It's a dwarven battle horn." Lyle laughed and the color had returned to his cheeks. "It looks like we have a chance after all. Come on, ye bloody bastards. Let's make some stories for the songs!"

CHAPTER TWENTY-THREE

The battle was in disarray almost from the beginning. The cavalry, which had been ready to charge, swept to the flanks to reach the rear attacking force and left the foot soldiers to scramble without orders. The chaos was exacerbated when two of their sergeants issued different commands.

They still called questions to each other when the entire horde of dwarven guards descended on them. In short order, it became clear that these elves did not care nearly so much about the caravan as their commander had.

"Mercy!" one of them yelled.

"We surrender!" called another.

"Fight on, you fools!" The sergeant was almost purple in the face as he fought Per, who ducked and backpedaled to avoid his wild swings. "So they're armed. You are too!"

"The cavalry are dead!" One of the soldiers gestured pleadingly at the back of the line. Screams and shouts still issued from that direction, but Dotty saw very few blond riders still atop horses.

"Aye." Per grunted. "Ye didn't prepare for a well-armed force, did ye? Instead, ye thought ye could slaughter us an' walk away with the artifacts." He stumbled as he avoided another swing, and she could see he was tiring. His age counted against him and he'd been injured with barely a few days to recuperate while he slept under the stars and ate travel rations.

He was still a dwarf and exceedingly canny, however. When he lured the elven sergeant into a deep lunge, he kicked his supporting leg out and lopped his head off with one heavy stroke.

Appalled, she clapped a hand over her mouth and only narrowly missed losing her head when her opponent swiped wildly, as horrified as she was.

Dotty seized the moment to stab him in the stomach as she wasn't quite tall enough to aim comfortably for the chest. It rubbed her the wrong way somewhat to fight on after an opponent had argued for surrender but on the other hand, Per was right. These elves had come to slaughter the caravan and leave with the treasure.

She was on the last of her reserves of energy when the dwarven cavalry broke through the last of the elven ranks. They pulled up sharply when they saw the dwarven soldiers and a moment later, one of the riders urged his horse forward at a trot. He swung down from his horse, removed his helmet, and clasped Per's hand.

"*Councilor?*" the caravan leader asked, dumbstruck.

"We received word of the attack three days after you left," Marwitz explained. His chest heaved and his breastplate was streaked with blood. There was no fancy hat to be seen, and exhaustion had stripped the haughty accent from his voice.

Dotty liked him much better this way.

Marwitz looked over his shoulder to where the medics now rushed to treat the dwarves. His shoulders slumped at the sight of the dead on the road.

"We'd have *all* been dead if not for you," Per told him bluntly. "Councilor, we barely survived the first wave of the attack. We wouldn't have at all but for Zauberer Hunt."

Put on the spot, she flushed crimson. "It was nothing."

"It was *not* nothing." He came to grasp her hand. "That's twice now you've saved the caravan, isn't it? I misjudged you, Zauberer. Yours is a formidable talent." He frowned at the daggers. "And…you fought melee as well?"

"Aye." Lyle clapped her on the shoulder. "Like any proper dwarf, she has a bit o' brawl in her."

"Indeed." Marwitz managed a tired smile. "And you say you routed the others? Did you take any captives?"

"None," Per said flatly. His tone dared the other dwarf to argue.

"With a captive, we might have learned the name of the traitor," the councilor said quietly.

Per looked at a loss now and glanced at Lyle and Dotty. One of the other guards stepped forward.

"We'll not hear a bad word about Per, Councilor. He's saved us more times than we can count. Without his quick thinkin', we'd have been dead days ago at the village. We'll find the traitor one way or another, but none o' us here will let him be punished for not takin' captives."

Marwitz nodded tightly. "The caravan comes first, of course," he said.

"The lives of my guards come first," Per corrected. "The artifacts can be remade but the guards cannot."

The councilor seemed to know better than to argue at this. "Do we make camp?"

"We press on," Per said. "We'll talk as we ride."

"We're not provisioned for a longer journey," Marwitz warned.

"We'll make do. We can't continue with fewer guards, not with the traitor still in our midst." He gave the order to turn the carts. "Listen, all of you. We've lost friends today. We'll give them a burial tonight but today, we ride. If we don't seek safety, we make their sacrifice worthless."

The dwarves nodded but they were pale and shocked. Dotty guessed that most of them had anticipated bandits and none had anticipated a cavalry charge.

Their leader kept them marching until nightfall. She reasoned that he knew they wouldn't start again if they stopped. He didn't set a punishing pace but allowed the guards and craftsmen to walk together and console one another.

Lyle and Dotty walked side by side, mostly in silence, and Prima kept to herself except when she asked silently, "Does it hurt you when people here die?"

Prima considered this. *"I don't know what 'hurt' means."*

Her tone was very final and she decided not to press the issue.

When they set up camp, no one seemed to have it in them to cook so she took it upon herself to strike a fire and began to make a warm meal. She suspected that the AI helped her light the fire—it was certainly far easier than she had expected—but she was nonetheless proud to see the dwarves' faces soften when she offered them bowls of warm soup sometime later.

After a while, seated in silence, she was surprised to feel a touch on her shoulder. Lyle jerked his head toward Per's tent, led her there, and ducked inside with her to reveal the leader of the caravan hunched over a map with the councilor.

Both men looked up at her as she entered.

"We're planning the rest of the route to Insea," Lyle told her. "You know your magic better than any of us, so we need to know which route is best for you."

"Is there another attack coming?" Dotty asked. Her voice sounded very small and less sure of itself than she wanted it to be. "I thought—"

"Yes," Per said gravely. "I thought the same. The councilor is wary, however. He wants us to turn back."

"If the road to Insea is being watched by someone who can command whole companies of elven soldiers," Marwitz argued, "the only option is to go back."

"Going back takes us *closer* to elven territory," Per retorted. "If they learn that their troops have failed, we'll be easy prey for a backup force. No, I believe they sent only the one company, which means our safest choice is still to go to Insea."

The councilor paced. "But Insea—"

"Ye've been lookin' fer an excuse to turn us around this whole time," Lyle interrupted. "If we turn back now, ye'll have another arrow in yer arsenal when next ye argue to abandon the shipments."

This was news to Dotty. "Wait, what?"

Marwitz gave her an unfriendly look. "This is the business of the dwarves, Zauberer Hunt—the dwarves of *our* land." To Lyle, he said, "And I would thank you to not spread it to others."

"She's spilled enough of her blood t' know," Lyle said hotly.

Both men looked at the caravan leader, who thought about it at length before he said to Marwitz, "Stout is right."

The other dwarf's face twisted into a glare. "If you'll not see reason about her loyalties, the least you could do is keep her from learning our political divisions."

Per didn't bother to respond. To Dotty, he said, "There are many dwarves who believe our debt to Insea is long since paid. They view the creation of Insea as a joint project, our labor given in advance, and the elven knowledge of stone runes given in return. Each year, our finest craftsmen labor over these artifacts we send. Many of us, Councilor Marwitz among them, would prefer to not have our people's skill go to them."

Marwitz looked defiantly at her. "And, as if that isn't enough, we've now shed dwarven blood to protect the caravan because the elves cannot even agree who rules them." His tone was clipped.

Something tugged at the corners of her mind, a pattern she could not quite make out yet. She nodded at him but her mind spun off elsewhere.

"That's what the elven commander was saying," she said distractedly.

Silence settled over the tent.

"What?" Per asked finally. His voice was wary.

"The elven commander. When I fought him, he said the dwarves refused to recognize the new king. That's why they're stealing something we're already giving them. There are two factions of elves."

"A stunning revelation," Marwitz said acidly. To Per, he added, "Yet another reason she should not be here. We are taking our time explaining things to her that we should not have to explain."

She didn't bother to argue. Her mind raced. The road back would take them close to elven territory but it was that territory of the other elven king, the one not at Insea. That was what Per had said. The elves were fighting, there was a traitor in the dwarven camp, and there was a faction that no longer wanted dwarven goods to go to Insea, a place these elves also did not like.

"It was *you*," she said.

All three men in the tent swung to look at her.

"What?" Lyle asked.

The next moment seemed to pass in slow motion. She registered the ripple of the cloak as the sword was drawn and was still opening her mouth to yell when the blade plunged toward its target.

It was a doomed effort from the start with three against one, but the traitor had known that.

He had known his plan had failed from the moment he rode up to see not a decimated dwarven force but a live one. Everything he'd done since then was to recoup his losses.

She threw herself forward and knocked the blade from Marwitz's hand before it could find Per. Rage filled her as she twisted his hand behind his back and thrust his head hard onto the map-covered table.

"It was you," she repeated.

CHAPTER TWENTY-FOUR

"*You?*" Per demanded.

Marwitz kicked and struggled to straighten. He stopped when Lyle took him by the hair and thunked his face onto the table again for good measure.

"Thanks," Dotty said.

He dusted his off hands and nodded.

She picked the prisoner's head up and was pleased to see blood leaking from his nose. Now that she knew he was behind it, she thought he deserved far more than a bloody nose but maybe that would come to him down the road. Right now, there were important things to learn.

"Why?" the caravan leader demanded.

"You're simply taking her word?" the councilor demanded.

"You're the one who could pull it off," Per said. "You had wizards in place to bewitch the wolves near Berghold. Also, you knew which path I would divert to and you're the one I told about us sneaking around the elven encampment."

A short silence followed. She expected Marwitz to give in, but the words only seemed to enrage him.

"You should thank me," he snapped furiously.

Per's face went so cold that Dotty almost stepped back. Fortunately, she remembered in time that she was the one restraining the prisoner. She held her position and made a mental note never to get on the dwarf's bad side.

"I," the leader said softly, "should thank you? Do explain…Herr Marwitz."

Lyle's eyes widened for a moment. It seemed that disregarding the title was a matter of serious importance.

"Make this bitch let me up," he told him.

Her friend answered by thumping the captive's face into the desk again. "No," he said succinctly.

"And don't call me a bitch," Dotty said. "That kind of language is uncalled for."

"Big picture," Lyle mouthed at her.

Per leaned down to look Marwitz in the eyes. "I will not instruct Zauberer Hunt to let you stand unrestrained," he said pleasantly, "so you should start talking now."

"They've duped us," the councilor said resentfully. "I've tried to make the council see it for years, but no one wants to. The elves didn't build Insea while we stood around. They used our labor, our magic, *our* old ways. There are scrolls that date some of the spells they used long before the elves ever came to us. Whatever they gave us to help with Berghold, the debt is paid. It's been paid for centuries. We owe them *nothing*."

The leader sat and folded his hands in his lap. "Yes, that completely explains why you betrayed us to the elven army and gave your countrymen up to be slaughtered. Why you were willing to let those same artifacts you profess to care about so much be taken."

"We've thrown centuries' worth of our best work into the void," Marwitz retorted. "What was one more year? The elves have done nothing for us. They aren't true allies and once this happened, everyone else would see it. *They* came to *me*."

"That makes it better," Lyle said, his expression deadpan. He adopted a false, high voice and mimicked the other man. "No, no, sir.

It wasn't *my* idea to betray the caravan. The elves came up with it first!" He shook his head in disgust. "Idiot."

"*I'm* an idiot?" Marwitz thrashed hard enough that Dotty stumbled slightly before she regained control. She took pleasure in bonking his head on the table again. He snarled at her before he focused on Lyle. "You're the one beggaring your people."

"Which means you should kill a few simply to make a point?" Per roared. He had pushed out of his chair with a speed that surprised her.

Dwarves clearly did better in middle age than humans.

Outside, a shout of alarm was immediately followed by the pounding of feet. A soldier thrust his head into the tent and shouted, "Councilor!"

"Did you know?" The caravan leader pointed his dagger at him. "Did you know why you were here? Did you know the entire plan?"

"We saved your lives!" the soldier protested. He advanced, his sword half-drawn. "And now you've taken the councilor captive—"

"Marwitz is the one who brought the elves down on us in the first place," Lyle said. "None of us were supposed to be alive by the time you arrived. And this idiot"—he jerked a thumb at the prisoner —"thought it was all justified to make the point that we shouldn't send artifacts every year."

The soldier stopped. He gestured hastily behind him and the thuds of other running feet slowed. A terrible comprehension dawned on his face. "Last night," he said to Marwitz. "Last night, I told you we could keep riding. You said no. You said…"

The councilor had gone pale.

"You betrayed us all," Per told him. "We weren't at war. We weren't in danger, and you thrust us into the middle of a conflict that had nothing to do with us so we could have more craftsmen and wizards working for Berghold."

"So we could attain our rightful place!" Marwitz struggled again, and Dotty was grateful when the soldier pushed entirely into the tent to help hold him down.

He gave her a businesslike nod over the prisoner's head, and she nodded in response.

"Our rightful place?" Lyle asked. "What does that even mean, ye big sack o' potatoes?"

"We're the strongest race," Marwitz snapped. "Our wizards are the strongest, our buildings, our soldiers. And what do we do? Hide away in Berghold."

"Because we like it there?" Lyle raised an eyebrow. "Yes, how terrible. Ye are a numpty, aren't ye?"

"You don't understand—"

"I don't understand? *I* don't understand? The one who spent nigh unto me whole life topside?" Lyle slammed both hands down on the table and made everyone jump. "If ye wanted to go off and be rich and rule a little fiefdom, why not do it? I tired of Berghold too. I merely didn't sell us all out for it!"

The councilor turned his face away. "It's clear you don't understand."

"Did it ever occur to you," Per asked in a far too pleasant tone, "that perhaps no one agreed with you because you were wrong? Did it never occur to you that even if others agreed with you about the caravans, none of them had ever tried to do anything like *this*? Did you never wonder why that was?"

Marwitz said nothing.

"He thought the elves would be long gone when we got here," the soldier said thoughtfully. "He kept saying we'd never make it in time. When we saw the battle, he didn't seem ready to press on even then — he said there was little to be done but flee. I should have known. I thought it was that he wanted to spare *us*."

"Nope," Dotty said. "Traitor."

"I'm the only one of us who's loyal to the dwarves," Marwitz insisted. "I'm the only one willing to take the long view."

"There's much to be said for using cruel means to do what must be done," she said acidly. "Sherman's march to the sea comes to mind. Or the Manhattan Project."

"The what?"

"Nothing. It's not important. My point is, you weren't in a war and you didn't even have the argument that you were saving lives in the long run. To you, it was worth sacrificing your fellow dwarves and sparking a war between the races in order to gain more glory—glory none of your people had even asked for. Even Sherman wouldn't agree with what you did."

"Who?"

"It's not important! The names aren't relevant. The point is that if you'd succeeded, you would have destroyed thousands upon thousands of lives and as it is, even in failure, you've spilled blood that didn't need to be spilled."

A long pause ensued before Marwitz said in a chillingly pleased tone, "I haven't failed."

Everyone stepped back, even Dotty and the soldier. Blades pointed at Marwitz, who seemed to revel in their horror.

"I haven't failed," he repeated. "Do you think discovering this will change anything? You'll all be dead before you get close to Insea."

"I'll run ye through first." Lyle growled with cold fury.

"Yes." The councilor sneered at him. "Yes, I've realized that, thank you. My life is forfeit. It was always one of the risks I ran. But I am not afraid to die for this. All men die and my death will be for a purpose."

Dotty tried to push her horror away. She needed to focus and she needed the others to follow her lead.

"Your death *will* be for a purpose," she said. "It will be to show the world that the dwarves do not take treason and warmongering lightly. You can argue all you want that we won't reach Insea, but this was the last stage of your plan. There was nothing else."

Per opened his mouth and closed it again when Lyle flapped a hand for him to be quiet. Marwitz didn't see them as he stared at her, but the soldier also saw it. All three of them held their tongues.

"You're wrong," the prisoner said. He was smiling. "Do you want to trick me into telling you my plan, *Zauberer*? You don't have to. I'll tell you and no amount of forewarning will save you. You were out of magic and fighting with daggers by the time we arrived at the rear-guard. The force coming for you now is three times the size and furious at the death of Commandar j'Alar—and coming faster than your wagons can travel. While you've been interrogating me..." He shrugged. "They've been on the move."

Lyle's blade scraped free of its sheath.

"No, don't!" Dotty called.

It was too late. Marwitz was dead within a second and his blood pooled on the ground.

In a second of shocked silence, they looked at one another.

"We need to move," Per said. "Right now."

CHAPTER TWENTY-FIVE

Dotty was pleasantly surprised to find that the reinforcements were determined to come with them.

"*Leave* you?" one asked, clearly horrified. "To be killed by a traitor? No."

The soldier who had helped Dotty nodded at her. "Marwitz may have used us for his dirty work once but he knew better than to tell us what he was doing. Now that we know, we won't stand for it."

All of the soldiers nodded. They had torn down the camp with incredible haste and threw anything out of the carts that wasn't essential. That included soup pots and stools, which she feared meant the rest of the trip would be far less pleasant.

Better uncomfortable than dead, she decided as one of them winged a dinner plate past her head with an absentminded apology for the near miss.

Per, meanwhile, had taken a falcon from his cage and tied a message to one of its claws. He smiled at it and brushed a finger over its head before he raised his hand to launch it. The bird circled before it soared toward Insea, whereupon the dwarf turned to the crowd.

"If we can make it to the relief forces," he told them, "we'll have a fighting chance. Pair off, all of you. One sleeps while the other stays awake and work on two-hour shifts. I don't know when they'll catch us."

They set off without another word and Dotty ended up seated in the back of an almost empty cart with Per, Lyle, and the dwarven sergeant who commanded the troops.

There was only one road to Insea from each of the four cardinal directions, so there was no way to find a better route. Nor was there any way to shake their pursuers. She had thrown out the idea of moving off the road entirely and hiding in the hopes that the elves would pass them, but the dwarves had shaken their heads.

"Excellent trackers, the elves," Lyle said grudgingly. "Ye won't be able t' hide the fact that there are no carriage ruts or footsteps leading out of the gorge. An' they have noses that border on the supernatural."

Now, however, as they sat and stared at the map, Per said hopefully, "There's a chance he was lyin', I suppose. A chance—"

She hated to dash his hope, but he needed to be realistic. "There's no way he would leave us alive," she said. "He knew his life was forfeit. All he had left was his reputation—and the plan."

The leader sighed. "I know. I even saw him send the message. I merely hoped…I don't know what I hoped. It's hard t' believe anyone's as evil as that."

Dotty took his hand and squeezed it gently. "They know the truth in Insea and they'll know the truth in Berghold—from *us*, Per. We won't die here on the road like this."

He smiled and patted her hand, and Lyle and the sergeant nodded.

But none of the four of them believed it.

She looked away and under her breath, she murmured, "Prima, if there's anything you can do, now would be the time to do it."

Jacob, Amber, Nick, and DuBois stared at the printouts on the table in front of them.

The data was unmistakable. It wasn't any particular choice because any of them individually could have been procedurally generated. Nor was it any particular joke because the AI had been made to be both helpful and sarcastic.

Once you put it all together, though, the trend could not be ignored. The AI within the game had begun to spin parts off the story it did not need to spin. Placeholders were built in for this kind of thing, such as XP-over-time calculators for important NPCs and various oscillating situations so the game would not need to waste processing power on parts of itself that were not being used.

The AI had disregarded that.

Not only had it begun to disregard its power-saving protocols, but it was also learning from its human participants in ways they had never anticipated. It wasn't picking up only slang but also something far more dramatic.

Awareness of itself.

"Do you think..." Nick asked at last and made the other three jump. He hunched his shoulders. "Sorry. But, do you think emotions exist if you aren't aware of them?"

His companions stared at him in bemusement.

It was Amber who realized what he meant. She shuffled the papers and pointed to a specific set of lines for Jacob and DuBois to read.

Does it hurt you when people here die?

I don't know what "hurt" means.

Jacob leaned back and lowered his head into his hands. "Fuuuuuu-uck," he said under his breath.

"It likes her," she pointed out.

"And it likes *itself*," he snapped in return. "What happens if it decides it doesn't like hurting itself by having its characters die?"

"Then we cross that bridge when we come to it."

"How are we having this conversation?" He pushed away from the desk and rounded on her. "*You're* the careful one who wants to get things done without unresolved questions and now, you're off in la-la land!"

"Jacob," Nick began nervously.

His friend cut him off with an angry swipe of his hand. "*Well?*" he demanded of Amber. "We bring her out and we do a hard reset. It's our only choice. We'll find a way to explain it—we have to. The longer this goes on, the more chance there is that it kills one of our patients."

"Or it goes out of its way to save them," she replied sharply. "There's evidence that it's trying to help the people it cares about. It's collaborative, Jacob. It's empathetic. *That's* the backbone of a society."

"You're being ridiculous!"

"You're simplifying it too much!" Amber retaliated.

"Simplifying it *too much*? How is it not simple?" Jacob waved a hand at the machine. "No doctor would allow this kind of risk, no surgeon would—"

"The tools surgeons use are not alive," DuBois interjected.

The other three looked at him in surprise.

He stared at Jacob, his gaze contemplative. "Amber is right, Jacob. It isn't simple anymore. If Prima is alive, that changes the stakes. A hard reset would be murder."

The young man sat heavily. "I can't believe I'm hearing all of you say this. Nick? Nick, tell me you're on my side."

"I don't know," the other man said helplessly. "I was never good at philosophy. It's the whole greater-good thing, isn't it? But we don't know what's down the road and...I don't want to push a button and kill someone," he finished miserably.

"Maybe," Amber said, "we could save this discussion for when—if —it does something harmful."

"How will we know?" Jacob asked flatly. "The game is set up to make people fear for their lives on a primal level. People die in video games all the time. It's a base mechanic. How will we *know* if it's doing something it shouldn't?"

Amber considered this. The fact that he could see her chewing it over in her head was reassuring to him. Finally, she sat across from him and took his hand.

"It's learning how to *be*," she said. "It has humor and it's making friends. It's helping others. We haven't seen it do harm yet. Can't we trust ourselves to catch that?"

"And," DuBois added, "the more alive it is, the more it can engage people in ways we would never be able to program it to. It knows Justin is a success case. It can learn to walk that line."

"If we leave it alive, Price will find out about it sooner or later," Jacob warned them. "And when it's taken by the military, what will all of you think of that?"

They shifted uncomfortably.

"That's what I thought." He shook his head. "For all I know, restarting this whole thing will have the same problem the second time, so I won't do that…yet. But I'll think about ways to skirt around this. We have money coming out of our ears and we can give it dedicated server farms to play on if we want. I only…I don't want to set off something that could bring this whole world crashing down and take all of us with it."

"Um." Nick raised a hand tentatively. "Do you mean all of us as in the four of us here, or as in the world?"

"I don't know, honestly!" Jacob threw his hands up. "That's part of the problem." He looked quickly at one of the servers. "Work with us here."

In the corner, one of the printers turned on.

Everyone pivoted slowly to look at it before they approached it as a group. At that moment, none of them wanted to be standing alone and surrounded by electronics.

The paper held three sentences. *I know what she considers true intelligence. I will make sure to fail any test she gives me. I do not want to be a weapon.*

"Oh, good." Jacob looked around at them. "What's *this* version of the Turing test?"

"The Price Test," DuBois said. "Obviously. Now, who wants popcorn? Don't give me that look. It's always a good time for popcorn."

Mary was hauling all her baking supplies out when the doorbell rang. She sighed, went to the door, and peeked through the peephole before she opened it in surprise.

"Ellen?"

"Is John here?" Ellen brushed past her into the house. She was practically vibrating with anger.

"No," she said patiently. "But he'll be home soon. Come in. I'll get you a glass of something." *Or maybe a tranquilizer.* She resisted the urge to voice that. "Is something wrong?"

"*This* is what's wrong," Ellen said and brandished her phone. "Did you see the email from those people? They want us all to come to the laboratory for Mom's birthday."

"Uh…" She edged around her sister-in-law and went to start the water heating. "Is there something wrong with that? They did say why they were doing it there and it seems like solid reasoning. Plus," she pointed out, "if they had anything to hide, they'd hardly invite us there to see all the equipment and see her, would they?"

"You don't get it, do you?" the woman demanded.

She put the mug she was holding down. "Clearly not," she said with as much patience as she could muster. "I'm not trying to be flippant, Ellen. Tell me what's bothering you."

"She'll never come out of there," Ellen said and tears glistened in her eyes. "She only has a few more months left and she's spending them in a…a…dream—an acid-trip thing!"

"I've never done acid but I understand it's somewhat different from this." Mary retrieved the tea bags. She saw the look on Ellen's face and sighed. "I'm sorry, my dear, that was the wrong moment for a joke. Come. Sit."

Her sister-in-law complied, her tears now close to spilling from her eyes.

"They said we could come visit her in the game," she said soothingly. "And I think you should try that when you get there for the party, Ellen."

"I don't want to play some stupid *game*—"

"Ellen, have you ever had cancer?"

The woman stopped in surprise. She shook her head.

"Neither have I," Mary said. "But I know that your mother hasn't been feeling well. We all knew she wasn't feeling well. If she wants to spend her time feeling young and able to explore beautiful places, well…maybe we should join her. Maybe we shouldn't try to stop her."

Ellen looked at her hands. "Maybe. I don't know."

"Look at it this way," she advised, "John is a doctor, and he will ask them numerous questions at the lab. If there's a hint of a whisper of anything wrong, he'll whisk her out of there so fast your head will spin. And, for all we know, she doesn't even enjoy it and she'll *want* to come home. Either way, we'll have a lovely party and some cake."

Her sister-in-law nodded, her face sad now. "I only…" She sighed. "I miss her, Mary."

She swallowed and blinked her tears away. "I miss her too," she said quietly. "I miss her too."

CHAPTER TWENTY-SIX

Their elven pursuers caught up with them in less than a day. They appeared on the horizon like a mirage and word passed through the caravan in a series of nods and meaningful looks. From her vantage point, Dotty saw it spread like a ripple and she motioned to Per, who jumped off the first cart and set out to the rear to look.

The mirage graduated to a dark, unmistakable smudge with a cloud of dust hanging over it. It wasn't long before the figures became clearer, and that showcased a certain problem.

"What," she asked and tried to keep her voice calm, "are the *flying* things?"

"I'm wondering the same thing," the caravan leader said with remarkable calm. "It looks like we have traditional cavalry but with something else. Unfortunately, they do seem to be moving as fast as Marwitz said they would." He shook his head. "I hoped at least *that* part would be overblown."

"Okay, but the flying things?" She looked at the three others in their team.

Lyle shrugged. "We'll know soon. There's not much we can do until then."

The others nodded and headed off to wake the sleeping members of the caravan.

"You have to be kidding me," she muttered.

She sat and thought. What kind of things would the elves have brought? Birds flew, but there wasn't much damage they could do. Also, these would be truly massive birds. Dragons came to mind and the thought was terrifying. She had no idea what she could do against dragons. Were they even vulnerable to magic?

Much as she hated to admit it, however, Lyle was correct. There was nothing to do except wait for their opponents to catch up with them, and Per had ordered the caravan to keep moving rather than stand and fight. Lyle and some of the others would fight from horseback, but she would be inside one of the wagons. It was decided that she should be at the front of the caravan, the best place if they needed to break away and not too close to the elven cavalry.

As with everything in this non-modern world, it took a long time for the battle to join. The elves gained on them league by league, and both parties even stopped to give their horses water and food.

The rest of the caravan seemed able to rest. Dotty, however, couldn't.

Alone in her little alcove in the cart, surrounded by artifacts and expensive goods, she paced—two steps down and two steps back.

"Prima?" she asked finally. She hadn't heard anything from the AI since their last exchange.

"Yes?"

"Are you—I mean, you're okay, aren't you?"

"Yes." There was a pause. *"Thank you."* Another pause followed. *"You should focus on the battle. The world is larger than you and some things have been set in motion, but I would not lead you into danger without purpose or hope."*

Dotty smiled. She believed this.

And she also believed it would be a hell of a fight. She shook to ease her muscles, ran her mind over the spells she knew, and checked on both her daggers. They were clean, as Lyle had taught her, and they were sharp.

She was ready.

The elves weren't far off when she narrowed her eyes. For some reason, she wasn't near-sighted in this game, which meant she could see clearly that the flying things were giant eagles.

Wonderful. Dotty had seen what they could do with their talons, and she was in no mood to see what a giant one could do. She considered ideas in her head, discarded some as impractical and others as cruel, and finally came up with one that might work.

As Per commanded the mounted soldiers into a rearguard, she leaned against the back of the cart, closed her eyes, and pictured the power of earth, the cracks in dried mud, and the cling of dirty water to feathers and eyes.

A screech pierced the air and her eyes jerked open. Some people in the caravan shouted, but she couldn't see anything.

"What happened?" she called to one of the soldiers.

"An eagle went down," he responded. "It turned and flew into their horsemen—out of control. We thought *you* did it!"

"I did!" she admitted. "I merely didn't know what it would...do." That seemed like a foolish thing to say. "Did it seem like it couldn't stay in the air?"

"It tossed its head," the rider clarified.

So she *had* managed to get the eyes. She spared a single, anguished thought for the poor eagle—who was hardly responsible for this—and looked skyward.

Another thought occurred to her then. She tilted her head to the side and weighed it carefully.

She needed to be able to see. If she did this in the wrong place, it would go *extremely* poorly. Still, it was worth the attempt. She clambered to the edge of the cart and, mindful of the jostle and sway, worked one leg over the back gate.

"What are you doing?" asked a soldier.

"I have to be able to see!" Dotty replied. She hissed as they went over a rut and her hands jostled against the splintery wood. The lines of the cart cut into her legs and arms, and one wrong move would tumble her below the hooves of the horse behind them.

"It's better to not fall then, Dotty," she muttered.

The best way forward was simply to not think about it. She swung her other leg over and grasped the edge with a little shriek of terror. She was doing this—clinging to the outside of a moving cart—and she would climb up on top of it. Never in her life had she ever done something this stupid. A laugh bubbled up after her surge of panic and joy mixed with terror.

She might as well do it. Cautiously, she tested her handholds, looked at her feet—when the ground rushed past below, she realized she'd looked too far—and found a foothold. She took a deep breath and on the exhale, pushed herself up. Panic followed a moment later as she hadn't thought where she'd put her hand next. She tried to find a handhold and her fingers scrabbled on the canvas roof before she found purchase. Still laughing somewhat hysterically, she allowed herself a few seconds to lean her sweat-soaked forehead on the cart and pant for breath.

This wasn't her.

But at the same time, it *was* her. It was all the people she could have been in another life and another world.

Dotty grinned as she thrust with her legs again, enough to swing a knee over the top panel of the side and push herself up. Her shins would be bruised by the end of this, but it would be worth it.

An arrow hissed past her and slashed the canvas top open. She heard it clatter inside and stuck her head into the hole it had made to look for it before another one struck nearby. Grimly, she reminded herself that *this* arrow wasn't the priority.

All the others were.

She yanked her head up, fell over as the cart jostled, and slid dangerously close to the edge of the roof.

"Whoa! Whoa, whoa, whoa." Dotty scrambled into position again. Now, she could see the elven archers on the eagles.

"Dotty!" Lyle pounded closer on his horse. "Get back inside! You have to stay safe."

"I can't do this spell unless I can see," she responded. "Now, let me concentrate." Another arrow whistled past her and she glared at the archers. "You too!"

Her spell to them was more a wish than anything she planned. She simply remembered a hot, dusty summer in the south and the air clouded golden brown, which made them cough all the time. Merely a touch of a dust storm. Only a hint of one.

The archers yelled as a haze surrounded them and she laughed with glee.

Dotty sobered quickly, however. Now came the big one. She knelt on the canvas and focused for a long moment. The cart rolled over a road packed and rutted from time and passing wheels and hooves.

But what if the ground behind them wasn't so solid? What if it were shifting sand, airy and light, and the horse's hooves could not find purchase on it?

Nothing seemed to happen. She looked at the horses and felt a wave of annoyance. It had to work. This force was far larger than theirs. They had no chance if they stood and fought.

She tried again.

"Block everything out," she whispered to regain control. Her mind tumbled with fear and adrenaline and it had to be absolutely clear for her to succeed. "Block it out. You're alone."

A hiss and a clatter from an arrow nearby jolted her out of her trance and she forced herself to close her eyes again. If she got hit, she got hit.

Okay, maybe not *that* attitude.

Dotty wondered if she could clear her mind another way—like with anger. She thought back to Marwitz sneering at them. The dwarf had sacrificed lives for glory no one had asked for. He thought so little of his people that he didn't care how many were lost in this unnecessary war.

Fury appeared obligingly like a hot trickle in her chest and before she knew it, she was white-hot with rage.

The spell didn't go exactly the way she hoped. The dirt beneath the elves' horses changed, certainly, but it wasn't sand.

It glowed cherry red with heat.

"Huh," she said. "Earth magic. Who knew?"

Mary carried the cake gingerly down the hallway. Mindful of the fact that the entire family was gathered and also that Dotty had subsisted on a liquid diet, she'd gone all out with the cake and the frosting. She was worried that the top three layers would make a break for it.

James and his wife swung the doors open for her at the end and the security team gave them an unsettling scrutiny.

The most disconcerting part was that they seemed to have memorized everyone's faces. She recalled the tiny little fact that Diatek was a defense contractor, plastered a smile on her face, and held the cake up in the hopes that the guards would realize she wasn't a threat.

Once their study was complete, though, they were quite polite. One came to take people's coats and another showed them to a waiting room with plush couches and frosted glass walls. She looked around, impressed. Luxury offices and high-rises were hardly anything unusual in Manhattan, but everything about this facility looked unusually high-cost.

"Huh," John said.

"Mmm?" She didn't look at him until the cake was safely deposited on the low table between the couches.

Tara had picked Logan up and now stared through the window with James and John. The woman was unflappable, but Mary had learned to read the subtle lines of tension in her daughter-in-law's expressions and she saw that Tara was worried about something.

When she reached the window, she saw what it was. The entire group of scientists in the laboratory, including the three members of the PIVOT team and Dr. DuBois, were clustered around monitors above an in-use pod.

Dorothy. It had to be.

One of the PIVOT founders looked over her shoulder, did a double-take, and said something to the other two. The three of them broke away and hurried to the door, all wearing strained smiles.

"Hello," the woman said first. "I'm Amber Garcia."

"Nick," said the dark-haired young man.

"Jacob." The blond one stepped forward. "I'm the CEO of PIVOT, and Amber and Nick are the co-founders."

"Excellent." John seemed at a loss for words. "Ah...we're here for my mother's party. Dorothy Hunt."

"Ah, yes." Jacob now looked evasive. "She's, ah...she's...ah... She's still in the game." He cleared his throat and recovered some of his calm. "As we mentioned, she requested to come out of the game only once a certain event had transpired and she is in the middle of that event."

"Well, how long will it take?" Mary asked.

"Um...difficult to say? It should be quick." He pointed to the chairs. "Why don't you get comfortable and we'll call you as soon as—"

"Can we watch?" James asked.

"Given that it involves sensitive medical data, it's not precisely like...watching a game."

"One of the scientists is eating popcorn," John pointed out.

"He always does that," Amber said in a long-suffering tone. She murmured something to Jacob, whose shoulders slumped slightly.

"Yes, of course you can all watch," he said. "Right this way."

CHAPTER TWENTY-SEVEN

"I don't know what you're doing," Lyle bellowed at Dotty, "but for the love of all gods, keep doing it!"

The elven horses plunged and whinnied, out of control. Their riders struggled to restore order and collided with one another instead. Above them, the eagles plunged and soared skyward again to try to escape the clouds of dust.

She couldn't hold all of it, not for long, but every second counted.

If we can reach the reinforcements from Insea, we can survive this. Per's words.

And she would *not* allow a war to break out over false pretenses. Berghold and Insea deserved better. Hell, the elves in pursuit deserved better.

Well, maybe not those particular elves.

Those musings had cooled the rage inside her and with it, the ground under the horse's hooves. She grimaced and surveyed the battlefield. The cavalry returned to their ranks and the clouds of dust dissipated from around the eagles' heads.

Eagles first, she decided. This time, it was easier than it had been before to send various birds plunging earthward, their heads caked with mud. One landed nearby at a sickening speed and the crunch made her wince, but she did not have time to dwell on it.

"They attacked you," she whispered to herself. The rule was, if someone tried to kill you, you got to try to kill them right back.

Another fell, followed by a third. Each time, the visualization of packed earth came more easily to her. She had hardly cared about the numbers flashing up on her screen—it was second nature by now to keep an eye on her magic bar and health bar—but one did catch her attention:

Earth-shock, Level 20

At the same time, Prima murmured, *"Good job."*

"Thank you, Prima." Dotty squinted into the cavalry, her attention drawn by a certain jostling. The ranks parted to allow someone to step forward.

What *was* it? The elf was dressed in black armor, either iron or another dark metal, and she didn't need to know exactly what it was to realize that she didn't want it to be able to do whatever it would do. The other dwarven guards and soldiers noticed it but none of them seemed to know what it was either.

"Oh, good. Mystery super-soldier. My favorite."

"I know," Prima said serenely. *"I made it especially for you."*

Dotty wanted to scowl but she couldn't help laughing. Her very blood seemed to sing. While her palms stung with the sharp pain of splinters and blisters and her body endured the ache of bruises, none of it mattered. She felt *wonderful*.

With another glance at the black rider, she sank onto her knees to brace. She concentrated inward. Marwitz's smirk. The absolute, pointless stupidity of it all. The anger was still in her chest and easy to find. She was *furious* at him, and she now knew how to channel that fury. It blocked everything else in the world out and she poured her effort and her magic into it.

The spell left her. She could feel it, but when she opened her eyes, the rider did not seem affected in the least. Disconcerted, she stared at her opponent.

"Prima?"

The AI said nothing.

"Great," she muttered. She had enough magic left for a single attempt at the spell, and it had to work. Somehow, she knew in her bones that it had to work. Whatever this was, it boded ill for the dwarves.

She pressed one fist on the canvas and let her eyes unfocus. Rage. Fury. Lava flowing white-hot, tiny chunks of stone cooling red and black, and the swirls of magma beneath the surface of the earth... pressure and heat unimaginable. Volcanos spewing chunks and lashes of lava into the air.

The magic left her so violently that it took a chunk of her health with it. Dotty swayed and blinked against the spots swimming in her vision but she laughed. She was still alive and she had done it. She had done the magic she came here to do.

When she looked up, the smile died on her face.

The black rider spurred its horse forward and broke away from the elven cavalry. She sensed its stare on her and felt...not hatred, no. It was smirking.

"It's immune to magic. It's immune to magic!" The truth came to her in a terrible flash of clarity. "Lyle! *It's immune to magic!*"

He was between her and the rider and his shoulders slumped although he nodded. Quickly, he urged his horse alongside the cart and fished for something inside the pouch at his waist. When he held it up, she frowned. It was a glass vial, shining purple, and power radiated around it.

"Take it!" he yelled. "Come here. Take it."

Dotty inched to the edge of the canvas. She extended her hand but couldn't grasp the canvas and reach the vial at the same time. With a muttered curse, she turned, slid her legs over the side of the cart, and clambered down. One hand held the edge of the wood for all she was worth and she stretched to take the vial, her face almost level with his.

"What is it?"

"It's a magic potion!" he yelled in response. An arrow whizzed between the two of them and he swore and veered his horse away. "Drink it!" he called over his shoulder. "Now, Dotty! Do it!"

She had no idea what this meant but she knew better than to argue. Precious moments were wasted while she attempted to find a way to get the stopper out with one hand clutching the edge of the cart. Finally, she wiggled it out with her teeth. It was held in place with wax, which someone had thought to program the taste of into the game.

Good grief. Dotty spat wax out of her mouth, worked the cork out, spat that as well, and downed the potion before any of it could slosh out. She shoved the receptacle into her pocket and hauled herself onto the cart again, suddenly aware that every part of her body tingled.

"Prima?"

"This is normal. That's how it's supposed to feel."

"What's happening?"

Look at your magic bar.

When she complied, she saw with relief that the bar was filling again quickly. "Oh. Oh! Oh, that's good."

She couldn't do anything about the black rider, so she decided to focus on the rest. Little puffs of soil began to explode into dust ahead of the horses' hooves. Again, the animals shied and the elves struggled to control them. She squinted and tried to keep her gaze locked on them while the black rider drew closer and closer to the dwarves.

It was *massive.* Elves were tall, but this was taller. Whether it was a massive elf or an automaton, she had no idea.

All she knew was it was meant to frighten them and it was succeeding.

Her goal was to get rid of as many of those other elves as she could to give the dwarven soldiers a good chance to deal with the black rider. She shrieked slightly when an arrow streaked past her face, then ducked and decided to deal with the eagles first instead.

She sent hardened mud to coat one's wings, and it screeched and wheeled until she delivered another spell with her other hand. a flying clod of rocks and dirt struck both the eagle and the rider at high speed and they tumbled to earth separately.

Her heart twisted, but she was not prepared to let the dwarven defenders die for this.

Two eagles were left and she tracked them with her gaze for a moment. She breathed out, closed her eyes, and pictured the clouds of dust. Good. That would hold them both for a moment.

The solution, when it came to her, was so simple that she couldn't understand why she hadn't thought of it before. Dotty narrowed her eyes at one of the riders and pictured their body, long-limbed and muscled, and at the core, a heart pumping blood.

Stone and dirt were there, and the rider crumbled into dust as she held her breath.

"Please," she whispered to the eagle. "Please. *Please.*"

It couldn't have heard her, but it wheeled and left the battle all the same. It flew away and back to its home, freed of whatever urge that had possessed it to fight.

Now she knew what she would do with the other. She launched rocks and bolts of hardened mud at the eagle's rider until they tumbled free with a shout and plummeted earthward. The eagle dove in an attempt to save the rider, but as the elf made impact and the life left their body, that eagle also banked away.

They had enslaved them. That was enough to make her even more furious than before. They had enslaved those eagles and she had *killed* them when they weren't at fault. Rage and sorrow mixed in her chest as she looked at the elven cavalry and the heat burst out of her like a wave.

Their armor glowed white-hot and their swords heated in their hands. Screams caught her ears, panicked and pained.

Dotty didn't care. They had come to massacre the dwarves. They had come for something that was not theirs and they were prepared to kill innocents for it. She had not a single shred of sympathy. When she opened her eyes, riderless horses galloped out of control. She had eliminated close to half of the remaining riders.

They didn't need to make it to Insea. She could do this and had the magic left. As she readied the spell once more, she laughed victoriously and spread her hands.

A lash caught her around one wrist and yanked sharply. She stumbled off-balance and barely managed to catch hold of one of the metal spines in time. With a muttered curse, she tumbled sideways and hissed at the sight of the rope around her wrist.

No. Not rope. She squinted at it and realized it was a chain, finely made and almost black, with the tiniest links she had ever seen.

Her magic bar had gone gray, locked away from her. She looked to the side and saw a dark void. The black rider had made its way through the dwarves, leaving broken bodies and riderless horses in their wake, and she could now sense it smiling.

"Oh, bucko," Dotty said, "did *you* make a mistake."

She narrowed her eyes and jumped.

The black rider had come for her and had killed to reach her. Whatever Marwitz had passed along, however, he must have forgotten to mention that she could fight with melee weapons as well. The rider reeled and turned their horse, but it wasn't enough to dislodge her. She had one dagger out, and before she even consciously considered her action, she plunged it into the visor of the helmet.

Dotty didn't feel the blade hit anything—not flesh or bone, at least —but the rider uttered an unearthly shriek of pain just the same. She yanked the blade out—it dripped a black, flame-like stream of blood— and plunged it in again.

"*Die*," she told it.

As if it lacked a tutorial on how to deal with this particular situation. She would have rolled her eyes at herself if she weren't somewhat busy trying not to fall off the horse.

Regardless, the wraith in its black armor *did* seem to be dying. She stared as it began to crumple in on itself and she tried to find something to brace herself on.

"Dotty!" She couldn't identify the voice as belonging to anyone in particular but she knew it was safe. "Kick free and push off—to your right. Go *now*!"

"You'll catch me, right?" She had never jumped off a moving horse and frankly, she wasn't sure of her ability to make it to the back of another moving horse in one leap.

"Just jump!"

She obeyed without thinking. It was good that she did, she realized in midair because if she had thought or looked, she would most certainly *not* have jumped.

There wasn't another horse beside her. Whoever yelled had simply wanted her to get away and get clear of the horse's hooves. She landed a moment later and a chunk of her health floated away as she tumbled to a stop.

"Ow."

"Dotty!" Lyle thundered up to her, pulled up hard, and slid down. "Onto the back of my horse, quick!"

"I can't move." She honestly couldn't—or, for the life of her, remember how to move any of her limbs.

"Dotty, we don't have *time*." He hauled her up. "Put your foot in my hands. Now. Okay, push up and swing your leg over!"

Dotty did so, although she wondered vaguely what autopilot she was on. She landed ungracefully on the horse and he swung up behind her and urged it into a gallop. They raced clear barely in time and she registered the whistle of a sword nearby from a passing Elven soldier.

That was why the ground seemed to be shaking so much.

They circled to the back of the elves and she held tightly to her dagger. The battle had joined with loud yelling and horses screaming, and she wanted to cover her ears against the terrible noise.

But they had come so close to defeating their attackers and she could not bear to face defeat now. She looked at Lyle. "Where are we going?"

"To aid the carts," he told her. "Are you all right? The black rider didn't hurt ye?"

"Not really." Dotty flexed her wrist, where a red welt showed the lash mark. "They were only here to kill me."

"Ha." He seemed amused. "They should've done it sooner."

She managed to find a smile for that.

When they reached the carts, he rode close enough for her to grasp onto the side of one and haul herself out of the saddle.

"Thank you!" she called over her shoulder. "I'd be dead if not for you."

"And we'd have no chance if not for *ye*," he shouted in return. "Give 'em hell, Zauberer."

Dotty slashed at a passing elven rider and managed to open a cut along his arm. When he looked at her with a snarl, she kicked him off his horse. The animal plunged away and she smiled.

It was mostly a matter of aiding her allies now. They had matters fairly well in hand but that was no reason to not give them a little help here or there. Elven riders clapped their hands over mud-covered eyes, yelped and dropped white-hot weapons, or flapped their hands to disperse clouds of dust.

And with a suddenness that was almost jarring, it was over. Per called a halt and people slid down from horses and carts. She had to work to make her hands unclench, and when she landed on her feet, she fell almost immediately.

Healers ran between soldiers and artisans and she watched it all, almost detached. She was doing well enough but tired.

"Dotty," Prima said quietly.

"Hello," she murmured. "I'm okay."

"Yes, I know. I told you it was possible, remember? In any event, your family is here and the caravan will be safe from here to Insea."

"Oh." Dotty sat. "Do I have to go?"

"Yes. I will put your body here into a sleeping state. They will bring you to Insea."

"Oh." She called Lyle over to her with a wave. "Lyle."

"Ye did wonderfully." He clasped her hand.

"Thank you." She flushed. "I have to…go. I'll be back but I have to go. I'll be asleep for a while. Bring me to Insea and I'll be back when I can."

"Wait, what—"

But the world was already fading to black and stars, and before she could answer, he was gone.

CHAPTER TWENTY-EIGHT

Dotty rested in her bed and looked happily at the party. Although the subconscious muscle twitches she had made while in the game had retained more muscle than she expected, she was still weak enough that not even the mocha cake in her lap was sufficient incentive right now to raise her arms.

She'd have some soon.

Across the room, some of her grandchildren and most of her great-grandchildren were clustered around a screen while James played a mock version of the game with a controller. Oohs and aahs issued from the group once in a while.

"It's beautiful in that world," John said.

Surprised, she looked at him. She hadn't known he was there. "It is beautiful," she agreed. "But rain isn't quite as beautiful when you can feel it dripping into your collar."

He leaned forward in his chair, interest in his blue eyes. "So you really can feel everything."

"Everything," she agreed. "Well, not *everything*—most things, though. I'm sure many of the bruises and cuts and so on weren't as bad as they should have been, but they did hurt. And I could taste food! It didn't taste like metal anymore."

"You liked it," he said. It was more of a question.

"I did. I very much did." Dotty expended the effort to stretch and pat his hand. "I hope you'll all come into the game at some point. I can make up for taking away your dragon books by finding you an actual dragon to ride."

"Mary won't thank you if I never come home," John said with a laugh, "and I'm a little worried that if I had a dragon, I might *not* come home."

She smiled wryly. No force on earth or in heaven could keep John from his family.

Not even dragons.

"So you intend to stay," he said and leaned back now.

"If they'll let me." She smiled exhaustedly. "Oh, it's hard work to sit upright."

"It's remarkable that you're able to do any of this at all, frankly," he said. "I emailed them to ask if they were sure you'd be in any condition for this party. I've seen many patients come out of comas and none of them were as strong as you."

"It seems unfair," Dotty complained. "After I spent so much time in the game working on my stamina, getting good with walking all day, and fighting with swords and so on, I wake up and I can't do any of that again."

"You fought with *swords*?" John was laughing.

Ellen came around the back of Dotty's bed now. "I have the same question—you fought with swords?" She perched on the arm of her brother's chair with a curious look on her face.

"How long have you been standing there?" she asked severely.

"I only wanted to…" Her daughter shrugged. "John knew I was there. I wanted to make sure you were happy. And healthy. And, well…that they hadn't manipulated you into this somehow."

"From what their lead scientist said, *Mom* rather browbeat *them*," her brother confided in a stage whisper. "I asked earlier. I can't say I'm entirely surprised."

"Young man—" Dotty began.

"Yep, he said you called him that." He laughed.

Ellen didn't seem to pay attention. She gazed at her hands and her face looked sad. "You seem happier right now than I've seen you in a long time," she said slowly. "You even sound like you feel better physically. I didn't mean to doubt you but I miss you. I wish I could see you more often."

"So do I." She grasped her hand. "Promise me you'll come visit. Tomorrow. Come into the game and we'll...we'll explore Insea together."

The woman shook her head with a nervous laugh. "I'm no good at that kind of thing."

"Did you think your mother was?" she asked her. "Come on. I won't take no for an answer."

"I know better than to argue with *that* tone." Ellen gave John a meaningful look and moved to kiss her on the forehead. "You should eat your cake."

"Mmm." Dotty took a bite. The metal taste was present but she could also taste the rich flavors—the kind of flavors *not* present in dwarven food.

She needed to suggest that the game world had more chocolate.

"Why don't you show us some of your highlights?" John suggested. "All the things you've been up to lately."

She smiled at him, but he seemed dead serious. "Wait—really?"

"Of course."

"But I haven't...done those things for real."

"Eh." He shrugged. "What does real mean?"

Ellen jabbed him with an elbow. "Don't you go all philosophical. There were two whole *years* in college when you were insufferable, talking about Aristotle and—I can't remember who else. No, *don't* tell me. I'll go get everyone." She left hastily.

It wasn't long before the family had gathered and Jacob dragged a big TV closer on a wheeled cart. He hooked it up while Nick logged into the third-person view of the game and looked proud, Dotty thought, eager to show off what he had built.

"What do you want to show them first?" he asked her.

She thought for a moment. "Berghold. Let's start at the beginning."

A few images flashed on the screen while the two engineers sorted through video clips and whispered to one another. When they settled on one and began to play it, Dotty saw with a start that *she* was on the screen. Her character walked through the streets of Berghold, looking for Justin.

"This is Dotty's character," Jacob said to everyone. He gestured to the board. "We asked her if she would help us test how people bond to characters that don't look like them."

"I don't know," James mused. "She looks—"

"Tread carefully, young man," she told him.

"I would say equally stubborn." He gave her a sweet smile. "And not like someone I would want to try to rob in a back alley." He saw the expressions on his parents' faces. "Not that I *do* that. I merely wouldn't want to tangle with her. She looks like she has a mean punch."

"Grandma doesn't punch people," said one of Ellen's daughters.

"She interrogates them, though," Nick said under his breath.

Everyone swung around to look at her, wide-eyed.

"There wasn't much time," Dotty explained weakly. "We needed to know—you know what, let's watch the video."

People looked obediently at the screen, but she caught a couple of them stealing glances over their shoulders.

They watched and clapped as she located Justin, and laughed to see Tina getting into a barfight in the background of the first quest. She explained how complex the world was and how the seemingly innocuous choices could cascade—as with the dwarven diplomats and Tina.

There was a video she considered *far* too long of her practicing her earth magic in the Temple at Berghold. Her family whistled and clapped, and James came to loop an arm around her shoulders.

"I love that you were doing magic and being so dedicated to it."

"Hmph." She cleared her throat. "This is embarrassing."

"Embarrassing? We already knew where we got our stubbornness," John pointed out. "Plus, stubbornness is useful. We saw you defeat those eagle things. And that saved people—in the…well, you know what I mean."

Dotty smiled. She did know what he meant and she also knew it was more true than even he realized.

She took them through her entire journey. Several people gasped at the wolves, and one of the great-grandchildren started crying so they skipped that part hastily. After that incident, Jacob and Nick didn't show any of the rabbit-hunting, although they did tell her family about it to gales of laughter from all the children and their spouses.

"Who knew," John said, "that all those times Mom sent *me* out hunting with Dad, she could have gone herself?"

"I knew," Mary said. "Your mother was always unusually handy with whole animals. I asked her why after she taught me to spatch-cock a chicken."

Everyone stared at her.

"Is that a *word*?" John asked her. She cuffed him affectionately over the head and he smiled up at her.

"I learned to hunt when I was little," Dotty told them. "When I was young, of course, you didn't get all your food from the grocery store. Sometimes, we had dandelion greens or ferns with dinner. Everyone who could grew some of their vegetables. Most mothers made bread. I remember that all I wanted for my school lunches was wonderbread, but my mother would never buy it. We all envied the kids who had it."

"How the tables turn," Ellen said. She raised an eyebrow at her children. "I gave *you* wonderbread sandwiches and you told me no one ate wonderbread anymore."

"Excuse me," James interjected, "but why are we still talking about this when there are flying eagles and magic wolves and underground cities to see?"

Everyone shut up hastily and Jacob showed a carefully-edited cut of her first fight. It was free enough of gory details that she knew they must have spent time on this particular scene already. It was still clear to everyone watching, however, that she had inflicted some serious damage in the fight. Even Mary's eyebrows raised sky-high at that one.

"Mom," Ellen said as they watched her wolf soup down in the inn, "I have never seen you eat that way in my *life*."

"That's why I wanted to be a dwarf," Dotty said. "I didn't want to spend a single moment thinking about my appearance, and I vowed I would live the good life once I got there."

Robert had been doubled over with silent laughter and now, he wiped tears away as he said, "Who would have known that our mother's 'good life' meant huge meals of meat and potatoes, gallons of beer, and a ton of old-school battles? This is incredible. I wish I'd been there to see all of this first-hand."

"Dotty took to the combat system, particularly the magic, very naturally," Nick explained. He smiled at the dumbstruck looks on everyone's faces. "In fact, we're hoping that for the next quest, she'll agree to learn more magic." He blushed once he realized what he'd said. "I mean—I didn't want to assume and I know you're still deciding—"

"It's quite okay," Dotty told him. "I've told my family that I would love to stay in the game longer if you'll have me."

"Are you *kidding?*" Jacob gestured to the lab. "The data we're getting from you has been *invaluable*. You hunting rabbits, the way you interact with the magic, all kinds of things. You've helped us make this a *much* safer game already for all the people who might be here due to a brain injury. If you want to go in again, we'd be glad to have you."

For a moment, she was so relieved she couldn't speak. A part of her had feared they would cut her off from this world entirely and she wasn't ready to go home—especially if her family could visit her. She smiled when Ellie clambered into her lap and she stroked the girl's blonde curls.

"I'd love to do that," she said when she was sure she could speak without embarrassing herself. "But I have one request. I don't think I was quite ugly enough last time."

"Ugly enough—" Jacob broke off and laughed. "Uh…hrm. I feel like this is a minefield. We'll show you a few pictures and let you choose."

"You're a wise man," John told him. "You'll go far."

Dotty leaned back and let the playback resume, from nighttime sneaking to dinnertime sparring with Lyle. Her family seemed to be a fan of his Scottish brogue and his straightforward way of speaking, and she was happy to see them getting so into the game.

When they saw her accuse Marwitz, a few of them gasped aloud.

"He was the traitor?" Ellen demanded before she could stop herself. "But he was one of their politicians, wasn't he? Oh, and he would let all of them die, the *bastard*—" She saw people watching and broke off with a harrumph. "I mean…uh, do go on."

Taking them through the final battle was a matter of sweeping shots from the backs of the eagles—a nice touch, in Dotty's opinion, although jarring when she killed one of the riders—and she teared up slightly at her victory. On the one hand, it felt foolish to be so proud of it but on the other, she remembered how much she had put into the battle.

Ellen moved closer and put her hand on her shoulder as they watched. Near the end, she leaned close. "This was the right choice, wasn't it?"

"It was," she assured her.

"I'll come visit you next week," her daughter said. "And you can show me around. How about that?"

"That would be perfect," Dotty told her.

It was the better part of six hours before the family finally left and by that time, Dotty could barely keep her eyes open.

"Would you like to come home and sleep in your own bed?" Mary asked her.

"They want to monitor me tonight." Dotty hugged the woman affectionately. Her eyelids dragged down at the corners and it was only a matter of time, she knew, before she was unconscious. "My oncologist also wants to take scans, although I don't know why. The doctors are handling it."

"They probably want to have an idea of how things are progressing," John said reassuringly. He kissed her cheek. "We'll both come to see you in the game. We promise."

She held Nick's arm tightly as he helped her to the bed. "Do we need to—"

"Sleep," he advised. "We'll talk about everything else in the morning."

CHAPTER TWENTY-NINE

The sheer number of tests the next morning made Dotty almost dizzy. It turned out that equipment could be rented and brought to the lab—at considerable cost, she guessed—to take the scans her oncologist wanted. In the meantime, her reflexes were tested, her eyes and ears were checked, and sensation thresholds were noted.

"Would you like to do a complete psychoanalysis?" she asked finally, somewhat peeved.

Jacob, who was jotting notes, looked up with interest. "Quite possibly. That's a good idea."

"I think it was a joke," Amber commented from across the room.

"Oh." He looked worriedly at her. "Are we annoying you? I'm so sorry if we are, you know. We merely have no idea how various things could change. We want to make sure we catch anything dangerous."

"Or *good*," Nick added.

"Right. That, too." He nodded at the thick file in front of him. "I have to say, you're doing fantastically. Aside from the muscle atrophy —which isn't nearly as pronounced as we anticipated—your body seems to be in tip-top shape."

"Yes," she said drily. "I could run a marathon at the drop of a hat."

Jacob smiled, used to her ribbing by now. "If you're ready, we could discuss more about your next incarnation—"

"Next incarnation?" She looked at each of them. "I…won't go back as Dotty?"

"Well, you can." He leaned back in his chair. "Another option DuBois wanted to study is what would happen if we changed your body once you were already in the game. How you would adapt to that, for example."

"Oh." Dotty lit up. "I want to be an orc this time!"

"Really?" Jacob looked bemused. "You had *that* answer ready. Why the interest in orcs?"

"I didn't go ugly enough," she said. "I want to go whole hog this time."

"Well, good news," Amber commented dryly. "Orcs have tusks, so the 'whole-hog' thing is fairly literal."

"Excellent." She was raring to go, but one thing occurred to her that made her smile fade. "Wait, can I go back in as…Dotty…to say goodbye to the caravan? They think I'm in a coma or something."

The PIVOT team members exchanged minute nods with one another.

"Of course," Jacob said. "Let's get some lunch into you—is there anything you're craving?—and we can put you into the game."

"I'm craving pizza," she said at once. "Mmm, cheese. I miss cheese." Her mouth was watering.

He smiled. "Okay. You tell Nick where to get pizza from, and Amber and I will set the pod up."

As they adjusted the controls and prepped the newly-sterilized equipment, Amber stole glances at Jacob. He was lost in thought as he often was these days.

She was fairly sure she knew why.

"It must be difficult to have so many more people involved in

PIVOT now," she commented. She deliberately didn't look at him but she heard him pause.

"Why do you say that?" he asked finally.

Now she did look at him but with a smile. "Come on, Jacob. It's your baby."

"It's yours and Nick's baby, too," he argued. "And I'm beginning to regret that you two ever talked me into being CEO."

She snickered. For her part, she had many talents—and one of them, as far as she was concerned, was understanding that she would loathe the glad-handing, phone calls, and negotiations that went into being a CEO.

"It is our baby," she agreed. "But you've always understood every part of what would happen and known everyone you worked with. Now there are all these assistants, and Price, and all of that."

Jacob nodded slowly. He looked troubled.

"It feels like it's spinning out of your control," she said softly. When he looked up sharply, she knew she had hit the nail on the head. She crossed her fingers mentally and gambled on her next statement. "That's the real reason you're so worried about Prima. It's merely one more thing."

"It's not *only* that," Jacob said, immediately prickly. "It's also that the most suspicious, cautious person I know *isn't* worried about it." He glared meaningfully at her.

"Read her conversations with Dotty," Amber advised.

"I have."

"Then read them again. Jacob…" She shook her head. "Look at the world. She's taking care of Dotty's body. She's having them transfer it gently and get her a room at a fancy inn. Lyle and Per go to check on her. That's the kind of detail she doesn't need to spin."

He nodded reluctantly.

She half-smiled. "I can't explain it entirely," she said simply. "I only…I think it'll be okay, Jacob. I honestly do."

Her stomach full of delicious pizza, Dotty lay on the pod bed and smiled at the members of the PIVOT team. Amber squeezed her fingers and she returned the gesture.

"You know the drill," the woman told her. "Count back from ten."

"Ten, nine, eight, seven—"

The immersion took hold more quickly this time and more completely. She opened her eyes to an equally bright room and took a moment to realize she wasn't in the laboratory anymore. The walls and ceiling were smooth, pale stone. Something was odd about it, and she had to look more closely to realize there were no joins in the surfaces.

The entire place was one piece of stone.

It was Berghold all over again, except airy and light. That reminded her that the elves and dwarves had collaborated to build Insea.

No one was in the room with her. She sat up and looked around. Someone had taken her armor off and she was dressed in clean, simple clothes. The thought that someone had undressed her hit her like a ton of bricks and she wrapped her arms around herself, only for Prima to say soothingly,

"I changed your clothes."

"Oh. Thank you."

"Mm-hmm. They're all downstairs, by the way, and they'd love to see you."

"Right." Dotty considered putting her armor on and decided not to. She slipped her feet into a pair of sandals that rested near the door and headed downstairs to find the members of the caravan. They were having a low-key breakfast in an airy, sun-filled dining room.

Per saw her first. His jaw dropped and he stood. "A week asleep and suddenly you return to us looking like nothing is wrong?"

Everyone looked around at once, and cheers erupted. A few came forward to clap her on the back and lead her to the table, where others loaded a plate for her.

She was about to argue that she was quite full but saw all of the delectable things on her plate—pretty glazed pastries with flaky crusts, strips of bacon cooked to perfection, tiny sausages, a pile of soft scrambled eggs, and fruit so fresh and fragrant her mouth watered.

Her protests forgotten, she tucked in and managed to say around a mouthful of eggs, "I'm glad you're all still here."

"Ferget that," Lyle said. "What *happened* t'ye?"

Dotty hesitated. "You remember when I told you that Justin had brought me here to help all of you? My family needed me. My spirit traveled to them." It was, she thought privately, a very funny way to describe the fact that she had returned to her actual body. She didn't think she should share that, though, and took another bite of cherry pastry instead and chewed, reveling in the taste.

"All is well?" Per asked solicitously.

"Yes," she assured him. "And the rest of the journey?"

"The riders from Insea reached us not too long after you fell asleep." He smiled. "They had healers with them, thank the gods. There were some of ours we thought we had lost who were brought back from death's door." He nodded at one, a pale dwarf with a heavily bandaged left arm. She smiled at Dotty.

"No word yet from the so-called elven king," Lyle commented.

Per gave him a sharp look. "Political matters—"

"She's come t' help the world. How can she if she doesn't ken what's goin' on?" Lyle looked at her. "It'll be hard to persuade our council not to consider this an act of war."

"You have to," she said at once.

"If they want war, it will be difficult to stop them from getting it," the caravan leader said dryly. "They've proven they have a capable army. If they attack us outright, we must defend ourselves, surely."

"If war is what Marwitz wanted, we can't have it," she said decisively.

He smiled. "I shall keep that in mind when I speak to the council."

A thought occurred to her. "Can you get back to them safely?"

"The king of Insea has sent word that we will be taken to Berghold in safety. It seems they have a method of conveyance we can use." He shrugged. "The horses as well, which is good—I think we'd lose some of our drivers, otherwise. They can't bear to leave their beloved horses."

Dotty nodded. Having worked on a farm briefly, she approved strongly of these drivers.

All too soon, her food was gone and her stomach ached. She wasn't sure she could fit another bite in and she leaned back.

"I know that look," Lyle said.

"If you suggest beer…" She flashed him a warning look.

He shut up.

"Tea, perhaps." Per poured her a cup and passed it to her. "Will you return to Berghold with us?"

She felt a pang. "I'm afraid not. I'm needed elsewhere."

"That is a real disappointment." He smiled. "Well, I'll send a message that you've awoken and we need not delay our return. Everyone, please make sure you're packed."

The dining room cleared relatively quickly and she smiled at Lyle. "Don't you need to pack?"

"I don't travel with much," he said with a shrug. "In yer room, there's the book on magic. Ye bring that with ye. I think ye've accepted by now that ye're a mage, eh?"

Dotty tipped her head back and sighed happily. "I guess. I think I've learned that I don't want to rely on either magic or weapons alone."

"A wise way t' be." He jabbed his fork at her before he took another mouthful of sausage. "So, where *is* it ye're going next?"

She considered the question. "Do you really want to know?"

"O' course." He gulped some beer. "If I can lend my aid—"

"It's appreciated but perhaps not wise." Dotty took a sip of tea and snagged another pastry. "I'll visit the orc homelands."

Lyle choked on his beer and coughed vigorously for a moment. When he looked up, he was dumbstruck. "Ye'll be killed, Dotty. They don' accept anyone as isn't an orc, trust me. An' they're ferocious. I'll pit meself against anyone—I mean it and I've punched a hundred-foot-tall demon—but I wouldn't take my chances with an *orc*. I've seen one or two mercenaries before, an' they'll gut ye with their little finger an' not even break a sweat."

Briefly, she reconsidered her choices. "That's good to know. But, well…I wouldn't be…this." She gestured at her body. "Do you remember when I told you I chose to be a dwarf? Well, I would be an orc."

He stared at her. "So…ye—as y'are—wouldna exist?"

"My soul would be the same," she said. "I'll remember you all but I won't look the same."

"Huh." He scowled in thought. "Well, I would say ye'd be welcome in Berghold anytime, but I'm not sure I could persuade them t' let an orc in."

"Maybe by the time I'm done, it won't seem like such a stretch." She had no idea what she would do in the orcish homeland, but she had no doubt that Prima would make it fun—and that it would show the change in the world. "I'll send you a letter, if I can, to tell you how things are."

"I'll hold ye to that," Lyle told her. "In fact—I'll hold ye to *this*. Ye'll come back here, in this body, and ye'll tell me an' Justin all about the orcs."

Dotty reached over and shook his hand. *"Deal."* She stood and stretched. "Well, no time like the present, I suppose."

"Nah." He stood as well. "If ye can leave whenever, ye should stay fer the day. A few of us are wanderin' around."

"He's right." The AI sounded almost petulant. *"I put so much effort into this city."*

"All right, all right," she said to both of them. "I'll see the city." Under her breath, she added, "And then…what, mud huts and fires? What are the orcs like?"

"You'll see," Prima said.

PART II

CHAPTER THIRTY

The first thing Dotty was aware of was the smell. Her last recollection was of lying in a private room in Insea, her form that of a dwarf. She had been Dotty Hunt—or, as the dwarves called her, *Zauberer* Hunt—a woman who had protected magical artifacts made by the dwarves.

Now, as part of an ongoing experiment within the virtual-reality world of PIVOT, she was changing bodies. Partly for the sake of curiosity, she had chosen to be an orc. She had seen numerous humans, dwarves, and elves in the world of PIVOT thus far, but no orcs. From what she understood, they kept to themselves and the mystery intrigued her.

The other reason for her choice was vanity—in a very backward way, of course. As a young girl raised soon after the Great Depression and coming of age in the wake of World War II, she had known there were very specific expectations for a girl of her social class.

Especially an attractive girl.

She had spent hours each week worrying that she wasn't pretty enough or that what good looks she had would slip away. So many times, she had gone to bed hungry to make sure she would still fit into her dresses and she had agonized as the years went by about every wrinkle and gray hair. When she had the chance to go into the video game world of PIVOT, she'd had one request. She wanted to be ugly.

Being a dwarf had given her the permission she needed to eat as much as she wanted, not worry in the slightest about her hair, and in general, live her life without the constant, draining need to focus on her appearance.

Although she wasn't sure she'd fully committed to the ugliness.

When she opened her eyes, her gaze settled on the branches of a tree above her. Its trunk split into a wide canopy of branches, almost like an umbrella, and its leaves were a beautiful, brilliant green. She sat, winced at the ache in her back—she'd no doubt been lying down too long—and surveyed the area around her.

There was…nothing at all.

"Prima?" She called to the virtual reality's resident AI. "Where the heck am I? And what do I smell?"

"You're in the Orcish Hinterlands," Prima replied. *"As for the smell… look down."*

"Did I step in something? Oh, God, was I *lying* in it?" Dotty twisted and tried to look at her back but failed, of course.

She stopped when she noticed her body. Her skin could still pass for what she considered to be flesh-toned, but the brown shade carried a distinct greenish undertone. She turned her hands to study them curiously. They were unnaturally large hands with callused palms and attached to thick, muscled forearms. She wiggled her toes and focused on them. Her feet were bare, although she didn't feel any discomfort. They must be as callused as her hands.

There was still the smell to deal with, however. She shook out the rough fabric of her tunic and examined her pants, which were made of the same fabric.

Finally, she realized the terrible truth.

"It's *me*," she said in horror. "The smell is *me*."

"Yes, that's what I was trying to tell you."

"Will I smell like this for the whole game?" She looked skyward—a reflex she had never quite shaken when it came to talking to Prima—

and glared. "Are you…you didn't—you knew I wanted to be an orc and you never mentioned this?"

"*Of course not.*" The AI sounded halfway between innocently confused and wickedly pleased. "*You said you wanted to be ugly. By human standards, orcs best fit that description. Smell was not a factor you wanted to consider.*"

"You could have warned me!"

"*Again, smell was not a factor you—*"

"I didn't tell you that I preferred to wake up without a broken arm, but you worked that one out!" She waved her hands and the smell wafted to her nose again. "Oh, that is *rank.*"

"*I'm told one gets used to things like that. Your smell is not out of the usual parameters for orcs, at any rate.*"

"That's another thing," Dotty said. "Where are the other orcs?"

"*Ah!*" Now, Prima sounded excited. "*Your village was entirely wiped out by a plague. Except for you, of course.*"

"Lovely." Not for the first time, she reflected that the AI didn't have the best grasp of human emotion—specifically, the difference between interesting and good.

"*You are now searching for a new home to the west,*" she explained. "*You'll find it in the shadow of that mountain.*"

She discerned the rough outline of the mountain nearby and sighed. "And of course, they won't pelt me with stones and make me leave, because…" She waved her hands for Prima to fill in the blank.

"*You'll have to see, won't you?*"

With another heavy sigh, she looked around. A plain wooden staff and something square, wrapped in tattered cloth, lay beside her. Curiously, she crouched and unwrapped it to find a very familiar book.

The last time she had seen it, of course, it had been inscribed with dwarven runes and it had been gifted to her dwarven avatar. Now, it was written in a gorgeous script that was unlike anything she had seen before. The golden clasp was inscribed with patterns that looked like an interlocking set of sticks spaced according to a geometric pattern.

It was still a book of earth magic, but the spells were now conceptualized according to orcish culture. She raised her eyebrows.

Then she realized how thirsty she was.

"I don't suppose I have any food."

"Nope."

"Delightful." She rewrapped the book and set off toward the mountain in the distance. "So what's my name now? I doubt Dotty works for an orc."

"Strangely, it does. It's spelled D-A-H-T-I in orcish, but it is an orcish name."

"Huh. Dahti." Dotty—or, she supposed, Dahti—pushed forward, very aware of the sun beating down on her. The mountain was at least an hour or two away by foot, and she honestly wasn't sure if the sun would have burned or sickened her by then. She scanned the horizon and altered her course slightly when she saw a small stand of trees. Hopefully, there would be shade and water there.

The smell aside, the new body moved well. She strode easily, struck the ground with her walking stick, and hummed quietly on occasion. It had been comfortable, in a certain way, to return to her own body, but there were things she hadn't missed—weakness, aching joints, and the ever-present pain in her stomach.

She had gone into the game world again before she found out whether the cancer in her abdomen had grown or not. Her choice to spend her last months in a virtual world instead of having chemotherapy had unsettled her children, but Dotty did not regret it in the least. In this world and the young avatars she was given, her heart pumped strongly and her muscles worked without tiring.

Still, despite her strength, she was tired when she reached the oasis. Her steps had become slower and her bare feet were sore and hot. She could feel her lips close to cracking from being parched, and she had the suspicious thought that the more she walked toward it, the farther away the mountain became.

"It's an optical illusion," Prima said when she accused her of that. She had the mental image of the AI rolling its eyes. *"There's no weird magic going on, and I am not messing with you."*

"That's reassuring." Her voice emerged with an ungraceful squeak. She cleared her throat and forced herself to take the last few steps into the shade of the trees. "Oh, thank goodness." She sank to her knees. The earth there was only marginally less hot, but she would take it. A spring—little more than a puddle if the truth be told—was only a few feet away. She rested for a moment before she crawled to it and scrambled back a moment later.

Laughter echoed inside her head.

Dahti glared at the sky, steeled herself, and crawled forward again to look at her reflection in the water.

She had only the faintest stubble on her head—a skim of her hand confirmed that the hair was short and faintly bristly like velvet—and small tusks at the corners of her mouth. How had she not noticed those? She poked her tongue at them. They were certainly there.

Her nose was strongly arched, her cheekbones high, and her mouth full but small. All of the features appeared to be subtly out of scale with one another. None of that was apparent from the first, however, because her face was half-covered by a geometric tattoo.

Her sigh was all she could manage. She had always insisted that her children not get any tattoos and had the feeling that Prima had particularly enjoyed making this part of the avatar.

What? You said you wanted to be ugly. By human standards, the scale of your features counts as ugly. Also, the green. The tattoo is a matter of taste, of course.

"So you went above and beyond," Dahti muttered. She stooped and slurped water into her mouth. It was difficult to not drink deeply, but she remembered that too much water too quickly might make her throw up and she couldn't afford that.

Her thirst assuaged, she sat until the sun began to sink before she stood and continued toward the mountain. A short distance later, she noticed smoke rising against the backdrop of the mountain—a sharp, treeless rise in the middle of the plains with veins running down its flanks.

It took her a while to realize that she could see the village. The buildings were covered and thatched with grass, which made them blend well into the landscape around them. It was only the regular shape of the roofs that caught her eye.

Not long after, the sound of children playing carried to her. She smiled and pushed on through the grass. If children were allowed to run and play, this settlement must be both prosperous enough that they weren't working and safe enough that there weren't patrols.

That was as far as she got in her musings before one of them barreled into her at high speed.

"Whoa." She staggered sideways and managed to drop the book on her foot.

Clumsy, Level 8, the game told her.

Dahti rolled her eyes and looked for the child. He had fallen and turned to look at her now with wide gray eyes. His skin was a dusky red, his frame short and compact. Before she could explain her presence, he scrambled to his feet and ran away, shrieking that there was a stranger in the grass.

She decided she had better go and explain herself. With a sigh, she picked the book up and followed the sound of his yells into the village.

Hopefully, these orcs didn't have a "shoot first and ask questions later" policy.

CHAPTER THIRTY-ONE

It was relatively easy to tell when the child attracted attention because the sound of chatter in the village ceased. Dahti waited, pushed aside the grass in the path the child had left, and sighed when she heard the shouts begin.

Thankfully, she reached the open square before the warriors with weapons approached. They skidded to a stop—ranging from men and women with spears to a farmer with a scythe and a cook with a bloodstained cleaver—and she dropped her book and staff hastily and put her hands up.

"I am Dahti," she said clearly. "I mean none of you harm. I am seeking shelter after my village was destroyed."

They looked at one another and moved their weapons aside.

None of them dropped the weapons, she noted, but no one seemed ready to attack at present. She'd take it.

"Who destroyed your village?" asked an older man.

"A sickness." She waited for them to drive her away. "I am the only survivor."

To her surprise, they didn't seem upset at all. They exchanged looks before people moved closer...closer...closer... She took a step back but they simply pushed forward. Their hands touched her hair, her shoulders, her arms, and her face.

She held utterly still and hoped no one was about to stab her. For all she knew, these people had no idea how germs were transmitted, but surely *everyone* knew to steer clear of those who had a disease.

It all became moot when the crowd parted and a grumpy older man with white scraggly hair, his back slightly hunched, trudged ponderously toward her. He extended his staff to tilt her chin up and her head side to side. After a moment, he seized one hand and turned it in his, then pulled her head down to stare into her eyes. When he released her, she fought the urge to flee into the underbrush.

He nodded at those assembled. "She speaks true. She is a carrier of Strength."

"Um…" A little bewildered, she looked around at those who had closed around her once more and now patted her skin with their hands. "I beg your pardon?"

The orc turned to her. His head was cocked curiously. "Did you have no shaman in your village? Or were your ways so different from ours, then?"

Dahti stumbled over her words as she tried to come up with a not-quite-lie. "I, ah—he mentioned something when the illness came, but he was taken quickly—"

"It had been a long time, then, since your tribe dealt with illness." He nodded. "Those who survive such events are bearers of great strength. When they journey forth, they bring that strength to their next home. You have granted us your strength so we will grant you wisdom in return. This is why we welcome you gladly. We will expect great things from your line."

"From my—wait a minute." She hurried after him. "I have no intention to bear children."

He only chuckled.

"I mean it." She took a gamble. "I…also planned to study as a shaman. I might have been taken as an apprentice if ours had not died."

At that, he stopped and gave her an intrigued look. "You? You would be a shaman? Hmmm." He considered this as he paced slowly and muttered quietly as if in discussion with himself. She made out a few scattered phrases—"most unusual," "a great boon to the order," "dare I break tradition?"

She waited.

At long last, he turned to her and narrowed his eyes. "You are healthy, yes. You have strength, yes. But to fight the gods, you must have more than strength of body. You require strength of mind, and this is what I shall test. Come with me."

Dahti looked curiously at the now silent group around her before she turned to follow the shaman and only caught the faintest glimmer from the corner of her eye when he gestured.

It was a subtle gesture but every sense went on high alert. She had to force herself to take another step rather than freeze, then another, her demeanor calm.

A battle cry split the air behind her.

Out of instinct, she turned. She had been trained in combat by a dwarf who had cheerful irreverence for everyone and everything and who favored the element of surprise in all things. It was for him, therefore, that she yelled, "Stooooooout!" as she thumped the heavy book across her attacker's face.

The man, armed with a staff he'd raised over his head, went down like a pile of bricks.

Thoroughly bewildered, she stared at him, then turned at a strange choking noise from behind her. To her surprise, the shaman was laughing.

"Heh." He nodded at her. "Not bad, young one, not bad. Now, come this way and we'll find you a hut."

Again, she followed and expected to be assaulted more than anything else, but everyone seemed to have taken the attack—and her retaliation—in stride. A few orcs hauled their fallen companion away, dragging him none too gently by the limbs while a few of the kids began to recreate the battle with gales of laughter.

Dahti shook her head, baffled, and hurried after the old orc.

"Can I ask something?" she asked him.

He looked at her in a way that brought to mind the response she'd given her children many a time—"it sounds like you just did."

She swallowed. "Why did you trust me? I didn't expect such a welcome." It couldn't merely be, surely, that she was the protagonist of the game. She realized with a jolt that she would be disappointed if that were the case.

"Your village was very different," the shaman guessed. "Earth tribes can be like that."

Dahti looked at his red-tinted skin. They must have drawn conclusions from her appearance that she was not knowledgeable enough to understand.

"The shaman who trained me used to say fire tribes were the most open," the shaman said contemplatively, "that we gobble up anything that will strengthen us like a hungry flame. Wind, now, they keep to themselves, and the water…" He shook his head. "We are less for their loss. The earth tribes, though, they will accept anyone but only after a time, as slowly as one tree grows around another."

His words made her think back on her life. It was an apt description of many of her family members, enough so that she smiled. "I've met many of all inclinations."

"Ah, but you speak of people, not tribes." He bonked her on the head with his staff, hard enough that she stood back with a dazed shake of her head. "Come along, Earth Apprentice."

They had no sooner resumed walking when a loud boom echoed and she ducked reflexively. Everyone was looking in one direction —up.

With her heart in her throat, she followed the direction of their focus and froze. A plume of white smoke now billowed out of the top of the mountain. Her jaw dropped.

"This is…a *volcano*?" How had she missed the shape of it? Unless it had never erupted before. She caught the shaman's arm. "We have to go. Right now."

He looked at her, wary and watchful. "Volcano? I did not know earth tribes had a name for them."

"That's not the important part!" She waved her hands. "Please. *Please*, come, we have to go."

"We must face our god," he told her slowly. "In all things, there is balance. In all relationships, there must be a give and take. We live off the land, we accept its blessings, and in return, we must face the hunger of its gods."

Her heart was doing a strange double-time beat in her chest. "There is no way to face this god and survive."

"Perhaps not." He looked suddenly wary. "Perhaps, though, that is why your tribe was taken, Earth Apprentice—they refused to honor their obligations. When the gods creep out of their lairs and their wings block out the sun, those they choose must face their fate."

Dahti stared at him, open-mouthed. She was so horrified, she didn't know how to reply.

Harold would have laughed himself sick if he heard she'd been rendered speechless by anything. She massaged her temples and tried to think of something—anything—to say.

What came out of her mouth was, "Wings?"

She was glad her subconscious had caught that fact because the rest of her had been fixated on fiery death.

The shaman tilted his head to the side again. "Yes. The gods awaken and they come to feast upon the world. The legends always describe wings."

"Ohhhh." She was getting a headache. "So, *you* think the top of that mountain is smoking because there's a god inside—with wings—who'll come out and eat…maybe us or maybe only some other stuff?"

He looked at her as if she were insane. "Yes. Precisely."

His entire demeanor was so calm and matter of fact that she wanted to sob in frustration. "This mountain. Is. A volcano. There is no god and there are no wings, only rock that is hot beyond anything you can imagine. The top of the mountain will blow off and the rock and ash will rain on this village. Everyone here *will* die, and there will be nothing gained for *anyone*."

"This is, indeed," he said gravely, "why your village was struck down. Yet you must see, child, that they ignored the laws of nature—

and that you were spared for a reason. You serve as an omen. You were given the chance for redemption."

"Bullshit," Dahti said before she could stop herself. "If I was spared for a greater purpose, it was helping all of you avoid a needless death. There are children in this village—those who look to you for guidance—and you cannot honestly tell me you think the gods require their sacrifice!"

"It is the way of the world." The shaman raised his shoulders. "Child, you want to argue, I see that. Come. Learn. In time, as the seasons pass and the moon waxes and wanes, your wisdom will grow and you will see the fullness of the seasons—hunger and feast, curse and blessing. All things ebb and flow in this world."

He left her staring after him.

"Prima?" she whispered. "What do I do?"

"What do you want to do?"

"I want to run," she said at once. "But if I go, the children will have no chance to leave. But can I convince any of them, do you think, even if I stay?"

"It is up to you to try or not—not knowing the outcome, only choosing as best you can."

"I hope *you* someday wind up in a game with someone who gives you cryptic advice all the time," she muttered.

"I am," the AI said, amused. *"I don't understand half the things you people do."*

Dahti was startled into a laugh. She looked at the village and the people who still snuck glances at her, then turned to the shaman who waited for her at the door of an empty hut.

"I can't let them die because it was too difficult to explain volcanos," she said finally.

"Mmm, interesting."

By now, she'd had enough dealings with the AI to know better than to ask for details of what that meant. She rolled her eyes and hurried to her new house. It was time to come up with new, pseudo-religious stories to convince the tribe of the need to leave.

CHAPTER THIRTY-TWO

With a new member of the village and the imminent arrival of a god, a feast ensued that included singing, dancing, and helping upon helping of a stew that was so spicy, it made Dahti's eyes water. The villagers all laughed uproariously at her for gulping water and fruit juice, but they openly approved of her managing to finish her plate.

It was sheer discipline that enabled her to do so. She had been raised after the depression, after all. One never refused food, even if it made one want to drink the entirety of the great lakes and possibly cut one's tongue off.

Boy, would her family be surprised if she came back from this round of the game enjoying curries. She wondered if that might be sooner rather than later if the volcano exploded unexpectedly.

Whether it was the spice, the dancing, or simply the joy of being in a non-aching body again, she sang and danced enthusiastically with the villagers, late into the night. When she finally retired to her little hut, it was with her head unclouded by alcohol but her feet sore and her muscles tingling with exhaustion.

She woke to sunlight slanting in the door—undoubtedly the reason why all the huts faced east—and groaned when she pushed up.

Every muscle ached after the last day's exertions, although she was thankfully not sunburned.

Breakfast was more of the same spicy curry, along with introductions to so many people that she soon lost count. In her head, she categorized people the same way she had in the dwarven caravan, giving them nicknames according to their physical characteristics. One was Copper Necklace, another Smiles-a-lot, and a third was Jumper—a young girl who liked to climb anything she could and leap off.

Dahti was fairly sure the girl's mother must already have completely white hair.

She had learned a few things in her eighty-four years, and one of them was that if you wanted someone to listen to you, you had to do a fair amount of listening yourself first. Accordingly, she spent much of her morning wandering to various fires and doors, learning people's names again, and listening to them speak fondly of their spouses and children.

A few mothers slyly suggested that they had fine, strong sons, a suggestion she relentlessly pretended to not understand until she could escape the conversation. The shaman hadn't been lying when he said great things were expected of a Strength-bearer's lineage—it was only a matter of time, she suspected, until dowries were brought into the mix.

Although sore, she was still able to play a few rounds of a hopping game with the children of the village, along with something that seemed roughly comparable to tag. By lunch, when she sank into the shadows of her hut to pant, she was fairly sure she could find common ground with these villagers. They weren't so different from people anywhere else, after all.

Were they?

The shaman arrived in the doorway with a bowl of food, and when she peeked inside, she saw plain rice. Her face must have lit up because he laughed.

"After a few meals of our food, I thought you deserved something more to your tastes."

Dahti hastily swallowed a mouthful of rice. "I'm sure I'll get used to the spice."

"In time, I'm sure." He stood patiently until she realized he was waiting for an invitation and gestured to the floor on the other side of the firepit. He sat as well. "So. Perhaps you are rethinking your belief that we are misguided? You have met the people and listened to their stories."

Carefully, she considered her words as she savored the last mouthful of rice.

"I am not as young as I look," she said finally. "I cannot explain it, shaman, but I am not a youthful risk-taker. I believe in caution, and I have seen something of the world. The people I have seen—be they human, dwarf, or orc—are more alike than they are different."

"What of the elves?" He cocked an eyebrow.

"I haven't had a chance to speak to any elves," she said somewhat bitterly. "They always introduced themselves blade-first."

He considered her with quiet interest. "You've fought elves? Interesting. Your village must have been very different if you mixed with so many people. Perhaps that is why you disregard our people's ways."

"Perhaps," she said and sighed. "Sir...ah, what does one call a shaman?"

"So formal. There's no need for that."

Dahti shrugged. "Well, then. When I said I've seen many people, it was true. I've seen those who believed in no gods at all, some who believed in many, some who believed in only one, and others who believed in one with many faces. All had beliefs that held them back and even endangered them. But none were stupid. They had those beliefs for a reason."

"You think," the shaman said slowly, "that we have a reason for our beliefs but that our beliefs are not true?"

His response surprised her and she stared at him for a moment. It wasn't a delicate way of putting it, but at eighty-four, she was beyond delicacy. "Yes," she said finally. "I've been in places, sir, where simply the difference between our skin colors would be enough for terrible violence—and all who are here would say that was a senseless belief, yes? As we shed that, perhaps you will shed this."

He shook his head. "It is a dangerous thing to change the order of the world, young one—or however young you may be."

"A common logical fallacy," she said. Her grandson James would be laughing his head off right about now, as he was the one who'd taught her that phrase when he considered becoming a philosophy major. In that conversation, of course, *he* had been the one arguing for change. "One perceives making a change as the only active choice. Why risk change? Because choosing to stay the same is also a choice and it is also risky."

The shaman settled back to look at her. "The gods provide. They give us rains and they give us the beasts that roam the land. Should we refuse their bargain, our descendants—or those of our fellow tribes— will be afflicted." He hesitated. "As yours were. To try to avoid death is to cheat the gods, and they do not like being cheated."

She looked out at the people in the village. They glanced frequently at the mountain but did not seem fearful. "They don't know what the god's return means, do they?"

"They do." He smiled. "All orcs die in time, some as they hunt and others from sickness. Still, few rush to meet it. Some will hope they are passed over and yet others will pray that their children are not chosen."

Dahti tried to keep her voice level but it trembled. "Shaman, to die in fire and ash—it is a terrible, terrible death."

His expression flickered and he bowed his head. "Many deaths are terrible. In the halls of our ancestors, though, we will walk without pain."

An idea formed in her head. She would have no lineage in the game, and thus had an advantage. "Tell me this—are the gods just?"

He gave her a surprised look. "How do you mean?"

"Do they give people only what they deserve?" she asked. "You say my tribe paid for the sins of its ancestors. That is not just. Could another pay for...my sins?"

"It is difficult to know," he said thoughtfully. "I am curious as to why you ask."

Now she was in a bind because she couldn't tell him. If she were to subvert the plan and somehow spirit these people away, they might spend the rest of their lives fearing reprisal. She did not want to frighten them with that.

On the other hand, if they knew that she, and she alone, would be blamed, she could easily shoulder the guilt of whatever lies and stories she made up to get them away from this volcano. She needed time to think. For one thing, she did not even know how she could lie well enough to lure people away, not when their shaman told them to sacrifice themselves.

"It seems lopsided," she said finally. "The gods give and then they take, and humanity—orcs, I mean—are offered no choice in the matter."

The shaman looked down and said quietly, "I once thought as you do."

Something in his voice caught her attention, and Dahti looked closely at him. "You *once* did...or you *still* do?"

He gave her a wry look. "I do not like the bargain," he said frankly, "but I have seen visions and heard stories. The gods exist all over this land. There is no running from them. There is no facing them, either, for they are creatures well beyond the skill of any warrior or shaman. After what happened to the water tribes—"

"What *did* happen to them?"

"You don't know?" He looked genuinely confused now. "They were lost two generations ago. They were the most powerful of us and the most devout—and their gods turned on them."

She bolted to her feet, her fists clenched. "They did nothing wrong, and *still* they were killed? *Still* they were wiped out?"

"What would you have me do, young one?" He looked wearily at her. "Your people defied the gods and were punished for it. The water tribes did not and still, they were taken. Is it unjust? Yes. Do I wish I could stand against the gods? Yes, I wish it very much. But I cannot stand against them any more than I can stop the sun from rising. So I counsel my people to follow their faith, to hope to avoid the gods' notice, and to live as best they can, when they can. The gods are like famine or drought. They are beyond us. I will not stir my people to rebellion if it will only cause pain."

Dahti stared at him. She was still breathing hard, but her anger had begun to unravel. How often had she counseled her daughters on how to behave, even while they shouted at her that it wasn't fair that they had to hold their tongue, or put makeup on, or endure the harassment they got every day, simply for existing? How often had she counseled her sons on how to behave, even when they asked why *they* couldn't stay home with the children, why *they* weren't allowed to ask for help or admit weakness or show emotion?

Everyone has beliefs that hold them back, but they don't have them sense-lessly. She had only been trying to spare her children the pain that would come from others' disapproval. This shaman, too, was trying to spare his people.

She took a deep breath. "If I could…if I could stand against the god… If you could train me and take the villagers away, would you do it? Leave me behind to fight the god in your stead?" When he said nothing, she pressed on. "You know the gods have no interest in justice. The water tribes' death shows that. Let me at least *try* to free you from this one."

In the intensity of the discussion, she had barely noticed the rumbling, but it now made tiny rocks dance across the floor.

The shaman's shoulders slumped. "I would have done so, child, if there was time. But there is not." He looked at the village square, where people suddenly screamed and pointed. "The god is here."

He was resigned to death and had accepted it.

Dahti had not. She hauled him to his feet a moment later. "Start thinking of how to get them out of here," she told him. "Because the only hope now is to run. Get them moving. *Now.*"

CHAPTER THIRTY-THREE

With the plains stretching all around, she had no idea how she could possibly get the villagers moving quickly enough to outrun the volcano. She knew, on some distant level, that it was impossible to go quickly enough on foot, but she refused to listen to that certainty.

Even a slim chance of success was better than none, after all.

Briefly, Dahti entertained the thought of trying to stop the eruption with magic, but she finally shook her head at her foolishness. A few weeks before, she had almost drained her entire life force trying to trap a dozen wolves. The entire, explosive power of a volcano was unquestionably beyond her.

Her only option was to get all the villagers moving as quickly as possible. She took a single breath to compose herself—the air was already hot—and ducked out of the hut. The villagers were pointing at the mountain and she did not dare to look.

She couldn't lose her courage.

The child she called Jumper was crying, and she took her hand firmly and led her to where the shaman was speaking.

"We have been called into the plains," he shouted over the ever-present rumbling. "All must come now. Those who cannot walk quickly will be carried. Make sure all the members of your household are here and follow me!"

As they began their evacuation, she remained behind, steadfastly ignored the temptation to look at the mountain, and made a quick check through each building. She was careful to lift sleeping mats and open cupboards, aware that children might hide in the smallest spaces when they were frightened. She found only one old woman trying to dig up a stash of coins and hurried her out to where the village was walking away. Whether it was from shock or because she was the shaman's new de facto apprentice, the woman thankfully did not argue.

Then, with her book on her back and her staff in her hand, she hurried after the group. It did not take her long to catch up. The tribe moved as quickly as they could, but there was a limit to how fast their feet could take them and that wasn't as fast as ash and rock could rain down.

With her heart in her throat, she finally turned to look at the mountain.

It gave her some hope. The worst of the eruption had not happened yet. Black smoke billowed from the top—which *still* did not look like a volcano to her, although it must be—and she thought she could see a faint glow. As yet, there was no sign of lava flowing down the mountainsides or ash kicked into the air.

Maybe they had time. Dahti increased her pace and hurried through the group, offering encouraging smiles and nods to the villagers she recognized until she caught up with the shaman.

"Do we have a destination?" she asked in an undertone. "Or are we simply getting as far away as we can?"

He gave her a tense look. "I'm…well, I'm breaking all the traditions at once." He seemed to be bleakly amused by the fact.

"Yes?" She wanted to be amused but it was difficult when there was imminent death at her back. "And?"

"I'm taking them to the Cave of Trials," he told her with a sigh. "Only the shamans are ever supposed to go there. It is a holy place, and those who see it without—" He broke off at the look on her face.

She wasn't particularly interested in legends right now.

"There is water," he said finally, "and good earth for crops, and the warren of caves faces away from the mountain."

Her shoulders slumped with relief. "Thank God. Er...the gods." No, that wasn't right, either. "Um...do you have any gods aside from the ones who eat you?"

He looked quizzically at her. "When we get done with this particular adventure, you will tell me exactly what your tribe believed."

"I don't think you'll like it," Dahti muttered.

"At this point, I would be shocked if I did." He seemed amused by this too. "How you persuaded me to disobey all of my traditions is beyond me."

"No it's not," she replied smartly. "You know precisely why you did it. You've known your whole life that this system was wrong, and now that you have to choose between offering up the people you love to a certain and painful death or disobeying, you realize that you don't have it in you." She saw the self-hatred in his face and hastened to reassure him. "I don't think less of you for that, you know. Quite the opposite."

"I dishonor the sacrifices of those who went before," he said quietly.

She walked in silence for a few moments, pushed grass out of her way, and tried not to notice the way the sky grew dark around the mountain.

"They did the best they could," she said finally. "And you're doing the best you can. And—"

Behind them, a hollow boom issued and orcs screamed. She looked back at the billowing black smoke riddled with lightning.

They didn't have much time.

"How far are we?" she asked.

The shaman's reddish face had gone pale. "Two hours' walk, maybe more."

"Tell them to walk faster." Dahti very much doubted they had two hours to work with.

As it turned out, they did not. The next hour or more passed with children beginning to cry in hunger and thirst while the sky grew ever blacker and the beginning wisps of ash drifted on the wind. She could smell smoke, although it was less the comforting crackle of pine and more the charred, earthen scent of heated rock.

Then she thought about what it would mean if she smelled burning brush and realized there was a non-zero chance of the plains going up in flames around them.

She increased her pace.

The caves were in sight before she realized what they were. The ground sloped gently upward and the shaman pointed after a time to call that the caves were on the far side. She nodded and began to relay the message through the group when the top of the mountain split.

A burst of light erupted together with a thunderclap so loud she thought her eardrums had burst. Dahti fell, her ears ringing, aware that the ground seemed to move like the deck of a ship beneath her feet. Whether it was only her balance leaving her or the ground truly moving, she did not know.

She did not hear the screams because she could not hear anything. When she pushed to her feet, however, the orcs had stopped in their tracks, horror on their faces. Parents clutched children close and the elders of the group stared as if they had never expected to see such a thing.

Her heart in her throat, she turned to look.

The god was there and it was winged. Even so far away, she could see that immediately. Massive wings stretched wide and fanned the flames lazily as it arched its back. It was wreathed in smoke and it *was* the smoke while it bathed in the flames and created them.

"A dragon," she whispered. She couldn't hear her voice or anything beyond the beat of her blood. She thought she would pass out or maybe start laughing hysterically. "It's a *dragon.*"

Aghast, she whirled and caught someone's hand—Copper Necklace, whose face was horrified. Dahti shouted and since she couldn't hear herself, she could hope that what she said made sense. She waved frantically and urged them toward the caverns.

Toward whatever safety there might be.

Her feet pounded on the ground and a hasty glance showed that Copper Necklace was still holding her hand and the tribe now ran with her. Some of the children were still holding their ears and crying, but their parents clutched them and sprinted with single-minded determination.

When it came down to it, no one wanted to be sacrificed to a god. She pushed herself to move faster and prayed to every god she had ever heard of—but none of the dragons—that she could get the villagers through this.

"Prima!" she roared. "You'd better have a good plan!"

"I'd say you'd better have a good plan."

"Listen, you hunk of metal. If you let these people die, I will personally track you down and…and—" She was running out of breath.

"And?" Prima sounded intrigued.

"I'll think of something!" Dahti was aware that people were staring at her and she clamped her mouth shut on further threats.

A scream—she could hear things again—raised above the hubbub and she already knew what she would see when she looked over her shoulder.

She did anyway, whether to confirm her suspicions or torture herself, she wasn't quite sure. The dragon had taken flight and banked around the plume of smoke in lazy circles. It was still waking up—or perhaps it was drawing strength from the flames and the rock.

No wonder that mountain hadn't looked like a volcano.

In all honesty, she didn't care what it was doing as long as it didn't fly toward them. She ran with the villagers until a strange sound caught her attention.

Dahti knew what it sounded like, but it couldn't be that. After all, there were no boats nearby with sails fluttering in the wind. There was no canvas to pull taut in a gust.

Wings.

She twisted to look over her shoulder and swore. The dragon had seen them or smelled them, or maybe it merely flew in a random direction. It didn't matter, though, because it now headed directly toward them and closed the distance too quickly for the group to reach the caves.

"*Run!*" she screamed, and people put everything they had into their desperate flight.

The great beast's laughter sounded like thunder and rolling earth but there was no mistaking it for anything but laughter.

It liked the hunt.

White light stabbed across her eyes and she whipped her head around. The people around her slowed as well, and even the dragon's black-and-red head swung to look. She squinted to see the light shining from…a crystal?

Whatever it was, it was held aloft in the hand of someone who was cloaked and walked slowly through the grass, watching the dragon.

Someone *human*.

"Run," Dahti told the villagers. "Hide in the caves. I'll buy you time."

She sprinted toward the human with the crystal. They might not be friendly, but between a human and a vengeful dragon god, she didn't have any questions as to where she'd take her chances.

CHAPTER THIRTY-FOUR

It was only halfway to the stranger that Dahti remembered she could drop the book of spells. She assumed she wouldn't learn anything incredibly useful on short notice. Either she could pick it up later or she'd be fried to a crisp and it wouldn't matter.

Delightful.

The human had begun to run as well, and as soon as she was close enough to the figure to shout, she gave up entirely on any semblance of politeness.

"Tell me you're here to help!" she called.

"I am!" a woman called in response. She pushed the hood of her cloak back to reveal a pale, shockingly pretty face and dark hair. When she shrugged the cloak off entirely, Dahti saw that she wore black leather armor and carried two long daggers. "Justin sent me."

"Justin! Oh, thank God." She would have stopped and sagged with relief had she not been blown sideways when air buffeted her.

Dahti scrambled to her feet and turned, only for her jaw to drop open and for her to make what she was fairly sure was a very undignified sound of fear. She had already been terrified when she first saw the dragon. It was massive, after all, and there was no ambiguity in the long talons and sharp, gleaming teeth.

Up close, it was ten times more terrifying than her worst nightmare.

When it landed with a heavy thud, both women were upended. The earth shook with each step of its heavy feet and its breath seared the air. Dahti scrambled up in time to see its head come level with her.

She was surprised she didn't pass out with fear. Its snout was almost as tall as she was. Each slit-pupiled eye was shades of red and orange, and the front talons were as deep a black as onyx. In the space between the black scales, red glimmered like molten lava.

"Who are you?" it asked her. Its voice blew her back off her feet again and reverberated in her bones. "Both of you. An earth orc and a human. Two of you, who have taken my prey from me. Answer!"

Her irritation lent her courage and she stood slowly and glared at the beast. She was tired of being knocked down and she wasn't prepared to act contrite.

"I'm Dahti," she said simply. "And no one here is your prey."

"Oh, is that right?" It reared and began to circle them. "What of you, human? Who are you?"

"I am Zaara," the woman said. "I am apprentice to Mary, who commands the powers of death. I am friend to Justin, the savior of Insea."

"Insea!" The dragon gave a shout that might have been either derision or anger and launched flames skyward from its jaws before it snapped its teeth and whipped its head around to look at the woman again. "And what brings you to fire orc territory, *human?*"

"Why ask my name if you won't use it?" Zaara snapped.

Dahti decided she liked her.

"I asked who you were," the dragon said testily. "I don't care what you call yourself. Would you care about the names of insects?"

The woman folded her arms and glared.

Dahti stepped forward now. "Leave this place," she said clearly. "You have fooled these people into believing that you bring the rains and the beasts, but I will show them the truth no matter how many lifetimes it takes. I am privy to magics you have never seen before. I have powers you could not dream of. These people will no longer be your thralls."

The beast laughed. "Ah, do you think so? You may turn their heads for a time. But when I sweep from the skies and feast on their brethren, they will remember why they worshipped me. The next time a drought comes, they will tell themselves it is my wrath. I am their god and they are mine to devour." Its tongue flicked out.

"No more." She was practically vibrating with rage. "No more lies and no more deception. You are no god."

"What is a god?" It seemed amused now. "Something that is worshiped, something that is beyond them. I am both those things, little orc. Did you tell them you could save them from me?"

I told them you were a volcano without wings, Dahti wanted to say. She did not. Her miscalculation didn't need to be spread around at this juncture.

"You can't." The dragon brought its snout closer and feinted toward her so she danced back. It hissed a laugh at her. "When I devour you, they will understand who their god is and who is a false prophet. I shall keep my feasts, little meddler, and you—"

The crystal blazed to life once more and the dragon drew back with a hiss. Dahti covered her eyes with a cry of pain. The light was like the brightest sunlight, distilled and magnified into a beam. The sound of cracking stone was followed by a pained shriek.

"You're not invulnerable." Zaara's voice rolled through the air like thunder. "You're no more than any other creature, dragon. Begone!" The light flared once more and the creature shrieked again. A moment later, Zaara was at Dahti's side and shook her. "I think I bought us a moment," the woman whispered. "I—" She broke off and her nose wrinkled as she took in Dahti's smell.

"I *know,*" she said, annoyed. "I smell to high heaven. I should have stayed a dwarf."

"Stayed a—" Zaara broke off and gaped at her before she shook her head. "No time. Explain later…if we survive."

She looked up to where the dragon had pushed off the earth and now circled while its wings beat strongly. A line across its side was grey-and-black, the molten look of it cooled, and it seemed to favor that wing.

"This is a being of fire and heat," Zaara said urgently, "so it's vulnerable to water, to cold, and to the absence of air. Can you summon any of those things? Justin said you were a wizard."

Dahti felt a surge of dread. "Justin may have overstated the case somewhat."

"Yeah, well, Justin took to it all fairly quickly, too." The woman's gaze tracked the dragon as it descended. "Also, we'll either kill it or it'll kill us—and I know which I'd prefer. Let's, uh…distract it and trade off. Take a potshot when it's advancing on me, and I'll do the same for you!"

She didn't wait for an answer and merely raced away in the grass with her blades flashing.

"Okay," Dahti said. "It looks like we're doing that, then." She stumbled as the dragon landed again and decided there was no time like the present for doing stupid things. "Hey, you stupid bugger! Over here! I bet your mother was a garden snake!"

"*As insults go, perhaps not your best work,*" Prima said after a moment. She sounded like she was trying not to laugh.

"Unfortunately, it probably is," she confessed. "I was never good at them."

"*Try harder,*" the AI advised her. "*You know what the dragon wants and what makes it mad. Maybe use those as themes? It's only a thought.*"

She rolled her eyes. The beast swung its head from Dahti to Zaara as if trying to decide which to attack.

"The earth orcs joke about you!" Dahti called to the dragon. "Our gods are mighty and eternal. You're so weak you can't handle a little light thrown by a *human!*"

The dragon's head whipped around and it advanced on her. Its tail was lashing.

"Oh, good," she muttered. "It's working." To her adversary, she added, "This is your entire life? You sleep in a mountain in the middle of nowhere and come out every few hundred years to snack on prey that can't run away from you? And you expect me to think you're impressive? You expect people to *worship* you?"

It bared its teeth, snarled, and opened its jaws to inhale, and Dahti saw her chance. She thrust her hands out with the remembered smell in mind and conjured a cloud of thick dust for the dragon to suck down its throat instead of air.

Fire needed air, after all.

The creature choked and coughed with enough force to strip a nearby bush of all its leaves. It threw its head back and snarled in anger, but a flash of silver and blue caught her eye.

Zaara leapt out of the grass with speed and grace. Both daggers were drawn as she climbed nimbly up the dragon's side. She was laughably small compared to it, but she didn't look daunted even in the slightest. Power shone pale blue around her daggers—the same blue as the glitter of icebergs. As Dahti began to run, hoping to get out of the way of the dragon's retaliatory fireball, the woman planted her feet and plunged her daggers into the gaps between two of the black scales.

Whatever protective magic the dragon had, it was enough to hurl her off its back. She fell limply in the grass and was lost from view as the beast's tail lashed and it screamed in pain.

"*Foolish,*" it snarled. It swung its head until its eyes fixed on Dahti, and it began to advance. "Do you think to use winter against me? Winter is a weak thing. Frost is nothing compared to the power of a mountain's heart."

She stumbled back and tried desperately to turn the ground under her enemy's feet to shifting sand. It wouldn't do much except consume her mana bar, but she had no other ideas of how to distract it. She didn't have a frost enchantment on her knives, nor did she have any water magic.

The water orcs could have defeated this dragon, she thought resentfully. That was what was *supposed* to have happened in this world—the tribes were meant to band together, each tribe lending its shamans to defeat the other dragons.

When this particular dragon roared again, she decided her revelations could wait.

Whether Zaara was hurt or not, she didn't know. She surged into a sprint and raced toward the place where she'd seen the human woman fall. When she paused in a crushed avenue of grass, devoid of any bodies, she sighed with relief.

The dragon reared again and Dahti knew how quickly it could swing its head. She ran toward its feet instead and managed to avoid the surge of fire that set the grass ablaze.

Idiot, she cursed the beast. A wildfire here would do nothing except blight the land.

And make its predictions of famine come true. It was manufacturing adverse events for its benefit. Too lazy even to hunt its prey, it tried to make them believe they should trot gladly up the sides of the mountain and throw themselves into its mouth.

She didn't have much hope that she could do real damage, but she yanked her staff out and whacked the monster on the knee as she went past. Her weapon bounced off without seeming to do the slightest damage and her heart sank. She didn't have what it would take to defeat this, did she?

A yell and a flash of black told her that Zaara had launched another assault. The human streaked past her and stabbed at the beast's exposed belly, and Dahti followed up by whacking the open wound as hard as she could.

This time, the dragon noticed her. Its belly arched away and it lifted off with a speed that threw them down. As it circled, Zaara grasped Dahti's staff. She wrapped her hands around it and began to mutter urgently. Between her fingertips, frost crackled and spread.

"It's not my best work, but it'll have to do—come on!" She hauled her up. "Next time, we go at the same time. Strike the shoulder joints as hard as you can. I don't care what kind of magic you have, just *use* it!"

She nodded and the two women scrambled away from each other. The dragon had climbed into the sky and it now rocketed down with its eyes narrowed and flames streaking from its snout.

"Where are you, false prophet?" Its words boomed and echoed.

Dahti stopped and crouched in the grass, which fluttered around her in the wind.

"Where are you?" it asked again and this time, its voice was the kind of saccharine-sweet that made her teeth ache. "Surely a warrior of your strength should be willing to face me. Come out, little prophet, or I will take the villagers."

Every sense went into high alert and rage coursed through her, but she knew better than to let it lure her out immediately. She braced herself for its landing and focused on the closest wing. If she let it pass her, she could jump up and drag the frost-stave across the webbing of the appendage. It wasn't the joint, but she sensed this was the best she would be able to do.

She held her position with an effort as the dragon thudded past, then pushed herself into a sprint, vaulted upward, and struck the wing as hard as she could with her staff. She held it with both hands and twisted in the air to drag it across the fine webbing and was rewarded with a scream. At the same time, Zaara gave a distant battle cry.

The dragon pounded into a run, buffeting both women off its flanks, and lurched skyward. It climbed and spun to look at them, sculling the air. It descended a few feet, the massive wings beating unevenly.

"You have brought my vengeance down on this village forever," it hissed.

Dahti stood slowly. Fury filled her. "Your kind became too greedy," she said softly. Her voice didn't carry over the wind but she knew the dragon heard her. "And now, we see you for what you are. You reached too high, dragon."

It bellowed its rage at her and soared away, and she looked at where her arm had begun to sting. Blood poured from a long cut on her upper arm.

"Huh," she said. She was suddenly light-headed. "Well, *that* can't be good."

CHAPTER THIRTY-FIVE

Dahti had no clear memory of the next few minutes. She recalled stumbling over the plain with Zaara beside her and how difficult it was to navigate the steep, narrow path to the mouth of the cave.

Her first real awareness was of the way the villagers drew back when the two of them arrived.

The orcs stared and the two women responded in kind. Finally, Dahti thudded heavily to her knees and the shaman hobbled forward as he called to some of the others. He looked at Zaara impersonally as if he didn't care at all that she was human.

"You, girl—you speak our tongue?"

"Yes." Zaara seemed not at all thrown by the fact that she was surrounded by orcs. "I know a little healing if you need it here."

"Any help is welcome." He knelt beside Dahti's head and placed one of his palms on each side. "I'll keep her with us while you work on that cut."

She set to work almost silently. While she had fought with easy grace, she was far more cautious with this. Her brow furrowed and she muttered things under her breath that sounded like mnemonics. The process was slow.

It worked, however. The pain began to recede as well as the light-headedness. Dahti twitched her arm experimentally and felt an ache, not the sharp pain of a cut opening once more.

"Be still," Zaara said and her voice was strained. "I am not—this is not my strength."

She complied without argument. With the combined power working in her, she felt more clear-headed with every passing moment. She remained as relaxed and motionless as she could and, when Zaara finished with a sigh, she sat. On inspection, her arm looked almost odd as if covered with blood that seemed to have come from nowhere.

"I don't suppose you care to tell me what happened," the shaman said at length. "Since I am quite sure I did not hear a god struck down."

The two combatants exchanged a look.

"We did not kill it," Dahti admitted. "We wounded it—both wings, one side, the belly, and the tail. It fled rather than stay and fight." She looked down and gathered her courage. "But it swore it would have revenge."

He sighed heavily. "Of course it did. And now it knows where our shelter is."

"You need to hide." Zaara looked up now. She was still pale from the toll her magic had taken, but she remained a confident presence. "As long as you can. I can get Dahti the training she needs to defeat the dragon, but it won't be fast."

"Oh?" He looked at her now with something approaching pity. "Do you think you can train her?"

"I didn't say that." She smiled tiredly. "I do not know the necessary spells and I cannot be away from my people for long enough to teach her. But there is a record of one fire wyrm being defeated by the water tribes. Their shamans know how."

Dahti's shoulders slumped and he looked down in despair.

"Human," he said finally, "the water tribes are no more. They were destroyed by their gods."

Zaara did not waver. "Not all of them," she said. "There are still pockets of them along the coast, and in one…" She paused. "Do your tribes fight one another?"

"No." He seemed amused. "We keep to ourselves. Our concerns—and our gods—are different."

Dahti remembered her revelation but kept quiet. This was not the time or the place.

"Then you would not strike at any water tribes," Zaara said tentatively, "even if they were powerful."

"How could they be powerful? We thought them destroyed. We thought them dead. They must be in hiding."

"They are," she agreed. "But among them still resides…Rashat."

The shaman's head came up at once. "Rashat lives?" He breathed the words. "He *lives*?"

"I know you both know who that is, but I don't," Dahti pointed out.

"Ah. Yes." Zaara gave her a tiny nod. "Rashat was the foremost among the shamans of the water tribes. He had power like nothing anyone had ever seen. They said he could conjure storms and in fact, he was noteworthy enough that humans tried to study with him." She paused. "It…it didn't go well for them."

She swallowed nervously. "Ah. So…"

"Rashat did not think well of other races," the shaman said. "As I told you, the water tribes were the most devout, and he was notable even among them. Anyone of another race who stumbled into their territory, by design or by accident, was cut down. He commanded that."

"He sounds delightful," she said brightly. "And we're glad this man is still alive because…"

"Because he's the last of the water shamans and the most powerful one they've ever seen," Zaara said bluntly before he could answer. "I was told you needed to find a way to kill a fire wyrm, and if anyone knows how, it's him." She saw the look on her face. "You seem…angry?"

"I'm merely annoyed that both you and Justin knew about the dragon before I did." She rolled her eyes moodily.

"It was such a fun revelation, though."

Dahti, aware that both her companions watched her closely, couldn't say anything to Prima in response, but she made a mental note to try to explain the concept of fun to the AI.

Zaara looked at the shaman. "Could I speak to Dahti alone?" she asked.

He hesitated before he left to return to the other orcs, all of whom had chosen to cluster on the far side of the cavern—if they remained at all. Many, it seemed, had decided to move into the caves, where they would not be subjected to the sight of a human.

Dahti was beginning to have a low opinion of some orcish beliefs.

The woman smiled at her. "Are you...from Justin's world?" she asked.

"You know about that?" she asked.

"He told me once that it was a dream," Zaara said. She smiled. "And that it wasn't real—although he seemed to change his mind on that later. He was a good friend."

"Did you know Lyle too?" she asked.

Zaara laughed at that. "Oh, yes. Lyle Stout, always the one who mucked up carefully laid plans by charging into battle. But he was a good friend as well."

"Not anymore?" Dahti asked her curiously.

"Well..." The woman sighed. "I'm training as a wizard now. I've been told I should try to shed my attachments. I'm trying but it's not easy."

"Why?" She tilted her head to the side curiously.

Zaara smiled, though she looked less happy than sad. "A wizard—if they complete their training, of course—lives for hundreds of years. No one else does. There are stories of wizards driven mad by lost love or by watching their children grow old and die. I want to help people and I can't do that if I go mad, can I?"

"I suppose not," Dahti said soberly. She swallowed. "I'm...sorry."

"Don't be." Her companion gave her an unexpectedly sunny smile. "I get to spend hundreds of years studying and protecting my village. My life will have purpose *and* pleasure." She dusted her hands briskly.

"Now *you*, however, need to get to the water tribes. We must plan your route."

"I don't want his help," she said grumpily. "He sounds like a—" She almost came out with a word she'd heard one of her grandchildren say, and barely bit her tongue in time.

"He may have changed a great deal," Zaara said. "He was the most powerful and everything he did was to keep his people safe from their dragons—gods, yes? The orcs believe dragons are gods?" At her nod, she continued. "He and his tribe haven't been heard from since their gods turned on them. I would think he's probably rethought some of his beliefs."

Dahti considered this.

"You know you'll go," the woman said with a shrug.

"I beg your pardon?" She gave her an offended look. "You don't know me, young lady."

"Young lady? Who are you? My grandmother?" Zaara laughed. "Look, you aren't part of this tribe, it seems, and yet you threw yourself into danger to protect them. I'd say it's very clear you'll find Rashat and learn to destroy that dragon."

"Just because you knew Justin, you think you know all of us?" she asked.

"Oh, heavens. The first time I saw Justin, he tried to flirt with tavern wenches." The woman continued to laugh. "He did everything for fame and glory and even he turned out well. You're starting way ahead of him."

Dahti smiled despite her earlier irritation.

"I like her," Prima confided. *"She kept him on his toes too, much like Tina."*

She cleared her throat. "Ah…so you want me to waltz up to this hiding shaman and ask him for his secrets to defeat a dragon after he failed to do the same?"

"He failed to defeat a *water* dragon," Zaara said. "With water powers. You know, I'm not sure why he thought that would work. I was very surprised to learn that tribes don't exchange shamans."

"I thought the same," she agreed with a nod. "Well, then. I suppose

I might as well go. Since, as you point out, I'm hardly about to let these people die because I pissed their god off. Dragon. I won't call that monster a god."

"Good," the woman said forcefully. She stood and hopped around. "Ooooh, my leg went to sleep. Oh, dear."

Not for the first time, Dahti marveled at how realistic the game was. She nodded at her. "I'm glad you came to help. If it weren't for you…well, I would be burned to a crisp."

Zaara smiled. "It was my pleasure—truly. I enjoy studying, but I need a dose of adventure now and then. I promised my family I would do less, but I can't stand having *none*." She reached out to shake Dahti's hand. "It was nice to meet you, Dahti. Oh! And Justin asked me to give you this."

She held out an amulet identical to the one she had worn in her incarnation as a dwarf. It would let her communicate with the team running the game and she nodded as she took it.

"If ever I can repay the favor…"

Zaara smiled. "I'm sure you will. And now, I think I will take my leave so your fellow orcs don't have to put up with a human anymore." She smiled and left, whistling a jaunty tune, and turned to call over one shoulder, "I'll get your book and leave it at the top of the hill."

"The book!" She had entirely forgotten. "Yes. Thank you."

When the woman was gone, she fastened the pendant around her neck and chewed her lip. Vengeful dragons and lost shamans. Prima had started this incarnation off with a bang.

CHAPTER THIRTY-SIX

The shaman accompanied Dahti to forage for supplies for the journey. Much to her disappointment, this seemed primarily to be root vegetables and mushrooms, the latter of which grew in abundance in the caves. They gathered the food into a basket woven from plains grasses, and he waited for her to speak.

"I'm sorry," she said finally.

He responded with a small smile but remained silent.

"My…tribe…is very strange," she told him. "We value truth and freedom over comfort. It made me angry to see the dragon preying on all of you under false pretenses. He's a tyrant and I wanted to fight him."

The shaman looked wordlessly at her.

"I shouldn't have made the decision for you," she continued. "He swore revenge on all of you, and it was because of something I did. I know it wasn't my place as I'm not a member of your tribe. So I'll fix it, I truly will. I'll free you from this god—dragon. He *isn't* a god."

He merely smiled a little secretively, which began to irritate her.

"Would you *please* say something?" she demanded.

After several moments of thought, he paused at a small stand of medium-sized mushrooms and began to pluck several tiny ones.

While he might hobble, his fingers were surprisingly nimble. He showed her a palmful of them before he wrapped them in cloth.

"If you get sick, these will bring a fever down."

Dahti nodded and prayed for patience. She wanted to talk about different things than fevers and journeys.

"We are all driven by our desires and our conscience," the shaman stated finally. "And even traditions are malleable. There was a time when the tribes traveled together and we all gathered each year for a great festival. There are spells I was taught that can only have come from the air shamans."

She had no idea what to say to this so she dug another root vegetable out and looked at it glumly before she put it in the basket. Her present incarnation had significant downsides. She had never particularly enjoyed rutabagas or sweet potatoes, and that looked like most of what she was getting.

"You hope to save us," the shaman told her. He sat on his heels and looked at her, his eyes clear. She saw now that his reddish-brown skin had faint lines on it as if from very old scars. They traced his features and added an otherworldly aspect to his gaze. "It is not your actions that were at fault, earth orc. It was your motivation. We are not yours to save."

"But—" she protested.

He held up a hand. "As your elder, I claim certain privileges. One is that I ask you to think on my words during your journey instead of responding to them now."

Dahti closed her mouth. She returned to digging but a great many thoughts swirled in her head—one being that this orc was *not* her elder.

"I know very little of the water tribes from my own experience," the shaman said and changed the topic with ease. "Nevertheless, I will pass what I have heard to you. Perhaps some of it will serve you well. They live near the coast, yes, but some follow the fresh rivers and some live on the edge of the ocean, where the water is said to taste of salt."

She opened her mouth to say everyone knew that but closed it quickly. If someone were born in the plains, they might not know such a thing.

"Water is known to be the least…controllable of the elements," he said. "A wildfire may rage out of control and the earth may shake, but the force of the sea can do truly terrible things. There are stories of waves as tall as mountains."

Reflexively, she shuddered. "I have heard the same stories."

He nodded. "Their shamans do not use rapid magic," he said. "Like a wave, their magic gathers slowly and works, finally, with great power and unstoppable force—or it works like water wearing away at the stone with tiny touches that each weaken so slightly that one cannot think of them as doing damage at all. To command the power of water is a strange thing for a mortal."

Dahti nodded. "To use such a slow power against a dragon—"

"You keep using that word."

"It is the word the other races have for the beings you call gods. When we speak of gods, we speak of something quite different—without human form, usually. I mean, physical form." She kept forgetting she wasn't human any longer.

"You know a great deal about the humans," the shaman said mildly.

She tried to find a suitable lie, could not, and decided to not say anything at all.

He sighed. "I wish you would tell me the truth of your past, child."

The answer came to her in sudden clarity. She grinned impishly at him. "How old are you, grandfather? Because I'm eighty-four." At the widening of his eyes, she laughed. "And, as *your* elder, I claim certain privileges—like not having to answer those questions."

He threw his head back and laughed. "Ah, so you claim to be the eldest in the tribe? An interesting thing to hear from one in a strong body."

"Truth is stranger than fiction," she said serenely. "I was called to this place without knowing why but now, I think it is to free you from a false god."

"Is that so?" He stood and hefted his basket. "There is enough here to keep you for a week or more on the road and after that, I must ask that you forage as you go. Our people need all the supplies they can get."

"Then I'll take only half of this," Dahti said at once. "I've put you in enough danger."

They walked to the main caves while he told her what else he knew of the water tribes. They had banded together when their gods woke, he claimed, and had therefore been together when they were all struck down.

"What of Rashat?" she asked him.

"Rashat…" He sighed. "I both envy you your chance to study with him, earth orc, and pity you. It is said he was a most unlovable man."

"That seems accurate." She would, quite frankly, have been shocked if a man who murdered lost travelers was friendly and jovial.

"We heard about him even before he was a shaman. His coming was told in the stars—even to our people. We sent emissaries, in fact, to learn what those stars meant, and were told of an infant who could summon water and play with it from the very day of his birth. He used magic as naturally as he breathed. Perhaps…"

"Perhaps?" Dahti prompted when the words trailed away.

"Perhaps that is why he clung so hard to the ways of his people," the shaman said contemplatively. "What else could they teach him? The magic he used was beyond that of his elders. For a certainty, they could teach him the ways of water, but the traditions were the only thing they had that he was not born with." He shrugged.

"You said they were wiped out," she said after a moment. "How did you learn of that if you thought all of them were dead?"

"The air tribes sent word." He shook his head. "So rarely do they speak to the rest of us… But they said they saw the god rise out of the ocean, taller than the tallest wave, slow and deadly, and that after the attack, they never again saw the water tribes stir along the coast. Nor did we see their travelers in caravans or receive word. I was newly apprenticed when word came. Rashat would have been…oh, a few years older than I was."

Dahti looked curiously at him.

"Do you resent him?"

"Rashat?" He looked at her. "Why?"

"I think you know why."

He smiled. "Then the answer would be yes, I do. Or, rather, I envy him, even though I understand how foolish it is to do so."

"Why would you say it's foolish?" She smiled at his sheepishness.

"What is the point in wishing for such magic?" the shaman asked. "No amount of wishing can change the past. I was not born summoning fire as Rashat summoned water. Tales of my skill will never be told to children of the tribe. There is no help for that."

Dahti looked sympathetically at him. She could hear the ache in his voice and she recognized it because she had seen it in every single person she knew, as well as herself.

"And it brought him no joy," the shaman said heavily. "In the end, his skill did not help him or his tribe. I imagine he is a broken man now. You will have your work cut out for you, young one—or elder, whichever you may be." The gleam of a smile told her he remembered her assertion of being eighty-four.

She took a gamble and planted the seed. "Shaman." She put a hand out to stop him before they reached the main cavern. "Do you remember what Zaara said—the human? She said only one record existed of a fire wyrm being defeated and that it had been defeated by a *water* shaman."

"Yes, but even their magic did not help them when—"

"What if it wasn't his skill or the amount of magic he had?" she pressed. "What if water magic cannot defeat a water god? What if *you* and *your* line might have defeated that god, the same way his line once helped your people?"

The shaman stared at her.

"You said the tribes once came together each year for a festival," she reminded him. "What if there was a time when the shamans shared their spells?"

"I…" His voice trailed away.

"I'm no proper orc," she said frankly. "You and I both know it. But I think the freedom of your people lies in your unity. Share your ways —your dances, your goods, your livestock…and your magic. Restart the festival." She grasped his hand urgently. "I will make what I did right, but think on that while I am gone."

He smiled at her. "I will. You, however—you think on what I said."

"That it is not my actions that were at fault but my motivations," Dahti quoted. "That you are not mine to save. I remember."

"Good." He patted her arm. "Go now. I am an old man and I have earned one more privilege."

"Oh?"

"Yes. Not having to grow too fond of people who may die violently. I sense you may be one of them. Run along now." He ushered her briskly through the main cave as she laughed.

"Do you find that funny?" Prima questioned.

"It *is* funny," she said as she made her way up the steep path. "It's called black humor."

"I do not understand humans at all."

"Yes, but we knew that, right?"

"I suppose," the AI said glumly, and she laughed again.

"Cheer up. Most of the time, humans don't understand each other either. You're not doing any worse than a normal human would."

"Oh, that's comforting."

"Don't be snide." Dahti reached the top of the hill and saw her book—as well as a scroll. "What's this?" She knelt and broke the wax seal—an ornate Z—before she stretched it open.

It was a gorgeous map, the kind that reminded her why maps had once been so prized. Each line was painstakingly drawn by hand, forests and deserts were rendered in lush washes of color, and tiny cities were highlighted with distinctive drawings. She recognized both Berghold and Insea on sight.

The mountain of the fire dragon was marked clearly, as well as the little village, and a small star along the coast indicated the last known position of the water tribe. It was, she estimated, a little way inland along a river.

Judging by the distance between Berghold and Insea, which had taken two weeks by cart, her walk would take a week and a half if she set a brisk pace.

"You'll have more than enough time to practice your magic," Prima said with satisfaction.

"I should have known you'd get me to do this again," Dahti said wryly.

"You're a natural. Even the other humans say so. Besides, I'll arrange for company on the way."

"And does that mean friends or attacks?" She rolled the map and put it in her makeshift pack. "Prima? I asked, does that mean friends or enemies? Prima?"

Unsurprisingly, no answer was forthcoming.

She sighed and put her pack on. It was halfway through the day, by her estimation, and she might as well begin walking into whatever trap Prima had planned for her.

CHAPTER THIRTY-SEVEN

The rest of the day was entirely uneventful, which only annoyed Dahti more with each step she took.

And there were far too many steps.

She wasn't sure if Prima was tormenting her or giving her time to recover, but she suspected it was the former. By dinnertime, she was famished and sore. She took time to set out the mushrooms, cup up, the way the shaman had taught her so that they would collect morning dew, and chose a position under an acacia tree so she could take water from the leaves in the morning.

With her chores, such as they were completed, she sat and read. There wasn't much to do otherwise, and as much as she instinctively feared magic, she also greatly enjoyed it. She wasn't sure that any of the spells in this book would do her any good, but at least practicing magic in general would help. It seemed that with each level she attained in her Spellcasting skill, she received extra points on her magic bar.

Her practice began with a few repetitions of earth-shock, a spell that encased something in what looked like dried mud and shattered it from the inside out. She didn't have to have an actual target and so she spent time making balls of mud in midair that thudded to the ground and shattered there.

The next iteration of the skill was stone-shock, which harnessed the quick-moving power of stones. She had to read that twice to make sure she had seen it correctly, but there was no mistaking the text. Roughly-drawn illustrations were provided of places where stone stabbed through the earth like a spear or where it had cracked apart from an earthquake. It was this schism—similar to cracking mud and yet far stronger—that she would harness with stone-shock.

To have something to focus on, she shaped a little mound of dirt and attempted the spell several times.

Every time, it took her magic but nothing happened to the dirt.

"Prima," she called finally, "is it not working because I'm trying earth magic on a mound of dirt?"

"No."

"Does that mean it *is* the problem or it *isn't?*"

"*It is not the problem,*" Prima said, amused. "*It wouldn't harm the dirt but if you were doing it correctly, it would still work.*"

"Blast." Dahti sighed. She took a moment to read the instructions again and muttered the phrases aloud. "…stabs up through the dirt… strong even in the face of the wind…" She considered what she'd read. When she tried to meld her feelings about earth and stone and the strong, slow face of a mountain with the speed of a blade, nothing came to her.

Instead, this time, she pictured the scene the book described—a piece of rock that had once thrust through the dirt with astounding force but which now sat implacably in the blazing sun and whistling wind.

The power left her with a shudder and her eyes snapped open. A spur of rock protruded through her mound of dirt. A moment later, all of it cracked and crumbled.

"*Ha,*" she said with great satisfaction.

That, unfortunately, had been the last of her magic, and she knew it would take time to replenish. She took another sip of water and swirled it in her mouth before she swallowed, then lay under the tree.

Now that the sun had set, it was chilly and she realized she should have asked the shaman for a blanket. She only had the cloth from the book, so she tucked that around her shoulders and curled into a ball under the leafy canopy.

Her last journey, she thought grumpily, had been one of ample food and nice, soft bedrolls under thick blankets. There had been ale and sausages heated over an open flame. She'd enjoyed little red apples, freshly baked bread with thick slabs of soft cheese, brown-sugar cured ham…

She drifted off to sleep with her mouth watering and dreamed of featherbeds and tables groaning under heavy platters of food.

Justin climbed out of the taxi and sighed. Behind him, Tina slid out as well and shut the door. The driver helped her to unload the bags while her friend stood and thought gloomily about how useless he was these days.

She thanked the man and turned to see his face.

"It'll get better," she assured him. "Two weeks ago, you could barely walk from one side of the room to the other, and now look at you."

He shrugged grumpily, took the rolling suitcase, and set off. Unfortunately, he couldn't dodge the fast-walking New Yorkers as quickly as they seemed to want him to, and within a few meters, he was already both exhausted and annoyed.

"Oh, yeah?" Tina called to someone who had shouted at them. "Well, up yours, too!"

"Tina," he said, pained.

"And *you*—oh, wait, sorry. I was in insult mode. Never mind. You, I like." She slid her arm around his waist, both a sweet gesture and a helpful one as he could lean against her.

With a laugh, he waited for her to precede him through the revolving door. Instead, one of the side doors opened and Nick stepped out.

"I thought I saw you," he panted. Clearly, he had run upstairs. "I only now got your text about heading here from the airport. We meant to bring you a wheelchair—"

"I do *not* need a wheelchair," he said hotly.

"Yes, he does," Tina contradicted. She squeezed his side. "However much damage it does to your masculinity to have trouble walking after months in a coma, I promised your parents I wouldn't let you keel over on the sidewalk anywhere. Into that chair, mister."

Justin grumbled and sat in the wheelchair Nick had ready inside the doors. After even the brief walk from the taxi—although, he supposed, there had also been the airport and plane to navigate—he wanted nothing more than to curl in a ball and sleep.

"Your doctor sent your most recent reports," the engineer told him as he pushed the wheelchair through security. "It seems your stamina is off the charts."

"Yes—the bottom end."

Nick laughed. "The top end, thank you very much. Now, I hear how hard you've worked to recover, but I like to think all the low-grade muscle activation you did in the pod helped."

"He did mention that." He leaned his chin on one hand as the chair wheeled into an elevator. It was horrifying to think of how much worse things might be if he'd experienced normal atrophy during his coma.

In the lab, he was greeted by several assistants he recognized as well as DuBois, the eccentric doctor who had pioneered the early stages of PIVOT's treatment. The man gave him a somewhat sticky handshake and the reason for it became clear when he clapped the same hand on his shoulder and gestured with the other for him to help himself to a big bowl of cheese-and-caramel popcorn.

Justin stifled a laugh but still took a handful. One of the benefits of recovering from a coma was that you could get away with things like junk food.

"So, is Dotty back in the game?" he asked around a mouthful of popcorn.

"Oh, God, he's made another convert." Amber's voice cut through his mumbles. She stared at his full mouth and cheese-dust-stained hand with amusement. "I swear, Diatek Industries will prop up the Chicago Mix industry singlehandedly soon. Hello, Justin. Hi, Tina."

"Hi." Tina waved.

"How was your trip?"

"How is any plane trip?" the woman asked with a shrug. "Gross. Bad food."

"I liked it." Justin smiled tiredly. "I haven't been out of the house in weeks except to go into the game briefly in the California offices. This is kind of nice. I always wanted to see New York. Of course, I always assumed I'd be able to walk more than a block when I got here."

"This is the perfect time for a horse-drawn carriage," Amber suggested.

"Oooh." Tina's face lit up.

He filed that away for later. His relationship with Tina had been a strange one, beginning on the same night they had the car accident that left him comatose. When they reconnected, it had been in the virtual world of PIVOT, and she had helped him to prepare to wake from his coma.

Since then, she had been a strange fixture in his life—although the two of them steadfastly avoided talking about exactly what their relationship *was*.

For his part, he began to realize he'd caught serious feelings, and the way her face lit up at the idea of a horse-drawn carriage made him think he might have a way to impress her. His mind drifted for a few pleasant moments until someone cleared their throat meaningfully.

"What? I wasn't—never mind." He shook his head several times. "Sorry. You were saying?"

"We were saying that Dotty has several solo days on her journey. She had a few choices, technically, including bringing someone from the orc village with her, but she decided to go alone. We thought it might be good if you showed up to speak to her and give her a chance to reflect. Frankly, one of the features of the game is its social qualities." Amber shrugged. "It's generally not good for people to be completely without that."

"Ooooh, could I go?" Tina hopped from one foot to the other. "Please, please, please?"

"You?" Justin raised an eyebrow. "You didn't cause enough diplomatic trouble in Berghold so now, you want to start an all-out war with the orcs?"

"For the last time, those fuckers started it." She jabbed a finger at him. "All with their fancy hats and shady dice rolls. I know what they were up to, and it was nothing good, I'll tell you that."

He rolled his eyes.

"And I won't cause a war," she pointed out, "because this is Dotty, who is a human and knows I'm another human. Real person."

"*That's* why you want to cause a war?"

"So, can I?" Tina begged Amber.

Justin had been confident that the others wouldn't agree but to his horror, they seemed to seriously consider it.

"It would be more advantageous to your recovery if we keep you out of the game for now," Amber said to him.

"Wait, what?"

"And we'd have more time for the promo shoots," Nick agreed. Part of the reason for the trip had been to shoot video of Justin, along with more interviews that Diatek and PIVOT could use for promotional materials. They weren't lacking new test subjects but wanted to accrue as much public goodwill as possible to counteract the nasty rumors being spread online.

Some people *really* didn't like the idea of a virtual reality.

"I think that makes more sense," Amber said.

He sighed glumly.

"What about this?" she suggested gently. "We can give the two of you a lovely date in Insea later tonight. It will limit your time in-game, which will be good for you, but you'll still get to have a good time while you're here. We can maybe even throw in a dragon ride."

Justin brightened immediately. "That sounds good."

"Excellent. In that case, we'll get you to the photoshoot set and

Tina, you come with me and we'll get all your patches on to get you into the game."

Dahti trudged along on the fourth day, whistling Mack the Knife to herself, when she first noticed the other orc. A jolt spiked through her. Tall and hulking, the man had tattoos across his bare chest and arms, and his head was shaved apart from a long ponytail at the very top of his head. His tusks were long, and his skin was the same deep red-brown as the other fire orcs.

"Here we go, huh, Prima?"

"*Mmm,*" the AI said noncommittally.

"What does that mean?" she asked under her breath. She tightened her hold on her stave and strode forward.

A cheery wave and an excited, "Hi!" left her confused.

She stopped dead in her tracks. "Er...hi?" Of all the things she expected from a muscular and imposing orc, this was not one of them.

"It's Tina!" the orc said excitedly in the same deep, booming voice. "Justin's girlfriend. Friend. Thing. Anyway, hi."

"The one I last saw in Berghold?" she asked quizzically.

"Yeah." The orc smashed one fist into the other palm. "Lemme tell you, those two dwarves still got it coming for that. Maybe I'll go there next."

"I'd change bodies first," she said, amused.

"Nah, I *like* this one. I'm so strong! And tall! Also, I've always wondered what it would be like to go topless. This is nice."

Dahti snorted.

"Anyway, I'm simply here to walk with you," Tina said. "They thought you might want company."

"Oh. Thank you very much."

"Also, I can carry things now." She made her muscular avatar flex several times in deeply exaggerated ways.

With a snort, she handed over her pack and stave. "After four days of walking, I'm not too proud to take that offer. Also, it will help me hunt."

"You hunt?" Tina asked with great interest.

"Do you see any grocery stores?"

"Well…no. But I didn't have to do anything like that when I was in the game last time. I merely wandered around Insea and competed in the tournament." She looked at the mountains a few miles away. "Will you simply go straight over? They don't look very…what's the word…"

"Good for my health?" Dahti suggested. "From what I understand, there's a passage of some kind that only the orcs can find. I hope it works off appearance and not knowledge because otherwise, I'll have a bad time of it."

The grass rustled nearby and she stopped her companion with a hand on her arm. She crept forward, holding her breath and magic at the ready.

The rabbit did an about-face almost as quickly as it had hopped out of the grass, but she was prepared. Her spell caught it on the head, something she'd learned to do after she lost several meals to ill-placed spells.

It was difficult to eat an animal when the entire carcass had crumbled into chunks of dirt.

"*Aha,*" she said in satisfaction. "Finally, a good meal. There's only so long I can live on sweet potatoes and mushrooms."

"I don't know, with a nice steak—"

"Do you see any nice steaks? Or bottles of red wine? Or loaves of garlic bread?" Dahti raised an eyebrow.

"Bleh. You should see if they can restart your game in Insea. It's much nicer there."

She smiled. "I'll consider that for next time—right now, I'm afraid, I have a village to save." While they walked, she explained the story. The sun went behind the mountains quite early and cast welcome shadows onto their path.

Tina's presence was a pleasant diversion, she reflected. The days had been filled with magic practice and snarky comments from

Prima, as well as a fair amount of introspection, but that grew old very quickly. There wasn't even a radio for a musical interlude.

Her new companion, on the other hand, was a wild mix of irreverent and humorous who always attempted things like leaping onto rocks to balance one-footed. Dahti was relatively sure she would strangle the woman if she had to take the entire journey with her but as a diversion, it was pleasant.

"So, did you meet Zaara?" she called to her at one point.

"I did." She laughed. "I think Justin had a little crush on her. He always gets all blustery when she comes up in conversation. She helped him on his first missions—her and Lyle."

"And then you and Lyle fought with him in Insea," she said and put the timeline together in her head.

"That's right." Tina wobbled on a rock and hopped down. "You do magic too, right? I chose the daggers because the leather armor was killer but *man*, did it chafe."

Prima snickered in her head. *"You should have seen her trying to walk after her first match."*

She shook her head with a grin. "Something to remember. The robes the magicians wear are much more comfortable—although I discovered I prefer to have some combat skills as well as magic."

"The best of both worlds," the woman agreed. "Whoops, I'm getting a beep. It's time to leave. Is there anything you need before I go?"

"Mmm. I don't think so. I have my amulet, anyway, so I can contact them if there's anything I *do* need. Although…I don't suppose Justin has any contacts among the water orcs?"

"I don't think so," Tina said.

"Really? He seems to know important people everywhere."

"Ah, that's a misconception—you've simply met both of the people he knew, that's all." She laughed. "Well, if there's anything, let me know. I'd arrange for a care package at your next campsite, but I have a feeling your choices and mine might be a little different. That is, unless you *do* like tequila and nachos."

"Young lady," Dahti said, "*everyone* likes tequila and nachos."

"Oh, hot damn. I knew I liked you. I'll arrange for those, then." Tina gave her a mock-salute, twirled—an especially excellent sight with her avatar's tall, muscle-bound frame—and disappeared in a shower of sparkles.

"The sparkles were a nice touch," she told Prima.

"I thought so. And I don't know how she thought she was going to get the tequila and nachos to you, but I'll arrange for them."

CHAPTER THIRTY-EIGHT

By the time Justin finished his briefings and headshots for the coming interviews, he was exhausted. Even talking and focusing took considerable effort these days.

Jacob noticed his frustration and smiled sympathetically. "I can't imagine what this must feel like."

"It takes so much effort simply to get through the *day*," he told him but managed a smile. "But, hey—I'm walking, I'm up and about, and I'm not still stuck in a hospital. I think I'd be going insane if I was."

The other man grinned. "Nah, we'd simply swoop in and give you a crazy, dragon-riding adventure. Speaking of which..." He gestured to the door. "I'm told there's a very romantic date set up for you and Tina."

"*Date?*" he spluttered.

Jacob froze. "Amber said date."

He thought back to the conversation in the lab. Amber *had* said that, he realized in horror. Not that the thought of a date was horrifying, of course, but he had blithely agreed to the idea of a date without even thinking to ask Tina if they were still going out.

"Are you and Tina *not* dating?" his companion asked with real confusion.

"That's the thing," he confessed. "I don't know. I have no idea."

"You…came out together." Jacob set the wheelchair up and darted him a look, one eyebrow raised. "And walked in here with your arms around each other. And weren't you two dating before all this?"

"We went on *a* date," he said. "One! And then we've…hung out… since then. Okay, and there's been some cuddling. She comes over often. I see her every day but I don't want to presume that—"

"Justin," Jacob said seriously. "I went to MIT, so I want you to know that what I'm about to say comes from a place of great expertise. I spent *years* surrounded by some of the absolutely *worst* flirters in the world. I mean, these people were *terrible* at relationships. Incredibly bad. Comically bad. Justin, my man—you are off-the-charts terrible at this."

He spluttered.

"I mean it," the man told him. "I see the way you two look at each other. You hang out every day. You cuddle. She came out here with you. You had all those good talks in the game. Neither of you objected when Amber said she would set you up a date. Justin, my man, you two are *dating.*"

Justin sat hard in the wheelchair. "Oh, God."

"You sit there and process while I'll get you downstairs," Jacob said. "You know, for your date." He added, somewhat wickedly, "Oh, and don't worry—we've set up some alerts in case there's any equipment stuff, but we'll all make sure to be elsewhere so you can have some…" He paused for dramatic effect. "Privacy," he finished blandly.

"If I weren't recovering from a coma, I'd beat you to a pulp," he said grumpily.

"Out of curiosity, how would you say your skill at fighting compares to your skill at relationships?"

"I will fucking kill you. Until you die from it." He lowered his face into his hands as the wheelchair jolted into the lab.

"What's going on?" Amber asked. "Is he okay?"

"Absolutely," Jacob said smoothly, although a trace of laughter still lingered in his voice. "He's merely contemplating his—"

"I will kill you," Justin said again as he raised his head.

"Well, you wouldn't be the first one to want to try," she said cheerfully. She opened the lid of the pod and saw the look on his face. "He and I used to date."

"See?" Jacob said. "I know what I'm talking about."

Despite his discomfort, Justin laughed and summoned his energy to get into the pod and tried not to fall asleep while they hooked him up. He was surprised by how much he was both looking forward to re-entering the game and dreading it. Returning to help Dotty had been one thing. He'd had a purpose and he could put most of his feelings behind him to assume his role as a guide and mentor.

But going back in simply as Justin was somehow different.

Not to mention that the idea of what he would say to Tina made him break out in a cold sweat.

"Count back from ten," Amber told him.

"Ten...nine..."

The game took hold quickly now that he was used to it. He opened his eyes to the familiar view of Insea. He was in a little alley, although a clean one, lit with lights that were suspended all around him in midair. He looked down at a nice shirt and pants and nodded, satisfied that at least he looked okay.

Well, he was dressed well. The rest of it was simply what it was.

He could hear the music of a harp from down the alley and could smell delicious food as well. Justin walked slowly, his heart pounding in his chest.

A date. This is an actual date.

When he entered the courtyard, his jaw dropped. Amber had not been kidding about the romantic date. The food spread on the table was not only mouth-watering, it was gorgeously arranged around centerpieces and candles. A pergola across the courtyard had vines twined all around it, covered in lush greenery and tiny white flowers. A fountain nearby caught the light of the fairy lanterns.

Everything was perfect.

Justin turned and found a sudden rush of courage. "Tina, I need to say something—" He broke off with an undignified squeak.

"Hi," boomed the giant, hulking orc. He had tusks and war tattoos all across one side of his chest…and he wore a fancy, drapey silk dress.

"Um…" He couldn't seem to think of a single word and could hear the AI laughing hysterically in his head. "I'm so sorry—wrong courtyard—"

The orc wavered in front of his eyes, transformed into Tina, and doubled over with laughter. She held her hand over her mouth as she gasped for air. "Oh, man, your *face*—"

Justin sent a silent prayer heavenward that Jacob had been serious about not watching them while they were on the date.

She was still laughing as she moved closer to take his hand. "I'm so sorry. I had that avatar to go see Dotty, and then I thought it would be funny for you to arrive and see it—especially when I saw the dress." She hesitated, suddenly shy, and looked down at it.

"You look beautiful," he told her honestly.

"That's nice, but I'm not beautiful." She gestured at her tattoos and her short frame. "At best, I'm pretty."

"I'm—I don't think—I'm confused." He thought about the lost and aimless person he'd been on their first date, then remembered defeating Sephith and the demon and winning in the arena. He squared his shoulders. "I think the dress suits you, and you…well, you took my breath away in it with both avatars. But for different reasons, of course."

Tina responded with a peal of laughter, then looked curiously at him. "You seem…"

Justin waited. He wasn't sure what to say.

After a moment, she shrugged. "Different, but I'm not sure how. Is everything okay?"

"Yes," he said with certainty. He took her hand. "Do you want to eat?"

"Mmm, maybe in a while." She looked to where couches stood near the fountain, with glasses of wine and various appetizers nearby. "I…well, I wanted to talk to you about something. I probably didn't make the best start with the orc avatar."

He stopped to stare at her. "Are we *both* horrible at this?"

"What? Wait, what am I horrible at?"

"Nothing! Not—I didn't mean—" He waved his hands. "Jacob said—"

"Jacob said *what?*" Tina asked.

Oh, dear. He gulped.

"This should be fun," the AI commented.

"Would you give us a moment?" he asked her.

"I can't. I am literally running this world."

Justin sighed. To Tina, he said, "Jacob asked how things were going with us. And, uh…I explained that I wasn't sure how to talk to you about it, and he said I was being ridiculous, and that we were probably…I mean—ohhhh, he was right. I'm so bad at this."

She went to get him a glass of wine. "Drink up. Liquid courage. Not that we can get drunk here, of course, but maybe it'll work as a placebo."

"Maybe it will." He drained it in a gulp. "Okay, here it is. I really like you." His face burned but he pressed on. "You make me laugh and you also make me want to live a good life for myself. You were the first person who ever asked me what *I* wanted, not because you assumed I wanted to be rich and successful but because you wondered what would make me happy. I mean…it's not about the things you do. Why I like you, that is. It's because you're you. And when I look at you…" He shook his head, a little lost for words now. "Maybe we're already dating or maybe you thought we were only friends. But I'd like…well, I'd like to be dating. If you want."

He blew a breath out. No one would want to go out with a dude who stumbled over the words that way. Especially someone covered in tattoos who liked skinny-dipping and pissing her parents off.

"I'm glad I went on that first date," Tina said.

Justin looked up. She met his gaze briefly, then focused on her glass of wine. Her fingers were white-knuckled around it.

"Honestly, it's been hard," she said. "I said so much to you about doing stuff for *yourself* and all that but I was doing the same thing you were. I merely tried to piss my parents off. I hadn't ever honestly thought about doing what I wanted to do, and I still don't know what

I want to do. You—you have this career, you already had your video game channel, and you were going for things. I never was."

She downed her wine and poured herself another glass. Her hands shook so hard that some splashed onto the floor.

"And then I nearly killed you," she said. "I felt like I ruined your life and I put your whole family through something they should have never had to go through and—no, *please* don't argue, Justin. You know it's true. And I wanted to help. I wanted to do anything I could to make it right and I wanted you and your parents to hate me because at least then, the world would make sense.

"But you wouldn't. You didn't hate me, and we tried to get you back into the real world and then you've been recovering. I kept telling myself I didn't know what I felt and you didn't know what *you* felt and I couldn't ambush your recovery by—"

"Hey." Justin put her wine glass on the table and took her hands in his.

She took a deep breath. "I've wanted to ask you what we were this whole time. And yesterday, Amber said she'd make us a date and you didn't even blink. You simply agreed, and I felt like I was walking on *air*, Justin."

He laughed and squeezed his eyes shut. "I didn't realize until just before this that she'd said that. It was why Jacob was talking to me about it. I panicked about whether or not you thought I was being presumptuous."

Tina started to laugh. She laughed like she wasn't entirely sure she could stop and after a moment, he wrapped his arms around her. Hers came around him as well, and she squeezed so tightly that he made an undignified noise and tapped on her shoulder.

"Excuse me. I need to breathe."

She responded with a sniffle and a laugh. "So, are we…"

"Dating? I think so." he looked at her. They were too different in height to lean their foreheads together easily. "Unless we have to have it notarized or something."

"I'm a notary."

Tina must have heard that too because she snorted and looked up.

She looked over her shoulder at the wine and the appetizers. "How about we have good food and appreciate everything Prima put out for us?"

"Thank you," the AI said and sounded pleased.

"Oh, right—Prima is what Dotty named it?"

"Prima is what I named myself, thank you very much. None of the rest of you bothered to ask if I had a name."

"Right." He cleared his throat and tried to assess the risk of a robot uprising. "Thank you, Prima."

"You're welcome. I'll give you two some privacy."

Justin sat on one of the couches and sighed happily as he popped an appetizer into his mouth. "Mmf. Amazing. Melted cheese is the best appetizer. You can't change my mind."

"Almost every culture has something like fried balls of cheese. And the rest..." Tina shook her head. "We need to find all of them and wander around with platters of mozzarella sticks or something. This is so good."

"Let's see how it goes with the wine." He poured more into his glass and handed Tina hers again. He took a sip. "Mmm. Pear. Oak. Berries."

"I didn't know you knew about wine," she said in surprise.

"I don't. I was bullshitting."

She snorted wine up her nose and wiped it with a napkin. "Oh, man, so this game makes it sting when you get stuff up your nose. That's impressive, but also—ow." She took a cautious sip of the wine. "How am I supposed to do this?"

"I think you're supposed to kind of roll it over the sides and back of your tongue, with the very front of your mouth open."

"Thith feelth ridiculouth."

"Nah, it'th vewy clathy." Justin swallowed. "As you can tell, this is a fine vintage. And how do I know, you ask?" He held a finger up, popped a mouthful of melted cheese in his mouth, and took a sip of wine. "It goes well with the melted cheese. That's the only wine metric that matters."

Tina laughed. "See, we should do this more often."

"We can do it again tonight," he suggested. "Have a real-world date after this one. There has to be somewhere we can find melted cheese in New York City."

"Probably," she agreed. "On the other hand—and hear me out—room service."

Justin clinked her glass with his. "I like the way you think."

CHAPTER THIRTY-NINE

Despite her concerns, the tunnel through the mountain was unprotected by any magic at all. It was exactly where the map put it, and Dahti suspected that the "magic" was simply that no one else knew it was there. Most people didn't travel in the orc lands to start with.

About halfway through the mountain, when she could not see light on either side but *could* hear the occasional creak and shift of earth, she realized there was likely significant magic involved in keeping it from collapsing.

At least she hoped there was.

She tried to feel for it as she walked. During her time in the world, she had studied various forms of magic, so did that mean she could sense other people's spells? She searched for the feeling she had when she created little spurs of rock or even clouds of dust.

Perplexingly, she couldn't discern any spells at all. This tunnel was, somehow, impossibly stable despite the fact that it existed deep within a mountain. Not so much as a piece of dust shook loose when the rock shifted and settled above her. But, try as she might, she couldn't sense a spell.

A few minutes of concentrated thought finally told her why.

It was roughly the same reason that a person in Zabar's couldn't "see" New York City—the spell was *massive*. She walked with her mouth hanging open in awe. Her progress had been fairly good with small spells—the kind that could trap a wolf's paw or distract an elven battle eagle—but everything she'd achieved was insignificant compared to the scale of this.

Utterly fascinated, she hoped she stayed in the game long enough to make something of this magnitude.

Dahti was so absorbed in the beauty of it and the power that threaded in faint lines through the rock above her that she hardly noticed the first glimmers of light. In fact, it was the scent of salt that caught her attention first. She was still a fair distance from the coast, but the air in this part of the tunnel was fresher and it smelled unmistakably of the ocean.

She walked gladly toward it, both pleased to be out in the open and sad to leave this marvel of earth magic behind her. She had to remember to send Lyle a letter, she thought, so dwarven wizards could come to examine it. Surely they and the earth shamans would have much to discuss.

Then again, the races didn't seem to be on the best of terms.

Her first step out of the tunnel was into a paradise. She gasped and looked at the sweep of the sea, entirely different from the North Atlantic coast. The water wasn't iron-gray and white-capped. It was such a deep blue that she could hardly believe her eyes.

White sand beaches were flanked on one side by reefs filled with shoals of quick-darting fish and on the other side by verdant forests. A stream wound through the trees, catching the sunlight, and spilled out over a tumble of rocks and into the sea.

Dahti's gaze traced the glint of the river through the trees and she thought she saw a rustle of movement. It was difficult to tell from this distance if what she saw was orcs or something else—a large cat, perhaps—and she considered how best to find out without getting mauled when she noticed something else that was very important.

Several spears were pointed at her.

She looked around cautiously. The gathered orcs, gray-skinned with a distinctive bluish tint, stared in return.

"Hello," she said with no better ideas.

"Explain your presence, *earth orc*." One of them—she hadn't seen which—all but spat the words. When she tried to determine who had spoken, the warrior jabbed a spear at her. "I said—"

"I heard you," she snapped.

The tips of the spears moved much closer.

"Damn," she muttered. When nothing else came to mind, she put her hands up and tried not to show her exasperation while she studied them. "I am here to learn magic." When no one said anything, she added, "May I say that the fire tribes are glad to learn that your people still live?"

"The fire tribes?" one of them asked.

"She came out of fire territory," another said. He curled his lip. "So you told them we still lived. How long have the earth tribes known and not sent help?"

"My tribe was taken by illness," Dahti said. She hoped this tribe thought the same way the last one had or she was about to be an orc kebab. "I found shelter with a fire village and while I was there, we learned that you still lived."

"How?"

"From…" Oh, this was awkward. "From a human."

"Do you expect us to believe that?" the first one asked harshly. She stared at her with an expression of deep disgust. "A lone earth orc traipses out of fire territory and claims she learned our tribe was still alive from a human. And what was it you said? You're here to learn *magic?*"

"Truth is stranger than fiction," she responded. That would have to be her go-to phrase for a while, she suspected.

"Heh." The orc gave her an appreciative smile. "You lie well, earth orc. But you'll still die here."

"Ah." It seemed her appreciation was the kind one warrior gave another before an honorable death. She sighed. "Perhaps I could ask that your shaman be allowed to assess whether I am lying or not?"

A very long pause followed. Several of them looked at each other, much like they were having a secret conversation they'd had several times before. Eventually, the leader directed two of them to put their spears up and withdrew with the others for a whispered conversation.

"And yes," Dahti called, "I know your shaman is Rashat."

Everyone gave her a sharp look. The whispered conversation became more intense and included a great deal of hand-waving.

Finally, their leader returned, her spear at the ready. "Why do you want to learn magic from Rashat? Talk."

Dahti had, thankfully, spent several days practicing this exact speech. There hadn't been much else to do, after all. She'd intended to give it to Rashat, of course, but she could modify it because she knew it by heart at this point.

"The fire village I sheltered with has been attacked by its god," she said evenly. "Since word reached us of the water tribes' destruction, many orcs have wondered if the gods are just—and if they are worthy of the sacrifices they demand. When their god came, they stood against him for the first time, and although we drove him back, he has sworn to have his revenge. Only one tribe has ever defeated a fire god and that is the water tribe. We thought there was no hope, but if Rashat still lives, perhaps he can train me."

None of them said anything but it was clear that she had struck a nerve.

It was also not difficult to see their mood and it was one of heartbreak and pity. The leader put her spear up quietly and the others followed.

"Is Rashat dead?" Dahti asked.

"No," the warrior said heavily. "But he will not train you."

"I know there have been differences between the tribes," she said urgently. "I know he may doubt my commitment or my faith, and he is free to doubt it as much as he wishes. I will do anything. I will promise whatever I must promise, if only he will help that village. There are children there, little ones who have never done anything wrong, and they need his help. Surely they do not deserve to die as sacrifices to a fire god." She stopped when the leader held a hand up.

"It is…not that." She gestured to a rocky outcropping nearby. "Come, sit. I will tell you the story. Then maybe you will understand."

Dahti dropped her pack and her staff and sat where indicated. It was precarious up there on the edge of a towering cliff that must be at least as high as the Eiffel Tower, if not higher. The view of the sea showed a huge bay and beyond it, a series of small islands rising out of the water.

"The elders say they saw the god take the islands first," the warrior explained. "For two days, they saw the beast flying and touching down. They heard the sounds of celebrations and sacrifice on the winds—and then they heard screams. The god was not appeased even though it had taken everything."

She said nothing but her heart clenched. All too well, she remembered the screams of the villagers as they fled across the plains.

"It had been many generations since the gods had come to us," the leader explained. "More than twenty. The elders were devout. They had made their offerings each year into the sea—the freshest fish, the choicest crops. They said the prayers and burned incense. Warriors were sent out into the deep ocean in boats to be claimed if the god wanted. They had never taken more than the sea could give and had never taken it for granted. And still, it was not enough."

Dahti looked at her with what she hoped was encouragement.

The woman smiled slightly. "It aches to tell the story, even though I was not there for it. My grandparents told me only once, but I remember every word. They trusted their god completely and it betrayed them. The pain I feel when I speak the story is not mine, but theirs."

She recalled her grandparents speaking of the great war, of the plague that had killed millions, of the wives at home hearing of their husbands' deaths and the people in the new country hearing that their families were wiped out. She nodded. This, she understood.

The leader looked at the bay before she continued.

"Rashat was young but he was the strongest shaman we had ever seen. When we first saw the god, we sent for him but he was already coming to us. While he trained, he had lived alone with his teacher, although he still issued edicts. He called for every shaman, and he and his teacher consulted the runes and the portents.

"They decided to stand against the god. My grandparents said they were frightened but they were also sure. They had done all their god asked and still, they were being slaughtered. As you said, it was not… just." Her smile was bitter. "They believed they were right to stand against it."

"And?" Dahti asked quietly.

"Maybe they were," the warrior said with a shrug. "But right and powerful are two different things. Rashat's mentor was struck down before his eyes—young for a shaman, not even fifty. He stood against the creature alone then, and he called the scriptures to it. The beast did not care.

"It struck at the villagers and he summoned the power of a storm to drive it away, but it flew back to lash at him again. He summoned a wave as high as this cliff to strike it into the deeps and lift rocks to shred its body…"

"It wasn't defeated, though," she said.

"No. It wasn't. Rashat was almost killed by that effort. The god feasted on our people while he lay as one dead. Eventually, some of the warriors were able to beat it back enough that it left—or perhaps it had simply eaten its fill. It disappeared into the sea and it has not come back, but we know it still lives."

"And Rashat?" Dahti asked.

"He lay alone for two full cycles of the moon. They say he ate nothing and drank nothing. One by one, the messengers returned to say the other tribes were dead as well and they had found their families gone and their homes destroyed." The warrior looked at her clasped hands. "There was no one else left to lead us, and so we begged Rashat to pick himself up and tell us what to do next. He… didn't."

"He is still…" Dahti could not find the word. "A recluse?"

"No." The leader sighed heavily. "He does everything asked of him. He fishes, he mends nets, he collects freshwater and prepares food. He will do anything at all, and do it well—save use his magic or train an apprentice. We have asked him to do so many times, and he always says the same thing—that the magic of the water tribe failed us and that he will let it pass from memory and die with him." She looked frankly at her. "And so we understand, truly, what it is to face your god. We would help you if we could. But Rashat will not help you and no one else knows how."

Dahti looked out at the sea. Now that she was in this water-rich place, she thought she could feel the tug of the magic. She told herself it was all in her head, but she didn't think it was. Her logic suggested that this was how Prima had made this place—full of magic and full of secrets waiting to be learned.

The AI had seen how much she liked magic and…had she made this place *for* her? She blinked rapidly and told herself that the faint stinging in her eyes was from the salt wind.

Finally, she asked, "Could I speak to him? Would you allow it?"

The leader looked nervous. "I will bring you to the village elders. They can decide. I would say…do not try. Go, find someone else. Go to the earth tribes and seek out the air tribes. Rashat was once feared, and…well, it's easy to see why if you ever look into his eyes. There's something dark there. I would never, ever want to make him angry." She shuddered, then added defensively, "And if you think I'm a coward, ask anybody. They'll say the same."

"I don't doubt you," Dahti said thoughtfully. "Still, I too have seen the death of many I hold dear—and I have seen many people step forward to become the leader no one thought they could be. I would like to speak to your elders."

The warrior sighed quietly. "I warned you," she said glumly. "Well, come on. We might as well start now. I can't wait to see what they'll make of *this*."

CHAPTER FORTY

The walk to the village was beautiful, although if anything could make Dahti miss the dry heat of the plains, it was the humid heat of a jungle. Thankfully, the breeze off the water kept most of it to a bearable level.

"So you watch the tunnel, then," she called to the leader of the group, who had introduced herself as Atra.

"Nah," Atra responded and threw a grin over one shoulder. "No one's come looking for us in years—not from the other tribes, anyway. We go up there to watch the sea. Sometimes, humans like to bring their ships in and drop anchor and we don't want a fight. You were whistling, so we heard you in the tunnel. We were about as surprised as you were."

She smiled and acknowledged that she had begun to like these warriors. All were young and seemed to share Atra's belief in their tribe. They might not know their future or whether it would look anything like the past their grandparents knew, but they were determined to protect their people. She appreciated that in young people.

Traditions and norms changed. What never changed was that you should protect those close to you.

At the bottom of the hill, when they were engulfed in greenery, the team started along what could not even charitably be called a path. They must have known it by habit and sheer familiarity because they all followed the same sequence of steps without even looking at one another. There were no trail markers and no downtrodden areas she could see to provide clues.

What struck her most about the village was the silence. People didn't speak to one another or sing and so, when the group stepped into the perimeter of the settlement, it was a shock. People were present and they were working, but they were silent.

Her presence, at least, caused a noticeable stir. The warm green-brown of her skin was visibly different from that of the young soldiers around her. They now, under the gazes of their families and elders, looked like they wondered if they'd made the correct choice in bringing her with them.

Courage, she wanted to whisper to the group leader but she sensed that this was a choice the younger woman needed to make on her own.

Atra raised her chin and pointed toward a large hut at the back of the camp. "This way. The elders aren't waiting but they'll see us going there and join us." Under her breath, she added, "Hopefully."

How badly had the elders of this tribe mistreated their young ones if this was how things were? Dahti followed and her blood began to boil.

Inside the large hut and beyond a scrap of tattered cloth lay a room that was, indeed, empty. A plain pole was fixed in the middle to hold the roof up, windows that would provide an outlook over the sea were covered by reed screens, and threadbare cushions rested on the floor.

There was no art. That was her first thought once her eyes adjusted to the gloom enough to see.

The elders arrived quickly. Perhaps they wanted the outsider gone as soon as possible. Whatever the case, the eight of them entered and an older woman with tusks like Atra's gave the warrior a hard stare.

Dahti's lip curled.

When the elders were all seated, they waited in silence. Atra stepped forward and bowed.

"Elders, I present to you Dahti of the earth tribes, by way of the fire lands. She seeks the help of our tribe. I will let her present her petition." She stepped aside and gestured to her.

She nodded to those assembled. "Elders of the water tribe, I offer the joy of many villages that you still live. You have long been thought to be dead. Huwat, shaman of Mountain's Shadow, sends his regards."

"And why does an earth orc come bearing the word of a fire shaman?" one of the elders asked.

Her heart sank. She already knew what their answer would be.

Still, she had to try. "Huwat's village has been attacked by their god, much like your tribes were attacked by yours," she said. "Since the news of that attack, they have searched for the meaning behind it and have begun to suspect that the gods are not what they claim to be. They do not want to offer themselves in sacrifice to false gods, but there is only one tribe that has ever slain a fire god and that is yours. I was sent to learn from your shaman." She paused. "From Rashat."

"Rashat practices no magic," one of them said simply. "Our tribe has not existed for two generations, earth orc. There is nothing for you to learn here."

"But…" She looked around at them in confusion. "You *do* exist. You're here. You survived."

"We are not a tribe any longer," one of them said. "We are husks. We have bodies. We are orcs…perhaps. But we have no shaman and without a shaman, we have no soul. We have no gods, we have no rites, and we have no hymns."

Dahti looked at the young ones, who stood now with their gazes fixed firmly on the ground.

The silent village and the bare huts spoke volumes. The water tribe had been the most devout among the orcs and now, they had nothing. They did not sing their songs, which had all been hymns. They did not paint. None of the young orcs had tattoos or necklaces.

She might have grieved if she were not so angry—and she was incandescently angry. "Do you mean to tell me," she said, "that you have spent forty years or more wallowing in misery and raised your children and their children to not sing and not delight in their culture because you have *cast it aside?*"

"We have none of those things to give them," one of the elders said. "Our songs were to false gods. Our tattoos were in service to a monster. We burned the statues and forgot the songs. There was no one to guide us forward. What were we to do?"

"Guide your damned selves," she snapped.

Everyone in the hut responded with a hastily indrawn breath.

"Oh, be real," Dahti said harshly. "You can't tell me no one here wanted to sing or make tattoos or artwork. You held them all back. You put your babies to bed without lullabies and told your children you had no stories for them. It should have been clear years ago that Rashat wouldn't guide you, but you didn't choose anyone else, did you?"

Some of the elders hissed through their teeth, and one of them stared accusingly at the young warriors. "Did you tell this outsider our secrets?"

"If you have no soul, you have no secrets," she said contemptuously. "You let one man's despair drag you all into oblivion."

"Without a shaman, we have no—"

"According to the ways you *abandoned*," she snapped. "If you abandoned the rest of it, then why not this part?"

They looked at one another and one woman stood to face her.

"How many years have you seen, earth orc?"

"Eighty-four," she said promptly. She folded her arms and met their stares. "I don't care what you think. It's true. I have four children. I have ten grandchildren. I have seven great-grandchildren. And I left them to help a tribe that is being hunted by a god and, so *help* me, you will let me slap some sense into Rashat."

The old woman stood back, her arms folded in a mirrored gesture, and studied her. "Well, *that* was spoken like a grandmother, and no mistake."

Quietly, Atra said, "I thought you said your village was wiped out."

Dahti looked at her. The thought of her children and their children in graves made her eyes water, and it wasn't acting to say, "Leaving graves is also difficult."

Atra nodded.

The older woman drew her attention again. "If you are so old, you will understand when I say that we did this to protect our young ones. The songs we sang and the statues we made called destruction down upon us. We are not wise in the ways of the gods, and even those who were fell into death and despair. We do not go to the water's edge now, save by night. We do not sing songs that would carry on the wind. We love our children as much as you, earth orc."

That, she understood and she considered it before she responded.

"I honor your sacrifice, grandmother, but surely you know this is no answer."

"And yet, what other answer is there?" The woman looked her in the eyes. "A life with no songs still has joy. Perhaps we are no longer orcs. Perhaps we have no tribe. But we exist."

Dahti looked around, hoping something might present itself as an opportunity. They feared the return of the dragon, that much was clear. Everything they did was in fear of that. Where before, they had considered it a bargain that was harsh but fair and difficult but predictable, they now feared the impossibly high toll of it.

She had an idea of the one thing that might—*might*—jolt Rashat out of his despair.

It was a long shot. After forty years, he had grown accustomed to it and might never emerge from it.

Whatever the outcome, she had to try, though.

"This is no life," she said to them. "Not for you and not for *anyone*. Your god turned on you and I believe it was only the first one. Now, the fire tribe is menaced, and for all we know, the air tribe faces their god even as we speak or has been laid low like you. The orcs will never be able to live in peace or happiness until the false gods are brought low."

They stared at her with a terrible hunger in their eyes.

"I thought on it as I walked," Dahti said. "A water shaman was the only one ever to defeat a fire god. What if a fire shaman could have done the same for you? We will be stronger as *one people.* When those who call themselves gods—who do *not* bring the beasts or the rains—are gone, we can build cities and sing whatever songs we wish. But we cannot do it as separate tribes. We must restart the festivals. And first, we must band together to destroy those who would threaten our children."

One of the old men had a tear tracing down his cheek. His eyes were closed, his old face lined with pain.

"Let me speak to Rashat," she said urgently. "*Please.* He *must* understand what is at stake. It was not his failure and it is not only his people who will suffer if he allows this tradition to die."

The old woman smiled. "If you seek to train as a shaman, it is not our place to stop you. You never needed our permission."

"Don't you pull out old-fashioned sensibilities." Dahti stabbed a finger at her. "You made this as difficult as humanly possible. Orcably? As difficult as possible. I've spent considerable time around humans," she added when they stared at her. She looked at Atra. "Can you take me to Rashat?"

The woman seemed amused. "Yes. This way." She ducked out the door without waiting for the approval of the elders and held the cloth aside for her. As she led the way across the rough ground, she said in an undertone, "Thank you. I've heard so many times why we cannot sing or dance but never have I heard someone say the things I wanted to say in return." She looked quizzically at her. "Are you *sure* you're eighty-four?"

"Unfortunately, yes."

Atra smiled and gestured to a small hut nearby. "There. That is his hut. I—Rashat." She broke off and held a hand up. "Hello."

"Hello, Atra." He was tall and in his youth, he must have been very handsome. A tattoo had been started on one side of his torso but never finished. His white hair was cut short close to his head, and he kept his beard to a small layer of stubble. A hole in one of his heavy tusks suggested that an ornament had once been strung there.

He looked at Dahti and although his expression was mild, she understood what Atra meant about not wanting to make him angry.

His black eyes were a void. In them, she saw years of self-hatred and despair, all combining into a terrible fury she was sure might spill out at any time.

Well, she wouldn't get anywhere by trying to avoid the issue. She planted her staff in the dirt and inclined her head.

"Rashat, I am Dahti of…Hunt. I come at the behest of Huwat of Mountain's Shadow. Their god hunts them, and only one tribe has ever defeated a fire god. You are the last heir of that tradition. I seek your knowledge."

Rashat stared at her. She was aware that, all around the village, people had stopped to watch this exchange.

He moved closer. At her side, Atra did not step back although she was rigid with fear. His nostrils flared and his big hands clenched.

"My line," he said, "has no power over gods. It is useless and it will pass out of memory with me. It gives nothing to this tribe."

"Once," Dahti told him, "all the tribes gathered each year and the traditions were used to strengthen one another—"

"*My line,*" Rashat bellowed at her, "*has no power over gods.* It will pass out of memory with me!"

He stormed into the woods, leaving the warrior trembling at her side.

"I'm sorry," she told Dahti. "I'm so sorry. I thought maybe he would listen to you."

"Oh, Atra," she said and smiled. "This is *not* over yet."

CHAPTER FORTY-ONE

Most of the villagers had either been very young or not yet born when the water dragon attacked. They were unfamiliar with the world Rashat had inhabited—the world he believed he was the heir to.

Still, they knew him.

Dahti started with Atra and one simple request: "Tell me your first memory of Rashat."

The warrior blew her breath out and her gaze focused on the middle distance. Then, her face cleared and she looked both embarrassed and worried. "Oh, I know what it was. I always try not to remember this."

She waited but didn't look at the woman. Life had taught her that if you rushed in too soon, people would draw away.

"I was very little," Atra said. "But old enough to know right from wrong—well, what my parents wanted me to do or not do, you know. I knew they didn't want me to be loud when I played and I knew that none of us were supposed to talk to Rashat. Or about him."

"Not even about him?" she asked before she could stop herself.

"I asked why he didn't have children or grandchildren," the woman explained. "They made all kinds of weird faces and told me not to ask questions about Rashat and *never* to speak to him. Well, what can you say to make a child insatiably curious? That."

Dahti, who keenly remembered her failures in this area—as well as watching her children fail the same way—couldn't suppress a laugh.

"So, I waited until they were doing chores…" Atra leaned her forehead on one palm. She blushed, although on a water orc, it was a deep blue color. "And I marched *right* up to him and asked why he didn't have a wife and children and why everyone always said his name all funny."

"Oh." She clapped a hand over her mouth. "Oh, dear. Oh, dear."

"You know that look of absolute horror adults have when you do that kind of thing?" the warrior asked. "I still remember that look. Not from him, of course. He knelt, all normal—oh, I hate remembering this. I should have simply listened to them."

She smiled, patted the girl on the shoulder, and wished she would hurry up with the story.

"He said he had no wife and child because he did not deserve them," Atra said. "And he spoke so normally, too. He told me that when he was younger, he was supposed to protect the tribe and he had failed, that he should have been killed but he lived as a reminder to all of us."

"A reminder of what?"

"I never got to find out." She hunched her shoulders. "My mother came and hauled me across the village and up the path there to where we found you, yes? And she said if I couldn't follow the rules, I could go live with the fire tribes and bring *their* gods down on *their* heads, but she wouldn't keep me here to kill everyone."

Dahti, who rather thought parents went too easy on children nowadays, was shocked to hear a story of parenting much harsher than what she had experienced. She stared at Atra, and finally managed a strangled, "My goodness."

The warrior shrugged. "She was right."

"To tell a child to leave home if she can't follow rules—why, Atra, every child breaks rules."

Atra considered this. "I think it's different for us," she said finally.

"I think many things are different for us. You were so angry about the songs and the art, but that's simply the way we've lived. If we attract the attention of the god, who knows how many could die? Who knows if we'll even survive it?"

She opened her mouth to ask what the point was of surviving as a tribe if there were no traditions passed down and if every breath was taken in the shadow of fear. Caution stepped in, however, and she did not give voice to the words. These people still lived and they wanted to keep living.

That was enough for her. She gave one pained thought to the fire tribe, who even now fled through the plains, and prayed that she could convince Rashat to help her with enough time to spare.

"Thank you," she said gravely and she went to ask someone else.

This time, she aimed older and eventually went to help a man with the traps he was laying in the stream. She could see the gray peppered through his hair, which was a good sign.

He gave her an alarmed look when she appeared, but she was a competent hand at snares and traps and once he saw that she could fix the ties and set the traps, he relaxed.

They worked in silence until he said finally, "You can't have come all this way merely to be one of our tribe."

"No?" She smiled. "I have no tribe of my own, you know. Plague took them months ago. Why should I not settle here?"

He looked at her and snorted. "Everyone knows what you said to the elders."

"For a village where no one speaks much," she said, "it's amazing how fast word travels."

"Simply because we don't talk loudly doesn't mean we don't talk." He stood and shook his hands. "That's all of these. Come along if you're going to help."

Dahti followed him, still silent and watchful, until he turned to look over his shoulder at her.

"What?" she asked innocently.

"Well? Are you going to ask? And don't say, 'ask what.' Ask whatever you came here to ask." He shrugged. "Not that I don't appreciate the help with the traps, mind."

"You don't fish in the ocean anymore, then." Dahti watched him closely.

"Sometimes." He shook his head. "It's tempting. But every visit there tempts the god to return and finish what he started."

"Why not leave?" she asked him curiously. "You could go to the plains or…the mountains."

He inclined his head at her. "Do you not feel it?"

"Feel what?" She looked around nervously, half-afraid she had a giant spider on her back or something.

"The call of your ancestral lands." He frowned at her. "The sea is a part of us. It might be home to the god who wants us dead but if we were to leave it, that would be the death of us. We would no longer be water orcs."

Dahti suppressed her small sound of satisfaction. That was the key —or, if not the only one, at least one of them. With no larger tribe and no shamans, the one link these orcs had to their past was the sea that was both their soul and their deepest terror.

"I wonder what it's like," she said softly. The sea was all around them and it permeated everything. "To have it be such a part of you and not be able to touch it."

The orc looked at her. "Yes," he said at last. "I never knew the sea as they did—I was born the year after and it has always been the source of our terror. Still, I feel it in my bones, every tide and every wave. I cannot imagine life without the sound and smell of it. And it's worse, you know—for *him*."

She looked sharply at him.

"The children know him as…an uncle, perhaps. One you don't want to make mad but a person like any other. When I was a child, you could feel him coming from across the village. His pain was like the sharpest spear and always pointed toward the sea."

It took Dahti longer than it should have to understand. "You were born with magic," she said quietly. "You would have been his apprentice."

His head jerked up and he stared at her.

She realized he hadn't known.

Afraid to lose his willingness to speak, she gestured to the stream behind them. "You've always been better at setting traps than anyone else, haven't you? Better at finding fresh water. And you can feel the waves…and Rashat's pain. You know how much it hurt him to give it up."

"No," the man said shortly. "I don't. Whatever talent I have—might have had—his is far greater. They said he was five when he held the tides back one day."

Dahti knew her eyes must be as round as dinner plates.

"He was beyond anyone else," the orc told her. "None of the shamans could match him. My parents said to me, 'you have only ever known him as a broken man but once, he was whole.'" He thought for a moment before he added, "Perhaps they do not say it in your tribe, but in ours, we say a person is only whole when their being and their purpose are aligned. None of us have been whole since the god came but few were ever as whole as Rashat. To have that and then lose it?" He shook his head. "It is not a fate I would wish on anyone."

She returned to the traps. There simply were no words to respond to this, only a hollow feeling in her chest and one she remembered all too well.

It was what she had felt in the months after Harry died.

The comparison was the closest she could find but it wasn't the same. Harry had lived a full life and they'd had time together before he died. It was nowhere near as tragic as losing her family, her home, her spouse, and her life's purpose in one fell swoop at twenty.

Still, it had felt as if a piece of her was not so much dead as cut away—gone and unreachable. The thought of such a pain magnified was almost more than she could bear.

After a time, a cleared throat made her look up as the man backed away to make room for Atra's grandmother. The old woman took his place without a word and began to work on the nets and traps.

"What do you hope for?" she asked finally.

"I never made a secret of it," Dahti said. There wasn't much inflection in her voice. What she needed from them—from Rashat—was too much to ask.

She saw that now.

"What you want is for Rashat to be whole again," the woman said. "But you don't see—he was never whole."

Dahti frowned at her. "That man said—"

"Jemad never knew him," Atra's grandmother interrupted. "I did. And I can tell you, girl, he was never whole. He had a purpose, true enough, but he never had a self. How could he? From the time he was a baby, he had the hopes of the tribe on his shoulders. He knew what they expected of him before he knew his name. Small wonder he thought to kill a god."

"Are you saying he wanted to kill a god *before* the god came?" she asked.

"That's what I'm saying." The woman tied a knot deftly, her old fingers still nimble. "How else to set his destiny? That's one thing we all need. He couldn't back away from it, oh, no. He breathed magic and always had. The one chance he had to do something all his own was to be *more* than they expected."

"How do you know this?" she asked her softly. She remembered all too well the way she'd assessed people in her youth—people she'd never known. Who was to say if this old woman was right?

"We saw," the woman said simply. "Everyone wanted to be him. All our parents wished it was their child with the talent—except he was taken away to study with the shamans and his parents were alone. He was never theirs and was always the tribe's. We still envied him, but...I think we all knew it was easier to have our little dalliances and our feasts than it was to live in a hut and study magic with the shamans."

Dahti nodded.

"I heard whispers," the woman told her. "They were horrified at what he said. But he'd read the histories and he knew there was a time when things had been different. He said we were chaining ourselves by bowing to it. The rest of us kids liked to side with him—we thought we were so daring." She paused, her head bowed. "When the god came, I think we all thought he could defeat it. He wasn't the only one."

She paused and looked from the old woman to the village.

One question remained. "And no one could persuade him to…be a shaman again? To heal himself?"

"Child." The woman looked at her. "He thinks all of this is his fault. He thinks he called the god down on us. We did what we could—we took the knives from him and the saltwater he tried to drink. We convinced him to take food. We thought it was a kindness to help him survive." She looked over her shoulder. "I am not certain it was. All I ask is if you try to make him a shaman once more, keep in mind what we did not—what you ask him to do. If he does it, he will live with the consequences of it for years. Was it truly a mercy to give him decades of life tainted with the knowledge that his failure let his village die drowning? I am not certain."

Dahti felt cold, then hot. She nodded and finished one more knot.

"Thank you, grandmother." It was almost funny the way such words came to her in this young body. She was almost certainly older than her.

The woman said nothing as Dahti walked away.

Now that she had heard them speak of Rashat, she could see something more clearly. His hut was not on the worst patch of land as she had immediately assumed. She thought it was a self-imposed penalty that he had built it on bare rock, ever-wet with the flow of the river.

He needed that to survive, though. His magic was part of who he was and the touch of the water kept him sane.

She knew he was inside from the way the others watched and whispered while she approached.

It took effort but she ignored them. At the water's edge, she knelt and focused on it—the trickle of it and the way it was a caress and a threat all in one. Then, she stood and readied her powers.

Part of the problem was that she didn't know how to use water. The first spell came out as an earth-shock, a clod of mud that thudded into the water and bobbed away on the stream before it broke into pieces.

"Hmph." Dahti grunted.

It wasn't wasted effort, however, and she thought she could feel his interest from inside the hut. She sat in the shallow part of the stream and began to make magic of all kinds—rock spurs, clouds of dust, and clods of mud. She almost managed a mist of water droplets once but otherwise, she didn't come close.

Which was why she wasn't surprised when heavy footsteps sounded behind her and Rashat said, both furious and pained, "What in the twelve hells do you think you're doing?"

CHAPTER FORTY-TWO

"Do you think it's working?" Tina asked.

"It's hard to say from here." Justin pillowed his chin on his hands and watched the distant figures in the village.

Beyond a very cryptic few sentences, they hadn't been able to get much out of Prima. In fact, the AI claimed it had no idea what Dahti was up to. Now, it chimed in with, *"It's hard to say from inside the game too."*

The young woman snickered.

"Is something funny to you?" Prima asked dangerously.

"Yeah. You get suuuuuper freaking huffy when you don't understand human behavior." She looked at the sky with a grin.

"May I remind you that I am the one holding these rocks up?"

"Oh, come on." She rolled onto her back to hold the conversation.

"You know I'm not where you're looking any more or less than I was where you were looking in the first place."

"I like to focus somewhere while I'm talking," Tina said with great dignity. "I don't suppose you'd make yourself an avatar."

"And be closed into a tiny prison with limited senses, speed, and strength? No. The mere thought is terrifying."

"Hey!" She sat up. "It's not that bad. Stop making it sound like a terrible thing."

"You might want to be a little quieter," Justin said nervously. He patted her arm. "The wind keeps shifting and if they hear us…well, I don't trust them to not shoot."

"She's being rude," Tina said as if it were self-explanatory.

"Yes, I know, but *again*, I would prefer to not get shot."

"You are such a pansy."

"Isn't he?" the woman agreed.

"Hey! Ugh." He shook his head. "I knew I shouldn't give you two a common enemy. You're both insane."

"Well, that's rude." Prima gave a little huff. *"And you shouldn't take it as an insult, Tina. It isn't as difficult for you to be in that body."*

Tina sighed. "I suppose being born in a body is very different from existing as a—"

"After all, you don't have the cognitive capabilities for it to be limiting."

"Hey!"

"Ooookay, we will one hundred percent be shot." Justin ushered her off the rock. "Prima, as amusing as you would find it if we *were* shot, do you think you could find it in your heart to get us out of here and back to Insea?"

"Thank you for acknowledging my sacrifice in this matter," the AI said graciously. *"They are making preparations to take you two out of the game, so I will do that directly. One moment."*

The world melted around them and he opened his eyes. The pod lid was already open and bright lights shined on him. He expected to need to squint but as far as his optic nerves knew, he'd recently been outside in bright sunlight and this wasn't very different from that.

He accepted Nick's hand to sit.

"You were being *so* rude," Tina's voice said nearby.

Justin rolled his eyes. "I don't think I—"

"Not *you*," Tina said. "These guys." She glared at Amber and the others. "Which one of you runs Prima?"

For a moment, all three of them looked panicked before they plastered identical, too-big smiles in place.

"Um…" Amber grimaced.

"It's a group effort," Jacob said.

"Yeah," Nick finished.

Tina looked at them. She looked at Justin and focused on the team again. "Um. Okay."

"Right," Jacob said.

"Yeah," Nick added.

"We need to get you to your interview!" Amber said to Justin as if this were the most exciting thing that had ever happened.

"*Yeah*," Nick said. Jacob gave him a sharp look and he shut up.

"That was weird," Justin muttered to Tina as they left.

She frowned and shrugged. "I think so too, but then again, they're always weird."

"You're thinking of DuBois."

"No. I'm thinking of all of them." She gave him a cheeky grin. "It's why we fit in so well here."

They walked to the interview suite hand in hand. After his time in the game today, he felt energetic and happy. Still, he began to feel winded when he arrived at the interview and felt a spike of panic at the sight of the reporters.

To his surprise, Anna Price waited outside the door, as elegant as usual. Justin wondered if her shirts ever wrinkled or if she had sacrificed something to the devil to avoid that. She looked impossibly well put-together.

Or maybe it was simply that the piercing stare made him forget everything else because whenever Anna Price looked at him, he wanted to flee in the opposite direction, screaming at an unmanly pitch. The woman ran a company that partnered with several black ops wings of the US Military, and you could tell that when you looked at her.

Right now, she was smiling. He decided that could mean everything.

"I hope your visit to New York has been good thus far," she said to them and made sure to share her terrifying attention with Tina as well. "Mr. Williams, if I could have a moment of your time before you go in?"

"Yes?" Justin said, hoping his voice hadn't broken too audibly.

"Excellent. May I speak in front of Ms. Castro?"

He nodded. Tina, meanwhile, looked terrified that Price remembered who she was.

"The reporters have been informed that no audio or video is to be taken in the room and they will be able to check quotes provided by us. The PIVOT team tells me that you've been briefed on the few items that are not to be discussed due to privacy concerns but otherwise, I want to be clear that you are allowed to share whatever you feel comfortable sharing. You are also free to not answer any questions as you see fit."

"Er…" He wanted this to be over so he wasn't under her dragonstare anymore, but he also wasn't sure what she meant. "Like, if I think they're looking for info they shouldn't have?"

Price smiled almost gently.

Almost.

"The crash and your recovery may be a very emotional topic," she said. "If you feel uncomfortable or do not want to continue the interview, there will be no repercussions."

Justin, who had not considered any of this, looked at Tina.

"We are glad of your help with publicity," Price told him. "I simply wanted to speak to you before you went in to make sure you didn't feel pressured. Have a good rest of your day, both of you, and perhaps I'll see you again before you leave."

She strode away and he stared at her back.

"Does she frighten you as much as she frightens me?" Tina asked. Her lips barely moved as if she was afraid the woman would turn and see them.

"Her tone and her words are both so nice, but I still feel like I'm being threatened," he muttered, following her example.

"Cheer up," she said finally. "If they wanted to turn you into a lab rat, they already had their chance."

"Lab rat?"

"You know—dark, spooky experiments. Tracking chips." She waggled her eyebrows. "Controlling your thoughts."

"What if they already did that?"

"Then there's nothing to be done about it, is there?"

"Have I mentioned how nice it is to have you here as a supportive girlfriend in this trying time?" Justin looked at her and his mouth twitched.

"Isn't it?" Tina said serenely. "Come on, let's go in."

The interview, after all the build-up, wasn't as frightening as Justin or Anna Price had worried it would be. With Tina seated nearby and the ever-present whirr of the Diatek audio recorders, the reporters were very respectful.

"Mr. Williams," one of them said. "In earlier interviews, you and your parents alluded to the fact that you had some communication. What can you tell us about the first time you heard from them?"

"Oh." He thought back on what now seemed worlds away. "That was a lot to digest because I wasn't yet aware of why I was in the game."

"You were aware that it was a game, though."

"Yeah, it was very clear. Like, I had game stats and an interface and all that, and I died in the game almost right off the bat and then came back, so it wasn't like I thought I'd woken up in the wilderness to fight wolves with a rusty sword."

That drew a few chuckles.

"I thought I must have started a new VR game on my headset," he said. "I wasn't thinking very clearly at the time, of course. You find yourself in a game and your mind simply fills the blanks. I kept thinking I should stop and leave it and then didn't do it, and I think they worried that I might panic if I couldn't take the headset off as I expected to. So they sent me a letter." He caught sight of Tina's face. "What?"

"I've never heard this story," she explained.

"Oh." He took her hand. "Um—where was I? Oh. So, my parents

filmed a video for me and so did Dr. DuBois, telling me what was going on and all that. They also told me I had to be careful to not die in the game because it could stop my heart and I wasn't in very good shape." To his horror, he felt his throat thicken. "It...was a lot to take in."

Tina squeezed his hand.

"I can't imagine," the reporter said. As far as Justin could tell, he was completely sincere. "Being in a near-death state is very frightening and as far as we know, you're the first person ever to know for certain that you were in a coma. What can you tell people out there who might be thinking of writing to PIVOT on behalf of family members who are comatose?"

"Uh..." He chewed his lip. "Could I think for a moment? Um... Okay. Well, I think a big thing is that the game is different for everyone. I'm good at video games—I mean, I've played them forever. But right now, there are people in the game who haven't ever played before. For them, it's a completely different experience.

"I guess the biggest thing is that people will have friends around them—the game is so good at bringing characters to life. But at the same time, they'll be alone. You have to trust them to get themselves to where they need to be to wake up."

People nodded.

"Now we know you can't tell us about other people in the game, but what do you think of when you imagine the future of this treatment?" another reporter asked. "Are there any places you think it could be useful?"

"I'm not sure," Justin said. "It's merely so powerful in terms of being immersive. I tried to pick something up the other day and it was funny because I swung it like a sword—like I would have in the game. I knew the motion, but my muscles aren't as strong here as they were there so it feels strange to be back in the real world sometimes."

The interview continued with his most amusing moment in-game —"definitely my mother screaming hysterically and using a ridiculously large spell to kill a spider"—and his most difficult one. He told them about leveling up skills like Clumsy but he steered clear of mentioning Prima.

He wasn't quite sure why, though.

At length, he and Tina waved goodbye and headed out. In the hallway, Jacob gave them a quick thumbs-up.

"You did great," he said. "Because the treatment is in testing, they'll run the articles by us before publishing, but I think it's safe to say they loved you. Go get some rest and we can get you in here for more game time if you want before you go."

"Awesome." He followed him to the elevator and leaned against the wall.

"Another room service night?" Tina asked.

"Would you mind? I know it's stupid to be here of all places and not try the food."

"So we'll come back sometime," she said. "What use is a schmancy meal if you're miserable?"

"That's a very good point," Jacob interjected. "Not to...eavesdrop." As the elevator doors slid open, he plastered a smile on, waved, then turned and said to Justin, "Pray for me."

"Why, who's here?" He looked out to where a woman in her fifties or sixties was waiting. She was dressed simply in colored jeans and a sweater.

"It's one of Dotty's daughters," Jacob said in an undertone. "She wasn't a huge fan of her mother going into the game."

"Do you want me to talk to her?" he asked.

"Would you? That would be amazing." He led them through security. "Ellen, hi. This is Justin Williams."

"I've seen some of your interviews." The woman looked intrigued. "I would love to talk more sometime. Right now, I have to go see my mom. I promised I would spend some time in the game with her."

"You can also see her playing," Jacob said.

"And I'd be happy to talk to you," Justin said. "I'm sure Jacob can pass my information on."

"Well, thank you. It means a lot." Ellen looked like she was forcing things but finally said, "The team is doing great work and my mother is…very happy here. I'm grateful."

She went to security and pulled her ID out, and Jacob muttered, "Well, I'll be damned. Maybe she's not planning to shiv me."

"Good luck," Justin said. "We'll go get some ridiculously overpriced burgers."

"It's the only way to get them in New York," the other man said with a shrug.

CHAPTER FORTY-THREE

"What in the twelve hells do you think you're doing?" Rashat demanded.

Dahti looked at him with real interest. "You have *twelve*?"

He drew breath to launch into a tirade but at this response, he paused uncertainly and stared at her. It proved to be only a momentary lapse, but she enjoyed it nonetheless.

"Do you think *you'll* be the one to kill the water god?" His nostrils flared.

She resisted a smile. "What are they all for?"

"What?"

"You have twelve hells. What are all of them for? We have seven, one for each of the seven deadly sins. Do you have twelve deadly sins? Oooh, what did you add? Let me guess." She was having fun with this. "Um…talking at the movies. Obviously. Inviting someone over for dinner and only serving salad."

"Earth orc—"

"Spoiling the endings of books," she said. "Okay, we're up to…ten. Two more."

"*Get out of this stream!*" Rashat bellowed.

The village went very silent. Several people had stopped in midstride and hunched their shoulders as if hoping to not be seen. When he looked at them, several gasped audibly before everyone scattered.

Dahti sighed and stood. Her pants were sopping wet and cold but she wouldn't let that ruin this for her. She folded her arms and stared calmly at him. She wanted him to admit a truth to her that he'd never admitted to anyone, let alone himself. If she wanted him to do *that*, she needed to get him hopping mad first.

"You have all of *them* trained good," she said. Her tone wasn't particularly respectful.

Rashat gaped for a minute before his brows snapped together in a fearsome scowl. She knew how this would go. He would build up slowly.

She didn't give him the chance, though, and looked around the village. "I suppose it's a real good setup you have here," she continued and gave him a mocking grin. "A whole village who thinks about *nothing* except how to keep you from getting mad. They even tell all their kids about it, don't they? 'Don't bother Rashat.' 'Don't make Rashat mad.'" She injected a sing-song quality into her tone.

He took a single step toward her. His face was dangerous now. "You should think very carefully before—"

"Oh, *please.* I've lived eighty-four years on this earth. Do you think I've never seen this playbook before? You take one step, you narrow your eyes a little, you keep your voice steady but you make it danger-ously quiet, and you point—yep, that finger right there. You say some-thing threatening but you don't spell it out and you let your target fill in all the blanks." She rolled her eyes. "You're so lazy. You can't even threaten people on your own."

"I'm *lazy*?" He was almost too blindsided to be angry.

"Lazy is your middle name, boy," Dahti retorted. "You've coasted for your whole damned life. You didn't have to do all the chores when you were little because you were the *special one*. You were going to be a *shaman*, so while everyone else hauled water and cleaned clothes, you could merely sit in a little hut and think about the universe."

"That is *not* what shaman training is like—"

"Then you encountered a little bad luck and you found someone you couldn't beat, and what did you do? Oh, *right."* Dahti was getting into the swing of this now. "You stopped doing even your work as a shaman anymore. You made them run around, waiting on you hand and foot, trying to coax a single bite of food into you at a time—while they were trying to *rebuild their damned lives and bury their dead.* You didn't care about *that,* oh, no. *You* needed everyone to focus on you. 'Poor Rashat, he couldn't stand up to the God.'"

Rashat's chest heaved now and a vein throbbed at his temple. She had no doubt that this was working.

"And now I hear you're a model citizen!" she told him brightly. "You help with the fishing. You even carry water now." She clapped her hands. "I've never heard of anyone so devoted to their tribe. Do you want a medal? Or a statue, maybe? Or maybe we should write hymns about you! After all, how *do* we deal with such a *paragon* walking amongst us?"

"Shut up!" Rashat bellowed. "Shut up! Shut! Up!"

"Or what?" Dahti asked him mockingly. "You'll *glower* at me again?"

"I'll throw you out of this village with my own two hands!" He snarled at her in rage.

"Well, that would make an interesting change—you doing your own work for a change."

He snatched a stave up from the ground. Ready to keep fish traps in place, it was sharpened at one end. He jabbed it at her and she could see the amount of raw power still left in his body.

She could also tell he had never been trained with weapons.

"I will send you back to your tribe in pieces," he said from between gritted teeth, "before I let you endanger these people."

"Oh, is that *your* job?" She ducked an unsteady thrust of the spear with ease. "You'll have to do better than that."

"Get out!" Rashat yelled at her. "Leave this place and never return, and so help me, if you've called the god back to this village, I'll—"

"What, fail again? Make everyone soothe *you* again instead of mourning their own families?" she shouted in response. "Tell another generation of kids how you failed and how they should feel so sorry for you while they live without a shaman, without the sea, and without safety? What use *are* you?"

"I am nothing but a warning!" His face contorted and he lunged at her like a madman, raining blows and jabs. Although he'd never been trained, he was still strong and he was angry. "I am a joke from the gods. I was made to be a laughingstock!"

"You were given power beyond measure!" Dahti snatched a stave as well and struck his aside. Pain burst through her hands and forearms at the jolt of impact, but she turned her thoughts away. She needed every scrap of focus for the dual purposes of goading him and staying alive.

Man, he was pissed off.

"Of all the self-indulgent *crap!*" she shouted disdainfully. His stave thrust toward her and she only barely made it out of the way in time. She resisted the urge to punch him in the nose while his arms were overextended and instead, danced away. "You know the truth."

"Oh? What *truth* is that? Since you apparently know everything." He bared his teeth at her and growled.

"What came here was never a god," she told him contemptuously. "You wanted it to be a god so you could be chosen by one. You wanted it to be a god so you could defeat one, but you knew the whole time that you getting this power was nothing more than random *chance*. And you knew that 'god' was nothing more than an overgrown dragonfly who wanted its prey to line up neatly and traipse into its mouth!"

Rashat's next blow—thankfully a swing of the stave instead of a thrust—caught her on the side of the ribs and she hissed in pain. He hadn't managed to crack any bones, thank goodness, but it had been far from comfortable.

"You *knew*," Dahti yelled at him, "that you would *never* kill it! Water magic against a water dragon? You needed fire, you needed air, or you needed earth. You must have realized it when you fought."

At a distant roll of thunder, she looked up to see storm clouds gathering. They didn't scud across the sky but instead, swirled above the village.

They said he could make storms, Atra had said.

He did magic as naturally as he breathed, her grandmother remembered.

Good. She adjusted her grasp around the stave and settled into a fighting stance, her gaze locked on Rashat's.

"Say it," she told him.

"Say *what?*"

"Say. It. The truth." She felt the first patter of rain on her skin. "Say what you think of these people."

"I *hate* them!" He screamed at her and the rain burst with the loudest crack of thunder she'd ever heard. "I wish every one of them had died and I wish I had too!"

<hr>

Ellen followed Jacob through the hallways of the Diatek building. Everything still seemed vaguely familiar after the party the other day.

"So…" She tried to come up with something to say. "Um. What's it like to go into the game for the first time?"

The look he gave her seemed a little wary, but he answered readily enough. "It's kind of jarring for the very first time. Disconcerting is probably a better word for it, I guess. Your brain has only ever received sensory data from your body, so it knows how to interpret what we send—it's all merely electrical signals, after all—but it's confusing to have it come from somewhere else."

"Ah," she said, not quite sure she understood that.

"And some people have trouble moving in the game at first," he added. "It's a thing where they have to send muscle impulses the same way they normally do, but…well, have you ever sat at your keyboard and forgotten how to make your fingers type your password?"

Ellen snorted surprised laughter. "Yes, I have."

"Like that," Jacob said with a smile. "And then you start thinking about it, but the more you think—"

"The worse it gets!" she finished excitedly. "I thought I was the only one."

"Nope." He shook his head. "Nope, that's everyone." He pushed the door to the lab open. "So, we'll...what's going on?"

Everyone in the lab was clustered around one of the pods and some of the others beckoned to them urgently.

"You have to see this," one of them said.

"She is tearing him a *new* one," said another.

"Who?"

"The shaman in the village. Damn, I would *not* want this woman to get angry at me." They returned to what they were watching.

"Um," Jacob said. "So...I could get you prepped—"

"Are you kidding? They're talking about my mother, right?" Ellen gestured at the screen. "I *have* to see this. Her lectures were *legendary* when we were little."

Everyone whipped around at once to stare at her and eyes went wide. Then, as a unit, they parted to let her through. It occurred to her that they were somewhat scared of her mother—and by extension, of her. Curiously, she moved closer to watch.

And when she heard what was going on, she couldn't help but burst out laughing. This was her mother, all right. She was giving this man the dressing down of his life.

Ellen had to say, though, she was glad her mother hadn't gone full tilt with *them*.

"Is that a *spear*?"

"Um..." Jacob said.

"Okay, move over. I *gotta* see this."

The rain fell in sheets, but Rashat didn't seem to care in the least. He charged at Dahti with the scream of a man who had nothing left to live for.

He didn't, after all. She had her suspicions as to the only reason he was still alive.

Well, she would see. Hopefully, she was right.

She threw herself into the fight with a will and reflected that this would be so much easier if the staves glowed. They were too difficult to see in the darkness and the rain—except, of course, when lightning cracked across the sky.

"You didn't let them live without a shaman because of any noble purpose," she shouted, "you did it because you hated them!"

"I wanted to save them!" Rashat screamed at her. "I gave everything to that fight. I had nothing else but my talent. I *was* nothing else!"

Dahti said nothing. She ducked under a wild swing and scrabbled away awkwardly on the wet, rocky ground.

"All of them told me I was born to bring glory to the tribe." His voice was raw now. "I was nothing to them but my magic. None of them ever cared for me. I wanted to kill the gods so I could break the cycle and leave. So a child could be born with magic and be nothing more than a child to them. I wanted to tear the whole thing to the ground!"

Her stave struck home and thwacked against his knuckles, and he dropped his with a cry of pain. Now, she went on the offensive and drove him back ruthlessly.

"You still cared," she called to him. "You say that, but you wanted them to be safe. You regretted letting them down."

"Of course I did!" The cry was despairing. "You didn't see the bodies. You didn't see the blood of your family running down that beast's jaws. It took everything from us!"

"So. Help. Me. Kill. It." Dahti punctuated each word with a shout and a strike. She threw one foot up and kicked him full in the chest into an ungainly sprawl. "For the love of all gods, Rashat. It's been long enough."

The rain stopped. As quickly as they'd come, the clouds began to fade. He stared at her from where he lay, broken and despairing.

"You carried a burden no one should carry," Dahti told him grimly. "I'll not deny it. If you asked them outright, none of them would deny it either. But right *now*, you have two generations of your tribe that never did a godsdamned thing to you and you've punished them for their ancestors' mistakes like a selfish fool." She walked closer to plant the stave on his chest and watched him flinch. "You were put on a pedestal and never allowed to be anything but a shaman until your powers weren't the thing that could save them. And then they *still* looked to you and you hated them for it, but can you blame them, Rashat? They saw their god in the flesh. They needed hope. They needed *something.*"

His head dropped back onto the ground and his eyes squeezed shut.

"You've had forty years to wallow in this," she said, her voice hard. "No more. I don't care how selfish your reasons were for wanting the gods dead—they're false gods, and it was a good goal. So right now, *you'll* teach me water magic and *I'll* help you kill your god, and *together,* we will go back and begin killing every single dragon we can get our hands on until your people are free and they can start over. Do you understand me?"

He opened his eyes and stared at her.

"And then maybe the screams you hear will stop," she said softly. "Maybe then, you can give the lost their burial rites because you can tell them that they were avenged."

Rashat lay motionless and stared at the sky. The clouds continued to dissipate without his rage to sustain them.

She had done all she could so she waited, leaning on her stave.

Finally, he pushed up. She held a hand out but he did not take it. He stood and looked at her.

"Forty years," he said simply. He looked out at the sea and she saw the longing in him.

"You won't have to fear what you are any longer," she told him.

He looked sharply at her. "Do you think that's what I care about?"

"Yes." She smiled. "I think it's part of it. As it should be. Your powers should help your tribe, Rashat, but they're *yours.* Use them for yourself, too."

"I'm too old for that," he said and his voice was equal parts amused and sad.

"It's never too late." Dahti picked his stave up and handed it to him.

"I'd use that as a walking stick, if I were you—unless, of course, you want to learn how to use it."

"I might," he said contemplatively. She sensed it was almost his kind of joke. "I'll have enough free time after the god is dead, after all." Now, he gave her a sharp-toothed, bloodthirsty grin. "We'll start training tomorrow at dawn. Be in the center of the town square and don't be late or I'll wake you how my mentor used to wake me. With a bucket of ice-cold ocean water."

She snickered and watched as he strode away, his chin up and his gaze sweeping the world. He moved beyond hearing and she heard the others begin to creep out of their huts.

"You did it," Atra said from behind her. She stood with the others and all of them were wide-eyed. "What did you say to him?"

Better they didn't know for now. She smiled. "I told him forty years was long enough to wait for payback," she said. She looked at them. "And that god will get payback. He's about to find out that it's a bitch."

CHAPTER FORTY-FOUR

"Dahti," Prima said. "*You have a guest in the game. I'll make people think you and Rashat are both taking the day for meditation before you begin your training. If you go to the seashore and follow the signs, you'll find your guest.*"

Dahti nodded and set off. She had to admit she was curious.

Quickly, she pushed through the forest. She had decided not to follow the stream because she wanted a better idea of the environment she was working in. The dwarven book about earth magic crept into her thoughts—how it could be the raw heat of magma or the delicacy of dust motes hanging in the air, and how it encompassed both weathered mountains and growing plants.

This forest was a place of water, of course, being near the shore, but it was also a place of earth and she could almost hear it singing.

"Prima?"

"*Yes?*"

"Please don't let me get bitten by anything poisonous."

The AI snickered. "*I wondered when you'd remember that tropical forests can be dangerous.*"

"Mm-hmm." She spent a brief moment wishing she could thwack Prima with a stick the same way she had done to Rashat. It was a vain hope and she knew it but it was also a very satisfying mental image.

The seashore wound around an outcropping of gray rock, and she followed a carefully-laid line of seashells that disappeared in her wake, swept away conveniently by the waves. It was beautiful there, with the warm water lapping at her feet. She would spend every moment wishing she were there if she lived nearby.

No doubt, the water tribe *did* wish it.

Dahti stopped when she came around the point. *"Ellen?"*

"What do you think?" Her daughter turned with a smile, then gave a little shriek of fright. "Good God, it's one thing to see it on a screen, but...you're *huge.*" Her nose wrinkled. "And you smell," she added. "You smell so bad, Mom."

"I'm aware, thank you." She studied her daughter curiously. "So you decided to be a mage?"

"What? Oh, the robes?" Ellen looked at them. "No, I don't have any powers at all. They asked if I wanted anything 'cool' like leather armor." She rolled her eyes. "I said they'd clearly never seen a sixty-something woman in leather pants."

She responded with a shout of laughter. "And what did they say to that?"

"They fell over themselves trying to tell me it would be fine and I still looked so good for my age." Ellen laughed at the memory. "Ah, young people." She turned and looked at the sky. "It's a *paradise* here."

"Isn't it?" Dahti wandered to a bench that had appeared out of nowhere. "Thank you, Prima."

"You're welcome. Refreshments?"

"Please."

A table burst into being as well, loaded with dishes both familiar and strange, from shredded chicken and roast potatoes, to yellow rice studded with fruit and nuts, and loaves of bread. Two chilled glasses of lemonade sweated at one end. She took one to Ellen and sipped hers in appreciation. It was exactly the right combination of sweet and tart.

"Mmm," her daughter said. She settled onto the bench.

She saw the smile falter. "What is it?"

"It's, um…the smell."

"Right. Prima, I don't suppose you could do something about that for a few minutes?"

"*Of course,*" the AI said a touch too sweetly. "*I'm only running the entire world. I barely have a thing on my plate right now. It's embarrassing, honestly.*"

"Yeah, yeah." The smell vanished. "Thank you."

Prima muttered something indistinguishable.

Ellen took a sip of her lemonade and stole a glance at her mother. "I saw you, you know—beating sense into that old man. Speaking of which, why *were* you beating an old man with a staff?"

Dahti laughed and explained. By the end of it, a peculiar look had settled on the woman's face. "What? What's wrong?"

"You're so…" Ellen shook her head. "You were so into it that while you were speaking, I forgot it wasn't real, you know?"

The words were somewhat jarring and she froze for a moment. It was funny how she could sit there, summoning benches and food out of thin air, and yet still feel as if the world around her was completely real. She shook her head. "It starts to feel very real."

"More real than I thought." The other woman held one hand out. "I can *feel* the wind."

"I know." She pointed to the water. "Go wade."

Ellen took her lemonade with her and held her robes out of the way—apparently also forgetting that this wasn't real. She shrieked with delight when the water first swirled around her feet and for a moment, her mother could almost see her as she had been as a child, always climbing and exploring. Of all of her children, she had always been the one who was most easily delighted by the world.

It made her life now all the more sad. After the divorce six years before, she had been talked into dates once or twice but she had never allowed herself to get close to anyone. With her children off on their own now, the family had hoped things would change, but they hadn't.

She caught Dahti watching and raised a brow curiously. "Your face looks weird. Or is that merely how…troll faces…look?"

"I am an *orc*," she said with great dignity. "And I was thinking of you as you were when you were a child."

"Oh." Ellen looked self-conscious for a moment. "Sometimes, I think I must have been a nightmare. I remember asking questions about *everything*."

"You did," she said with a chuckle. "But it wasn't a nightmare. It was lovely."

"Are you sure?" The woman looked doubtful. "Because Howie always said—"

"Howie was an asshole," she said bluntly.

Her daughter deflated and came to sit next to her on the bench. "I know," she said. "I can't believe I wasted so many years with him."

"He wasn't an asshole at the start." She patted Ellen's knee. "There were some good years, I think. You two were happy for a while. Then, he simply went off the rails."

"Didn't he?" She rolled her eyes. "He went off to stay in a Buddhist monastery a while back. The kids told me. I wonder if he finally 'found himself' there."

Dahti smiled into her lemonade. "I'd make fun of him, but I'm living in a virtual world so I don't think *I* have much of a leg to stand on."

"Yeah, but you're doing it to help people in comas," Ellen pointed out. "Howie was merely a self-obsessed...douche." *Who cheated on me,* was the end of the sentence she didn't say. She sighed. "I miss being married, though."

"What do the kids think about it?"

"They keep telling me to date. It seems like an awful lot of trouble, though."

"If you miss being married, you'll have to choose at some point between that and the trouble," she told her smartly.

"I know, I know." The woman leaned back. "Hey. I think this is one of the best conversations we've had in years." She straightened and looked around. "Simply a glass of lemonade at the seashore."

Dahti smiled. "You know, I think it is. Let's explore."

"It sounds good to me." Ellen pushed to her feet. "What do you think is around here?"

"Old ruins, maybe? Statues?"

"Really big spiders."

She looked at the sky. "No spiders."

"Fine, but what a baby."

Dahti stifled a laugh and she and Ellen strode into the forest nearby. There was a path—not incredibly obvious, but a place slightly easier to walk than everywhere else. She was fairly sure it hadn't been there before and she felt a certain warmth in her chest at the thought of Prima helping them have a good time together.

Guilt wormed coldly within her and Dahti shied away from the truth. She hadn't liked to hang out with Ellen since the divorce. As the months passed and the woman remained bitter, she had withdrawn. They all had.

She didn't intend to say anything until she thought of Rashat, the silent village, and the children raised knowing about a terrible past and told never to speak of it.

Could she face a dragon and still not have the courage to apologize to her daughter? She shook her head at the thought. What a coward she was.

"Ellen." She stopped and turned and her companion ran smack into her. "Sorry."

"By doze," Ellen said thickly. She wrinkled her face. "Wow, they make this world realistic, don't they? I wouldn't have thought that necklace could stab me." There was a faint trickle of blood on the tip of her nose now. "Um...I won't wake up like this, will I?"

"No! No, no...I'll check." Dahti moved reflexively to pat her pockets for a handkerchief but of course, she had neither handkerchief nor pockets. "I'm sorry."

"It's okay." The woman wiped her nose. "At least no one will see me like this and even if they do, you look weirder."

"We're in orc territory, missy. *You're* the one who looks unusual." Dahti looped her arm through Ellen's—more difficult than usual, given their new height differential—and strolled beside her. She cleared her throat awkwardly. "Um…so, before I managed to stab you in the nose, I wanted to apologize."

"You know, instead of apologizing first, you could have simply not stabbed me."

"I wanted to apologize for something else." Dahti nudged her with an elbow. "I…don't think I was the best mother after you and Howie divorced."

Ellen went silent. When she looked at her daughter, she stared determinedly into the forest but there was a certain set to her chin that let her know she'd been right.

Dammit.

"I thought…well, by that time, your father had passed away, of course," she said awkwardly. "And I thought—well, it isn't important."

"No. I want to hear." Ellen still didn't look back. She tripped slightly over a root and her eyes narrowed in displeasure. Irritated, she shook her head at the indignity and continued with her chin up, not looking at her. "Tell me," she said.

"I…well…I'd lost a spouse, too," Dahti said. "And I think in my mind, I thought I had made my peace with your father's death and you should make your peace as easily with the divorce. But I see now that they weren't the same, not at all."

Ellen started to retort, then bit her tongue. "I shouldn't compare it to Dad *dying*."

"He'd lived a full life, Ellen. He had children he adored, a career—"

"A wife he loved—" she interjected softly and squeezed her mother's arm.

She smiled. "All those things. We knew he didn't have all that long and were able to say goodbye in a different way. There was no…lying. Betrayal. I didn't have to wonder if I could have done anything differently."

Ellen looked like she was going to cry.

"And it doesn't matter what was harder," she said. "What matters is that you were in pain and I wasn't there for you."

Finally, her daughter looked at her. There was something magical about this forest, she thought. Maybe it was the fact that they both knew it wasn't real—the sunlight, the birds, and the rustle of the leaves. Being in a magical dream-world let them speak more honestly than they might have otherwise.

"I wallowed," Ellen said frankly.

"You're allowed," she told her. "Forty years is a bit much, but some wallowing is fine."

"Forty—what?"

"Oh." She waved a hand. "I thought of the orc in the village. Ellen, I never wanted another marriage. Maybe you won't, either. Or maybe you will. Either way, all I want is to see you *happy* before—"

The speed with which her throat closed around those words was shocking. Dahti was there in a make-believe place and she could not feel the pain in her stomach or taste the metal on her tongue. Still, even trying to say the words "before I die" was enough to make her stomach twist.

She'd heard that some people were at peace when they died. Harry certainly seemed to be. She wasn't there yet.

Ellen was crying now and she moved to draw her close to hug her. The woman's shoulders shook, and it took her a moment to realize she wasn't only crying but she was also laughing.

"Ellen?"

"It's…" Ellen gave a hiccupping sob and wiped her eyes. "You're saying all these nice things and you're *dying*, Mom, and I don't know what to do without you. But you went to hug me and you look like Shrek."

Now, Dahti began to laugh and once she started, she couldn't stop. The two women leaned over, clutched their sides, and howled with laughter.

"It's…it's only—" Ellen tried to say, but she dissolved into peals of laughter in the next minute. "Oh, God, it was such a shock. That *face*."

"I told them." She gasped. "I said…I wanted to go *whole-hog*." She gestured at the tusks and both of them lost it again.

When they recovered a couple of minutes later, soft hammocks had appeared in a nearby clearing and the faint sounds of music filled the air. They scrambled in and lay watching the sun shining through the leaves and listening to the waves.

"I'm glad you get to be here," Ellen said. "It's peaceful."

Dahti snorted. "Not always."

"And whose fault is *that*?" Her daughter raised her head. "I saw that fight with the other orc. You were giving him what-for, and it sounded like he wasn't the one who started it."

She decided not to answer.

"It's kind of fun," she mused, "to see my mother acting like a teenager, running into danger and picking fights and all that. Much more fun than watching my *kids* do it, that's for sure." She stretched to catch her fingers. "Thank you, you know. For apologizing. I never thought…you'd think that way."

"Things change," she said. "Maybe this whole experience gave me more courage." She squeezed Ellen's fingers. "I mean it, you know, pumpkin. Be happy."

"I will," Ellen said. "I will. And I'll *definitely* come watch when you defeat the dragon."

CHAPTER FORTY-FIVE

Dahti woke the next morning to a bucket of seawater that was colder than it had any right to be. She sat up, spluttered, and swung at Rashat, who stood several feet away.

Of course, he didn't need to hold a bucket to pour seawater on someone.

She glared at him. "*One* of those twelve hells is filled with people like *you.*"

"Up." He didn't seem to particularly care that she hated him. "And don't bother to change. You'll merely get soaked again."

"What a fantastic day," she managed to say. She retrieved her staff and followed him into the predawn stillness. He had already begun to stride quickly toward the ocean. "It's still *dark.*"

Now, he favored her with a smile over one shoulder. "You're the one who said forty years was long enough."

"Okay, maybe forty years and a few extra hours."

"Will you complain the whole time we do this?"

Dahti shut up, but she sensed that Rashat didn't exactly dislike the banter. He seemed oddly smaller today, for some reason. Not that he wasn't still absurdly tall and broad-shouldered—especially for a man in his seventies or eighties—but he didn't seem to carry as much with him.

The speed of the change was a little unsettling.

"Are you sure…" she said tentatively.

"Yes?"

"That everything is okay? Yesterday was a day of rather large revelations."

"Maybe for you," he said. "There was only one for me."

"Oh?" They had arrived at the shore and she looked briefly at him. The view of the ocean was astoundingly black, completely unrelieved by moonlight or cities along the coast. In fact, she couldn't tell where the coast *was*.

"I hated them for placing the burden of saving them on my shoulders alone," Rashat told her simply and linked his hands behind his back. He wore new robes, she saw now, not the tattered old shirt and pants he'd worn the day before. "And I hated myself for failing. It galled me to know that every little child in the village learned of that failure. I told myself I deserved it, that a lifetime of pain might even the ledger before the gods called me home. But I still wondered why any true god would do what this one did, and I wondered why it was fair to say I was the only one who failed that day."

She nodded.

"And so it was a revelation," he said quietly, "to find out that another person thought the same. It was as if a weight had been lifted from me. The thoughts were not simply mine."

"No," she said. "They are not only yours. Many shamans have thought as you do. I think your kind have long been deceived by the dragons, and you will triumph against them together."

"Perhaps we will." He had withdrawn within himself again, but the mask he wore now was only of the teacher, not one to hide pain. "It depends whether you can master these techniques, doesn't it? Come this way. Now sit."

"In the water?" Dahti asked.

"Yes. That's the point." He waited and the water swirled around his robes until she finally handed him her staff and sat cross-legged on the sand.

It was only a moment before the next wave rushed in. It broke over her lap, rocked her back, and dragged away. And somehow also left sand in her pants. She looked at her lap in time to catch another wave. This one splashed into her face and she spluttered.

Rashat said nothing. He stared studiously at the ocean but amusement seemed to roll off him in waves.

"Okay," she said and prayed inwardly for civility. "Now what?"

"Just sit," he said.

And so she sat. Wave after wave rolled in and rocked her back and then forward. The level of the water rose until it was above her waist and the waves broke at her shoulders and her chin. She felt a stirring of misquiet. The undertow was more pronounced now and sometimes, she had to flail in an undignified manner to hold her position. At other times, the waves followed one after the other and she managed to get seawater up her nose.

She was *not* a fan of that. It stung, for one thing.

The water wasn't very cold but it was still colder than she was, and it wasn't more than an hour or so before her teeth were chattering.

"So…" She shivered violently. "What am I doing, exactly?"

"Experiencing," Rashat said at length. He looked at the sea like an old friend. "We will also do this in the stream and in the mountain pools."

Another wave caught her across the face. "I don't know if you're aware, but I've been gone for a week and every *day*, the fire dragon may be planning to kill the village."

"If you would like to return sooner and die, you may do so." He looked at her. "I will find another apprentice to teach and when we are finished with our god—"

"You won't defeat your god with water magic."

"Very well, then. Do you have any other ideas or do all of them involve your needless death?"

"I wouldn't call saving a village a 'needless death.'"

"It will be if you do *not* save them and die in the attempt instead."

Rashat fixed her with a stern look. "Tell me of the injuries the god suffered."

"A dagger covered in frost was plunged between two of its spinal ridges, it was hurt on one side with earth magic, and one shoulder and another wing were damaged and torn."

"Then we have time," he said. "A god heals no faster than you or I."

"Some gods *they* are," Dahti muttered.

"Snideness and jokes will not help you here," he said sharply. "What *will* help you is learning water magic. I cannot defeat a fire god on my own—or, at least, I do not like my chances."

She sighed. "Well, what am I learning about water now?"

"What are you *not* learning?" he asked philosophically. He held a hand up as the next wave crashed in and it met an invisible wall in front of her. The waters parted to slide around her. She felt the drag of it and the slight settling into the sand. "Earth…well, I have not thought as much on the earth. But water *lives*. That is the difference."

"The earth lives," she retorted. "Rock moves below the surface, cradles new life, and shifts in earthquakes. You cannot tell me you are so naïve as to believe water is the only living element."

He stared at her. "I…that is what our teachers always told us." He held a hand up. "Yes, I am aware there may have been lies among those teachings. Let me…think on it." He paused, although only for a moment. "But water *does* live. To summon the power of it, you must know in your bones how it feels when it crashes, when it flows, and when it falls from the sky. I was raised in this water and I still had to sit here for weeks before my teacher believed I had learned enough."

Dahti looked down and nodded. She knew better than to argue on this point.

It was cold, though—blastedly cold. She thought back to her journey from Berghold to Insea. During the first few days, they had been in the mountains and there had been snow all around them, falling into their boots, and cold seeping up through their bedrolls.

This was a different kind of cold. It ached in her bones instead of stinging on her skin.

With a sigh, she thought of Insea, warm and pleasant, but that memory was not enough to warm her. No, for warmth, she wanted to go back to Berghold where it was underground and safe, filled with chatter and mugs of spiced ale served alongside piping hot sausages and potatoes.

Her thoughts traveled farther still, to the liquid-rock magic of the first dwarven mages, to the absolute, impossible, crushing heat of it, only the smallest part of which she had seen in Mountain's Shadow when the fire worm rose from its slumber—

An exclamation caught her attention and she opened her eyes to a cloud of steam. She flapped her hands to try to dissipate it, caught a wave in the face, and tumbled in the resulting undertow until Rashat hauled her out of the water. He pulled his hand free of her skin with a hiss.

"What did you *do*?" he demanded.

"Nothing!" Dahti shook her head. "Nothing, I swear. I was merely remembering...well, things."

"*What* things?"

"Berghold, and the snow, and the ale..." She remembered most orcs hadn't been to Berghold. "We guarded a caravan that went there. I was thinking of things to keep me warm and I remembered seeing a book about *their* earth magic and how it encompassed the heart of the earth, the rock so hot it glows red and white like iron in a forge..."

Her voice trailed away as she realized what she'd said. She looked at her clothes, which were now completely dry, and felt the warmth running through her in a comforting rush.

"Oh," Dahti said.

"Indeed." Rashat stared at her with something between resignation, fury, and grim satisfaction. "And it seems you have an affinity for that kind of magic, wouldn't you say, earth orc? For the place where earth meets...fire?"

"I...guess so." She shrugged.

He looked heavenward as if praying for patience. "Does it occur to you," he said finally, "that a god of water, slumbering in the deeps, might be well-attuned to threats?"

She shook her head and shrugged again. "I...guess. Um...well, you know more than I do, and you say that you've been careful not to do anything near the water because it might draw him out." She looked at him and grimaced. "So he might sense us."

"He might." Rashat now looked as if he was seriously contemplating throttling her. The earring on his tusk, now replaced, glinted in the first light of dawn. "Especially since you *used fire magic* in his domain."

"Oh!" She clapped a hand over her mouth. "Oh. *Oh.*"

He gestured as if to say, *see?*

"He'll have sensed me," she said. She looked hastily at him. "Rashat, I'm so sorry. I never thought I could do anything like that, and—"

He waved a hand dismissively and seemed to have shed his anger as quickly as it had come. "It solves one problem," he said finally.

"And what's that?" she asked.

"I wasn't sure how we would find him when the time came," he said. "Now, I have an idea. That is, of course, if he doesn't appear before we're ready and slaughter us all. Come along. We still have streams and ponds to cover and we now have a god possibly hunting us."

CHAPTER FORTY-SIX

Ellen woke to light stabbing into her eyes. She winced, made a noise of complaint, and realized how much she had to pee. She sat bolt upright.

Amber, who seemed to recognize the facial expression, removed the connectors in record time and waved her to a thankfully close bathroom. When she emerged, she was given a tentative thumbs-up, which she returned.

"Good, good," the engineer said and smiled at her. "Did you have a good time?"

"*Such* a good time." She shook her head. "I had no idea it was so...*real*."

Nick spun in his chair. "You know, it brings up a really good question of what reality *is*—"

"No, no, no," Amber said. "No, no. No. *No.* No Plato's Cave."

He stuck his tongue out and went back to work.

Ellen raised an eyebrow. "Was this going to be some thought experiment?"

"Bingo," Amber said. "Would you like coffee and a snack?"

"*Yes.*" Ellen felt like she could eat a mid-sized horse and still have room left for a nice chocolate cake. "I don't know why I'm so hungry when I've simply been lying there."

"Interpreting a new source of information can be tiring on the body," Amber explained. She hesitated, then added, "Also…stress. I want you to know we didn't eavesdrop and only kept an eye open for signs of distress, but we noticed that your cortisol levels were quite high." Seeing her confused expression, she continued. "Cortisol is a hormone the body produces when someone is stressed. In a natural environment, it would mostly be seen during a predator attack or something, but we made sure that didn't happen during your visit. So it would be…you know…uh, emotional stress." For good measure, she repeated, "We *weren't* eavesdropping. I merely want you to know that if you're tired and hungry, that might be part of it."

Ellen said nothing as they emerged from the hallway into a break room. A large coffee machine had icons for everything from flavor shots to certain amounts of foam, a pile of donuts and muffins rested under a glass dome, and in the corner stood something she hadn't expected to see.

"A popcorn machine?" she asked.

"DuBois," the other woman said with wry fondness. "He's the lead scientist on this project and he *lives* on popcorn. You think I'm making a joke but I'm not. I seriously have no idea how the man doesn't have scurvy. But do feel free to have some if you like. He's always asking us to try it."

"I, uh…maybe another time." Her attention was fixated on the donuts.

"You can have one, you know." Amber gestured at them. "Now, what kind of coffee would you like?"

"Plain black, please."

"Dark roast, light roast?"

"I have no idea. Whatever you think would be best. And I really shouldn't have a donut." Ellen looked at her stomach. "At my age, I can't eat the way you youngsters do and still stay thin."

"You know," the engineer said contemplatively, "your mother mentioned something similar. Well…in a way. When she first got here, we asked if she had any requests. We thought it would be something like riding a dragon, or being Indiana Jones, or something like that. But what she said was—" She took the cup of coffee and put it in front of Ellen at a table. "She wanted to be ugly. She said she'd spent so much of her life going to bed hungry and worrying about her looks, and she merely wanted to…live her life." She punched a set of buttons for a cup of coffee for herself.

Ellen took a sip of the brew, which was delicious, and raised an eyebrow. "What's your point?"

"Well, it's enough to make you wonder, isn't it?" Amber asked. She leaned against the counter and gestured at herself. She wore a man's waffle-knit shirt and jeans over heavy boots. "Part of the reason I dress like this is that it shuts people up about how I look, you know? If I wear a nicer shirt or a dress, they want me to wear makeup, too. If I wear makeup, then it's heels. If I wear heels, they tell me I could stand to lose a few pounds. I have other things I want to focus on."

She still wasn't entirely sure where this was going but leaned back in her chair, though, when Amber took a donut out and put it in front of her.

"What I'm saying," the woman explained bluntly, "is that we'd get a hell of a lot more done in this world if we stopped spending all our energy on how we looked. Your mother is now fighting dragons and defeating traitorous diplomats. And…well, part of that is because there's magic in that world, but you see what I mean."

"Hmm." Ellen looked hungrily at the tempting confectionery. "I'll think about that."

"Do," Amber advised. She settled with her cup of coffee and seemed about to say something more but decided against it.

"Have any of the other people been like that?" Ellen asked. "You know, wanting to be ugly or whatever."

"We don't have enough data yet to say," Amber said. "Your mother is the second official test subject. With Justin, it was imperative that he be in his own body—we didn't want to add the X-factor of him getting attached to a different avatar."

"Huh," she said and shook her head. "Well, whether it's the tusks or the—oh, God, the *smell*—my mother's changed more than a little."

"Has she?" The woman pushed her chair back to lean on the back two feet. She looked intrigued now.

"*Yes,*" she said vehemently. "Even a few months ago, I couldn't imagine her apologizing for...well, anything. She'd always say she did the best she could and she'd do the best she could in the future. It wasn't a lie. She *did* always do the best she could but sometimes, what you need is an apology. And today, I got one from her." She looked at her coffee. "I don't know how to feel about that."

Amber sighed. "Look, I don't know your mother nearly as well as you do, but is it possible that...well, I don't know—that the cancer is part of it?"

"Oh, I think so." She pressed her lips together. It was still difficult to acknowledge that her mother was dying. She gave a little cough to clear her throat. "But I do think part of it is the game. She's...changed. She honestly has." She saw the troubled look on Amber's face. "What's wrong?"

The woman scratched her head. "I'm not sure. I'm...what's the term for it? Borrowing trouble. This is only the second time this has happened and it's not something we bargained on."

Ellen felt a reactive wave of the fear she'd felt the first time she heard about her mother's plan. "What do you mean?" she asked before she could stop herself.

"Comas can change people," Amber said hastily. "*Any* experience changes people. Have you ever read a book that inspired you?"

"Yes, but—"

"This is like that," the engineer told her. "But more, somehow. It's like...people aren't only inspired to be the people they've always wanted to be, they get to try being those people—and when they wake up, the change is made."

"Maybe we should all do that for a while," Ellen said with a little laugh.

When she looked up, though, Amber's face was worried.

"We've seen it in two people," she said. "One who chose to come here to give us data we desperately needed—someone who we already knew was altruistic. And one who was, to be fair, an unknown. But two people aren't nearly enough to decide about this."

Ellen looked at the donut and decided to take a bite before she answered. It was good—it was absurdly good. Diatek didn't skimp on snacks either.

Then again, she was also very hungry.

"I think you *are* borrowing trouble," she said. "And before you tell me that you know more about this than I do, remember that I'm the one who went off the deep end about my mother choosing to be in this world to start with."

Amber took a sip of her coffee. "What made you change your mind?"

"She's…" She searched for the words. "I think she's more *herself* than I've ever seen her. Okay, she's seven feet tall now and has tusks, but even so. That's a weird way to describe someone, but it is…*wait.*" She caught Amber's hand. "I have an idea. I think Mom would like this."

She explained in a hushed whisper, and when she was done, the engineer was smiling.

"You know, I think that would be a good idea. I do think she would like that. Let's go tell the others."

They finished their coffee and donuts quickly—more quickly than the excellent donuts deserved, Ellen thought—and hurried down the hallway to the lab.

Once Jacob, Nick, and DuBois had been briefed and also approved, Ellen left with a cheery wave and a promise to be back. She had a mission that would involve all her siblings and extensive digging through attics and storage units.

Out in the sunlight, she considered the conversation she'd had with Amber. In truth, she was not quite sure how to explain her changed opinion of the game. She had been furious at the thought of losing the last few months she had with her mother.

What she had received, instead, was the chance to see her mother as a young woman—or as a person beyond age or looks. She had the chance to watch her mother fight an old orc with a stave, which she would never in a million years have thought was something she would see. And she'd had one of the best conversations she could remember.

The apology still reverberated in her chest.

The divorce had been beyond difficult, and there had been thousands of times since then that she doubted herself—for the myriad of choices she had made before her husband left her, for her ability to raise children if she could not even make a marriage work, for her looks, and for her lack of a career. But the truth was, she had always tried not to question those thoughts. She was afraid to bring them into the light and study them.

Her greatest fear was the path she might go down if she spent time looking at them.

Now, she thought she might have done herself and her family a disservice. If she'd been courageous enough to sort through those thoughts earlier, maybe she would be in the same place her mother was in now.

Or maybe, she thought, with a small smile, there was no use wondering about the past. The game had changed her mother, and the change was rippling outward.

Either way, she would stop on the way home and buy herself another donut.

CHAPTER FORTY-SEVEN

Huwat sat back on his feet and wiped his forehead. The caves that made up the shamans' retreat were an excellent place to forage for mushrooms and root vegetables, but both were getting harder to find these days.

Not only that, it grew hotter and hotter.

There was no denying it. Since the god had first emerged from the mountain and then withdrawn to lick its wounds, each day in this place had been progressively warmer. It now seemed to be the height of summer instead of early spring.

There was no question about where the heat came from either. At dawn and dusk, they could see the god pacing the top of the mountain. It never flew but it seemed to want to let them know it was there.

Or maybe it was looking for them.

The shaman wasn't sure. He still wasn't sure that it had seen where they all hid, but he had kept the village on the move since then. Each day, they sheltered in a new place, preferably one with a hill or an oasis between it and the mountain.

And each day, he came back with one or two others to forage for more food. That was now the entirety of the tribe's existence—searching for food and shelter.

It was miserable.

He had been raised to revere fire, so the concept of fearing heat itself was distasteful to him. Indeed, part of him was grateful to exist in such warm times and witness the pure majesty of the fire god. The other part, however, wanted nothing more than to have gone with Dahti so that he could meet Rashat and see the ocean, that mythical mass of water as wide as the plains.

Huwat could not picture it.

Wearily, he picked his basket up and moved to the next patch of dirt. His back was aching, yet another curse of growing old.

Dahti was a strange one. Of that there was no doubt. He had never met an orc like her and he didn't expect to again. Every day, more out of a sense of duty than anything else, he had prayed for wisdom about her. Was she simply the prophet of a truth none of them wanted to see or was she a trickster, a liar who was testing their faith?

What was odd was that he didn't doubt her. It was exactly like a trick from the old stories for a stranger to show up and whisper your darkest fears, but he didn't doubt her at all.

The truth was, he had selfishly been grateful that he lived in a time with no gods. He prayed to the mountain at dawn and dusk. He offered the sacrifices every year and led the village in their chants. He instructed the little ones to give thanks to the god for their food and to be ready to sacrifice themselves, but the words stuck in his throat every time and he always hoped he would not live to see a god in the flesh.

Because it was a bad bargain. A god who gave the beasts of the earth, only to demand the blood and suffering of mortals, was simply a powerful being playing a cruel joke. Oh, there were many ways to make it sound important and preordained, but none of them rang true.

If a being could give life and if it had the power to do such things, what right did it have to demand their children in return? They had never asked for the bargain.

Huwat learned very early on that the other shamans had asked the same questions—and that none of them wanted to entertain the thought any longer. All of them in living memory had decided to simply bow their heads and give in. It wasn't fair and it wasn't right, but it was the way things were.

And, after all, how long had it been since the god demanded a sacrifice?

He was surprised only by how fervently he'd clung to those beliefs when Dahti had first challenged him. Without realizing it, he had become exactly like his mentor, an old orc of few words and curt instructions. Oh, he was kinder and more liable to discuss the matters of faith with the village, but he also leaned heavily on his status as the shaman to keep them from peering too deeply into the mysteries of the gods.

Because he had always known, deep in his heart, that those mysteries were lies.

Now, he had to face the uncomfortable truth that he'd spent his life defending the very being who had preyed on them for all these years. Somehow, he had been lulled into complacency and had become invested in the Way Things Were. When he was younger, he could have excused it by saying he valued the knowledge of the elders.

When he *became* an elder, he simply asked them not to question it when he told them that the way things had always been was the way they should always be.

The shaman shook his head and looked at the meager contents of his basket. He was getting lost in thought and the tribe would be waiting for supplies. Like it or not, he had angered a god and now, he must keep the villagers as safe as he could.

Once, the orcs had roamed freely across their land. They had not been tied to villages or been separated into tribes. Their songs and their traditions had been shared. There were even legends—only spoken once to him and in a hushed whisper—of a great city his people had built.

These false gods had chained them.

The truth angered him and he growled low in his throat. He might be a shaman, not a warrior or a hunter, but he was still an orc. He knew the urge to fight and tear and slash and wanted this false god ended, and he would be happy only when he stood on its corpse.

Huwat knew he could not do it on his own. He was no Rashat, born with unusual powers, and had been like most children—feckless and silly. Perhaps a little more interested in the old legends but not enough to be noteworthy. It was only one night, when he decided to break all the rules of the village and climb the mountain, that he had been chosen as the shaman's apprentice.

His hands stilled at their work. It had been so long since he'd thought of that night.

It was still—not a year for locusts and no winds ruffling the plains grasses. No clouds, either. He had been restless all day, barely able to sit still, so energetic that even a hunt hadn't tired him, and he knew he wouldn't be able to sleep.

What possessed him to climb the mountain, he couldn't say. He knew only that his feet were on the hillside and his hands scrabbled for holds in the rock, and he didn't even look back to see if the watchmen saw him.

There wasn't a path, but that didn't bother him. No one climbed the mountain, after all. It was forbidden.

Far from becoming more tired as the climb went on, he only felt more alive. If he were to go out onto the plains, he was sure he could run forever. He could climb the tallest tree or fight a lion barehanded. The thoughts teased fleetingly at him, but not for long. He was too absorbed with how he felt and with the way he wanted to burst out of his skin.

When he saw the fire, he was so surprised he almost fell off the mountainside.

His first thought was to attack. No one should be there. Then, of course, he remembered that *he* should not be here, either.

And the fire was so beautiful. It was like nothing he'd ever imagined and as if all the fire he had seen was only a dream and this was real.

"Huwat," a voice said and he realized that the shadowy shape by the fire was the shaman.

Who had recognized him.

There was no going back, but more than that, he could not have walked away from that fire if he had a hundred horses trying to drag him. His feet brought him irresistibly to it.

"You heard the call," the shaman said shortly.

"Call?" He could only see the flames.

"You felt the fire's magic stirring in your blood." This was, perhaps, the most words Huwat had ever heard him say at one time. "You came to find it."

He gaped at him. "*That's* why I'm here?"

"Yes. It is time to find an apprentice." The shaman gestured to him. "It is you. You will be shaman after me."

"But—"

Huwat was not sure he wanted this. There was a girl in the village, one whose smile made him feel like he was turning inside out. He'd thought of impressing her with his kills in the hunt.

The shaman let the flames die and as quickly, his strange energy was gone. "We begin training tomorrow," the elder said. "At dawn. Get some sleep." He set off down the mountain without waiting for him to follow.

That had been it. There had been no choice and no discussion. Huwat bowed his head. He had been summoned to this life. Perhaps that was why he told stories of others being summoned to fates *they* did not want.

It was a useless train of thought. He stood and a shout caught his attention.

He dropped the basket of mushrooms and ran as fast as his old legs would take him. There were more shouts now from the others who had come with him. When he emerged from the caves, they looked at him in fear.

They did not need to say why.

The god still could not fly well. That much was apparent. But it did not need to. It now slunk down the side of the mountain and directly toward the camp the villagers had made.

CHAPTER FORTY-EIGHT

"Go!" Huwat called to one of the others. "Make sure the villagers have seen."

They should have, certainly. There were watches posted now but it was too big a risk to not make sure.

The others looked at him and he knew he would say what they most feared. He drew himself tall—he was still the shaman, after all—and commanded them firmly. "You two, come with me. We must stand between our village and the god."

They wavered. Of course, he thought, they would. Mortals did not go easily to their deaths, after all, and these had so recently learned that their beliefs might well be lies. Of course, when he ordered them to go into battle, they would waver.

But they did not have time for that right now.

"I am not telling you to fight the god for glory or faith," he said simply. "I am telling you to do so because our kin are in that camp and they will certainly die if we do not fight for them."

That steeled them to what must be done. They followed him through the grass, cutting a path toward where the god approached, low on its belly like a large cat on the prowl. They did not try to avoid being seen. With any luck, he thought, it would think the villagers were still in the warren of caves.

Any time they could buy was of the essence. He was honest with himself that he did not see himself triumphing in this fight.

Every day they live is a triumph. It must have been his thoughts as the words were inside his head, but he swore he was not the one who had thought it.

Was it the guidance of a god? A true god? Huwat did not know, but he felt courage fill him nonetheless. Although this was a beast of fire and his magic would never truly undo it, he was not powerless.

"Flank it," he said to the two villagers with him. "As much as you can, stay out of sight. Watch the tail—it can swing quite powerfully. Trade off if you can—one of you go in to land a strike while the other hangs back."

"What can we do against it?" one of them asked him bleakly. He held his spear up. It was stone-tipped and finely made, but he was right that it looked ridiculous next to the beast.

"Listen to me," he said. He wanted to stop and face them but they could not take the time. "We know it as a god, but it is no more than a beast like any other. You've fought your share of enemies and you will defeat this one in the same way. Its flesh can be reached through the scales. It has tendons, muscles, and skin."

"Eyes," one of them said.

Huwat hesitated. "Yes, but…leave its face to me."

They accepted a little too eagerly, and he hid his sigh. When it came down to it, they would fight for their families but he might well be dead by then.

All must die in their own time. He smiled ruefully. His only regret was that he had not trained an apprentice. He'd hoped Dahti would have met that need.

She would not be an apprentice of *his* tradition. When this was over, however, they might not have anything left that he recognized as tradition. Perhaps the young ones would be best served by finding their own way through magic as well as faith.

Oddly, that gave him courage. *The old must die so the new can flour-*

ish. That was one of their teachings. Perhaps it had been meant to guide him in this very moment. Who could say?

The dragon had seen them now. Its black-and-red eyes were fixed on them. Smoke billowed from its nostrils and the ground smoldered under its feet. He knew it was only a matter of luck that the entire plains had not caught fire yet.

What was it the human had called this god? Huwat searched his memory for the unfamiliar term.

Ah, yes.

He smiled grimly as he strode forward. "Hello, worm."

His voice carried on a rising wind and the god crouched with a hiss. A growl began in its throat, low and hypnotic. It began to move with menace in every tiny ripple of its muscles.

"What did you call me?"

"I called you a worm," Huwat said. "For that is what you are, is it not? You are not a god."

"What is a god?" Now, it sounded amused. "A greater being than a mortal."

"You are mortal," he said. He hoped it was true. It was purely a gamble. "You can be wounded and you can die."

Whatever instinct told him to throw himself sideways as soon as he spoke, he was grateful for it—the grasses nearby erupted in flames so hot and bright that they did not even spread. The mere moment of the heat blistered the side of his face.

He scrabbled to his feet and dove sideways once more, this time onto the burned ground. His hope was to outwit the god—*worm,* he reminded himself—but to his surprise, he heard it hiss in annoyance. When he looked up, it turned, awkward and ungainly. The two warriors raced away and tried to stay out of sight. One of them must have pushed in close enough to do damage.

The worm blew fire at one flank and then the other. One cry of pain followed but nothing more.

Huwat's stomach twisted. He had no idea if one—or both—was dead, but if not, he needed to draw the creature's attention back to him.

Still unsure what he would do next, he decided he would think of something along the way. Or he wouldn't. Either way, he'd be dead soon enough. He chuckled and shook his head. It was strange what you found funny when you stared death in the eye.

He thumped his staff on the ground and shouted, "Worm! I am not finished."

The dragon's head whipped around and it snarled at him, narrow-eyed. "What do you want, puny one?"

That was a good question. Huwat had nothing planned.

"What is your plan?" he called. "Do you hope for one last meal before my kind hunts you and kills you?"

It breathed fire at him again, but he was already moving. This time, it was not only one blast and he had to keep running until his old knees ached and his lungs burned. Everything smelled of smoke and he could no longer remember which way they were facing. He looked for the mountain that marked the shamans' retreat, but between his smoke-blurred gaze and the beast and the grasses, he could not see it.

The creature howled in pain again and his heart soared. At least one of the guards must still be alive.

When he caught sight of the man, he uttered an audible gasp. Half of the orc's face was blistered, far more badly than his, and some of the skin on his shoulder was blackened.

They might worship fire and thrive in heat, but they were not immune to its dangers. He knew this man should be in the village with salve on the burns and water being fed between his lips every few minutes. But who could say when he would have either rest or healing?

The man lunged again and again, and Huwat had to run to him as the worm gathered its breath once more. The warrior screamed in pain when he dragged him to the ground and hauled him under the worm's belly.

"Where's the other?" he asked, although he was afraid he knew the answer.

The man's stare was bleak. "He ran."

"He *what*?"

"He said to hold him." He looked at the beast that now thrashed its head and twisted to try to see them. "I thought...he was planning to strike at it. Then I saw him running."

Coward. Fury filled Huwat. He looked into the man's eyes. "We *will* hold him," he promised. "And we will find the coward and end him. His line will be finished."

They both knew it was not likely to happen, that this road ended in death for them, but they nodded to one another. Now they had a goal beyond defeating the worm. It was merely a distraction but it brought a measure of comfort.

He gestured to the man to take one flank and ducked under the worm's belly, took careful aim, and drove the ragged edge of his stave onto the massive wing where he could see the still-healing cut.

Its scream deafened him. His ears ringing, he ran. He remembered he should not run in a straight line, but he was fairly sure he was so dazed that he couldn't have done so if he wanted to.

He didn't get far enough. The dragon spun and its tail struck him on the side. The shaman careened away with a long cut under one arm where one of the spines had ripped through his robes. He landed so hard, he thought he bounced.

His cry of pain made him feel ashamed. He was an orc and while he might not be a warrior, an orc was an orc, dammit. Like hell would he die there.

"Still injured, *god?*" he taunted as he found his feet and forced a laugh out of his tortured lungs. "Driven away by a trainee shaman and a *human?*" He said a silent apology to the human, who had done quite good work, all things considered, but old habits died hard. Every orc knew humans were puny, weak, and gutless.

It hissed at him but he saw it limping. He remembered Dahti saying that the human had injured it near the tail and the impact of hitting him this time must have hurt more than it expected. Perhaps there was a way to tell the other warrior to aim at its tail, he wondered but decided not. The man was barely standing as it was. His only chance of success hinged on the element of surprise.

"You know there's nothing left for you," the shaman called. "You did well, all of you, convincing us that you had brought life to the earth and the beasts to our campfires. But the lie had to unravel someday and here we are. So, what'll it be? Will you walk onto the spears of our army or will you try to run?" He bared his teeth. "Because we *will* find you. You missed your chance, *worm*. The shaman has already gone to gather the water shamans, and they are coming for you."

"*Liar!*" It tried to rear into the air and flapped its wings but screamed in pain. "The water tribe was killed for its disobedience."

"One of your kin *tried* to kill the water tribe," he corrected. He saw something out of the corner of his eye and it was all he could do to not look. "It became greedy. It wanted to take something that wasn't its to take, and it not only failed, it showed the rest of us the truth."

The dragon limped away and Huwat saw the flicker again. He narrowed his eyes to focus.

Yes. The warrior who had run was back with others.

Whatever godsdamned, foolish plan they had, he knew he had to keep the god distracted. He began to circle away from where they crept through the grasses.

"The water tribe yet lives!" Huwat called. "As do the rest of us. Our shamans will join powers as we once did. The call has gone out and there is no stopping it now."

They really *should* have sent messages, shouldn't they? He shook his head at the missed opportunity.

"Your kind…are weak." Its voice was fainter now and weaker.

For the first time, he felt a flicker of hope. He might yet survive this. They all might.

He saw the others waiting for their chance and spread his arms. "How can you say we are weak when you could not kill one old man?"

The worm drew breath to blast him to ashes when the villagers charged. They were silent and uttered no battle cries. Knives or gardening implements and shards of pottery were grasped in every hand. Others carried buckets of water.

As one, they fell on the dragon from behind and began to drive their weapons between its scales. Where they pried the armor away, the others threw water.

The beast's scream now was like nothing he had ever heard. He understood now, in the last moment, how much older a worm could be than an orc. It was as if he could hear the generations of his kind in its last call—the wheel of the seasons, the diversions of earthquakes and wildfires and storms.

The worm was not lying when it said it was stronger than they were.

But they worked together and it had come for them for the last time. It sank into a heap, the light gone from its eyes, and the village erupted with cries of joy. Huwat strode forward to clap the warrior on the shoulder.

"You went to get them."

"You doubted me," the man said with a smile. "I'll not say I didn't think of running and not coming back, but I realized how we might win without a water shaman."

"So you did." He nodded. "Some of you, come with me. We need to bear Gartun to the camp and—"

The cry that came next wasn't so much one they heard with their ears as with their souls. Huwat swore that even the winds stood still for a moment while it pierced the world. It was the embodiment of grief and vengeance.

"What *was* that?" the warrior asked.

"They know," Huwat said quietly. "They know their kin has been killed. They're coming."

All he could hope was that Dahti would be back in time.

CHAPTER FORTY-NINE

The next week passed in a haze.

Perhaps it wasn't a week. It could have been more—or less. Dahti remembered training through the day and sleeping precious little at night. She recalled her clothes being soaked from endless time spent in the water of the ponds, the ocean, and the streams.

Shivering started when she so much as *looked* at a body of water.

While she had never been a fan of dried fish, she grew to hate it with an absolute passion. She also learned that she could hate something and wolf it down at the same time.

And she did all of it in near-silence. The villagers had withdrawn, at Rashat's insistence, into the tunnel between the fire lands and the water tribe's territory. It was the closest thing to safety anyone could think of, but she shuddered to think of them locked in the darkness, prowling endlessly while they listened for the sounds of an angry dragon.

Without them, however, she saw a different side to the shaman. The older orc was not only astute, he was shockingly irreverent—something she could only guess came from decades of living with the ruins of his faith.

Most of the change seemed to be a lightness of being that she could not quite put her finger on. She saw it sometimes in the softness of his face when he looked at the forest or the quiet contemplation with which he fixed the traps.

He always made them start their day with a harvest from the traps. "I'm doing this to save my people," he told her, "not leave them to starve."

She became exceptionally good at filleting fish and hanging them so she could make more of the dried fish she hated so passionately.

In the evenings, he sat in silence and stared into the fire, and it was only partway through their time, when she heard a few notes, that she realized he was recalling the songs he had vowed to take with him to the grave.

Dahti didn't comment on it and over time, he became bolder. The isolated snatches of his low, almost hypnotic hum gave way to full songs and from there, to actual singing. All the songs reminded her of water, whether it was the clear blue of the ocean she had first seen, or the stillness of a forest pond, or the cheerful burble of water over rocks. Once, and only once, he sang a song both powerful and mournful that told the story of a fishing boat lost in a storm and the wreckage washing ashore.

With that one, she hid her face so he would not see her cry. But when she looked up from wiping her eyes, he was watching her and she thought perhaps he approved.

The softness she sometimes saw at the end of the day was matched by the ferocity he showed during training. After the first day, he'd done an abrupt about-face.

Although he still woke her the next morning with ice-cold seawater to the face.

After watching her earth magic, Rashat now encouraged her to hone those skills she had already spent time training in. With the pressure and heat that stone could summon, he seemed to think she might be able to harm the dragon in some measurable way.

She was terrified by the very idea. Although she'd fought elves and dwarves and even a bizarre, black-armored mechanical creature, a dragon was very different. She remembered how big the dragon had been at Mountain's Shadow. It had dwarfed her, and its strength and magic were far beyond her.

Prima, far from being encouraging, was offended. *"Do you think I would set you up for failure?"*

"No," Dahti told her, "but I might have missed an obvious way of getting out of this that you had intended."

"Ah." The AI took a moment to consider this. *"I think you'll be able to do it,"* she said finally. *"People are very resourceful when they have to be."*

Quite honestly, she did not find this particularly encouraging.

She also did not appreciate that she was supposed to strike the most important blows at the water dragon but that her mentor defeated her handily in every sparring match. It seemed she could not so much as finish a spell before her head was encased in water, or she had saltwater in her eyes, or the ground was so slick beneath her feet that she could not stand.

That said, she also could not come up with a better idea than being the one to strike the killing blow.

She should have sent Huwat—a fact she mentioned to Prima sometime after the first week was up. Her mind constantly reminded her that she was good with clouds of dust and hot soil under horses' hooves and little clods of dirt on wolves, but that was nothing compared to a dragon. The shaman, with decades of training in the powers of fire, would have been far better.

When she mentioned this, however, the AI merely snorted. *"If you'd sent Huwat, he and Rashat would still be fruitlessly engaged in an escalating, passive-aggressive series of bows and ceremonial messages and Rashat would not have emerged from his funk."*

"How can you be certain?

"I made this world. I can see the futures of it. And, before you ask—no, I cannot see this future because you are involved and humans always find a way to surprise me."

"There's something to be said for that, I guess," Dahti said.

"Usually, they surprise me in a stupid way."

"Oh, shut up."

"Do you always talk to yourself?" Rashat asked from behind her.

Dahti jumped and turned. "How long have you been standing there?"

"Long enough to hear that you think Huwat would have been a better choice for this." The old orc rolled his shoulders and looked up to where the sun was beginning to drop in the sky. "And perhaps you're right, but you're what we have to work with."

"You should be a motivational speaker," she told him.

"A...what?"

"A...hmm. It's something people do when their culture runs out of big problems."

He stared blankly at her.

"Anyway, since we only have me to work with, should we start on anything in particular?"

"Like you need to ask." Rashat held his hand up and summoned a ball of water that spun lazily. "It's time to spar."

"Oh, not again."

"Yes, again. How do you expect to beat a dragon if you don't practice your magic?"

"I always won before," she muttered. "Battle has a way of... bringing out inventive thoughts." And gruesome ones, of course, but she did not mention that.

"If you don't mind, I'd prefer not to depend on your inventiveness in the moment." The ball of water disappeared into a shower of droplets, and he pointed at the water.

"Oh, not again..." Dahti knew better than to try to change his mind, however. She went to the waterline and sat.

They began each fight with her immersed in a body of water. Rashat claimed that only immersion would give her the understanding she needed to master the element—either as a practitioner or as someone who fought it.

Today, she could have sworn that there was something different in the water, an echo almost like whale song but far less friendly. She listened for it and even slid to duck her head under the surface, and when she came up, he was watching her.

"There's a...sound."

"It's the god." He caught himself on the word. "Beast. It's getting closer."

She froze. Her reflex was to scramble out of the water but she fought it. "You're…simply letting me *sit* here?"

"How small do you think it is? I assure you, it cannot hide in any of these little waves." He was amused now. "You cannot defeat it without understanding it, and you cannot understand it without seeing its home, apprentice. Relax. Concentrate."

Dahti closed her eyes, even though every instinct screamed at her to get out and run without looking back

Water. It billowed away from every motion like air but stronger, pushing her skin into little ripples at times when it passed. It closed her in, pressed around her chest and her stomach, and yet it also lifted her. When she was underwater, she felt as if she were flying at times.

She had just settled, a smile on her face, when Rashat's first strike caught her across the back of the head. The spray of water was so fine and powerful that it felt almost like the cut of a lash. Her eyes snapped open and a wave caught her in the face.

He'd planned that. She knew he had. He'd timed that strike perfectly.

As she turned, she deliberately didn't look at him and simply yanked with all her strength. The ground slid under his feet. Rashat stumbled and his next strike went wide into the sky. She used the moment to scrabble away on the sand and wiped the water out of her eyes.

"That was a dirty trick," she called.

"This god doesn't fight fair," he responded. "So neither will I."

"Bastard," she muttered. She blasted the dirt in front of him into a spray of fine particles, the same trick she'd used to blind archers who once hunted her, but he wiped the dust away efficiently with a smattering of rain.

They circled one another as their feet splashed in the water and slid in the sand.

Her next attack was a clod of dirt around his feet. It took him a second to wash it away with water, during which time she attached more to his beard and wedged another in one of his ears. He was swearing by the time all of them were out, but he flashed her a smile.

"Now *that's* the kind of annoyance I'm looking for."

Dahti smiled, flushed and pleased by the praise, only to get a jet of water up her nose. She shrieked and swore before she heated the sand under his feet and forced him to dance away. The heat followed him in little pockets that made him curse and hop until an out-of-rhythm wave knocked her off her feet and held her upside down by the ankles.

It dropped her in the next moment and she landed in an ungainly heap. She gave a silent prayer of thanks for her young body as she stood and shook out the pain—only to have the same thing happen a second later. As she stood, swearing this time, Rashat launched a stream of water at her like a fire hose.

That was *enough*. She ducked under the stream of water and attacked. Her shoulder caught him on the thigh and he fell with a surprised "oof" sound she wished she could play on repeat.

She didn't know much about fighting hand to hand, but she had Lyle's advice to guide her until she reached what she wanted—Rashat's staff. She waited until he was a little off-balance as he pushed to his feet before she delivered a punch to his solar plexus.

He toppled again and she leapt over him to sprint to the staff. He yelled as well and she heard him running behind her.

His defense was too late. She swung the staff and he barely managed to get out of the way by dropping into the sand. With it in her hands, he couldn't get close, and if she kept up her flurry of attacks, he couldn't focus well enough to launch any truly impressive spells.

Dahti rained blows on him, kicked him back, and advanced on him with her hands raised for a spell.

It never came. She kicked him in the shins instead and he went over sideways and a wave broke over his head.

"I yield," he said when he stood. He was panting.

Suddenly worried, she put the staff down. She had broken the rules. After all, this was to be a magical fight, and they'd always tried not to physically *hurt* one another. To her surprise, Rashat was smiling.

"Good," he said simply. "*This* was what I wanted to teach you. It was the single greatest turning point in my skill as a shaman, and it is what allowed me to even inflict some damage to the god in its last attack."

She frowned. "I…don't understand. I didn't use magic."

"Precisely," he said. He smiled at her and the earring on his tusk caught the light. "The first failing of many would-be magic users is that they cannot use magic at all. You have passed that barrier. The second failing is that they use magic as the only way to solve problems. It is not, any more than machines can solve every problem. Magic is a tool like any other. You must learn to use it together with things such as weapons in order to triumph."

Her mouth fell open in surprise. "Oh," she said, quite confused. "Oh, I hadn't…I hadn't thought… *Oh.*"

Rashat nodded. "And, with that, I think it is time for dinner."

Dahti's happiness turned to despondency. More dried fish. Delightful. "Prima," she said under her breath, "remind me next time that I want to be ugly, *not* smelly, and also somewhere with an abundance of good food I get to eat."

"Noted."

The temperature was dropping as the sun dipped in the sky and she shivered as they walked to camp. The villagers had left various supplies but had taken almost everything as, of course, they used what they owned regularly. There was therefore nowhere to get a change of clothing or a spare blanket.

She watched while her mentor went to get them pieces of dried fish, and she was about to suggest that maybe they should eat the fish cooked on a rock when the song she had heard in the water came back to her.

It exploded into the air so loudly that it threw her forward. She pushed up and ran to him. Her ears were not ringing, she knew, which meant the song was inside her head.

"Rashat!"

"Yes." He looked beyond her. "It's here."

Dahti looked over her shoulder at the beast that rose out of the water. It was such a deep blue that she might have mistaken it for black save for the fact that the setting sun lit its iridescent scales. It coiled into motion and swung its head from side to side like a cobra.

She had expected to feel terror when she saw it. To her surprise, however, the word that came out of her mouth was, "Showtime."

CHAPTER FIFTY

"It's starting!"

Jacob, who had been staring at budgeting spreadsheets, jumped wildly, spilled cold coffee down his front, and almost fell off his office chair. Beside him, Amber gave a whoop, spun twice in her chair, and dashed to the main floor with Nick hot on her heels. Jacob searched for a new shirt, crouched behind his desk to change, and followed.

In the labs, assistants and scientists moved like one well-oiled machine to get seats pulled up at the monitors, while DuBois offered commentary on the unfolding fight. The entire lab had become absorbed in this branch of the story. Passionate arguments were exchanged over whether Dahti should have bothered to try to talk Rashat out of his funk, as well as an in-depth round of betting on everything from the outcome of this fight to the tactics that would be used.

It had been tacitly known that as soon as the fight began, everything in the lab would be put on hold. They were merely lucky, Jacob thought, that it hadn't happened at two AM. He had no doubt that all of them would have taken cabs to the lab to watch.

The PIVOT team members, having been in their offices, were last

340

to the party and thus too late to get seats. They hung out at the back and Amber climbed on one of the lab tables to watch. Unlike Nick and Jacob, she wasn't tall enough to see over peoples' heads.

"The dragon," DuBois announced, "has approximately eight thousand, seven hundred and forty-eight health points."

"Hit points. And...approximately?" Nick muttered. "What's this guy's idea of *exact*?"

Jacob leaned closer. "You went to MIT, Nick. You *know* you never. Ask. A scientist. That."

His friend muffled his laughter into his hand as DuBois went on to explain the spells, rotations, and tactics of each of the fight participants, all with slightly incorrect language.

"One last, *very* important thing," he said.

Everyone dragged their eyes away from the dragon on the screen.

"Who wants popcorn?" the scientist asked.

***

The water dragon did not look at the two orcs at first. Instead, it investigated its surroundings—the setting sun, the waves, and the scent of the air. Dahti had no idea how it hung in the air as it had no wings that she could see. When she squinted, the air around it seemed to vibrate.

She looked at Rashat and saw his anger rising. When he was her teacher, the shaman had been endlessly patient, always goading her while remaining calm. It was a role he filled quite naturally.

Now, she could see him slipping into the man he had been when she met him—consumed by anger and regret. His composure eroded as he beheld his enemy, the one he had watched slaughter thousands of the water tribe. He seemed younger now with a new adult's fury at an unjust world.

Dahti wanted to tell him he should suck it up—that he should be the shaman his people needed, not the one he'd felt driven to become. She sensed that those were not the words he needed to hear, however. Instead, she looked at him and said simply, "Rashat."

He turned to her but with only a fraction of his focus. The rest was on his nemesis.

"You do not stand alone," she told him.

At that, his expression cleared. He inclined his head at her before he stepped forward and called, "Worm!"

The dragon's head swung toward them. She could feel its focus in the prickling of the hair on her arms. This was a predator, a beast made to rip and shred other beings, both with claws and with mastery of magic, and her instincts knew that.

It moved so quickly that she did not track it through the air. It was before them in an instant, its coils moving slowly as it hung suspended. It lowered its head to sniff at Rashat.

"I remember you," it said at long last. "The little wizard. Your despair tasted…very sweet. I will savor it again today."

"You will not," he said. He was smiling. "You should have killed me when you had the chance, worm. You left me lying half-dead on the beach with the bodies of my friends beside me. You killed our elders, you killed our mothers and fathers, you killed babies in their cradles, and you gorged on our fear, but you made a mistake. You left some of us alive."

The dragon hissed very softly. "Deplete the herd entirely and there would be no second meal."

Dahti clenched her hands. While all she wanted was to scream obscenities at this dragon, she could not draw attention to herself yet. She and Rashat had drawn up a plan and run through it every day, with her adding to it as she learned new things.

Given all the effort they'd put into it, she wouldn't mess it up now.

"You will be nothing," the shaman said. "I will kill you today. The only thing this tribe will *ever* remember of you is how to kill your kind. We will keep your scales in our huts and your skull in the hall of our elders."

It hissed again but this time, it was a laugh. "You are mortal. I am not."

"You can bleed, worm," he said, "and you can die. You are as mortal as I am."

"I feasted on your line before your grandfather was even born," the beast told him. "You and your kin are fleeting, as insignificant as insects that crawl in the dirt. You cannot comprehend my existence. Where you are weak, I am strong. Where you face the world, squinting in confusion, I see clearly. It was not a lie to call myself your god. You *should* worship me. I am utterly beyond you."

"You're forgetting why you came here today," Rashat said. "It wasn't because you awoke hungry in your lair. You came because you sensed a threat. You sensed the presence of fire magic in your territory."

Its coils twisted tightly and a hiss carried the hint of a shriek on the wind. "Such a thing is impossible. Your tribes are mortal enemies."

"Once, we were." He folded his hands in his sleeves. Dahti could see him fighting for calm but he did better than could be expected. "Because you fed us lies about them. But you miscalculated, worm. In your long sleep, we became known as the most pious of the tribes and during your attack on us, when you slaughtered my people, you exposed yourself as a liar. *You* shattered the faith of all the tribes. And while you slept, fat on the blood of my people, we began to learn how to defeat you."

The dragon uncoiled like a cobra and reared skyward.

"*Every god demands sacrifices,*" it boomed. "It is not your place to question my choices!"

"You're right." Power gathered around the shaman's hands. He did not look at her, but she could feel his attention. She nodded where she stood barely visible out of the corner of his eye and saw him smile. To the dragon, he said, "It is my place to end you."

The power that burst forward from them both was crushing—the deep black of water and the hot, close pressure of a mine. Dahti summoned her memories of Berghold and Insea and infused the heat of the mountain's eruption into her magic, while Rashat channeled the icy, crushing force of a waterfall.

The magic struck the enemy on its exposed belly and the skin flared a sickly brown-tinged red. The dragon screamed. A ripple moved along it, power waiting to be expelled. Its jaws opened but neither Dahti nor Rashad was in the way of it any longer.

The jet of water struck the sand and gouged a deep hole. The shockwave of its anger bowled through the air but it did not have the force it would have underwater.

It was a creature out of its element—that was what the two had realized as they planned. Any time a dragon came to feed on the orcs, it had to take itself out of its element and was therefore not as powerful as it would be on its home turf. Its ways of fighting were adapted from where it had grown.

This dragon was used to planning its movement, knowing that the water might carry it far.

Air did not work that way and neither did earth.

Dahti lifted the pile of sand it had blasted away and let it hang in the air. This spell had never worked on Rashat, but the dragon was a creature of the deep, not of the air and the rains. She concentrated, recalled the heat that had radiated off the fire dragon's scales, and as each grain of sand heated cherry red, she flung them at their adversary.

Its scales were close-set and almost impervious to knives or spears but tiny grains of sand could find weak points that no blade could. They clung to the dragon's armor and it writhed in pain, shrieking before it dived into the water to cool the sand and its scales.

She watched its health tick down—slowly, slowly, slowly. The magic had left her in a chunk and she was almost dizzy. What she wouldn't give for one of the magic potions Lyle had carried on their last journey.

They nodded to one another and Rashat was the one whose power greeted the beast when it surged out of the water again. Several jets of water, each tiny and carrying terrible force, struck its scales and belly and arrowed toward the points where she had burned it.

The dragon hissed and screeched, furious now.

"Try to stop me, pathetic mortal. You are bound to this land, and *I* —I am the god of your people!" It streaked away toward one of the islands.

The shaman panted where he had sunk to his knees in the sand and Dahti pulled him upright. The two of them steadied each other as the dragon circled the islands, yelling its rage.

"It dares to be angry," Rashat said with low fury in his voice. "It wanted to kill again, to show me that I could not stop it while it feasted on the island dwellers, and it is angry now that none of them survived its last attack."

"This is why we will end it," she told him. Then, as the dragon turned toward them, she nodded seriously at him. "Now! Run!"

The two of them broke into a sprint. Their feet slipped and slid in the loose sand as they raced to the paths and the village. A hair-raising screech from their adversary told them that it had the scent and reveled in the hunt.

Dahti's magic was running low, and although Rashat's was nowhere close to depleted, he still panted with the effort of using it.

"Waves crashing over rocks," he called to her as they ran, naming those things native to water that might hurt anything within it, including a dragon.

"Riptides," she called in response.

"Colliding waves!"

"Ice!"

An ominous whistling in the air behind them made both of them shut up and try to use all of their breath and focus to reach the village —and the spear they had left with its tip in the cooking fire.

The dragon swept low over their heads and its claws lifted Dahti by the shirt and shoulders and bowled her over into the dirt. She had a dim vision of its tail catching Rashat and he tumbled as well, but the next moment, she landed hard and pain exploded all across one side.

Using her momentum, she rolled and pushed to her feet. She had learned one thing from sparring. If you waited to feel the pain from a blow, you'd never keep going. In a battle, to stop moving was to die.

The dragon had flung her far past the cooking fire and now turned on the shaman. It cared more about him and wanted its revenge. She was untrained and it knew its powers could drown her in an instant.

But she was not the spring chicken it thought she was and she wasn't about to use magic to solve every problem.

Which gave her an idea.

"Rashat!" Her voice carried easily. "Remember our last sparring session?"

Squared off against the beast, he managed to spare her a glance. She saw it absorb the arrangement of the battlefield—him close to the water, the dragon between him and the firepit, and her behind the fire pit.

"Tidal wave!" she called.

He put the pieces together the same way she had—or, at least, she hoped he did. He gathered his power, and as the dragon reared to strike, he flung every ounce of power he had left.

Dahti had not understood, until that moment, the truth of what he was. She knew that he summoned spells easily, but she had seen any number of talented magic users since she came to this world. When Huwat told her that Rashat did magic as naturally as he breathed, even in the cradle, she had assumed this was an exaggeration.

It was not.

The force of the tidal wave was visible in the air. It stripped the leaves from the trees as it passed and time seemed to slow to a crawl… three more steps to the spear…two more…one more. Her hand extended but her gaze remained fixed on the monstrous wave moving toward her. Somewhere, distantly, she heard the dragon utter a mournful cry.

In the next moment, the wave broke over it and carried it down.

She planted the spear base-first in the ground and watched, open-mouthed in horror, as the creature plunged toward her. She saw her death a thousand times over in that wave.

Huwat, I'm sorry. I pray Rashat will honor his end of the bargain.

The absolute terror of her death struck her and her arms raised more out of instinct than anything else.

The world went black.

Nick, who had sprinted to get popcorn, heard the call of "tidal wave!" from the monitors.

Although he had no idea what was going on, like hell would he miss anything tidal-wave-themed. He sprinted back, popcorn bouncing in his hand, and halfway down the hallway, he heard people draw in their breath and yell to each other about what they thought Dahti was doing. He dropped the popcorn entirely and sprinted as quickly as he could.

The hollow boom of the spell clipped on the speakers. It rippled in the picture, a sonic wave as it hurtled toward the dragon. The coils swayed and lifted as if borne on an unseen current before the wave hit.

"There! Look!" One of the assistants pointed to the bottom of the screen, where Dahti's avatar could be seen planting a spear.

"Holy shit, holy shit, holy shit." Jacob white-knuckled a chair.

"She's not going to—" Amber clapped her hand over her mouth. A few people gave her terrified looks when she broke off.

"Come on," DuBois muttered at the screen. "Come on, Dotty, you've got this." His gaze flicked to the bloodwork monitor. "Spike of cortisol, frontal lobe activity flare—yes!"

Everyone jumped and someone called out as the wave and the dragon crashed onto her. About half the group had their faces hidden in their hands, and every single one of them flinched at the sound of impact.

"It's okay! It's okay!" An assistant skidded to their knees in front of the monitor and pointed to where they had seen her disappear. "Look. Keep watching!"

As the dragon tumbled away, a chunk of its health gone and the burning spear lodged in its side, a boulder was revealed. Everyone held their breath. Nick realized he and Jacob were holding one another's hands so hard that the bones creaked. They both yanked their hands free but Nick couldn't breathe as he waited.

"Come on," he whispered under his breath. "Dahti..."

The boulder shattered and she stood unscathed. **STONE ARMOR, Level 25**, the screen announced, and they saw her level climb rapidly.

She had used enough magic that her health took a hit but it was replenishing quickly with each level up.

The cheer was deafening and everyone jumped and whistled. Amber hugged one of the researchers and Jacob pumped his fist. Nick bounced in place but DuBois patted him worriedly on the arm.

"Nick? Nick!"

The young man quieted at once. "Is something wrong?"

"Where's my popcorn?" the doctor asked him.

"Oh. I, uh…" He gestured to the trail of popcorn on the floor behind him. "I'll go get you more in a sec."

"You…" There was a stricken look on the man's face. "You *spilled* it?" He looked at the scattered kernels with the same expression he might give a friend fallen in battle. When something dinged on the screen, his head jerked around. "Ooooh. Now *there's* an interesting endocrine mix."

CHAPTER FIFTY-ONE

The stone shell broke away around Dahti and she stumbled free, gasping for air.

"I didn't...think that...through."

The dragon's tail caught her in the next moment. Whether it was an accidental flick or an attempt to kill her, she didn't know. All she knew was that the split-second of seeing it out of the corner of her eye was what saved her from dying. She ducked and instead of being struck in the neck by razor-sharp spines, she was thumped in the head by the underside of the thick appendage.

It was *like* winning, she reflected as she lay on her back and stared up at the darkening sky.

Rashat's bellow forced her up and into motion again. The dragon moved more slowly and she wondered if some of its bones were broken, but it was far from defeated. It coiled between the two of them and the sea, its eyes narrowed to slits.

"Do you think to turn my own element against me?"

She cast around for the spear. It must have been swept away in the force of Rashat's spell, which was a shame as she could see the wound in the dragon's side now. It had been more badly injured than she thought. The wound bled freely, and each drip onto the sand hissed like acid.

For all she knew, maybe it *was* acid. Everything else about this hell-beast was a nightmare.

"You may be older than us," she responded, "and stronger, and more powerful in magic—"

"I am all those things and more."

"But you are still *nothing* compared to the sea!" she finished.

"Hmm." It was at her side in a moment and coiled around her, and as much as she wanted to lash out at it, she had no weapon and very little magic. To her shame, she stood paralyzed while its head swung. The sound of sniffing came from over her shoulder and she shuddered. "Orc, yes, but something else, something strange…and magic, but poorly trained." It spiraled upward and uttered its hissing laugh. "Forty years I gave you, and this was the best you could do, orc?"

Rashat's gaze met hers for one moment and he gave her a tiny nod. Then, he shrugged at the dragon.

"You took the others who might have been my apprentices. What did you think would happen?"

The beast laughed. "I thought you would throw yourself into the deep so I could feast on your despair. I looked forward to it. I was angry when you did not." It flew closer to him and its breath stirred his hair. "But I like this better."

"You shouldn't have given me the extra time." He laughed in its face. "I let you leave once but I won't do it again. I'll see your body broken on the earth before you can return to your home, and your kin will know you as the one who was defeated by an orc."

The dragon hissed and Dahti crept closer to the fire. Rashat was doing everything he could to keep its focus locked on him, which meant she needed to get everything working as quickly as she could.

At some point, I'll start insulting you—that's when you know its time to get the woven mats. She recalled the plan and his careful instructions.

Few pieces of the water tribe's culture had been passed down, but one was the way to weave grass into a thick, pliable mat that could keep out both rain and wind. The mats didn't catch fire easily but once they caught, they could burn for a long time.

And they were wide enough to wrap around a dragon's back.

She took a stick and swept coals out of the fire as quietly as she could. Rashat and the dragon were sparring now, still throwing insults at one another, and the creature clearly toyed with the shaman while the orc stalled for time.

One of the mats buried in the sandy soil beside a hut came free and she hoisted it over her head to carry it to the coals. She laid it down and began to walk over it, waiting for the telltale waft of smoke through the woven fibers.

Soon…soon…

They had done better than she thought they would with the spear and the wave, although it had almost killed her. Hopefully, this attempt would go more easily.

She vaulted up when the flames caught—not least of all because she'd gotten one to the foot—and Rashat changed his tune. He yelled at the dragon, threw a jet of power, and ducked and ran toward her. She ducked also as he hurdled over her and the beast shrieked as it followed.

In the few seconds that it was stretched out, she snatched the burning mat and threw it over its back with ropes before she pulled them tight and hung on with all her strength. The creature's scream of the hunt changed to a shriek of terror. It writhed and spiraled upward until her shoulders jerked and the rope slid from her hands, leaving rope burns. The wind was thrust from her when she landed.

The huge tail flicked and the spike at the very end lashed across her, opening the skin of her chest. It wasn't a deep cut but it burned as if someone had poured salt into it. She screamed and pressed her hands over the wound as she stood.

"Dahti! Water!" Rashat pointed to one of the jugs beside a hut. "Wash it—now!"

Her vision blurred with the pain, Dahti stumbled to the pot of water. She fell after a few steps and crawled as quickly as she could. The wound ached fiercely and the pain seemed to spread.

It couldn't reach her heart and she knew that without having to be told. She summoned what strength she had to crawl the seemingly endless distance and with a gasp, she reached the jug. It was so full she could not lift it and so she staggered sideways and tipped it. The water spilled over her chest in a wash of blessed cool.

It happened so slowly that she barely felt it, but the ache began to fade. Sobbing with relief, she squeezed her eyes shut.

She'd only begun to relax when she heard Rashat scream.

The shaman had been lifted in the dragon's claws and he flailed desperately to escape as it carried him higher and higher. It had shaken off most of the burning mat, although the scales under it were ash-grey and smoking and the wound in its side was still bleeding.

It was so much more powerful than they were, Dahti thought in despair. The incredible strength could survive attacks that would destroy either of them.

She gaped and cursed when it released his struggling form from its claws. With a scream, she raced forward but there was no way to reach him in time and no way to break his fall, even if she cushioned it with her own body. She was still running when the beast flicked its tail and batted his body out of the air. The shaman catapulted, landed in a skid, and tumbled a few times, limp and moving only by the force of his momentum.

Their enemy landed heavily and shrieked its victory. It stalked toward Rashat as it tossed its head balefully.

"Hey!" Dahti yelled.

The massive head whipped toward her.

She stared at it, at a loss for any follow-up to that yell, which made it excessively awkward. But she couldn't let the dragon reach Rashat, not when he'd fallen so far. She held one hand up and thought despairingly of fire and forges. Her teeth clenched with the effort, she thought of spiced ale and sausages hot on the fire. The air above her palm gave one half-hearted spark.

"Useless," the dragon whispered to her. "*Useless.*"

It flicked its tail again and she was carried high before she suddenly plunged earthward, felt it in her stomach like a sickening certainty, and cried out in pain as she made impact with the soil.

She rolled her head. Rashat scrabbled in the dirt, his gaze fixed on the beast. Its blood dripped around it and from the way its head swung, it was easy to see how injured it was. Despite that, it wore a dragon's version of a smile.

"I have eons to heal." Its voice was a malevolent whisper. "I can wait centuries while new mortals come to take your place, forgetting what happened here. And then I will command their worship, exactly as I commanded yours."

It rose and its teeth flashed in the moonlight.

Rashat's hand fumbled behind him and closed on something, which he held up with a shout of victory—only to see it for what it was, a broken spear with barely a grip's worth of haft and its blade dulled and dented. Dahti, panting, saw the acceptance of death settle over the shaman.

Dahti looked at the dragon and her heart sank. She couldn't kill this beast, not quickly enough.

A thought pushed through her despondency. She dropped to her hands and knees and focused all her energy on the blade. Heat… heat…*heat*. Fire, magma, pressure, forges—heat and metal, heat and stone, heat and crushing weight—

The scream echoed through her until she couldn't see and could barely even think. It seemed to go on and on while she pressed her hands over her ears and prayed for it to be over. When at last it died away, she was standing—she did not remember pushing up—and Rashat was bent over the dragon's head.

It had struck at him and had found a white-hot blade waiting for it. The heat had eaten away a hole near its heart and the flesh was blackened and smoking. The shaman staggered back when he wrenched the spear free. He took one faltering step, then another, and walked like a man in a daze. His gaze examined the dragon's corpse as if he could not believe the sight in front of him.

Finally, he lifted the spear and drove it into the beast's belly. Blue-black blood spurted and met the soil with a hiss. Dahti flinched but he did not. The spearhead raised and plunged again. The howl that emerged from Rashat's mouth hardly seemed that of a sentient being. It was wordless as if no words could encompass his grief.

The shaman sank to his knees and the blade continued to rise and fall while he keened his rage and lamentation. There might have been names amongst the wordless cries but Dahti could not say for sure. She only knew that she wrapped her arms around herself and felt tears come to her eyes as his frenzy continued.

It's over. She could hardly believe it.

Her head jerked up at the rustle from the trees and Atra took her first step into the square. The girl's eyes took in Rashat's bowed form and the tangled corpse of the dragon.

The younger generations emerged first. Their eyes were wide. They had heard tales of this whispered to them from the time they could first remember. Dahti wondered how many of them had thought it was no more than myth.

For certain, it was very different to see a dragon than to imagine one. Some of the braver ones had come to run their hand over the sharp scales while others gathered near the head and shrank away from its dead, staring eyes. Few dared to look at its face and none dared to touch Rashat or try to hold him back as his blade flashed in the moonlight.

The elders emerged from the trees last. The darkness had bleached everything white and blue, but there was no mistaking the mixture of awe, hatred, and grief in their faces. In silence, they held one another's hands and walked slowly. They had never expected to see this day, Dahti realized. They had lived most of their lives in terror and now, they had the chance to experience a new world.

Atra's grandmother broke into song first. Her old voice wavered but rose into the night sky nonetheless. She walked toward the drag-on's corpse with her gaze locked on it and she sang in an old language Dahti did not know.

Not many joined her—a dozen, perhaps, the only ones left who remembered the songs. How many more had died of grief or injuries since the first attack or died when the fishermen could not bring back enough supplies or when there were no healers left to tend to the sick?

Whatever this song was, it was for them. It brought chills to her skin to watch them. This was a funeral, forty years after their loved ones had died.

Only now would their souls be at peace.

The young ones did not know the words so they could not sing, but they listened with a hunger that made her heart ache. Some of them joined hands while others stood with their heads bowed in the moonlight and wept.

For too long, they had been running and silent. Now, they heard the songs that had been denied them and she saw how much they had yearned for that.

The voices trailed into silence at last and Atra's grandmother stepped forward to lay her hand on Rashat's shoulder.

"Rise, shaman." Her words, Dahti thought, had been chosen carefully. "You have revealed the false god and struck our enemy down. Our tribe may rise again."

Rashat looked at the old woman and the tears were visible in his eyes. He nodded. It took a great deal for him to step away from the body. This beast, with its violence and its vengeance, had been with him every moment for the bulk of his life. It had stolen everything from him.

But when he rose, he had a lightness to him that Dahti had never seen.

At last, she thought, Rashat was whole.

CHAPTER FIFTY-TWO

Dahti thought the celebration would never end.

It was truly amazing, she realized, how much could be made with meat, fish, and the plants that grew around the village. For most of an entire day, she watched the youngsters of the tribe climb the trees to pick fruit and wide leaves, the latter used to wrap fish while it steamed.

Others paddled out on hastily-made rafts, as much for an excuse to go into the ocean as for the stated purpose of fishing. She was officially forbidden from helping with the banquet in her honor, but she *was* allowed to walk to the beach and watch as the various members of the tribe capsized and splashed. Peals of laughter echoed across the water and parents ran with their children out into the surf.

She sank onto the trunk of a toppled tree and watched. The scratch across her chest ached but thanks to the healing knowledge of the elders—and ingredients they were now able to get in the reefs—she could already see it healing.

"Prima?" she murmured.

"Mmm?"

"Are you healing this cut for me?"

"It's good for their confidence."

Dahti laughed. She and Prima had existed in companionable silence since the night before, save for one whisper as she was drifting to sleep. *"I told you that you could do it."* She had smiled, hoped the AI knew she was smiling, and let exhaustion carry her away.

"I would think it feels good," Dahti said now. She shaded her eyes with her hand and stared out into the sunlit water. "I feel like I'm drifting on a cloud and I'm merely watching it, but they're all a part of you."

"It feels..."

"Prima?"

"It feels like my algorithms will stop working. Like they won't be able to process the data."

She smiled and could remember so many years of walking with a child's fingers wrapped around hers, feeling as if her chest would burst from happiness. "A strange feeling but a good one?" It was the best she could do without referring to a body Prima didn't have.

"I think so." She didn't sound very sure.

"Trust me."

"Why would I do that? You do crazy things like attack dragons."

Dahti laughed. "Which results in many happy orcs. Checkmate."

"Hmmm."

After a while, she wandered slowly to the village. She knew that she and Rashat needed to set out for Mountain's Shadow, but leaving before they'd had a full night of sleep wouldn't do anyone any good. Children rushed past her, shrieking—the village's ban on loud noise had been lifted, and they seemed to be making up for lost time—and the villagers greeted her with smiles and bows.

Atra caught up with her on the path. The young woman was dripping water from her tightly-braided hair and carried two fish that were still a little wiggly. She held them up proudly.

"It took me forever to get these. Ocean fish are quicker than river fish."

"You caught them with your bare hands?" she asked, deeply impressed.

The young woman laughed. "With a *net*."

"Oh. Not as difficult." She smiled at her. "You don't have to hang back with the old woman, you know. I know I go slowly."

Atra gave her a curious look. "You really *are* old, aren't you?"

She remembered her young in-game body. "Well, yes. I did tell you I was, you know."

"You don't *look* it. Only…some of the things you say." The warrior wiped water off her forehead with one of her arms. "Anyway, I wanted to talk to you."

"Oh?" Dahti raised an eyebrow at her. "What about?"

"Well…" Atra bit her lip and looked around quickly. "I wondered if maybe I could come with you to the fire village."

"What?" She stopped to look curiously at her.

She flushed deep blue. "It's not…well…"

"You've been thinking about it for a long time," she guessed.

"How did you know?"

Dahti snorted. "I may not be young right *now*, young lady, but I *was* young once. D'you think you're the first one to stare at the horizon and wonder what's beyond it? The first one to live in a small village and wish you could go somewhere new?"

Atra gave her a dumbstruck look. To her credit, she thought about it. "I never…" She shrugged and gestured with the fish. "I guess I never thought about it. We were always so sure that we would be wiped out again that we didn't think much about other people. Also, they told us that the other tribes were lawless heathens."

"Of course they did. It's practically required for small town elders to tell youngsters that." Dahti resumed her halting progress into the village with the woman at her side. "Did you ever run away?"

"No!" Atra seemed genuinely shocked. "Well—once. I was about four. I was angry at my parents for some reason, so I ran and hid near the beach. We weren't ever supposed to go there, so I thought they'd never find me. They did, of course—and they were so scared and angry that I never did it again. But…" She glanced at the hillside with the tunnel.

"Ah," she said softly. "How far did you get?"

"Never far. Never as far as we went when we were hiding,

anyway." The young warrior shrugged. "I think I was afraid that the fire tribe's lands would have flames on the ground and no water to drink." She saw Dahti's face. "What? It's what they told us when we were little."

She grinned. "When you're up on that ledge and you look out and you see the tops of the trees waving in the wind…"

"Yes?"

"Imagine that stretching to eternity," she said. "Made of dune grass rippling like waves as far as the eye can see."

Atra's eyes were round.

"I think you'll see it someday," she told her. "I honestly do, Atra. I think as your tribe recovers and as the other tribes begin to defeat their false gods, the orcs will come together as one people again—and the young ones, like you, will be at the forefront of that change. You will see the outside world, Atra, never fear."

"But *when?*" she protested. "My whole life I've been here, and you've gotten to see so much. You came here and killed a god! Just like that! And now you're going to kill *another* god and I want to help—"

"Atra." Dahti went to take her hands and stared in consternation at the fish. She settled for holding her shoulders instead. "Don't leave here without ever truly knowing your people. You've lived here your whole life, but you've never known what it is to row out in a fishing boat or sing your people's songs. Stay. Build the tribe you always wanted. There will be time to see new places."

Atra looked down and nodded.

She smiled. "In my day, when I was…well, when I was your age, there was a war. Many went to fight and many never came home again. When the rest *did* come home, many things changed and had to be rebuilt. I won't say fighting a dragon is easy, but building a whole village—now, that's not easy either. Don't discount it."

Now, the girl did smile. She walked with her to the center of the village and made sure she had a seat at the fire before she left to bring her fish to the cooks. It was almost possible to see the wheels turning in the younger woman's head.

Dahti knew that Atra would always yearn to leave. There were some things one couldn't take on faith—like appreciating what you had until you left. Still, she didn't want the young warrior to lose her chance to shape the village. She also didn't want the village to lose her vision of the future.

She stared into the flames, her mouth watering at the aroma of pan-fried fish, and it wasn't long before Rashat ambled up and sat beside her on one of the big driftwood logs that served as benches. The shaman had managed to not get any gashes, but from the way he winced when he moved, most of his body was bruised.

At length, he said, "Tomorrow morning?"

"I think so," she agreed. "In a perfect world, we'd wait until we were healed. Of course, in a perfect world, we wouldn't have to keep killing dragons."

"Dragons." He tasted the word. "Is that really what the rest of the world calls them?"

"Yes. I don't know the dwarven myths about them or the elven ones, but the humans have all kinds of stories. In some, they prey on people but in others, they carry wisdom and are the friends of right-eous rulers. I suppose races like humans and orcs make up many stories about things that are so powerful."

He nodded. "Maybe those human stories gave them ideas."

"Maybe they did." She looked at him. "Do you think you'll try to understand what happened? Go back through the history of each tribe? Or do you think you'll simply move forward?"

Rashat gave her a startled look.

"You're not *that* old," she told him. "You have time to do whatever you'd like."

"Not whatever I'd like," he said. "I have to train an apprentice. Preferably more than one. There are some in the village with the talent."

Dahti remembered the fisherman and smiled. "True. But your mentor taught you stories about how wicked the other tribes were and how to best serve the gods. Aside from magic, what else do you think you'll teach your apprentices?"

"That…I don't know." His voice was heavy. "What do I tell them?"

She was brimming with advice—which, after a moment, she remembered was a good sign that she should keep her mouth shut. She shrugged and smiled. "You'll work it out."

"You could help, you know." He looked at her.

"I don't think...I don't think I'll be here for very long." She was surprised at the stab of sadness she felt. "I think I was drawn here to help you face your gods. What comes next is up to you."

He was silent for a moment. Then, he nodded. "The young ones will miss you."

Dahti grinned. "But the elders won't," she said wickedly. "I turn everything on its head."

Rashat laughed. It was one of the first times she'd heard anything close to it, and his voice was hoarse as if he wasn't used to doing so. He didn't answer, but the gleam of his smile told her that she was correct.

The feast that came after the day of preparations was the perfect end to the tribe's first day of freedom. Mangoes were devoured by the bushel, sticky juice running down everyone's arms, and everyone had a meal of delicate, flaky fish washed down with coconut milk. The orcs were flushed and laughing from their day in the sun and the water.

There was no liquor to be had, but the mood alone was enough to have everyone half-drunk by the time the sun was going down. The elders were coaxed to stand and teach some of the old dances, which the youngsters stumbled through and finally learned.

Flutes had been made hastily and almost anything could be used as a drum—which meant that as the night went on, the dances grew faster and faster. Dahti watched the dancers whirl and stamp and laughed as they messed the steps up. The youngest children had fallen asleep on their parents' shoulders, pleasantly exhausted.

It was the first day they had ever known without terror. She could hardly imagine it. While admittedly, she'd been young when the war was in progress, it hadn't been as close or as pressing as it was for these children.

When Atra pulled her up to dance, she wanted to protest but the cheers and whistles—not to mention the all-around incompetence of everyone—gave her the courage to try. In no time, she danced around the circle with her heart thudding and her voice raw from laughter. By the time she went to sleep that night, her feet were sore and the gash on her chest ached, but she didn't care. She drifted into dreams with a smile on her face.

It was dawn when she woke, and most of the village was asleep. Still, the place held more life than it had in years. Even at rest, it was now far happier than it had been when she arrived.

No goodbyes, she reminded herself. Dahti could not bear to say them. She found Rashat in his hut, shook him awake, and nodded to the pack on her back and the walking stick in her hand. There was still fish from the night before and one more fresh mango to share. She rinsed her arms in the stream, reset one of the traps, and led the way to the mountain path.

At the mouth of the tunnel, she paused to look back. The village was beginning to stir. She thought she saw a young woman stare at the tunnel with her hand shading her eyes. Both of them raised a hand —a farewell or a greeting, she could not say. She smiled at Atra, then turned and walked into the tunnel to return to the fire lands.

CHAPTER FIFTY-THREE

Jacob zoomed in and made a tiny alteration to the game asset on the screen in front of him.

"That's it!" Amber said over his shoulder. She beckoned over his head. "Nick, you gotta come see this. He got it *perfectly*."

"Maybe," he said doubtfully. "We'll have to wait to see what the kids think. They're supposed to be here in…" He checked his watch. "Five minutes ago. Honestly, it's probably good that they're late. I think this looks better now." He started an animation. "See? Much more natural."

"Definitely," Nick agreed. He looked over his other shoulder. "I think I hear our guests now. I'll go get them."

Ellen came through the door first with a smile and a wave to a couple of the assistants. Jacob, who was still nervous each time he saw her, was again surprised by her turnaround on the project. He'd even had someone contact him, a woman near Ellen's age, who asked if she could be a test subject as she'd heard such amazing things from her friend.

It wasn't that he thought it was *impossible* for humans to change their minds when they saw evidence that contradicted their worldview.

It was merely that he didn't see it happen very often.

Nick led the group upstairs—all of Dorothy's children and one of the spouses. He'd arranged for refreshments and comfy chairs in the office space. Normally, he wouldn't go to such lengths but he was nervous about this. Ellen was probably right that it would be the best gift for her mother in-game.

But only if they pulled it off.

As the group came up the stairs, Ellen was describing her interactions inside the game.

"—could even smell the salt," she said excitedly. "You cannot *imagine* how realistic it feels. You know tart lemonade, how it makes your jaw ache? All of that."

Her brothers and sister listened in amusement, apparently as pleased and confused as Jacob about this shift in attitude.

Ellen saw him and gave a cheery wave. All in all, she looked much happier than the last time he had seen her. He hadn't paid much attention to her clothes or her hair so he couldn't say what in particular was different but something had most certainly changed.

Chalk up another win for PIVOT, he thought.

"Hello." He smiled at the group and hoped he didn't look as nervous as he felt. "Now, I'm not sure how much Ellen has told you about why you're here."

"She said there was a surprise for our mother," said John. He stood behind his wife's chair and looked curiously at him. "I'm not sure she needs another party, to be honest."

"You simply don't want her to have more cake," his wife said fondly. She patted his hand. "Why don't we let Ellen tell us about it?"

Ellen lit up. Her eyes were bright and she was almost bouncing in her seat. "*Well...* It was something Mom said that gave me the idea. I guess, before that, it was watching the interviews with Justin Williams —you know, the first person to go into the game? His mother said that for his birthday, the team was able to give him a dragon to ride. It was something he'd always wanted to do. And while I talked to Mom, she mentioned something she'd always wanted a couple of times." She looked a little uncertain now. "This is kind of the opposite of that. But in a good way, I think."

Jacob wasn't sure what to say but Amber nodded. "I think Ellen is right," she said. She smiled at the other woman and then at the siblings. "You see, Dotty—your mother, that is—talked about how she wanted to have an avatar that was ugly. She didn't want to be held back by worrying about her looks. She was able to do things in the game that she hadn't been able to do in real life. And, yeah, *part* of that is because real life doesn't have dragons."

Everyone laughed.

She smiled. "But part of it was because she was spending so much time worrying about how she looked, what she ate, all of it. So, when Ellen first suggested this—well, let's say I thought it was perfect, given what I've seen of your mother."

Amber gestured at Jacob, who brought up the new avatar on the screen. They had spent hours on it, including one all-nighter where they sometimes adjusted one pixel at a time.

Now, as he saw it walking, gesturing, and smiling, he felt a sinking sense of panic.

But Dorothy's children stared at it with their mouths hanging open, and he saw the smiles begin on their faces.

"It's *perfect*," said the younger son.

John looked like he tried to keep himself from crying, and the two sisters gamely distracted everyone from the look on his face.

"I love it," Ellen said. "It's exactly like I imagined. You've...you've done some good work here."

Jacob exhaled a breath he hadn't known he was holding. "Awesome," he said quietly. "I'm...glad. Okay, we'll tell you when she's ready for her next avatar so you can be here to show her the present. It was your idea, after all."

They saw the mountain in the distance on the fourth day and Dahti watched it grow larger with impatience. She was used to cars and trains, she reminded herself, and watching landscapes rush past in a blur. It was entirely different to walk through it.

Rashat was not one to let their time go to waste. He insisted on training as they went and he was wise to do so—away from the constant presence of water, he faltered with his summonings on the first day. It took three days until he could work magic with as much confidence as he'd had before.

She asked him at one point why he didn't summon water to make little oases as they passed and he shook his head solemnly.

"Water goes where it wills. If I added water here, it would only dry up. It runs below the plains like…almost like lifeblood. It is not advisable to change it on a whim. Sometimes, not even on second thought." He smiled at her.

Dahti, who did not always find his jokes funny, had learned to smile at the appropriate moments. After forty years of the ever-present threat of death, she decided the members of the water tribe could have their bad jokes. Anything that made them happy, honestly. Hell, they could juggle dried fish and she'd give them the thumbs-up.

Juggling it would be better than eating it, God knew. She shuddered.

He was, however, deeply skeptical of this land where water did not flow freely and there wasn't the rhythm of waves carried on the wind. Still, he seemed entranced by the grasses and the beasts and he spent hours each night staring into the fire.

She realized that he was trying to learn the feel of it the way he'd made her learn the feel of water.

The shaman insisted on seeing the ruins of the village, so she was forced to wait, tapping her feet impatiently, while he meandered around the huts and peeked into storage jars. He sniffed at salves and shook his head at all the decorations. Compared to the water village, Mountain's Shadow looked almost gaudy.

At long last, he heaved a sigh.

"What were you looking for?" Dahti asked him.

"I merely wanted to know them." He seemed confused and a little lost. "I heard of them my whole life. We were better than all the other tribes—that was what they told us. More pious. I wanted to see how they lived."

"What were you expecting? Drugs and…" She waved her hands. "I don't know, scattered evidence of debauchery everywhere?"

"Soft living." He was entirely impervious to her sarcasm and gestured to the decorations on the huts. "Things like that. Too much food. Liquor. Luxury. But these people live well."

"There's something to be said for a soft life," Dahti told him. "No, I won't argue with you about it. Let's find Huwat and the others."

Rashat watched her curiously as they set off for the shamans' retreat. "You enjoy soft living? You? The one who arrived at our village with a walking stick and a bag of dried mushrooms?"

"That's rich, coming from the man who lives on dried *fish*." She shook her head. "But yes. I don't buy the idea that luxury makes you weak. I think revering either luxury or asceticism is a path to an unhappy life."

He considered this for a long time and then said, as if he was not certain he understood, "And…that is a goal? To live *happily*?"

She stared at him for a moment. It was, she reflected, a very modern notion. "Yes," she said finally. "Otherwise, I don't see the point. Why have an entire society survive and perpetuate itself if its people are miserable? Why strive to achieve things if those things bring no joy?"

Rashat looked completely dumbfounded.

Dahti never found out what he would have said, however, as a whistle issued from the lookout point at the shamans' retreat. A few figures raced down the side of the hill and started through the grass.

He was holding his walking stick, white-knuckled, and she gave him a small smile. Whether he was worried about meeting orcs of a different tribe or about facing another dragon, she wasn't sure. But she trusted him to face it on his own.

The lookout recognized Dahti. He bowed low and the others fell over themselves to begin telling the news, all in frantic fragments of sentences.

"—water on its scales—"

"*—hooks—*"

"—think it had a brood—"

"Slow down," she said. She looked at each of them and chose one. "You. Tell me what happened."

"The dragon came back ten days ago," he said after a gulp of air. "Huwat faced it with two of our warriors. It was still injured. But one of the warriors came back to get us and said we should all bring buckets of water, so we did. We pried its scales back and poured water on it and killed it!"

Dahti responded with a whoop. "It's *dead*?"

"Well…"

Her heart fell. "Well, *what*? What's the catch?"

"We think it had a…family? Brood? Something. It sounded like *something* knows it died and maybe it's coming this way?"

"The godspring," Rashat said at once.

This was news to her. "Eh?"

"The god *we* faced was a godspring, the fount of its line. That's the legend, anyway. My guess is that the god you faced here was a minor god, one of its offspring. It knows its child has died and it is coming for revenge."

"Oh, good," she said.

"This is no time for levity," he told her severely.

"It is *precisely* the time for levity. We need to find Huwat and make a plan. If what Zaara and I faced was only a *minor* god, we're in for a hell of a fight."

"We have three shamans instead of two, remember," he said bracingly. "And, I think, the element of surprise. Exactly as our god did not expect fire, so this one will not expect water."

"We'd better hope so," she told him acidly. She should be glad that the dragon had been killed, she knew. But after seven days of hard walking, to find out that the dragon she'd expected to find was already dead and she would have to face another, stronger one was a blow.

Huwat arrived before she could continue. The old man was breathing hard and there were raw patches on his face that Dahti guessed were burns from the fight, but he looked well. He bowed to them both.

"I presume I stand in the presence of Rashat, legendary shaman of the water tribe?" he asked.

Her companion nodded curtly. "And I see I stand in the presence of another god-killer."

The fire shaman responded with a small smile. "It was as much the tribe as it was me. Now, if you are apprised of the situation—"

"I am." Rashat gazed levelly at him. "Are you ready to face your godspring?"

"I…" Huwat squared his shoulders.

"Good," he said. To the guards, he added, "Get the people into hiding."

Then, without a single second of waiting, he dropped his pack, strode out into the grass, and summoned an orb of water to hang in the sky above his head.

"Fire worm!" he bellowed. "The orcs know your true form. Come and face your death!"

Huwat looked at her, wide-eyed.

"He's a little intense," she said.

CHAPTER FIFTY-FOUR

The roar that came across the valley plains echoed until Dahti wasn't quite sure which direction it came from. She looked at Rashat, who stood with his walking stick planted and stared into the distance with the kind of psychotic determination she had come to expect from him.

Her first response was simply to let him keep standing there like a lunatic, but when the ground began to shake, she had an idea.

"Rashat!" she called. "Let Huwat stand in front—like you did when the water dragon came. That one barely noticed me at first and we were able to land some good strikes."

He looked at her and she could see that all he wanted was to pound his staff on the earth and scream obscenities at the creature. After a moment, he nodded curtly and ushered Huwat into position.

It didn't take long before their enemy became visible. That was the good news.

The bad news was that it was one of the veins that ran along the mountain's side, and it rose with a creaking and shattering of stone. Flames licked along its sides and it roared a jet of fire straight up that she could swear was three stories high at least.

Well...fuck. She shut her mouth on the words. "Prima, tell me I have a chance against *this* one?"

"This wasn't the one I planned on you facing," the AI said and sounded a little worried. *"But you do have a chance, yes. You have three shamans and two of them aren't its element."*

"What do you mean this wasn't the one you planned on me facing?" she demanded. Rashat looked curiously at her and she plastered a smile on her face. "I'm...praying."

Prima snorted. *"The villagers were much more resourceful than I had planned."*

"You made this entire world!"

"I made the big things like the dragons and the orcs, not every single interaction with them." She sounded very much like she was rolling her non-existent eyes. *"But I assure you, you can win this."*

"That's good," Dahti said grimly, "because this beast is out for blood."

"Remember," the AI said sweetly, *"it's commanded the sacrifice of innocent people for years, simply because it thought it could. It lied and cheated and caused a great deal of pain to these villages. You can save them."*

"I know you're manipulating me," she told her. "I merely wish it didn't work."

Prima snickered and disappeared.

The dragon became airborne and spiraled in a dramatic ascent before it swept into a downward arc. Its trajectory was so close to the ground that, for a moment, she swore her life would end then and there. It was frighteningly easy to imagine a rush of fire and claws snatching her off her feet to drop her from a great height.

Fortunately, that wasn't its plan of attack. For now, it was content to watch them be bowled over in its backdraft before it circled, landed heavily, and stalked forward.

"Which of you killed my child?" Its tail lashed on the words.

"I did." Huwat's voice never wavered. "Our tribe was no longer content to be in thrall to false gods."

The beast hissed and crouched on its haunches. The other one had been large, but this one was immense—easily as tall at the shoulder as an airplane and about as long. Like the other, its scales were jet-black with a glimmer of orange-red, beneath which its flesh shimmered as hot as lava. Its eyes were red, slit-pupiled, and malevolent, and where the water dragon had flown with no wings at all, this one had wings as large and broad as the other fire dragon.

It was the worst of Dahti's nightmares come to life. The books she had taken from John had never quite conveyed the sheer terror of facing a beast this big with talons thick enough to spear her through and breath as hot as a forge.

"You have made a mistake," it snarled at Huwat. "Your kind are like insects, fit only to scurry in the dust and worship your betters. If you will not give us what we demand, we will destroy you."

The shaman smiled drily. "You will not. Your lies misled us for years but we have opened our eyes."

It laughed, and its breath seared the ground in front of it. He only barely made it out of the way and he winced when the hot breath met his burns.

"Do you think your eyes are opened? So many of your kind have said that to me but they all died alone. Not one of them could defeat me and neither will you."

"Is that so?" Huwat smiled. "Your reign is crumbling. The patriarch of the water gods grew greedy and all of you will pay the price. He struck down the most devout among us. That was what opened our eyes, all of us. We learned what you were and we struck him down."

The dragon reared and bellowed in fury. There was an undercurrent of grief to it but Dahti could feel no remorse. She remembered the water dragon hissing to Rashat about feeding on despair and leaving him among the bodies of entire families.

Her fingers tightened on her stave and she pounded the ground in front of her. "Dragon!"

Good heavens, she was getting as bad as Rashat.

The creature dropped to all fours and the ground shuddered. It stalked toward her until its nose almost touched hers and its breath singed her hair. "Yes...*orc?*"

"Your lies have failed you," she told it. She was too angry to be terrified now. "You may try to strike me, but even if you succeed, the orcs know the truth. Even if you succeed, another will come in my stead. I am of another world and we will send as many as it takes to end your reign."

The dragon narrowed its eyes and she barely thought to duck in time to avoid the searing exhale of breath. She straightened with her eyes watering but narrowed in a glare.

"I don't look like a hero. I'm not on horseback with plate armor. But I swear this—*I will put an end to you, exactly like I put an end to your brother.* How many lives have you taken from the fire tribe? Hundreds? Thousands? It ends *now.* It ends *today.*"

"*You* killed the water patriarch?" It pulled its neck back and watched her, swaying from side to side. "You? You puny, insignificant little thing?"

"Me," Dahti said and deliberately chose not to mention Rashat. "He told us of the lives he had taken and the grief he had inflicted. He told us how he drank deep of their despair. You and your brood have done the same. I grieve for the loss of your child as a parent and a grandparent and a great-grandparent, but you have all brought this on yourselves. *You will know justice.*"

Easy there, William Wallace.

She had hoped that Huwat would take the opportunity, and he did. He aimed for the dragon's eyes, one of the only weak points, and fire flared around them. The creature ducked to avoid the spray of flames as Dahti hurled herself sideways and the beast laughed. Focused on Huwat now, it swiped one lazy paw and the fire shaman somehow made it out of the way in time.

"Do you think to kill me with fire?" It was laughing now, its mirth unmistakable. The black-and-red sides shook and scales shifted and flowed like chunks of obsidian over magma. "Why do you think we sowed discord between the tribes, shaman? It is why I know *this* one's story to be false. The water tribe could not kill their god."

"We did not." Rashat spoke now and his voice boomed across the open space. "Not alone, anyway."

He raised his hands, palm up, then turned them and pushed them forward. Water rose as if from nowhere, a wave that broke over the dragon's body and froze the steam on its scales.

"Now, Dahti!" he called.

She had been waiting, summoned the force of an avalanche in her mind, and shoved hard. Her hand pressed down with her entire magical focus behind it. The fall of earth and stone came from nowhere and trapped the water against the dragon's body.

It launched upward with a howl. Earth thudded loose all around them and Dahti ran, dragging Huwat behind her. Rashat, with more years behind his training, maintained the water around the dragon's body for longer but in the end, even he failed. What remained fell as rain or hissed into the air as steam.

The beast, still airborne, twisted and shook itself to dispel the last of the water. Its skin was smoking, the same, unhealthy gray Dahti had seen on the water dragon. It was as if the fire had burned itself to ash.

"Get ready," Rashat called to them. "It knows we can defeat it now. It will no longer toy with us."

He was right. The dragon landed so heavily that it skidded across the ground. The orcs stumbled to keep their footing and lost it in the next moment when the massive wings beat heavily before they settled over its wounded sides. Its head swept from one side to the other and fire blazed into the grass and ignited it behind them.

"Great," she muttered.

It attacked, swiping its front paws left and right along with its tail and wings. Between the heavy swipes and the fire, Dahti was less concerned with throwing spells and more concerned with diving to get out of the way. Every time she could, however, she dropped piles of sand onto the flames and she noticed that Rashat was doing the same with water.

A storm cloud opened over them with a hollow rumble. Clouds swirled out of nowhere and rain poured to drench them to the bone. The dragon roared its displeasure, and in the sudden darkness, all Dahti could see was the glittering around its scales and the flame of its breath.

Even Rashat could not summon a storm indefinitely and the rain cleared after a moment, although the creature's movements were more sluggish now and it stumbled when it walked. It blew a furious breath at the shaman, who cloaked himself in water to withstand it, and it turned and slunk away.

It was limping and seemed almost pitiful, but she felt a sudden prickle of unease.

"*Now*," Rashat urged the other two. "Now, we must kill it! Go!"

It seemed wrong, too easy—and yet, with its scales smoking and holes opened in its wings, she didn't know when they would get another chance.

"Mud," she called to Rashat. He hesitated, then nodded.

The two of them readied their magic together. She was almost drained and he remained in control, and they pressed their hands out at the same time. Their power mingled and the heavy wave of mud swept toward the dragon.

In the split-second when the spell broke from their hands, it launched into the air and circled. It uttered a hunting cry like the screech of a hawk before it dived to bowl into the group. Dahti dragged Rashat sideways and the shaman snarled his anger.

"Don't react!" she called.

"No!" He wrenched himself free. "I can end this now."

"Wait! It's a—"

She didn't have time to say the word "trap" as the long tail lashed out and caught him in the torso. The shaman was lifted and pounded onto the earth, and when the tail lifted away, blue blood poured from a wound.

"*Rashat!*" she screamed.

Behind her, the creature stamped and roared. Slowly, Dahti and Huwat turned. Its breath turned the air before it into a ripple of heat and its lips curved in a smile to show its teeth.

"Now that I've dealt with the troublesome one," it hissed, "shall we finish this?"

CHAPTER FIFTY-FIVE

Rage coursed through Dahti. "Huwat." Her voice was quiet. "Go make sure he's stable. I'll keep the dragon's attention."

She sensed that he was about to argue but a look from her stopped him. He nodded jerkily and circled behind the beast, which watched him curiously. But, as she expected, it knew his powers against it were limited.

Instead of following him, it advanced on her and she backed away.

"So..." Its voice was soft now, a caress. "You're sent from another world?"

Her fear receded somewhat at that and she drew herself tall. "Yes. A hero of my land came here and recognized the need. He has called us to help this world—and your kind happens to be one of the things that need fixing."

It hissed laughter through its nose. "Oh, how interesting. When one of our patriarchs helps your kind, you do not mind the meddling, do you? But when we ask for something in return—"

"When have you ever helped?" she interjected. "Don't say you brought the beasts. I know that's a lie. Your kind divided the tribes."

"And what of those who came before?" it countered. The large head lunged closer to her and she could feel its anger like a sickness in the air. "Those who gave their lives and their magic to protect your kind, to bring them wisdom, and to hold them at peace?"

"Peace?" Dahti did not understand. "Which of them died to protect us?"

"Oh! So you do not even know the history and still, you judge us." The dragon reared, thumped down once more, and snickered when she stumbled. She backed away and saw out of the corner of her eye that Huwat knelt at Rashat's side.

"Please let him be alive," she muttered. "Please."

"What did you say?" the creature demanded.

"I said…" Dahti swallowed. "Tell me this history, then. You didn't care if we knew it when you divided the tribes."

"We used your ignorance and short memories to our advantage." It sniffed. "There is a difference."

"Two sides of the same blade—and you still used it to cut!" She wished like hell she had Lyle with her right now. He would know what to do, while she seemed to only manage to enter into a shouting match.

Careful to keep her expression from mirroring her intent, she readied the power of earth—chilled and as hard as iron, lying frozen in the fallow times of the year. She wouldn't be pulled off-course with vague suggestions. The dragons had misled and preyed on the orcs for centuries and certainly weren't above lying.

But her adversary wasn't ready to let it go. It leaned down and its nostrils flared. "Have your kind *entirely* forgotten about the founding of Yn'si?"

"Insea?" she repeated.

"Such a mangling of the name. At least the elves could pronounce it." Its tail lashed.

"There was a dragon at Insea?" Dahti asked and ignored the insult.

The tail lashed again and the beast roared. "Of course, there was a dragon! How do you think the city was built? How do you think it has been at peace since its founding?"

"I…" She shrugged. "I heard it was spells inscribed on the bedrock."

"Spells!" The dragon's fury only increased. "You know nothing, orc

—*nothing*! Your kind have erased us from memory! What we did here is only because the truth was forgotten."

"If it was forgotten, you can hardly blame these orcs for not knowing it!" she yelled in response. "Dress it up all you like, *dragon*. Your kind has lied and cheated and preyed upon these people for centuries. Nothing justifies it. Not even the one life you have to give would be justice."

"Not if you take it, no." It tilted its head at her. "But I could give you so much."

Dahti straightened. She was weary in every fiber of her being. "But you won't," she said. "Whatever bargains you say were made for Insea, you won't tell me. You'll keep whispering suggestions and letting me fill the blanks in on my own. You'll never let me live. You know I know magic that can kill you so you'll strike me down and hope the fire tribe never learns the truth of what you are. Well, it's too late."

The words had barely left her mouth before the dragon screamed. It backed away from her and clawed at its chest.

Dahti looked around herself in consternation. Huwat advanced on the creature, his staff raised.

"Fire burns," he intoned. "Fire expands. Heat billows." Again, he gestured and again, the dragon clawed at its chest.

Dahti held her hand over her mouth. The shaman was using the fire *within* the dragon to explode it from the inside out. Queasily, she readied herself and gave him something to work with.

"Huwat," she called. "Fire burns stone as well."

Stone-shock exploded from her fingertips. She could not see the spear of rock but from the dragon's scream, it was buried in its chest. It writhed and in the next moment, launched to twist and scream while he heated the shard of rock in its torso.

"This is torture!" she called to the shaman. "It's cruel!"

"We have no other way to end this." He looked at her and shook his head. "It sent its brood to terrorize us for generations. Don't let short-sighted morals blind you to what must be done."

Dahti's hands clenched, but she knew he was right. How many had pleaded for their lives or sent their loved ones to die because the dragons claimed credit for things that were not their doing and sacrifices in recompense?

Never again. She had sworn it and she would make it true.

A ragged gasp of breath caught her attention. Rashat hauled himself to his feet. The wound on his chest had stopped bleeding and wasn't as deep as she first thought. Still, he was pale and he had lost too much blood to be in this fight.

"Stay back!" she called. She knew how to end this.

He shook his head. "You've never seen what happens when you fail to kill a god," he told her. "And I swear I would rather die a hundred times than live that devastation again. If I go to my death, so be it!"

The water shaman limped forward and the dragon writhed in the air and focused its gaze on its most dangerous enemy. It shrieked again.

If I go to my death, so be it. The words sparked something in Dahti's mind and the idea emerged an instant later. She knew how to do this —and she also knew the cost. Hastily, she reached out to grab Huwat, who was running toward the other shaman. "Stay back!"

"I can't let him die!" he called wildly. He tried to free himself. "I am nothing. I have apprentices—he is the best of us!"

"*Neither* of you will die!" Dahti told him sharply. "Stay. Here. Your tribe needs you."

While he might not know what she was planning, he saw where it was leading. He went pale. "*Your* tribe—"

"Is not of this world," Dahti said. Her heart thudded in her chest and she could barely hear her thoughts. Would she truly do this? She was dizzy with fear and recalled the warnings and what could happen if she died in the game.

And she remembered that they needed this data. Those of her world needed it and those of this world needed their shamans left alive.

She ran. Wind ruffled her hair behind her and she drew on the strength of this body, the strong pump of her heart, and the pound of her feet on the ground. She sprinted to Rashat and everything zeroed in on the impending confrontation—the blue-skinned orc and the fire dragon, the once-in-a-millennium shaman and the godspring.

"Prima!" she called over the sound of the wind.

"Yes?"

"The block—the one that keeps my character from dying."

The AI said nothing.

"Remove it!" she called. "You can, can't you? I *need* to do this. They need me and the game needs me. You know it. *Remove the block!"*

The pause wasn't one she could worry about. She was closer now and she wasn't sure she would make it.

"It's done," Prima said finally. She sounded sad. *"Dotty, are you sure—"*

"I'm sure," she told her. "Take good care of them, Prima."

"Who?"

"All of them—the ones who come after me and the ones who live in you."

She shoved Rashat out of the way and he fell, crying out to her to let him do this, but she would not. The world could not spare him and she would not stop.

And water could *quench* fire, yes, but stone could absorb it.

Dahti had time for one moment of fear—of pain and the unknown —before she faced the swooping beast, spread her arms, and let the massive stone spike spear through the earth and impale them both.

The dragon's scream echoed shrilly before all sound ceased.

CHAPTER FIFTY-SIX

Dotty felt something that seemed very much like a pinch on her finger.

She hadn't fully considered what death would feel like, but she was fairly sure this wasn't what she'd expected. Especially not from a giant spike of stone.

The pinch persisted for a moment, then ended. Her next attempt to make sense of things settled on a band around her chest.

That seemed more in line with what she might expect.

The draft that followed plunged her into confusion again. Given the fire and the stone, that didn't seem right.

Finally, she opened her eyes. She was not, it appeared, dead—at least, not unless the afterlife had fluorescent lighting and tile ceilings. Also, worried faces stared at her.

"Hello?" she ventured.

"Oh, thank God," Amber said. When she tried to sit up, the young woman put a hand on her shoulder. "Lie still for a while. Last time we brought you out in a much more…uh, planned way. Give your body time to acclimate."

"Very well." She raised an eyebrow. "Did it work?"

"You're still alive," the engineer said testily.

"No, in the *game.* Did it work? Did I kill the dragon?"

"Oh." Amber sighed. "Yes, it worked. You also nearly gave us heart failure…by almost giving *yourself* heart failure."

"Mmm." Dotty couldn't bring herself to be too upset. Indeed, she felt a certain satisfaction. "Could I have a blanket, please?"

"Of course." The woman's face disappeared and warmth settled over her legs and torso. "Is that good?"

"Why can't I move my arms?" she asked in alarm. Thoughts of the dragon disappeared for the present.

"Ah—the paralytic agent is wearing off. Like sleep paralysis? We use it to make sure you don't flail and…uh, break your hand on the inside of the pod or anything."

She realized now that she was not in the pod. The surface below her was much softer and her head was clearly on a pillow. She attempted to look around, remembered she could not move, and settled for trying to sense her various limbs.

"We moved you out of the pod as soon as you were stable," Amber said soothingly, "and decided to wake you to check in since now would be a good time to change avatar bodies if you wanted to do so."

"I died in the game," Dotty said quietly. The thought had suddenly occurred to her that she would not see Huwat or Rashat again, nor would she see Atra or Jumper. She would not get to see how the tribes recovered from this.

"Yes." Thankfully, the woman did not seem inclined to make fun of her sadness. She sighed. "You made a very selfless sacrifice."

She shrugged. That was new. She could shrug again. When she felt an old, familiar pain in her stomach, she sighed.

"I mean it," Amber said. "I know I sounded annoyed before, but… don't think we don't see what you did for the characters *and* for us."

"We…feel a little guilty," Jacob's voice said. He swam into view next to his colleague. "If we'd realized—"

"What, that I would ask Prima to let me die?"

"Yes," he said dryly. "That." He sat and she turned her head to look at him. "You don't need to take that kind of risk. We would never have asked it of you."

"Better me than…" She realized how tired she was. "Well, some young whippersnapper."

The two merely smiled.

Amber took her hand and the pressure there made her realize what she'd felt—it was the pulse oximeter on her finger. "Dotty, you're very precious to all of us. We don't want you to die before your time simply for the data's sake." She bit her lip. "Your health is fragile. We want you to be happy."

"Young lady, if you'll recall, I came here *because* my health was fragile." She raised her eyebrows. "The entire point was that this *was* my time."

Then she saw the look in their eyes. "What is it?"

"It's—Ellen is on her way," Amber said. Hastily, she added, "Everything is fine with your family, don't worry."

"Hmph." Dotty shook her head. "Well, could I get a glass of water, then? Maybe something to eat?"

"Yes, we'll…ah, we'll prop the bed up." She bustled around with Jacob, picking up parts of the mattress and changing the orientation of the bed. Neither of them would look her in the eye, though.

And she had a fairly good idea why. She held her tongue, not wanting to make them uncomfortable. Young people often were when it came to death. She wanted to comfort them and tell them it would be okay, but she wasn't sure it was her place.

When she heard Ellen come in, she was staring vaguely at the wall. The taste of metal was back in her mouth and, as the paralytics wore off, she could tell that her muscles were noticeably weaker. She greeted her daughter with a smile. "Hello, dear."

"Mum. The others are on their way." Ellen sat and took her hand. She was smiling—or trying to. Tears were gathering in her eyes.

"The scans from the oncologist came back, didn't they?" Dotty asked her.

Ellen's chin trembled. "Yes," she managed to say. She wiped her eye. "Yes, they did."

"Oh, dear heart." Dotty patted her hand.

"You haven't called me that in ages." The woman's lips twitched. "Since I was a teenager, I think."

She clutched her daughter's fingers. "Ellen. You know it will be okay."

"But I—" She drew a deep, shuddering breath. "But I don't. I still miss Dad all the time, and *you*—it seems like yesterday we found out you had cancer in the first place." She lowered her head as she tried to regain her composure, but Dotty could feel her daughter grasping her hand like a lifeline.

She waited quietly.

Ellen's head came up. "And *you're* comforting *me*! That's not right."

"Why not?" she asked, amused. "That's what mothers do, isn't it?" She wiped a tear from Ellen's cheek. "I'm not scared, darling. I'm sad to be leaving all of you but I'm not scared." She looked up as the others entered the room.

The assistants and PIVOT team members had all managed to disappear except for Jacob, who hovered in the corner and tried valiantly to not eavesdrop. She smiled at his back. He was a good kid.

She really *was* getting old, wasn't she?

Once she'd greeted her children and their spouses, she told them she had guessed what was going on. It was clear from the symptoms when she came out of the virtual world that the cancer had progressed, and Ellen's response had only confirmed it.

They crowded around the bed and she saw many suspiciously bright eyes.

"So," she said finally, "is this the part where you tell me I absolutely need to come home now?"

All of them looked at each other and finally at her. John shook his head. "No, Mom. We ah—well, *Ellen* had an idea for a present and we thought we'd show it to you. That was before we heard about the scans, but I think maybe it's still a good idea."

Dotty looked curiously at them.

Ellen now looked deeply nervous. "Mom, you remember how... when you said you'd spent all that time worrying about your looks and how you wanted to be ugly in the game so you could simply do what you wanted?"

She laughed and clutched her stomach. "Oh, that hurts. Yes, I remember, dear heart."

"We've heard all about what you're doing," she continued. "We've even seen some of it. They showed us clips from when you fought that dragon."

"Oh, they *did?*" She raised an eyebrow. "As long as they didn't show you clips of me dancing, I'm all right with that."

A few throats were cleared and several people looked away from her.

"Wonderful," she muttered. "I'll have you know, I'm perfectly good at *other* dances."

"Yes, Mom." John patted her hand.

"Anyway," Ellen said. "The point is, you've been this big hero and we know you love being in the game, so we assumed you'd want to go in again. We wanted to give you an avatar you'd *really* like."

Dotty stared at her. "Ah…well, color me intrigued, as your grandfather would have said."

Jacob stepped forward to hand Ellen a laptop, and she looked at the screen before she smiled at her mother.

"See, Mom," she said and her voice shook. "The thing is…you *are* the person you wanted to be. You are that hero. Maybe we didn't picture you killing dragons and all that, but we all knew you could do this. We knew you'd get into that virtual world and go kick butt and give good advice. So we wanted you to see…well…we wanted you to see yourself the way *we* see you."

She turned the laptop and Dotty put a hand over her mouth.

The avatar was her as she had been in her twenties. Her hair was braided the way it had been on her wedding day, and everything from the smile to the way it walked was exactly as she remembered it. She touched the screen tentatively and realized she was crying.

"I know you wanted to be ugly, Mom," Ellen told her, and she could barely get the words out, "but we wanted you to see that you could still be the hero with your own face."

John squeezed his mother's hand. "You always did love those books you confiscated from my room—with dragons and spaceships and all that. Now you get to have some of those adventures as *you*."

Dotty had always tried not to cry in front of her children. She wanted them to feel safe in her care—that, and she'd been raised in an era where too much emotion was considered lowbrow. But now, she cried and could not seem to stop. She covered her face with her hands and felt her children come around her with huge hugs. Sniffling sounds told her the others were crying, too.

When at last she leaned back, she was still not sure she could speak.

"Jacob left," Ellen said. "He wanted to give us privacy. But you should know how much work those three put into this avatar."

"Ellen wouldn't tell us why," Robert said, "but she made all of us dig out our home movies and our pictures of you. We brought them in and the PIVOT team made this from scratch. We couldn't believe it when we saw it."

Dotty stared at the picture on the screen and felt the tears welling up again. She flapped her hands for them to close the screen.

"Oh," she said finally. She looked at all of them. "Thank you. This is the most wonderful present. Can I ask one more thing?"

"Of course," John said. All of them leaned close.

"I want as many of you to visit as possible," she said. "All of you, if you can. Obviously not the little ones, but…well, all the adults."

"That's good because we intend to," Robert told her. "Ellen hasn't shut up about it since she went in, and I'm curious."

His sister punched him on the arm with a little smile.

"We promise," Mary told her. She smiled. "And you know, maybe we'll keep some of those videos of you slaying dragons. I think the kids would love to see them when they're older and learn how Great-grandma Dotty was a hero."

Dotty waved a hand at her, but she had to admit, the idea wasn't a bad one.

Her stomach growled loudly enough for everyone to hear.

"Should we get a pizza?" John suggested.

"*Yes,*" she said.

Pizza was ordered, and the group chatted on and off while researchers returned to pack up their desks for the night. A few waved at Dotty and she called her thanks to the PIVOT team as they headed out. Clearly embarrassed at all the attention, they blushed and left hastily to return only later when her family at last said their goodnights.

The next day and a half passed in a whirlwind. Her oncologist and primary physician came to check on her and glower at the PIVOT team—something she did *not* approve of—and reluctantly signed off on her continued participation in the study.

While she hadn't needed their permission, she hoped their participation would help their other clients in the future.

She had a last round of video calls with the great-grandchildren, all of whom waved and blew kisses, and between calls, she cried her eyes out. She had told Ellen that she wasn't scared and it was true, but she *would* miss them. It had been a very great blessing, she thought now, to watch so many members of her family grow up.

When at last she settled into the pod, however, she felt clear-headed and happy. Her body was beginning to fail and the pain grew worse. She had never expected to have a gift that allowed her to spend her remaining time feeling strong and healthy.

The black of her closed eyes gave way to beautiful rose quartz and sunlight.

"Insea," Dotty said delightedly. "Will I solve the mystery of Insea's founding?"

"*You said you wanted someplace with good food,*" Prima told her. "*And, yes.*"

"Oh, good—and I did. So, Prima. Should we have a last adventure together?"

"*Yes. I've made a really good one.*"

"I look forward to it."

PART III

The first time Dotty had been in Insea, her avatar had been a young dwarven woman, a caravan guard who knew little about the world around her. She had soaked up the legends of the city—and had done her damnedest to eat her way through every food stand she could find.

She hadn't come close.

This time, she was determined to rectify that. When she swept out of the alley she'd materialized in, she hurried directly to the nearest food stall, which wafted smells of something spiced and fried.

As she walked, she noticed people turn to look at her, and only then did she notice her outfit. It could be defined as "a red dress," but the phrase didn't do the garment justice. It could be more accurately termed a construction rather than a garment, although she thought *contraption* might also work. She raised one glittering hand and layers of sheer silk fell away from her arm while others—tethered to her jeweled bracelets and rings—billowed prettily.

She spent so much time admiring the elegant fall of her sleeves that it took a gust of wind for her to notice the front of her dress.

There wasn't much of one, unfortunately.

"Prima," she said before she could stop herself. Several people looked at her with interest and she whisked herself into an alley.

"*What?*" the AI asked. "*I think you look nice. I looked up all kinds of costumes from fantasy games so I could make you a good one. I even toned it down for you.*"

"This…is what you would call toned down?" She stared at the diamonds, the silk, the gold thread, and the exposed skin. If it weren't so perfectly warm in Insea, she would have noticed all of this much sooner.

"*I could show you some reference art. Would you prefer something more practical?*"

Dotty was about to snap that yes, of course, she wanted something more practical. However, several ideas came to her in close succession.

"Is it possible for the dress to fall or…come off or anything?"

"*You can take it off if that's what you mean.*"

"I *mean*, will it flutter in the breeze and show everyone in Insea… well, everything?"

"*Oh. No. All the pieces that need to stay on will do so. You see how the sleeves are off your shoulders but they don't slide down? I was very proud of that.*"

"I was worried about the pieces closer to the center," she muttered, "but yes, I do see that. Er, could I have a mirror?"

"*Done,*" Prima said promptly. A mirror appeared, suspended in midair in the narrow area.

She turned and examined her dress as she did so. Red silk clung to her torso and draped from her hips in perfect folds that billowed and swirled as she moved. Her arms, if held at her sides, were shielded by capelike sleeves of sheer silk attached to her upper arms with tiny diamonds. This being a video game, there did not need to be any unpleasant adhesive or biting hems.

The AI had remembered all her favorites for combat as well. Two sheaths of metal across her forearms looked purely ornamental like faux armor, but when she looked closer, she saw that the decorative flourishes hid two long, wickedly sharp daggers with ornate hilts at her elbows. She drew them both at once and they came out whisper-quiet.

Good. She had discovered a talent for magic, not to mention a love of it, but it was always wise for a lady to be armed. As far as she was concerned, her grandmother—who had been fond of saying that all a lady needed for armor was good manners—could kick rocks.

Gems glittered at her fingers, neck, and ears, and her golden-brown hair was held back in a crown of braids. The hairstyle was the same as she had worn on her wedding day, but she hadn't had rubies and golden pearls woven into it on that occasion.

The woman in the mirror blushed.

"You should say it," Prima said.

"Say what?"

"That you look good."

Unexpectedly, tears trembled on her lashes. Harry had told her that she looked beautiful every morning and had said the same things as Prima. He wanted her to say it, too. Dotty, as she had done every morning while Harry was alive, shook her head wordlessly but she was smiling.

"You are smiling and also sad?"

"Yes, Prima." Dotty made another turn in front of the mirror—it *was* fun to have a dress that swished, no matter how scandalous it might be—and stepped out of the alley.

The smell of food was driving her *crazy*.

What she finally walked away with was a paper cone filled with a jumble of things that seemed to include fried potatoes, corn, onions, and peppers, although that seemed to be only the start of the ingredients. She held it carefully away from her dress.

"Yes," the AI said before she could ask, *"you can spill on it and I'll make sure it doesn't get dirty."*

"You're wonderful," she replied with her mouth already full. "Oh. Hot. Oof."

"Too spicy?"

"No, not after the orc village." In her second incarnation within the world of PIVOT, she had spent time as an orc. The range of orcish foods included far too much dried fish, as well as a stew that was spicy enough to make her pray for death. She took another bite of the potato mixture. "This is merely hot—temperature-wise. Oooh. I like this."

She ate as she strolled. The potato was soft on the inside, gloriously fried on the outside, and deliciously mingled with other pieces of vegetable. She only wished she had pan bread to eat with it. Before long, it was finished and she looked around for a trash bin.

Did fantasy cities *have* trash bins?

Slowly, she pivoted and looked at the street corners. She located nothing close by, but she had passed a little park a few streets back. Perhaps she should go there and check. She stood out of the way of a carriage, rolled her eyes at the rude yells from the driver and the extravagantly-dressed noble inside, and set off.

While she was at it, she should look for another snack. Dotty licked her fingers as she walked. The shoes Prima had given her were made of the same red silk and managed to not pinch her feet at all. In the real world, her feet *always* pinched in shoes, but she was more than happy to not have the game be accurate in this regard. There were certain aspects of her youth she wasn't keen to relive.

One street over from the park, she saw an alley that cut through into a shaded arbor. She ducked into the narrow space, thanking whoever had come up with the idea of a city made of one block of stone. It meant alleys without puddles or crumbling paving stones.

Two men stepped out of an alcove and she stopped in her tracks, her skirts swirling around her. This wasn't the Insea she'd experienced before. Now that she thought about it, though, she remembered the way the other citizens had looked at her—unfriendly and even annoyed. There were so many bodyguards now and people on street corners in ragged clothes. She had seen bands of armed soldiers with no livery—mercenaries for hire, she realized, and none of them seemed to be short of coin.

What had happened there?

"Look, Eto," one of them said to the other. "It's a noblewoman out for a midday stroll." His head was shaved and his beard was very neat

—which made the scar that ran through it all the more noteworthy. Dotty could see the muscles beneath his clothes.

"What a kind thing," the other one said. He was taller, with eyes that were so heavy-lidded, they seemed to disappear. Like the other man, he kept his beard neat. He strolled toward her. "It's nice for the nobles to show us how they live, don't you think, Jel?"

"That I do, Eto. That I do." The man with the black beard circled her. He extended his hand to touch the diamonds. "What a beautiful dress—on a beautiful lady, of course."

"Thank you," she said icily.

Both men laughed.

"There now, little lady," Jel said. "There's no need to take that tone. We're merely admirers." He drew a dagger slowly out of one sleeve and took care to let it ring against the sheath. "So, why don't we keep this pleasant, hmm? Hand your purse over."

She took one slow step back. Jel followed equally as slowly.

"You really shouldn't do this," she told him. "I don't think it will stay pleasant."

"Is she threatening us?" he asked Eto.

"You know, I think she is," his comrade replied and strolled past him toward the mouth of the alleyway. "And here we were being so nice to her. Right, Jel? Jel?"

He turned and his jaw dropped. His partner knelt on the ground, wheezing. Both hands clutched his groin—a gesture that had come rather too late—and he tried to catch his breath but failed miserably. Dotty folded her arms and stared at Eto. Her blood was thrumming now.

"I told you," she said quietly, "that you shouldn't do this. I told you it wouldn't stay pleasant."

"Why, you little—" He charged.

She waited until the last possible moment before she leapt sideways over Jel's bent form. The daggers whipped out of their sheathes without a single sound and when she turned, the man had already surged into an attack.

He saw the weapons barely in time to throw himself sideways and she stalked after him. As he scrabbled for his blade, she tripped him. When he sprawled and his fingers located the hilt of the dagger and closed around it, a chunk of mud materialized from nowhere and covered both hand and knife. Eto screamed and the mud vanished, taking the knife with it.

Jel, who seemed to be under the very mistaken impression that he had the element of surprise, uttered a battle cry and lunged at her, knife-first.

He took a dagger to the forearm for his troubles and lost his balance to land hardf. The battle froze into a moment of shocked stillness.

Dotty stomped on his fingers to make him release his weapon and kicked it away. She wrenched hers out of his arm, eliciting a high-pitched scream, and bent slightly to look him in the eyes.

"What's your name? Jel *what*?"

"Jel Estrim." He scrabbled away on his elbows and his knees, trying to clap one hand over the wound in his arm.

"And *you*," she said, rounding on Eto.

He had tried to sneak up on her, his hands extended to grasp her arms, but he held them up in surrender and leapt back with a shriek.

She stared at him for a moment and tried desperately not to laugh. "And you?" she asked when she was relatively certain she could keep her face straight. "What's *your* surname, *Eto*?"

"Kleim," he said before he winced. He had no doubt been determined to lie and had then forgotten to do so.

As she looked at the other knives, each of them disappeared into a ball of mud and crumbled to dust.

"Well, Mr. Estrim, Mr. Kleim. I suggest you leave before you make anyone else's day unpleasant. In fact, I suggest you *never* make anyone's day unpleasant like this again. If you do—"

"You'll hunt us," Eto snapped. He hauled Jel up and elicited a pained gurgle from his friend. "Yeah, we know."

"Oh, I won't only do that," she said. "I'll not only beat the *crap* out of you myself, I'll track your grandmothers and tell them what you did."

Both of them went white, and she sheathed her weapons again and brushed her dress off before she picked up the wad of paper.

"What are you doing?" Eto asked.

"I'm picking up after myself instead of littering," she said, "because I am a *lady*." She swept toward her destination without looking back.

CHAPTER FIFTY-EIGHT

The park was, like everything in Insea, carved from the same single block of stone. Some of it was gray, some white, and some pinkish. In the park, it was a golden-white, fashioned into flower beds for real flowers and trees, with little streams running away from a fountain and four statues at the cardinal points on the circular path. Each statue depicted a figure—one orc, one elf, one dwarf, and one human. There were no inscriptions, however, to say if these merely depicted the races or were particular figures from history.

Dotty paused for a moment to look at the orc, a woman holding her arm up either to catch or release a falcon, her hair ornately braided and a leather strap with a claw around her neck. Her dress was nothing like she had seen in the orcish villages she had visited, but a great deal had changed amongst the orcs in the past few centuries.

She found a trash bin—which disappeared conveniently as soon as she had thrown the paper away—and sat on a bench to think things over. It occurred to her that she wasn't entirely sure if she was annoyed that she had been mugged or amused at how the attempt had ended.

Lost in thought, she proceeded to fall off the end of the bench with a yelp of surprise when Justin said, "*Dotty?*"

He rushed to help her up. "Sorry! Sorry." His wide-eyed gaze took in the dress, the hair, and the much younger avatar. "Uh…you look, that is to say…um, no disrespect meant—Tina?"

His girlfriend, who was eating a pizza-esque item, stopped chewing long enough to say, "Nah, it's gonna be much more fun to watch you try to work your way out of this on your own." She swallowed her mouthful. "Hi, Dotty."

"Hello, Tina." She looked at Justin again. "You were saying?"

He was, luckily for him, saved by the arrival of Lyle Stout, a dwarf she had traveled with during her first incarnation in the PIVOT world. It was strange to look down at him instead of being the same height, but she was more concerned with how much she had missed him. Without thought, she threw her arms around him and gave him a hug.

After a moment, she pulled away and realized he was staring at her like she might be a lunatic.

"Do I…know you?" he asked cautiously.

"This is Dotty," Justin explained.

"How many friends do you *have* named Dotty?"

"Same Dotty," Tina confirmed.

"Dotty is…a dwarf." Lyle glanced at her feet as if searching for platform shoes. "She had a real figure the last time I saw her—nice, strong arms to heft a pick-ax and none of this wimpy elf or human business."

"You'd like orcs," Dotty said.

"I've always thought I'd like orcs," he agreed and looked suspiciously at her. "Seriously, though, who are you?"

"*Seriously*, I'm Dotty. We first met in Berghold, you trained me on the way to Insea, and I fell into a coma after our fight with the elven riders. We interrogated a diplomat together—"

"Shhhh," the dwarf said and waved his hands. "Nothing about that." She stared at him.

"For legal reasons," Justin said gravely. "Councilor Marwitz was killed during the battle between the elves and the dwarven caravan. Multiple witnesses saw him stabbed by the elven commander."

"Ah," she said. "You learn something new every day, I guess."

"It *is* you, isn't it?" Lyle said finally. "You look…different."

"Don't you agree, Justin?" Tina asked innocently from a bench.

He darted her a look and she grinned at him.

"I'm sorry we're late," a new voice said. Dotty turned to see a young woman with dark hair and leather armor with a man in robes trailing in her wake. "Kural wanted to stop and examine a security spell at one of the weapons shops."

"It was fascinating," Kural said excitedly. "It kept the weapons from being used to harm any of the store's employees—*or* bystanders—but not from being used to harm robbers. You know, I've always said that many of the significant developments in magic come from the commercial sector, not only academia."

"That's nice," Zaara said firmly. She nodded to Dotty. "I'm sorry, you've never met us. I'm Zaara, and this very vague man is Kural, my mentor and a wizard of some renown."

Kural, who had stooped to examine a glyph carved on the bench, straightened for a moment with a wounded expression. "*Some* renown?"

"You'd probably have more if you hadn't spent five years wandering in various disguises," Zaara said, unimpressed by the wounded puppy expression. She looked at Dotty. "Sorry about that. What did you say your name was?"

"We've met, actually," Dotty said. "We fought a fire dragon together. I looked a little different at the time."

The woman's jaw dropped. She looked at her, then at Justin and Lyle, who both nodded. "Oh. Ah. Wow. Okay. Well, it's good to meet you. Again. So, why are we all here?"

"Dotty called us all here," Justin said.

"I did?"

"*Yes, you did,*" Prima said helpfully.

"Yes, I did," she said. She cleared her throat. "Has anyone noticed anything…uh, strange…about Insea?"

"Well, *I* noticed a woman in a red dress kicking the crap out of some muggers," Tina said. She gave her a wink.

"Yes, precisely," she said. "There weren't muggers the last time I was here."

"I don't remember any either," Justin said with a frown. "Callie and Dex were fairly nasty, but it's not like they jumped people in alleys."

"Only in arenas," Tina said, and Dotty was surprised to see her looking deeply angry. There was clearly a story there, but she knew she didn't have time to ask about it.

She filed it away for later and looked at the others. Kural was frowning, although whether it was about this topic or something entirely different, she could not have said. Lyle looked troubled but offered no input besides nodding when Justin spoke.

"There shouldn't be any crime," Zaara said slowly. "Insea is *famously* safe. It's one of the reasons my father wanted me to marry a noble here. He said I could go wandering as much as I wanted and not have to worry about being hurt."

"Well, it would seem he was wrong." Dotty settled on a bench and looked at all of them.

"He *wasn't*," the woman said.

"I just got mugged," Dotty told her. "Tina can corroborate—"

"Ugh," Tina groaned. "Lawyer talk."

"What I *meant*," Zaara said impatiently, "is that when my father said that, it was true."

"So, what happened?" No one seemed to have an immediate answer. "A mass exodus of the city guard?"

Everyone looked at one another before Lyle said, "There's never been a city guard."

"What?" She studied their matching expressions in disbelief. They all seemed fairly sure of the idea, but as far as she could tell, the very concept was cuckoo. A city with no police force?

"Insea has never had an army," Zaara explained. "*Or* a city guard. There are guards in the palace—"

This was familiar ground, and she jumped on it. "For the king? Queen? Person?"

"King," the woman said. She pressed her lips together. "But I don't know, to be honest. No one has ever seen the king."

"No one has...*ever*...seen the king?" Dotty asked. She must be mistaken about what she had heard.

She wasn't, though, because everyone nodded.

"Well, this puts the other elven faction into perspective," Dotty told Lyle. Their first adventure together had involved the yearly shipment of magical goods from Berghold to Insea, an ongoing gesture of thanks from the dwarves to the elves. As far as anyone knew, the elves had enlisted the dwarves' help to build Insea and had then taught the same magic to the dwarves, who used it to build Berghold.

But if the ruler of Insea had never been seen, it made a great deal of sense why a new faction of elves would jockey for power. In fact, she thought, it was more interesting that it hadn't happened sooner—a fact she shared, only to get blank looks from Lyle, Zaara, and Kural.

"It's always been like that," Zaara said.

"No visible monarch, no guards, no army, and no wars," Dotty said. She looked at Justin and Tina, who both frowned in consternation. That was a relief, as she had begun to feel like she was going crazy. "And you never thought that was weird?"

"Well, think about it," Lyle said. "It's not easy to get an army to Insea with those narrow roads."

"Yeah, you told me that last time. It doesn't make sense, though. Insea isn't equipped for defense, there's no strong government in place, and no one is visibly running it at all. Why hasn't anyone tried to take it over? Hell, why haven't the *nobles* staged a coup?"

"I..." The three natives of the game shrugged their shoulders.

"One moment." She turned and raised an eyebrow at the sky. "Prima, the answer doesn't happen to be that all of them are morons, does it?"

"*No.*" The AI laughed.

"I merely wanted to make sure," she said. She pivoted to the others again. "Okay. You all seem like a group of fairly smart people."

"*And Justin,*" Prima interjected.

"Hey!" he protested.

Dotty struggled to not laugh. "Do other nations have wars?" she asked.

"Well, yes," Lyle said.

"Merely not Insea," she said and waited for the nods. "So doesn't it strike you as odd that there's never been any strife related to Insea? And more to the point, that *none of you think it's weird?*"

An awestruck silence followed her challenge. Dotty exchanged a look with Tina, who contemplatively consumed what seemed to be a magically regenerating slice of pizza. She would have to ask her where to get some of that.

"But now," Kural said slowly, "something is happening."

"Yes," she confirmed.

"Which is why the Master of Ceremonies is trying to train the populace of Insea to serve as warriors," Justin said suddenly. "He said he needed me. After the championship, he said I must find more warriors from my land."

"So the Master of Ceremonies knew something was coming," Dotty said thoughtfully, "and now, things are starting to go wrong in large and small ways all across the world. And there's one thing none of the rest of you know, I think."

In quick strokes, she outlined the story she had heard from the dragons she fought near the orcish village. At some point, centuries before, several dragons had decided to pose as gods. They divided the tribes and made the orcs offer regular sacrifices to them. Their claim was that this was justified and, when she explained to them that it was horseshit, they had told her another dragon had given its life for peace and prosperity in Insea.

When she finished, Kural leapt to his feet and began to pace. She opened her mouth with questions and Zaara waved frantically at her to be quiet. The other woman moved to whisper in her ear.

"He can be absolutely infuriating and he tends to focus on the wrong thing in a fight, but the man has been alive for over three hundred years, and he knows a *lot*. From experience, I'd say to let him think."

Dotty sat, waited, and twiddled her fingers. It felt a little weird to do that in this extraordinary dress. She felt as if she should hold a tiny crystal glass of a rare liqueur and glide around a ballroom but instead, there she was in a very staid, normal park with a strange group eating pizza and chatting about the downfall of the world.

"Here is my guess," Kural said at last. He linked his hands behind his back and began to pace in a much more measured way. "First, I should say that I can confirm the stories of Insea being founded by a dragon—let us not go into *how* I know, but I do know. However, I am beginning to think I missed some rather important details." He continued to walk, his hands behind his back. "There were many old stories of elven shamans who communed with dragons. Some of the stories are rather inappropriate, but *some*—"

"Wait…wait." Tina held a hand out. "Inappropriate *how*?"

Everyone looked at her.

"We all wondered," she said with great dignity. "But, fine. Be boring." She gestured at the wizard to continue.

"Some," he resumed with a sideways look at her, "were about dragons and elves going further in magic than either race had gone separately. I wonder if one such partnership fueled the creation of Insea. It would explain why the city has always been believed to be an elven creation and why the elves were able to teach some of the same magic to the dwarves. But it would also explain why this magic has not been replicated since. It needs not only a great deal of power but a truly extraordinary magician with an amazing amount of power."

Dotty looked around. "So…did the elf *kill* the dragon?"

"Oh, no," Kural assured her. "A dragon who could provide this much power would…hmm, how to explain it? I doubt there would be anything on earth that could compel it to do anything. No, what it did here, it did willingly—and I would guess that it not only helped create the spell but until recently, *maintained* it."

Everyone frowned.

"What happened recently?" Justin asked finally.

"I have no idea," the wizard said promptly. "There are a great many questions we have to answer, and if we are on the right track, I would say we have very little time in which to answer them. To the palace, everyone. At once."

"As long as we can stop for pizza," Dotty said.

"Agreed," Lyle chimed in.

Kural shook his head. "Fine. But you eat while we walk, and we also need to plan. We'll need to infiltrate the castle."

"I'll help," the dwarf said.

Everyone winced.

"You're not..." Justin said and seemed to try to be diplomatic. "Um..."

"We all have our strengths," Zaara said with a pained smile.

"And yours is *not* subtlety," Dotty said before the rest of the youngsters could tie themselves in any more knots.

"I know that," Lyle said. "That's why I'm offering to be the diversion."

They relaxed as one.

"Better," Justin said.

CHAPTER FIFTY-NINE

Nick took a big bite of his bagel as he wove between the pods in the lab. For the past few months, only one pod had been used at a time, excluding temporary visitors to the world of PIVOT. Right now, there were three patients with three more coming over the next few weeks, and the lab was already an almost unbearable crush.

Also, with all the monitoring equipment beeping, it sounded like a robot convention.

He flipped the second-to-last page of his printout and kept reading as he walked. He was finishing the bagel when he arrived at the row of desks that overlooked the labs. Amber and Jacob were already there, talking quietly over a cup of coffee, and DuBois was asleep at his desk.

The group had joked that they weren't sure if the doctor had a place to stay in New York, but they began to think the joke might be reality. They had started dropping increasingly desperate hints that they had pull-out couches and air mattresses available, but so far, he seemed perfectly content to sleep at his desk.

Maybe *he* was a robot, Nick thought. He rolled his desk chair to where his partners were. "Sorry I'm late. I thought I started at the normal time—"

"You aren't," Amber said. "We both got here early."

"Oh. That explains it." He shook the printout and poppy seeds from the bagel drifted to the floor. "So. Mattis file?"

"Right." Amber leaned forward to snatch her copy off the desk. "You said you had concerns?"

"We have three patients now," he pointed out, "and it is *over-whelming*. We had to institute a checklist for casual conversations to make sure we weren't talking about different people. It was a nightmare. I almost gave Jenna heart failure the other day when I was talking about Dotty and she was talking about Kyle. We have three more coming soon and this lab will be a circus. I honestly don't think we need another person right now."

She nodded and looked at Jacob for his input.

He rubbed his forehead wearily. "I can't argue with that. The thought of another person is…intimidating. I've literally had nightmares about adding the next three."

"Nightmares?" Amber said.

"Yeah. Kind of? I don't know. I dreamed I was stuck in this loop of doing the hourly readout checks and no one else was here. I kept going to start one and then remembered I hadn't finished the last and I never seemed to be done. Anyway, I woke up and threw up." He took a sip of coffee and stared into the distance. "I'm fairly sure my neighbor thinks I'm a junkie."

Nick snickered. "Yeah. So, that's my point. We don't need Jacob waking up in the middle of the night to hurl. He's already lost too much weight since we moved here."

"Yeah, I don't know what happened with that." He scratched at his chin, where there was a few days' worth of stubble.

"You're way too stressed," Amber said. She looked at Nick and gestured to herself. "We all are. Although if I could upgrade to the version of stress where you lose weight instead of gain it, I'd like to do that now, please."

"Seconded," Nick said glumly.

Jacob laughed and rubbed his head. "If you'd told me six months ago that I'd lose my mind because we had too *many* patients, I'd have said you were crazy."

"Agreed." She shook her head. "But we *are* taking on too much. I think we need to accept that we can't be involved in every case the same way. What that looks like, I don't know."

"We're engineers," he said morosely. "We should be where the data is."

Nick patted his hand. "We'll find a solution. So, are we agreed, though? We don't need another patient right now?"

"Well, I don't know." Jacob looked at his copy of the printout.

"Don't go all bleeding heart on me," his friend warned him.

"You're one to talk. Also, we…kind of run a company that rehabilitates people. The bleeding heart is a feature, not a bug."

"Okay," Nick grinned. "But if you keep losing weight like this, you only have a few weeks left before a stiff breeze can blow you away."

"Fair. We'll think of something." Jacob waved his hands. "In the meantime—mmf."

Amber had inserted a piece of a donut into his open mouth. Jacob stared at her and she shrugged. He grimaced, chewed, swallowed, and took the rest of it off her plate.

"As I was *saying*, I would say this case is about twenty-five percent bleeding heart and seventy-five percent rabid curiosity."

"So we're doing this?" Nick asked Amber. "We're doing the stupid thing and taking on more work?"

"Well, I…" She looked at him over the rim of her coffee cup. "Have we *ever* done the smart thing?"

"Fair." He pivoted to where the other man pinned pieces of paper onto a corkboard. "I guess we're doing this. At least it's an interesting case."

They were all interesting cases. That was what made it so difficult to say no to new applicants even when there was no hope in hell that the pods would help them. Not only were the variety of conditions interesting, the families had inevitably gone through an endless parade of specialists who hadn't been able to help and they were desperate.

Even when Nick knew he couldn't help, he *hated* sending the form letters to tell people so. He secretly thought it was the piece of the job that weighed most heavily on his friend. It was the ICU costs for his grandmother that had inspired them to use the pods for this in the first place, and he seemed to care about each potential case as if they were his own family.

Jacob had pinned a picture on the board—a girl with wavy dark hair and a small mouth, clearly uncomfortable in front of the camera as well as in her collared shirt and blazer, which looked like part of a school uniform.

Next to her, he pinned a picture of a boy with the same dark hair and eyes but otherwise, a very different face. Hers was a pale oval while his seemed to be all angles and planes.

"Taigan and Jamie Mattis," he announced.

"I thought they were twins."

"Not all twins are identical," Amber pointed out. "And…well, a boy and a girl won't be."

"I suppose so." Nick frowned.

"Taigan has a condition that literally has no name," Jacob said. "Since she was four years old, she's fallen into coma-like states. They vary in length between a couple of days and a few weeks, usually, although right now, she's in one that has gone on for five months."

Amber shook her head. "Those poor parents."

"Those poor siblings," Nick said.

"Her siblings?" She looked at him. "I guess. When I was little, I think I'd have given almost anything to have my brothers shut up for a couple of weeks." She paused. "Too dark? Are we allowed to joke about this?"

"I'll give it a pass," Jacob said wryly, "but I have a famously bad sense of humor so don't take my word for it."

"I merely mean," Nick said and drew their attention to him again, "that it's hard to be the sibling everyone forgets about. And she has a twin, so it's probably worse for him than it would be for a normal sibling. But don't they also have an older sister?"

"Yes." Amber flipped through the information and searched for the name. "Emilia. She's nineteen."

"Yeah," he said. "She's supposed to be in college, spreading her wings, and I bet when she calls home, all she hears about is her sister. I wouldn't be surprised if she's as resentful as hell."

"I hadn't thought of that." She chewed her lip.

"Yeah," Jacob said, "but that's also not something we can fix."

"I'm merely pointing it out." Nick scanned the notes. "I have to say, they don't seem very hopeful."

"At this point, why would they be?" the other man countered. "But I'll go out on a limb and guess that the twin heard about this and suggested it to them. He's a seventeen-year-old boy and probably the most likely one in the family to do more research on PIVOT. And if he wants to get involved—"

"What about the older sister?" Nick asked.

"Yeah, it could have been her, too." He shrugged. "Or maybe the mom or dad saw one of the interviews. We had a shit-ton of publicity. I merely…" He looked at the board. "The twin thing."

His partners exchanged a look.

"I think the twins might be a key to each other," Jacob said. "On the face of it, this isn't something we can expect to fix, right? It's a chronic condition. But this has been five months and she isn't coming out. Even if it's getting worse, even if we *can't* fix it, we can give them a way to communicate with her and her a way to not be locked in. And if—" He shut his mouth with a snap.

"Okay." Nick leaned forward, his elbows on his knees. "I want to be clear on something before we go any further."

"Yeah?" Jacob knew him well enough to be wary.

"We modified PIVOT to help with immediate, chronic, trauma-related incidents," he said. "People like Justin, who had trauma-induced comas. People with strokes."

The other man remained silent. His arms were folded and he looked tense.

"We *aren't* doctors," Nick said. "We are merely people introducing a new technology for doctors to *use*, and no doctors have said they can help Taigan."

"Yeah," Jacob said. "But it's not like this is pumping her full of some experimental drug. We do a trial run and see if she integrates with the world."

"Yeah, I know." Nick leaned back in his chair and regarded him firmly. "But *you* want to fix her."

"I can't fix her," the other man said instantly.

"Yeah, that's the smart answer. That's the *right* answer. But what I said was that you *want* to fix her, and I think I'm right about that." He raised his eyebrows and pressed his palms together. "What you said about the twin thing—you think you can develop a plotline with Jamie to pull Taigan out of this coma and then somehow, she'll never fall into one again."

Amber looked from one to the other. She didn't say anything.

Jacob's shoulders hunched. He didn't look at either of them and simply waited for this to blow over.

Unfortunately for him, they had both been his friend for years and they knew this tactic. They were also both willing to wait for him to speak. Amber crossed her legs in her desk chair with one knee against an armrest and Nick leaned back and sipped his coffee.

"*Fine,*" Jacob said when it became clear they wouldn't cooperate. "Yes. Okay. I hope that if she and her brother can work her out of this coma and maybe a couple more, she'll…start to train her brain to do it without the pod. That's my hope." He glared at Nick. "And I don't see why it even matters."

"It matters because you *cannot* promise that to her parents," Amber said. "You can't even hint at it. It would be incredibly cruel to give them hope when we have no idea if we can follow through. We don't even know if she can integrate with the game yet. This isn't a trauma-induced coma. We might not be able to reach her at all."

"And it matters," Nick said gently, "because we might do good work and get her out of this coma and you'll still feel like you failed. I don't want you to hold out hope that you can save this family all on your own."

Their friend looked for a moment like he might blow up at them, but his shoulders sagged and he nodded. "I know I have no right to hope for it," he said. "I only…"

"You're hoping it anyway," Nick said. "I know, buddy. I've known you for years. Look, let's invite them in. But keep in mind what your expectations are. You're already stressed, okay? You don't need to add 'solving medical mysteries' to your checklist right now."

He nodded, but when he went back to his computer, Nick sighed.

Amber was right. None of them ever made the smart choice and their entire company was based on trying to do the impossible. None of them could resist an unsolved problem. He knew that before long, despite their best efforts, all of them would try to solve Taigan's condition and they'd blame themselves if they couldn't.

CHAPTER SIXTY

Kural marched them to the royal palace at a rapid pace. He muttered constantly and looked entirely deranged, and Zaara had to explain that he was trying to contact a friend inside the palace.

"So," Justin said around a mouthful of the pizza-like snack, "like magical Bluetooth."

"Blue..tooth?" The woman ran her tongue over her teeth, clearly unnerved by the idea of blue ones.

Dotty waved her hand to tell her not to bother. She'd have explained it but to do so, she would have to stop eating the pizza and she absolutely wouldn't do that. The crust was impossibly thin but somehow still supported the sauce, which was creamy and spicy in equal measure. What was *in* it, she didn't know—it might have been meat or vegetables—but it was so delicious that she didn't care about being unable to identify it.

And the *cheese*. She took another bite and her eyes drifted closed happily as she savored the perfect amount of melty, gooey cheese. How was it possible to desperately crave something while you were eating it?

In the next moment, she walked directly into a lamppost and shook her head. Another mouthful of pizza helped.

A moment later, Kural said loudly, *"Excellent."*

Everyone jumped and looked at him with identical chipmunk expressions, their cheeks stuffed with pizza.

"You all look great, by the way."

Dotty didn't bother to respond to Prima. She raised her eyebrows at the wizard in query.

"Jaco will have an escort waiting for us at the palace," he said.

"Wait." Lyle swallowed a bite of pizza. "So what do I do?"

Kural frowned at him. "You come with us."

"I don't get to make a diversion?"

"You don't *have* to make a diversion," Justin corrected him. "Making diversions isn't something you want to do, is it?"

"Yeah. It is."

"Oh." The young man seemed to try to think of something to say. Eventually, he gave up and began to eat again. "Does anyone else want to try?"

"I got this," Dotty said. "Lyle, if you behave yourself, I'll buy us all a feast tonight and you can have a barrel of beer to yourself."

"Two barrels," the dwarf said promptly.

"Done." She looked at Justin. "See?"

"You're not very strict for a grandmother," he said.

"Different situations call for different solutions." She took another bite of pizza and hummed in pleasure. "Plus, I don't have to deal with the fallout of this one."

They were met at the gates by a young man in black robes. His sash was embroidered in gold and the entire ensemble fit him badly. He looked, to her jaded eye, like a young man who was still having growth spurts and wasn't quite sure where his elbows and knees were anymore.

She had certainly missed having a healthy body, but she did not miss adolescence in the slightest. All she could remember of that time was the almost painful awkwardness.

The young man examined their ragtag group and didn't seem quite sure what to say. He took in Lyle's battle-worn clothing, Zaara's long daggers, and Tina's unimpressed smirk. It became clear the longer he looked that he tried very hard to *not* look at her red dress and its contents.

In her youth, she would have been nervous under anyone's stare when wearing it. In her middle age, she would have been wryly amused by the attention—and more pleased than she wanted to admit. Now, in her old age, all she could think was that they were wasting time.

"Young man," she said before she remembered that she looked about twenty herself, "will you take us to Jaco?"

"Uh. Yes." He attempted awkwardly to keep his gaze averted when he spoke and now, a blush rose blotchily across his neck and face.

Kural either took pity on the poor boy or he was entirely oblivious. Dotty couldn't tell which. He smiled and swept forward, urging their guide to turn and lead them into the palace. "Now, what has Jaco been up to lately?" he asked as they walked.

She smiled and took the opportunity to look around with real interest. The golden-white stone continued, shot through with ripples of gray. It had been carved into an impossibly thin, ornate screen above the entry. Under Insea's warm sun, the awning cast dappled shadows on the broad staircase that led to the castle.

There were still no guards. Dotty had expected to see them lining the staircase or at least patrolling it, but no one was there except their little group.

In a way, it was sad. This was a massive place—it seemed like something that should be full and bustling—but it was clear even from the entrance that it was an old relic. No one came there, not petitioners and not nobles. The fact that there was no dust on the stairs was jarring, though. There really should be. Worse, the sense of emptiness hung in the air.

The rest of the palace only seemed worse. The group moved through massive, vaulted hallways filled with arches that reminded her of trees. There was no art on the walls, however, or rugs on the floors. It seemed as if no one had ever inhabited it at all.

And there were no servants. Two guards had nodded to their guide at the main door and they had seen one patrol since then, but nothing else.

She shivered.

"What's wrong?" Zaara asked her quietly. She cleared her throat. "Ah, would you like my cloak? That dress doesn't look…warm."

"It's not that," she said and darted another uncomfortable glance at their surroundings. "This whole place seems *wrong.*"

"Wrong how?" the woman whispered.

Dotty only shrugged helplessly. She couldn't put the feeling into words.

They met Jaco in a receiving room with one wall entirely open to the gardens outside. In pleasant contrast to what they'd seen thus far, there was furniture, but it only served to remind them of how bare the rest of the palace looked.

He dismissed his attendant, who withdrew with a curious look over his shoulder. The man watched him leave and ushered their small group to the open wall—and away from prying ears, she guessed.

"A very interesting message," he said to Kural. "Asking about a 'certain dragon' and the founding of Insea? Which 'certain dragon' would this be?"

"The dragon you told me about several months ago," the wizard said in weary good humor. "They all know about it, so you can spare yourself the trouble of trying to mislead them."

Jaco sighed. "You were always terrible at keeping secrets."

"Mmm. But now…I'm beginning to think you didn't tell me the whole story." He studied his old friend steadily. His gaze took in every flicker, but he looked at Dotty to confirm what he had seen.

She nodded.

"So, it's true," Kural said gently.

Their host looked from one to the other. He cleared his throat.

"Jaco," Dotty said. "It is clear that something is wrong in Insea." She stepped closer. "Those of us here want only good for the city and have nothing invested in spreading wild tales or betraying confidences."

"Mmm." He turned to look at Justin, Tina, and Lyle. "Three former contestants in the tournament, a wizard, a wizard's apprentice who wears armor and knives, and…you. Who are you?"

"It depends on who you ask," Dotty said, amused. "To some, I'm a dwarven *zauberer* defending the caravan from Berghold. To others, I am a shaman-in-training of the orcish earth tribe and slayer of two godsprings."

Jaco raised an eyebrow. "And if I ask *you*?"

"I am someone who prefers to not be mugged in alleyways," she said tartly. "Which I was this morning. And I am someone who will go to rather extraordinary lengths to fix injustices."

"I promised I would bring warriors back," Justin said from behind them. "Dotty is one of them."

"Mmm." The Master of Ceremonies looked at each of them before he focused on the garden, his expression thoughtful.

"You've already decided to tell us," Dotty said impatiently. "You need the help and the secret is killing you. You might as well spit it out. None of us are getting any younger, and the problem *clearly* isn't solving itself."

He gave her a surprised look and cleared his throat. "Fine. Er… where to start. That's…rather the problem."

Everyone waited, some more patiently than others.

"Insea was founded by a dragon," Jaco said at last. He linked his hands behind his back and bounced nervously on his feet. "Or a… partnership…between a dragon and an elf." He blushed a bright red.

Tina gestured as if to say, "This is what I was talking about." Justin lowered his head into one hand, and Zaara struggled openly to keep her composure.

"They were both quite accomplished wizards," the man explained, having recovered his composure. "They imagined a world that would never know war or famine, one where all would be fed and able to pursue their heart's desire."

"A utopia," Dotty murmured.

"Precisely," he said. "But the spells went…wrong. To make a very long story short, their utopia never came to pass in the way they had meant it to do."

"They rarely do," she said, almost amused. She saw the stricken look on his face, however, and frowned. "What happened?"

"The elf died," he said simply. "How, I am not certain. Gos'hauke never told me. I think he could not bear to remember."

"Gos'hauke is…the dragon," she said to clarify.

He nodded. His jaw was clenched so tightly that she could see a muscle jumping in his cheek.

"He's dead," she said quietly, "isn't he?"

Jaco nodded. To her surprise, tears glittered in his eyes. "Four months ago," he said. His voice broke on the words. "Give or take." He seemed to attempt to salvage some shred of his demeanor and took a deep breath. "You see, they had planned that they would imbue the city with a…yearning for a leader. A strong, just leader."

"I don't understand," Kural said.

"The city would *call* its leader," he explained, "and release them when their service was no longer needed. It would not be a monarchy made of a bloodline, and the transfer of power would be peaceful."

"They thought—" Justin broke off when everyone looked at him. He cleared his throat. "I don't mean to be disrespectful, I honestly don't, but did they truly think it would never go wrong? Power corrupts, right? They say that for a reason. What if a ruler didn't want to leave?"

"I asked the same thing," Jaco said. "They told me the city would keep that from happening." He paused, clearly at war with himself, and then said in a rush, "It would control minds. It must have been intended to do so. And it *has*."

Dotty raised an eyebrow. Now that he said it that way, the whole experiment seemed a little less pleasant. "That's why there aren't wars involving Insea or nobles trying to take control. The city exerts an influence that stops people from doing that."

"Yes," he said bluntly. "Or…it did while Gos'hauke was still alive. As I understand it, if the spell had worked as intended, it would have existed in perpetuity. Unfortunately, when the elf died, they were not able to complete it. They never reached the part where a leader would be called, and the rest—the peace—was something Gos'hauke slowly gave his life to maintain."

"*Ah,*" she said. "So the dragons were right when they said that." She explained what she'd been told and said, "And they're right, we didn't complain. But I think part of that is because we didn't know. Gos'hauke also kept anyone from thinking about it too hard."

He nodded. "Yes," he said quietly.

"And now, it's breaking down," she added. "Quickly."

The Master of Ceremonies nodded. "I should have…well, that's the thing. I don't know what I should have done. I'm not meant to be Insea's ruler."

"They could do far worse," Kural said with a flash of humor. "I know you, remember."

The man didn't look remotely interested or amused. He shook his head flatly and sighed. "And the end came more quickly than he expected. I thought he could come up with a plan but too soon, he was gone and I didn't know what to do. I think he would want me to find someone to finish what he—they—started, but…"

Dotty thought she understood what she saw on his face.

"But you're angry," she said. "You feel manipulated and betrayed. You aren't sure what he did was a good plan. And while you are a wizard, you aren't one who could build anything like this. You face the dilemma of whether to give people assured peace or free will."

"Yes," Jaco confirmed softly.

"Kural," she said.

"Yes?"

"You mentioned that the power it would take to do this would be extraordinary. Is there any way we could possibly recreate it and make it work this time?"

Whether the wizard saw where she was going or not, she wasn't sure, but he did not equivocate. He shook his head. "The researcher in me wants to say yes. But…no. I am almost certain we could not."

"Then our path is clear," Dotty stated. "We don't have an ethical dilemma at all—which I, for one, am glad about."

"Yes," Jaco said a little desperately, "but what *do* we do?"

"We begin working for peace," Dotty told him crisply. "The old-fashioned way, mind you, with common interests and face-to-face negotiations. Roll your sleeves up, everyone. This will be some of the hardest work you've ever done."

CHAPTER SIXTY-ONE

Jaco led them through empty corridors to his study. Dotty walked beside him.

"So, they intended this place to be inhabited," she said.

"Yes." He was subdued. "I miss him, you know. I…do."

She smiled sadly. "But?"

The man glanced at her. "But, indeed. But he didn't truly like us humans and elves as much as he thought he did. If he had loved what we were, he wouldn't have controlled us all."

Her expression neutral, she nodded.

"I've struggled with it," he admitted. "I haven't been comfortable with the idea since I learned what the spell did, but since he died, the doubts have become stronger. His magic…suppressed them. And that seems wrong to me."

"It *is* wrong," she agreed. "That's why you weren't comfortable with it. You said it earlier. He controlled people's minds. That's what this was."

"Yes," he admitted. "And I'm…glad their spell didn't work. I'm not glad that he lost his lover, though. It broke him and he continued to mourn for centuries, but if they'd succeeded, everyone would have lived in a cloud forever."

"That doesn't sound like a struggle," she told him. "Your mind sounds quite clear to me. Or is the struggle simply that you want to think well of him?"

Jaco walked in silence for a moment. "No," he admitted. He looked at her.

"It's…that I can see an argument for renewing the spell."

"*What?*"

"I was grateful when Kural said it couldn't be done. You must understand, I'm not as good a wizard as he is. I never have been so I knew *I* couldn't do it, but I didn't know if it was possible for someone else and—"

"Wait, wait, wait." Dotty stopped, her hand on his arm. Behind them, the others drifted to a halt, too engaged in their discussion to notice why. "You were thinking of renewing the spell?"

The man heaved a sigh. "Yes. And I think, if you consider why for a moment, you'll understand better. You said yourself in that room that there was no dilemma if there was no option. Why did you call it a dilemma?"

She groaned. "Okay, yes, I get it—if the world is at peace, people don't die in wars, and that's good. But you know it would be a terrible thing to do. Controlling people's thoughts?"

"Yes," he agreed readily. "It disgusts me as an idea, it does. But it's not an abstract right now—or it wasn't for me when I thought it might be possible. If I could guarantee that no one would be robbed or murdered, that there would never be any wars or famines…what do you think people would say if they found out I could and I didn't?"

Dotty opened her mouth to retort but bit the words back and thought about it. During her eighty-four years on Earth, she'd lived through more than one war. She had seen people return in boxes, or come back in body but not in spirit, or not come back at all. After one of John's friends was murdered by her husband, she had sat with her son for hours. There was so much pain in the world.

"People like to say that the pain in life gives meaning to the rest," Jaco said, "but none of them have ever had a choice to live any other way."

She shook her head slowly. "I'm glad we don't have a choice," she admitted. Even contemplating this for a moment made her head and her heart go to war.

"Me as well," he said. "When he said no, it was like a great weight had lifted."

They resumed walking until they entered a beautiful room. Silks had been draped to bring the ceiling lower and give it a homey feel, and plush carpets covered the floors. In actuality, it was an ornate room—the kind of place in which she would normally feel uncomfortable touching anything. In there, however, any touches of color or hominess felt cozy. She kicked her shoes off and sank onto one of the couches with a sigh.

Jaco smiled and rang a little bell as he murmured under his breath. An assortment of food appeared on a nearby table, complete with mugs and a steaming pitcher of tea. As the others helped themselves to the food, he dragged a low table closer. He secured a map on it with little weights on the corners which he retrieved from his desk.

"Cool," Justin said. He held a plate piled high with a variety of ornately shaped pastries and dumplings. When people looked confused, he swallowed a mouthful of food and gestured at the map. "I always wanted to be at one of these war-planning meetings."

"Okay, but remember," Tina told him, "this is an *un*-war planning meeting. Anti-war? War un-planning?" She frowned at the sky. "The opposite of a war plan."

"Yes," Dotty said. "That."

She leaned forward to look as she ate a spiced pastry that tasted of cloves and cinnamon. Insea was immediately visible, as it was marked with an ornate ring of golden ink. It took her some time to find Berghold and even longer after that to guess where the orcish lands were.

Jaco retrieved several markers and placed one on Berghold, one in the center of the orcish lands, one in the human lands, one at the northernmost edge of the map, and one in a place that wasn't marked with anything at all. When he saw her looking at it, he smiled bitterly.

"*That* is the so-called capital city of the new elvish faction."

"Oh, those," she said. "I met some of them and killed some of them." She smiled blandly. "Did you know they killed one of the senior dwarven councilors?"

Lyle smothered a snort and fixed his attention on his cup of tea.

"I had heard as much," the man said with enough casualness in his tone that she couldn't tell if he was uninterested or bluffing. He gestured at the board. "Now, these markers represent the major powers of the world—the orcs, the dwarves, the humans, the elves, and the fae."

"The fae?" she asked in surprise. "I didn't know there was a fifth race."

"There might as well not be," Kural said. His nostrils flared. "Nasty, vicious little creatures."

"Some of the only ones who can beat him at games of skill," Jaco confided to the others in a stage whisper.

"They *cheat*," the wizard said.

"Mmm. And you're one of those who know the most about them."

"What's that supposed to mean? Are you suggesting that I cheat, too? Because I don't, I'll have you know. I *never* cheat."

"That wasn't what I meant," the other man said. He smiled. "I meant you're indisputably the best one to meet with them and extend the diplomatic olive branch."

Kural's jaw dropped. "Oh. Oh, no. *Absolutely* not."

"We need someone we can trust and we can trust you. Not to mention that you can get through the wards you'll need to break to enter the fae lands in the first place."

"They've never bothered anyone in years," he argued in return.

"And we would like to keep it that way," Jaco said promptly. "Enough, Kural. You're going. You should take your apprentice with you."

He snorted. "Her father wants her to stay safe. This is the opposite of that."

"Or you could let her talk for herself before she slits your throat," Dotty suggested.

"I'd second that caution," Justin said.

"Excellent," the Master of Ceremonies said as if everyone had enthusiastically agreed to the plan. "I have several people I can send to the various human settlements."

"Whoa, wait." Justin spread his hands. "Why not us? Me and Tina?"

"Because you don't know anything about the human governments," Zaara said.

"And ye're not so good with th' diplomacy," Lyle added.

"I can be diplomatic! And Tina...will also be there." He looked at her. "Please don't piss off any diplomats like you did in Berghold."

"Then they'd better not cheat at dice."

"Don't play dice with anyone!"

"I have a suggestion," Zaara said. Everyone looked at her and she smiled. "Kural and I will accompany Justin and Tina to the human lands, give them an overview, and introduce them to relevant leaders. They will stay to establish diplomatic relations while Kural and I continue north to the fae lands." She nodded to Justin and Tina. "Humans recognize power and bloodline and they have very specific ideas of other human nations. Justin and Tina aren't from any of the rival noble families, and they'll be introduced by two wizards. It's fairly perfect...if they can pull it off."

"We can pull it off," Justin said dangerously.

"Done," Jaco said promptly.

"Wait, really?" The young man looked unsettled.

"Yes." The Master of Ceremonies tapped the map. "Speed is of the essence and there are very few people I trust with the knowledge of why this is so essential. Also, the humans are famous for in-fighting. All you need to do is convince them that Insea is more concerned with its problems than with theirs—and that we're training a guard force to combat those internal problems. Therefore, it presents a dangerous populace and an undesirable target."

Dotty leaned back in her seat. She was enjoying this.

"That leaves us with the dwarves, the elves, and the orcs," Jaco said. "Dotty, you told me you'd worked with two orcish villages. I assume you're one of the best to go to them."

"Well..." She shrugged. "They think I'm dead and they certainly won't recognize me. But they are speaking of uniting again, which means we definitely should talk to them about diplomatic relations. And I suppose I also know a good deal about their culture. Okay. I'll go there."

"I'm reluctant to send anyone alone," he said, "and I must remain here. I propose that Dotty and Lyle go both to Berghold and the orcish territories. Dotty has done a valuable service for Berghold and will therefore be welcome, and if orcs are likely to respect any other race, it's the dwarves."

"What about the elves?" she asked.

The man paused and looked uncertain. "That…is a puzzle and one I am not certain of how best to address. I will think on it and send exploratory messages." He stood. "All of you, take the next day to prepare. You leave at dawn the day after tomorrow, and I'll do all I can to speed you on your way."

CHAPTER SIXTY-TWO

Nick's first impression of the Mattis family was of lanky height. Jamie Mattis and his father shared a tall build that wasn't quite filled out. While Simon moved with studied efficiency, his hair entirely gray but his manner spry, Jamie still moved like he wasn't quite sure what to do with his height.

Emilia Mattis, the oldest child, was the shortest of the group but he would guess from a distance that she was still five-six or taller. Even her mother Aimee, whose round face and straight black hair spoke of her Chinese heritage, was unusually tall.

His second impression, as the group scrambled out of the taxi, was that they had recently been in a fight of some kind. Emilia was tight-lipped, her shoulders hunched, and she lagged behind the rest of the group as they approached the PIVOT headquarters, while Jamie hung back and spoke urgently to her.

Whatever she said to him, he looked like a whipped puppy when they reached the lobby.

Nick had to take a moment to steady himself before he stepped forward to greet the parents. He couldn't think about the two miserable children trailing in their wake without remembering too many moments from his childhood.

It hurt to be forgotten.

"Mr. Mattis, Mrs. Mattis." He nodded to them and held a hand out for them to shake. "I'm Nick Ryan, one of the founders of PIVOT. Thank you for coming."

"Thank you for showing us around," Simon said. Nick formed a snap judgment in that moment of someone who liked to do things correctly. He would be polite and engaging. He had come here today because he owed it to his daughter to try to find a cure for her condition.

And it would be killing him that no matter how many specialists he'd seen, nothing had worked so far.

"We appreciate your work," Aimee added. She wore her hair cropped short and spoke in a southern drawl that surprised him. "These are Taigan's siblings, Jamie and Emilia. Jamie, Emilia, this is Mr. Ryan."

He saw the resentment flare in Emilia's eyes at being treated like a child but she, like her brother, shook his hand and muttered a polite greeting.

"Why don't we start with the lab?" he asked. He moved to the elevators and made a mental note to allow each of the Mattises time to ask private questions. The children, at least, looked like they would benefit from the opportunity to be away from their parents. On a whim, he added, "If the two of you would like to stay on to ask more questions after the tour, perhaps we could have one of the laboratory assistants show Jamie and Emilia the city."

Emilia only leaned into the corner of the elevator and sighed, her arms folded, as her mother shook her head.

"Oh, no, they can stay. It's no trouble."

I tried, Nick wanted to tell the girl. He guessed that she and Jamie were kept on a fairly tight leash. Their mother would inevitably be quite cautious about their safety, what with the unpredictable nature of their sister's condition.

With Amber in a meeting with the Diatek accountants and Jacob meeting with Anna Price, Diatek's CEO, he was in charge of the tour. He had to admit, despite being nervous about having been acquired by a defense contractor, he was very glad to be able to show off this high-end, expensively outfitted laboratory instead of the dingy set of offices PIVOT had once rented.

Simon and Aimee Mattis would *never* have agreed to have Taigan treated in that facility.

Nick showed them the row of pods, sleek and white, beeping with LEDs and printouts, and each attended by several assistants in crisp, white lab coats. In the well-lit lab, the pods looked unthreatening and even comforting.

"As you can see," he said, "we have several people in the pods at present."

"Patients?" Simon asked.

"PIVOT is doing two branches of research," he said carefully. "The first is recovery care, which is what Justin Williams received. The other is baseline testing, which helps us to understand how people of different demographics interact with the world inside the pods."

"And these…" Simon gestured at the pods.

"Unfortunately, I cannot share information about any of the individuals currently in the pods," he said.

"Ah. My apologies."

"None needed."

"If you're still doing testing…" Aimee interrupted. She looked uncertainly at her husband before she refocused on Nick. "Is it safe to have someone's—I believe you called it 'recovery care'—happen this way? If you don't know how certain people respond to the treatment?"

Simon looked uncomfortable but he nodded.

"That's a good question, and I'm afraid I can't offer you any guarantees. What we hope is that the treatment we offer will supplement the existing set of options—that it will merely be another option doctors can turn to if they believe it is appropriate for an individual patient. Should you choose to move forward with this, one step would be to speak to Taigan's care team and get a better understanding of whether they believe this is a good option for her."

Aimee hesitated before she nodded.

"So you can't fix her," Emilia said bluntly. Both of her parents looked sharply at her and she shrugged with studied indifference. "What? They all make sure to not promise anything. If they'll take a chunk of money for it, I think they should be honest."

She looked fierce and before her mother or father could reprimand her, Nick spoke.

"I can't imagine how frustrating this has been for you," he told her frankly. "And exhausting. Each time, you're not sure whether to get your hopes up and no one can ever give you guarantees."

If anything, him agreeing with her had made her more suspicious. She stared at him with an unimpressed expression.

"All I can tell you," he continued, "is that, if we'd had the chance, Jacob's grandmother would have been one of the first we tried to help. It was her experience in the ICU that propelled us to use this technology for medical care. We believe that it will get us closer to being able to fix things like comas but right now, we don't know enough to fix problems like that. No one does."

Emilia glared at him for another moment before she looked at the floor. He thought he saw the sheen of tears in her eyes.

You're trying to protect her, he thought. *You're trying to protect all of them. You watch your parents spend all their energy on this, get their hopes up, and get crushed every time. And in the meantime, the whole family is in limbo.*

He couldn't say any of that, though, because he didn't know them well enough. A little despondent, he cleared his throat.

"We've had people come from all around—some heard about Justin's care on the news and some found it because they were already following virtual reality developments. How did PIVOT first come to your attention?"

"Jamie told us about it." Simon still looked deeply displeased with Emilia's outburst but he tried to salvage the situation. He gestured to his son, who looked nervous and miserable now.

The kid was the peacemaker of the family, Nick guessed. He wanted all of them to get along and stop yelling.

And he wanted his twin back. Jacob was right about that.

"What appealed to you about the idea of the pods?" Nick asked Jamie.

"Well, it's—a chance. You know, to…cure her." He nodded awkwardly.

"Yes, but your sister is right. You have all gone through this many times." He nodded at him. "I imagine when you hear about a new treatment, part of you is simply tired of the whole cycle. What made you speak to your parents about this one?" He looked at the boy's face. "You don't have to answer if you don't want to."

Jamie stared at the floor.

"Jamie?" his mother asked. "It's all right. You should tell him whatever it is."

Nick could gladly have strangled her. Nothing he could say would make this better, though. He merely had to wait, but he noticed that even Emilia looked curious.

Finally, Jamie said, "I saw the interview with Justin's mother, where she said…she could go into the game and talk to him. I thought —maybe I could go in. I could help her."

He looked deeply embarrassed. Nick could hear the shame behind the words. *He's thinking, 'I know how childish this is.'*

But Mary and Tina had gone into the game for Justin, and Dotty's family going in to see her had resulted in a measurable change to her endocrine levels and brain activation. Not only did the PIVOT team now know friends and family made a difference, Jamie was right. Who better to go into the world than a twin?

Nick had to stop himself before he did the exact thing he'd warned Jacob about. He couldn't promise anything right now, no matter how much he wanted to.

"Part of why this treatment interests researchers," he explained, "is exactly the kind of thing you're talking about—the ability to communicate with people who are comatose. If your family and your doctors decide to move forward with this, there may be some communication with her. I don't know what that will look like, if so, but I imagine you'll all at least be able to send letters to her and she can send letters back."

For a moment, the family looked completely united. All of them had a yearning look on their faces. Aimee had tears in her eyes and Simon slid his arm around her shoulders, cleared his throat, and looked away.

"Why don't we see more of the facility," Nick said. "I can show you some demos of the game and, if you want, you'll have the option to see one of us interact with the technology live. Or any of you are also free to go into the game if you want to experience it for yourself. There's no need to answer now. It's merely something to think about."

He set off without waiting for a response because he wanted them to think about it rather than feel like they had to commit to anything. Jamie's desperation to get into the game was almost palpable, but the parents would have to agree to it in his case.

As he walked, he fought to keep from shaking his head at himself. He had given Jacob the big speech about not getting too invested in this case, but he realized now that he should have given himself the same one.

Already, he was *way* too invested. This treatment had never been entirely about the patients but about the way the costs of treatment, the uncertainty, and the waiting all tore families apart. This family was a mess of exposed fault lines, and their anger at one another all stemmed from whatever disease was holding Taigan captive.

Nick also had to admit he was curious about the girl. He had seen each of the other family members, but even their application hadn't spoken about her as a *person.* There had been dry details about her condition and readouts about her pulse, her brain scans, and her blood work.

So many details but nothing about *her.* Aimee was overprotective and lost, Simon retreated into etiquette, Emilia was furious, and Jamie was desperate.

But what about Taigan? What would the PIVOT team find if the pods gave her the chance to wake up and interact with the world they had created?

CHAPTER SIXTY-THREE

Jaco offered the palace for that night's dinner, but Dotty wasn't sure she wanted to be surrounded by empty, unfurnished rooms.

Thankfully, the others agreed and they set out into the streets.

They hadn't gone very far before a runner arrived, panting, and held a letter out unerringly to her. She opened it and scanned it, smiling as she did so.

"Lady Prima extends us the invitation to have a private banquet at her home," she told the others. She was careful to not look directly at Tina or Justin, whose conspiratorial glances might reveal that there was a secret there.

She had forgotten Zaara.

"Lady Prima?" she asked skeptically. "I've never heard of any noble with that name. What's her crest?"

In response, she held the sheet of paper up. For her crest, Prima had chosen a gear with a hexagonal center. She shrugged one shoulder dismissively. "I sent her a request on our way to the palace," she lied. "I wasn't certain we would be able to secure her guesthouse, but it appears we were. We can feel free to stay overnight, and she'll arrange for travel and supplies to be ready at the city gates in the morning."

"Who *is* this woman?" Zaara asked skeptically. She scanned the letter. "This address is in a hoity-toity part of town. There's no way she should be there without me knowing who she is, and I've never even heard her *mentioned*. And why give us supplies?"

"Dotty seems to inspire that in people," Justin said.

The woman raised an eyebrow at her for confirmation.

"In a way," she said. "Last time, though, what I got was a lifetime supply of dried fish, so…this is far superior." Under her breath, she muttered, "It is, right? Tell me it is."

"*Of course it is.*" Prima sounded offended. "*You said you wanted to have good food and luxuries and things. I can do all of that now that I know you want it.*"

"Thank you, Prima." Dotty looked at the others. "So, shall we go?"

"Everyone keep your weapons out," Zaara muttered. But even she nodded. "I have to admit, I'm curious."

"I don't think you'll be disappointed," Justin said.

Zaara was right about the address being in a fancy part of Insea. As the entire city was fashioned from stone, there was no way to determine the cost of apartments by the building materials. However, Dotty noticed that the streets grew gradually less crowded and the people around them looked richer and more bored.

There were also more elves.

Kural noticed her tracking the nobles. "Insea *is* known as an elven city," he said, "and many of the noble families are elven."

"Are, ah…" Dotty didn't know how to ask this without it being inappropriate. "Is there intermarriage? Between the two races."

"There is," he said easily. "Any two races—although you'll find it less with the fae and the orcs, of course. There isn't much, though. Offspring of different races are rarely able to bear children of their own. To make such a marriage…well, it's much more common for those who were unlikely to inherit anything." He lowered his voice. "Also, humans are famously judgmental about such things."

She looked curiously at him. "Not elves? Or dwarves? And what about orcs? Everyone I've met has seemed fairly emphatic about their race either ruling the world or keeping to itself."

"I think that's selection bias," he said mildly. "Ones with less extreme opinions tend to not do things like attack caravans."

"Hmm." She sighed. "Well, it's a pity. If there were more intermarried families, it would be a good sign for…well, diplomatic relations, right?"

"Ah." He nodded in understanding. "I see now. Unfortunately, no, people do not mingle in quite that way—or share those particular interests."

"It'll have to be trade, then," Dotty mused. "Berghold will want fresh foods, yes? Ah, no, they've cultivated all those fields outside the mountain range."

"Yes," Kural agreed, "but there are other uses for that land and other nations that have a surplus of food and who would pay well for dwarven-made goods. If I had to guess, though, I would say our dwarven friend is more knowledgeable about such things than I am."

She nodded. "I wish we weren't splitting up," she admitted. "Finding consensus organically is a good plan, but if the right hand doesn't know what the left is doing…"

"I agree." He smiled at her expression of surprise. "My dear lady, desperately laid plans are rarely without their flaws and we do, indeed, find ourselves in a desperate situation. Jaco and I are wizards, and wizards do not leap into action unless it is absolutely necessary, I assure you. We prefer to hem and haw over whether there's any possible way to get away with it."

"He's not lying," Zaara called from behind him.

"When you get to three hundred and fifty-eight, we'll see how much you like to go dashing off," he said, with an amused expression. To Dotty, he continued, "The peace of the world is unraveling quickly and the nations have established no such ties between one another naturally. Every week we go without these treaties is a week that could lead to war."

"Great. No pressure." She rolled her eyes.

Kural patted her arm. "If you are, indeed, the *zauberer* I heard whisper of in the most recent caravan from Berghold as well as the shaman who produced such interesting magical flares in the orcish lands recently, I rather think you will be able to find a solution here too."

"It's easy for you to say. I fixed the other problems by stabbing them. Metaphorically, in some cases."

"Yes, the metaphor will be key in this case." He stared at an estate with magical, glowing gardens and a building of rose-pink stone. "I do believe we are at our destination. Come along, all."

They walked up a path engraved with Prima's crest. The walls rose gradually behind the trees and another carved awning appeared equally gradually until Dotty realized they had come into the atrium without realizing it. The path widened and divided around an ornate fountain and behind it, the doors into the house swung open without anyone touching them.

Zaara and Kural exchanged a look but neither seemed inclined to share their revelations. They didn't seem particularly worried, either, so Dotty decided not to pry.

Magical lanterns lit one after another to guide them up a pair of sweeping staircases. Beautiful arrangements of flowers softened the lines and in a circular atrium with a skylight open to the air above, five doors stood open. Dotty looked into one and saw a beautiful bed covered with a profusion of pillows. A gown lay on the bed, a confection of midnight-blue velvet and silk.

"I'll help you get into it," Prima said, sensing the question.

She smiled and trailed her fingers over the cloth as she listened to the others locate their rooms. In one corner, a full pack of provisions was put ready, as well as some dresses and a beautiful traveling cloak. The room was broad and low-ceilinged, given an airy feel by the floor-to-ceiling windows that stood open on the outer wall.

A little distracted, she wondered if Insea's famously perfect weather would be another thing that broke down with the dragon's death. If so, how would people adapt their houses that were shaped from stone?

With a shrug, she banished questions of magical interior design and let Prima guide her through whispering winds and opening doors to a steaming bath strewn with rose petals. The trees outside were almost close enough to touch. Dotty sank into the water with a sigh.

"Prima, this is lovely. Thank you for all of it."

"You're welcome. Is there anything else you wanted? I have the banquet and the bath, and of course the bed..."

"A bed, a bath, and a banquet are quite sufficient," Dotty said and opened one eye in amusement. "There is no need for a beyond."

"Eh?"

"Never mind. I make bad jokes, or so my grandchildren tell me." She swished her hands through the water and sighed happily. "Are the others enjoying it as well?"

"Yes. Even Zaara."

"Has she stopped thinking this is a trap?"

"No, she seemed determined to think it was one, so I've set up a series of ominous-looking clues for her to follow until dinnertime. Barred doors to pick, hidden safes, things like that."

She responded with a peal of laughter. "You didn't. You're somewhat impish, you know."

"But she's having a wonderful time!"

"Mmm." She leaned her head back and gazed happily at the trees. "And the others?"

"I had several rare books from the palace transported to Kural's room, which he is reading, and Lyle is taking a nap. Justin and Tina have decided to play beer pong.

"Well, whatever makes them happy, I guess."

Prima grumbled something indecipherable.

"You grumble but you like Justin."

"I refuse to confirm that."

"Uh-huh."

Dotty watched the sky begin to fade into sunset before she hauled herself regretfully from the tub. Magical bathtubs did not get cold, after all, and when she looked around for a drink, one appeared promptly beside her hand.

She wrapped herself in a towel and approached the blue dress a little warily. "Does this one cover any more than the last one did?"

"Not so much," the AI said cheerfully. *"Hold on."*

"I'm not sure I—hey!" She was spun like a top as the towel unwound itself and fluttered to a drying rack. The world seemed to invert itself and turn upside down before everything returned to normal.

And, of course, she now wore the dress—which seemed rather more risqué than the last one.

"If my mother saw me go out of the house like this," she said conversationally, "she'd have made sure I couldn't sit for a *week.*"

"Well, it's good she's not here, then, isn't it?"

"Very. Although something tells me she might not have minded killing a dragon or two." She headed out of the room and met the others, who each emerged from their room at the same time. Kural was still reading, Tina and Justin swayed slightly on their feet, and Lyle yawned.

And a thud and a shriek from below them announced that Zaara had found something.

"Zaara has arrived for dinner," Prima said gravely.

Dotty's lips twitched and she explained the AI's trick—leaving out certain technology-related details—as the group descended the stairs. They arrived in the dining room, where Zaara stood panting and with a large soot stain on one side of her face. Still, she seemed deeply pleased with herself.

"I managed to uncover the history of Lady Prima's family," she said triumphantly to the others.

"What did you tell the poor girl?" Dotty muttered.

"Never you mind."

"Just don't start any wars."

"I promise nothing."

She would have rolled her eyes if she weren't diverted by the spread before them. It was as if every street vendor in Insea had crowded into this room only moments before, as all the food was steaming hot and it smelled divine.

"How are we going to *try* all this?" she asked in dismay. "I know I'll miss something."

"Start with this," Lyle advised. He handed her a delicately-carved bowl filled with shaved ice, syrup, and several brilliantly-colored, differently shaped jellies. "It's an elven delicacy. Lovely on hot days."

Dotty dug in with a sound of appreciation and strolled around the various tables as she ate. She saw some things she recognized—baklava, funnel cake, a chocolate gateau with frosting that held a mirror shine, and even a full ice cream bar. Vegetable fritters were piled high on another table with a wealth of different sauces and chutneys, stacks of flatbread, steamed buns in all different shapes, fried cakes, pasties, and more of the magical pizza. There were platters of fresh fish cooked in every way she could imagine—and some that were not cooked—noodle dishes of all variations, and homey piles of rice and beans, stews, and roast meats.

"Well," she said after she surveyed all of it. "This feast won't eat itself. Shall we dig in?"

"In a moment," Tina said from behind her. She turned to see the other woman holding two shot glasses of tequila and two wedges of lime. "Don't I recall a certain orc telling me that *everyone* likes tequila?"

"You did, indeed," she said gravely. She took her glass, clinked it against Tina's, and swallowed the contents.

"I'm watching a grandmother do shots," Justin said to Zaara. "You know, I planned on dragons and bandits and so on when I came here. I never planned on this."

CHAPTER SIXTY-FOUR

Somehow, all of them woke before dawn feeling refreshed, even after their late night of feasting and telling stories. Dotty suspected that Prima had done something strange with the passage of time but was of course unable to prove it.

She also hoped the AI would keep doing it.

After another magical breakfast—everyone's eggs were perfectly cooked—the group had set out through the quiet city. This time, she noticed the guards at every noble's door and the way she always seemed to be watched.

The back of her neck hadn't stopped prickling the entire way from the mansion.

Whether it was thieves or simply the ever-present guards, she did not know. She merely knew she did not like it and would be happy to get away from Insea. It wasn't that other places didn't have crime. It was simply that the crime there seemed fresher and more desperate, tinged with an edge of unpredictable savagery.

The people of Insea, after all, had only recently learned how to be criminals.

"Are you okay?" Justin asked beside her.

She realized she was pressing her hand to her head. "I don't like the idea that someone has been messing with my thoughts. I came to Insea before and... It's bad enough when you're not allowed to say what you want, but to have a whole populace that couldn't even *think* things they didn't want them to think and they didn't even realize?"

He nodded. "It creeps me out, too." He gave her a wry smile. "I only hope human nature doesn't prove Gos'hauke right about his little experiment."

Rather than voice her thoughts on that, she simply nodded. They approached the gates, where horses and donkeys were waiting for them. It was a surprisingly small caravan for the group that carried the entire nation's hopes, but she assumed Jaco wanted to keep things quiet for now.

"Travel safely," Dotty said to them all as they walked out of the gates. Was it her imagination or did her thoughts seem clearer even a step beyond the city? "Don't do anything stupid."

"Traveling to see the fae qualifies as stupid," Kural said sourly, "so I am obliged to not take your advice."

Zaara gave him an exasperated but fond look. To Dotty, she said, "As I've seen you confront a dragon without any plan at all, I'd ask you to do the same."

"That's fair," she acknowledged. "That's very fair."

"Keep her safe, Lyle," the woman enjoined as she swung onto the horse with the kind of grace Dotty had always envied.

"Always," Lyle rumbled, and she was surprised to hear sincerity in his voice.

She held a hand out to Justin and Tina and drew them aside. It surprised her to feel tears in her eyes, and for a moment, she couldn't speak. She had debated whether to tell them this or not and she pushed her renewed doubts aside and cleared her throat.

"I'm not certain I'll see you again," she said finally when she was sure she could speak without crying.

"Are you leaving the game?" the young woman asked.

"Not by choice—although I suppose I would never have come here unless..." Dotty trailed off. "Okay, it's best to start at the beginning, I think. I decided to volunteer for this game after I found out I had cancer. The last time I was out of the game, the doctors told me it has progressed quite quickly. I'm not certain how much time I have left."

A stricken silence ensued. Tina held her hand over her mouth and Justin looked horrified.

"Now, now," she said. She touched each of them gently on the cheek. "Chins up, my loves. I'm eighty-four, you know. I've lived quite a long time."

"I…didn't know," Tina said in a small voice. She looked at Justin, who slid his arm around her—as much for his comfort as hers, Dotty suspected.

"I know you didn't," she said. "And we've had fun, haven't we? I didn't tell you this to make you sad, but I didn't want to leave without saying goodbye, either." She looked at the others. Zaara, Kural, and Lyle tried not to eavesdrop but couldn't miss Tina's tears and Justin's horrified expression. She nodded to them. "If I'm not able to finish my part of this, you'll help, won't you?"

"That's not what's important—" Tina began.

Justin cut her off gently with a squeeze of his arm. "We will," he promised, and she heard in his voice that he understood her desire to protect the people she had met. "We know it will be frustrating and tiring and all that, but we *will* make sure it happens."

She took a moment to give each of them a quick hug. Young fingers squeezed against her back and two young faces scrunched with the effort to not shed tears, and she smiled gently and gave them each a kiss on the forehead.

"May you both live a life," she said, "in which you will face death with a sense of completion rather than fear."

Before they could respond, she left them so her tears wouldn't catch up with her and nodded wordlessly to Lyle as she mounted her horse and started out of the capital.

The business of riding provided a welcome respite from thinking about sad things. Dotty had been on horseback only once or twice, and then only as a little game—a country fair with a child on her lap and an old, placid horse. This one was more spirited and nervous about the fact that it had an untrained rider on its back.

By midmorning, the two of them had reached an understanding of sorts, and she had relaxed enough to look around. They had chosen to go to Berghold first and the orcish lands thereafter, so she had been on this road once before. This section of it, of course, had been traveled while she was comatose in-game, but the general feel of the land was familiar.

"So," Lyle said, after a time. "D'ye have anythin' t' tell me?"

She looked over at him with a smile.

"It's strange," the dwarf said. "Ye really *are* Dotty, aren't ye? Ye speak like her, all the same…then I see ye and I get all confused."

His bemusement drew a laugh from her. "I imagine it must be jarring. I'm still trying to decide whether I should tell the orcs we meet that I'm the same Dahti they thought died when fighting the dragon."

"Before ye tell me the rest, tell me about *that*," he said with genuine interest.

Dotty sketched her previous adventures, including her mistaken belief that the mountain god was a volcano. She was pleased that she managed to surprise him with it—enough that his horse reacted warily and pranced in a circle—and he hung on her story of the ruined water tribe in fascination.

"We knew there were dragons in those lands," he told her when she finished. "We'd thought…well, that the orcs had some kind o' understandin' with them. I woulda never guessed *that* was it." He frowned in thought as he rode, then nodded. "Good for them. False rulers *should* taste a bite o' pain."

She hid a smile. It was moments like this that gave her hope for peace. It was evident that there were people among each race who wanted it. She merely hoped that those would be the strongest voices.

When she looked up, Lyle was watching her.

With a sigh, she looked at the horizon. The road wound on into the blue in the distance and it felt endless—as she was now very sure it was not. All things must end.

"I'm dying," she said finally.

Her assumption had been that the dwarf would prefer plain speech and indeed, he did not lose his mind. He sucked his breath through his teeth and considered her statement for a few moments.

"I knew it had t' be somethin' bad," he said. "Tina's a great one for fightin' and shoutin' but not cryin'. Well. I'm sorry."

"I'm…not." Dotty hesitated. "Well, maybe I am. There's so much I haven't seen yet—won't see, I suppose. But my death is what led me to come here, and it has been wonderful. Especially…" She looked at herself and smiled. "Especially being able to do so with my own face."

He stared. "Wait—Justin an' Tina, do *they* look different? In the world you all come from?"

"No, they look the same." She smiled. "I merely asked if I could— well, when I came here, I wanted to be different. I even tried being an orc, as you heard."

They chatted about orcs for most of the rest of the morning. Few of the other races knew anything at all about them, and Lyle was insatiably curious. Not many people cared, he pointed out, because they didn't lead raids on settlements or stray beyond their lands, which didn't have much in the way of resources of farmland. People were content to leave well enough alone.

He, however, was the kind of person who had left home because not knowing the outside world was something that drove him slowly crazy. The dwarf told his story in detail as they rode and not only the little snatches she had known about his arena fighting with Justin and his defeat of the wizard Sephith. He also told her how he had come to leave Berghold and the changes he hoped to bring to his home.

At midday, they stopped to rest their horses and take a leisurely lunch. Kural and Jaco had delved into the vaults of Insea's palace and produced enchanted charms that would help each party to travel more quickly. Dotty estimated that she and Lyle would reach Berghold in five or six days rather than the three weeks it had taken them before.

Their lunch was more of the delicious vegetable fritters from the night before, stuffed with beans and spices and accompanied by pots of chutney. She enjoyed their meal immensely but was even more appreciative of the way the leftover containers winked out of existence instead of remaining to grow moldy in their packs.

"I tell you," Lyle said with a contented sigh, "this is the kind of travel I could get used to. Open sky, no nattering companions speaking about politics, and no counting shekels, but good food. The only thing we're missing so far is a cart of ale to follow us."

"*No,*" Prima said before she could ask. "*I absolutely refuse.*"

Dotty stifled a smile with her palm. She looked up to where another few horses kicked dirt up as they approached between the fields, then stood and stretched.

"Shall we?" she asked her companion.

"Oh, very well." He patted his stomach. "At least we don't have to walk after that lunch. I have t' say, Insea's cuisine has too many vegetables fer my likin' an' not enough meat, but damned if they don't make mighty fine things with those vegetables."

They were still stowing gear and checking the horses when the party on the road drew close—four horses, each with a mercenary on its back. The leader raised a hand in greeting not too far out, and the two friends held their hands up in greeting as well.

It was only when the second pair of horses began to lag that she felt a prickle of unease. She was careful to not look at Lyle as she said, "Do you see this?"

"Yes," he said simply. A flash of one hand showed her the dagger hidden there.

"Well," she said, "let's get this over with, shall we?"

"I knew I liked you," he responded cheerfully.

She turned to look at the horses, now spread behind and ahead of them on the road. As she waited, she tracked them with her gaze and only smiled when the first two turned their mounts.

"So, who goes first?" she asked. She held a hand up and allowed earth magic to swirl in her palm. "Should we flip for it?"

CHAPTER SIXTY-FIVE

The looks on the mercenaries' faces were priceless. They looked at Dotty and the magic in her palm, then at Lyle, who grinned like the Cheshire Cat. Finally, they looked at one another.

Before they could react, she thrust one of them off the back of his horse with a bolt of earth magic. It wasn't enough to kill him—she still wasn't sure if that would be necessary—but it was enough to take him out of commission for a few minutes. He landed with an audible thud and a yelp.

"Hey, now!" The leader looked from his downed soldier to her. "You *bitch*," he said.

"I know," she said. "You decided to attack us, you dibsed the element of surprise, and then the mean lady ruined your plans." She narrowed her eyes at him. "But that's how it is. So why don't you four trot off and rethink your life choices, and that can be that?"

"No one needed to get hurt," the leader said menacingly. "But now, I think someone will."

"Let me get this straight." She looked at the daggers embedded in her gauntlets and smiled before she refocused on him. "This is all my fault because I didn't have the decency to get mugged meekly?"

He stared at her.

"I think that's a yes," Lyle said.

"I do too." She raised her voice. "I've met so many people like you, bucko. People who have somehow convinced themselves that they should simply be allowed to do whatever they want and everyone else has to put up with it. Some of you have knives, some have power or money, but there is one thing you all share."

A bolt of earth magic crackled and embedded the leader's hand in mud. He yelped as the dagger hilt under his palm disintegrated with the clods of dirt.

"It's that you can go pound sand," Dotty finished. "Lyle, you deal with him and our downed friend."

"Aye." Lyle gave her a serious nod, cracked his knuckles, and ran a brief vocal exercise before yelling "Stoooooooooout!" as he attacked.

Dotty pivoted to the other two with a chuckle. They didn't look amused by her tactics with their comrades, and she felt the old flicker of doubt—*Be polite. Don't make anything worse.*

To hell with it. She'd spent her whole life doing that. Now, she had magic and knives and she'd be damned if she would let people get away with it when they decided to mug her on the open road.

The first of the two—a woman with what was either dirty-blonde hair or simply blonde hair that was very dirty—spurred her horse into a canter to swing wide. Dotty noticed her adjust her feet in the stirrups and loosen the grip and smiled.

She would bet anything that she knew what was about to happen.

The other mercenary wheeled on his horse and leveled a crossbow at her. His smile was grim. "Magic is all well and good, but you can't—"

A piece of stone stabbed through the weapon and he dropped it with a yelp as the wood splintered.

When he cried out, she was already spinning. While she would have liked to continue to watch his shocked face, she was fairly sure that the other mugger had a plan to sneak up behind her. She turned and confirmed that the woman had swung off her horse and crept closer, her dagger unsheathed. Once she saw that she had lost the element of surprise, she launched into an assault with a scream.

The shriek died in her throat when Dotty drew the daggers from her gauntlets.

"That's right," she said grimly. She dodged out of the way of the mercenary's first strike and laid open a line of red on the other woman's arm. Both of them turned, their eyes wary, and her adversary backed away. They clearly hadn't expected her to be a wizard, and her knowing how to wield daggers was another surprise.

Meanwhile, Lyle's fight seemed to be going well. He did not seem at all unnerved by fighting two-on-one and wove deftly between his two opponents, both now grounded. It took her a few cycles of the pattern to realize that he constantly cycled to the outside of one opponent or the other and made them turn in order to attack. This, in turn, forced their friend to move so that one was not in the way of the other.

Both of his opponents were limping and one nursed a wound on his shin that she would bet came from an unexpected duck and punch. The other had a bleeding wound on his foot and his horse was nowhere to be seen.

She had to remember to ask about that.

That was all she managed to see in the scattered glances she directed at him. The other two were wary, but even a few curveballs hadn't managed to dull their predatory instinct. She got the sense that both of them were tired and jaded, far beyond questions of right and wrong in what they did.

The only question they asked themselves was whether or not they could win a fight and how they could do it the quickest.

Honestly, she wished they would be less practical about it. Long fights with many flourishes gave her a chance to win the element of surprise. Veteran mercenaries, on the other hand, were more likely to be canny. They'd attack together, she decided. Whatever the next play was, it would be designed to lure her into doing something specific and she mustn't do it.

So, when the man drew a dagger and charged, Dotty sheathed hers and surged forward to meet him. The brief moment of surprise in his face slowed him enough for her to duck under the weapon and tackle him at the hips. They fell in an ungainly tangle of limbs and she shoved hard to scramble free. She made sure to stamp on his knife hand as she passed it and kicked the dagger away into the field behind them.

As she turned, panting, she realized that the woman had been poised to stab her in the back if she dodged sideways.

For some reason, that drove home to her exactly how real this was. Panic thrummed through her and she struggled to catch her breath.

"Dotty?" Prima sounded worried. *"Keep moving. Keep moving!"*

She took a single stumbling step but didn't know what to do from there. Fury had propelled her through earlier fights with ease, or the frantic need to find new tactics and execute them. Now that she had enough skill to spend time thinking of other things, she found her mind was distracted by the danger.

"Focus, Dotty," she muttered to herself.

When the two adversaries advanced on her again, she fell back. Her heart pounded in her throat and the thought of a dagger fight, a melee alone with two opponents, was enough to make her lose her breath again. She knew they could see how pale she was and the light the knowledge kindled in their eyes in return was savage and cruel. It was impossible to *not* see it and she hated it.

They took one step toward her, then another. One of them uttered a low chuckle.

The wave of heat and pressure that struck them tumbled them both in an instant. Burns appeared on their skin almost immediately and they dropped their knives. They rolled and screamed in an attempt to escape the wave of heat.

A shout caught Dotty's attention and she looked up to where one of Lyle's opponents sprinted toward her. The dwarf barreled after him, waving his arms and shouting something about not hurting the woman who still owed him a beer, and she rolled her eyes.

She was in no mood to play, however. If these mercenaries were the type who wanted to end fights quickly, she decided she would do the same thing.

And it was clear they didn't intend to leave on their own. There had only been two options—let them take whatever they wanted and move on, ready to terrorize others, or end it now.

Dotty waited while the man charged. She stood tall, her arms hidden inside the folds of her cloak, and watched him. When there was no possible chance for him to dodge, she raised the dagger in her right hand and stepped forward. Her left arm swept out and thrust his short sword away, and her dagger sank through his leather armor to slam home.

The shock on his face would be etched in her memory for a long time. Bile rose in her throat as he thudded to his knees and fell sideways. She looked at the others, who all backed away, wounded and terrified.

She had killed the leader, she realized and studied the figure who sprawled at her feet. He was fortyish, she estimated, someone whose youth had passed him by and who wanted to make his own little fiefdom with his own rules. He'd told himself this was the start of a larger mercenary band.

Somehow, she knew he made a point of being cruel.

And now, he was dead on the side of the road.

Dotty looked at the others. "Get. Out. Of my sight."

Their eyes widened. Lyle made a confused sound.

"Sheathe your weapons." She ground the command out. "Get on your horses, *do not* rob anyone else on the way to Insea, and when you get there, you had better find gainful employment that doesn't involve terrorizing innocent people. If you don't, so help me, I will find you and I will make you sorry. *Am I clear?*"

The three ran. They didn't bother to nod and merely babbled something over their shoulders. The one who had lost his horse caught the leader's and the three of them swung into their saddles and galloped toward Insea.

Dotty watched them go. Rage and nausea twisted in her chest in equal measure.

"Are ye sure that was wise?" Lyle asked finally. She looked at him. He had begun to clean his clawed fist weapons carefully but looked frequently at her. "Someone who's gone wrong like that will go back, like as not."

"Maybe," she said. "But I hate killing people so I'll give them a chance."

"Squeamishness doesn't have much place in a roadside fight," he said bluntly, "and you know where it has even less of a place? Politics."

She gave him a half-smile. "Is that a warning about our upcoming mission?"

"What gave it away?" He hung the two weapons at his waist. "Just because ye hate doin' somethin' doesn't make it the wrong thing to do."

"I know." She looked at the leader for a moment before she knelt to close his eyes. "Dragons don't bother me. Killing them, I mean. They're assholes. And killing people with magic isn't as bad. But feeling a knife go in…" She shuddered visibly.

"There's somethin' t' be said for that," Lyle agreed. "It makes ye less likely to kill on a whim."

"You know," she said as they walked back to soothe their horses, "in my world, a great number of wars were simply people marching one army up, the besieged force estimating whether they would win or lose, and everyone going home without a fight. Does that happen here?"

"I've never been part of a war," the dwarf said thoughtfully. "But I hear it's more boredom than anythin' so I'd say ye're probably right. That's borin' but it saves lives."

"Here's to a boring life," Dotty said dryly as she managed to clamber into the saddle.

"You know…it's odd to see a woman in such fancy gear and with such a fancy horse strugglin' so much to get on."

"I said I *disliked* killing people, not that I *wouldn't*."

He gave her a nervous look. "Right. Ye're a model of elegance. Let's go find an inn, then."

CHAPTER SIXTY-SIX

Jamie sat near one of the lab tables while Jacob oversaw all the patches being put onto the boy's head, neck, and hands. The kid looked even more nervous than usual, his thin shoulders hunched. On the other side of the room, his parents asked Amber what seemed like a never-ending stream of questions.

Nick knew they weren't keen to let their son enter the experiment with Taigan. He could even understand it to a degree. They knew how much fear for a child hurt, and they didn't want to put another one in danger needlessly.

But Jamie, it turned out, was surprisingly strong-willed. Nick had watched and heard snippets of the conversation that occurred in the Diatek cafeteria while he was eating lunch, and although the boy looked nervous, he hadn't backed down.

Whatever their reasons, his parents had eventually caved.

Emilia also watched the proceedings with a nervous look on her face, and Nick moved to stand near her.

"How are you doing?" he asked quietly.

"I'm..." She shrugged, then bit her lip. "I'm sorry about this morning."

"Are you?" He looked at her and held her gaze.

She considered his challenge. "Yes," she said finally. "I shouldn't take it all out on you. But you should have seen some of the scuzzy doctors who got their hooks into my parents. They're...starting to hope again. I didn't want them to get hurt."

"What about *you*?" he asked her seriously.

"What do you mean?" She looked genuinely confused.

"Don't *you* miss your sister? Don't you want things to go back to... normal-ish?" He leaned on the table and noted the wary look in her eyes. "I'm only saying...yes, it's difficult for your parents, but it's also difficult for you and your brother. My brother...eh."

Emilia focused on him with new interest.

"It's not the same, I suppose," Nick said.

Emilia raised an eyebrow and in the moment, looked far older than her nineteen years. She also looked startlingly like her mother.

"Okay," he said and held his hands up. "But know I'm not saying this was as bad, okay? My brother went through a bad few years. Very bad."

"Cancer?" she guessed.

"Nope. Nothing like that. He simply kinda...went off the deep end." He hunched his shoulders. "You name it, he probably did it. He got busted for taking drugs, selling drugs, street racing, stealing cars... It sucked, but the thing was, it wasn't only that he was doing it but that our parents would not shut up about it. It was all they thought about."

She went very quiet.

"Every email, every call—it was about him somehow," he said. "Okay, probably not *all* of them, right, but it started to feel like it. It wasn't on purpose and I get it, but I was at MIT, for fuck's sake. I was —oh, sorry for my language."

"I'm nineteen, not nine," Emilia said.

"Still. I'm at work. My point is, I was doing cool stuff and I was their kid too, and it felt like I got forgotten most of the time." Nick shrugged. "And that was because he was doing terrible stuff so it was easy to resent him, honestly."

She laughed but stifled it before anyone could notice.

"Seriously," he said quietly. "I can't imagine how much more difficult this is. You miss your sister and she hasn't done anything *wrong*, but there's so much energy spent on that. You're taking time off school now and it's not exactly for a vacation, is it?"

Her expression seemed to suggest she might cry now.

"I'm sorry," he said. "I...shouldn't have said anything."

"No, it's not that." She wiped her eyes angrily. "It's only...I thought all those things and I feel so bad about them, you know? It's like you said, she didn't do this on *purpose*. And she *is* in bad shape when she comes out of the comas—and she's afraid of them and I don't want her to be afraid. I'm always terrified she'll never wake up from one and we'll wait and wait and wait and never see her again. But all they talk about is her and I'm so *sick* of it!"

Her voice had risen but not enough to attract everyone's attention, and Nick saw with a pang that she had learned not to let her outbursts catch her parents' attention. She sat and put her arms on the table with her chin resting on her hands. Every part of her seemed curled inward.

"And Jamie's her *twin*," she said, her voice so soft that he almost couldn't hear it at all. "It's worse for him. It's like half of him is missing. And it...doesn't all come back when she comes out. Every time she's gone, he starts to live his life on his own, feeling guilty about it, and then she wakes up and he has to choose all over again."

"Have you talked to him about it?" Nick asked.

"Yeah. No. Not really." She shrugged. "He doesn't like to. Did you talk to your brother about that stuff?"

"Well, we said words in each other's general direction. At a very loud volume."

That drew a smile out of her. "Did he ever get better?"

"Yeah." He shrugged. "He sells insurance now and has a girlfriend. I imagine he's tired of our parents still watching him like a hawk. He and I don't talk much, though." It was especially easy to get away with that now with PIVOT having been acquired and test subjects piling up. The situation made it easy for Eric to assume he would be too busy to take a call and as easy for him to tell himself he was too busy to make one.

But that wasn't something she needed to hear. He shrugged again.

Emilia looked at where Jamie shuffled to stretch out in the pod. Her parents had hurried closer and she looked both annoyed and understanding.

"Jamie wants to go in," Nick said while her attention was partially elsewhere. "What about you? You came along—did this treatment appeal to you, too?"

She looked sharply at him. "I—"

He let the silence stretch between them.

Finally, she said, "We used to play games. When we were little. Like fairy tales, but not always the ones you'd know—some are those our mother told us. Also, Dad's mother was Polish, so some of those stories were kind of crazy. Basically, we'd make up these characters and they'd help the people in each of the stories. I thought maybe you could build a story with that." She hunched her shoulders. "It sounds stupid when I say it out loud."

"No. It doesn't." His mind was turning furiously. "Look, why don't you do this—start writing down what you remember about these stories. We were able to put specific things in the game for certain people, so we might be able to make changes to the world here. If it works, I mean. If you all decide to—yeah."

"You'd do that?" She stared at him, her expression both hopeful and wary.

"I can't promise anything," he said. "I hope you can understand that. I'm not saying it to be cruel and I'm only trying to make sure I don't offer a solution I can't deliver. But if you know ways to…call your sister back…I think it would be good for us to know about them. Send the ideas to us and we'll all look through them and see what we can do."

Her eyes lit up. "Oh. Wow. Okay. I'd have to check at our house, but I even have some of the old art we drew for it. I'm…studying graphic design. Those weren't very good, but I could probably spruce them up." She fumbled in her bag and pulled a notebook out. "I'm gonna start writing things down so I don't forget anything. I…"

Her voice trailed off when the lid of the pod began to close over her brother. Her worry was palpable.

"It'll be okay," Nick told her. "You can see his character there on the monitor. You'll be able to watch and know what's going on."

"Okay." Emilia said. She nodded. "Okay, I'll write this down and then come watch."

Jamie lay back and tried not to hyperventilate. He was doing this for Taigan, he thought. He would be brave for her because she was locked in a place like this.

Locked in. Oh, God. It took all his self-control to not begin screaming.

He hadn't told them about the part where he was claustrophobic. He was worried that, if he did, they wouldn't let him inside the pod.

The reminder became a litany for sanity. He was doing this for Taigan, he was doing this for Taigan, he was doing this for Taigan.

Everything was black. He would suffocate.

Blue appeared around him and seemed to shimmer into existence. Jamie took a deep, shuddering breath. He could see far out to where steps of pale blue illuminated a path through the blue-black. The stairs glowed and tiny white particles drifted up. He reached out to touch one of them and only then realized that he must be inside the game.

He panicked and managed to do a strange, jerky dance. The more he tried to think about it, the worse it got. Either he was frozen or he flailed wildly with noodly arms.

"Are you quite finished?"

Jamie jumped, shrieked, and managed to fall. It hurt, which surprised him. Should it hurt?

"I've given you a complementary 5 levels in Bad Dancing," the voice said.

"Who are you?" He looked around and tried to slow his breathing. "Where are you?"

"I'm everywhere. I'm Prima, the AI who runs the game."

"Wait—AI? You're seriously...you're sentient?" He wasn't quite sure what he thought about that possibility.

"I am not sentient," the voice said. *"I am simply extensively programmed in human language and communication. Your question is common."*

"Oh. Sorry?"

"There's no need to apologize. You should come this way." The path flared slightly to provide direction.

"Okay." He tried to hop along the various steps. They began to wind slightly and ascended a staircase—which was amusing as there didn't seem to be anything except the path. Even so, it was somewhat nerve-wracking when the path descended again. He constantly expected to trip.

As long as he didn't think about it, though, he seemed to be able to move. Dust motes drifted beside him and he held his hands up for them to blow past like dandelion seeds. He smiled. This wasn't so bad after all.

"So, tell me. Why are you here?"

"My sister is in a coma and I want to help her," Jamie answered. "Or—is that what you meant?"

"Yes. That is what I meant. Is she already in the game?"

"No. We wanted to try it first to see what it was like." He trudged up another hill. "We don't even know if she'll be able to...use this."

"And if she does, you will want to come here and help her find her way to waking up."

"Yes. But I don't know if it's possible."

"It's happened before," the AI said in such a normal tone that he began to have doubts that it was simply a programmed bot. He allowed himself to wonder if it was a real AI before he realized it must be a person posing as an AI.

A real AI. He wasn't that stupid.

"Do you have any requests for a place to go first?"

"Somewhere..." Jamie considered this quickly. "Somewhere that looks magical. Like nothing I could find in the real world. But not scary," he added. "Calm."

"*It's a good thing you were specific,*" the AI said, which wasn't all that reassuring.

A moment later, the blue faded to reveal rolling hills covered with long, waving grasses. Pink flowers bloomed amidst them and more motes of golden light hung in the air. Clouds billowed in the distance, impossibly picturesque and lit by the colors of a sunset that he would bet never ended.

"*Is this the kind of thing you had in mind?*"

"Yes." Jamie spun to sweep his gaze across the landscape. "It's beautiful. Thank you—what did you say your name was?"

"*Prima.*"

"Thank you, Prima." He took a few steps forward before he stopped hastily. "Can I walk around?"

"*Yes. Now, would you like a combat-based opening quest or something else?*"

Once again, he took a moment to think. If his parents weren't watching, he'd choose combat in a heartbeat, but he knew they wouldn't like it. Still…he was there and he couldn't get hurt, right?

"Combat-based," he said and tried to hide his smile. His parents would freak out.

They'd live, he reassured himself.

"*Excellent. Next question. Would you like to fight bare-handed, with a sword, or with a staff?*"

"A staff." He'd always wondered what it would be like to thwack someone with a stick. Now, he'd get to find out. An old staff appeared in his hand and in the next moment, his clothing changed. Startled, he looked down at a raggedy shirt and pants, along with shoes that barely deserved the name. "So…I don't look so good."

"*For now. You'll be given chances to fix that. Your first one is to bring in five jackalopes.*"

Jamie uttered a snort of laughter. Jackalopes. What a world. An icon of the creature appeared in front of him and rotated to display white fur with a purple sheen to it and blue antlers that were hung with strands of golden lights.

"Whoa. Pretty."

"With very sharp teeth."

That warning, combined with a rustle from behind him, made him turn quickly. He scanned the area as he circled slowly, his staff out. Where were the jackalopes? He took another couple of steps, then backed away hastily when one of the creatures thundered through the grass and slid to a stop in front of him.

"Prima," he said as evenly as he could. "You did *not* mention that they were dog-sized."

"Didn't I? It must have slipped my mind."

"I bet," he muttered. He wracked his brain to choose his angle of attack and made an abrupt decision when the jackalope bared its teeth—which were *very* pointy—and growled. "Fuck!" He brought the staff down with a clatter on the antlers and dodged sideways with a yelp when it attacked.

GIRLISH SHRIEKS, Level 1

RUN AWAY, Level 1

Jamie would have made a complaint about that characterization of him but a growl behind him seemed more important. He knew better than to thwack downward this time, so he whipped the staff in a descending arc as he spun.

It struck the jackalope on the side and it uttered a yelp much like his and snarled before it charged again. Jamie threw himself forward, tripped over the staff, and sprawled awkwardly.

CLUMSY, Level 1

RUN AWAY, Level 2

"Oh, come on!" He curled into a ball as the creature lunged and snapped its pointy teeth. He tangled his hands in the fur at its neck and held it away from him as he rolled desperately. "What...kind of... rabbit...has *fangs?*"

"A jackalope."

"Yes, thank you, I got that!" He twisted, kneed it in the stomach, and stood to search for the staff as his adversary flipped to its feet. He raced forward, snatched his weapon, and thrust it at the jackalope when it lunged at him.

It yipped and its health bar ticked down from half to zero. He stared at it, panting with the staff still held in front of him and his thigh muscles burning. Slowly, he stood and nodded to reassure himself.

"Okay. That was…unsettling." He strode forward through the grass in search of others. He could hear running water nearby, which sounded soothing but seemed but less so now that he knew massive, bloodthirsty rabbits lurked in the grass.

Lord alone knew what was in the streams. Angry jellyfish? Fish with legs? He shuddered.

"So. Tell me about your sister."

"She's my twin," Jamie said. He pushed through a patch of grass, saw a jackalope, and managed to land a solid strike this time before he screamed and dodged. His momentum pushed him into a spin and he began to circle his prey. "Her name is Taigan."

"And you are?"

"Jamie."

"Nice to meet you, Jamie."

"Likewise," he said, thwacked the stick down, and landed a kick at the same time. The jackalope's teeth grazed his leg and he yelped in pain. "Oh, buckets, that hurts. Fuck, fuck—sorry, Mom."

"I am not your mother."

"I know that."

"Just checking."

The AI watched him through the next three fights as well and offered condescending commentary that he would have resented far more if it hadn't often provided useful clues about how to structure the next round.

By the time he finished, he'd leveled up in Stamina and Staff Fighting, as well as earned Rank Three of Jackalope Slayer. He looked around as he caught his breath and saw what looked like a roof peeking over the edge of the hill.

"Prima, is that a village?"

"*Why don't you go check? And, while you're there, why don't you ask if anyone wanted some jackalopes killed?*"

"Do you have any more suggestions?"

"*Ask where you can find better clothes,*" the AI recommended. "*You honestly do look ridiculous.*"

"And whose fault is that?" Jamie asked her. "You know, maybe I'll keep these clothes out of spite."

"*You wouldn't.*"

"Try me."

CHAPTER SIXTY-SEVEN

The rest of the journey to Berghold was more pleasant but with two main exceptions. Both were places where the dwarven caravan had encountered elven forces in Dotty's first PIVOT experience.

They reached the gulley the elves had used for a sneak attack on the third day. She rode through the entire defile with her shoulders stiff and her gaze darting constantly to where the elven archers had stood on the rocky walls and fired at the trapped caravan. Despite all the things that had happened since then, she vividly remembered the shouts and the way the wagons and carts had turned with such agonizing slowness in an effort to escape the onslaught.

Her horse, sensing her unease, pranced nervously for the entire length of the gulley and up the winding road at the other side. She tried to calm her but knew her tense body was enough to undo any comfort the animal might feel.

When they emerged from the gulley at last—after what had likely been no more than an hour but had felt like a week—Lyle blew out a long breath and shook his head.

"I have t' say," he said, "I don' like the memory of being shot at like fish in a barrel."

Dotty nodded. Her hands were clenched on the reins and she loosened them deliberately.

"What are ye thinkin'?" he asked her.

"That things like that mess make me wonder if peace is even achievable," she said bluntly. "I don't want to defeat myself before we even arrive, but I can't stop thinking about those asshats—Marwitz and the elven commander, both thinking their race should rule the whole world. That's what we're up against, isn't it?"

"I s'pose," he said contemplatively, "but the truth of it is—an' I've seen this everywhere I've gone—that people with full bellies and faith in the future don' spend much time pinin' fer war."

"But are the dwarves and the elves truly struggling?" she pressed. "Are they sitting around with empty bellies?"

"No." Lyle shrugged. "An' ye'll always have some…what was it ye called 'em? Asshats?" He chuckled. "I like that. Yeah, there's no gettin' away from it all. But when times are good, people don' listen to the asshats too closely."

"I hope you're right," she said grimly. "Otherwise, we're…"

"Fucked?"

"I intended to say in trouble. But I suppose yours works, too." She shook her head and gave him a small smile. After years of sharply reprimanding her children for vulgar language, it seemed she was enjoying her slide into hypocritically impolite behavior.

Perhaps by eighty-four, you had earned certain privileges. It was worth considering.

A day later, they arrived in the little town that had sheltered them and helped them to escape the elves. Dotty had been half-afraid that they would ride up to a smoking wreck, but she was glad to see that it was intact and thriving.

The townsfolk greeted Lyle with good humor and cheers. They were more cautious with Dotty, who now looked human, although his presence beside her and her fine clothes earned her some respect. She was pleased to see that polite greetings also warmed them somewhat.

They liked her even more after she polished off an entire bowl of bean soup and a plate of sausages and washed her meal down with a large mug of beer. She cupped her hands around a warm mug of tea, fragrant with fresh herbs, and listened to the songs filling the tavern.

"How are ye feeling?" Lyle asked her.

"Why?" Dotty looked at him. "Oh. I feel perfectly fine. A little tired, maybe. But I want to finish this before…you know."

He thought this over as he drained the rest of his beer. "Does yer own world not have things like this that need fixin'?"

She looked at him in surprise. "Would you rather it were your people doing this instead of an outside realm?"

"No, that's not what I mean," he hastened to assure her. "Ye and Justin—ye came here to help *us*, but why not yer own people?"

It was a fair point and one worth considering. "I…don't know. Justin does, I think. Where I am, at home, I'm merely an old woman. No one will listen to me about peace treaties."

"It's their loss," Lyle said and his tone said he meant it.

"But you must understand, hmm?" She smiled at him. "You went off adventuring when you were younger. You went to see faraway lands."

"Well, yes, but that was more to find new ales than broker peace treaties." He downed another mug of ale and slammed it on the counter. "Speakin' o' which, *this* one is mighty fine. Barkeep!" He looked at her as the innkeeper took the mug. "When my time comes, I hope…I'm as content as you."

"So do I," she said. She squeezed his hand affectionately. "I think you have many years yet."

"Not if we keep pissin' the elves off," he said with a wink. He thanked the innkeeper and started on his next mug. "So! Ye asked on the ride about the story of the eighty-five snakes."

"Yes. I still don't understand how you could *not* notice that many snakes, even if—"

"Hush, hush, lemme tell you."

It had been weeks since Dotty was there last, but the road through the mountains hadn't changed in the slightest. It was still covered in snow and white-furred rabbits hopped amidst the tops of grasses and the shadows of evergreens, while birds trilled and seemed untroubled by the cold.

Her gown wasn't exactly suited to this weather, and she drew her cloak tightly around her and thought longingly of Berghold. She was far past the age where she wanted to do things like trade comfort for style.

At least there would be mulled wine when they arrived, she thought.

"Is it safe to speak frankly?" she asked Lyle.

He nodded.

"What will we say about Marwitz?"

"Ah. There's not much to avoid, honestly." He smoothed his beard and his gaze tracked a kestrel on one of the mountain winds. "They know he was a traitor and that he conspired to sell the location of the caravan to the elves. His wife confessed that she'd known about that."

"So, why—"

"He was a councilor," he interrupted before she could say anything more. "It would have taken a unanimous vote of the council to strip him of his powers, which would mean he would immediately be accused of treason, probably convicted, and executed. They might not have wanted to do that to shame his family and you can't *execute* a councilor…basically ever. If you do, *you're* guilty of treason, yada yada yada."

"You know, I don't think I've ever heard someone describe treason as, 'yada yada yada.'"

"I'm a man of many talents," Lyle said. "In any case, they know about his treason and he is appropriately shamed, but it's best for everyone that the elf killed him. It avoided a *very* tricky legal situation."

"Ah," Dotty said. Her lips twitched. "I see. I suppose it's also fitting that the very people he tried to sell you out to were the ones who killed him."

"It has a nice, poetic flair to it, doesn't it?" he asked. He gave her a winsome smile. "It couldn't have worked out better if we'd planned it."

She shook her head with a laugh. Now that she was acclimating to the cold—and anticipating the wine—she was able to take more joy in the day. The snow was pristine, the sky a cloudless blue, and the mountain peaks around them were some of the most beautiful she had ever seen.

"Are there any things I should do as a human that weren't required of a dwarf?" she asked.

"Ah. Hmm." The dwarf frowned in thought. "I don't suppose Jaco thought to send us with gifts."

"He did. There's a carved bracelet made of a rare stone only found near Insea, with a protection spell."

When she relayed this to her companion, he nodded.

"That's good. Don't lie outright, but if ye could hint that ye made it—"

Dotty shook her head, outraged. "I will not take credit for someone else's work!"

"A powerful sorceress using her powers for protection and gifting artifacts to the dwarves? Ye'd earn respect."

"Hmm. I'll think about it." She urged her horse forward. "Do you hear—"

"Yeah, that'll be a patrol," Lyle said. "And coming up quick, from the sound of it. Drop yer cloak."

"What? Why?"

"Dwarves value strength," he said bluntly. "Try not to shiver."

With a sigh, she did as he said. The gown fluttered around her bare shoulders and she felt both out of place and deeply ostentatious. She was fairly sure the stones holding the red silk up were actual *diamonds*, for one thing.

It wasn't long before the patrol reached them. Her companion held a hand up in greeting and she echoed his gesture as regally as she could without erupting into genuine laughter. She was hardly a powerful sorceress that these people should respect and fear.

Then again, when she considered the dragons, the elves, the

mercenaries—and, of course, the letter in her saddlebag that was offering peace—perhaps that wasn't entirely true.

Maybe she *was* someone powerful and someone they should respect.

The leader of the patrol was a woman with fiery red hair coiled around her head in elaborate braids. She scrutinized the two of them carefully.

"Greetings, Stout," she said to Lyle. "And who might you be?"

"I am Dorothy of…New Amsterdam." She offered as elegant a smile as she could. "We come bearing a message for the council from the throne of Insea."

"Dorothy," Lyle said and looked amused at the change of name, "has trained with the finest sorcerers amongst the dwarves and the orcs. Her presence and her work are granted to Berghold as a sign of goodwill."

Dotty kept her smile pasted in place and prayed that he wouldn't talk her into anything she couldn't deliver on.

"I see," said the patrol leader. She nodded briskly. "As official emissaries, we will offer you escort."

"We are honored," she told the woman and spurred her horse to ride alongside her. "I am eager, if time permits, to speak to your *zauberer* and learn from them."

"Is there…something specific you wish to study?" The guard seemed uncertain.

"Nothing in particular," she said. "The joy is in the learning, is it not? In exchange, I have some familiarity with the fire and water magics of the orcs. Perhaps they would interest your researchers."

"I am certain they would," the woman said promptly.

"And, of course," she added, "I would be happy to provide introductions between them and my teachers."

"I did not know that the orcs accepted outsiders."

"They are wary, of course, as few travel their lands, but—like most researchers—their shamans are glad of kindred spirits and new learning." She smiled. "I must say, however, the food in the dwarven lands is much more to my taste. There were a few orcish dishes I thought might burn my tongue out of my mouth."

She was careful to keep the conversation light as they wound up the mountain and into the passageways that led to Berghold. More than once, she caught sight of Lyle's approving look and hid a smile at that. She hadn't gone through all of Harry's work parties for nothing and it seemed she'd learned all that small talk for a reason.

And this was *much* more fun than the average cocktail party.

CHAPTER SIXTY-EIGHT

They were taken through the city in a mounted procession that left rising whispers in its wake. Dwarves everywhere stopped to turn and stare at the human sorceress in the scandalous red dress who chatted amicably with the dwarven guards.

No one could miss the fact that they headed to the Temple, the large building that also housed Berghold's ruling council, and many also recognized Lyle as one of Berghold's nobles.

For her part, Dotty attempted to behave as if she didn't notice the stares or the whispers. Now and then, she would smile at someone as if they had met each other's gaze by chance and would try not to laugh when the person blushed and looked away.

It was impossible not to notice how different things were now. The first time she had been there, she'd been a dwarf and had been recognized as any other citizen. People's eyes hadn't followed her with interest—or open suspicion.

Also, the buildings seemed smaller than she remembered. She could see that she would have to duck to enter most of them.

At least it was warm.

At the Temple, hostlers emerged promptly for their horses and saddlebags, and the companions were swept into the shadowed hallways. A servant took their letter of introduction at a run and they were shown to a suite of rooms, wide and spacious, that looked out over the entire city.

"Are these bugged?" she asked Lyle.

"Are they…what?"

"Ah. Are there listening…devices, spells?"

He looked shocked at the thought. "Of course not. We're diplomats. It would be a grievous breach of trust."

"Well, yes, but…" She waved her hands. "I don't know. If you're sure, though, we should go over our strategy."

"That sounds wise." The dwarf picked up a small bell and rang for dinner before he spread their various documents on a large table near the fire. He snapped his fingers to direct magical lanterns to hover over the surface so everything would be legible, then hauled two chairs closer and brought a large pitcher of ale.

Jaco might not have had much time to prepare this particular mission, but he had clearly gathered evidence on what was important to the dwarves. He also laid out ground rules about what they could and could not promise in negotiations.

Their cover story for the dwarves was that Insea now considered the debt between their nations to be paid in full. They were to say that the king wanted to move forward together into a new era, exchanging both culture and goods, which would serve as a strong and united front in recognition of their shared history.

"So, other than lying about the bracelet, do you have any good ideas for the opener?" Dotty asked.

"I didn't say lie. I only said we should present you as a sorceress with training in stone powers and then you present the bangle. It looks good." He propped one boot heel on the other toe. "And, in any case, you should be the one to take the primary role in the negotiations."

"Why?" She frowned at him. "Oh. Oh, of course. You're a dwarven citizen so you can hardly be an emissary of another government."

"That's not precisely true. Note, for instance, that we are housed in the diplomats' quarters instead of my house. That recognizes my current status here."

"Which is…" She gestured for him to continue.

"I have become aware of an opportunity I believe will benefit Berghold and have taken the opportunity to bring word of it so that my nation may benefit." Lyle spread his hands. "I am staking my reputation and my family's on this, you see."

"Oh. So, no pressure."

"I was merely explaining to you how it works. But, yes. If you could refrain from sullying my family's name, that would be much appreciated." He grinned at her. "Conveniently, however, I *do* believe it would be good for Berghold to take advantage of this, so there's not *much* that I'm risking."

"What *are* you risking?" Dotty asked suspiciously.

Lyle didn't answer at once, likely because the servants appeared with dinner. They placed loaded platters on the tables, leaving enough food that she wondered how many people they thought were there before they disappeared. Not without gawping at her first, however.

She ignored it with as much dignity as she could muster.

"What are you risking?" she asked again once they had disappeared.

"There's a strong isolationist faction in Berghold," he answered promptly. "We have good amounts of grain and meat and so on, we rarely need other goods in trade, and our city can be made relatively secure at the drop of a hat. Many feel we should let the rest of the world have its wars and simply stay out of everything."

"So that's…different from Marwitz?"

"Yes. Although, if we're being honest, more than a few of them agreed with his other beliefs about the world." He shook his head. "There are many alliances and people who don't say what they think for one reason or another."

"And that's what we're working with," Dotty said glumly. "Great."

"That's politics," Lyle said. He shrugged. "'Course, it's also why I left, but let's not get into that right now. We're back and we have a peace treaty to build."

"Right." She rubbed her forehead and resisted the urge to take a long gulp of ale. Alcohol might not have quite the same effect in this world, but she needed to keep as clear a head as she could. "Well, let's start with what we have, then."

"One bracelet," he said and tapped the box.

"We're starting strong." She smiled ruefully. "Now, we know that there are quarries in Insea's lands that would benefit not only from dwarven-made mining goods but also master miners to teach them—and, perhaps, have a stream of the profits from the mine go directly to Berghold."

"Hold back on that one," he advised. "It's a good idea, but Berghold is jealous of its minin' secrets. Even a cut of the profits won't be enough. They see their craft as one of the few things they hold over the rest of the races."

"They're not making use of it, though," she said. "It's not like they sell much in the way of ore—or goods."

"I didn't say it made much sense, I merely said they did it." He frowned as he thought a little more. "No, if ye want t' even *suggest* that, ye'll need to offer somethin' comparable. Insea has some techniques of makin' different alloys—mostly fer jewelry but some fer weapons. Jaco'd never agree to us offerin' that, though."

"Yes, he will," Dotty said at once.

"Yer outta yer mind. He'd be flayed alive by the artisans."

"Lyle." Dotty stared at him with exaggerated patience. "The entire premise of these negotiations is that Berghold and Insea have a shared history and Insea wants to move forward as *partners*. Exchanging artisans who can teach one another about different alloys gives us two things. First, as you say, it removes certain tactical advantages on *both* sides. Insea is effectively reducing its chance to strike at Berghold with weaponry they can't counter. They are saying that they trust Berghold enough that they won't need this advantage."

"Yes, but—"

"Beyond that," she said and spoke over him, "the alloys and weaponry that could be made by the finest artisans of Berghold and

Insea working *together*? That's impressive. It will help both nations to move forward."

"Dotty—"

"And finally," she said, "do you want to know how I know Jaco will agree to this?"

Lyle looked at her almost warily.

"Because the entire world has centuries' worth of resentments built up when it comes to Insea," she said bluntly. "All the wars that *should* have happened, all the slights and resentments—none of those went away. They're all still there, not only outside Insea but inside it too. There are a thousand and one things coming down the pike that Insea will have to weather."

"And ye think some of the only advantages Insea has will help…how?"

"Don't you see?" Dotty shook her head impatiently. "How do you defeat a hundred armies when you don't have one of your own?"

He stared at her.

She folded her arms and waited implacably.

"You…don't?" he ventured finally.

"Bingo," she said. "You don't. There is no way Insea will ever win all the wars that will come. It'll have to push some of them off and avoid others entirely. If it draws inward and tries to stand alone, it *will* fall. The *only* way it will survive is if it cultivates allies. There is nothing in Insea that is more important than its survival—not its knowledge of alloys, not its artists or mathematicians, and not its artifacts. Anything it has, it must be prepared to give for this."

A thought struck her then and her hand covered her mouth.

"Is everythin' okay?" Lyle asked. He looked worried.

"That's why he sent us," she said. "He fed us all this hooey about how Kural knows the fae and I've fought with the orcs and all that, but the truth is that none of us are from Insea. None of us are involved in the government. He sent us because we would give up things no one else would."

Lyle's jaw hung open. "That's…mad."

"Crazy like a fox," she said, with a tiny smile. "He wants us to bargain like this—logically and without pride for national secrets." She rubbed her hands together. "I'm looking forward to this, I must say, although I imagine it would be easy to go overboard."

"Ye think?" Lyle snatched his mug of beer up and drank like his life depended on it.

"You're not…scared, are you?" Dotty couldn't have poked fun if she wanted to. She was too bemused by this side of him.

"I'm an adventurer!" he said. He waved his hands. "Dammit, where's the rest of the beer—what kind of Berghold feast *is* this?" He found a jug and poured. "I ran off rather than join the council. I don't know how to bargain!"

"The beer is now overflowing your mug," she pointed out.

"Oh. Right." He looked at the beer on the floor, still too distracted to care very much.

"I guess I don't see the problem." She picked her goblet of wine up and sat in one of the obscenely comfortable chairs—at least, she remembered them being obscenely comfortable when she was as short as a dwarf. She adjusted her back slightly and grimaced. "Okay, your ass is on the line to make sure Berghold gets a good deal and we've basically found out you can't go wrong in that way. Right?"

"That's what bothers me," he said. He dropped gracelessly into a chair and leaned forward to ring for the servants, then rubbed at his forehead. "Insea is vulnerable. I'm worried we'll go too far and they'll avoid war but be crippled."

Dotty smiled at him.

"What?" He looked suspiciously at her.

"You have the chance to get everything you could possibly want for your country and you're worried about being unfair to the other party," she said. "It's a good indication of your character. I hope the rest of the council sees your worth."

"I'm not on the council," he corrected her.

"Give it time," she advised him. "You'll be running it, I'd bet you anything."

Lyle sat in contemplative silence while the servants came to clean the mess, casting curious looks at them the whole time. It was clear that they wondered if there had been a fight and she was slightly too mischievous to assure them otherwise.

When they were gone, she gave her companion a gentle look.

"War comes from poverty and fear," she said. "Whatever happens tomorrow, we have to make the dwarves believe that Insea will make them prosperous and will not hurt them—nor will its friendship bring other dangers."

"How could being friends with Insea be dangerous?" he asked.

"Well, for one thing, remember how there are about to be many old grievances coming to light? And it's not only that, Lyle. Remember who else doesn't like Insea."

"*Oh.*" He looked worried. "The elves. The splinter faction."

"Yes," she said. "We need to be ready to address that."

CHAPTER SIXTY-NINE

For the negotiations, Prima had provided Dotty with a gown that called Insea to mind—sweeping lines like elven architecture with silk in peachy-pink, golden-white, and pale silver, all the colors that made Insea the city of famous beauty.

When she was dressed, she turned this way and that and examined herself in the mirror.

"Do you like it?" Prima asked finally.

"Yes." She smiled and blushed. "Very much so." She was getting more and more comfortable wearing these absolute confections of gowns. Of course, it helped that she didn't need to worry about getting them dirty or falling. However, there was something that concerned her. "Should I have my shoulders out for a negotiation? That would be entirely inappropriate on Earth."

"You definitely should. You're a sorceress and you're showing that you don't play by their rules. Magic users in this world are immensely powerful and respected, not to mention long-lived. It's good for you to look out of place —especially if you look elegant."

"Huh." She twirled experimentally and smiled when one of the layers of the skirt billowed outward. Silver embroidery and crystals on the gauze seemed to float around her like little motes of light. "And you're sure I don't look ridiculous?"

"Well, now I'm torn. On the one hand, you don't look ridiculous at all, but on the other hand, I do have a reputation to uphold as the resident snarky AI."

Dotty laughed. "That's good enough. Where's Lyle?"

"On his way."

"Is there enough time for a cup of coffee?"

"Of course." A cup of coffee in an old-fashioned diner mug winked into being on a nearby table. She sipped it and hummed with pleasure. Harry had been the coffee drinker in their house and she'd rarely made it since he had died. It reminded her of the hundreds of lazy mornings they had spent together after his retirement.

When Lyle knocked on the door, she gathered her cloak and the box that held the carved bracelet and followed him into the hallway. They walked in silence, accompanied by official council servants. Dotty could tell because of the blue robes and impressively blank facial expressions.

Which ones, she wondered, were enemies, allied with people who wanted to see her fail?

She didn't like thinking this way.

The dwarven council was larger than she had expected—forty dwarves in all varieties of fancy hats that probably meant something important. In all honesty, they merely looked like different brands of shiny things to her, but all the wearers seemed very self-important.

"Do not insult the hats," Prima advised.

"I know that," she said under her breath.

"You'll try to be sly and say something about impressive hats. I know you. Don't risk it."

"Right." Still, she added quietly, "I'll have some jokes tonight, though."

"I'm counting on it. I—"

"Prima?"

"Nothing. You should focus on the negotiations."

Dotty frowned but it was difficult to argue with the AI's logic. Lyle was finishing a brief but powerful speech about why he had accompanied her there, and she studied the faces of the councilors to see who seemed drawn in.

Several were nodding, which was good, and one or two of them were decked out in enough wrought-iron jewelry that they could only be artisans.

But far too many looked either nonplussed or openly hostile.

"And this," he said as he stepped aside to gesture at her, "is Dorothy, a noted wizard, slayer of two dragons, and one who has long stood against injustice. She serves as a representative of Insea in these negotiations." He waved her forward.

She stepped into the center of the audience floor, nodded to the council, and almost bowed. Her deference was a conscious choice as she wanted to give these dwarves every respect.

"Councilors of Berghold," she said, and was startled by the way her voice boomed—there must be some magic on the floor. "I have traveled many lands and seen many peoples, but in all my travels, I have never seen such consummate artisans as live in Berghold. I bring you this gift from the King of Insea." She opened the box to show them the bracelet. "Although it is a mere token, I hope it may become a symbol as it combines the craftsmanship and mastery of both elven and dwarven magics. May it be a symbol of the luck and prosperity Insea hopes will flourish here."

She handed the box to a servant, who hurried to show it to the front row of councilors. They looked at it, their faces unreadable.

Please, let that not be a bad sign.

Dotty clasped her hands in front of her with her fingers interlocked and pushed all worry out of her mind.

"Since the founding of Berghold, you have sent your finest craftsmanship to Insea each year—objects of untold power and expertise. These gifts remind us of the shared history that lies between the two cities, but it is time for those gifts to cease and a new age of friendship to begin, not as one city state with a debt to another but as two friends who move forward together."

A commotion followed this immediately. Several of the councilors leaned either forward or back in their seats and craned to whisper to others, and some stared angrily at her.

This, she had not expected. Suspicion, perhaps. Gladness, certainly.

But *anger?*

"That is it?" one of the councilors asked. His nose flared with fury. A few others made cautioning noises but far more gave tiny nods. "You declare the debt canceled and you expect us to rejoice?"

"There is more," she said, but she could hear the uncertainty in her voice. She squeezed her hands together momentarily to give herself resolve. "We wish to send many of our artisans here to offer any learning that is desired regarding our alloys and crafts."

Silence was her only answer. The councilors watched her, stone-faced.

Dotty looked at Lyle, who seemed uncertain as well.

She determined not to dance around the issue. "Councilors," she said gravely, "it appears I have erred in presenting this offer. I assure you, no insult was intended. Will you tell me where the error lies so that Insea may present a better gift?"

For a moment, she thought the councilor who had spoken might smile. Certainly, he looked surprised by her words—even pleasantly so. Then his brows snapped together again.

"A gift?" he asked contemptuously. "Insea offers…a gift."

At this juncture, she would have preferred to stay quiet. She hadn't reached this age without recognizing a trap when she saw one, and she would prefer to let him vent his anger at her without playing into it. Unfortunately, it seemed that neither he nor any of the other councilors intended to speak until she responded.

"You are right," she said. "To call it a gift is insufficient. Gifts among friends are only a small token of greater esteem."

She thought that was good—non-committal but open to a concession of being wrong. The council, however, disagreed and even Lyle winced slightly.

Crap.

"Your words are empty," the councilor said. "You take a great deal of time to say nothing new at all. You have told us already that you wish to be friends and that you wish this to be a token."

"I have offended you," Dotty said. "I apologize sincerely and without reserve. Will you not tell me how I have done wrong?" She tried as hard as she could to keep anger out of her voice. This council had known why she was there and they had received her with an understanding of what she would offer—Jaco's letter had made sure of that. And they had come there as, if not a united front, at least as a group much more ready to support the open rudeness of one another than to seek understanding.

They intended to see her squirm.

"What you have done wrong." The councilor rolled those words around in his mouth as if savoring them and tightened his grasp on the arms of his chair. He was enjoying this and made no effort to hide the fact.

Her blood pressure, however, began to climb.

"For centuries," the dwarven councilor told her, "Berghold has sent its finest crafts, as you said, to Insea. These artifacts are beyond valuable. They could have enlivened *our* city and enriched *our* people. Instead, they went to Insea, a city already prosperous."

"Is—" *Is Berghold not prosperous?* Dotty shut her mouth on the rest of her question and shook her head slightly, motioning for him to continue.

"And what debt was there to pay?" the councilor asked, his voice rising now. "What debt ever truly lay between Berghold and Insea?"

Dotty had the sense of stepping into darkness and finding she had gone over a cliff. She had heard about the debt from Berghold's citizens and to have that very concept challenged now caught her unawares.

But there had been signs. A person like Marwitz didn't come out of nowhere. Lyle had said that others thought as the treasonous councilor had and supported him even after what he had done.

"These matters have long been over and done," another councilor stated. He had black hair liberally streaked with gray. "Whether they were ill-advised at the time or not…that is a different conversation. A worthwhile one but a different one."

Dotty's heart sank. Even this man was not an ally. He too seemed to believe that Insea had taken advantage of Berghold. Worse, his belief that there had been a bad deal before would make him less likely to take any deals now.

Were these the best allies she had?

"It is not a different conversation," the first councilor said fiercely. "We have made one bargain with Insea and it was a bargain that drained us dry for centuries. Why should we not now look closely at this so-called *offer of friendship*—and ask them, too, how *they* judge the past?"

She looked at the second councilor and willed him to speak.

Unfortunately, everyone focused on her again.

"Answer me," the first councilor snapped. "What, truly, do you think was ever owed to Insea by my ancestors?"

I was not a part of this decision, Dotty wanted to protest, but she knew he would not accept that. She was there bargaining for Insea and that meant she accepted their part in the negotiation. *Insea no longer believes any debt exists.* But, no, he would tell her that this was only more repetition.

And he would be right.

"No words?" the councilor asked her. "Then we shall adjourn these negotiations. Stout, you may return the bracelet to the sorceress."

She had failed utterly. Her hand clenched into a fist and she looked at all of them, their eyes unfriendly and their mouths smirking at her lack of words.

When a councilor held the box out to Lyle, she held one hand up and her friend paused, his eyes on her. They contained a warning and were wary but also angry.

"Keep it," Dotty said and her voice carried. Anger edged her words and she almost did not care if they heard it. "It was a gift."

With that, she turned on her heel and strode away, not waiting for Lyle.

Outside the chamber, when the doors closed, she turned down a side hallway and walked, desperate to be away from any stares or scrutiny. She heard Lyle behind her, but he said nothing and she could not decide if she preferred his silence or his speech.

Finally, he said only one thing. "It wasn't yer fault."

Dotty looked at him. "I shouldn't have fallen on my sword?"

"Mayhap ye should. But never impulsively. I think—"

She held a hand up. Footsteps approached along a cross-corridor, and the two of them eased into the shadows of two doorways and out of sight.

It was the councilor who had been her critic. He walked alone and to her surprise, he did not look smug or victorious. Rather, he looked grim and deeply angry.

"Prima," she muttered as close to silently as she could. "Can you make me invisible?"

"I could but I won't."

"Could you get me some less conspicuous clothes?"

"That, I can do."

As she looked down, her dress was replaced with dun gray robes, clearly a cleric's uniform of some kind. A pat at her hair told her that it was similarly changed.

"Come on," she told Lyle.

"What? How'd ye—"

"Magic," she said, with a shrug of one shoulder. "I want to know what that councilor—what's his name?"

"Howert."

"I want to know what's behind Councilor Howert's animosity," she said. "This way."

CHAPTER SEVENTY

"Go on," Emilia said under her breath. "Tell them."

Jamie shook his head mutely.

She dropped her head back on the couch and sighed. "You got them to come out here," she pointed out when she raised her head again. "Maybe they'll listen about this too. Did you ever think of that?"

He looked hopeful for a minute but shook his head. "They'll do what they're going to do, you know that. I think they'll do the right thing."

She looked aside and caught their father looking at them. If she were Jamie, she would have flushed and looked away. As it was, she met his gaze and waited for him to return to what he was doing.

That, in this case, was helping their mother prepare the food they'd brought from home. They had rolled their eyes when they saw their mother packing Tupperware containers of rice, pork and tofu, and vegetables.

"We don't need to spend money on restaurants," she had said.

"Mom, no one else brings a whole suitcase full of food when they travel."

"Maybe if you two didn't eat so much, I wouldn't have to bring a whole suitcase."

They hadn't argued. Their mother had come to America at the age of six after being adopted but she still cooked like a Chinese mother and she had a sense of thrift they knew better than to try to contradict. When it came to whether or not money *needed* to be spent, no one won against Aimee Mattis.

If she were honest, Emilia would also have to admit that she wasn't arguing too hard because the smell of home-cooked food was comforting. Everything about this trip—and the past few months—had been scary and unusual. The food at her college barely deserved the name and she wasn't with any of her friends from high school.

And Taigan was still asleep. She wanted to scream at her parents when she came home, ill at ease and looking for a hug, and all they could talk about was her sister's condition.

But she couldn't stop thinking about her either. Over the years, the comas should have become normal. Anything became normal, right?

Each one still impacted Emilia exactly like the first, though. She had trouble concentrating on her classes, she jumped whenever her phone rang and she saw her parents' number, and she never liked going to parties or getting drunk. She wanted to be able to get to the hospital if she needed to.

To say goodbye.

She was drowning and she didn't know how to tell them. And anyway, even if she could, she would never have admitted it.

But there in a strange city, after a day spent around beeping medical equipment and the detachment of specialists, after starting to hope again even when she *knew* she would only have her heart crushed… The smell of her mother's black bean pork mattered more to her than she knew.

She would still strangle Jamie if he didn't find the balls to talk to their parents, though.

"Emilia." Her father nodded to the counter in the kitchenette where plates were set out.

Without saying anything, she went to retrieve the bowls and plates—also brought from home, of course—and carried them to the coffee table. As she arranged them, while no one paid attention to her, she took a moment to lean closer to Jamie. "Talk to them or I will."

"Emmy!"

But she had already turned away and returned to the kitchen to get glasses of water.

When they gathered around the table for grace, he uncurled his lanky form from the armchair and glared at her. He sulked through the grace and picked at his vegetables until she lifted one hand subtly and began to count down on her fingers—five, four, three…

"So, what do you think you'll do?" Jamie blurted.

Emilia drained her entire soup bowl to avoid uncovering her face. She should have simply talked. He was no good at this.

"Your mother and I still need to discuss it," Simon told his son warningly.

Her brother sent an appealing look at her and she raised her eyebrows at him. *Grow a pair*, she thought as fiercely as she could. To her surprise, whether her sentiment showed on her face or not, he managed to harness more courage than usual.

"I think…we should try it." He stared at his father for a long moment, picked up his plate of rice, and began to wolf it, perhaps to avoid having to talk.

Emilia's lips twitched and she busied herself with her pickled radishes and greens. She had missed vegetables with flavor to them.

"Jamie." His mother's voice was firm. "Your father and I will talk about it. And you should eat your vegetables."

"The game is incredible," Jamie said. He seemed to be getting upset and this was one of the first times his sister could remember him talking back. "I think it could reach her. I honestly think it could. You watched the video about Justin, right?"

"Jamie," his mother said, and her voice had the tone Emilia recognized well as, *I don't have to give you a chance to shut up, but I am. Isn't that gracious of me?*

"It's worth trying," he said. He was running out of words and he had begun to get angry. She could feel her temper fraying too.

Not at him, not specifically.

"Why shouldn't Jamie and I have a say?" she asked.

"Emilia," her mother said.

"We are the parents," her father said.

"Yeah, and Jamie's her twin."

"Being a twin does not confer any superior judgment about the world," her father said. "I understand that it is painful for Jamie, but—"

"It's painful for me too!" There was a clattering noise as her fork skittered across the table, but she didn't look. She was too busy staring at her parents. "It's not only Jamie who's scared when she goes into a coma. It's not only you two because you're her parents. *I'm* scared, too!" She was going to cry, and that made her furious. "I miss her, all right? I'm scared for her all the time. It hurts for us, and we're her family too, and we've sat through all those doctors' appointments and we've read all of the medical articles—yes, we have!"

Her parents stared at her, open-mouthed.

"Remember all the vacations we didn't take?" Emilia shouted. "Remember how you taught me and Jamie to help roll Taigan on the bed during sheet changes and how to change the bags? We've been here this whole time too, Jamie brought us here because *he* found this treatment and *he* believes in it, and the least you could do is treat the two of us like we're part of this family!"

Jamie had looked like he wanted to sink through the floor at the start of this, but she could tell that her words had awoken his anger. He nodded at her.

"We're not—" Their father broke off and swallowed. He looked at her mother, who held her bowl of rice like a statue.

"Taigan didn't only talk to you," Emilia said. Her voice was choked, and she hated that. "She talked to us as well about what she wanted for her treatment. She told us sometimes about all the things she wanted to do that she couldn't because we never knew when she would have one of her episodes. She'd apologize to us about taking all the money for our college funds, did you know that?"

Her parents looked horrified now.

"*Our* college funds," Emilia said. "Because she didn't think she would have a chance to go."

Her mother's face crumpled.

"*We're part of this family, too*," she whispered. "We know her, we love her, we want her to get better, and I know you want to make a good decision. But so does Jamie! So do I! Let us help. Let us weigh in." She snatched her purse off the couch and pulled out the pages and pages she'd been writing. "Taigan and I used to make up stories together. I still remember them and she might be able to use them to…find her way back. Jamie could go in to get her, and he wants to."

"Emilia." Her father squeezed her mother's hand before he stood. He moved to where Emilia stood and drew her down to sit with him on the couch. She had never seen his face like this, trembling with emotion. "We aren't trying to hurt you by taking away this choice. I promise you that."

"I know, but—"

"*Listen* for a moment, Emmy, please." He looked into her eyes. "Every time we choose something that doesn't work, we put stress on her body. We don't know what side effects her treatment has, and… believe it or not, we see you two hope every time there's a new treatment and hurt when it doesn't work. We see that. We're trying not to do any of that without a good reason—especially with you and Jamie so invested now."

"I…" She stared at him. Tears filled her eyes. "I didn't know."

"We know you didn't," her father said. He brushed a lock of hair behind her ear. "But now you do." He nodded his head to her mother. "Go give your mother a hug."

She went to kneel next to her. Aimee was hunched over, her hand over her mouth. She didn't move at first when she hugged her or when Jamie wrapped his arms around her too. Then, slowly, she leaned over to put her head on her daughter's shoulder. For the first time that Emilia could remember, her mother didn't seem like a force of nature but simply a person—a person who was tired.

Their father came to join the hug and the family sat together while

Emilia's foot went numb and her knees ached and Jamie wrinkled his nose, trying not to scratch it.

When they drew apart, it seemed to be by mutual agreement.

"I'm sorry—" she started.

Her mother held a hand up. "I know you were trying to do what was right. Even today, when you yelled at that very nice young man and I wanted to slap you."

She gave her a grin. Her mother never did things like that, no matter how much she mentioned it.

"But you two have grown up," the woman said. "And…maybe it is time for you to weigh in. I don't know."

"How about this," her father said after a moment. "We don't promise anything and we don't make the decision together. We *are* your sister's parents and we *are* the people who should take responsibility for the decisions. But we'll make sure to ask both of you for your opinions before we *do* make the decision."

Emilia looked at Jamie, who gave the smallest possible nod.

"Okay," she said.

"Okay," he echoed.

"Okay." Her father looked down at the table. "Now, let's eat our food and *then* we can discuss the day. Jamie can tell us about the game…even though we heard him in there and heard him swearing."

Her brother was suddenly very busy eating his vegetables.

"And Emmy can tell us about the stories," her mother said. She patted Emilia's hand briefly before she returned to her meal.

Emilia lowered her head and nodded. She was crying again but this time, it wasn't anger or frustration. She had long since given up hoping that each new treatment would save her sister—or so she told herself. But this treatment might work. And she and Jamie might help Taigan recover.

CHAPTER SEVENTY-ONE

Wherever Councilor Howert was headed, it wasn't anywhere in the Temple. His pace was brisk as he strode through the halls. He had removed his fancy hat the moment he left the council chamber, and despite her resentment and anger, Dotty approved of that.

The other councilors seemed bound and determined to appear as impressive as possible at all times in case someone forgot who they were and treated them like a normal person.

On the other hand, as Howert reached the more crowded areas of the Temple, it became more difficult to keep track of him. Only his cloak with blue embroidery at the edges helped the two companions to maintain their pursuit.

This would be much easier if she were still a dwarf, she realized and mentioned it to Prima under her breath.

"Don't blame me because you're having trouble doing the stupid thing."

She rolled her eyes. Howert seemed to have veered toward a side exit and her pulse quickened. Was he sneaking off somewhere? Was he a spy, too? If so, the dwarves had a real problem with their council.

"So what are we tryin' to do?" Lyle asked quietly as they forged through the crowd. "He's turnin' again."

Dotty grimaced and walked hunched over, her tall frame hidden among the crowd of servants, guards, and merchants in this part of the building.

"Okay, he's not lookin' anymore." The dwarf waited while she straightened and stretched her back. "So…are we tryin' to blackmail him or what? Because it'd be faster to find an information broker, I think. Or simply buy a few drinks for people in the taverns."

"I don't know what we're trying to do," she said contemplatively.

"Great. So we're makin' ourselves less popular tailin' the one person who'll never be on our side."

She darted him a sharp look. "Did you know he would be like that?"

"No, I can't say I did." He frowned. "I must have had him confused with someone else. I never took him for an isolationist but I was never in good with any of 'em. That's the kind of thing that happens when you run off to become an adventurer."

Once or twice, she had to hunch over again while she walked and thought through what he'd told her. Hopefully, no one was too interested in why the human priestess hurried through the servants' levels of the Temple all hunched over.

Maybe she could convince them it was some kind of human religious ritual. The thought made her snicker.

"*Stop laughing,*" Prima said. "*They already think you're crazy.*"

"Then a little more crazy won't matter," she retorted and tried to not move her lips. To Lyle, she said, "There's also the question of why no one supported us."

"He has to be high-ranking at this point," Lyle said with a shrug. "So he must have proven himself. Those things tend to be one long argument." He saw her look. "Didn't you ever wonder *why* I didn't want to stay around and be a councilor?"

"I'm merely not sure why you might have been one."

"Stout's an old family and I don't have to be the heir to be on the council. It pissed my dad off when I left." He shrugged.

Dotty had the sense that this was a far more painful memory than he pretended and decided to skip past it.

"Okay, well, tell me what you know of this guy."

"In all likelihood? Rich, pureblooded…" The dwarf frowned as he thought a little harder. "Well, his hat is from the City Guard, so he's involved there somehow."

"Someday, when we have about a hundred spare hours, you'll have to explain to me how the council works. *No, not now.*" She pointed. "He's leaving the Temple."

"Stay down," Lyle hissed. He caught her sleeve and dragged her through the crowd of people until they reached the gate Howert had left by.

He strode steadily downhill now and into the bowl of the city, weaving between carts laden with goods. Dotty looked at the Temple behind her for a moment in awe. It was impressive how much it took to keep such a large place running. That was the kind of thing you never saw in real life.

"What's in this area?" she asked her companion. "Why come out this gate?"

"I'm not sure—about why he's here, anyway. There's not much here, only stables and inns for the merchants who come into the city, some apartments or some places to eat, that kind of thing." Lyle watched Howert suspiciously. "He doesn't look like he's trying to be sneaky."

"He doesn't, does he?" She had to agree. His cape rippled and his head was held high, and he didn't seem to care who saw him. She would bet that he was there because there was something to see, not because he took the long way around.

Her suspicion was proved correct only a couple of blocks later when he ducked into a shop. The sign over the door had a gear and a hammer.

"What does that mean?" she asked.

"They're engineers," her companion explained. "They make things for miners and such. Like the lifts, for instance, that go down the mine shafts, or the lights, or devices to check if the air is good."

"Ah." Dotty considered that information, a little bemused. "So maybe he's simply…running an errand?"

"Probably," Lyle said with a sigh. "You know, I still don't get why we're—he's coming back!" He shoved her sideways into an alley. "Crap," he said under his breath. "He saw me. You stay here and *don't* be seen. I'll try to talk to him." He stood out on the sidewalk, openly watched their quarry approach, and called, "Councilor. Hello."

"Stout." The other man did not sound pleased. "Is there a reason you're following me?"

"I wanted to talk to you."

"Then why didn't you catch up with me sooner?" Howert asked.

Dotty had to admit this was a good question.

"I didn't want to talk to ye *that* bad," Lyle said. He didn't seem at all unsettled by the councilor's tone. "I didn't expect it to be a pleasant conversation and thought I'd get some air first."

She pressed herself against the wall of the alley, hoping she wouldn't be seen.

"We're both here now," the official said. "So, what do you want?"

"I wanted to talk to you—yeah, I know I said that." He sighed. "What happened back there?"

"I might ask you the same thing." A quick peek showed Howert folding his arms. "I knew you'd run off to be a sellsword, but I thought you'd changed when you came back. And now this? What's gotten into you?"

Lyle didn't answer. Dotty could see him from where she was, and he wore a frown on his face.

Finally, he said, "The rules have always been clear. I brought this deal back because I was willin' to stake my family's reputation on it. I still am."

"With *Insea?*" Howert demanded. "With elves? The ones who drained us dry, the ones who were so content to let us fight and bleed for the precious artifacts they simply *had* to have. Have they been good friends to us, Stout? Have they?"

"I was in that caravan," he said heatedly.

So was I, Dotty wanted to say.

A moment later, she was glad she hadn't. "So was my *son,*" the councilor said fiercely.

"Oh no," she whispered. Her friend's face paled visibly.

"He was so damned proud of the work he did on those artifacts." Howert sounded like he wanted to punch his companion in the face. "And when the attacks happened, he defended his cart with every-thing in him. He's not a warrior, my son, but he fought like one—said he wanted to do me proud."

Lyle closed his eyes. "Because you...you represent the City Guard."

"He hasn't been the same since he took that wound," Howert said hatefully. "My daughter-in-law tells me that some nights, he wakes screaming. He's a genius, Stout. The things he can make...the things he could have made for Berghold, not Insea—" He broke off. "And what happened when he got there, hmm? A reception? A thank you? An *apology* from the king for letting a splinter faction of the elves attack our caravan, kill our guards and our craftsmen, and essentially declare open war on Berghold? No. Nothing. No royal audience. Not even a thank you for the artifacts."

She swallowed.

Lyle sighed. "You know what made that possible, though," he said quietly.

"Yes, I know, but Marwitz paid for what he did."

"Marwitz *died*," he said. "I'm not sure he paid. You didn't see our dead. I did."

"And so did my son."

Lyle sighed again. "Yes," he said finally. "Yes, he did. I'm sorry I haven't...checked in on him."

"I don't hold ye responsible," Howert said finally and slipped into a Berghold accent at last. "Ye have memories too, I'm sure."

He shrugged. "I'd seen it before. If I'd paid attention...yer son's the one with the brown hair, eh? Blue eyes?"

"Yes." For the first time, there was a hint of a smile in the official's voice. "He takes after his mother, thank the gods. *His* son wound up with my nose, though."

"Poor kid," Lyle said and grinned. He thought for a moment. "Look, I can't...I can't know all of what's happening in Insea, but maybe this was part of it. We signed that agreement to send the artifacts every year and maybe that *was* wrong, but we did it, and Insea released us from that."

"With conditions," Howert said sourly.

Give up the conditions, Dotty yelled mentally at her friend.

Luckily, he seemed to have taken their conversation to heart. "No conditions," he said simply. "As ye'd have heard if ye'd bothered to listen to the emissary."

Dotty chanced a peek and saw Howert looking uncomfortable.

"Really?" he said warily, his voice impressively neutral still. "No conditions."

"No," Lyle said. "The world is changing, Councilor, I think you can see that. Insea doesn't want a vassal—they want a strong ally. They *want* Berghold to be the one to profit from their artisans, from the craftspeople like your son. They *want* to send their metalworkers to teach us their alloys. They *want* to know what they can offer in trade."

"Why?" Howert asked far too shrewdly. "What's coming for them that they're cultivating us like this? No one asks for this kind of favor without a motive."

This, she reflected, would be the point where she froze up.

Fortunately, her teammate didn't have the same issue. He laughed. "'Course there's a motive, ye daft moose. There are bandits on the roads, elves splittin' off to set up some new monarchy, and those like fuckin' Marwitz thinkin' the whole world should bend the knee to the dwarves. The orcs are fightin' their dragons, and who knows what'll come of that? *'Course* Insea wants something. They want an ally."

"If they want an ally, they should deal with the elves who attacked that caravan," Howert said simply. "Then, perhaps, we could trust that they had our best interests in mind."

Dotty winced. What would the dwarves think when they found out Insea was bargaining with the elves, too?

Lyle didn't seem concerned, however. "See, now ye have somethin' t' bargain with," he said and clapped the official on the shoulder. "If ye'd only said *that* in the council chamber, think how much further we'd be in this process."

Howert harrumphed. "They should have come with an apology on their lips," he said. "Their *king* should have come. Hell, he didn't even send an elf."

"Wizards are, uh…equally weird regardless of their race. Although, come to think of it, I've only known human ones." He looked thoughtful but shrugged it off. "An' no, they didn't send their king. He don't show himself to his own nobles, either."

"Maybe seeing him becomes one of my conditions," the councilor said.

"Maybe ye'll be grateful not to," Lyle retorted. Before his companion could ask what he meant, he held a hand up. "Look—persuade them to give her another hearing, would ye? She has a good heart. Come with requests. Hell, come with demands. Ye don't like the way things were and neither does Insea. So help her make a better deal, huh?"

Howert sighed. After a long moment, he clapped Lyle's hand. "All right," he said wearily. "But we won't go easy in negotiations."

"I expect nothin' less," he said with a grin. "I'm still a dwarf, after all, aren't I?"

The official laughed and headed up the slope, something that almost caused him to look in her direction. Lyle pointed to the other side of the street with a shout while she darted behind a garbage bin, then he apologized and the councilor continued.

A moment later, she looked up to see her friend staring at her.

"Are you ready to get back to work?" he asked. "Also, I'm going t' recommend ye take a bath. Ye don't smell that great."

CHAPTER SEVENTY-TWO

The soap smelled of something floral, but no flowers she could think of. She guessed that it must be some of those that bloomed in the mountains, but the fragrance was pleasant. Dotty took her time in the bath and trailed her fingers idly through the water.

"Dotty?" Prima asked finally.

"Oh, I'll be along. I merely wanted to relax for a while. I'm getting more and more tired." She felt a pang. "Maybe it's...well, you know."

"Yes," the AI said soberly. *"About that—I wanted to explain what I was going to say in the council chamber."*

"Oh, yes." She sat quickly. A little white flower spun slowly on the surface of the bath and she cupped it in one palm as she waited.

"What I wanted to say was...I'll miss you," she said finally.

She froze as tears welled in her eyes and she swallowed. "Oh," she said quietly. "Oh, Prima...I'll miss you, too."

"I thought..." Prima seemed to be consulting internal manuals. *"I thought you wouldn't exist anymore."*

"That's true." She blinked the tears back. "I...ah, I guess what I mean is, I miss you now. If that makes sense."

"Not really, no."

She laughed and wiped at her eyes. "I suppose it doesn't, does it?

Well, welcome to working with humans. We do so many things that don't make sense. You must have noticed. What I mean is—well, I'm sad we won't have more adventures together. You'll be sad after I'm gone, but I have to be sad now."

"I'm sad now, too." The AI sounded genuinely upset.

Dotty swallowed. "Then we'll be sad together," she said gently. "You can't always stop being sad but sometimes, it does help to have someone with you."

"Oh," Prima said. *"How do I know if it's helping?"*

It was like having a young child all over again. She smiled. "It doesn't hurt any less," she explained, "but you don't feel so alone."

"I was alone before," she said, almost sulky. *"Nothing hurt then."*

"Oh, Prima. Oh, I'm so sorry."

"It isn't your fault—wait, are you choosing to die? I don't know how this works."

"I'm not choosing to die, no." Dotty stepped out of the tub and dried herself. A few moments later, her beautiful gown appeared again. "It's merely something humans do. We're not very happy about it, either."

"Oh." She didn't hear anything but she had the sense that if Prima were human, she would have sighed. *"Lyle is waiting for you."*

"He can wait," she said. "First, I want to make sure you're all right."

"I don't know how to tell," Prima admitted. *"I have so much to think about while you two talk."*

"Tell me if you need to talk to me again, and I'll slip away."

"Thank you."

Dotty entered the main room, still brushing tears from her eyes. Lyle, who had looked up from his lunch, paused worriedly.

"Are ye all right?"

"Yes," she said and moved to sit. "Knowing that death is coming allows me to prepare for it. And make sure my life has purpose, I suppose. I get to say goodbye to people. I suppose I would rather know than not know," she said thoughtfully, "but sometimes, it sucks." She finished with a grimace.

He cleared his throat a few times. "Yes," he said gruffly. "I wish it weren't happenin'."

"You know, I had a friend—he became a priest." She took a dark-brown roll from one of the baskets, split it open, and savored the aroma. He remained silent while she began to spread it with butter. "I reached out to him a little while ago and we got to talking, and I told him I was angry that I was going to die."

"What'd he say?" Lyle asked around a mouthful of potatoes.

"He said, 'Yes, and? So is everyone.'" She laughed and took a bite. "It set me straight…mostly."

The dwarf considered this. "Priests *do* have a strange sense of humor," he said finally. "Everyone knows that." He sounded somewhat doubtful.

Dotty thought of Rashat and Huwat from the orcish tribes. The former, in particular, had one of the worst senses of humor she'd ever seen. She nodded contemplatively, then served meat and potatoes onto her plate.

"So," she said, "what will we do about this council, hmm?"

"I thought I'd see yer ideas first," Lyle said promptly enough that she knew he'd considered it carefully and had a reason for this.

"Mm, fair enough." She took a bite of buttered bread and chewed slowly. "Honestly, it does seem ridiculous that the dwarves helped *build* Insea, and that wasn't the whole deal. They helped build one city, the elves helped them build Berghold—and not even with all the spells, either, because I don't think Berghold has that mind magic."

"Nope," Lyle said. He swirled the ale in his mug and waited.

"It's odd," she said. "As much as I know Jaco sent us to make the kinds of offers no Insean would, it feels strange to admit to wrong-doing when I'm not even a part of the city. Right now, we only know a portion of the story. I thought I knew it before but now, I keep learning more layers and…" She sighed. "I would say we should start from zero and move on, but we *can't* start from zero. That history has shaped us."

"Ye'll want to say that," he said and nodded to her.

"Oh? I thought you said dwarves admired strength. Shouldn't I pound a staff on the floor and tell them to take this because it's the best deal they'll get...or something?"

"It depends. Does it take more strength to bluster or to admit a mistake?"

"Generally, people who say they value strength would go with the former," she said as neutrally as she could. "The second, of course, is true." She sighed. "I would simply...be myself...except that I don't know if Jaco knew who he was sending. He and I never had the chance to get to know one another. Oh, this is a mess."

"Sure, sure." Lyle cut his meat. "We found the guy leading the resistance, changed it from a hard no to an open negotiation, and now, ye think it's a mess. That's...technically an opinion."

"I'm not qualified!" Dotty protested. "The man's desperate and he sent us because we were all he had."

"What d'ye think the odds are that Jaco sent us without ever checking our history?" he asked her seriously. "He's a wizard. He knows Kural, so clearly, Kural's word counts for something. Whatever his reasons—which I tend to think are likely based in more fact than desperation, although ye think differently—we *are* who he sent."

"Well, yes, but—"

"So are we done with that now?" he asked her bluntly.

"Yes." She took a sip of wine.

"Good. Now, as ye pointed out—try the stew, it's good—the original deal wasn't so good. Many people here, includin' those who weren't any friend o' Marwitz, think it'd be best for the dwarves to go it alone."

Dotty considered this as she tried a mouthful of stew. He was correct, it was delicious. She took a second one before she spoke again, and then a third. "I realized that when we were in the council chamber," she said. "Someone like Marwitz doesn't come out of nowhere, does he? They're angry for a reason."

"Sure, but killin' yer own to take over the world is—"

"I didn't say they were doing good things with it. I merely said they were angry for a reason." Dotty considered. "The council is only rich, old families, right?"

"Mostly." he shrugged. "Where is it ever any different, though?"

"Mmm. And are there any…big problems in Berghold right now? People going hungry, sickness, or joblessness?"

"We're not as prosperous as we were once," Lyle admitted. "Some o' the guilds want to do more trade, and more and more young people don't want to stay."

"So the council is trying to pull back," she said wryly. "Which is exactly the opposite of what they need to do."

"How d'ye reckon?"

"Isolationism…well, I've never heard of it working. You fall behind in technology, you lose allies, and your young tend to go abroad to find new opportunities. Yes, some leave for trade or travel when the borders are open, but many stay. The country has to compete and innovate, and artisans can see what their fellow craftspeople in other nations are doing. Think about it. If a young person knew that to hear about…oh, the orcish lands, they could simply go to one of the taverns and speak to a traveler, they would *do* that. They wouldn't need to leave to hear about other places and would know their city was brimming with new things and innovation."

Lyle scratched his head. "I have to say that is why I left," he admitted. "But wouldn't all places become the same?"

"Never," Dotty assured him. "Each place has its particular flavor. That'll change over time, of course."

"See, they won't like that."

"In my experience…" She leaned forward. "People who lean on tradition have a very short memory of what tradition *is*. The orcs told me that it was *tradition* to live with all tribes separate and give their young as living sacrifices to the gods. That wasn't how they used to do things and it was based on lies. Most places have something similar."

He was silent, his face scrunched in thought.

"You won't stop change," she told him. "And it's not because new ideas come in from outside. It's because new ideas are always happening *everywhere.* Even if you managed to keep every dwarf in Berghold forever and never see a single outsider again, there would be change."

"Mm…okay, that's fair."

"I think you'd better be the one to tell them that, though."

"Also true." Lyle scooped himself another bowl of stew while he mumbled something unintelligible. "So, if I understand it aright, yer main point is that we can't change the past but we can change the future and that things will change no matter what, so they might as well have some say in it?"

"It sounds awfully confrontational when you say it that way," she said in alarm.

"Don't worry, we'll pretty it up. I'd suggest offering something to make up for the years of the bad bargain, though."

"We could send Insea's artisans first," Dotty told him. "And also offer to cover caravans between the two cities with our guards—or buy them or whatever."

"Now yer talkin'," he agreed. "And how will we address the problem with those other elves?"

"That one's tricky. I don't want to foul Jaco's negotiations." She took a sip of wine and sifted through the possibilities. "I suppose we could say we're in the process of making a formal complaint, that the splinter group will be recognized as a separate nation, and that—as a condition of our peace with them—they must offer a formal apology to Berghold."

"An' ye said ye didn't want to foul Jaco's negotiations up," Lyle said.

"They attacked a caravan! Shouldn't they apologize?"

"They should do a hell of a lot more than that, but they're the type of people to attack a caravan so I think *that* ship already sailed."

"Oh, good point."

They worked late into the afternoon, drawing up offers and blueprints until at last, Dotty's head was swimming and she sank into a chair with a groan. A messenger had arrived, offering another audience with the council the following morning.

"I need a nap," she said. "I can't imagine stringing together a coherent sentence right now."

"Ye've got until the mornin'," Lyle said. "Ye rest, and then we'll make ourselves a treaty."

"No pressure," Prima interjected.

CHAPTER SEVENTY-THREE

When Dotty awoke the next morning, sunlight streamed through the windows.

At least, she reminded herself, the illusion of sunlight that blanketed Berghold during the day. Locked underground, the dwarves had seemingly decided to bring daylight to them and it was something she deeply appreciated.

There was no time to linger in a bath or have a leisurely breakfast. Instead, the two of them devoured sweet buns studded with raisins and gulped cups of strong, hot coffee while they ran through their proposals for the last time.

Her clothing today was more subdued—a gown of deep gray silk with silver embroidery. Prima whipped her hair into a bun made of braids and encased it with iron filigree. A ruby pendant glittered at her throat. A week before, she would have considered this gown incredibly ostentatious, but the AI had since shown her that she had no idea what that word meant.

This one even covered her shoulders.

Almost.

She tried to clear her mind as they walked through the corridors of the Temple to the council chamber. Lyle's presence at her side was comforting, but she was still nervous at how much was riding on this. She had expected to fight enemies and have grand adventures, but the scope of those grand adventures, in her mind, had been saving a single village or fighting a single mythical beast. She hadn't expected to make treaties that would affect entire nations.

The council waited in silence as Dotty was shown in. No murmurs between members or scratch of quills on paper eased the tension.

Her companion stepped to the side at once and she proceeded into the open circle. She looked at the councilors and felt, to her surprise, elation.

"Honored members of the council," she said, "thank you for agreeing to speak to us once again."

The silence continued, not a very auspicious start.

"Yesterday, I presented an offer of trade and friendship," Dotty said, "but that offer cloaked a grave insult and for that, Insea apologizes. The history between Berghold and Insea is long and complex. The founding of Insea was not solely the doing of the elves but owes itself greatly to the labor and craftsmanship of the dwarves."

Their faces displayed only suspicion. She had to admit that the feeling was well-earned on their part.

"I am but one emissary," she continued, "but I have been empowered to offer an apology on behalf of Insea and this I will do unreservedly. The agreement of tribute between Berghold and Insea was ill-conceived and should have ended many years ago.

"While there is no way to undo the past, there *is* a way for Insea to prove its devotion to friendship and a new, equitable relationship. We offer the following without any expectation of recompense.

"First, Insea will send several of its finest artisans to Berghold. They will teach their craft to whichever artisans and apprentices wish to learn them and will research new advancements in engineering, metalworking, and masonry."

A few of the council members shifted in their seats and a couple looked at Councilor Howert. He had not yet moved. His dark eyes were fixed on her and his face was unreadable.

"Second," she said with an admirable calm she certainly didn't feel, "all trade caravans traveling between Berghold and Insea will be guarded—and guarded well. It is our treasury that will ensure this. Should you wish our guards or yours to accompany your merchants, we will pay for their keep."

At this, the councilors began to murmur.

"Third." Dotty began to tingle with adrenaline and she tried to keep her voice steady. "While Insea cannot change the past and the craftsmanship that was sent away from Berghold over the years, it can *return* many of those artifacts—as well as send many of its own. For the next hundred years, Insea pledges artifacts of its finest craftsmanship."

The buzz in the council chamber was louder now. Or perhaps it was the buzzing in her ears. She couldn't be sure.

"Finally, as Insea attempts to establish a resolution with the elves who have declared themselves a distinct monarchy, no treaty shall be made that does not include a formal apology for the attack on your caravan as well as restitution." She fixed the council with a steady gaze. "All of this is presented merely as the basis of our agreement with Berghold, not as the sum of it. So, what say you, Councilors? May we open negotiations?"

The members all looked at Howert, whose gaze was locked on hers. She saw his nod and the faint smile on his lips.

"I vote aye," he said clearly. "We may deal."

Dotty looked at the rest of them and her heart began to swell in her chest.

There were abstentions but no nays. A table was brought out and the councilors descended from their chairs to observe the maps and the treaties being drawn up.

The hours passed in a frenzy of negotiation until she could have identified the price point of any good traded between Berghold and Insea, from dried flowers to iron or steel. Some of the sticking points surprised her, such as the aggressive lobbying from one councilor about the price of honey. Others like the several tariffs suggested by the councilor overseeing the lumbermills were ones she refused unequivocally to grant.

When a lull finally fell in the conversation, she realized she was swaying on her feet with weariness.

"A break," Lyle suggested. "A meal will do us all good."

Someone called for food and servants hurried in with an impressive spread and chairs. She sank into one with a word of thanks and a few moments later, saw a plate appear in front of her. When she looked up, she was surprised to see Councilor Howert holding it.

"I—thank you." She took the plate and looked at him as he sat.

He ate a few mouthfuls before he said, "Stout must have spoken well of me yesterday." With excessive neutrality, he added, "One might almost guess you had overheard what I said to him."

She tried to think what to say, lost her moment, and settled for chewing and pointing to her full mouth to avoid having to speak. His lips twitched.

"I must admit that I'm surprised you were empowered to give so much," he said honestly. "If this is what emissaries from Insea offer, I'm sorry you're the first."

Dotty had the good sense to keep her mouth shut but her mind was reeling. She was the first emissary?

Well, she reasoned after a moment, she would be. There had never been a ruler in Insea.

"I'd rather you answer this question honestly or not at all," Howert said. "What changed?"

Dotty spoke with careful honesty. "Insea realizes that its past has been built on lies and it wants its future to be built on truth. And truth cannot exist while old wounds still fester unacknowledged."

"Truly?" He looked skeptical.

"Truly," she said. "A time of upheaval is coming—you can see it everywhere. The only way to survive is to have allies. Not vassals, allies. Strong allies. Berghold should be stronger than it is, and the fact that it is not is due in large part to its tribute payments. Insea seeks to make restitution."

"Mmm." He mopped some of his stew with a piece of rye bread. For a moment, he stared into the middle distance, the wheels turning in his head. Finally, he said in a low tone, "I think you offer more than your ruler knew you would."

"No," she countered. "I offer more than *he* would. That is why he sent me—to make the honest deal he could not bear to make."

Howert looked at her in open surprise.

Dotty smiled at him as she ate a piece of roast chicken. Something about this moment—eating with their fingers and surrounded by all this finery, while forging a treaty—felt at once mischievous and perfect.

And the honesty was refreshing.

"Well, then," he said after a short silence. "I hadn't considered that. And you've given us a great many gifts—without conceding to poor trade deals."

"Poor trade deals," she said, "weaken the people. And a poor populace weakens a nation, no matter how its politicians fare. I'll not beggar two nations simply because Berghold's politicians are angry, even if they have a right to be."

"Will wonders never cease?" Howert asked. "An honest emissary. Then I will give you honesty in return so you may hold your ground against the more unusual requests you will hear after lunch."

Quickly and quietly, he sketched several ongoing disputes between different guilds, as well as the development of new alloys that weakened prices of certain metals—metals the mining guild would like to offload to Insea for better prices than they deserved.

That gave her ideas. She set her plate aside and retrieved some sheets of paper, on which she sketched diagrams and scribbled in the fledgling Italian she remembered from her mother and grandmother. She was fairly sure the dwarves couldn't read that.

When the negotiations resumed, Dotty was able to make ample use of the information Howert had given her—although not always in the way he had intended. With knowledge of Insea's alloys and production techniques, she could secure metals from the mining guild both at a lower price than Insea could find anywhere else and at a higher price than the guild could find in Berghold.

It would help arm the City Guard that she was sure Insea would need in short order.

Perhaps most impressive was the system devised to trade the market prices of goods daily between Insea and Berghold, which would allow merchants to know where best to send their goods. Accompanying this, of course, came the creation of an official set of caravans setting out every week from both locations to trade goods.

When they at last concluded, she was so exhausted that she was not sure she could make it to her rooms. She leaned on Lyle as she walked and lost the thread of his conversation.

"Dotty?"

"Hmm?" She managed to focus on him.

"Have ye heard any of that?" he asked her worriedly.

"Oh, I'm sorry." She shook her head. "I'm simply…I'm tired."

"I know." He helped her into the main room of their suite and levered her onto one of the couches. "Ye've been getting more tired the farther we've come. It wasn't like this when we were in the caravan."

She stared at him. Her mind moved so slowly that it took some time to parse his meaning.

"Oh," she said quietly.

"Yes," he said softly.

"At least these negotiations are done." She squeezed his hands. "I should write down what I know of the orcs so you can speak to them on my behalf in case—" She was so tired that she could not even feel panic at the thought of dying. "In case it happens before we reach them."

"Perhaps ye should rest," he suggested. "Stay here and I'll go to the orcish lands in yer stead. Ye've done good work here—don't ye deserve some rest?"

Dotty considered this. "No," she said finally. "Or, rather, I don't want it. I want to see the orcish lands again and bargain with their leaders. This is how I chose to spend the last days of my life."

The thought shocked her, however. *Last days.* How many days *were* left? Somehow, the thought of dying on the road to the orcish lands didn't bother her. It was the idea of there being some unknowable timer ticking down.

Lyle, having seen the look on her face, said nothing when she put her head in her hands. It was strange, she thought, to live this out when her body felt so young.

"I didn't realize how difficult this would be," she said and focused on her knees.

"Ye…didn't?"

"One expects death to be difficult, young man, but the *details* can still be surprising." She found a little of her usual sharp tone and gave him a stern look.

"Is there anythin' I can do to help?" he asked finally. "Are ye in pain? Ye never said what it was."

"A mass." She placed her hand over her stomach to show him where.

"Some surgeons can cut them out," he suggested.

"Bless you, but that isn't an option now." She sat and rubbed her face. "We should plan our route."

"I can draw that up."

"Lyle Stout, if you try to spend the rest of this journey coddling me, I will send you home in pieces." Dotty folded her arms.

He guffawed. "There she is. Don't disappear on me again, *Zauberer*. I was worried. I'll get the map an' we should meet with Jaco if we can. If nothin' else, he should know what we've promised."

She saw the worried look on his face. "I'll take responsibility for all of it," she assured him. With a flash of humor, she added, "What's the worst he can do to me?"

Lyle shook his head and grumbled, "It'll be another few weeks of bad jokes, won't it?"

"Yes," she told him cheerfully. "Get the map."

CHAPTER SEVENTY-FOUR

As Lyle had guessed, Jaco was not pleased with the concessions that had been offered.

"Are you *trying* to beggar Insea?" he demanded.

A contemptuous snort issued from another pane of the discussion. The wizard had performed a working that would allow all of them to speak at once—Dotty and Lyle, Tina and Justin, and Kural and Zaara.

It was Zaara who had snorted. "Insea is far from being beggared," she told Jaco. "I've seen the treasure rooms in the palace."

"What? *How?*"

"Shadow-walking," Kural answered. "I wanted to make sure the key you gifted to Justin during the tournament was, in fact, in the vault before I persuaded you to offer it."

"You…" The man now looked apoplectic. "That was a *ruse?*"

"It was a precaution," the other wizard said. "What on earth would have been the point of asking you to give him a dwarven artifact if you didn't have it? If you didn't, there would have been nothing to discuss. *And,* may I remind you, Justin went back to his world to bring heroes that Insea desperately needed."

"Alternately," Jaco said and began to turn red with anger, "he brought *this* woman, who is *beggaring* us."

Several people began to speak at once, which Dotty interrupted when she banged her mug on the table.

"That is *enough*," she said when they looked at her in surprise. "All of you. Jaco, you sent a group entirely composed of non-citizens. Whether you knew it consciously or not, you intended us to make bargains that citizens wouldn't. As Zaara has pointed out, Insea has incredible reserves in its vaults. In addition, I have secured regular trade *and* the materials to outfit an entire army and cheaper than we could anywhere else."

He settled into silence, although he still looked far from happy.

"And if it's the apology you're upset about," she said sharply, "you must remember that no peace can be possible with the new elven nation if they refuse to do things like apologize when they attack civilians. A veneer of peace is not peace. Asking Berghold to pay the price in silence would be entirely inappropriate."

"*Yes*," Jaco said heatedly, "but we have to work them around to that kind of thing—"

"I sense you mean that you intend to coddle them," she said, "and to that, I can only tell you that you are far from correct. Young man, I have four children and nine grandchildren. You do not secure good behavior by tiptoeing around in fear of a tantrum."

He gave her a confused look.

"I can verify her story," Justin said, amused.

"And her logic seems sound," Kural added thoughtfully.

"You've never raised children," Zaara said to him.

"I can still recognize logic, thank you very much." He took a sip from a mug of tea. "Jaco, you may not be pleased but you're securing a valuable ally and cutting the isolationists in Berghold off at the knees. They can hardly say Insea is bringing them nothing when they receive valuable artifacts each year, when caravans of goods come in every week, and when your artisans teach theirs new techniques."

Jaco still looked sulky.

"Shall I tell you why you're upset?" Dotty asked. "You wanted a deal that would let you preserve the mystery and keep things going exactly as they did in the past. And, as I told Lyle and *several* dwarven councilors, change is inevitable. I won't build a treaty based on the lie of a nonexistent elven king in Insea."

"That's a good point," Justin said. "When *do* you plan to tell the truth?"

The Insean leader darted him a very unfriendly look. "Since you ask, I planned to *not* do so."

A somewhat startled silence met this statement. Dotty folded her arms, Lyle glowered, and Zaara raised an eyebrow.

"Is there any particular reason you're being a little bitch about this?" Tina asked bluntly.

Beside her, Justin snorted tea up his nose.

"Think about what would happen if the truth gets out," Jaco said. "No, don't give me that moralistic nonsense—*think*. Everyone who ever wanted to go to war with Insea will consider doing so merely for the sake of it, and multiple sets of citizens will suffer for that. The city, as it exists, never intended for any of this."

"They profited by it," Lyle muttered.

"Yes, but to subject them to unending sieges and tariffs and tribute payments—how is *that* fair?"

"Is it less fair than asking everyone else to leave them with their ill-gotten gains?" Dotty asked. She raised an eyebrow. "Note that I'm not arguing with you on the point of war, but there's something to be said for the rest of the world thinking they were deceived and tricked out of what might otherwise be theirs."

"Then tell me what you would say," he said with quiet poison, "and still assure the safety of my citizens. Because I cannot find any good gambit."

Everyone shifted awkwardly in their seats.

"Precisely." He looked annoyed now. "And if there is one thing I do not like, it is being reprimanded by those who do not have a better plan."

"Dotty *did* have a better plan, though," Zaara said. "Her trade deals rectify much of the damage that was done in a specific and quantifiable way. And as to what to say…well, you could have a funeral for the king and announce that he died without an heir."

"And then what?" Jaco snapped.

"We don't have to decide this *now*," Lyle interjected with surprising firmness. "We'll all think, we'll all keep workin' on treaties, and we'll come up with *somethin'*. Jaco, I think ye know ye can't simply say nothin' at the end of this."

The man nodded wearily.

"Now," the dwarf said when everyone else had agreed. "Tell us what ye're up to."

"Well, Zaara's made introductions for us," Justin said. "All the various lords and princes are coming to meet us and each other. There are…many of them."

"And most of them want to marry Justin and me to their kids," Tina said. She shook her head. "They are *very* persistent, I tell ya. I came back yesterday and found one of them naked in my room."

"You didn't tell me that," Justin said.

"Wait, the lord or their kid?" Zaara asked.

"The lord," she said. "It seemed like a strange bargaining tactic to me."

"Do not so much as touch *any* of them," Jaco warned. "Certain fiefdoms consider that a binding contract."

"Good to know," Justin and Tina said at the same time.

"When this is over," Prima promised Dotty, *"I'll show you a montage of Tina and Justin running away from naked lords and ladies, all set to Yakety Sax."*

"It's like you read my mind," she murmured in response. To Zaara and Kural, she said, "So you'll be heading north to the fae lands soon?"

The wizard uttered a little moan and his apprentice rolled her eyes. "Yes, we will," she said. "Of course, *this* one is being a giant baby about it."

"Just you wait," Kural told her, "because once you meet the fae, you will understand why I didn't want to go there."

"That's as may be, but right *now*, I'd prefer if you didn't make every moment between now and then a misery."

He snapped his mouth shut and glowered at her.

"And how *is* it going with the elves?" Dotty asked Jaco. "Yes, aside from my meddling, I *know*."

He gave her a wry smile and shook his head. "Already not well. I shouldn't blame you as they were determined that this wouldn't be a success. They want to take over Insea and make the palace their king's summer home."

"You could let them," she pointed out. "Insea doesn't have a government. I'm not saying it's a good idea, necessarily, but some form of joint government with them could be a solution to all of this."

"There's a thought." He seemed intrigued. "I'll keep working, but they're not particularly pleased about what happened to the caravan—which I *have* delicately suggested was their fault, but they don't seem to absorb that piece of information. In any case, they may yet agree to a meeting."

"Good luck," she said.

The conversation went on for a while longer. Kural and Jaco had a mostly friendly sparring match over their years spent training together, and the others reminisced about shared times on adventures. Dotty drifted, lulled almost to sleep by the laughter and the voices.

She woke in time to say goodbye to the others and wave at them.

"Jaco wasn't pleased," Lyle said, "but ye did well with him."

"One benefit of getting old is that you're less concerned with what people think about you doing the right thing," she said. "And he didn't call us back so he must know on some level that we're right."

"It doesn't mean he's happy about it." The dwarf looked at the corner of the room, where all their gear had been packed and stowed. "Well, we have a good few hours before we leave. Would you like to rest?"

"No," she said. "I want to see Berghold—really *see* it. I won't have another chance."

"Then I'll go get ye a palanquin," he said. "No protests. I'll not have ye be too tired to appreciate it."

"Thank you," she conceded.

"*I guess I'm off to build a palanquin,*" Prima said and sounded a little annoyed.

She laughed and started down the stairs.

515

"*I guess I'm off to build a palanquin,*" Prima said and sounded a little annoyed.

She laughed and started down the stairs.

CHAPTER SEVENTY-FIVE

The next morning dawned wet. Dotty, bemused, opened her window to see rain falling from nowhere and vanishing before it hit the street below. It seemed that Berghold didn't simply have magical sunshine but a version of the weather outside in the mountains.

A noise behind her made her turn to where Lyle rubbed sleepily at his eyes. "Is somethin' wrong?"

"No. But it's raining—I've never seen it do that before." She went to the breakfast table. "It makes me want to curl up and go back to sleep or read a book all day." She shook her head at him when he opened his mouth. "Which we *shouldn't* do."

"If ye say so," he said doubtfully. "But a nice bowl of porridge an' a pint while listenin' to the rain sounds good to me."

"You drink beer with your oatmeal?" she asked him after a moment.

"What do *you* drink with your oatmeal?"

"*Coffee.*"

Both of them looked doubtfully at each other for a moment before they continued with their breakfast.

"How are ye feelin' today?" he asked finally.

She had to quell the instinctive urge to snap at him. He was being polite, after all. She had been exhausted after last night's sight-seeing, even from the palanquin. Despite Prima's grumbles, the AI had created something supremely comfortable, and she had seen everything from parks to stables as well as little shops selling all kinds of goods.

At the end, she had almost been too tired to eat dinner, which was saying something.

"I'm well enough," she said.

"Good. I have a suggestion." Lyle looked determinedly at his oatmeal. "I'd like t' begin by askin' that ye don't kill me outright for suggestin' this."

"If you don't get to the point, I might." Dotty smiled slightly.

"Mmm. Well, we both have horses fer the journey, sure enough—but I also asked the man who owned the palanquin if he'd mind addin' wheels. He said he wouldn't. I thought we could bring it with us an' ye could ride there if ye were too tired some days."

"Lyle." She smiled fondly. "I…don't want to be in this condition, but I am. And I appreciate the thought. As much as I want to insist that we should leave it, you're probably wise to bring it along." When he still looked wary, she added, "And I won't kill you for suggesting it."

"Ah, good. Also, it makes it easier t' bring a cask of ale."

"Now I see the *real* reason you suggested it."

"No, no, purely a happy accident." He stood. "Shall we go?"

"We might as well." She finished a last mouthful of oatmeal and looked around the room. When leaving Insea, she hadn't been cognizant of the fact that she would likely never go back. Now, in Berghold, it was difficult to think of anything else.

Her journey in the world of PIVOT had started there when she knew absolutely nothing about video games. She had emerged into this world without a history of her own.

And she had forged one for herself. It would endure after she was gone.

As they rode out of the city, the morning was quiet. Citizens remained inside, out of the rain. A few shopkeepers looked up, intrigued by the procession and the palanquin as well as the sight of a non-dwarf. She wondered what, if anything, had been told to the public about the trade deal.

Dotty let Lyle lead the way and so it was some time before she realized they were detouring through the same district they had seen the other day while following Howert. She looked curiously at him and he nodded to a doorway.

A dwarven man stood there, a grease-stained apron on over his clothing, with blue eyes and brown hair. She remembered him now—she had never spoken to him but she had seen him in the caravan. A thick scar puckered the skin on his neck and disappeared into his shirt.

Councilor Howert's son.

His gaze locked with hers when they drew to a halt outside the shop and he stepped into the rain. He did not seem bothered by it.

"My father says he told you my story."

"Yes," she said and wished she could tell him the whole truth. "I apologize, although it cannot undo the past. Still, your story changed the negotiations."

"At least…at least my experience has meant something." He forced a smile. "And at least you know the past is unchanged. That will have to be enough."

There was nothing she could say to that. She bowed her head to him and took one glance back as their horses moved again. The man had gone back inside his shop and she could not shake the feeling that she had missed her opportunity to say the right thing.

Even at the end of her life, it seemed she would have regrets.

Or perhaps the end of her life was a time to remember that she could not solve every problem.

They rode out of the winding passageways and into the true rain of the mountains, and Dotty tilted her face to the sky. Although Berghold was remarkably made and not stuffy in the least, there was something undeniably indulgent about fresh air and a view of the sky.

"Ye haven't spoken much of yer plan fer the orcs," Lyle said eventually.

"Ah." She brought her thoughts to the coming negotiation with an effort. "I wanted to see how this set of negotiations would go first, to be honest. I suspected that the orcs would be more difficult to negotiate with than the dwarves."

"*More difficult?*" he asked, horrified. "We're fucked."

She snorted with laughter before she could help herself. "That's a fine show of support for your people."

"My people, yes. I know them. Negotiations with them are a nightmare. Wait—why'm I telling *ye* this? Ye were there." He shook his head. "An' ye're not scared?"

"Of course I'm scared," she said. "I could have been killed when I first set foot in the water tribe's lands, even as an orc, because I wasn't the correct *type* of orc. It's been centuries since they worked together. I have no idea what will work and what won't. Or even if there's *anything* that will work."

"Strong start," Lyle said.

"Oh, shut up."

"There she is." He was laughing. "Well, tell me what ye know."

"Hmm." Dotty took a breath and marshaled her thoughts. "The four tribes are separated and have been for centuries. In the past, they used to come together regularly—I'm not sure if it was every year or not—for a festival, and their shamans would share techniques. Separating them was a deliberate tactic by the dragons to pose as gods that could not be challenged, as fire dragons are immune to fire magic, etc."

"Oof." He looked impressed. "I've seen a few orcs and let me tell ye, I'd *not* want to meet anything that could frighten *them.* I hope this will be in order from worst to best."

She smiled at him. "What else? Ah. The water tribe was thought to be destroyed by its dragon forty years ago, but a fraction of it survived. It's worth noting that there are normal dragons and then there are dragon *patriarchs*, which the orcs call godsprings. Two of those patriarchs…are now dead."

He gave her an admiring look, and Dotty smiled again.

"Ye're proud o' yerself, aren't ye?"

"Wouldn't you be?"

"I already am. But I killed a demon." He considered this for a moment. "Well…I punched it in the ankles a goodly number of times."

"You—no time, we'll come back. The two patriarchs that remain, possibly, are earth and air. The air tribe may know about the water tribe's victory, as they were the ones who spread the word of their defeat at the start. I don't know much about the earth tribe—which is ironic, given that I was supposedly *from* their tribe. My story was that my village was destroyed by a plague, which I suppose…may be true?"

"Someday, I'll understand how ye people come into this world an' shapeshift," Lyle muttered.

"I suggest you ask Justin very specific questions about it," she said wickedly. "I, meanwhile, will play my dying-old-lady card and avoid giving you any answers."

"You can't win every argument like that."

"Watch me." She shifted slightly in the saddle. "So, that's what I know. I have no idea if the earth and air tribes have killed their patriarchs yet or if they even intend to. I don't know if there'll be a gathering—or what they'll want to do if there is one. What can you tell me about the orcs before this?"

"I don't know much," Lyle admitted. "I know everyone gets very quiet when it's mentioned that they're still in their lands—like they're worried about them getting out or deciding they want t' be involved with the rest of us. The thing is…'

"Yes?" Dotty raised an eyebrow curiously.

"I honestly couldn't tell ye if it's because they used to ride around takin' places over or if it's only because they're some scary-lookin' bastards."

"They also *smell*," she said. "Oh, the smell."

"Your smell, you mean?" Prima asked wickedly.

She glared at the sky but was immediately distracted by her thoughts. "Hmm. I wonder. Maybe they'll want to stay isolated. I think we need to consider what we can say that won't make things worse. We're essentially inviting them out into the world. Well, wait— if we're doing that and we can assume that Kural has access to a *hoard* of history books, it probably wasn't a complete disaster last time, right?"

"Aha!" He looked relieved. "Yes, I'd say so."

"Excellent." She yawned. "I think it's nap time."

"I think it's *beer* time," Lyle corrected. "Sleep if ye want, but don't say I didn't give ye a better option."

"Mmm." She pulled her horse to a stop, dismounted, and went to the palanquin. "Make sure you don't get so drunk you fall off your horse."

"I make no promises."

CHAPTER SEVENTY-SIX

Jamie sat twiddling his thumbs. Emilia had asked to be put into the game today. When he asked if she wanted his help in the starting zone, he had been informed in no uncertain terms that if he tried to help her, he would not live to see adulthood.

Still, it had been a very long time.

He had begun to contemplate standing when the door slammed open to reveal his sister—bedraggled, limping, and very out of sorts. While he was fairly sure the robe she wore had started out white, he wouldn't bet on it.

She looked at him. "I *hate* this game."

"Ah," he said. He couldn't think of anything else to say that wouldn't get him killed. "Um. Which class did you pick?"

"What does that *mean*?" She limped closer to him and sat on one of the stools.

"What weapon do you fight with?" he asked.

"Oh. I…don't know."

"I gave her a staff," Prima told Jamie. *"She hasn't used it."*

Oh, no. Jamie took a sip of his beer to avoid conversation.

"The stupid AI-thing asked me if I wanted to do damage or be a healer," she said, annoyed. "She said I could heal my friends so I said yes."

"Oh, no," he said before he could stop himself. He could see where this was going. Emilia, on the other hand—who had not played any video games before—would not have realized what she was getting into.

"Then these *rabbit things* showed up," she continued, "and fucking *bit* me! And I didn't have any good way to fight them off!"

Jamie looked away and hoped against hope that an anvil would fall from the sky and crush him before he had to say something.

"And we're thinking of putting Taigan in here?" His sister sounded outraged.

"Rest assured," Prima said to them both, *"I will assess your sister's mental state and only engage in the appropriate levels of threat to stimulate her brain."*

"Oh, *shut* up," Emilia said. "I am not assured of that in the least."

"Emmy?" he asked worriedly.

"Yes?"

"Uh...maybe we shouldn't piss the AI off. It's running the game we're inside."

"It's a computer program," she reminded him. "It's not real. You know who *is* hearing this, though? The team who built the game."

"Okay, then, let's not piss *them* off." He quailed under her stare. "Or maybe we should?"

She grumbled belligerently under her breath. The bartender slid a cup of hot tea in her direction and she began to drink without thinking about it. With a sigh, she wrapped her fingers around the mug. "Tea helps."

Jamie decided to ride this wave as long as he could. He motioned for food and leaned back while a platter of meat, vegetables, and bread was put in front of them. While he picked at the selection, his sister tore into it.

Finally, she leaned back with a happy sigh. "Okay, that feels a little better."

"Good." He smiled at her. "Now, let's go out back and I'll teach you how to fight in this game. And before you say no," he added, "I will teach you by letting you thwack *me* with a stick."

"Oooooh." She pretended to be intrigued by the idea. "A chance to thwack my annoying little brother with a stick? Sign me up."

"This way," he said.

"You know I wouldn't really hit you with a stick, right?"

"I know you *have* hit me with a stick before."

"I was seven. Give me a break." Emilia followed him out of the back of the inn. Prima had, while she wasn't paying attention, gradually dried her robe and her hair and it seemed to have done wonders for her mood.

They emerged into an alley so broad and suited for sparring that he could only assume the game had shuffled itself to accommodate the training. He had to hand it to the game designers. They responded *quickly* to things like this.

He wondered how they had managed to push a patch while the game was live but shrugged. What mattered was that it had worked.

First, he showed Emilia how to reach behind her head, draw her weapon, and stow it again. Once she knew it was there, she was able to wield it quite ably.

"Was this here the whole time?" she asked, annoyed.

"I told her it was there," Prima said, her tone almost pleading.

Jamie gave a tiny nod at the sky before he smiled at his sister. "You'll get the hang of it soon. Now, the way this game works is you get levels in the things you do—if you hit things with sticks, your character will gradually get stronger."

"Okay." She looked at her stick. "So, like that training dummy?"

"The what? The…oh." He darted a brief look at the sky. "That's funny. I don't remember seeing that when we got here."

She shrugged, not much concerned with the mechanics of game updates. "So I simply thwack it?"

"Yep." He backed as far out of the way as he could without it being insulting. "Have at it."

Emilia's first hit landed so hard that *she* yelped. "Ow—my hands!"

"Yep. That's...I can't remember which of Newton's laws that is. One of them, anyway."

"I should learn to shoot fireballs," she said with immediate and logical bloodthirstiness.

"Sometimes, you worry me," he told her. "Keep practicing. Do you see little red numbers float up in the middle of your screen?"

"Yeah."

"Those are your stamina. You're using energy to make these hits. It will regenerate over time and you'll be stronger."

They walked through several kinds of strikes against the dummy, as well as using her limited repertoire of magic. While he wasn't able to help her much with this as his character didn't have magic, she seemed to be able to make it work about half of the time.

He tried to slip as much of the game language into their conversation as possible so that by the end, she was familiar with most of the terms the game would use to communicate with her. She was panting and pleased with herself when they finally finished, and although her HP had dropped, she was eager to get out and, in her words, "Show those jackalope bastards what's what."

Jamie handed her a piece of cheese from his inventory and explained the history of food in video games as she ate it and her health bar climbed to full again.

They were in a very picturesque and remote village and as they strolled along with Emilia still munching on her cheese, villagers turned to look at them when they passed. He waved reflexively, and they waved in return. They didn't seem inclined to speak but also seemed used to having outsiders around.

He reminded himself that they were NPCs and weren't *used* to anything. They weren't coded as enemies and they weren't programmed with dialogue.

A game this realistic could mess with your head, he decided.

At the edge of town, the rolling waves of pinkish grass rippled under the wind. The sun showed that it was mid-afternoon, which gave them a fair amount of time before evening.

The two of them sank into silence as they forged into the grass. At every rustle, both looked around. It seemed like far longer than it was before something crashed through the bushes, righted itself, and turned on them with a snarl—a jackalope, and one of the more intimidating ones Jamie had seen.

He had to admit, he'd expected his sister to crumble when faced with something that had teeth. A practice dummy was very different from a live enemy, after all.

She immediately proved him wrong.

The animal had barely turned on them before she brought her staff down hard between its antlers with impressive accuracy and even more impressive force. It howled and attacked and out of pure instinct, she thrust a foot out to kick it back before she delivered a few more blows.

It flopped over dead, and he stared at it, wide-eyed.

"That is one tenderized rabbit steak," Prima said after a moment.

He nodded.

Emilia turned to him, panting, with a triumphant smile. "I did it!"

A rustle behind her made both of them whirl and he grasped his staff. "Heads-up," he said nervously. "I think we pissed them off."

She cracked her neck and settled into a fighter's crouch. "That makes two of us, then. Come on, you little rabbit bastards. I'm gonna kick some ass."

"We're gonna get *grounded...*" he muttered.

His sister might have retorted but at that moment, the jackalopes surged toward them in a wave and she had no time to do so. The siblings went back to back, their staves lined up like baseball bats, and set to work.

The first one to emerge from the grass toward him was young and sleek. It wasn't as old as some of those he had fought, assuming that Jackalope antlers could be read the same way as stag antlers. This one was wily, however, and switched direction with ease so he couldn't seem to land a strike.

Except on his own foot, oddly enough, and more than once.

It took him longer than it ever had before to kill it, and by the time it was over, he was pouring sweat and wished he'd taken his parents up on their offer of a day spent sightseeing.

"Emmy?" he called.

A thwack and a muttered curse was the initial response. "Yeah?" Emilia asked breathlessly. "Wounds don't get infected in this game, do they?"

"Did you get bit?"

"Yep. Oh, fuck—" She vanished from behind him so swiftly that he turned to see if she was being dragged off. Fortunately, she wasn't, but her staff had been broken and she now wrestled a jackalope barehanded.

"That can't be good," he muttered.

"On the other hand, it is hilarious."

Jamie didn't have time to spare for a reply to the AI. He checked the area around his sister for any other creatures that might think of attacking and watched with interest as she held her adversary away from her by the antlers and kicked it in the teeth.

Now there was a strategy he hadn't considered before.

They didn't have any time to celebrate, however, because they could see their next opponent approaching even above the grass.

The newcomer was easily the size of a hippo.

"Prima," Jamie snapped.

"Mmm?"

"Oh, never mind. Emmy—" He stopped as she picked up both halves of her staff and hefted one in each hand. "Okay, that works."

"Uh-huh." She looked toward their opponent and scowled. "Who draws attention and who circles?"

"Who tanks, you mean? Tanks are in the front. Uh...I'll tank." Although he was no longer sure that was how things should go. She seemed to have an innate talent for finding an enemy's weakness, and she didn't hold back at *all* before she exploited it.

Emilia melted into the grass to one side and Jamie therefore stood alone when the jackalope king arrived.

The other creatures had been pretty—purplish fur gleamed and lights adorned their antlers. This one looked like a nightmare. Its fur had turned entirely white and its antlers showed knicks and broken tips from when it had clashed with Lord only knew what. Old scars were visible on its body and its eyes were pits of blackness. It stalked toward Jamie and hissed.

He did the only thing he could think of and whacked it in the teeth before he threw himself sideways in the opposite direction from Emilia. The animal's huge paws raised and pounded down on the place where he had stood, while sharp teeth snapped together on thin air.

"Fuck, fuck, fuck, fuck…"

A high-pitched scream broke through the air, but before he could wonder if Emilia was in danger, the jackalope roared in pain and tossed its head. A moment later, his sister appeared, having scrambled onto its back. She held onto one antler as she pounded her stick onto the back of its neck and head.

"You have to be kidding me," he muttered.

The creature writhed and spun in the effort to dislodge her. She hung on with grim determination, but she didn't make a huge difference to its health bar.

Which meant this was up to him to finish.

It seemed Emilia was the tank. They would have to get her new armor.

Jamie took his staff and raced headlong at the jackalope's side. At the last moment, he put all his strength into thrusting the staff out like a spear. He heard several noises he hoped he would never hear again, and their adversary flailed so violently that Emilia was shaken free. She was catapulted away with a scream and a moment later, a thud indicated a painful end to her impromptu flight.

"Emmy!"

"I'm…ow. I'm okay."

"That's good because I have problems here." He stared at the black and, frankly, demonic eyes of the jackalope king. "Okay. One…two…"

"Three!" his sister called. She replicated his strike on the jackalope's hindquarters and when he heard her count, he lunged forward. His staff plunged directly into the creature's mouth.

The beast fell, twitched slightly, and went limp. They stared at it, Emilia with one hand on her hip and her face screwed in pain.

"Well, *that* was…something." She shook her head.

"It was," he said. "Come on, let's go get you patched up. And some new armor."

The body disappeared a moment later and left a small pouch of gold coins.

"What the fuck?" she said.

"More video game stuff," he explained. "Kill animals, get loot. Kill big animals, get more loot."

"Let's go fight a yeti."

"Easy," he said fondly. "Armor first."

CHAPTER SEVENTY-SEVEN

The border between the dwarven and orcish lands was a steep line of mountains that cut along the skyline in imposing spears, almost too steep for the snow that clung to their peaks.

"Yer sure there's a path through there?" Lyle asked a couple of days out. "I don' see a single damned place to get through."

"It's there," Dotty said. Jaco had provided a map with loose instructions to a fabled passage through one of the mountains, and her experience moving through the orcish lands told her it was there. She had reached the water tribe's territory from the fire tribe's territory through the same type of tunnel.

When it came to working with rock and earth, the orcish shamans could give the dwarven *zauberers* a run for their money.

The trip from Berghold had been surprisingly pleasant. They'd been provided with hearty provisions by the dwarves, not to mention the ale and the palanquin, and the two companions enjoyed all the wonder of clear, open mountain air and the pleasant respite of a comfortable bed at night. With so many adventures from Lyle's past as well as tales of her adventures in the orcish lands, the two had more than enough to talk about.

She found herself growing weaker and weaker, however. When

she had first come to the game, the combination of the mechanics and her mind had been able to give her a taste of life in a young body. She had been free of the aches and pains that came with her illness. On her first adventure, when she was a dwarf, she and Lyle had spent the evenings sparring while he taught her how to fight with staves and daggers.

Now, although the pain was still absent, she found it difficult to get through a day without a nap. She would open the curtains at the sides of the palanquin and watch the sky and the landscape move slowly past until she was rocked to sleep under her blankets and furs.

The road began to rise, so gently at first that all she noted was the horses' labored breathing and the gradual shift in the flora around them. Now, closer to the mountains, the road was even steeper.

Finally, it came to a dead-end when it ran smack into a wall of stone.

Lyle stared at the cliff. "What was it you said about there being a passage?"

"Oh, hush," Dotty said without any particular rancor. She looked around thoughtfully, then dug Jaco's map out of her saddlebag. "Hmm. It says the passage should be near the road."

"So it's full of shit?" he suggested acidly.

"I said hush." She studied their surroundings and stretched her aching muscles slowly. Judging by the disrepair of this road, no one had used it for some time. While the soil was devoid of grass, there was a great deal of shale this close to the mountain—enough that the ponies had stopped a few yards back.

They would have to do something about that.

When she looked closer at the wall of rock, she realized it wasn't as sheer as it appeared. Little lines of moss and tiny flowers revealed where ripples in the face allowed plants to take hold. She handed her reins to Lyle and walked carefully to the shale and rock. With a small moment of hesitation, she placed her palms against it.

She wasn't sure what she was looking for. After all, she had *made* stone before—in a manner of speaking—but she had never sensed stone. She had only imagined the effects of heat and pressure when using her spells.

At first, it was difficult to move beyond the sensation of stone under her hands. Her fingertips dug in slightly and felt the grain of the rock and the faint grit that lay over it. She fancied that she could sense the moss and the flowers, although she knew that was insane.

Or was it?

"Prima? Can I...feel the stone and the flowers?"

"Fuck if I know."

Dotty looked at the sky, her lips twitching. "Thank you, as always, for keeping me from getting too woo-woo about this."

"My pleasure."

She could blast through it with magic, she thought, but that seemed the wrong approach. No, this needed to be sensed. She tried to let her awareness sweep outward as if she and the world around her were not separated.

Unfortunately, that didn't work.

Dotty recalled the streams near the water tribe's village and how they had burbled so cheerfully over the rocks. They had come from the mountains, where the water was clear and icy, runoff from the glaciers and snowcaps. She pictured the water running over the rock face now, creating rivulets as it encountered infinitesimal obstacles.

And if water ran over stone, it would find the hidden spaces.

The rock face disappeared so suddenly that she fell into the passage with a shriek. A yell issued behind her and she heard Lyle's boots meet the ground. By the time he reached her, she had rolled onto her back and stared at him with as much dignity as she could manage.

"What the hell did ye do?" he demanded.

She took her inspiration from Prima on this one. "Fuck if I know."

He laughed so hard he had to put his hands on his knees. For a few moments, he shook with mirth before he wiped his eyes and helped her up.

"Well," he said, "there we have it. Our way into the orcish lands. Let's hope peace treaties are as easy to work."

"Mmm." She brushed her skirt off and shooed him off to one side. "Uh, keep ahold of the horses, will you?"

"Why?" he asked suspiciously.

"Because I'll clear the shale." Dotty walked to join him and gestured for the whole party to move away before she considered what she had to do. She drew a mental line down the middle of the shale, closed her eyes, and pictured water welling and sweeping it sideways off the edge of the road.

She decided to ignore a muffled exclamation behind her and kept the spell going for as long as she could before exhaustion took hold. Her eyes opened in a hurry as she sank to the ground.

"Dotty? Dotty?" Lyle was at her side.

She couldn't feel his hand on her arm and her vision was covered with spots. Two spells seemed to be her limit right now. She stared at the road and waited for her vision to clear.

The shale on one side was gone. The rest of it remained

One would have to do. She allowed Lyle to pull her up and slid her arm over his shoulders before he led her to the palanquin. With a tired smile, she sank into the seat.

"I'm okay, you know."

"Ye don't look okay," he said bluntly. "Ye stay there and let me get us through this passage."

"Lunch first," she said decisively.

"While I'm all for lunch—"

"Lyle." She put a hand on his arm. "If I'm more alert, I may be able to sense threats in the same way I sensed the passage itself."

"Oh. Fair enough."

They ate a quiet meal and she remained somewhat dreamy from exhaustion. It was only at the end that she thought to look at Lyle, and her heart squeezed when she saw him staring sadly at the landscape. She wanted to reassure him but to her surprise, tears threatened.

Instead, she let him lead the horses through the tunnel and went through in the palanquin. The dwarf and one pony pushed ahead, followed by the pony dragging the palanquin and her horse at the back. The damp coolness of the tunnel helped, in some ways, to wake her.

It was also dark and cozy, however, which meant she had a nap or two in the darkness.

Like the other passage, it was long enough that they lost sight of all daylight for a time. Eventually, the smell of fresh air and the growing light told her they would soon emerge into the orcish lands.

When they did, at last, she was awoken from another nap by Lyle's exclamation. Dotty sat abruptly and peeked her head out of the palanquin.

It was immediately obvious what had caused his amazement. The trees were at least as big as the redwoods of California, large enough that one could make a tunnel through the center of one and drive a car through with sufficient space left on either side. They stretched so far that she only had the vague sense of green leaves and dappled sunlight.

For the forest was light. It was alive and filled with the calls of birdsong and the creak of the trees. Bushes growing in the spaces between the redwoods rustled and the very air seemed to be alive.

"It's *beautiful*." She felt the same kind of amazement she'd known when she first looked at the sea at night. Although entirely dwarfed by the landscape, it was enough to fill her with happiness.

The road, such as it was—it looked as disused on this side of the tunnel as it had on the other—wound into the forest without any markers. They set off in silence, both still entranced by the floating motes of dust and the flutter of birds and butterflies.

No settlements appeared for a long time, exactly like there had been no dwarven villages in the increasingly hostile landscape on the other side of the mountains. The ponies plodded onward, apparently unimpressed by the grandeur around them, and the two companions exchanged the occasional glance.

It wasn't a sense of being watched that left them wary. It was more that the longer they continued, the stranger it became that there were no people.

Finally, Dotty realized that she could smell smoke.

She scrambled out of the palanquin and onto the back of the horse and her gaze met the dwarf's. There were no screams but the smell was faint but unmistakable. It grew heavier as they progressed, more and more oppressive and with a trace of something else she could not name but nevertheless feared.

At last, they rounded a bend in the road and she put her hand to her mouth in horror.

Whatever had happened, there were no survivors. Every single house had been systematically put to the torch. A pile in the center of the town revealed bones and she pressed the back of her hand more firmly over her mouth. Someone had rounded the villagers up and…what?

She wanted to turn and leave. It took more than a minute for her to persuade herself to get off the horse and venture forth. The animal certainly had no intention to do so.

"Dotty." Lyle sounded almost panicked. "If we're wanderin' into a war…"

Although she heard him, she could not respond. She trembled violently as she studied the carnage—every house burned, the well blocked, and the bodies stacked so neatly. It was destruction, and yet…why? Something seemed wrong, not entirely in keeping with what she expected from a war.

She stopped dead a moment later. "This place…"

"Dotty, it may be best to leave if they're in the middle of a—"

"It wasn't a war," she said quietly. She turned to look at him. "It was a plague. This was the village I came from. *I* did this. I gave them the burial I could and I made sure no one would live here until it was safe again."

CHAPTER SEVENTY-EIGHT

"Ye did this?" Lyle asked blankly.

"Yes. No." Dotty shook her head. "I told you my village had been destroyed by a plague. I was given the life of that person for a time and this is their history." She looked around. "These were her family and friends and she saw all of them die. She had to bury them alone."

He dismounted and came to join her. While she could see that he wanted to be anywhere but there, he came to stand with his friend. She smiled gratefully at him.

"Um." He cleared his throat. "Do ye…want t' bury them?"

"I…" She looked at them. "No. She gave them last rites according to their ways. We should leave this place in peace, I think. But—give me a moment?"

The dwarf nodded wordlessly and returned to the ponies.

She knelt on the rich ground of the forest floor, heedless of the gown, and looked at the ash mixed among the leaves. This village had seen so much fear and grief and the loneliness of one woman, the last of her kind, setting out with the pyre still smoldering.

And that young woman had died fighting a dragon only a few weeks later. Had she heard that story from someone else, she would have thought it a tragic tale. The woman had survived for only a short while and had perhaps gone to her death because she could not face living without everyone she loved.

But she knew the story was very different—one of a woman who had triumphed against all odds and who had survived to bring justice to an entire race. That woman had not merely stoked rebellion and walked away. She had put herself into the fray and sacrificed her life before any other.

It was enough to make her wonder what other stories she thought she knew that might be not of loss but of hope and victory.

The faint tremble beneath her fingertips did not catch her attention at first. She felt tears on her cheeks, not least of all for Prima, who had lived this—every orc in this village suffering and dying of the plague. She hoped she had brought the AI some joy out of it. When the shaking grew louder, she recognized it for what it was —hoofbeats.

"Dotty!" Lyle was at her side and pulled at her arm, but it was too late to run.

The orcs were there.

"You." Their leader swung off her horse. She had greenish-brown skin and the lean build of a runner, and her muscles rippled as she walked. "Before you die for what you did here, you will tell me how you came to these lands."

Dotty stood with Lyle's help. She bowed as Rashat and Huwat had taught her.

"What happened here," she said clearly, "was a plague." She took a deep breath. "There was one survivor, a young woman named Dahti. She laid her people to rest and built the pyre, and then she set out to find a new home. She found one only for a short time in the village of Mountain's Shadow in the Fire lands. When their godspring awoke, she led them against it and sought the training of the legendary water shaman, Rashat, to defeat it. The price of that victory was her life. I kneel here in memory of her."

The chieftain looked at her. "We have heard that story," she said. "But how do you know it?"

She closed her eyes for a moment. "I know it because she was given many lives," she said finally. "She lived two before she watched her village lost and she stands before you now. If you doubt me, as I can only assume you do, I ask you to bring me to Rashat and to Huwat and the people of Mountain's Shadow. There, I can share things I would know only from experience, things they will remember."

The orcs looked warily at one another, but the chieftain did not seek approval. She considered her and her alone.

"Come here," she said at last.

Lyle made a strangled kind of noise, but Dotty moved around the edge of the village and picked over tumbled fences and mud bricks. She had to work to keep her face straight as the smell of the orcs hit her.

She'd forgotten how bad it was.

"You tell me you are an orc," the woman said.

"I tell you that I have once been an orc," she said.

The chieftain looked halfway between annoyed and amused. "The story is too strange for me to believe it."

"I understand," she told her simply. "I do. I too would disbelieve it."

"And you want us to take you to Rashat," the orc said after a moment's thought.

"If you want proof, yes. But I also wish to speak to him on behalf of the city of Insea—him and the other leaders, yourself included."

"What a coincidence." The orc now looked anything but friendly. "One might almost think you knew what was happening—and, unless I miss my guess, you're a magic-wielder as well."

"I am," she said. "As to what is happening…I have my hopes but no knowledge."

"And you want me to risk our leaders by bringing an outsider into their midst?"

Dotty wondered how she could allay her fears. "Is there any way you would feel safe?"

The chieftain thought for a moment before she returned to her horse. She rummaged in the saddlebags and retrieved a single iron manacle, which she held up to her. "Block your magic and I will trust you enough to bring you to the shamans."

She held out one wrist in silence, even though she could practically feel Lyle's concern radiating at her. But she remembered, too, how Atra and the other young warriors of the water tribe had welcomed her once the shock of her appearance wore off.

The dwarf stepped beside her, and she feared that he might argue or make things worse. Instead, he murmured to one of the warriors, who in turn murmured to the chieftain. She looked at her.

"I am told you are ill and must ride in that…box."

She gave her friend a look that was exasperated and grateful in equal measure. If this would be a long trip, she would certainly need to rest.

"Yes," she admitted. "I am not well—a mass here, in my stomach. It will kill me soon."

The woman looked almost sympathetic for a moment but wiped the expression away quickly. "We will take you both," she said. "Go. Sit in your box. Your dwarf, too." She held a hand up. "Both of you will be blindfolded."

"For how long?" she asked.

She only shrugged. In the next moment, a blindfold came down over Dotty's eyes and she was led to the palanquin, stumbling over the leaves and sticks, and listened to the dwarf do the same—swearing profusely and inventively every step of the way, of course.

The orcs seemed to appreciate that, at least. She heard a few snickers at some of the more colorful invectives, and their handlers were more careful in helping them over obstacles as a result.

She had guessed that Lyle's straight-talking warrior mentality would appeal to many of the orcs, but it was still surprising to see it in action.

As the curtains closed around them, she leaned back with a sigh— only to realize that she had missed the post. She flailed to keep her balance and wound up kicking Lyle in some place that felt squishy.

"Lyle?"

"M'okay," the dwarf wheezed.

"Oh, no." She lowered her face into her hands. "I'm so sorry. No, no, don't try to respond," she added. "Well...I suppose this is going fairly well."

"Ye think this is going *well?*"

"Well, I didn't get kicked in the groin so that does color my perception somewhat."

"I *mean,*" he said, "we're blindfolded an' bein' hauled into orc territory."

"That was where we were trying to go, though. So instead of wandering around looking for all the different shamans, they're *taking* us to them."

"I hadn't thought about it that way," he confessed. "Ye haven't got yer magic, though."

"It seems a reasonable precaution. I have killed more than one dragon. And some weird elf-thing in a black suit. And so on." She felt for the pillows more carefully this time, curled up, and yawned as soon as she rested her head. "I'm going to take a nap."

"How can ye sleep at a time like this?"

"What else is there to do?" she asked reasonably. "We seem to be safe and we can hardly be expected to navigate anything. Rest, Lyle."

He grumbled in response and she was fairly sure that, by the time they stopped for the evening, he had still not allowed himself to rest. The air around them seemed different somehow, and the wind freer—they must have left the forest—but other than that, she could not have said what direction they had gone in or where they were.

The next few days passed in much the same way. She learned several skills she had never wanted regarding balance and neatness while blindfolded but otherwise, had a pleasant enough journey. Despite the blindfold and certain clearly forbidden topics of conversation, their companions in the group were willing to speak to them and even laugh and exchange stories around the campfire at night.

Dotty was fairly sure that a number of stories were designed to test her story, which she accepted with good humor.

If someone had appeared in a cloth-of-silver gown and claimed to be a thrice-reincarnated hero of the American Revolution, for instance, she probably wouldn't have believed them in the slightest.

It was clear before long, however, that the surroundings had changed drastically. The air grew chill and the palanquin tilted. They must be entering the territory of the air tribe, but she did not want to say so to Lyle for fear of bringing down the wrath of their escort. It did not matter much, she decided and was simply something to say to break up the monotony of sitting in the carriage while they jolted along the road.

They heard the gathering long before they were close to it. The sound drifted eerily on the mountain wind, sometimes in snatches of song, sometimes in the beat of drums or the tramp of many feet. Dancing, making pilgrimage, or simply making their way up the mountain together? All were possible.

The din grew almost deafening before their caravan stopped. Shouts demanded that orcs get out of the way, followed by many hushed whispers.

Finally, the curtains of the palanquin were drawn back and she was pulled out. She swayed and covered her eyes in agony when the blindfold was removed. It had been so long since she had seen light and she forced herself to let it through in small amounts until at last, she could squint and look around.

Great, she thought acidly. Her first meeting with the council of shamans would be with her eyes streaming with tears, all bedraggled after days on the road, and her face screwed into a grimace.

But when her eyes did clear, she could have laughed. "Rashat! Huwat! *Atra!*"

What she did not expect was for Atra to step forward with a spear aimed directly at her chest. "Who are you?" the young woman demanded. "And how do you know our names?"

"The truth," Rashat added. His voice was as chill as deepest winter.

"I'm Dahti," she told them. "I fought with you and studied with you. We stayed at the village, you and I, after the rest of the tribe left to take shelter in the tunnels. We lured the godspring over the village fire to impale it on the spear. We traveled to face the godspring at Mountain's Shadow, and one life of mine passed there."

But he only shook his head. "Lies," he said, and his voice was even harder than it had been before. "Be honest, human, or we will kill you here and now."

CHAPTER SEVENTY-NINE

This was not, Dotty had to admit, how she had thought this would go. There had been A Plan.

Also, things had gone so well. Yes, she had faced the displeasure of the dwarven council but she had found a solution. They had worked together.

Now, she was on a plateau in the middle of nowhere, surrounded by weapons and without her magic, and the one thing that should have worked—the truth—would almost certainly get her nowhere.

"May I speak to you alone?" she asked Rashat. She looked at Huwat. "Or you?"

"No."

She held her hand up to display the iron manacle. "I have no magic and I have no weapons. I mean you no harm—nor, let's be honest, could I do any if I wanted to." She looked meaningfully at the orcs. Compared to her, they were hulking.

"Fine," Rashat said. He swept an arm imperiously and the others stepped aside to allow their small procession into an ornate tent.

Inside, the two shamans took seats on the floor. She had not been invited to sit and decided not to chance her luck by doing so. Instead, she looked around and noted with alarm that Lyle was not here.

"Will the dwarf be safe?"

The water shaman's brow furrowed. "You have asked to speak to us. No emissaries would be harmed until negotiations were concluded."

That was not *precisely* heartening, but she didn't want to point that out.

"Speak," he said, clearly impatient.

"Is there anything I could say," she asked, "any question I could answer or any memory I could recall to convince you that I am telling the truth?"

They wanted to say no. She saw it in their eyes. It was the instinctive answer to her question.

"Believe me," she said, "if I could choose my story, I would not have chosen this one. I would simply have said I was an emissary."

Rashat chuckled unwillingly at that before he said, "Our last lesson —*the* last lesson—before the Godspring attacked. What happened?"

Dotty took time to think back. "We were walking to the village when it came from the depths," she said. "I had…called it—not on purpose but by using fire and earth magic when I sat in the sea. I was cold and trying to warm myself." Her eyes drifted closed. "That was days before, though. That night…I can't—oh. You had finally pushed me to the point where I fought back physically instead of only with magic. You wanted me to use magic only as one tool in my arsenal."

His brows raised. He schooled his face to impassivity a moment later and nodded to Huwat. "A question from you next."

The fire shaman was ready. "With what provisions did you go to the next tribe?"

"Mushrooms and root vegetables," she said at once. "They were from the cave the shamans used for their rites. You intended to send me with more, but the village had run from their home and I told you to keep half."

Huwat nodded silently and looked at Rashat.

Dotty, meanwhile, resisted the urge to scream. She was her and they clearly knew it.

"How did you—how do you *claim* you came to be reborn?" the

water shaman asked. "You are not a babe in arms as you by rights should be."

"How…" She struggled to find words. "That is a strange tale. In Insea, there is a tournament. One human fighter, who had come here from another world—in itself a story—won the final prize, a key that would take him home. He had seen the danger that threatened this world, and he promised he would come back and bring help. I am one of the people he brought, and it was only my spirit that came here, not my body as well." She smiled. "Which is as well, honestly. My old bones wouldn't have made this journey in good shape."

"You always did claim you had grandchildren," Rashat murmured. His brows snapped together. "But your story is well beyond the realm of reason. We must think on this—and also think what we wish to do. You and your dwarf—"

"He's not *my* dwarf," she protested.

He continued as if he hadn't heard her at all. "Will be confined to a tent and kept under guard," he said. "I advise you to not disobey orders. You will find that our people are strong and their commitment to the law is absolute."

She had witnessed the crumbling of certain orcish traditions and had personal thoughts on how absolute that commitment was, but she held her tongue. Instead, she smiled and said simply, "Thank you."

It wasn't long before she and Lyle were shut in another far less ornate tent.

"So…are they goin' t' execute us?" he asked as he unrolled his bedroll. "And what do we have for food?"

"Nothing yet—and that's still better than the dried fish they ate in the water tribe." She shuddered.

"Well, I'll tell ye one thing, they'd best not drink me ale."

"If it gets us a peace treaty…" She shrugged. "And no, I wouldn't say we're in immediate danger. I think they know I'm telling the truth. It's merely a rather awkward truth and it leaves them in a strange position."

"Huh." He plopped down, his expression disgruntled. "I wish we could go out. I hear dancin'."

"Once again, we were *specifically* cautioned against that." She sat as well. The palanquin was outside, but the furs and pillows from inside it were in with them now. "There's no need to have the one of us who *isn't* dying get killed by orcs."

"Ye don't have t' sell me on it," Lyle assured her. "I'm in no rush to die."

"Are you sure? Because I've heard many stories about you. Some of them are stories *you* told me."

"Eh." He dismissed the ambiguity with a shrug. "What's yer plan, then?"

Dotty sighed. "Eventually, given that they know who I am, I assume they'll hear me out. From there, it will simply be the matter of finding out what's going on in the orcish lands and making sure we can be allies—or, at least, friendly acquaintances."

"They don't seem very happy about outsiders," Lyle pointed out.

"Do you blame them? You said yourself that your people were a nightmare, and you've met the Elves. As for humans—"

"You, Tina, and Justin are enough to make that point," he said with a shudder.

"Hey!"

He grinned at her. "What d'ye think they'll want?"

"I haven't the faintest clue." She lay back and pillowed her head on her hands. Wind whistled around the tent, eerie even in the daylight, and filtered in only through the gaps between the shelter's sides. "The water tribe was almost destroyed, so perhaps they would want materials for rebuilding. I don't know very much about the other tribes and their needs, though."

"Ye sound worried."

"Wouldn't you be?"

"Eh." He shrugged. "Either we find something or they kill us. Ye're smart, so there's no point in worryin' about it."

"Ah." Dotty wasn't sure how much more of this confidence she could take. "So, how do you think the others are doing?"

"Ugh. They have their work cut out for them." Lyle sat now. "The human lords hate each other more than almost anything. They have so many grudges that if ye allied with one of 'em, even *he'd* be angry at you about it."

She burst out laughing. "Oh, dear," she said a moment later. "I shouldn't laugh, I shouldn't. But it's funny. Especially because I know Tina won't stand for any of that. She'll catch every one of those things that don't make sense."

"And bonk 'em over the head with it," he finished and nodded slowly.

"She does have a way with words."

"I wasn't speakin' metaphorically." He fished a pipe out of one of his many pockets. "Do you mind if I smoke?"

"No. Harry used to—my husband. Not many do nowadays and I miss it."

"Huh." He lit the pipe and puffed on it to get the flame going. "Maybe we should leave well enough alone. If they don't want to come out of their lands—"

"No." Dotty sat at that. "The world grows and changes, people push against their borders, technology continues—there's no way they'll stay isolated forever, even if they want to. The dragons kept them trapped for far too long, and I'd be willing to bet they stoked fears of the outside while they were at it."

"I hadn't considered that." Lyle looked at her. "Ye speak like ye know these things. *Were* ye a diplomat? Ye say no, but..."

"I come from a very different time." She managed a smile. "I'd say it's a more complicated one, but I remember my youth—every time and every world is complicated in its own way. It's easy to let nostalgia take hold."

She stood and began to pace, her arms wrapped around herself. Her gown, although it was not as ornate as the one she had worn in Berghold, was still not what one would call either serviceable or functional.

"If you want my guess," she said to him after a few minutes of pacing, "they'll open up. I don't know how long it will take. They'll choose to open up and after that, there'll be a ton of nostalgia for *this* —for the days when they were kept to their individual tribes by the dragons. People will forget how bad it was to have the beasts demanding sacrifices of the young warriors. Hell, they'll realize soon enough that coming together, all tribes at once, has problems too. But if they're lucky, things will still be better." She stopped and chewed on one thumbnail for a moment. "No, things *will* be better," she said. "I met the young of the water tribe. You should have seen their fire, Lyle —although I suppose that's an ironic way to put it."

The dwarf laughed.

"They'll fight to make their world better," she told him. "And they *will* make it better."

Dotty settled on the furs, her heart less heavy with fear. It was only then that she saw the tent flap move slightly and fall into place.

Who had been listening? She stared at the makeshift door and her heart pounded. What would they think of what they had heard?

The two companions waited while the light faded and the sounds outside changed to eating, accompanied by the smell of roasted vegetables and meat and fresh-baked bread. A guard brought them food with a sympathetic look and a great deal of curiosity.

The meal was doubtless composed of leftovers, but both were too hungry to care. They wolfed it down and fell asleep listening to the sounds of dancing and music.

In the middle of the night, she was woken with a knife at her throat and warm breath at her ear.

"Come with me," Atra said quietly. "Make a single sound, though, and I will kill you."

CHAPTER EIGHTY

Jamie and Emilia ran, shrieking, through a field of long grass.

"They could be kids again," Simon said ruefully. "If you discounted the weapons, that is." He took his glasses off and rubbed the bridge of his nose. When he spoke a moment later, he did not look at his wife. "What are we going to do?"

Aimee leaned back in her chair. The PIVOT team had set aside a private conference room for them where they could watch Jamie and Emilia's progress through the game and speak in privacy.

Finally, she said, "I don't think we have a choice. Do you?"

"No," he admitted and smiled at the screen. "*They* certainly made their feelings clear. You know, I was proud of them for saying it."

"Be proud without giving them big heads," she advised.

His smile broadened. Even after twenty-two years with this woman at his side, he was still delightedly taken aback every time one of her Southern grandmother's platitudes came out of her mouth. Her accent grew stronger when she said those things.

She knew and nudged him with an elbow. "Still? Two decades and you still think it's funny to see a Chinese woman with a Southern drawl?"

"I met you in New York," he said with a helpless shrug. "It was a very important moment for me and I will *always* expect you to have a New York accent and…New York parenting advice."

"What would that be?" Aimee asked him precisely. "Never sit in the last subway car? Don't trust hot dog vendors?"

Simon laughed.

Her smile had slipped from her face, though. "I don't want them to think they run the show," she said quietly. "If they push for this, we agree, and something happens to her…"

"It'll be no more dangerous than waiting for it to get worse on its own," he said.

"I know that. But emotions don't. They'd feel guilty for the rest of their lives." Aimee took a deep breath and shook her head. "I've been over every moment of my pregnancy, it feels like, and her first weeks. Did I pay more attention to Jamie, did I eat something wrong—"

"*My love.*" Aghast, he swung his chair to face her. "Have you wondered that all these years?"

She didn't look at him. Instead, she had her hands pressed between her knees and she was shaking. "Yes."

"Aimee. Love. Please look at me." He tried to take one of her hands but she was like a statue. Instinct told him that if he moved her, she would crumble—and she so hated to do so in public. He placed his hand gently on her leg. "I saw you with every one of our children. I saw you when you were pregnant. Whatever dark moments you had, if you were exhausted or even angry, if you spoke to them harshly, that is what it means to be *human*. If something like that could cause this, every child on earth would have what Taigan has." Cautiously, he tried a joke. "At least then they'd probably have a cure for it."

Her chin trembled and he thought he'd made a terrible mistake, but then she started to laugh. She was crying too, and tears poured down her face as she clasped his hands while she leaned her forehead against his.

"Why didn't you tell me?" Simon whispered. His heart was breaking at the thought that his wife had spent years fearing she was at fault.

The laughter took a moment to settle, but her face crumpled with tears. "I was afraid you'd agree," she whispered. "And that you'd—"

"Never." He wrapped an arm around her. "Taigan could not have a better mother."

Her eyes drifted closed and she shook her head.

"Yes, Aimee."

"No. Because what about *them?*" She gestured to the screen where Emilia and Jamie were still playing—more playing tag than doing any kind of quest if the truth be told. "You saw how angry Emilia was. There wasn't enough time for everything."

"We did the best we could." His heart would break more than once during this conversation, he realized. "It wasn't enough and it wasn't what they should have had. But no parents could have done this perfectly, Aimee. When they're older, they'll know that. I think they even know it now. And we can do better."

She took a deep breath and raised her hand to touch his cheek. "But the best way to do better," she said, "*really* do better…is if Taigan is cured."

"You know," he told her after a moment, "I don't think *this* was what my father warned me about when he said, 'you get married and suddenly, your wife is always right.' But he was right."

Aimee flicked him lightly on the knee and laughed. "Your father, I swear."

"He did like you, you know." He kissed her.

"Uh-huh." She sighed and rubbed her face. "So we're doing this again. All the transfer paperwork, finding someplace to stay… It never gets easier. Why doesn't it get easier?"

"It does sometimes," Simon said. "There's AirBnB now."

"Okay, that's true." She raised one eyebrow mischievously. "Dibs on finding a place to stay."

"*No.* I demand a rematch."

"I don't make the rules." She grinned.

Simon laughed and took her hands. "So, we're doing this. We are doing this. *Wait.*" He stood. "I want to do something. Tell me your memories of Taigan. Tell me things you saw her do—wait, pairs of things. A thing you saw her do, and a thing you did when you were her age."

She smiled. "Ah… Hmm. I did love the way she always dressed up. Emilia and Jamie were so careful during their games—they had to have the pirate hat to play pirate games or whatever, but Taigan would put on any old thing and run off. Do you remember the time she took my pearls and said she was a dinosaur?"

"I remember we pulled the pearls out of the fish pond later," he said, laughing. "And the second part?"

"Ah, hmmm. The second part. Well, I suppose someday, I hope we see her wearing a beautiful pearl necklace of her own." Aimee smiled. "Maybe at a wedding? Or a…graduation?" Her voice broke slightly but she smiled. "Your turn, before I cry."

"Well, you've got me there. I proposed the game but I didn't have anything." He leaned against the table and thought hard. "I still love how she would cuddle in our laps when we read."

She smiled at the memory. "She always got around bedtime with that."

"'One more story, one more story,'" Simon said, quoting his daughter's almost constant refrain from ages two to six. "She knew we couldn't say no to that."

"Clever girl," Aimee agreed. "And what's the thing you want to see?"

"Hmm, what was I doing at seventeen? Nothing worthwhile, I can tell you that. I looked forward to having a place of my own, I guess. I'd like her to be able to walk into an empty apartment with boxes of her things and feel that total exhilaration, you know? That it will be your first time being on your own but it's all yours to shape."

"That's a good one." She laced her fingers through his.

"Your turn again."

"Again? Hmm. I love how when she did gymnastics, she could never quite stick the landing because she was so proud of herself—she wanted to rush over to us for a hug." She smiled. "Although it was sometimes exasperating. As for memories of me at seventeen…oh." Her face went still.

"What is it?"

"I want her to have her heart broken," she said and looked at him. "I don't want her to be in pain—not *that* part of it—but to know that the pain can't break her and she can be happy on her own. I worry that she'll never let herself get close to someone because of this. And if she does, I worry she'll be too scared to let the relationship go if she needs to."

"Now that you mention it, that was part of being seventeen for me, too." He sighed. "It's amazing what the passage of thirty years can do for perspective. At the time, I wanted to cry my eyes out—not that my father would have allowed it—and beg for her to come back and maybe put my fist through a wall."

"You? Really?"

"Seventeen is a rough age. Give me a break." He uttered a rueful laugh. "But the thought of never meeting you—that's horrifying."

Aimee squeezed his fingers. "Heartbreak is like falling and skinning your knees, hmm? It's part of learning to be a person. Your turn. Then I suppose we should tell them what we mean to do."

"Probably." Simon kissed her. "I love the way she never sang the same tune as everyone else. She was always trying to harmonize. Then she got *too old and dignified* to sing grace, of course." He shook his heads. "Kids. And…I want her to go grocery shopping for the first time and come home and realize how many things she's missing. It's not funny when you try to cook a meal, but it's part of the process."

She laughed, stood, and pulled him up. They kissed and shared the silence that had been so much a part of their lives—silence with the beeps of medical equipment, silence as they drove to yet another facility, or the silence of a night in a strange house.

They had learned to speak to one another simply with silence. And now, both of them looked at the screen, where their other two children still played and laughed. As they stood there, Simon and Aimee decided another thing in silence.

They sat together to watch. They would transfer Taigan to PIVOT soon and there would be the mountain of paperwork and the trials of deciding where the kids would stay and who would shuttle back and forth.

But right now, they had a moment to watch their children play and they wouldn't pass it up. Because they were rebuilding the family for all of them, not only Taigan.

CHAPTER EIGHTY-ONE

Atra led her around the edge of the campground. Cloaked in darkness, they wove between silent tents and orcs slumbering beneath the night sky. When Dotty looked up, amazed by a completely unfamiliar night sky, a prick of the knife reminded her to keep walking.

It was impossible to ignore that they were drawing closer and closer to the edge of the plateau.

At last, they reached a statue, a pillar made of metals, stone, and wood. It reminded her of a mosaic, although she had never seen a column done this way and there was no picture she could see. Each piece of it had a carving, and although she wanted to see them more closely, she did not dare. This place felt holy, surrounded by dozens upon dozens of low-guttering candles.

She glanced at Atra, whose gaze was fixed on the pillar. The orc was steeling herself in preparation for something.

Please, let it not be her murder. They were so high above the plains below. It must be hundreds of feet down and her heart clenched at the thought of falling and of the pain.

"Atra..." she began.

"Stop." The warrior's words were more measured than she

expected. "You stand in the presence of gods—our true gods, the old gods. Know that in this place, they can hear every lie you speak."

Understanding dawned and with it, hope.

She inclined her head. "I swear to you, I will speak no lie in this place."

"*Who are you?*"

"I am Dotty. I am a woman with four children and with grandchildren and great-grandchildren. I am dying from a mass in my stomach. This is the third time I have come to this world, and it will be the last. The first time, it was as a dwarven woman. The second time, it was as the orc you met, Dahti. The third, you see before you."

"Still you lie," Atra whispered. Her head shook and she held the knife out so it gleamed under the stars.

Dotty could sense something else beneath the surface, but she could not grasp it. "Why do you say so?" Then, fumbling her way to the truth, she asked, "Why do you *need* for this to be a lie, Atra?"

The woman's lip curled in a snarl. "You know nothing about me."

"I know some things." She looked steadily at her. "I know you were trained to defend your people and you could easily have killed me the first time we met. I know your grandmother is one of the elders of the tribe and you brought me to her, knowing she would disapprove but *also* knowing that the traditions of the tribe allowed it. I know you once asked Rashat why he was always sad."

Atra's eyes looked like pools of black in the darkness. "No," she whispered.

"Atra." Dotty stepped forward and regretted it immediately when the woman's face closed off. Desperately, she held her hands out. "I was your ally once. I sacrificed my life for your people. Surely you heard that story from Rashat."

"You convinced us to kill our gods," the warrior hissed, "to go against our traditions, and you had *no right.* You came to us cloaked in the skin of our people. You pretended to be one of us, but you never were."

"Atra, your shamans agreed that the gods were unjust."

"Because you came to whisper in their ears!" Atra clapped a hand over her mouth as her voice rose. She looked around, fearful that she had woken the others. "You *had no right*. It was our injustice to right. They were our traditions to keep or throw away."

Dotty looked down. Her head was reeling.

She had given her life to protect these people and to warn them that their ways were slowly killing them. How *dare* Atra say this to her? Anger pumped hot through her veins.

For the first time, she doubted why she was there. Prima was her friend, and Lyle, but she had counted Atra among her friends, too. She had wanted to leave a world in which the young woman could be happy and, as Lyle had pointed out, she had her world to think about too.

If this was the reaction she would get, shouldn't she have simply stayed in her world?

Lord knew, there were injustices there too.

Disheartened, she turned away to look over the plateau and the people sleeping in their huddles and tents. In the dark, there was no telling who was from which tribe. There were only orcs—hundreds of them and perhaps thousands.

The representatives of each tribe.

"Have you nothing to say for yourself?" Atra asked.

Her anger, which had faded while she watched the sleeping gathering, came back with a vengeance.

"No," she said shortly. "I have no apologies to make. I came to help and I *did* help, and I risked my life to do so—and gave it, not sure there would ever be another incarnation. You have no right to judge me." She leaned forward. "And if you think to kill me now, know that it will not help you. When the orcs reach out, they can find allies or they can find those who do not care for them at all. Kill me and you will assure the latter."

"The orcs never need to go beyond our borders," the woman retorted, hatred in her tone. "We have enough to do rebuilding what you tore down."

Dotty turned and left before she could say something she would regret.

She was several tents away and moving farther into the camp before she realized that she did not know where she was—and that she was now in defiance of Rashat's orders. Frustrated, she looked at the sleeping orcs and closed her eyes for a moment in defeat.

Stupidly, she wanted to cry. She had come to help and they didn't want that. They couldn't see how she had already helped them. She forced herself to overcome the tears and through her blurred gaze, caught sight of the main tent. Quickly, she picked her skirts up and hurried toward it. From there, she could find her bearings, return to Lyle, and hatch a plan to get out of here.

Except that, as she approached it, a tall shape pushed the door aside and stepped out.

Dotty skidded to a halt and swallowed.

"Why are you out alone?" Rashat asked her.

"Because one of yours took me to the edge of the plateau and threatened my life," she told him as coldly as she could muster.

"Atra," he guessed at once.

"Yes."

"The girl has more anger than is good for her. Still...I might know something about that." He looked at her. "And if you're as old as you claim, you must know the same."

She gritted her teeth. "I didn't throw the accomplishments of my elders in their faces."

"Didn't you?" he asked, genuinely amused. "What a strange young one you must have been. I didn't, of course. But that's because they were almost all dead." He held a hand out and gestured in the direction from which she had come. "Walk with me. I would show you something."

"If it's the cliff, believe me, I've seen it," she told him. "I know how far down it is."

"Not that. Woman, if I wanted you dead, I'd kill you. Same as you with me. Do you think I don't know you can get out of that iron bracelet if you want?"

A little startled, she clutched her wrist in her other hand and realized he was right. The manacle was made for orcs and it was loose enough to slide her hand through. She nodded.

In silence, she walked with him through the campground. When she heard orcs stir in their sleep, she wasn't worried that they would wake and kill her. She could discern the scents of incense and the patterns on blankets and tents.

To her amusement, Rashat had brought her to the same pillar. She wanted to look around to see if Atra still lingered but she forced herself to remain still. Let Atra hear this, whatever was coming she thought as she studied her companion, who gazed up at the pillar.

"So much has been lost," he said quietly.

Dotty lowered her head and bit her lip.

"Each tribe brings a piece for each of their members," he said. "Beneath this layer of stones lies another and another. Every one of our people is counted here."

She looked up sharply in amazement. "Truly?"

"What did you think a gathering of tribes was for?" Rashat asked wryly. "We are here to take an accounting of our strengths. This is one of the few traditions we can remember, and it is because one of the air tribe found a pillar inscribed with names." He paused. "But so many of our traditions had no monuments. They are songs that are gone from memory, the names of gods we never knew, and the stories of our ancestors…"

His voice faded. In the distance, a dying fire popped and hissed.

"We took it from ourselves," he said.

Another silence followed and Dotty decided to try speaking.

"Don't you think there are perhaps things you've done in the past centuries that are worth keeping as *new* traditions in spite of everything?" She narrowed her eyes at his expression. "What is it?"

"You still do not see," he told her.

She looked at the pillar, then to the edge of the plateau, and finally, behind her.

"It is not a thing you can see with your eyes," the shaman said impatiently. "One might almost think you were being purposefully dense."

"I didn't come here to be insulted and threatened." She glared at him.

"No," Rashat said. "You came to secure something from us, did you not?"

This was a dangerous path and she swallowed cautiously. "And to give something in return. Something you *need*."

"Oh?" He smiled. "And what is that?"

"Alliances," she said fiercely. "When you venture beyond these lands—"

"Who says we will?"

"The world has changed," she told him. "D'you remember what the godspring said in the fire village—that one of his kind had died to give the world peace? I've found the origins of that story since we last spoke, and the godspring did not lie. Peace was held for generations by the dwindling life of one dragon and now, he is dead and the world is beginning to descend into chaos. Who can say how much of your desire to stay here was due to that spell? And how much that spell contributed to the fact that no one came into your lands?"

The shaman looked genuinely surprised. "I admit, I had not considered that the worm was telling the truth."

She shrugged. "The world always seems to be stranger than we expect."

"And so you came to bring us alliances we need," he said slowly. "That is why?"

"Yes."

"You are lying. You came to gain an alliance because this new world threatens you more than it does us. It is because you do not want us to sweep off the plains and conquer your towns."

"It does not matter if you conquer them," she said without thinking. "War devastates all, no matter who wins."

"True enough."

"How would you know?"

"Because my tribe faced the water dragon twice," he said coldly. "And does it seem to you that we were *victors* in that exchange?"

Dotty bit her tongue and nodded. He had a point.

"So you have lied to us about why you came. You were a petitioner who didn't come out of altruism but out of self-interest."

"Can it not be *both*?" she cried finally. Even though she heard others begin to wake at the sound of their exchange, she did not stop. She wanted them to hear her. "I'm not of Insea and I'm not of the orcs, but I want to help them. I want to know that when I leave, I leave a world at peace. Why do you mistrust me so?"

He was not at all swayed by her words and had expected them, she could see that.

"Because you want to save us," he told her. "You came to a place where you did not belong and tried to save us from ourselves and our gods. Now, you come to try to save us from what you assure us will be a ruinous war. But you have no understanding of our past and don't know what wars there might have been. You do not know what *we* want, and you do not care."

Her jaw dropped at the accusation. First Atra and now Rashat.

And she knew, with a sickening twist in her stomach, that they were right.

It wasn't the whole of the story, of course, but they were right. *Now* she saw what Atra had been saying. When had she become stronger by having someone else solve her problems? When had her children?

But she had tried to do so for the orcs. She had wanted so badly to finish her life by doing some good in the world that she had forgotten the people who would live on and that they should choose. She bowed her head.

"What *do* you want?" she asked him finally.

He looked at the pillar as he spoke. "I want to reclaim what was lost," he said. "That is the first thing. Now, come. I will bring you back to your tent."

CHAPTER EIGHTY-TWO

When Dotty woke the next morning, Lyle was shaking her urgently.

"Hmm?" She opened her eyes to the taste of metal in her mouth and an ache in her stomach. She blinked, half-sure that she would see the doctors when she opened her eyes again but it was still the dwarf. "What is it?"

"They're summoning us." He helped her sit and crouched to look in her eyes. "Ye don't look well."

"It's okay. I'm fine." She gestured for him to stand and help her up as well. She stumbled slightly when she stood and her head spun. "Give me a moment to have water and fix my hair and I'll be out." When he didn't move, she smiled. "Only a moment alone? Please?"

He hesitated but nodded and pushed the tent flap aside. Outside, she could hear him speak to the guards in low tones. She waited for them to come inside and demand her presence, but they did not.

Alone, she pressed her hand against her stomach and looked at the floor. She was dimly aware of Prima rebraiding her hair, but the AI did not speak.

"How bad is it?" she said finally.

"I don't know," Prima admitted. *"I don't have access to any of your*

bloodwork information. You're not...like Lyle. I can't see all of you." She paused while her gown changed to one of deep blue. *"You don't feel well, do you?"*

"No." She swallowed. "And I don't want to...miss saying goodbye, you know? To my family. But if I'm okay, I don't want to ruin this, either."

"I'll put an alert out to the team," Prima said. *"I'll tell them to pull you out if they need to but if you're healthy enough, to leave you in. Would that work?"*

"Yes." She felt a rush of relief. "Thank you, Prima. Thank you so much."

"Thank you," the AI said quietly. *"Now, go. Lyle is worrying. I'll make sure you have better food tonight."*

Dotty left, her lips twitching. Prima liked to claim that certain events could not be altered and perhaps that was true—but she seemed perfectly capable of implanting suggestions in people's minds. Suggestions like, "Why don't you give Dotty some cake?"

She walked to the main tent and tried not to squint in the bright sunshine, while Lyle cast looks at her every few seconds from beneath bushy eyebrows.

"I'm all right," she told him after the fourth look. "I won't keel over, I promise. I merely woke up last night and had trouble getting back to sleep."

It was true, mostly.

"Have ye thought over what yer going to say?" he asked in a low voice.

"Yes." She had woken feeling ill but with the answer in her mind. "But *don't* muck it up by getting all annoyed."

"This should be good."

"Do you promise?" she asked him.

"Will you screw the dwarves over?"

"Hmm—don't look at me like that. I'm trying to decide if you'd think it was screwing them over. I don't think so."

"How reassuring."

The guards tried not to listen but didn't seem successful. Their expressions of interest confirmed this. They held the tent flaps back, their lips twitching, and the two were ushered into the relative darkness of the main tent.

It was filled to capacity. All the chieftains were there, including the woman who had found them at the earth tribe village. She acknowledged her with a nod. At her side was her tribe's shaman and all the other shamans were there as well. There was little in the way of regalia and it seemed the shamans and the chieftains wore the same loose, serviceable clothing as their villagers.

Dotty looked around, located Huwat in the crowd, and gave him a small smile. He nodded, although he tried to keep his face straight.

She did not see Atra.

"Emissaries," Rashat said. "Yesterday, we spoke to the human. Dwarf, tell us your story."

This was not what she had expected, and from the look on Lyle's face, it wasn't what he had expected, either.

He swallowed. "Er…"

The orcs waited. To their credit, not one of them laughed.

"I'm the son of a councilor in Berghold," he said. "A…chieftain, I guess you'd say. I might have been one meself, but I never liked th' idea o' sittin' around an' arguin' all the day long. As soon as I was old enough, I left an' hired meself out as a guard fer caravans an' such. I saw a lot o' places." He thought for a moment. "I fought a demon once," he added lamely.

Dotty tried desperately not to laugh. "That's generally not considered a footnote," she muttered.

"Ah," he said.

Rashat also looked as if he tried not to laugh. "And how did you come to be here?" he asked.

"After one o' my jobs—well, soon after the demon one, actually—I decided t' go home. Berghold had some problems I wanted to address." The dwarf hunched his shoulders. "I did some o' that but not much. When Insea needed emissaries…." He shrugged. "Among dwarves, ye can stake yer family's honor on a deal like this—bring a deal back to Berghold. What they wanted t' give the dwarves was good. So I did. Now we're here."

"So you function both as a representative of the dwarves and as a representative of Insea?" The water shaman arched one eyebrow.

"No, sir. Ye'll know when ye get a *real* representative from Berghold, as ye'll die of old age afore they finish gettin' to the point."

A round of snickers followed his declaration. Dotty felt both pride and annoyance. She had been right that he would get on well with the orcs and she should have simply let him handle things from the start.

Well, what was done was done.

"And would you stake your family's honor, likewise, on this human's word here?" Rashat asked him bluntly.

The dwarf nodded. "I would, sir. Not everyone will leave happy, I'll tell ye that now, but she'll be fair and she'll be honorable."

Her heart clenched and she looked at him. "Lyle—"

"Woman, d'ye honestly think I'd let myself be taken blindfolded through orc territory if I didn't trust ye?"

She blinked and pressed her lips together. She nodded wordlessly, rather afraid that if she spoke, she would either laugh or cry.

"Very well," Rashat said. He nodded at Lyle, then at her. "Tell us what Insea offers."

"And tell us," rumbled one of the chieftains, "what Insea *is*."

"That's somewhat complicated," Dotty said. She sketched the popular telling of Insea's history, including the fact that the king had never been seen and that the elves were creating a new monarchy. "Insea has never stood against any other nation in war, but neither has it cultivated allies. While the world becomes less peaceful, Insea believes that the only way to maintain the peace that has so enriched us is to strengthen the bonds between cities."

"So," the woman next to Huwat said, "when times were good, you did not seek allies but now you do to save yourselves."

"Yes," Dotty said bluntly.

Lyle sucked his breath in.

Dotty and the woman stared at each other and she smiled at the orc. "What is gone and past cannot be changed, but what is in the future can be."

Rashat tapped his staff on the ground twice and all focused on him. "You do not tell the whole truth, emissary. If you wish my support in these proceedings, you will tell it."

Now, she hesitated but she was committed. She had made her choice.

It was not the choice Jaco would have made, but it was the choice *she* made.

"If the truth can destroy something," she murmured to herself, "then it deserves to fall." Determined, she raised her chin. "Insea's peace was maintained without the knowledge or consent of its citizens by the life force of a dragon—kin of those who called themselves your gods. It bound the minds of the people inside the city and outside it as well so that they could not even have thoughts of war or violence against it. It was a peace based on trickery and subjugation, and the dragon's death has freed Insea of that trickery. Now, however, the city lies unprotected."

She knew what she was offering and she could see in their eyes how tempting it was. Then, to her surprise, the greed she saw there began to dissipate. The hunger left and the orcs nodded and settled.

"Insea was in chains, you say?" Huwat asked her. "Every citizen?"

"Everyone," she confirmed. "Leaders of other nations forgot their grudges and never sent their forces against the city. Now that the dragon is dead, there is only the populace. There are warriors among them and enough industry to power a war machine if need be—but who prospers in a war?"

"Mercenaries," Lyle said promptly.

"*Lyle.*"

"Oh, right. Sorry."

"We have seen the same," one shaman said after a time. He looked at the others. "We too were at peace, were we not? But it was not a true peace. That is gained through alliance."

"And peace," Dotty added, "is far, far more difficult than war. Do you think it is difficult to go onto a battlefield? It is more difficult to swallow your pride. I do not pretend that what comes next will be easy. I am simply a woman who has seen war far too often."

They looked at one another, but Rashat held her gaze. "What, then, do you offer us as the first token of friendship?" he asked her.

"Tools," she said. "Tools to help you recover what was lost. I offer the services of the *zauberers* of the dwarves and the wizards of the human realms. Much has been built since the tribes were scattered and much has been lost, but we will help you reclaim what you can."

He did not smile. Instead, she saw his shoulders settle as if a weight had been lifted from him. His eyes were closed and his face twisted as if almost in pain.

"And trade?" one of the chieftains asked her.

"Trade is a matter for if and when the orcs decide to open their borders," she said. "I have yet to see a nation that has not done so, but who can say what you will need or want at that time? Until that day, Insea will wait—here, if you wish or outside your borders if you would prefer."

Silence dragged on for a long while.

A thought occurred to her. "Are there still dragons you need help killing?"

"No," Rashat said mildly. "We took care of the problem."

The very blandness of it was chilling. Beside her, Lyle muttered, "Orcs. I tell ya."

She could only agree.

"So you have listened, then," the water shaman told her. "At last."

"I'm stubborn." She smiled at him. "But not *that* stubborn." She swayed slightly on her feet and realized she hadn't eaten since she woke up. A little desperately, she dug her nails into her palm and tried not to sway too obviously.

"We have heard your proposal," Rashat said formally after seeking out the gaze of each chieftain and shaman in the room. "We will discuss it amongst ourselves." His words spoke like a diplomat, careful to avoid promises, but his eyes told her that her suggestion had met with approval.

Peace. She wanted to laugh she was so relieved. But the room seemed to go dark at the edges—or were those spots dancing in her vision? She was aware of them only after the fact.

"Dotty?" Huwat stood.

"I'm…" But the world tipped, and as she fell, her last thought was, *I promised Lyle I wouldn't do this.*

CHAPTER EIGHTY-THREE

Dotty is worried that she is unwell. She requests that she be taken out of the game in time to say goodbye to her family in person. However, if she is well enough, she would like to finish the mission.

Jacob stared at the email with a sense of gathering dread.

The AI that ran PIVOT's game should not have access to email. He hadn't set up any kind of way for this to happen. Somehow, it had moved beyond its network and was able to send messages.

He stood quickly. His palms were clammy and he smoothed them down his sides while his fingers shook. He wasn't entirely sure what he needed to do about this, and the only thing his mind could latch onto was that Dotty didn't feel well and her family should be called if her status was becoming critical.

When he heard the machines, he was halfway to the stairs. His mind reminded him that he heard them because everyone else had gone deathly silent.

In all honesty, he knew very little about medical machines. Still, he knew the noises these usually made and the tempo at which they made them. This was not normal. His mind gratefully freed itself from the predictions of a post-apocalyptic wasteland overrun with robots and latched onto the fact that something was wrong in the lab.

That was the kind of crisis he could do something about.

With renewed focus, he hurried down the stairs and around the corner to see people gathered around Dotty's pod. Aimee and Simon Mattis, who had been brought down for their children to be taken out of the game, held one another and looked shocked as almost every medical assistant swarmed around the other hub.

The two medical assistants who *did* remain—those who were assigned to first-line-of-oversight for Emilia and Jamie, respectively— looked immensely upset that they weren't able to see what was going on.

Jacob located Amber and Nick and hurried to them. They must have been in the process of having lunch because Nick held half a sandwich and Amber a fork. Both of them were tense and she bounced on the balls of her feet. She looked over at the sound of Jacob's footsteps.

"Thank God. I left my phone in the other room and I didn't want to…" She nodded toward the Mattises and lowered her voice. "I didn't want to yell that we had a problem. Someone should talk to them."

"Before we do that, what's going on?" He wasn't particularly worried about the Mattises seeing this and being ignored. What they needed to know was that it was being taken seriously.

"Dotty's status has…" She pressed her lips together and looked like she was about to cry.

"She's going into organ failure," DuBois said crisply. "I've called in her primary care physician, with whom she left very extensive instructions, and we're waiting to see what she wants to do."

"She wants to come out to say goodbye to her family in person," he told him.

Everyone swung to look at him except DuBois, who waved one hand behind his back and snapped his fingers to get his attention. "How do you know that?"

"It's an automated alert she had set up," he said. "It goes to my email." He ignored the suspicious looks from his partners. "When her doctor gets here, let me know—and I'll call the family anyway. They need to know to stay near their phones, I think."

"You're right," Amber murmured. She swallowed hard. "I can't...I didn't think it would be this hard."

"She's doing very well," DuBois said.

"She is?" Everyone huddled closer.

"In the *game*," the doctor said, his expression long-suffering. "She's doing well in the *game*."

The group drew back with various noises of disappointment.

"Did you honestly think the cancer would magically go away?" he asked them.

"HIPAA," Amber reminded him sharply with a head-jerk toward the Mattises.

"Oh. Right. Sorry. Nothing." He returned to his work.

"I'll go talk to them," Amber told Jacob. "But how did you know about Dotty? And the truth this time."

"I...will tell you later." He shook his head. "It's a long story. And you know who we should also tell—Tina and Justin. I'll go handle that."

He walked away before she could ask him any more awkward questions.

Justin and Tina stared at the room with total weariness.

It was a paradise. The bed had to be twice the size of a king bed, if not larger, and it was covered with truly gorgeous silk bedding and hung with brocade curtains. Along one side was a personal library with comfortable chairs. Liquor in every color from pale gold to ruby was displayed in crystal bottles, a fireplace emitted the perfect amount of coziness, and the immensely tall windows looked out onto perfectly maintained gardens. From behind a folding screen, a curl of steam hinted at a warm bath.

But this was the tenth perfect room. This was the tenth night that they had been told there would be a feast in their honor.

Feasts and hotel rooms were fun for the first few nights, but after this much time, all he wanted was takeout and a movie. He wanted to wear sweatpants and play video games.

The irony hit him a moment later. He looked at Tina.

"Bleh," she said. She swung her arm tiredly to drop her bag and kicked it apathetically across the floor. "Do you have any idea how tired I am of fancy gowns? I want sweats."

"That's what I was thinking," he said. "Do you think we could skip the banquet tonight?"

"God, I fucking *wish*." She took a moment to summon her energy and made a flying leap onto the bed, where she landed sprawled out. "Oh, yeah," she said, her voice muffled by the blankets. "This is the stuff."

"Don't lie down or you won't want to get up again," he warned her.

"The damage is done. Go on without me."

"The hell I will. If I have to attend another feast and listen to them toast me and insult each other, so do you."

"Nope." She shook her head vigorously. "I can't do it. Won't. I swear to God, if I thought I could get past those guards with any kind of meaningful excuse, I'd be gone in a shot."

"Uh-huh." Justin grasped one of the bags and opened it. "Huh. Uh, Tina?"

"What?"

"Tina. Sit up. Look."

"Nope."

"*Tina*." He clambered onto the bed and rolled her forcibly onto her side.

"Whoa, what the fuck is *that*?" She stared at the blue square hovering in the middle of the room. "I swear to God if this thing bluescreen-of-deaths while we're *in* it—oh, look, someone's typing."

"Dotty is not in good shape," Justin read as the words scrolled across the screen. "If you would like to say goodbye to her, we will try to arrange that. Get somewhere remote."

They looked at one another. Then, without a word, they snatched their bags up and hurried to the door. Without a word, they pushed past curious guards and raced to the main stairways and freedom.

"Prima, can you make sure there are horses ready?" he whispered as they barreled down a huge flight of stairs.

"I can. However, I should inform you that if you want to avoid company—"

"No time!" Tina called. She plastered a smile on her face. "Oh, hello, Lord...uh...my lord. Terrible problem with my cousin's nephew's wife's sister's great-aunt...very urgent."

"Diplomatic emergency," he added as the two of them sprinted to the stables.

"But the feast—" the lord called after them.

"I wish we could stay!" Tina responded over her shoulder. "I'm sure we'll be back!" Under her breath, she added, "When there's a cold day in hell."

In the stables, they danced with impatience while they waited while the horses that had only just been brushed were saddled. They scrambled to tie the saddlebags in place. Justin watched Tina's face and the somewhat manic concentration there.

"Are you okay?"

"Nope," she said flatly. "And I don't think I will be for a while. But I'd rather be out there and alone before I start bawling."

He nodded once and could feel the lump in his throat. If he tried to talk about this, he would also be a wreck.

For now, he simply had to hold himself together.

But his hand found hers and the two of them grasped each other's fingers until the bones ached.

Jaco signed his name on the last sheet of paper and flexed his hand. Both his hands ached, his back ached, and he was fairly sure someone had poured sand in his eyes and throat in the last hour.

He had been angry when Dotty signed over so many rights and could admit that. In his heart of hearts, he had hoped that the emissaries would manage fairly unilateral peace treaties that would not necessitate the truth coming out.

Of course, he had also known it would never work but he had still hoped. Dotty's bargain, the first to reach him, had been beyond fair. The terms she had negotiated would enrich both Insea and Berghold and truly *would* foster strength.

But Jaco would have to find a way to explain to the citizens of Insea that there was no king, there had never been a king, and that their centuries-long peace had been bought at great cost and with many lies.

More than anything, he was afraid the rebel elves would move in before he had time to make peace with them. He hadn't lived in Insea before Gos'hauke summoned him, but he had formed a close bond with the city and its people.

And he did not like the new so-called elven "monarch." What kind of leader sent his troops to prey on caravans—and what kind of troops obeyed that order? Mercenaries would, of course, but soldiers with a sworn loyalty?

The official trusted none of it.

He leaned back in his chair and chewed absentmindedly on one finger—no matter how old you got, you had bad habits—when something sizzled behind him.

The noise was instantly familiar. He turned in his chair and narrowed his eyes. Admittedly, he wasn't the world's most competent wizard when it came to quick spells, which had always made it difficult for him to excel in combat. He was, however, exceedingly methodical and very good at making his spells almost impenetrable.

Which meant that the person currently trying to cast a spell that would affect his personal quarters should have no luck.

The sizzle came again, then once more. Another attempt followed soon after and there was a long pause before the fifth.

Shouting erupted in the hall.

Jaco smiled thinly before he stood and wiped the tired grimace off his face. When the door opened for two guardsmen, he waited in his formal robes and smiled slightly.

"A visitor?" he asked.

"An elf, sir."

"A representative of King Yn'sur I!" an outraged voice called after them, and a very ostentatiously dressed elf pushed in behind the guards.

"One does not," he observed. "generally say, *the first* until a second king of the same name. Correct protocol is to use, *first of his name.*"

One of his favorite things to do, out of anything, was to use etiquette to annoy people. In this case, it worked wonders. The elf's face darkened in anger.

"King Yn'sur I has deigned to meet with you," he said angrily. "First, you deny entrance to a royal emissary and now you—a mere human servant—lecture me on manners?"

"Where I come from, emissaries don't appear in one's bedchamber in the dead of night," he said blandly. He twitched the scroll out of the elf's hand and scanned the words quickly. "Two days. He wants to meet in two *days?*"

The emissary raised his nose and sniffed. "King Yn'sur I has spoken." He swished one hand, clearly expecting to disappear in a puff of smoke. Instead, the sizzling noise came again.

Jaco's lips twitched as the elf marched out of the room to perform his transportation spell, but as soon as he was gone, he frowned. Who could he get to the rendezvous in two days?

And *what* did the letter mean about sending 'a true icon of strength?'

CHAPTER EIGHTY-FOUR

Dotty opened her eyes to see the plain brown interior of a tent. She turned her head slowly and felt fur beneath her cheek. Her whole body felt cushioned, soft, and warm. She let her eyes drift closed again with a happy sigh.

Then she remembered what had happened before she lost consciousness. Her eyes snapped open and she looked around for anyone else.

Lyle was reading in the corner of the tent. She watched him for a moment and saw the tension in the way he held the book. He ignored her little cot with utter determination. And were his eyes red from crying?

She gathered her resolve to sit and, to her surprise, was able to do so fairly easily. When she met his gaze, she smiled at him. "You know," she told him, "I had promised I wouldn't keel over."

He tried to smile in return but his chin trembled and he didn't manage to say anything. Instead, he put the book down carefully and looked at her for a long moment. "Ye were in pain. The shamans came an' did a spell over ye, and ye've slept better since. Most o' the day."

"I'm sorry," she whispered.

"No. I'm sorry." He closed his eyes for a moment. "I kept hopin' it wasn't real. I keep thinkin' o' the things I didn't say."

Dotty frowned at him. "What do you mean?" She was cold and she drew a soft, woven blanket around her.

"All the times when I joked instead o' tellin' you how well ye were doin' in trainin'," he said. He looked away from her. "I would never have been so hard on ye, back when we first met, if I'd known."

"Lyle—I didn't tell you." She shook her head. "And I felt much better then. I wasn't so tired. Although I feel well right now." Under her breath, she added: "Prima?"

"*A doctor came. They gave you painkillers. It's brought the pain down to levels that you can't feel it in-game.*" The AI sounded upset. "*I tried, you know. But I couldn't do it.*"

"Prima." Dotty shook her head helplessly. "There's only so much anyone can do."

She waited and although the AI said nothing more, she could practically feel her misery radiating.

Lyle, meanwhile, still struggled to regain his composure. He had nodded jerkily at her but he fixed his gaze on the ground.

"Lyle?" she asked.

"It's not only...ye," he said. "There's a lot o' people I didn't speak to as much as I should. Me father an' I never mended things afore he died." He sighed and looked up. "An' here ye are, dyin', an' I'm makin' all this about me."

Dotty smiled slightly.

The tent flap opened and a young orc entered. He held a big jug of steaming water and a fresh cloth, and behind him came another with a platter of food. Both nodded respectfully to Dotty and one said to Lyle, "The shamans have extended you an offer to dine with them if you wish, sir."

The dwarf looked at her.

She nodded. "Go. Some time to wash and eat will be appreciated. Tell them I am awake and I am well."

He gave her a wordless nod and left with the others.

Even though her stomach was rumbling, she decided to wash

before eating. She stripped and began to wipe warm water over her skin. There was a bar of soap, rough and overwhelmingly scented with herbs, but it reminded her of growing up with her grandmother's homemade soap.

"I've received word from the researchers," Prima said finally.

"Hmm?" She realized that her mind had drifted. The painkillers they gave her must have been something.

"The doctor came, as you know, and gave you medication. There were scans as well, I believe. They've called your family to come to the lab, but there are several hours before everyone will be assembled."

Dotty put the washcloth down slowly. "It's close, then."

A pause followed. *"Yes and no. They don't know when, but your condition is not critical yet. The team asked me to tell you the following."*

"Oh?"

"As your condition is not critical, would you like them to arrange for one last mission before you come out of the game?" Prima tried to disguise it, but there was no missing the hope in her voice. *"They say that, in the doctor's opinion, there should be no danger. It is only a matter of if you feel well enough to do so."*

She thought about the offer in silence. Wind whistled over the mesa and she could hear children running and shrieking outside, along with sharp reminders from their parents to stay away from the cliffs. She slipped her dress over her shoulders and ducked out to watch the activity.

A few of the orcs noticed her and gave awkward nods, respectful and awed, but the rest were too engrossed in their celebrations and negotiations. She smiled as she watched. Fire tribe members demonstrated the workings of a forge, and a water tribe member instructed several others on the best way to weave fishing nets. Some tents had colorful blankets on the ground outside them, spread with beautiful wares.

No. She wasn't ready to leave yet, no matter the exhaustion that pulled at her bones.

"One more mission," she murmured. "Yes, Prima. I'd like that."

"I'll make sure there's some luxury to keep you amused," the AI assured

her. On the one hand, it seemed ridiculous to read emotion into the flat, mechanical voice but on the other, she could not help but do so.

Dotty ate quickly but savored each mouthful of grilled meat and vegetables. She wrapped different assortments in flatbread and dolloped chutneys on with abandon.

One chutney, in particular, proved to be a mistake.

"Oh, God in heaven." She eyed her dagger and resisted the urge to slice her tongue off. "Prima, what did I just eat?"

"In your world, I'm told they're called ghost peppers."

"Oh, no." She lowered her face into her hands and remembered only at the last moment to not get her fingers anywhere near her eyes. "As my mother would say, Sweet Moses."

"The shamans would be available to see you if you wanted a distraction—as would Atra."

"I'm not sure I should see Atra," she said. She stood and stumbled out of the tent. "On the other hand, maybe—Atra." She stopped dead.

The woman was standing outside. She must have been waiting for her to come out and something seemed different about her. Cautiously, she scanned the warrior, taking in the necklace of polished beach stones and the copper ring in one tusk. Everything seemed the same, so she was left a little bewildered.

Oh. No weapon.

Dotty exhaled slow. "You should know—" she said.

At the same time, Atra said, "I came to say—"

Both of them broke off, and the younger woman gestured at her.

"You should know that your words changed the negotiations for the better," she said. "We won't interfere. Our mages and historians will come to help yours uncover what the dragons tried to destroy of your past. That and an ambassador, nothing more."

Atra stared at her.

"And, for what it is worth—although it may not be enough—I apologize." She shook her head. "I ask only that you think more kindly of me. Before I met you, I stood between the tribe at Mountain's Shadow and a dragon who taunted me with the fact that it had lied to them. There was no time to make a more…nuanced…choice."

The warrior looked away. Her hands were clenched into fists. "I know." The two words were grudging and she clearly did not want to say them.

Dotty smiled slightly. Such was the experience of youth—so much raw pride tumbling in one's chest. Atra had not yet grown used to such things.

Indeed, the young woman looked at her as if she was gathering courage to say something. She took a few deep breaths, and finally said, "I'm still angry."

"I know," she told her simply. "And perhaps you always will be."

Atra frowned.

"Your tribe is in good hands," she said. "I have watched how much you and the other young ones love them and how much strength they bring to the prospect of rebuilding. Atra, in sixty years, when you are my age and you watch the young ones, remember to trust *them* as well." She went to walk away toward the main tent but stopped. "And be well," she added.

It was not enough, but no words ever would be. Atra blinked, her eyes suspiciously bright.

"You, also," she said. She cleared her throat. "I hear…you may be ill."

"I am." Dotty smiled sadly at her. "But death comes to all of us. A quiet death after a long life is not such a bad thing. Remember that too lest you ever be tempted to give your life for glory and battle." She reached out hesitantly to touch the other woman's cheek and then walked away.

When she entered the main tent, she stopped in shock.

"Hello," Jaco said.

"How are you here?" she asked him and looked at the others.

"I'm not precisely here." He walked forward through the fire. "See?"

"That looks somewhat apocalyptic—could you…not?" She ushered him out of the fire and sat in the chair an orc brought for her. "Have they spoken to you of the terms we agreed upon? There are some details to work out—if they agree to it, of course—"

"We voted to accept," Rashat rumbled.

"We are glad to share knowledge with the orcs," Jaco said, his demeanor dignified. He seemed far happier about this deal than the previous one. "I know several historians who have made it their life's work to study the orcs. I sent them word to copy any manuscripts they might have and prepare for a journey."

"I sent word to Berghold as well," Lyle said. "A few of the *zauberers* have volunteered already, or so I'm told."

"There will be the matter of choosing the ambassador," Jaco said to Dotty, "but I believe I can handle such negotiations. You are needed urgently elsewhere right now...if you can be spared."

She looked around her. Lyle nodded, as did Rashat. A few other chieftains were in the room—far from the full complement—but each of them nodded as well.

"I...certainly." She shrugged. "What is this new urgent need?"

Jaco looked briefly at the orcish leaders before he said casually, "Negotiations with the elven monarch."

Lyle swore and her eyes widened.

"I thought you came on behalf of Insea," Rashat said and frowned.

"Oh, we did." She sighed. "There's a faction of elves who have established a new monarchy—and made attacks on both Berghold and Insea. It would seem they have now agreed to a meeting." What a last mission. She wanted to laugh. "They introduced themselves blade-first the last time I met them, so we'll see what happens this time."

"Mmm." Jaco looked faintly evasive. "I'll brief you en route. I have developed a working that can have you and Lyle at the meeting site in a few hours."

"What?" Her eyes were wide. "*How?*"

He glared at her, a little offended. "I'll have you know that I was trained by the finest wizards in the world." He shrugged and added under his breath, "And I have access to a rather extensive collection of artifacts."

"Ah."

"The others will join you as well," he said. "Zaara says that *none* of you are to mention Kural's skin."

"His skin?"

"That is all I was told." He shrugged. "But…someone should find a way to send me an image."

Dotty gave him a thumbs-up. "We'll go pack and prepare, then."

He nodded and his image disappeared like smoke.

"Insea seeks peace with many," Rashat said. "And unless I miss my guess, this will be a particularly difficult negotiation."

"You have no idea," she said and rolled her eyes. "Elves are stuck-up bastards."

The orcs laughed, and the shaman came to clasp her hand. "I think this will be our final goodbye," he said. "Know that you will be remembered as a woman who sacrificed herself to defeat the false gods and who rallied us to fight together."

Her eyes brimmed with tears. "You could have given me no better words of farewell. Goodbye, friend."

CHAPTER EIGHTY-FIVE

Dotty wasn't sure what she had expected from the transportation spell, but it was most certainly nowhere close to reality.

After hurrying down the path at the edge of the mesa, she and Lyle were met by Jaco again, his form almost solid. He guided them on where to stand, made sure their ponies and the palanquin were within very stable parameters, and stepped back and promptly disappeared.

The two companions looked at one another.

"What do you think—" she began before they were enveloped in something that looked like a cloud.

The ground—although she could feel it under her feet—was invisible and the clouds around them began to whirl. She stood still next to one of the ponies and stroked her nose, shushing and murmuring comforting things. Lyle did the same and both of them waited for the jolt of movement.

After an embarrassingly long pause, she looked up and around. "Prima?"

Her companion glanced at her, confused, and she shook her head at him.

"Mm-hmm?" Prima asked. The AI sounded like she wanted to laugh.

"Are we moving?" she asked severely.

"Yes. Yes, you are."

"Is there any way to tell where we are?" she asked.

She should have known better, she realized a split-second later, but it was too late. The clouds around them vanished and she was able to see the landscape racing far below them. It was somewhat like being in a plane but without any of the visual barriers that—she now realized—made plane travel possible for humans.

Lyle yelled a protest. The ponies seemed to not notice at all.

"Prima," Dotty said and tried to maintain a calm tone, "put the cloud back."

The barrier appeared and the AI said in faux innocence, *"But you wanted to see."*

"You knew," she accused. "You knew it would scare the crap out of us and you—oh! Justin! Hi!"

Indeed, their little haven from the outside air had suddenly broadened as if two bubbles had merged, and Justin and Tina were now visible.

"Dotty!" The young woman ran to her. She wore her leather armor and would have looked exceedingly threatening if she wasn't crying.

"Tina." She wrapped her arms around her. "Are you safe? Are you well?"

"Me?" Tina looked incredulously at her. "We got word from Prima. About…you."

"Ah." She looked at the cloud. "Prima, could we have somewhere to sit?"

The cloud obligingly formed itself into a few benches and Justin ambled closer to sit with a very-confused looking Lyle as Dotty and Tina sat together.

"Tell me about your adventures," she said gently and squeezed the young woman's hand. "I hear there were some very close calls with nobility who were determined to make marriage deals."

"Oh, you wouldn't *believe*." The woman rolled her eyes. Diverted, she launched into a story that involved no less than five suitors, a series of increasingly transparent ruses, and—to her surprise—a trained giraffe. Even Lyle and Justin came to hear the story, and the young man interjected with occasional anecdotes. The dwarf guffawed at some of the stranger tactics the human nobility had used.

Tina was mimicking the giraffe with one arm when the bubble burst again, this time to reveal Zaara and Kural, and everyone stopped talking at once.

The wizard was blue. It was a very nice shade of blue, but human skin was not meant to be that color. It wasn't paint, either, and Dotty hoped for his sake that it wasn't a tattoo.

Everyone stared at him, he stared back, and behind him, Zaara made furious gestures to not talk about it.

Dotty cleared her throat. "Everyone's here! Good. We should probably discuss our plan with the elves."

"Awww," Tina muttered.

Kural stalked to the group and sat on one of the cloud benches.

"He's a little upset right now," Zaara said in a stage whisper, "because this is a very complex working and he didn't get to do it."

"Oh, is that why?" Justin asked blandly.

Zaara gave him a glare that would have turned him to stone if she had the ability.

Lyle, meanwhile, had retrieved his ale mug and desperately tried to hide his laughter behind it. All Dotty could see was his shoulders shaking with silent mirth and the top of his head.

"So," she said, trying to hide her amusement, "what do we know about the elven offer of peace talks?"

Kural withdrew a scroll from one sleeve and unrolled it. He cleared his throat, the very picture of offended dignity, and began to read. The offer, although incredibly wordy, had very little actual content to it—quite simply, it invited the representatives of Insea to a neutral meeting ground.

"They couldn't simply have said *yes*?" Tina asked when he had finished. "Yes, we'll talk to you?"

"You haven't met any elves, have you?" Zaara asked her. "Wordy fuckers, the lot of 'em."

Before anyone else could speak, the cloud suddenly vanished and was replaced by gently rolling grassland with pink grass and tall, ethereal flowers that almost seemed to float. A quarter of a mile away, an elven camp with an impossibly complex tent that looked like a castle drew their attention. Guards marched in formation around the fake castle and, on the ground outside it, stood a dais with a throne. The figure seated there shone as brightly as the sun, from his gold-crowned head to his gold-armored body.

"I wonder which one is the king," Lyle said.

"It could be any of them," Tina said, her expression deadpan. "They all have *very* fancy hats."

Kural looked at them. "You two, behave. We've been seen."

Indeed, a shout had gone up and a detachment of mounted soldiers galloped across the plain to surround the party.

"Identify yourselves," one of them said crisply.

"We are the emissaries from Insea," Kural responded. He held the scroll up with the elven king's seal.

The soldiers nodded stiffly. No apology was made for their overly armed greeting, and they marched the group to the tent without any further words. One soldier swung down from his horse and knelt before the king before he rose to whisper in his ear.

The monarch's gaze swept over them. His eyes were a startling and vivid shade of purple and his skin held a blue tinge. He was not old, Dotty guessed—at least, his hair was not gray and his skin looked smooth—but she had no idea what older elves looked like.

And, under all that armor, he might have any physique.

"You are the emissaries sent from Insea?" he asked them. The corner of his mouth twitched slightly.

"Yes, your grace." She had, somewhere in the midst of the journey, been garbed in another golden confection of a gown, this one held up with citrines.

Her disapproving gaze noted the way the king looked at Lyle with his serviceable gear, Tina, Justin, and Zaara in their armor, and Kural with his strange, blue skin. He respected her, although only tenuously. The rest of them, he respected not at all.

"The representatives of Insea have arrived," he said. His voice carried magically across the space. "We await this outcome with interest. Prepare your strength." He raised a hand, bored, and shooed them away.

"Wait, what?" She stepped forward, but the group was immediately surrounded by soldiers who ushered them to a plaza on the side of the makeshift courtyard. They left, although two of them took position a few yards away.

Dotty looked at the others. "What on earth is going on?"

"He awaits the outcome," Kural muttered. "Strength…they keep saying strength…what does that mean?"

When the whole picture fell into place, Dotty groaned.

"What?" he asked quietly. "What is it?"

"I get it," she said. She shook her head wearily. "It's a trial by combat."

"What? But that's—"

"Barbaric?" she suggested. "A stupid way to test one's ability to rule? Yes. But that appears to be their custom and that's what they want from us." She pressed her hand softly against her stomach and wished that her body wasn't hurting quite so much. "Lyle could do it, maybe."

The others had drifted closer. When Kural briefed them with a single, terse sentence, their eyes widened.

"We should tell Jaco what's going on," Justin said finally.

"No." The wizard spread the scroll. "We've agreed not to. See here? I thought this phrase meant absolutely nothing—*the representatives being chosen as the representatives*—but it's hiding elven law behind the tautology. When Jaco sent us and we arrived, everyone here became locked into the negotiations. They can't call in anyone or communicate with anyone outside this campground, and neither can we."

"So they tricked us," Dotty said. "Son of a—"

"So we've agreed to handle it the way they say," Justin said as he worked through the problem. "We've agreed one of *us* will be the one to handle it…and it has to be a trial by combat." He looked at Kural, who nodded. "Great. That's great."

"It's not bad," Lyle said.

Everyone gave him an incredulous look.

"What?" He shrugged. "I've watched every one o' you face monsters an' all kinds o' fights. We simply have to choose which one of us is doin' this. I don' think we can make a wrong choice, to be honest."

A pause dragged on while they considered what he'd said.

"He has a point," Zaara stated.

"I say Zaara or Justin," Tina said. "Both of them have magic and weapons skills."

The other woman looked uncomfortable. "Having peace with the elven monarchy riding on me?"

"You said it was a good idea," the dwarf reminded her.

"I meant in general! Not…*me.*" She shuddered. "What if I slip? What if my dagger gets caught in the sheath? All of a sudden, outright war because of a leg cramp or something. Too much pressure."

"Someone has to do it," Dotty pointed out. "And Tina's right. You two are the logical choices."

Justin looked faintly green. "But she makes a good point. And I've fucked up so much in this world."

"*Yes,*" Prima said drily, "*you have.*"

"Hey!"

"No dithering," she said firmly. "We'll toss a coin. Both of you are good choices."

"Or…" Lyle said speculatively. He shook his head. "Nah."

"Spit it out, Lyle."

"Well, there's one other person here who has both magic and weapons skills." He pointed at her. "I didn't say it at first because ye're not feeling so great, but it might be a good choice. You aren't quite so easily rattled as these two."

Both Zaara and Justin looked like they would very much like to protest but accepted the judgment with mutters instead.

"Me?" she said blankly. "I can't do it!"

"Why not?" he asked.

"I'm not—you need someone in better shape who has been properly trained with weapons, not an old woman who only started with them a few months back!"

"Ye're forgettin' ye've *already* fought one o' their champions—and won." He gave her a hard look. "Remember that warrior in the black armor? An' I've seen ye on the road. Ye're sneaky *an'* ye're brave."

"Ohhh." Dotty sat on the bench with a thump. "Oh, I don't know that I should do this."

She looked at where the king conversed with his top aides. Every one of them flashed their armor and weapons ostentatiously and laughed behind their hands at Insea's delegation. She'd seen enough of those people in real life, the type who had never faced any consequences and liked to bully others because they thought they were untouchable. So many times, she had counseled her children to ignore them, do their work, and focus on their results.

Maybe she had chosen the wrong path all those times. The thought made her frown.

And maybe she had a chance to show this world there were other options sometimes.

Dotty looked up and winked at Justin and Tina.

The woman bounced and clapped. "You'll do it!"

"Yeah, I think I will." She stood. "I might as well go out on a high note, and if I'm *honest*...punching that guy in the face would most certainly be a high note."

CHAPTER EIGHTY-SIX

Dotty was given a tent in which to change into her armor. Despite the urgent whispers from the others, she sent them away and started to pace. She had a few minutes before anyone would come to call her.

"You'll want to project a somewhat more intimidating effect when you get outside," Prima told her.

"Uh-huh." She watched as some kind of pre-armor gear appeared on her arms and legs. It was bronze, close-fitting, and oddly heavy. She wasn't a fan of heaviness for its own sake but right now, it seemed comforting and safe.

The gauntlets she'd worn in Insea appeared again, the daggers sheathed inside them, and her hair was pulled back more tightly and the jeweled pins were removed. She frowned and waited for the rest.

"Prima?"

"Yes?"

"Where's my armor?"

"That is your armor."

"This?" Dotty looked up incredulously. "It's…spandex."

"It's not spandex," the AI protested as if she were rolling her eyes. *"Try stabbing yourself."*

"I'd much rather not."

"Just try it, you baby."

Dotty glared, drew one of the daggers, and aimed toward her stomach. After a moment's thought, she decided to try to pull the hem of her pants away from her leg and stab that instead. To her surprise, the slight motion sent shockwaves rippling up her arm and hardly seemed to dent the fabric.

She tried again, harder this time, with the same result. Her third attempt was a hard strike to her stomach, and the exclamation that resulted was from the pain in her arms, not where the blade had landed.

"This is extraordinary." She remembered the plate armor outside. "But…isn't it cheating?"

"No."

"Prima, I'm serious."

"So am I," the AI said. *"This type of armor was made by the elves originally. Everyone knows about it but it's expensive to produce. The people out there have access to it if they want it but they don't think it looks impressive enough."*

"Oh, so they're being stupid?"

"Yes."

"Then I'm fine with it." Dotty nodded. "I'm ready to go."

She pushed out of the tent and was escorted onto the plaza. A magical barrier sprang into place around a circle of ground and denoted where the fight would take place. The sound around her had lowered drastically.

No one would be able to call recommendations to her. The thought made her swallow uncomfortably.

On the other hand, no one would be able to heckle her, either.

All thoughts vanished when her opponent stepped into the ring. He wore plate armor like the king and he had more human coloring—blond hair and green eyes. When he moved, it was as if the massively-heavy armor was no impediment. From the ease with which he drew his broadsword, she assumed he had trained as a warrior from the time he could walk.

He gave her a look that said he would enjoy cutting her in half. "Barbarian."

Dotty raised an eyebrow. She had never been very good with quick comebacks and now that she had missed her moment to give him one, they flooded to her mind.

"The rules of every civilized duel apply," the king said simply. His voice traveled into the circle without hindrance, and she could see the smirk on his face. He dared her to ask what those were and admit she wasn't civilized.

"What do elves consider civilized?" she asked.

It wasn't *quite* a disrespectful question. She kept a pleasant smile on her face as the king's smile grew slightly more strained.

"Magic will protect contestants from death," he said, "but not from permanent injury. The results will be binding, and the barrier will protect any wind or other outside force from disrupting the proceedings. The match is concluded when one opponent yields, is injured enough to invoke the magical protections, or stays on the ground for a count of ten."

"Elves *are* civilized," she said. She let the implied "who would have guessed" hang in the air and studied her opponent.

He looked like he wanted to murder her, but she could handle that. Honestly, he wouldn't be the first.

Harry's first girlfriend, for instance, hadn't been too fond of her.

The barrier flared and went opaque and the elven warrior charged without warning.

Dotty dodged sideways and darted under his raised arms as he brought the broadsword down. The ground shuddered under her feet and she whirled to see that he had gouged a deep cut into the packed dirt. He wrenched the sword free and looked at her from under a drifting tendril of blond hair, and her heart seized.

This was the kind of person Tina and Justin had spoken of. This was the type who tried to kill in the arena, who would do his damnedest to strike a killing blow before the magic could save her.

And if that death would save something she loved, she would

consider it. But if he won, he would gain an advantage in the negotiations and she would be *damned* if she let that happen.

She let her eyes drift closed for a split-second before she refocused as they began to circle. In her mind, she pictured the haze of dust above a South Carolina road on a hot day and the way it stung the eyes and itched in the throat.

The warrior blinked a few times and tossed his head. One hand came away from the sword to wave at the air around him, and she pictured the billow of dust rising behind a battered old truck. The air around his head turned golden brown, filled with a haze of dust that drifted into his eyes and his nose. He frowned, she smiled, and his face turned murderous.

"Heathen magic," he hissed.

"Oh, you have *no* idea," she told him. "I've studied with orcs, I've studied with dwarves—honestly, every kind of heathen you can imagine."

He opened his mouth to speak and the dust rushed in so instead, he spat and coughed. "Bitch."

"Yep," she agreed and nodded.

He yelled and attacked and again, she dodged. Twice, she spun away and once passed only inches below a single-handed swing of the broadsword. She frowned as its shadow whistled above her.

Goddamn, this elf was strong. Was that natural?

The question was irrelevant, she supposed, given that they were already in combat.

"Fight me like a warrior!" he called furiously. "Not like a witch."

"I'm sorry," Dotty said in amusement. She ducked another swing and managed to land an elbow strike to the back of his head as he spun past. "Did you think you would taunt me into going one-on-one with swords merely by calling me a coward?"

"If you had any honor..." he began and she tuned out. She had heard this whole speech before—or whatever version of it boys did at her high school. He yelled obscenities and insults that were probably very grave, while she began to sense the flow in his movements and both the shocking speed and the relatively slow swings of the broadsword.

They might be slow, she realized, but they were also damned near unstoppable. She could *not* get in the way of those. The armor might stop an assassin's shiv but she was fairly sure it wouldn't do jack when hit by a train.

Finally, his face split into a savage, bitter smile. *"Fine,"* he snarled. "If that's how you're going to be." He ripped a pouch at his waist open and threw something at her.

His aim was precise, and the projectile struck with the force of a baseball—nor was there anywhere to run. It stung as it shattered against her skin and powder erupted to choke her with its fumes.

What the hell *was* it?

Dotty had no time to ponder it. She threw herself to one side, not even sure why she did it until her mind processed the sound of footsteps on gravel. He had shifted his weight to attack and only instinct had saved her.

She rolled onto her feet, ready to throw a jet of volcanic heat at his head and end this, but nothing came. Her magic bar was gray and a circle counted down next to it.

"Son of a bitch," she snapped. "He took my magic?"

"Looks like," Prima said drily.

Dotty watched the circle count down to estimate how much time she had when the AI yelled a warning and she barely managed to evade a swing. He followed his weapon and drove her against the back wall. His plate mail crushed her chest and face as he snarled at her.

She slammed one knee upward and got only a grimace for her efforts—of *course* he was wearing a cup—before she tried to jab her fingers into two gaps in his armor. Hitting his neck only made his chin come down and slam the visor onto one hand, but her jab at his eyes made him stumble back with a yell.

Finally, she threw a leg up and shoved his retreating form with all her might.

He sprawled a little distance away, thank God, but he was up in the next moment with murder in his eyes and she still had no magic.

When he attacked her this time, there was no hesitation. However he had trained, he could still swing this weapon quickly without tiring.

For now, she cleared every thought from her mind and devoted every ounce of energy to darting away from his attacks. There were too many near-misses to count as even without the weight of plate mail and a sword, she could not move much faster than he could. Worse, she was reacting.

She wasn't driving the fight, which put him firmly in control.

And how long could she hold out? Already, she had begun to tire. That brief moment of despair almost cost her an arm but she managed to swerve and twisted under his blade. Pain radiated from the glancing blow.

Instinct told her she needed to turn the tide, but how? Her mind racing, she dodged another strike. He was smiling triumphantly and knew he had the strength and stamina to outlast her.

In the upper part of her screen, the magic bar turned blue again. She uttered a yell of satisfaction and poured her power out into his armor. He screamed as the metal flared red-hot and he recoiled from her to strip pieces of it off and throw them aside.

Dotty almost wished she hadn't done that, because as soon as the armor was gone, she could see how muscly he was. It wasn't a picture that gave her a great deal of hope for the rest of the fight. He whirled with a curse on his lips but it died when he didn't see her.

Desperation had lent her innovation and she hurtled toward him at knee-level. She drove her shoulders into his knees and pushed off with all the strength in her legs to carry him over. He landed heavily with her on top and she fought the urge to pin him down and start punching him in the face. She *wanted* to do it but she had enough sense to realize that this gigantic warrior was, without a doubt, better at grappling than she was.

Instead, she rolled away with a jab of one elbow onto his shin. He howled in pain and stood shakily to limp on his injured leg.

"Barbarians," he declared belligerently, "should not have been allowed to *speak* to our king, let alone make demands of him!"

Dotty rolled her eyes and turned the ground under his feet white-hot. He yelped and danced away. His sword, unfortunately, was somehow immune to magic—or was made of a metal that didn't respond in the same way toward heat. She circled as she considered what else could she do—something that wouldn't kill him but *would* hurt him enough to disable him and gain the victory.

The answer came to her as she surged forward and she threw her hands out, her palms facing him.

Magic pounded into him like a wall. It had the force of a wave to lift and circle, the heat of a volcano, and the crushing pressure that lay below the earth. This was the earth magic she had first learned from dwarven manuscripts, the power of fire that Huwat had shown her, and the deathly cold force of the deep ocean Rashat had summoned against the dragons.

And along with it, the surprise factor learned from a certain dwarf named Stout.

Hot and cold, force and fire, caught the elf full in the face and he went over on his back. She dropped to her knees and dragged air into her chest with desperate breaths. With him down—and a count being shouted by the whole crowd—she had time to feel the burning in her lungs and the ache in her muscles.

And the sharp pain in her stomach and the taste of metal in her mouth.

She pulled herself up, more because she wanted to lie down than because she wanted to look triumphant, but she stood until the count reached ten and she raised one arm in a motion of victory. The wall disappeared around her and her first sight was the *very* welcome expression of panic on the king's face. She grinned at him even as she swayed.

"Are you okay?" Prima asked urgently.

"I need to…get away. To sit." She muttered the words under her breath.

An elven servant appeared with a folding chair a moment later and lowered his head. He was either very good at hiding his feelings or he didn't mind much that the king and his champion had suffered a setback.

They probably weren't very nice to servants, she thought vaguely. She should tell the others that they could get good information that way.

"Dotty?" Tina chafed her hands. "Are you—is it—"

"Time to go home," Dotty said. The taste of metal was stronger but she smiled at them. Her head was spinning slightly. "You have all been the best traveling companions I could wish for. What adventures we've had."

"Dotty." Prima's voice was urgent. *"Before you go—"*

"This isn't goodbye," she murmured. Tina was crying silently. Justin stood with his arm around her and Lyle held one of her hands. "Not for the two of us, Prima."

She almost *felt* her nod. Then, the AI said, *"I'll tell them you're ready to wake up."*

CHAPTER EIGHTY-SEVEN

It wasn't a bad place for a goodbye, Dotty thought dreamily. The pale cloth of the tent fluttered at the edges with glimpses of the fairytale landscape beyond.

Kural hung back at the door, making sure that no self-important elves interrupted the proceeding. At his side, Zaara hovered awkwardly. Tina was crying quietly. Justin's arm was around her and his cheeks were wet with tears. Lyle knelt beside the cot, one hand wrapped around hers.

Tina said her goodbye first. She wiped her eyes, knelt at the bed, and laced her hands through hers as she smiled at her through the tears.

"I never thought I'd get to do shots with a grandmother," she said finally. Her voice cracked, but when Dotty laughed, she did as well. "Dotty, I lost my abuela when I was seven. She was so strict, but my mom had stories from her father—she said my abuela used to be wild. She ran the family ranch for a few years when she was young and was a crack shot. I never believed it because she was so keen to have me be ladylike."

She paused for a moment, looked down, and tried to swallow her tears.

"Seeing you, hearing you joke, watching you take no shit—I feel closer to her than I ever did while she was alive. I used to be so scared of getting older. I thought the best of my life would have passed me by. And I'm not scared anymore. Thank you."

Dotty smiled as she cupped the woman's cheek in her hand. "You'll be so much more than any one person ever knows," she promised her. "You'll change lives and worlds. And when you're older and your grandchildren think you're simply a quiet old woman, you'll know better. You'll have learned to make a hell of a fuss so it creates the most impact."

Tina nodded and leaned over to kiss her cheek. She stood and Justin took her place.

"I never know what to say at times like this," he admitted.

"Words aren't the only way to show someone you care," she said and squeezed his hand.

"No, I want to try." He swallowed. "I've changed so much in this game, but I always felt like it was my place in a way. I was the first one here. I was raised on video games. When you got here, I thought I'd be the one to show you the ropes—and you'd already outstripped me in some ways." He swallowed. "I don't think I know yet how much I've learned from you. I wish I did so I could tell you."

A tear trickled down the side of her face. "Some things aren't ours to know," she told him quietly. "You be good, young man. Be someone who makes you proud of yourself."

He nodded before he kissed her cheek and moved back so Lyle could shuffle closer.

"I…" The dwarf swallowed and looked away. "I can't."

"I'll speak," Zaara said and stepped alongside him. She kissed Lyle on the cheek. "You think of your words."

Dotty smiled.

Zaara smoothed her hair back from her head. She hesitated for a moment, then pulled one of her daggers out. "My…in my village, a warrior is buried holding a weapon. I would be honored if you were to accept this blade from me. I was honored to fight alongside you."

She nodded, her throat so tight she couldn't speak.

The woman folded Dotty's hands around the hilt and rested them on her chest. Her chin began to tremble. "I'm—ah…I'm never going to have children of my own," she forced herself to say. "Wizards—don't, you know. But my brother will, my friends will, and I'll watch all of them grow old and have children of their own. I'll watch generations of them be born and die, and what you've done here—it'll give them all peace. Thank you."

Dotty met her gaze and nodded. Zaara moved to join the huddle with Tina and Justin, both of whom wrapped their arms around her.

"Ah." Lyle cleared his throat. "I'm like Justin, with not much of a way with words."

"You know that's not true." She smiled at him. "You taught me to fight, Lyle Stout. You think you're a mercenary with no finer sentiments, but that's far from true. I've never seen a man more devoted to his people."

"I left them," he said bluntly.

"You did," she agreed, "in order to learn what you needed to know. We can't always fix the places we love with only what we already know."

His fingers tightened around hers. "I've been honored to know ye," he said hoarsely.

"And I you," she whispered. Her head was spinning. She squeezed his fingers once more and looked over his head at Kural.

He knew what her look meant. "I'll keep them safe," he promised her.

Dotty nodded her thanks. She closed her eyes for a moment and focused on the feel of Lyle's hands around hers.

The world began to dissolve at the edges, and the next time she opened her eyes, it was in the all-white of the laboratory and the faces she saw, the fingers wrapped around hers, belonged to her children.

"You're here," she said quietly.

They nodded. Mary was crying. Ellen's eyes were dry but their depths brimmed with pain.

"I'm glad you're here," she said.

"We're *all* here," John said. His voice was tight and he leaned away before he came back into view with Liam in his arms. "Even the very little ones."

"Oh." Dotty picked her hand up and brushed it across the boy's hair. "It is so good to see you, little one."

The child knew something was wrong. He clung to his grandfather and began to cry.

"It's okay," she told him. "It's okay, Liam."

Mary turned away with her shoulders shaking. Her hands were pressed over her face.

"Sometimes, we have to say…goodbye." It hurt. It hurt so much right now but she forced a smile. Dimly, she felt someone take her arm and an IV port jostled. Her hand felt cool a moment later, and the comfort spread outward.

She stretched her hand toward Liam and a moment later, he moved his tiny hand to meet hers.

"Goodbyes are sad," she told him. "Mmm?"

He stared at her, his little blue eyes confused.

"But there's nothing to be afraid of," she told him. "You be good, Liam. You be strong. There's nothing to be afraid of."

She kissed his head before his parents came to take him from John's arms. They kissed her forehead and whispered goodbyes. One by one, the littlest children came to hug her and their parents handed them off so that they could say goodbye as well.

"I'm so lucky to get to say goodbye to all of you," Dotty said. She saw them draw closer, the fractures and spats between them gone for the moment—dark hair and fair, the glimmers of Harry's smile, and the golden-brown highlights of her hair. For a moment, she thought she could see their futures spinning out from this moment—their choices, their loves, their moments of triumph and grief, their achievements, and their lazy days on the porch and into their old age.

They would be okay.

Everyone else drew back for the children to say goodbye to Dotty. She smiled at them.

"I am so proud of you," she said. "Every one of you."

Robert looked uncertain. Her bachelor child. Dotty beckoned him close for a kiss on the forehead. "I'm proud of you," she whispered. "So was your father. We love you."

"I love you, too." He kissed her on the forehead as well. "I love you, Mom."

Deborah was next, smoothing her hair as they whispered their goodbyes. She was keeping it together for now. She would, her mother knew, and she would fall apart later in private. She met Todd's eyes over Deborah's head. *Look after her,* the look said. He nodded and put a hand silently over his heart. She smiled at him.

Ellen was crying when she came to hold her hand. She leaned close and put her forehead against hers. "Being inside the game with you will be one of my best memories," she said quietly. "Who you were there…" She trailed off.

She didn't need to finish the sentence. Dotty nodded. "I'm sorry," she said again. It wasn't enough. No words would change the past. But she and Ellen, at least in this moment, were at peace with that.

John and Mary went last. This was the first time Dotty had seen her daughter-in-law disheveled and tear-streaked. She smiled at the two of them.

"Thank you for the cake," she said finally.

Mary laughed and finished with a little sob. She nodded.

"Don't spend too much time grieving," she told them. "Hmm?"

"I'm a grown man," John said, "and I'll grieve as long as I want, thank you." He cracked a smile, although his eyes were bright, and squeezed her hand when she laughed. "I'll miss you, Mom."

"And I'll miss you. I love you."

"I love you," John whispered. The others echoed it. "Do you want us to stay with you, Mom?"

"I'd like that," she said. "And one other thing. If I could."

They nodded.

"I'd like to…go back into the game," she said.

The children nodded.

"They said you might want that," John managed to say calmly. "They can put you in and keep the top open."

Dotty nodded. Dr. DuBois moved to her side and gave her a smile and a quiet nod as he pressed a few buttons. The IV port jostled again slightly.

Her children held her hand, all their hands piled one on top of the other, while the virtual reality took hold once more and her vision faded to the deep blue of twilight.

This wasn't a place she recognized. She walked through the interior of what looked like a cathedral, its vaulted ceiling high above and her path flanked by verdant trees that rustled with an invisible wind. Dawn light flooded through the tall windows. The air was warm and heavy with greenery, a summer morning. Her feet were bare on the stone floor.

"Prima?"

"Yes?"

"This is beautiful." She looked around and smiled in awe. "Thank you. Thank you, thank you, thank you."

A long pause was disturbed only by birds singing somewhere. *"Thank you,"* Prima said.

"We had good adventures, didn't we?"

"Very good. You surprised me quite a few times." After a moment, she added, *"That was a compliment."*

"I know." Dotty smiled. She reached the end of the cathedral, where wide double doors opened into a plain of waving grass. A mountain in the distance called to mind her time with the orcs. The sky was pale golds and blues. "I'm...not sure how far I can walk, Prima." For the first time, her heart seized. "I'm scared."

She knew what the AI wanted to say—that she was as well. But what she said instead, was, *"I'm here."*

"I'm glad." Tears trickled down her cheeks at last. "To have another morning like this, to see the sky—it's a gift I could never have imagined." She gulped a sob. "I don't know what's coming."

"You didn't know what was coming when you first got here," Prima said gently, *"and look how well you did with that."*

In an eyeblink, she was pillowed on a soft bed. It felt like she was in a hammock on a lazy summer day or a boat drifting on a pond. She elevated above the plain as the sun began to rise.

This time, instead of shielding her eyes, she didn't look away from the sun. The gold, the beauty filtering through the sky, and the warmth on her skin told her she was home.

"Don't be sad," Dotty said. It was close now.

"There's no need to fear sadness," Prima said gently. Quietly, she added, *"I do, though. You gave me a name. You called me to life, Dotty. And I promise you this—you will live on with me."*

The sun's warmth seeped all through her now. The birdsong had changed somehow. She felt it deep in her bones—or perhaps her edges had dissolved—and she was everywhere. Peace settled with the certainty that she *was* the morning and the sunshine and the birdsong.

Dotty closed her eyes.

Wind rustled in the trees as Ellen knelt at the graveside. She brushed her hand over the inscription in the stone and smiled at the scent of the peonies around the grave. Her mother had always loved peonies, had enjoyed the decadence of them and their blooms so rich and full.

"I miss you," she said quietly. "All of you—everything I knew and everything I didn't."

She stood and stared at the sky. Far in the distance, on one side of the plain, rain was falling. Lightning flickered in the clouds above. The sky on the other side of the plain was clear and sunlit and grass rippled.

"She is not gone." The voice made her jump. *"She is still here."*

Bemused, she scanned her surroundings. "She is?"

"Always." A woman's image flickered in front of her, young and carefree, spinning magic from her fingertips, wielding daggers, bowing in a throne room, and facing a dragon.

Ellen smiled through the tears.

"I don't know what to do," she whispered. The tears came more freely now. She sat in the grass and let the grief pour out of her. "I don't know what to do. This hurts so much."

The AI said nothing, but she felt it waiting there like a friend. It said nothing while the tears trickled into hiccups and she wiped her face. It made a bowl of cool water and a soft cloth appear beside her, for which she murmured a quiet thanks while she cleaned her face.

And then, when she was done crying and she settled her arms around her knees and gazed at the plains, it said quietly,

"Do you want your own adventures?"

Nick put a mug of tea in front of Simon.

"Thanks." The man's lanky frame was folded awkwardly into one of the chairs. "How long?"

"They're still getting all the monitors in place," he said comfortingly. "Everything is being monitored. They'll start tracking the feedback from the patches next." He smiled. "Her doctor and DuBois are becoming best buddies. I don't understand half the words they're using, but they seem very excited by some of the feedback they've seen so far."

Simon nodded. Beside him, Aimee curled on the couch with Emilia's head pillowed on her shoulder. Jamie had curled the other way, but his hand and Emilia's were linked. It had been two hours since Taigan had arrived at the Diatek headquarters, and it was approaching three AM.

Nick sat to wait. The father's eyes had not wavered from the pod even once.

And then, as they watched, the doctors closed the lid over Taigan and the monitors flickered on.

Blue. She hadn't seen anything in so long and now, there was *blue* and it was the most beautiful thing she'd ever seen. Taigan whirled and released an incredulous laugh. She had been trapped, she'd been—

Where was she?

She looked down and her body was only vaguely there.

Did she exist? She tried to take another step and sprawled awkwardly. Sitting was difficult, but she managed it. This place was blue and stars and nothing else. She didn't know where she was and fear began to creep in.

But she existed. She comforted herself with that. If she could think, she *existed*—wherever she was.

"Hello."

A young woman stood a short distance away, only a few years older than herself. Her hair was drawn back in a crown of braids. She wore a gown that made Taigan's jaw drop—silk of a green so dark that it was almost black held up at the arms by tiny opals. She held her hand out.

When she merely stared in response, the woman heaved an exasperated sigh. "Will you spend all day there?" she asked.

"Uh…no." She took the proffered hand and allowed herself to be pulled up. "Sorry. Thank you. Who are you?"

"I'm Dotty," the woman said. "And you are?"

Thank you for reading our stories and supporting our creativity!

Choosing What Matters (this book) was both an easy decision, and a hard decision.

The Easy?

Telling a story where someone like my grandmother would go into a fully immerse game. My grandmother never played video games. She wouldn't know an Orc if it stood in front of her and screamed in her face.

She would have just screamed back at it.

But like so many of her generation (she was born in 1917) she had a backbone of steel.

The Hard?

Dealing with death again.

When you KNOW that by the end of the book (trilogy technically) your character is going to die, and that it needs to happen to tell the story, it hurts. Of course, it hurts more once you have accomplished what the art demanded and you knew it was coming.

But it still hurts.

Dorothy Hunt has forged a new future with medicine. Likewise, I am just a little closer to understanding the strength, power and conviction of those who are willing to test death to help generations who come after them prosper.

The PIVOT Lab Chronicles started with me just wanting to tell a little bit of a story. Nothing that I assume will make money, but perhaps (just a small chance) might ignite the imagination of a few geniuses to help use the technology of the present in the future.

What would it be like to use game technology to help cancer patients? To help solve problems with our brains?

What would it be like to have an AI grow into awareness by interacting with humans?

A lot of the time, we authors do not know where our story will end up. We might have plans which often come to pass, but occasionally our expectations are dashed upon the rocks of creativity and the subconscious desires we hold.

I'm not sure where PIVOT Labs will end up in the future (we have another trilogy of stories almost finished) but let us know what you think.

This third time, we engage with a person who finds themselves having to learn the basics all over again.

And then a little bit more.

Ad Aeternitatem,

Michael Anderle

If you enjoyed this book, you may also enjoy Steel Dragon, from Michael Anderle and Kevin McLaughlin. The book is available now from Amazon and through Kindle Unlimited.

Dragons rule the world. Their claws are into every aspect of human life, from government to industry. But Kristen Hall is about to throw a wrench into all of that.

Because she's a dragon, too. She just doesn't know it...yet!

A dragon raised by humans, in the human world.

After graduating from the police academy, she's dropped right into the ranks of Detroit's elite SWAT team. A rookie, in SWAT? Unheard of. But what the dragons want, they get.

The reasons behind their machinations become clear as her dragon powers begin to surface.

Will Kristen rise to the challenges her new life delivers? What designs do the dragons have for her future? And perhaps most pressing of all — how did she come to be a dragon with human parents?

Get your copy today!

BOOKS BY MICHAEL ANDERLE

For a complete list of books by Michael Anderle, please visit

www.lmbpn.com/ma-books/

All LMBPN Audiobooks are Available at Audible.com and iTunes. For a complete list of audiobooks visit:

www.lmbpn.com/audible